Clive Cussler

Clive Cussler grew up in Alhambra, California, and attended Pasadena City College before joining the Air Force. He went on to a successful advertising career, winning many national honours for his copywriting. Now a full-time bestselling author, he has also explored the deserts of the American Southwest in search of lost gold mines, dived in isolated lakes in the Rocky Mountains looking for lost aircraft and hunted under the seas for shipwrecks of historic significance, discovering and identifying more than sixty. Like his hero, Dirk Pitt, he is also an avid enthusiast of classic cars. He is married with three children, and divides his time between Colorado and Arizona. *Sahara* has been a remarkable No. 1 bestselling success around the world. Dirk Pitt's adventures continue in *Inca Gold*, another worldwide bestseller, available from HarperCollins.

'Dirk Pitt has never been more entertaining. An ecological thriller with sideshows, and some most imaginative escapes and close calls . . . terrific escapist adventure.'
New York Daily News

'Clive Cussler's hero Dirk Pitt is made of strong stuff, handling the improbable with nerves of steel . . . he is one of the best adventure heroes around.'   *Today*

'Cussler champions ecological issues with verve and continues his love affair with history . . . great fun, putting Beau Geste swashbucklers against the vilest of villains.'
Publishers Weekly

'Amazing feats of derring-do . . . non-stop action . . . refreshing escapist entertainment.'   *Washington Post*

BY CLIVE CUSSLER

CLIVE CUSSLER

SAHARA

HarperCollins*Publishers*

HarperCollins*Publishers*
77–85 Fulham Palace Road,
Hammersmith, London W6 8JB

www.harpercollins.co.uk

Paperback edition 1994
This production 2013

Previously published in paperback by Grafton 1993
Reprinted three times
(A Grafton special overseas edition published 1993)

First published in Great Britain by
HarperCollins*Publishers* 1992

ISBN 978 0 00 793063 0

Set in Times

Printed in Great Britain by
Clays Ltd, St Ives plc

In deep appreciation to
Hal Stuber, Ph.D. (environmental chemist),
of James P. Walsh & Associates, Boulder, Colorado,
for sorting out the hazardous waste
and keeping me within acceptable limits.

SAHARA

The Gauntlet

CONFEDERATE STATES SHIP TEXAS

April 2, 1865
Richmond, Virginia

She seemed to float above the ghostly evening mist like a menacing beast rising from the primeval ooze. Her low silhouette stood black and ominous against the backdrop of the trees along the shoreline. Shadowy, phantom-like images of men moved across her decks under the eerie yellow glow of lanterns as moisture trickled down her grey, sloping sides and dripped into the sluggish current of the James River.

The *Texas* tugged at her dockside mooring line as impatiently as a hound about to be unleashed for the hunt. Thick iron shutters covered her gun-ports and the 6-inch armour on her casemate showed no markings. Only a white and red battle ensign atop the mast behind her smokestack, hanging limp in the damp atmosphere, signified her as a warship of the Confederate States Navy.

To landsmen she looked squat and ugly, but to sailors there was a character and grace about her that was unmistakable. She was tough, and she was deadly, the last of her peculiar design that set sail on a cruise to extinction after a brief but enduring burst of glory.

Commander Mason Tombs stood on the forward deck, pulled a blue bandana from a pocket, and dabbed at the dampness that seeped inside the collar of his uniform. The loading was going slow, too slow. The *Texas* would need every minute of available darkness for her escape to the open sea. He watched anxiously as his crew swore and strained while they manhandled wooden crates across a gangplank and down an open hatch on the deck. The crates seemed unusually heavy for containing the written records of the four-year-old government. They came from muledrawn wagons deployed near the dock that were strongly guarded by the battle-weary survivors of a Georgia infantry company.

Tombs turned an uneasy eye toward Richmond, only 2 miles to the north. Grant had broken Lee's stubborn defence of Petersburg, and now the battered army of the South was retreating toward Appomattox and abandoning the Confederate capital to the advancing Union forces. The evacuation was underway and the city was filled with confusion as riots and pillaging swept the streets. Explosions shook the ground and flames burst into the night as warehouses and arsenals filled with supplies of war were put to the torch.

Tombs was ambitious and energetic, one of the finest naval officers in the Confederacy. He was a short, handsome-faced man with brown hair and eyebrows, a thick red beard, and a flinty look in his olive black eyes.

Commander of small gunboats at the battles of New Orleans and Memphis, gunnery officer on board the fighting ironclad *Arkansas*, and first officer of the infamous sea raider *Florida*, Tombs had proven a dangerous man for the Union cause. He had assumed command of the *Texas* only a week after she was completed at the Rocketts naval yard in Richmond, having demanded and supervised a number of modifications in preparation for an almost impossible voyage downriver past a thousand Union guns.

He turned his attention back to the cargo loading as the last wagon pulled away from the dock and disappeared into the night. He slipped his watch from a pocket, opened the lid, and held up the face toward a lantern that hung on a dock piling.

It read eight-twenty. Little more than eight hours left before daylight. Not enough time to run the last 20 miles of the gauntlet under the cloak of darkness.

An open carriage pulled by a team of dappled horses rolled up and stopped beside the dock. The driver sat stiffly without turning as the two passengers watched the final few crates being lowered through the hatch. The heavier man in civilian clothes slouched tiredly while the other, who was wearing an officer's naval uniform, spied Tombs and waved.

Tombs stepped across the plank onto the dock, approached the carriage, and saluted smartly. 'An honour, Admiral, Mr Secretary. I didn't think either of you would have time for a farewell.'

Admiral Raphael Semmes, famed for his exploits as captain of the Confederate sea wolf, *Alabama*, and now commander of the James River squadron of ironclad gunboats. nodded and smiled through a heavily waxed moustache and a small goatee protruding beneath his lower lip. 'A regiment of Yankees couldn't have kept me from seeing you off.'

Stephen Mallory, Secretary of the Confederate States Navy, stretched out a hand. 'Too much is riding on you for us not to take the time to wish you luck.'

'I've a stout ship and a brave crew.' said Tombs with confidence. 'We'll break through.'

Semmes' smile faded and his eyes filled with foreboding. 'If you find it impossible, you must burn and scuttle the ship in the deepest part of the river so that our archives can never be salvaged by the Union.'

'The charges are in place and primed,' Tombs assured Semmes. 'The bottom hull will be blown away, dropping the weighted crates in the river mud while the ship continues a safe distance away under full steam before sinking.'

Mallory nodded. 'A sound plan.'

The two men in the carriage exchanged strange knowing looks. An awkward moment passed. Then Semmes said, 'I'm sorry to lay another burden on your shoulders at the last moment, but you will also be responsible for a passenger.'

'Passenger?' Tombs repeated grimly. 'No one who values his life I trust.'

'He has no choice in the matter,' Mallory muttered.

'Where is he?' Tombs demanded, gazing around the dock. 'We're almost ready to cast off.'

'He will arrive shortly,' replied Semmes.

'May I ask who *he* is?'

'You will recognize him easily enough,' said Mallory. 'And pray the enemy also identifies him should you need to put him on display.'

'I don't understand.'

Mallory smiled for the first time. 'You will, my boy, you will.'

'A piece of information you may find useful,' said Semmes, changing the subject. 'My spies report that our former ironclad ram, the *Atlanta*, captured last year by Yankee monitors, has been pressed into service by the Union navy and is patrolling the river above Newport News.'

Tombs brightened. 'Yes, I see. Since the *Texas* has the same general shape and approximate dimensions she could be mistaken for the *Atlanta* in the dark.'

Semmes nodded and handed him a folded flag. 'The stars and stripes. You'll need it for the masquerade.'

Tombs took the Union banner and held it under one arm. 'I'll have it run up the mast shortly before we reach the Union artillery emplacements at Trent's Reach.'

'Then good luck to you,' said Semmes. 'Sorry we can't stay to see you cast off, but the Secretary has a train to catch and I have to return to the fleet and oversee its destruction before the Yankees are upon us.'

The Secretary of the Confederate navy shook Tombs' hand once more. 'The blockade runner *Fox* is standing by off Bermuda to recoal your bunkers for the next leg of your voyage. Good fortune to you, Commander. The salvation of the Confederacy is in your hands.'

14

Before Tombs could reply, Mallory ordered the carriage driver to move on. Tombs raised his hand in a final salute and stood there, his mind failing to comprehend the Secretary's farewell. Salvation of the Confederacy? The words made no sense. The war was lost. With Sherman moving north from the Carolinas and Grant surging south through Virginia like a tidal wave, Lee would be caught between the Union pincers and forced to surrender in a matter of days. Jefferson Davis would soon be broken from President of the Confederate States to a common fugitive.

And within a few short hours, the *Texas* had every expectation of being the last ship of the Confederate navy to die a watery death.

Where was the salvation should the *Texas* make good her escape? Tombs failed to fathom a vague answer. His orders were to transport the government's archives to a neutral port of his choosing and remain out of sight until contacted by courier. How could the successful smuggling of bureaucratic records possibly prevent the certain defeat of the South?

His thoughts were interrupted by his first officer, Lieutenant Ezra Craven.

'The loading is completed and the cargo stored, sir,' announced Craven. 'Shall I give the order to cast off?'

Tombs turned. 'Not yet. We have to take on a passenger.'

Craven, a big brusque Scotsman, spoke with a peculiar combination of brogue and southern drawl. 'He'd better make it damned quick.'

'Is Chief Engineer O'Hare ready to get underway?'

'His engines have a full head of steam.'

'And the gun crews?'

'Manning their stations.'

'We'll stay buttoned up until we meet the Federal fleet. We can't afford to lose a gun and crew from a lucky shot through a port beforehand.'

'The men won't take kindly to turning the other cheek.'

15

'Tell them they'll live longer –'

Both men swung and stared toward the shore at the sound of approaching hooves. A few seconds later a Confederate officer rode out of the darkness and onto the dock.

'One of you Commander Tombs?' he asked in a tired voice.

'I'm Tombs,' he said, stepping forward.

The rider swung down from his horse and saluted. He was covered with road dust and looked exhausted. 'My compliments, sir. Captain Neville Brown, in charge of the escort for your prisoner.'

'Prisoner,' Tombs echoed. 'I was told he was a passenger.'

'Treat him as you will,' Brown shrugged indifferently.

'Where is he?' Tombs asked for the second time that night.

'Immediately behind. I rode out in advance of my party to warn you not to be alarmed.'

'Is the man daft?' muttered Craven. 'Alarmed at what?'

His question was answered as a closed coach rumbled onto the dock surrounded by a detachment of riders dressed in the blue uniform of Union cavalry.

Tombs was on the verge of shouting for his crew to run out the guns and repel boarders when Captain Brown calmly reassured him. 'Rest easy, Commander. They're good southern boys. Dressing up like Yankees was the only way we could pass safely through Union lines.'

Two of the men dismounted and opened the door of the coach and helped the passenger through the door. A very tall, gaunt man with a familiar beard stepped tiredly to the wooden planking of the dock. He wore manacles that were attached by chains to his wrists and ankles. He studied the ironclad for a moment through solemn eyes, and then turned and nodded at Tombs and Craven.

'Good evening, gentlemen,' he spoke in a voice pitched slightly high. 'Am I to assume I'm to enjoy the hospitality of the Confederate navy?'

Tombs did not reply, he could not reply. He stood there

16

rooted with Craven in blank disbelief, their expressions matched in total mystification.

'My God,' Craven finally murmured. 'If you're a fake, sir, you're a good one.'

'No,' the prisoner replied. 'I assure you, I am the genuine article.'

'How is this possible?' Tombs asked, completely unprepared.

Brown remounted his horse. 'There's no time for an explanation. I have to lead my men across the river over the Richmond bridge before it is blown up. He's your responsibility now.'

'What am I supposed to do with him?' Tombs demanded.

'Keep him confined on board your ship until you receive orders for his release. That's all I've been told to pass on.'

'This is crazy.'

'So is war, Commander,' Brown said over his shoulder as he spurred his horse and rode off, followed by his small detachment disguised as Union cavalry.

There was no more time, no more interruptions to delay the *Texas*' voyage to hell. Tombs turned to Craven.

'Lieutenant, escort our *passenger* to my quarters and tell Chief Engineer O'Hare to send a mechanic to remove the manacles. I won't die as commander of a slave ship.'

The bearded man smiled at Tombs. 'Thank you. Commander. I'm grateful for your kindness.'

'Do not thank me,' said Tombs grimly. 'By sun up we'll all be introducing ourselves to the devil.'

Ever so gradually at first, then faster and faster, the *Texas* began to steam downriver, helped along by the 2-knot current. No wind stirred, and except for the throb of the engines, the river ran silent. In the pale light of a quarter moon, she slid across the black water like a wraith, more sensed than seen, almost an illusion.

She seemed to have no substance, no solidity. Only her movement gave her away, revealing a spectral outline gliding past a motionless shore. Designed specifically for one mission, one voyage, her builders had constructed a marvellous machine, the finest fighting machine the Confederates had put afloat during the four years of war.

She was a twin-screw, twin-engined vessel, 190 feet in length, 40 feet of beam, and drawing only 11 feet of water. The sloping 12-foot-high sides of her casemate were angled inward at 30 degrees and covered with 6 inches of iron plate backed by 12 inches of cotton compressed by 20 inches of oak and pine. Her armour continued under the waterline, forming a curled knuckle that extended out from the hull.

The *Texas* carried only four guns, but they had a vicious bite. Two 100-pound Blakely rifled guns were mounted fore and aft on pivots that allowed them to be fired in broadside while two 9-inch, 64-pounders covered the port and starboard.

Unlike other ironclads whose machinery had been stripped out of commercial steamer, her engines were big, powerful, and brand new. Her heavy boilers lay below the waterline, and the 9-foot screws could push her hull through calm water at 14 knots, the nautical equivalent of 16 mph — tremendous speed unmatched by any armoured ship in both navies.

Tombs was proud of his ship, yet saddened too, knowing that her life might well be short. But he was determined that the two of them would write a fitting epitaph to the closing glory of the Confederate states.

He climbed a ladder from the gun deck and entered the pilot-house, a small structure on the forward section of the casemate that was shaped like a pyramid with the top levelled off. He stared through the eye slits at the darkness and then nodded toward the strangely silent Chief Pilot, Leigh Hunt.

'We'll be under full steam the entire trip to the sea, Mr Hunt. You'll have to bear a sharp eye to keep us from running aground.'

Hunt, a James River pilot who knew every bend and shoal like the creases in his face, kept his eyes focused ahead and tipped his head upward. 'What little light comes from the moon is enough for me to read the river.'

'Yankee gunners will use it too.'

'True, but our grey sides blend with the shadows along the bank. They won't pick us out easily.'

'Let us hope so,' Tombs sighed.

He climbed through a rear hatch and stood on the casemate roof as the *Texas* reached Drewry's Bluff and surged through the moored gunboats of Admiral Semmes' James River Fleet. The crews of her sister ironclads, *Virginia II*, *Fredericksburg*, and *Richmond*, sick at heart as they prepared to blow their ships into the air, suddenly broke into wild cheering as the *Texas* swept past. Black smoke spewed from her stack and obscured the stars. The Confederate battle flag stretched out taut in the breeze from the ship's forward thrust, presenting a stirring sight that would never be seen again.

Tombs doffed his hat and held it high. It was the final dream that would soon become a nightmare of bitterness and defeat. And yet, it was a grand moment to be savoured. The *Texas* was on her way to becoming a legend.

And then, as suddenly as she appeared, she was gone around the river's bend, her wake the only sign of her passing.

Just above the Trent's Reach, where the Federal army had stretched an obstruction across the river and dug several artillery emplacements, Tombs ordered the United States colours raised on the mast.

Inside the casemate, the gun deck was cleared for action. Most of the men had stripped to the waist and stood at their guns with handkerchiefs tied around their foreheads. The officers had removed their coats and quietly strode the deck in their undershirts beneath suspenders. The ship's surgeon passed out tourniquets and instructed the men on how to apply them.

Fire buckets were spaced about the deck. Sand was spread to soak up blood. Pistols and cutlasses were issued to repel boarders, rifles loaded with bayonets fixed on their muzzles. The hatches to the magazine rooms below the gun deck were opened and the winches and pulleys readied to hoist the shot and powder.

Pushed by the current, the *Texas* was doing 16 knots when her bow crushed the floating spar of the obstruction. She surged through into clear water with hardly a scratch on the iron ram bolted to her bow.

An alert Union sentry spotted the *Texas* as she slipped out of the dark and fired off his musket.

'Cease fire, for God's sake cease fire!' Tombs shouted from the roof of the casemate.

'What ship are you?' a voice from shore came back.

'The *Atlanta*, you idiot. Can't you recognize your own ship?'

'When did you come up river?'

'An hour ago. We're under orders to patrol to the obstruction and back to City Point.'*

The bluff worked. The Union sentries along the shore appeared satisfied. The *Texas* moved ahead without further incident. Tombs exhaled a deep breath of relief.

He'd fully expected a hail of shot to lash out against his ship. With that danger temporarily passed, his only fear now was that a suspicious enemy officer might telegraph a warning up and down the river.

Fifteen miles beyond the obstruction, Tombs' luck began to run out as a low, menacing mass loomed from the blackness ahead.

* General Grant's Union army supply port on the James River.

20

The Union dual-turreted monitor, *Onondaga*, 11 inches of armour on her turrets, 5½ inches on her hull, and mounting two powerful 15-inch Dahlgren smoothbores and two 150-pounder Parrott rifles, lay anchored near the western bank, her stern aimed downstream. She was taking on coal from a barge tied to her starboard side.*

The *Texas* was almost on top of her when a midshipman standing on top of the forward turret spotted the Confederate ironclad and gave the alarm.

The crew paused from loading coal and peered at the ironclad that was hurtling out of the night. Commander John Austin of the *Onondaga* hesitated a few moments, doubtful whether a rebel ironclad could have come this far down the James River without being exposed. Those few moments cost him. By the time he shouted for his crew to cast loose their guns, the *Texas* was passing abeam, an easy stone's throw away.

'Heave to!' Austin cried, 'or we'll fire and blow you out of the water!'

'We are the *Atlanta!*' Tombs yelled back, carrying out the charade to the bitter end.

Austin was not taken in, not even by the sudden sight of the Union ensign on the mast of the intruder. He gave the order to fire.

The forward turret came into action too late. The *Texas* had already swept past and out of its angle of fire. But the two 15-inch Dahlgrens inside the *Onondaga*'s rear turret spat flame and smoke.

At point blank range the Union gunners couldn't miss, and didn't. The shots struck the sides of the *Texas* like sledgehammer blows, smashing in the upper aft end of the casemate in an explosion of iron and wooden splinters that struck down seven men.

* The original *Monitor* was only the first of her class. Almost sixty more were built of varied design as late as 1903.

At almost the same time, Tombs shouted an order down the open roof hatch. The gun-port shutters dropped aside and the Texas poured her three guns broadside into the *Onondaga's* turret. One of the Blakely's 100-pounder shells crashed through an open port and exploded against a Dahlgren, causing a gush of smoke and flame and terrible carnage inside the turret. Nine men were killed and eleven badly wounded.

Before the guns from either vessel could be reloaded, the rebel ironclad had melted back in the night and safely steamed around the next bend in the river. The *Onondaga's* forward turret blindly fired a parting salutation, the shells whistling high and aft of the fleeing *Texas*.

Desperately, Commander Austin drove his crew to up anchor and swing around 180 degrees. It was a futile gesture. The monitor's top speed was barely above 7 knots. There was no hope of her chasing down and closing on the rebel craft.

Calmly, Tombs called to Lieutenant Craven. 'Mr Craven, we'll hide no more under an enemy flag. Please hoist the Confederate colours and close the gun-ports.'

A young midshipman eagerly sprang to the mast and untied the halyards, pulling down the stars and stripes and sending up the diagonal stars and bars on a field of white and red.

Craven joined Tombs atop the casemate. 'Now the word is out,' he said, 'it'll be no picnic between here and the sea. We can deal with army shore batteries. None of their field artillery is powerful enough to make more than a dent on our armour.'

Tombs paused to stare apprehensively across the bow at the black river unwinding ahead. 'The guns of the Federal fleet waiting for us at the mouth of the river are our greatest danger.'

A barrage burst out from shore almost before he finished speaking.

'And so it begins,' Craven waxed philosophically, as he

hurriedly retreated to his station on the gun deck below. Tombs remained exposed behind the pilot-house to direct the movement of his ship against any Federal vessels blocking the river.

Shells from unseen batteries and musket fire from sharpshooters began to splatter the *Texas* like a hail storm. While his men cursed and chafed at the bit, Tombs kept the gun-ports closed. He saw no reason to endanger his crew and waste valuable powder and shot at an unseen enemy.

For two more hours the *Texas* endured the onslaught. Her engines ran smoothly and pushed her at speeds a knot or two faster than she had been designed. Wooden gunboats appeared, fired off their broadsides, and then attempted to take up the chase as the *Texas* ignored them like gnats and dashed past as if they were stopped in the water.

Suddenly the familiar outline of the *Atlanta* materialized, anchored broadside-on across the river. Her starboard guns poured forth as their lookouts recognized the unyielding rebel monster bearing down on them.

'She knew we was coming,' Tombs muttered.

'Should I pass around her, Captain?' asked Chief Pilot Hunt, displaying a remarkable coolness at the helm.

'No, Mr Hunt,' answered Tombs. 'Ram her slightly forward of her stern.'

'Smash her to the side out of our way,' Hunt replied in understanding. 'Very well, sir.'

Hunt gave the wheel a quarter turn and aimed the *Texas'* bow straight toward the stern of the *Atlanta*. Two bolts from the ex-Confederate's 8-inch guns drove into the rapidly approaching casemate, cracking the shield and pushing the wooden backing in almost a foot and wounding three men by the concussion and splinters.

The gap quickly closed and the *Texas* buried 10 feet of her heavy iron prow into the *Atlanta's* hull and then drove up and through her deck, snapping her stern anchor chain and thrusting her around in a 90-degree arc as well as forcing her deck under the river's surface. Water gushed into the Union ironclad's gunports and she quickly began to slip out of sight as the *Texas* literally rode over her.

The *Atlanta's* keel sank into the river mud and she rolled onto her side as the widely churning screws of the *Texas* spun within inches of her upturned hull before thrashing into the clear. Most of the *Atlanta's* crew rushed from the gun-ports and hatches before she went under, but at least twenty men went down with her.

Tombs and his ship hurtled on in their desperate effort to reach freedom. The running battle continued as the *Texas* shrugged off the constant fire and the pursuing Union gunboats. Telegraph lines strung along the river by Federal forces hummed with news of the ironclad's approach as a mounting wave of chaos and desperation increased among army shore batteries and navy ships determined to intercept and sink her.

Shot and shell continuously plunged against the *Texas'* armour with thumps that made her shudder from bow to stern. A 100-pound bolt from a Dahlgren mounted high above an embankment at Fort Hudson bashed into the pilothouse, stunning Chief Pilot Hunt from the concussion and leaving him bloodied from fragments that flew through the viewing slits. He gamely stayed at the wheel, keeping the ship on a straight course in the middle of the channel.

The sky was beginning to lighten in the east, when the *Texas* thundered out of the James River past Newport News and into the wide estuary and deeper water of Hampton Roads, scene of the battle between the *Monitor* and the *Merrimack* three years before.

It seemed the entire Union fleet was lined up and waiting for them. All Tombs could see from his position above the casemate was a forest of masts and smokestacks. Heavily armed frigates and sloop-of-wars on the left, monitors and gunboats on the right. And beyond, the narrow channel between the massive firepower of Fortress Monroe and Fort Wool that was blocked by the *New Ironsides*, a formidable vessel with an ironclad conventional hull mounting eighteen heavy guns.

At last Tombs ordered the ports opened and the guns run out. The *Texas* was finished making no show at resistance. Now the Federal navy would feel the full fury of her fangs. With a great cheer, the men of the *Texas* cast loose and trained their guns, primers in the vents, the locks thrown back, and the gun captains poised with the lanyards.

Craven calmly walked throughout the ship, smiling and joking with the men, offering words of encouragement and advice. Tombs came down and gave a brief speech, sharp with barbs at the enemy and optimistic about the thrashing that tried and true southern boys were about to dish out to cowardly Yankees. Then with his telescoping glass tucked under his arm, he returned to his post behind the pilothouse.

Union gunners had plenty of time to prepare. Code signals to fire when the *Texas* came in range were run up. To Tombs, as he stared through his glass, it seemed his enemies filled the entire horizon. There was a terrible quiet that hung over the water like a spell as the wolves waited for their quarry to sail into what looked to be an inescapable trap.

Rear Admiral David Porter, thickset and bearded, his flat seaman's cap set firm, stood on an arms chest where he could oversee the gun deck of his flagship, the wooden frigate *Brooklyn*, while studying the smoke from the approaching rebel ironclad in the early light of the coming dawn.

'Here she comes,' said Captain James Alden, commander of Porter's flagship. 'And she's coming like the devil straight for us.'

'A gallant and noble vessel going to her grave,' murmured Porter as the *Texas* filled the lens of his glass. 'It's a sight we'll never see again.'

'She's almost within range,' announced Alden.

'No need to waste good shot, Mr Alden. Instruct your gun crews to wait and make every shot count.'

Aboard the *Texas*, Tombs instructed his Chief Pilot, who stood gamely at the helm ignoring the blood that dripped from his left temple. 'Hunt, skin the line of wood frigates as close as you dare, so that the ironclads will hesitate to fire for fear of striking their own ships.'

The first ship in the two lines was the *Brooklyn*. Tombs waited until he was within easy range before he gave the order to fire. The *Texas*' 100-pound Blakely in the bow opened the engagement as it threw a fused shell that screamed across the water and struck the Union warship, shattering the forward rail and bursting against a huge Parrott rifled gun, killing every man within a radius of 10 feet.

The single-turreted monitor *Saugus* opened up with her twin 15-inch Dahlgrens while the *Texas* was bearing down. Both solid shot struck short and skipped across the water like stones, sending aloft huge cascades of spray. Then the other monitors, the *Chickasaw*, recently returned from Mobil Bay where she helped pound the mighty Confederate ironclad *Tennessee* into submission, the *Manhattan*, the *Saugus*, and the *Nahant* all swung their turrets, dropped their port shutters, and opened up with a tremendous wave of fire that found and battered the *Texas*' casemate. The rest of the fleet joined in and boiled the water around the speeding warship into a seething cauldron.

Tombs shouted through the roof hatch to Craven. 'We can't hurt the monitors! Answer their fire with the starboard broadside gun only. Rotate the bow and stern pivot guns to fire against the frigates!'

Craven carried out his commander's orders and within seconds the *Texas* replied, sending shells exploding through the oak hull of the *Brooklyn*. One shell burst in the engine room, killing eight men and wounding a dozen others.

26

Another swept away a crew feverishly depressing the barrel of a 32-pounder smoothbore. And yet a third burst on the crowded deck, creating more blood and havoc.

Every gun of the *Texas* was busily engaged in destruction. The rebel gunners loaded and fired with deadly precision. They hardly had to waste precious seconds aiming. They couldn't miss. Yankee ships seemed to fill up all vision beyond the gun-ports.

The air of Hampton Roads was filled with the thunder of discharged round shot, exploding shells, conical solid bolts, grape and canister, and even musket balls potshotted by Federal marines perched aloft in the yards. Dense smoke quickly shrouded the *Texas*, making it difficult for the Union gunners to get a good sight. They fired at the muzzle flashes and heard the ring as their shot struck Confederate armour and ricocheted out of the smoke.

It struck Tombs that he had sailed into an erupting volcano.

The *Texas* had now passed the *Brooklyn* and gave it a parting shot from the stern pivot that passed so close to Admiral Porter that its air suction caused him to temporarily lose his breath. He was fighting mad at the rebel ironclad's ease of deflecting the broadside the *Brooklyn* threw at her.

'Signal the fleet to encircle and ram her!' he ordered Captain Alden.

Alden complied, but he knew it was a long shot. Every officer was stunned by the ironclad's incredible speed. 'She's going awfully fast for one of our ships to hit her squarely,' he said bleakly.

'I want that damned rebel sunk!' snarled Porter.

'If by a miracle she gets past us, she'll never escape the forts and the *New Ironsides*,' Alden soothed his superior.

As if to punctuate his statement, the monitors opened up as the *Texas* passed free of the *Brooklyn* and broke into the open ahead of the next frigate in line, the *Colorado*.

The *Texas* was being swept by a screaming bedlam of death. The Union gunners were becoming more accurate. A pair of heavy solid shot struck just aft of the starboard gun with a tremendous blow. Smoke burst inside the casemate as 38 inches of iron, wood, and cotton were crushed 4 feet inward. Another shot pounded a massive crater below the smokestack, followed by a shell that struck in exactly the same place, breaching the already damaged armour and exploding inside the gun deck with terrible effect, killing six and wounding eleven men and setting the shredded cotton and shredded wood on fire.

'Hells bells!' Craven roared, finding himself standing alone amid a pile of bodies, his hair singed, clothes torn, and his left arm broken. 'Grab that hose from the engine room and put out this damned fire.'

Chief Engineer O'Hare stuck his head up through the engine room hatch. His face was black from coal dust and streaked with sweat. 'How bad is it?' he asked in a surprisingly calm voice.

'You don't want to know,' Craven yelled at him. 'Just keep the engines turning.'

'Not easy. My men are dropping from the heat. It's hotter than hell down here.'

'Consider it good practice for when we all get there,' Craven snapped back.

Then another great fist of a shell smacked the casemate with a huge, deafening explosion that shook the *Texas* to her keel. It was not one explosion but two, so simultaneous as to be indistinguishable. The forward port corner of the casemate was chopped open as if by a giant meat cleaver. Massive chunks of iron and wood were twisted and splintered in a blast that cut down the crew of the forward Blakely gun.

Another shell sheared its way through the armour and exploded in the ship's hospital, killing the surgeon and half the wounded waiting to be tended. The gun deck now looked like a slaughterhouse. The once immaculate deck was blackened from powder and crimson with blood.

The *Texas* was hurting. As she raced across the killing ground she was being pounded into scrap. Her boats had been carried away along with both masts and her smokestack riddled. The entire casemate, fore and aft, was a grotesque shamble of twisted and jagged iron. Three of her steam pipes had been cut through, and her speed had dropped by a third.

But she was far from disabled. The engines were still throbbing away and three guns yet hammered havoc among the Union fleet. Her next broadside whipped through the wooden sides of the old side-wheel steam frigate *Powhatan* and exploded one of her boilers, devastating the engine room and causing the greatest loss of life on any Union ship this day.

Tombs had also suffered grievous wounds. A piece of shrapnel had lodged in one thigh and a bullet had gouged a crease in his left shoulder. Still, he insanely crouched exposed behind the pilothouse, shouting directions to Chief Pilot Hunt. They were almost through the holocaust now.

He gazed ahead at the *New Ironsides*, lying across the channel, her formidable broadside loaded and trained on the rapidly approaching *Texas*. He studied the guns of Fortress Monroe and Fort Wool, run out and sighted, and he knew with sinking heart that they could never make it through. The *Texas* could not take any more. Another punishing nightmare and his ship would be reduced to a helpless, stricken hulk unable to prevent its total destruction by the pursuing Yankee monitors.

And the crew, he thought, men no longer caring about living, men oblivious to everything but loading and firing their guns and keeping steam in the engines. The ones still living had gone beyond themselves, ignoring the dead and doing their duty.

All gunfire had ceased now, replaced by an eerie silence.

Tombs trained his glass on the upperworks of the *New Ironsides*. He spotted what looked like her commander leaning over an armoured railing, staring back through a glass at him.

It was then he noticed the fog bank rolling in from the sea through the mouth of Chesapeake Bay beyond the forts. If by some miracle they could reach and disappear into its grey cloak, they could lose Porter's wolfpack. Tombs also recalled Mallory's words about putting his passenger on display. He called through the open hatch.

'Mr Craven, are you there?'

His first officer appeared below and stared up through the hatch, his face looking like some ghastly apparition covered with black powder, blood, and scorched flesh. 'Here sir, and I damn well wish I wasn't.'

'Bring our passenger from my stateroom up here on the casemate. And make up a white flag.'

Craven nodded in understanding. 'Aye sir.'

The remaining broadside 64-pounder and forward Blakely went silent as the Union fleet fell behind and they could no longer train their sights on a good target.

Tombs was going to risk all on a desperate gamble, the final deal of the cards. He was dead on his feet and in pain from his injuries, but his black eyes burned as brightly as ever. He prayed to God the commanders of the Union forts had their glasses aimed on the *Texas*, as did the captain of the *New Ironsides*.

'Steer between the bow of the ironclad and Fort Wool,' he instructed Hunt.

'As you wish, sir,' Hunt acknowledged.

Tombs turned as the prisoner slowly climbed the ladder to the roof of the mangled casemate, followed by Craven who held a white tablecloth from the officers' ward room on a broomstick.

The man seemed old beyond his years. His face was drawn and hollowed under a gaunt pallor. He was a man who was used up and exhausted by years of stress. His deep-sunken eyes reflected a compassionate concern as they surveyed the bloodied uniform of Tombs.

'You have been badly wounded, Commander. You should seek medical care below.'

Tombs shook his head. 'No time for that. Please move to the roof of the pilothouse and stand where you can be seen.'

The prisoner nodded in understanding. 'Yes, I see your plan.'

Tombs shifted his gaze back to the ironclad and the forts as a brief spurt of flame, followed by a plume of black smoke and the scream of a projectile, burst from the ramparts of Fortress Monroe. A great spout of water rose and hung white and green for an instant before falling back.

Tombs rudely put his shoulder to the tall man and shoved him onto the top of the pilothouse. 'Please hurry, we've come within their range.' Then he snatched the white flag from Craven and waved it frantically with his good arm.

On board the *New Ironsides*, Captain Joshua Watkins stared steadily through his long glass. 'They've broken out the white flag,' he said in surprise.

His first officer, Commander John Crosby, nodded in agreement as he peered through a pair of brass binoculars. 'Damned odd for them to surrender after the lashing they gave the fleet.'

Suddenly, Watkins pulled the glass from his eye in growing disbelief, checked the lens for smudges, and not finding any, retrained it on the battle-scarred rebel ironclad. 'But who on earth — ' The captain paused to refocus his glass. 'Good God,' he muttered in wonder. 'Who do you make out atop their pilothouse?'

It took much to disturb Crosby's steel composure, but his face went totally blank. 'It looks like . . . , but that's impossible.'

The guns of Fort Wool opened up and water spouts gushed

in a curtain around the *Texas* almost obliterating her from sight. Then she burst through the spray with magnificent perseverance and surged on.

Watkins gazed, fascinated, at the tall, lean man standing on the pilothouse. Then his gaze turned to numbed horror. 'Lord, it is *him!*' He dropped his glass and swung to face Crosby. 'Signal the forts to cease their fire. Hurry, man!'

The guns of Fortress Monroe followed those of Fort Wool, pouring their shot at the *Texas*. Most went high, but two exploded against the ironclad's smokestack, gouging huge holes in the circular walls. The army artillerymen desperately reloaded, each hoping their gun would deliver a knockout blow.

The *Texas* was only 200 yards away when the commanders of the forts acknowledged Watkins' signal and their guns went silent one by one. Watkins and Crosby ran to the bow of the *New Ironsides* just in time to get a distinct look at the two men in bloodied Confederate navy uniforms and the bearded man in rumpled civilian clothes who cast a steady gaze at them and then threw a tired and solemn salute.

They stood absolutely still, knowing in shocked certainty that the sight they were witnessing would be forever etched in their minds. And despite the storm of controversy that would later rage around them, they and the hundreds of other men on the ship and those lining the walls of the forts never wavered in their absolute belief of who they saw standing amid the shambles of the Confederate ironclad that morning.

Almost a thousand men watched in helpless awe as the *Texas* steamed past, smoke flowing from her silent gun-ports, her flapping flag shredded and torn and tied to a bent railing post. Not a sound or shot was heard as she entered the enclosing fog bank and was forever lost to view.

Lost

KITTY MANNOCK'S FAIRCHILD

October 10, 1931
The Southwest Sahara

Kitty Mannock had the odd feeling that she was flying head-on into nothingness. She was lost, utterly and hopelessly lost. For two hours she and her flimsy little aircraft had been knocked about the sky by a severe sandstorm that shrouded all visibility of the desert below. Alone in that empty, invisible sky, she fought off strange illusions that seemed to bloom out of the surrounding brown cloud.

Kitty tilted her head back and looked up through the upper windshield. The sun's orange glow was completely blotted out. Then, for perhaps the tenth time in as many minutes, she dropped her side window and peered over the edge of the cockpit, seeing nothing below but the vast, swirling cloud. The altimeter read 15 feet, high enough to clear all but the most prominent sandstone plateaus of the Adrar des Iforas, an extension of the mountainous Ahaggar range of the Sahara Desert.

She trusted to her instruments to keep the plane from slipping into a spin. On four occasions since entering the blinding storm, she had noted a decrease in her altitude and an increasing change of heading, sure signs she was beginning to circle toward the ground. Alert to the danger, she had recovered each time without incident, banking until the needle inside her compass quivered back on a southerly heading of 180 degrees.

Kitty had tried to follow the Trans-Sahara motor track, but lost it soon after entering the sandstorm that rolled without warning from the southeast. Unable to see the ground, she had no idea of her drift and could not tell how far the wind had pushed her off course. She turned west, compounding her drift, in a vain attempt to fly around the storm.

She could do nothing but sit alone and plunge on across the great ocean of menacing, featureless sand. This was the stretch Kitty feared most. She calculated that she still had another 400 miles to fly before reaching Niamey, the capital of Niger. There, she would refuel before continuing her long distance record-setting dash to Cape Town in South Africa.

A weary numbness was creeping into her arms and legs. The never-ending roar of the engine's exhaust and its vibration were beginning to take their toll. Kitty had been in the air almost twenty-seven hours since taking off from the aerodrome at Croydon, a suburb of London. She had flown from the cold damp of England into the dry furnace of the Sahara.

Darkness would fall in another three hours. The unfavourable wind from the sandstorm slowed her airspeed to 90 miles an hour, 30 off the 120-mph cruising speed of her old, reliable Fairchild FC-2W, a high-wing monoplane with an enclosed cockpit and cabin, powered by a Pratt & Whitney Wasp 410-horsepower radial engine.

The four-passenger aircraft had once been owned by Pan American-Grace Airways and flew scheduled mail stops between Lima and Santiago. When it was taken off the route in favour of a more advanced model that could carry six passengers, Kitty had purchased it and installed extra gas tanks in the passenger compartment. She then proceeded to set a long-distance record from Rio de Janeiro to Madrid late in 1930, the first woman to fly the Southern Atlantic Ocean.

Another hour passed while she fought to stay on her planned compass course against the buffeting wind. Fine sand seeped into the cabin and invaded the tender membranes of her eyes and nostrils. She rubbed her eyes but merely aggravated the discomfort. Worse, she could no longer see. If she became blind and could not read her instruments, it was all over.

She pulled a small canteen of water from under her seat, uncapped it, and splashed water on her face. She felt refreshed and blinked her eyes furiously, the wet sand trickling down her cheeks and drying within seconds under the harsh heat. Her vision returned, but her eyes felt as if they had needles sticking in them.

Suddenly, she sensed something, a tiny instant in time or a sound that was out of sequence, or perhaps a slight tick of silence amid the wind and exhaust of the engine. She leaned forward and studied the instruments. Every dial showed normal. She checked the fuel cocks. Each valve was in its correct position. Finally, she wrote it off to a foggy mind.

Then the infinitesimal blip in sound came again. She tensed, all her senses tuned to her ears. The sequence between the abnormal and the normal came faster now. Her heart sank as she recognized a misfiring sparkplug in one of the engine's cylinders. Then the sparkplugs cut out one by one. The engine began to cough badly now as the tachometer needle slowly slipped backward.

A few moments later the engine stopped dead and the propeller swung still. The abrupt silence from the exhaust manifolds hit her like a shock wave. The only sound that came was the moaning rush of the wind. Kitty had no doubts. She knew absolutely why the engine had failed. The constant barrage of sand had choked off her carburettor.

The first few seconds of surprise and fear passed quickly as Kitty took stock of her limited options. If she somehow made a successful landing, she could wait out the storm and probably make repairs. The plane began to settle, and she eased the control stick forward to begin her glide to the desert below. It would not be her first dead-stick landing.

She had at least seven under her belt, having crashed on two of those occasions and walked away from each with little more than a few cuts and bruises. But she had never attempted a dead-engine landing in the dim half light of a sandstorm. Gripping the control stick tightly in one hand, Kitty pulled on a pair of goggles with the other, dropped the side window, and tilted her head out.

Down she flew, unseeing and trying desperately to imagine what the ground was like. Though she was certain most of the desert was reasonably flat, she also knew there were hidden gullies and high sand dunes waiting to smash the falling Fairchild and its female pilot. It seemed to Kitty that she aged five years before the barren terrain finally flashed into view little more than 30 feet below her undercarriage.

The ground was sandy but looked firm enough for her wheels to roll over it. But best of all, it looked invitingly smooth. She flattened her glide and touched down. The Fairchild's big tyres struck, bounced twice, three times, and then rolled effortlessly through the sand as the airspeed fell off. Kitty had sucked in her breath to give a cry of joy as the tailwheel settled down, when all of a sudden the ground fell away in front of her.

The Fairchild sailed off the sharp edge of a bluff and dropped like a rock into a deep, narrow dry wash. The wheels crunched into sand and the undercarriage collapsed. The forward momentum threw the plane into the far wall of the wash in a splintering thud of collapsing spars and tearing fabric. The propeller shattered as the engine was shoved back, breaking one of Kitty's ankles and twisting her knee. She was jerked forward. Her safety straps should have held her upright, but she had forgotten to tighten the buckles and her upper body was thrown forward. Her head slammed against the frame of the windshield and she was swept into darkness.

*

The news of Kitty Mannock's disappearance flashed around the world a few hours after she was reported overdue for her fuel stop at Niamey. A large-scale search and rescue operation was impossible. It was to be a meagre effort. The region of the desert where Kitty went missing was mostly uninhabited and rarely seen by humans. There were no aircraft within a thousand miles. An army of men and equipment simply did not exist in the desert in 1931.

A search was launched the following morning by a small mechanized unit of the French Foreign Legion stationed in what was then the French Sudan at the oasis of Takaldebey. Assuming she came down somewhere along the Trans-Sahara motor track, they worked north, while a few men and two autos from a French trading company at Tessalit worked south.

The two search parties met on the motor track two days later without sighting wreckage or flares in the night. They fanned 20 miles on either side of the track and tried again. After ten days of finding no sign of the lost pilot, the commander of the Legion detachment was not optimistic. No man or woman could have lived that long without food and water in the sun-scorched desert, he reported. By now Kitty would have surely died of exposure.

Memorial services were conducted for one of aviation's most beloved fliers in every major city. Considered one of the three greatest women pilots along with Amelia Earhart and Amy Johnson, Kitty was mourned by a world that had thrilled to her exploits. A lovely woman with deep blue eyes and black flowing hair that fell to her waist when released, she was the daughter of wealthy sheep ranchers outside of Canberra, Australia. After graduating from an advanced girls' school, she had taken flying lessons. Surprisingly, her mother and father supported her urge to fly and bought her a second-hand Avro Avian biplane with an open cockpit and 80-horsepower Cirrus engine.

Six months later, against all pleas to stay home, she had island hopped across the Pacific to Hawaii and landed to the cheers of a huge crowd who had waited anxiously for her arrival. With sunburned face and oil-stained khaki shirt and shorts, Kitty wearily smiled and waved, stunned at the unexpected reception. She went on to win the hearts of millions and became a household word for her record-breaking flights across the oceans and continents.

This was to have been her last long-distance attempt before marrying a girlhood sweetheart who was a neighbouring rancher in Australia. After mastering the air, the lustre had strangely worn off and she was looking forward to settling down and raising a family. She had also found what so many others had experienced in the pioneering days of aviation; there was glory but few paying jobs for pilots.

She had almost cancelled the flight, but stubbornly persisted in seeing it through. And now the aviation world waited for word of her rescue with a hope that faded as the days wore on.

Kitty remained unconscious until dawn the next morning. The sun was beginning to scorch the desert when she struggled from the depths of blackness and focused her eyes on the splintered stub of the propeller. Her vision came blurred. She tried to shake her head to clear the fog and gasped from the pain that stabbed her head. Gently, she touched her forehead. The skin was unbroken but a large knot rose along the hairline. She checked for other injuries and discovered the cracked ankle that had swollen inside her flying boot and the twisted knee.

She unbuckled her safety harness, pushed open the cabin door, and carefully climbed from the plane. Limping a few paces, Kitty sank slowly onto the sand and took stock.

Fortunately, there had been no fire, but the faithful

Fairchild would never fly again. The engine, three of its cylinders cracked on impact with the ravine slope, was bent upward on a crazy angle. The wings were amazingly intact as was the airframe, but the undercarriage had been mashed flat with the wheels bent outward.

So much for making repairs and continuing on. Her next problem was to determine her location. She had no idea where she had come down. She judged she had fallen in what they called in Australia a billabong, a dry stream-bed that is filled seasonally. Only the sand in this one probably hadn't seen water in a hundred years. The sandstorm had died, but the walls of the small gorge where she lay were a good 20 feet high, and she could not see the landscape beyond. Better she didn't. It was colourless, desolate, and ugly beyond description.

She felt a sudden thirst, and the thought of water reminded her of her canteen. She hopped back to the cabin door on one leg, leaned in, and pulled it from under the seat. Its capacity was only half a gallon, and it was less than two thirds full. Kitty realized she'd be lucky if it lasted her more than two or three days and dared not take more than a few sips at a time.

She decided she had to make an attempt at reaching a village or the motor track. It was suicide to stay near the ship. Unless an aircraft flew directly overhead, the Fairchild could not be seen. Still shaky, she stretched out under the shade of the plane and resigned herself to her predicament.

Kitty was soon to discover the incredible contrast of temperatures in the Sahara. During the day, the air climbed to 120 degrees F (49 degrees C) and dropped to 39 degrees F (4 degrees C) at night. The agonizing cold of the night was as torturous as the daytime heat. After suffering twelve hours of burning sun, she scraped out a burrow in the sand and crawled into it. Then she huddled in a ball, shivering and sleeping fitfully until dawn.

In the early morning of the second day, before the sun began to beat down, she felt strong enough to launch her preparations to abandon the airplane. She fashioned herself a crutch from a wing strut and made a crude umbrella from the wing fabric. Using a small set of tools, she removed the compass from the instrument panel. Despite her injuries, Kitty was determined to strike out for the motor track. She felt she had no alternative.

Feeling better now for having a plan, Kitty took her logbook and began writing the first page of what was to be the account of her perseverance and heroic attempt to survive under the worst conditions imaginable. She opened the entry by describing the crash and sketching her intended trek south down the billabong until she found an easy climb to the rim. Once in the open, she planned to head due east until she picked up the motor track or ran across a tribe of wandering nomads. Then she tore out the page and attached it to the instrument panel so that rescuers could follow her trail in the unlikely event the plane was discovered first.

The heat was rapidly becoming unbearable. Her situation was made even worse by the walls of the gully that reflected and magnified the sun's rays like an open crematorium. She found it difficult to breathe and had to fight off a terrible urge to drink her precious water in large swallows.

One last act before she set out. She unlaced the boot on her fractured ankle and tenderly removed it. The pain forced a soft groan from her lips, and she let it ease before binding the ankle in her silk flying scarf. Then with the compass and canteen attached to her belt, the umbrella held high, and the crutch snug under one arm, Kitty set out under the onslaught of the Sahara sun, limping gamely across the sand of the ancient riverbed.

The search for Kitty Mannock continued off and on over the years, but neither she nor her plane were ever sighted.

No clue turned up, no camel caravan came across a skeleton in the desert that was dressed in the old-fashioned flying togs of the thirties, no wandering nomad stumbled on the wrecked airplane. Kitty's total disappearance became one of the great mysteries of aviation.

Rumours of Kitty's ultimate fate grew and spread over the decades. Some claimed that she had survived but was suffering from amnesia and living under another name in South America, and many thought she was captured and enslaved by a tribe of Tuaregs. Only Amelia Earhart's flight into the unknown caused more speculation.

The desert held its secret well. The sands became Kitty Mannock's burial shroud. The enigma of her flight to nowhere would not be solved for another half a century.

PART ONE

Frenzy

1

May 5, 1996
Asselar Oasis, Mali, Africa

After travelling through the desert for days or weeks, seeing no animals, meeting no humans, civilization, no matter how tiny or primitive, comes as a stunning surprise. To the eleven people in the five Land Rovers, plus five tour driver/guides, the sight of a man-made habitat came as a great relief. Hot and unwashed, tired after a week of driving across pure desolation, the adventurous tourists on the Backworld Explorations' twelve-day *Across the Sahara Safari* were only too happy to see humans and find enough water for a refreshing bath.

They sighted the village of Asselar sitting in barren isolation in the central Sahara region of the African nation of Mali. A sprawl of mud houses clustered around a well in the dry bottom of what must have been an ancient riverbed. Scattered around the outskirts were the crumbling ruins of a hundred or more abandoned houses and beyond them the low banks that dropped below the alluvial plain. From a distance the village was almost impossible to see, so well did the time-worn buildings merge with the austere and colourless landscape.

'Well, there she is,' pointed Major Ian Fairweather, the safari leader, to the tired and dusty tourists who exited the Land Rovers and grouped around him. 'You'd never know to look at her that Asselar was once a cultural crossroads of western Africa. For five centuries it was an important watering hole for the great trade and slave caravans that passed through to the north and east.'

'Why did it go into decline?' asked a comely Canadian woman in halter top and brief shorts.

'A combination of wars and conquests by the Moors and the French, the abolition of slavery, but mostly because the trade routes moved south and west toward the seacoasts. The death blow came about forty years go when its wells began to dry up. The only flowing well that still supports the town has been dug nearly 50 metres deep.'

'Not exactly a metropolitan paradise,' muttered a stout man in a Spanish accent.

Major Fairweather forced a smile. A tall, lean ex-Royal Marine who prodigiously puffed on a long filtered cigarette, he spoke in clipped, seemingly rehearsed tones. 'Only a few Tuareg families that gave up the nomadic tradition reside in Asselar now. They mainly subsist on small herds of goats, patches of sandy soil irrigated by hand from the central village well, and a few handfuls of gemstones gleaned from the desert that they polish and carry by camel to the city of Gao where they sell them as souvenirs.'

A London barrister, impeccably dressed in khaki safari suit and pith helmet, pointed an ebony cane at the village. 'Looks abandoned to me. I seem to recall your brochure stating that our tour group would be "enthralled by the romance of desert music and native dancing under flickering campfires of Asselar." '

'I'm sure our advanced scout has made every arrangement for your comfort and enjoyment,' Fairweather assured him with airy confidence. He gazed for a moment at the sun setting beyond the village. 'It will be dark soon. We'd better move on into the village.'

'Is there a hotel there?' asked the Canadian lady.

Fairweather stifled a pained look. 'No, Mrs Lansing, we camp in the ruins just beyond the town.'

A collective groan went up from the tourists. They had hoped for a soft bed with private bathrooms. Luxuries Asselar had probably never known.

The group reboarded the vehicles, then drove down a

worn trail into the river valley and onto the main road leading through the village. The closer they came the more difficult it was to visualize a glorious past. The streets were narrow alleyways and composed of sand. It seemed a dead town that reeked of defeat. No light was seen in the dusk, no dog barked a greeting. They saw no sign of life in any of the mud buildings. It was as though the inhabitants had packed up and vanished into the desert.

Fairweather began to feel uneasy. Something was clearly wrong. There was no sign of his advance scout. For an instant he caught a glimpse of a large four-legged animal scurrying into a doorway. But it seemed so fleeting, he shrugged it off as a shadow from the moving Land Rovers.

His merry band of clients would be grumbling tonight, he thought. Damn those advertising people for over-exaggerating the allure of the desert. 'An opportunity to experience a once-in-a-lifetime expedition across the nomadic sands of the Sahara,' he recited under his breath. He'd have wagered a year's pay the copywriter had never ventured past the Dover coast.

They were almost 80 kilometres from the Trans-Sahara Motor Track and a good 240 from the Niger River city of Gao. The safari carried more than enough food, water, and fuel for the remainder of the journey, so Fairweather kept open an option to bypass Asselar should an unforeseen problem arise. The safety of Backworld Explorations' clients came first, and in twenty-eight years they had yet to lose one, unless they counted the retired American plumber who teased a camel and was kicked in the head for his stupidity.

Fairweather began to wonder why he saw no goats or camels. Nor did he see any footprints in the sandy streets, only strange claw marks and round indentations that travelled in parallel as though twin logs were dragged about. The small tribal houses, built of stone and covered with a reddish mud, appeared more rundown and decayed since Fairweather had passed through on the last safari not more than two months ago.

Something was definitely amiss. Even if for some odd reason the villagers had deserted the area, his advance scout should have met them. In all the years they had driven the Sahara together, Ibn Hajib had never failed him. Fairweather decided to allow his charges to rest for a short time at the village well and rinse off, before continuing some distance into the desert and making camp. Better keep a guarded eye, he thought as he pulled his old Royal Marine Patchett submachine gun from a compartment between the seats and tucked it upright between his knees. On the muzzle he threaded an Invicta silencer, giving the weapon the look of an extended pipe with a long curved shell clip protruding from it.

'Something wrong?' asked Mrs Lansing, who along with her husband rode in Fairweather's Land Rover.

'Just a precaution to scare away beggars,' Fairweather lied.

He stopped the four-wheel-drive and walked back, warning his drivers to keep a sharp lookout for anything suspicious. Then he returned and drove on, leading the column to the centre of the town and passing through the narrow and sandy streets that were laid out in no particular order. At last he stopped under a lonely date palm that stood in the middle of a spacious marketplace near a circular stone well about 4 metres in diameter.

Fairweather studied the sandy ground about the well in the last light of the day. It was surrounded by the same unusual tracks he'd spotted in the streets. He stared down into the well. He barely saw a tiny reflection deep in the bowels of the sandstone. He recalled that the water was quite high in mineral content that gave it a metallic taste and tinted it a milky green. Yet, it had quenched the thirst of many lives, human and animal, over the centuries. Whether it was hygienic for the uninitiated stomachs of his clients did not concern Fairweather. He merely intended for them to use it to rinse the sweat and dust off their bodies, not drink it.

He instructed his drivers to stand guard and then showed the tourists how to hoist a pigskin bucket of water by use of an ancient hand winch tied to a frayed rope. The exotic image of desert music and dancing by flickering campfires was quickly forgotten as they laughed and splashed like children in a lawn sprinkler on a hot summer afternoon. The men stripped to the waist and slapped water on their bare skin. The women were more concerned with washing their hair.

The comical scene was eerily illuminated by the Land Rover's headlights that threw their cavorting shadows on the silent walls of the village like film projectors. While Fairweather's drivers watched and laughed, he walked a fair distance down one of the streets and entered a house that stood next to a mosque. The walls appeared old and time-worn. The entrance led through a short, arched tunnel to a courtyard that was littered with so much human trash and rubble that he had difficulty climbing over it.

He shone a flashlight around the main room of the structure. The walls were a dusty white, the roofs high with exposed poles over a stick matting, much like the latilla viga on the ceilings of Santa Fe architecture of the American Southwest. The walls were indented with many niches for keeping household goods in, but they were all empty, their contents scattered and broken around the floor along with jumbled furniture.

Because nothing obvious appeared to be missing, it looked to Fairweather as if vandals had simply trashed the house after the occupants had fled, leaving all their possessions behind. Then he spotted a pile of bones in one corner of

51

the room. He identified them as human and began to feel extremely uneasy.

In the glimmer of the flashlight, shadows formed and played weird tricks on the eyes. He swore he saw a large animal flit past a window to the courtyard. He removed the safety on the Patchett not so much from fear as from a sixth sense of the menace that was forming in the darkening alleyways.

A rustling sound came from behind a closed doorway that opened onto a small terrace. Fairweather approached the door quietly, stepping softly around the debris. If there was someone hiding inside, they went silent. Fairweather held the flashlight in front of him with one hand and gripped the submachine gun, muzzle aimed forward, with the other. Then he kicked the door open, knocking it off the hinges onto the floor where it threw up a cloud of dust.

There was someone there all right, or was it *something*? Dark-skinned and evil, like a demon escaped from hell, it looked like an animal-like subhuman, swaying on hands and knees, staring insanely into the beam of light through eyes that were as red as burning coals.

Fairweather instinctively stepped back. The thing reared up on its knees and lunged at him. Fairweather calmly squeezed the trigger on the Patchett, holding the butt of the gun against his flexed stomach muscles. A rapid stream of 9-millimetre, 100-weight-grain, round-nose bullets spat from the muzzle with the muffled sound of popcorn popping.

The hideous beast made a ghastly retching sound and collapsed, its chest almost blown away. Fairweather stepped up to the huddled form, leaned over, and beamed his flashlight on it. The body was filthy and completely naked. The wild eyes were staring sightlessly, a bright red where white should have been. The face was that of a boy, no more than fifteen.

A fear struck with such shock, such stunning force, that Fairweather was for several moments numbed with the realization of the danger. He knew now what made the odd tracks in the sand. There must have been a whole colony of them that crawled through the village. He turned suddenly and began running back to the marketplace. But he was too late, far too late.

A wall of shrieking fiends burst from the evening dark and tore headlong into the unwary tourists at the well. The drivers were swallowed in the seething tidal wave before they could cry out an alarm or put up a shred of defence. The savage horde came on hands and knees like jackals, pulling down the unarmed tourists and snapping at any exposed skin with their teeth.

The horrible nightmare, illuminated by the headlights of the Land Rovers, became a frenzied press of writhing bodies with the terrified screams of the panic-stricken tourists mingled with the banshee shrieks of their attackers. Mrs Lansing gave a tortured cry and disappeared in a tangled mass of bodies. Her husband tried to climb on the hood of one of the vehicles but was pulled down into the dust and mutilated like a beetle under an army of ants.

The fastidious Londoner twisted the head of his cane from a hollow sheath, revealing a short sword. He flayed about him viciously, temporarily keeping the mob at bay. But they seemed to possess no fear and quickly overwhelmed him.

The area around the well was choked solidly with struggling humanity. The fat Spanish man, blood streaming from several teeth wounds, jumped into the well to escape, but four of the crazed killers jumped in after him.

Fairweather ran up and crouched, firing the Patchett into the surging attackers, careful not to shoot one of his own people. The mob, unable to hear the silenced gun, ignored the unexpected gunfire and were either too crazed or too indifferent to realize a score of their number were being cut down around them.

Fairweather must have shot nearly thirty of the murderous crowd before the Patchett spent its last shell. He stood helpless, unseen and unnoticed as the uncontrolled slaughter slowed and eventually ceased as his drivers and clients were all slain. He could not comprehend the suddenness that turned the marketplace into a charnel house.

'Oh God,' he whispered in a tight, choked voice, watching in cold horror as the savages set upon the bodies in a cannibalistic frenzy, gnawing at the flesh of their victims. He went on watching with a morbid fascination that slowly transformed to anger and outrage at the sickening tragedy being played out before him. Fairweather was caught in the nightmare of it, powerless to do anything but stare at the horror.

Already the butchers who weren't tearing at the hapless tourists were smashing the Land Rovers. Hurling rocks through the windows, shattering the glass. Venting their insatiable savagery on anything that was foreign to them.

Fairweather stepped back into the shadows, sick at the thought that he was responsible for the deaths of his men and clients. He had failed to provide for their safety and unknowingly led them into a bloody disaster. He cursed his impotency to save them and his cowardice at not dying with them.

With great force of willpower, he turned his attention away from the marketplace and began running through the narrow streets, through the ruined outskirts, and into the desert. To warn other desert travellers of the massacre that awaited them at Asselar, he had to save himself. The distance to the next village to the south was too far to reach without water. He settled instead for the motor track to the east, hoping to find a passing vehicle or a government patrol before he died under the blazing sun.

He took a bearing on the north star and settled down to a fast walk across the desert, knowing his chances of survival were next to nil. Never once did he turn and look back. He could see it all clearly in his mind, and his ears still rang with the agonized screams of the dead.

2

May 10, 1996
Alexandria, Egypt

The white sands of the empty beach flared beneath the bare feet of Eva Rojas, the fine grains sifting between her toes. She stood and gazed at the Mediterranean Sea. The deep water was dyed cobalt blue, becoming emerald as it shallowed, and then fading to aquamarine as its waves fanned out on the bleached sand.

Eva had driven her rental car 110 kilometres west from Alexandria before stopping at a deserted section of beach not far from the town of El Alamein where the great desert war of World War II was fought. Parking off the coastal highway, she collected her tote bag and walked through low dunes toward the tide line.

She wore a coral one-piece stretch jersey bathing suit that fitted her like a second skin. Her arms and shoulders were covered by a matching top. She stood gracefully, lightly, and her body was firm, the limbs slim and tan. Her red-gold hair was tied in a long braid that fell down her back almost to her waist and glistened under the sun like polished copper. She stared from Dresden blue eyes that glowed from a face with smooth skin and high cheek-bones. Eva was thirty-eight but could have easily passed for thirty. She would never make the cover of *Vogue*, but she was pretty with a vibrant wholesomeness that men, even much younger men, found very appealing.

The beach appeared deserted. She stood poised, turning her head and staring up and down the shore like a cautious deer. The only other sign of life was a Jeep Cherokee, painted turquoise with the letters NUMA on the door, sitting about a hundred metres up the road. She had passed it before pulling over and parking. The Jeep's occupant was nowhere to be seen.

The morning sun had already warmed the sand, and it felt hot to her naked feet as she walked toward the water. She stopped a few metres short of the water's edge and spread out a beach towel. She checked the time before dropping her watch in the tote bag. Ten after ten. After applying a number 25 sunscreen lotion, she stretched out on her back, sighed, and began soaking up the African sun.

Eva still suffered from the lingering effects of jet lag after the long flight from San Francisco to Cairo. That and four days of nonstop emergency sessions with physicians and fellow biologists over the strange outbreaks of nervous disorders recently discovered throughout the southern Sahara Desert. Taking a break from the exhausting conferences, she wanted nothing more than to immerse herself in a few hours of rest and solitude before travelling through the vast desert on a research mission. Gratefully, as the sea breeze soothed her skin, she closed her eyes and promptly dozed off.

When Eva awoke, she glanced at her watch again. It read eleven-twenty. She had been asleep an hour and a half. The sunscreen had held sunburn to a light shade of pink. She rolled over on her stomach and gazed around the beach. A pair of men in short-sleeved shirts and khaki shorts were slowly walking in her direction along the water's edge. They quickly stopped as they spotted her observing them and turned as if staring at a passing ship. They were still a good 200 metres away, and she took no more notice of them.

Suddenly, something caught her eye in the water some distance from shore. A head with black hair broke the surface. Eva held a hand over her eyes to shade the sun and squinted. A man with a dive mask and swim fins was snorkelling alone in deep water beyond the breakers. He appeared to be spear-fishing. She watched as he dived out of sight, remaining underwater for so long she thought he was surely drowning. But then he resurfaced and continued his hunt. After several minutes, he swam toward shore, expertly catching a breaking wave and body surfing into the shallows where he stood up.

He held a strange-looking spear gun with a long barbed shaft and surgical rubber attached to its ends. With his other hand, he carried a group of fish, none weighing less than 3 pounds and attached by a stainless steel hoop that hung from a belt and ran through their gills.

Despite a deep tan, his craggy face didn't bear Arabic features. His thick ebony hair was plastered down by the salt water and the sun sparkled the drops of water clinging to the matted hair on his chest. He was tall, hard-bodied, and broad-shouldered, and walked with a loose grace that was impossible for most men. She guessed him to be close to forty.

As he passed Eva, the man coolly flicked his eyes over her. He was close enough so that she could see they were an opaline green, set wide with a clear glimpse of the white around the iris. He stared at her with such direct candour that it seemed to reach into Eva's mind and mesmerize her. Part of her was afraid he might pause and say something, the other part wishing he would, but his white teeth showed in a devastating smile as he nodded and walked past her to the highway.

She watched him until he disappeared behind the dunes in the area where she had seen the NUMA jeep. What's the matter with me, she thought, I should have at least acknowledged his attention with a smile in return. Then she dismissed him in her mind, deciding that it would have been a waste of time since he probably couldn't speak English anyway. And yet, her eyes shone with a light that had not been there for a long time. How odd, she thought, to feel young and excited by a strange male who gazed at her for one brief moment, and who would never pass her way again.

She felt like going into the water to cool off, but the two men strolling along the beach had approached and were passing between Eva and the surf so she modestly decided to wait until they had passed on. They didn't have the fine features of Egyptians, but the flatter nose, darker almost black skin, and matted curly hair of people who lived on the southern fringe of the Sahara.

They stopped and furtively looked up and down the beach for perhaps the twentieth time. Then suddenly, they were upon her.

'Get away!' she screamed in instinctive reaction. She frantically tried to fight them off, but one, a slimy-eyed, rat-faced man with a thick black moustache, brutally grasped her by the hair and twisted her on her back. A cold fear shot through her as the other man, whose tobacco-stained teeth were etched in a sadistic smile, dropped to his knees and sat across her thighs. The rat-faced attacker straddled her chest, his legs pressing against her arms, forcing her deep into the sand. Now she was pinned helplessly, totally, unable to move little else than her fingers and feet.

Strangely, there was no lust in their eyes. Neither man made any attempt to tear away her swimsuit. They were not acting like men intent on rape. Eva screamed again, high and shrill. But her only reply was the surf. There wasn't another soul to be seen on the beach.

Then the rat-faced man's hands closed over her nose and mouth, and he began to smother her calmly and purposely. His weight on her rib cage added to the constriction of air. The supply of air to her lungs was completely cut off.

Through the hypnotic spell of terror, she realized with horrified disbelief that they intended to kill her. She tried to scream again, but the sound came muffled. She felt no pain, only blind panic and shocked paralysis.

She tried desperately to tear away the unrelenting pressure on her face, but her arms and hands were gripped as if in a vice. Her lungs demanded air that wasn't there. Blackness began to creep into the edge of her vision. Desperately, she held onto consciousness, but she could feel it slipping away. She saw the man who was sitting on her thighs peer over the shoulder of her murderer, realizing his leering face was the last sight she would ever see.

Eva closed her eyes as she approached the brink of a black void. The thought that flashed through her brain was that she was having a nightmare, and that if she opened her eyes it would be gone. She had to struggle to lift her eyelids for one final look at reality.

It *was* a nightmare, she thought almost joyously. The man with the stained teeth wasn't leering anymore. A thin metal shaft was protruding from both his temples, much like a novelty arrow that fitted over the head and looked as if it had been shot through the skull. The assailant's face seemed to collapse and he fell backward over her feet, his arms spread wide in crucifixion.

Rat-face was so intent on smothering the life from Eva that he didn't notice his friend had fallen away. Then for one second, maybe two, he froze as a pair of large hands materialized and tightly clamped around his chin and the top of his head. Eva felt the pressure over her nose and lips die as her assassin threw up his arms and furiously tore at the hands that were gripping his skull. The utter unexpectedness of this new development only added to the unreality of the nightmarish shock in Eva's mind.

Before blackness closed over her, she heard a crunching sound, like a person biting down on an ice cube, and she had a fleeting glimpse of the killer's eyes, wide open, protruding, staring sightlessly out of a head that had been twisted around in a full 360-degree circle.

3

Eva awoke with the hot sun on her face. She awoke to the sound of the waves pounding the African shore. When she blinked open her eyes, it was the most beautiful sight she had ever seen.

She groaned and stirred, squinting at the dazzling beach, the peaceful sun-splashed panorama of scenic beauty. She sat up suddenly, her eyes widening in fear, terrorized by the sharp recall of the attack. But her killers were gone. Had they really existed? She began to wonder if she had been hallucinating.

'Welcome back,' said a man's voice. 'For a while there I was afraid you lapsed into a coma.'

Eva turned and looked up into the smiling face of the spear-fisherman who was kneeling behind her.

'Where are the men who tried to kill me?' she asked in a frightened voice.

'They left with the tide,' the stranger answered with an icy cheerfulness.

'Tide?'

'I was taught never to litter a beach. I towed their bodies beyond the surf. When I last saw them, they were drifting toward Greece.'

She stared at him as a chill swept through her. 'You killed them.'

'They were not nice people.'

'You killed them,' she echoed dumbly. Her face was ashen and she looked as if she was going to be sick. 'You're as cold-blooded a murderer as they were.'

He could see she was still in shock and not reasoning

sensibly. Her eyes were filled with revulsion. He shrugged and said simply, 'Would you have preferred I hadn't become involved?'

The fear and revulsion slowly left her eyes and was replaced with apprehension. It took a minute for Eva to realize that the stranger had saved her from a violent death. 'No please, forgive me. I'm acting stupidly. I owe you my life and I don't even know your name.'

'It's Dirk Pitt.'

'I'm Eva Rojas.' She felt oddly flustered as he smiled warmly and gently grasped her hand in his. She saw only concern in his eyes and all her apprehension fled. 'You're American.'

'Yes, I'm with the National Underwater and Marine Agency. We're doing an archaeological survey of the Nile River.'

'I thought you had driven off before I was attacked.'

'Almost, but your friends made me curious. It struck me odd that they parked their car a good kilometre away and then walked across a deserted beach directly toward you. So I hung around to see what they had in mind.'

'Lucky for me you're the suspicious type.'

'Do you have any idea of why they tried to kill you?' Pitt asked.

'They must have been bandits who murder and rob tourists.'

He shook his head. 'Robbery wasn't their motive. They carried no weapons. The one who was smothering you used his hands instead of tape or a cloth. And they made no attempt at rape. They were not professional assassins or we'd both be dead. Most unusual. I'd bet a month's pay they were only hired hands for someone who wanted you dead. They followed you to a secluded spot intending to murder you, and then force salt water down your nose and throat. Afterward, your body would be left at the high-tide line to make it look like a drowning. Which would explain why they tried to smother you.'

She said hesitatingly, 'I can't believe any of this. It seems so purposeless and makes no sense at all. I'm only a biochemist, specializing in the effects of toxic materials on humans. I have no enemies. Why on earth should anyone want to kill me?'

'Having only just met you, I can't even guess.'

Eva lightly massaged her bruised lips. 'It's all so crazy.'

'How long have you been in Egypt?'

'Only a few days.'

'You must have done something to make somebody pretty mad.'

'Certainly not to any North Africans,' she said doubtfully. 'If anything I'm here to help them.'

He stared thoughtfully into the sand. 'Then you're not on vacation.'

'My work brought me here,' Eva answered. 'Rumours of strange physical abnormalities and psychological disorders among the nomadic peoples of the southern Sahara were brought to the attention of the World Health Organization. I'm a member of an international team of scientists who have been sent to investigate.'

'Hardly fodder for a murder,' Pitt admitted.

'All the more puzzling. My colleagues and I are here to save lives. We pose no threat.'

'You think the plague in the desert is due to toxins?'

'We don't have the answers yet. There isn't enough data to draw conclusions. On the surface the cause appears to be contamination sickness, but the source is a mystery. No known chemical manufacturing or hazardous waste sites lie within hundreds of kilometres of the areas reporting the symptoms.'

'How widespread is the problem?'

'Over eight thousand cases have erupted across the

African nations of Mali and Niger in the past ten days.'

Pitt's eyebrows lifted. 'An incredible number for so short a time. How do you know bacteria or a virus isn't the cause?'

'Like I said, the source is a mystery.'

'Odd that it hasn't been covered by the news media.'

'The World Health Organization has insisted on a news blackout until a cause has been determined. I suppose to prevent sensationalism and panic.'

Pitt had been glancing around the beach from time to time. He spotted a movement beyond the low dunes bordering the road. 'What are your plans?'

'My scientific team leaves for the Sahara tomorrow to begin field investigations.'

'You know, I hope, that Mali is on the verge of what could be a bloody civil war.'

She shrugged unconcernedly. 'The government has agreed to keep a heavy guard around our researchers at all times.' She paused and looked at him for a long moment. 'Why are you asking me all these questions? You act like a secret agent.'

Pitt laughed. 'Only a nosy marine engineer with dislike for anyone who goes around murdering beautiful women.'

'Maybe it was a case of mistaken identity?' she said hopefully.

Pitt's eyes travelled over her body and stopped at her eyes. 'Somehow, I don't think that's possible –' Pitt tensed suddenly and stood, staring at the dunes. His muscles tightened. He reached down and grabbed Eva by the wrist and pulled her upright. 'Time to go,' he said, dragging her at a run across the beach.

'What are you doing?' she demanded, stumbling after him.

Pitt didn't answer. The movement behind the dunes had become a wisp of smoke that was thickening as it rose in the desert sky. He knew immediately that another killer, or perhaps more, had set fire to Eva's rental car in an effort to trap them until reinforcements could arrive.

He could see the flames now. If he had picked up his speargun . . .? No. He didn't fool himself. It was no weapon against a firearm. His only slim hope was that the assassin's comrade was also unarmed and hadn't seen Pitt's Jeep.

He was right on the first count, wrong on the second. As they crested the last dune, he saw a dark-skinned man holding a burning newspaper in one hand that was rolled up in a torch. The intruder was absorbed in kicking out the windshield in preparation of incinerating the interior of the Jeep. This one was not dressed like the others. He wore an intricate white headdress that was swathed in such a way that only his eyes showed. His body was draped in a flowing caftan-like robe that swirled around his sandalled ankles. He failed to notice Pitt bearing down on him with Eva in tow.

Pitt halted and breathed the words into Eva's ear. 'If I screw up, run like hell for the road and stop a passing car.' Aloud he shouted, 'Freeze!'

Startled, the man twisted around, his eyes wide but menacing. In the same breath as his shout, Pitt lowered his head and charged. The man thrust the burning paper in front of him, but Pitt's head had already driven into his chest, breaking the sternum with the accompanying sharp snap of cracking ribs. At the same time, Pitt's right fist swung up into the man's crotch.

The menace in the man's eyes bulged into a look of shock. Then a strangling, tortured gasp escaped his gaping mouth as the wind burst from his lungs. He was thrust backward, and his feet left the sand as Pitt's wild attack lifted him in the air.

The lighted torch flew over Pitt's back and landed in the sand. The man's expression went from shock to pain and terror. His face congested and flushed crimson as he was thrown backward and collapsed. Pitt quickly knelt over him and searched his pockets. There was nothing, no weapons, no identification. Not even a few loose coins or a comb.

'Who sent you, pal?' Pitt demanded, grabbing the man by the neck and shaking him like a Doberman with a rat.

The reaction was not what Pitt expected. Through the torment and agony, the man gave Pitt a sinister stare — a stare, Pitt thought, curiously like a man who had had the last laugh. Then the dark-skinned man grinned, showing a set of white teeth with one missing. His jaw dropped open slightly, and then appeared to clamp down. Too late Pitt realized that his adversary had bitten into a lethal rubber-coated cyanide pill. It had been concealed in the man's mouth as a false tooth.

Foam seeped from the man's lips. The poisonous pill was very powerful and death came quickly. Pitt and Eva watched helplessly as the strength melted from the man's body. The eyes remained open, blank and glazed in death.

'Is he — ?' Eva broke off and then tried again. 'Is he dead?'

'I think it's safe to say he's expired,' Pitt said without a shred of remorse.

Eva held Pitt's arm for support. Her hands felt cold under the African heat and she was shivering from shock. Her eyes were stricken. She had never watched anyone die before. She began to feel sick but somehow managed to control her stomach.

'But why kill himself?' she murmured. 'For what purpose?'

'To protect others connected with your failed murder attempt,' Pitt answered.

'He'd willingly take his own life to remain silent?' she asked with disbelief.

'A loyal fanatic to his boss,' Pitt said quietly. 'I suspect that if he hadn't taken cyanide on his own, he'd have had help.'

Eva shook her head. 'This is insane. You're talking a conspiracy.'

'Face facts, lady, someone went to a lot of trouble to eliminate you.' Pitt stared at Eva. She looked like a small girl who was lost in a department store. 'You have an enemy who doesn't want you in Africa, and if you expect to go on living, I suggest you take the next plane back to the States.'

She looked dazed. 'No, not while people are dying.'

'You're tough to convince,' he said.

'Put yourself in my place.'

'Better yet, your colleagues' shoes. They may be on a hit list too. We'd better get back to Cairo and warn them. If any of this is tied to your research and investigation, their lives are also in danger.'

Eva looked down at the dead man. 'What do you intend to do with him?'

Pitt shrugged. 'Throw him in the Med with his friends.' Then a devilish smile rode his craggy face. 'I'd love to see the face of their ringleader when he learns his assassins have gone missing without a trace and you're still walking around as if nothing happened.'

4

Company officials at the Backworld Expeditions offices in Cairo realized something was wrong when the desert safari group failed to arrive in the fabled city of Timbuktu on schedule. Twenty-four hours later, pilots of the aircraft that was chartered to return the tourists to Marrakech, Morocco, flew a search pattern to the north but saw no sign of the vehicles.

Fears intensified after three days passed and Major Fairweather had still failed to report in. Mali government authorities were alerted and they cooperated fully, sending out military air and motorized vehicle patrols to backtrack the safari's known route across the desert.

Panic began to reign after the Malians failed to find any sighting of people or the Land Rovers during a concentrated search lasting four days. An army helicopter flew over Asselar and reported seeing nothing but a dead and abandoned village.

Then on the seventh day, a French oil prospecting team, pushing south along the Trans-Saharan Motor Track, discovered Major Ian Fairweather. The sky over the flat, rock-strewn plain was open and empty. The sun burned down and baked the sand so that the heat waves shimmered and danced. The French geologists were astonished when a distorted apparition suddenly appeared through a wavering heat mirage. One moment the image seemed to float free, and then expand and retract to grotesque proportions in the hot, freakish air.

As the range closed they distinguished a figure waving his arms like a crazy man and stumbling directly toward them.

Then he staggered to a stop, swayed like a small whirlwind, and slowly crumpled into the sand face first. The shocked driver of the Renault truck nearly braked too late and was forced to swerve around the fallen man, halting in a flurry of dust.

Fairweather was more dead than alive. He was badly dehydrated and the sweat on his body had crusted into a fine layer of white salt crystals. He soon regained consciousness as the French oil men slowly trickled water past his swollen tongue. Four hours later, his body fluids restored after drinking almost 2 gallons of water, Fairweather thickly croaked out the story of his escape from the massacre at Asselar.

To the one Frenchman on the prospecting team who understood English, Fairweather's tale sounded like a drunken fabrication, but it also rang with urgent conviction. After a brief discussion, the rescuers carefully lifted Fairweather into the back of the truck and headed toward the city of Gao on the Niger River. They arrived just before dark and drove straight to the city hospital.

After kindly seeing that Fairweather was comfortably bedded down and attended by a doctor and nurse, the French thought it wise to inform the Chief of the local Malian Security Forces. They were asked to write a lengthy report while the Colonel in command of Gao headquarters apprised his superiors in the capital city of Bamako.

To the Frenchman's surprise and indignation they were detained and jailed. In the morning an interrogation team arrived from Bamako and grilled them separately about their discovery of Fairweather. Demands to contact their consulate were ignored. When the oil geologists refused to cooperate, the interrogation turned ugly.

The French were not the first men to enter the city's security building and not be seen again.

When supervisors at the oil company headquarters in

Marseilles received no word from their oil exploration team, they became concerned and requested a search. The Malian Security Forces made a show of sweeping the desert again but claimed to have found nothing but the oil company's abandoned Renault truck.

The names of the French geologists and the missing tourists from Backworld Expeditions were simply added to the list of outsiders who disappeared and perished in the vast desert.

Dr Haroun Madani stood on the steps of the Gao hospital, beneath the brick portico with its unfathomable designs running around the top of the walls. He stared nervously down the dusty street running between the seedy old colonial buildings and the single-storey mud brick houses. A breeze from the north blew a light coating of sand over the city, once the capital of three great empires but now a decaying relic of French colonial days.

The call to evening prayers drifted over the city from the high-towered minarets that rose above the mosque. The faithful were no longer summoned to prayer by a Muslim holy man, or muezzin, who climbed the narrow steps inside the minarets and wailed from the balcony. Now the muezzin stayed on the ground and offered the prayers to Allah and the Prophet Muhammad through microphones and loudspeakers.

A short distance from the mosque, a three-quarter moon reflected its beam on the Niger River. Wide, scenic, its current slow and gentle, the Niger is a mere shadow of its former course. Once mighty and deep, decades of drought had lowered it to a shallow stream, plied by fleets of small sailing ships called pinnaces. Its waters once lapped at the base of the mosque. Now they sluggishly flowed nearly two city blocks away.

The Malian people are a mixture of the lighter-skinned descendants of the French and Berbers, the dark brown of the desert Arabs and Moors, and the black Africans. Dr Madani was coal black. His facial features were Negroid with deep-set ebony eyes and a wide flattened nose. He was a big bull of a man in his late forties, beefy around the middle, with wide square-jawed head.

His ancestors had been Mandingo slaves who were brought north by the Moroccans who overran the country in 1591. His parents had farmed the lush lands south of the Niger when he was a boy. He was raised by a major in the French Foreign Legion, educated and sent through medical school in Paris. Why or how this came about he was never told.

The doctor stiffened as the yellow headlights of an old and unique automobile swung into view. The car rolled quietly down the uneven street, its elegant rose-magenta-coloured body oddly out of sync amid the dismal and austere mud structures. There was an aura of dignified elegance about the 1936 Avions Voisin sedan. The design of the coachwork was an odd combination of pre-World War II aerodynamics, cubist art, and Frank Lloyd Wright. It was powered by a six-cylinder sleeve-valve engine that provided smooth silence and simple endurance. A masterwork of uncompromising engineering standards, it once belonged to the Governor General when Mali was a territory of French West Africa.

Madani knew the car. Almost every city dweller of Mali knew the car and its owner, and they shrank in nervous foreboding whenever it passed. The doctor observed that the car was followed by a military ambulance and he feared a problem. He stepped forward and opened the rear door as the driver braked to a perfectly noiseless stop.

A high-ranking military officer rose from the backseat and unlimbered a lean body inside a tailor-made uniform whose creases could have cut cold butter. Unlike other African leaders who listed to port under a mass of decorated hardware, General Zateb Kazim wore only one green and gold ribbon on the breast of his army jacket. Around his head, he wore an abbreviated version of the *litham*, the indigo veil of the Tuaregs. His face bore the dark cocoa shade and sculpted features of a Moor, and the eyes were tiny topaz dots surrounded by oceans of white. He might have been borderline handsome if it hadn't been for his nose. Instead of being straight and even, it rounded to a point, overhanging a sparse moustache that stretched off to the sides of his cheeks.

General Zateb Kazim looked like a benign villain out of an old Warner Brothers cartoon. There was no other way to describe him.

He oozed self-importance as he pompously brushed an imaginary speck of dust from his uniform. He acknowledged Dr Madani's presence with a slight nod.

'He is ready to be moved?' he asked in a measured tone.

'Mr Fairweather has fully recovered from his ordeal,' Madani answered, 'and is under strong sedation, as you ordered.'

'He's seen and talked to no one since being carried in by the Frenchmen?'

'Fairweather has only been tended by myself and a nurse from a tribe of Tukulor who speaks only in a Fulah dialect. He's had no other contact. I also carried out your instructions and admitted him to a private room away from the open wards. I might add that all records of his stay have been destroyed.'

Kazim appeared satisfied. 'Thank you, Doctor. I'm grateful for your cooperation.'

'May I ask where you're taking him?'

Kazim flashed a death's head grin. 'To Tebezza.'

'Not that!' Madani muttered thickly. 'Not the gold mines at the penal settlement of Tebezza. Only political traitors and murderers are condemned to die there. This man is a foreign national. What has he done to deserve a slow death in the mines?'

'It matters little.'

'What crime has he committed?'

Kazim looked Madani up and down as if the doctor was merely an annoying insect. 'Do not ask,' Kazim said coldly.

A dreadful thought crossed Madani's mind. 'And the Frenchmen who found Fairweather and brought him here?'

'The same fate.'

'None will last more than a few weeks in the mines.'

'Better than simply executing them,' shrugged Kazim. 'Let them work out the little time left of their pitiful lives doing something useful. A stockpile of gold is good for our economy.'

'You're a very sensible man, General,' said Madani, tasting the bile of his servile words. Kazim's sadistic power as a judge, jury, and hangman was a fact of Malian life.

'I'm happy you agree, Doctor.' He stared at Madani as though he was a prisoner in the dock. 'In the interests of our country's security I suggest you forget Mr Fairweather and erase all memory of his visit.'

Madani nodded. 'As you wish.'

'May no evil befall your people and goods.'

Kazim's thoughts were clear to the doctor. The words from the nomad-greeting ritual struck home. Madani had a large family. So long as he kept his silence they would live in peace. The alternative was not a vision he wished to dwell upon.

A few minutes later, an unconscious Fairweather was carried out of the hospital on a stretcher by two of Kazim's security guards and placed in the ambulance. The general gave Madani a casual salute and stepped into the Avions Voisin.

As the two vehicles moved off into the night, a chilling fear coursed through Dr Madani's veins, and he found himself wondering what terrible tragedy he had unwillingly participated in. Then he prayed that he would never know.

5

In one of the mural-walled suites of the Nile Hilton, Dr Frank Hopper listened attentively from a leather sofa. Seated in a nearby matching chair on the opposite side of a coffee table, Ismail Yerli puffed pensively on a meerschaum pipe whose bowl was carved in the likeness of the head of a turbaned sultan.

Even with the universal sounds of the busy Cairo traffic seeping in through the closed windows to the balcony Eva could not bring herself to accept the nightmare of her brush with death on the beach. Already her subconscious was blurring the memory. But Dr Hopper's voice pulled her thoughts back to the here and now of the conference room.

'There is no doubt in your mind these men tried to kill you?'

'None,' Eva answered.

'You described them as looking like black Africans,' said Ismail Yerli.

Eva shook her head. 'I didn't say black, only that their skin was dark. Their facial features were more sharp, more defined, like a cross between an Arab and an East Indian. The one who burned my car wore a loose-fitting tunic and a thick, intricately wrapped headdress. All I could see were his ebony eyes and a nose shaped like an eagle.'

'The headdress, was it cotton and swathed about the head and chin several times?' asked Yerli.

Eva nodded. 'The cloth seemed enormously long.'

'What colour was it?'

'A deep, almost ink blue.'

'Indigo?'

'Yes,' replied Eva. 'Indigo sounds about right.'

Ismail Yerli sat in silent contemplation for a few moments. He was the coordinator and logistics expert for the World Health Organization team. Lean and stringy, immensely efficient, and with an almost pathological love of detail, he was a smart operator with an abundance of political savvy. His home was in the Mediterranean seaport of Antalya, Turkey. He claimed Kurdish blood, having been born and raised in the Asia Minor hinterland of Cappadocia. A lukewarm Muslim, he had not been inside a mosque in years. Like most Turks he had a massive thicket of coarse black hair complemented by bushy eyebrows that met over the nose and were supplemented by a huge moustache. He displayed a humorous disposition that never quit. His mouth was always stretched in a smile that was a decoy for an extremely serious temperament.

'Tuaregs,' he said finally.

He spoke so softly that Hopper had to lean closer. 'Who?' he questioned.

Yerli looked across the coffee table at the Canadian leader of the medical team. A quiet man, Hopper said little but listened long. He was, the Turk mused, the complete opposite of himself. Hopper was big, humorous, red-faced, and heavily bearded. All he needed to look like the Viking, Eric the Red, was a battle axe and a conical helmet sunk on his head with horns curving from it. Resourceful, precise, and laid-back, he was regarded by international contamination scientists as one of the two finest toxicologists in the world.

'Tuaregs,' Yerli repeated. Once the mighty nomadic warriors of the desert, who won great battles against French and Moorish armies. And perhaps the greatest of all the romantic bandits. They raid no more. Today, they raise goats and beg in the cities bordering the Sahara to survive. Unlike Arab Muslims, the men wear the veil, a cloth that when unwrapped measures over a metre in length.

'But why would a tribe of desert nomads want to do away with Eva?' asked Hopper to no one in particular. 'I fail to see a motive.'

Yerli shook his head vaguely. 'It would seem that one of them, at least, does not want her, *and* − we have to heavily weigh this possibility − the rest of the health teams investigating the outbreaks of toxic poisoning in the southwestern desert.'

'At this point of the project,' said Hopper, 'we don't even know if contamination is the culprit. The mystery malady could be viral or bacterial.'

Eva nodded. 'That's what Pitt suggested.'

'Who?' Hopper asked for the second time.

'Dirk Pitt, the man who saved my life. He said somebody doesn't want me in Africa. He also thought you and the others might be on a hit list too.'

Yerli threw up his hands. 'Incredible, the man thinks we're dealing with the Sicilian Mafia.'

'Most fortunate he was nearby,' said Hopper.

Yerli exhaled a blue cloud from his meerschaum and stared at the smoke thoughtfully. 'More like opportune, considering the only other body on miles of shoreline had the courage to face a trio of assassins. Almost a miracle, or . . .' he stretched out the pause, 'a preconceived presence.'

Eva's eyes widened in scepticism. 'If you're thinking it was a setup, Ismail, you can forget it.'

'Maybe he staged the act to frighten you back to the States.'

'I saw him kill three men with my own eyes. Believe you me, there was nothing staged about it.'

'Have you heard from him since he dropped you off at the hotel?' queried Hopper.

'Only a message at the front desk asking me to have dinner with him this evening.'

'And you still think he was just a passing good samaritan,' Yerli persisted.

Eva ignored him and looked at Hopper. 'Pitt told me he was in Egypt for an archaeological survey of the Nile River for the National Underwater and Marine Agency. I have little reason to doubt him.'

Hopper turned to Yerli. 'That should be easy enough to check out.'

Yerli nodded. 'I'll call a friend who's a marine biologist with NUMA.'

'The question is still why?' muttered Hopper almost absently.

Yerli shrugged. 'If Eva's attempted murder was a conspiracy, it may well have been part of plot to instil fear and force us to cancel our mission.'

'Yes, but we have five separate research teams of six members each heading for the southern desert. They'll be spread across five nations from Sudan to Mauritania. No one forced us on them. Their governments asked the United Nations for help in finding an answer to the strange sickness sweeping their lands. We are invited guests, certainly not unwanted enemies.'

Yerli stared at Hopper. 'You're forgetting, Frank. There was one government who wanted no part of us.'

Hopper nodded grimly. 'You're right. I overlooked President Tahir of Mali. He was very reluctant to allow us inside his borders.'

'More likely General Kazim,' said Yerli. 'Tahir is a puppet head of state. Zateb Kazim is the true power behind the Malian government.'

'What's he got against harmless biologists trying to save lives?' asked Eva.

Yerli turned up his palms. 'We may never know.'

'It does seem a timely coincidence,' said Hopper softly, 'that people, especially Europeans, have been vanishing with

77

some regularity in the great emptiness of northern Mali during the past year.'

'Like the tourist safari that's making the headlines,' said Eva.

'Their whereabouts and fate are still a mystery,' added Yerli quietly.

'I can't believe there's a connection between that tragedy and Eva's attack,' said Hopper.

'But if we assume that General Kazim is the villain in Eva's case, it would stand to reason his spies ferreted out the fact that she was a member of the Malian biological studies team. With that knowledge in hand, he ordered her assassination as a warning for the rest of us to stay clear of his camel park.'

Eva laughed. 'With your fertile imagination, Ismail, you'd make a great Hollywood screenwriter.'

Yerli's thick eyebrows pinched together. 'I think we should play safe and keep the Mali team in Cairo until this matter can be fully investigated and resolved.'

'You're overreacting,' Hopper said to Yerli. ''How do you vote, Eva? Cancel the mission or go?'

'I'll risk it,' said Eva. 'But I can't speak for the other team members.'

Hopper stared at the floor, nodding his head. 'Then we'll ask for volunteers. I won't cancel the Mali mission, not with hundreds, maybe thousands, of people dying out there from something nobody can explain. I'll lead the team myself.'

'No, Frank!' snapped Eva. 'What if the worst happens? You're too valuable to lose.'

'It's our duty to report this affair to the police before you run off half-cocked,' Yerli persisted.

'Get serious, Ismail,' said Hopper impatiently. 'Go to the local police and they're liable to hold us up and delay the entire mission. We could be bound in red tape for a month. I'll not walk into the clutches of Middle East bureaucracy.'

'My contacts can cut the red tape,' pleaded Yerli.

'No,' Hopper said adamantly. 'I want all teams on board our chartered aircraft and in the air toward their designated locations as scheduled.'

'Then we're on for tomorrow morning,' said Eva.

Hopper nodded. 'No hang-ups, no rainchecks. We're going to put our show on the road first thing in the morning.'

'You're needlessly endangering lives,' murmured Yerli.

'Not if I take out insurance.'

Yerli looked at Hopper, not comprehending. 'Insurance?'

'Actually a press conference. Before we leave, I'll call in every foreign correspondent and news service in Cairo and explain our project with special emphasis on Mali. Of course, I'll make mention of the potential dangers involved. Then, in light of the international publicity surrounding our presence in his country, General Kazim will think twice before threatening the lives of scientists on a well-publicized mission of mercy.'

Yerli sighed heavily. 'For your sakes, I hope so. I truly hope so.'

Eva came over and sat down by the Turk. 'It will be all right,' she insisted quietly. 'No harm will come to us.'

'Nothing I can say will talk you out of it? You must go then?'

'There are thousands who might die if we don't,' said Hopper firmly.

Yerli stared sadly at them, then bowed his head in silent acceptance, his face suddenly pale.

'Then may Allah protect you, because if he doesn't, you will surely die.'

6

Pitt was standing in the lobby of the Nile Hilton when Eva stepped from the elevator. He was dressed in a tan poplin suit with single-breasted jacket and pleated pants. The shirt was a light shade of blue with a wide Botticelli tie of deep blue silk with black and gold paisleys.

He stood casual and loose, his hands clasped behind his back, head tilted slightly to one side, as he studied a beautiful, young, raven-haired Egyptian woman in a tight-fitting gold sequin dress. She was sweeping across the lobby in a blaze of glitter, hooked arm in arm with an elderly man easily three times her age. She jabbered every step across the carpet. Her ample bottom swung back and forth like a melon on a pendulum.

There was nothing in Pitt's expression to suggest lust. He stared at the performance with a detached sort of curiosity. Eva walked up behind him and placed her hand on his elbow. 'You like her?' she asked, smiling.

Pitt turned and looked down at her through the greenest eyes she had ever seen. His lips raised in a slight crooked grin that Eva found devastating. 'She *does* make a statement.'

'Is she your type?'

'No, I prefer quiet, intelligent women.'

His voice was deep with a mellow quality, she thought. She smelled a faint aroma of men's cologne, not the pungent variety brewed by French perfume companies for fashion designers' private labels, but a more masculine scent. 'I hope I can take that as a compliment.'

'You may.'

She flushed, and her eyes unconsciously lowered. 'I have an early-morning flight tomorrow, so I should get to bed early.' God, this is awful, she thought. I'm acting like a girl meeting her date for a freshman prom.

'A great pity. I'd planned to stay out all night and show you every den of iniquity and sin pot in Cairo. All the exotic spots unfrequented by tourists.'

'Are you serious?'

Pitt laughed. 'Not really. Actually, I thought it wise if we dine in your hotel and stay off the streets. Your friends might have it in their heads to try again.'

She looked around the crowded lobby. 'The hotel is packed. We'll be lucky to get a table.'

'I have reservations,' Pitt said, taking her by the hand and leading her into the elevator that rose to the posh restaurant on the top floor of the hotel.

Like most women, Eva liked a take-charge man. She also liked the way he kept his light but firm grip on her hand on the ride up to the restaurant.

The maitre d' showed them to a table beside a window with a spectacular view of Cairo and the Nile. A universe of lights sparkled in the evening haze. The bridges over the river were jammed with honking autos that fanned out on the streets and mingled with the horse-drawn delivery wagons and tourist carriages.

'Unless you prefer a cocktail,' said Pitt, 'I suggest that we stay with wine.'

Eva nodded and flashed a satisfied smile. 'Fine by me. Why don't you order the courses as well?'

'I love an adventurous soul,' he smiled. He studied the wine list briefly. 'We'll try a bottle of Grenaclis Village.'

'Very good,' the waiter said. 'One of our best local dry white wines.'

Pitt then ordered an appetizer dip of ground sesame seeds with eggplant, a yogurt dish called *leban zabadi*, and a tray of pickled vegetables with a basket of whole wheat pita bread.

After the wine came and was poured, Pitt raised his glass. 'Here's to a safe and successful field expedition. May you find all the answers.'

'And to your river survey,' she said as they clinked glasses. Then a curious expression came into her eyes. 'Just what is it you're looking for?'

'Ancient shipwrecks. One in particular. A funeral barge.'

'Sounds fascinating. Anybody I know?'

'A pharaoh of Old Kingdom called Menkura or Mycerinus, if you prefer the Greek spelling. He reigned during the Fourth Dynasty and built the smallest of the three pyramids at Giza.'

'Wasn't he entombed in his pyramid?'

'In 1830 a British army colonel found a body in a sarcophagus inside the burial chamber, but analysis of the remains proved it came from either the Greek or Roman periods.'

The appetizers were brought and they looked down at them with happy anticipation. They dipped fried slices of eggplant into the sesame seed dip and relished the pickled vegetables. While the waiter stood by, Pitt ordered the main course.

'Why do you think Menkura is in the river?' asked Eva.

'Hieroglyphic inscriptions on a stone that was recently discovered at an old quarry near Cairo show that his funeral barge caught fire and sank in the river between the ancient capital of Memphis and his pyramid tomb at Giza. The stone indicates his true sarcophagus, complete with his mummy and a vast amount of gold, was never recovered.'

The yogurt arrived, thick and creamy. Eva stared at it hesitantly.

'Try it,' goaded Pitt. 'Not only will *leban zabadi* spoil your taste for American yogurt, but it straightens out the intestines.'

'Curdles, you mean.' She played dainty and jabbed her tongue at a minute scoop in her spoon. Impressed, she began putting it away in earnest. 'So what happens if you find the barge? Do you get to keep the gold?'

'Hardly,' Pitt replied. 'Once our detection instruments have a promising target, we mark the site and turn the position over to archaeologists from the Egyptian Organization of Antiquities. After they obtain the necessary funding, their people will excavate, or in this case, dredge for artifacts.'

'Isn't the wreck just sitting on the bottom of the river?' Eva asked.

Pitt shook his head. 'The silt of forty-five centuries has covered and buried all remains.'

'How deep do you think it lies?'

'Can't say with any accuracy. Egyptian historical and geological records indicate that the main channel on the section of river we're searching has moved about 100 metres east since 2400 B.C. If she's on dry land near a bank, she could be anywhere from 3 to 10 metres beneath sand and mud.'

'I'm glad I listened to you, this yogurt is good.'

The waiter appeared deftly carrying a large silver tray with oval serving dishes. A spicy ground lamb cooked on skewers and crayfish grilled over charcoal were served along with a stewed kind of spinach green and a richly seasoned pilaf of beef, rice, raisins, and nuts. After consulting with the waiter who was so attentive he was downright patronizing, Pitt ordered a few pungent sauces for their entrées.

'So what sort of strange maladies are you going to investigate in the desert?' Pitt asked, as the steaming delights were dished onto their plates.

'Reports from Mali and Nigeria are too sketchy to make snap judgments. There have been rumours of the usual symptoms of toxic poisoning. Birth defects, convulsions or fits, coma and death. And also reports of psychiatric disorders and bizarre behaviour. This lamb is really tasty.'

'Try one of the sauces. The fermented berry complements the lamb.'

'What's the green one?'

'I'm not sure. It has a sweet and hot taste. Dip the crayfish in it.'

'Delicious,' Eva said. 'Everything tastes wonderful. Except for the spinach-like greens. The flavour is awfully strong.'

'They call it *moulukeyeh*. You have to acquire a taste for it. But back to toxin poisoning . . . What sort of bizarre behaviour?'

'People tearing their hair out, beating their heads against walls, sticking their hands in fire. Running around naked like animals on their hands and knees and eating their dead as if they suddenly turned into cannibals. This rice dish is good. What do they call it?'

'*Khalta*.'

'I wish I could get the recipe from the chef.'

'I think it can be arranged.' Pitt said. 'Did I hear you correctly? Those who are contaminated eat flesh?'

'Their reactions depend a great deal upon their culture,' said Eva, digging into the *khalta*. 'People in the third world countries, for example, are more used to slaughtered animals than people in Europe and the United States. Oh sure, we pass a road kill now and then, but they see skinned animals hanging in the markets or watch their fathers butcher the tribal goats or sheep. Children are taught early to catch and kill rabbits, squirrels, or birds, then skin and gut them for the grill. The primitive cruelty and the sight of blood and intestines are everyday events to those who live in poverty. They have to kill to survive. Then when tiny trace amounts of deadly toxins are digested and absorbed into their bloodstream over a long period of time, their systems deteriorate – the brain, the heart and liver, the intestines, even the genetic code. Their senses are dulled and they experience schizophrenia. Disintegration of moral codes and standards takes place. They no longer function as normal humans. To them, killing and eating a relative suddenly seems as ordinary as twisting a chicken's neck and preparing it for the evening dinner. I love that sauce with the chutney taste.'

'It's very good.'

'Especially with the *khalta*. We civilized people, on the other hand, buy nicely butchered, sliced meat in supermarkets. We don't witness cattle being brained with an electronic hammer, or sheep and pigs having their throats cut. We miss the fun part. So we're more conditioned to simply expressing fear, anxiety, and misery. A few might shoot up the landscape and kill the neighbours in a fit of madness, but we would never eat anyone.'

'What type of exotic toxin can cause those problems?' asked Pitt.

Eva drained her wine and waited until the waiter poured another glass. 'Doesn't have to be exotic. Common lead poisoning can make people do strange things. It also bursts capillaries and turns the whites of the eyes beet red.'

'Do you have room for dessert?' Pitt asked.

'Everything is so good, I'll make room.'

'Coffee or tea?'

'American coffee.'

Pitt motioned to the waiter who was on him like a skier attacking fresh snow. 'An *Um Ali* for the lady and two coffees. One American, one Egyptian.'

'What's an *Um Ali?*' asked Eva.

'A hot bread pudding with milk and topped with pine nuts. Soothes the stomach after a heavy meal.'

'Sounds just right.'

Pitt leaned back in his chair, his craggy face set in concern.

'You said you're catching a flight tomorrow. Do you still intend to go to Mali?'

'Still playing the role of my protector?'

'Travelling in the desert can be a murderous business. Heat won't be your only enemy. Someone out there is waiting to kill you and your fellow do-gooders.'

'And my knight in shining white armour won't be there to save me,' she said with a tinge of sarcasm. 'You don't frighten me. I can take care of myself.'

Pitt stared at her, and she could see a look of sadness in his eyes. 'You're not the first woman who said that and wound up in the morgue.'

In a ballroom in another part of the hotel Dr Frank Hopper was wrapping up a news conference. It was a good turnout. A small army of correspondents representing newspapers around the Middle East and four international wire services were besieging him with questions under a battery of lights from local Egyptian TV cameras.

'How widespread do you believe the environmental pollution is, Dr Hopper?' asked a lady from Reuters News Service.

'We won't know until our teams are in the field and have a chance to study the spread.'

A man with a tape recorder waved his hand. 'Do you have a source of the contamination?'

Hopper shook his head. 'At the moment we have no idea where it's coming from.'

'Any possibility it might be the French solar detoxification project in Mali?'

Hopper walked over to a map of the southern Sahara that was hung on a large display stand and picked up a pointer. He aimed the tip at a desolate region of desert in the northern section of Mali. 'The French project is located here at Fort Foureau, well over 200 kilometres from the closest

86

area of reported contamination sickness. Too far for it to be a direct source.'

A German correspondent from *Der Spiegel* stood up. 'Couldn't the pollution be carried by winds?'

Hopper shook his head. 'Not possible.'

'How can you be so certain?'

'During the planning and construction stages, my fellow scientists and I at the World Health Organization were consulted every step of the way by the engineers of the Massarde Entreprises de Solaire Energie who own the facility. All hazardous waste is destroyed by solar energy and reduced to harmless vapour. The output is constantly monitored. No toxic emission is left to be carried on the wind and infect life hundreds of kilometres away.'

An Egyptian television reporter thrust a microphone forward. 'Are you receiving cooperation from the desert nations you plan to enter?'

'Most all have invited us with open arms,' answered Hopper.

'You mentioned earlier there was reluctance on the part of President Tahir of Mali to allow your research team into his country.'

'That's true, but once we're on site and demonstrate our humane intentions, I expect that he'll have a change of heart.'

'So you don't feel you are endangering lives by prying into the affairs of President Tahir's government?'

The beginnings of anger stirred in Hopper's voice. 'The real danger is malaise in the minds of his advisors. They ignore the sickness as if it doesn't exist by letting it go officially unnoticed.'

'But do you think it is safe for your team to travel about Mali freely?' asked the correspondent from Reuters.

Hopper smiled a shrewd smile. The questions had turned in the direction he had hoped. 'If tragedy should occur, I count on you, the ladies and gentlemen of the news media, to investigate and lay the wrath of the world on the doorstep of the guilty party.'

After dinner, Pitt escorted Eva to her hotel door. She fumbled with the key nervously, unsure of herself. She certainly had the excuse, she told herself, to invite him in. She owed him, and she wanted him. But Eva played by the rules of the old school and found it difficult to leap into bed with every man who showed an interest in her, even one who had saved her life.

Pitt noticed the faint shade of red rising from her neck into her face. He looked down into her eyes. They were as blue as a South Seas sky. He took her by the shoulders and gently pulled her to him. She tensed slightly but offered no resistance. 'Postpone your flight.'

She averted her face. 'I can't.'

'We may not meet again.'

'I am bound by my work.'

'And when you're free?'

'I'll return to my family home in Pacific Grove, California.'

'A beautiful area. I've often entered a classic car in the Pebble Beach Concours d'Elegance.'

'It's lovely in June,' she said, her voice suddenly trembling.

He smiled. 'Then it's you and I and the Bay of Monterey.'

It was as if they had become friends on an ocean voyage, a brief interlude that planted the seed of mutual attraction. He kissed her softly, and then stepped back. 'Stay out of harm's way. I don't want to lose you.'

Then he turned and walked toward the elevators.

7

For a century of centuries Egyptians and the vegetation have fought to maintain their precious toehold between the pewter-blue waters of the Nile and the yellow-brown sands of the Sahara. Winding 6500 kilometres from its headwaters in Central Africa to the Mediterranean, only the Nile of all the great rivers of the world flows north. Ancient, always present, ever alive. The Nile is as alien to the arid North African landscape as it would be in the steamy atmosphere of the planet Venus.

The hot season had arrived along the river. The heat rolled over and settled on the water like an oppressive blanket pulled from the great sprawling desert to the west. The dawn sun came over the horizon with the fiery thrust of a poker, spawning a slight breeze that felt like a blast from an open furnace.

The serenity of the past met the technology of the present as a lateen-rigged felucca, manned by four young boys, sailed past a sleek research boat laden with state-of-the-art electronic gear. Seemingly little inconvenienced by the heat, the boys laughed and waved at the turquoise-coloured boat heading on an opposite course downriver.

Pitt lifted his eyes from the high-resolution video screen of the subbottom profiler and waved back through a large port. The oven outside bothered him not at all. The interior of the research vessel was well air conditioned, and he sat comfortably in front of the computerized detection array sipping a glass of iced tea. He watched the felucca for a few moments, almost envying the boys as they scampered about the small deck and unfurled the sail to catch the breeze blowing upriver.

He turned his attention back to the monitor as an irregular anomaly began to creep across the screen in coloured imagery. The vertical scan sensor of the subbottom profiler was recording a contact deep beneath the bottom silt below the moving water. At first it was merely an indistinct blob, but as the image was automatically enhanced the outline of an ancient ship began to materialize.

'Target coming up,' Pitt reported. 'Mark it number ninety-four.'

Al Giordino punched in a code on his console. Instantly, the configuration of the river along with man-made landmarks and natural features behind the shoreline flashed into view on an on-line graphics display. Another code and the satellite laser-positioning system pinpointed with precise accuracy the image's exact position as it related to the surrounding landscape.

'Number ninety-four plotted and recorded,' Giordino acknowledged.

Short, dark, and as compact as a barrel of concrete, Albert Giordino gazed through twinkling walnut eyes that sat under a wild mane of curly black hair. Give him a flowing beard and a sack of toys, Pitt often thought, and Giordino could have played a young version of an Etruscan Santa Claus.

Tremendously fast for a muscular man, he could fight like a tiger, and yet suffer the agonies of the damned if he was forced into conversing with women. Giordino and Pitt went back to high school together, played football at the Air Force Academy, and served in the final days of Vietnam. At one point in their service careers, at the request of Admiral James Sandecker, Chief Director of the National Underwater and Marine Agency, they were loaned out to NUMA on temporary status, a condition that had now stretched into nine years.

Neither man could remember how many times one had

saved the life of the other, or at least prevented a very embarrassing situation that usually resulted out of some sort of devious mischief. Yet their escapades above and below the sea had become legendary, resulting in a certain amount of fame neither relished.

Pitt bent forward and focused on a digital isometric screen. The computer rotated the three-dimensional image, displaying the buried ship in amazing detail. The image and dimensions were recorded and communicated to a data processor where they were compared with known data of ancient Egyptian Nile boats. In a few seconds the computer analysed a profile and made its call. Data on the vessel's construction blinked across the bottom of the screen.

'What we've got here seems to be a cargo vessel from the Sixth Dynasty,' Pitt read out. 'Built somewhere between 2000 and 2200 B.C.'

'Her condition?' asked Giordino.

'Quite good,' replied Pitt. 'Like the others we found, she is well preserved by the silt. Her hull and rudder are still intact, and I can make out the mast lying across her deck. What's her depth?'

Giordino studied his data-positioning screen. 'She's under 2 metres of water and 8 metres of silt.'

'Any metal?'

'Nothing the proton mag could detect.'

'Not surprising since iron wasn't known in Egypt until the twelfth century B.C. What do you read on the nonferrous scan?'

Giordino twisted a dial on his console. 'Not much. A few bronze fittings. Probably an abandoned derelict.'

Pitt studied the imagery of the ship that had sunk in the river forty centuries ago. 'Fascinating, how the design of the vessels remained virtually unchanged for three thousand years.'

'Goes with their art,' said Giordino.

Pitt looked at him. 'Art?'

'Did you ever notice that their art style stayed exactly the same from the First Dynasty to the thirtieth,' Giordino pontificated. 'Even bodily positions remained static. Why hell, in all that time they never figured out how to show the human eye from a side view by simply drawing it in half. Talk about tradition. The Egyptians were masters at it.'

'When did you become an expert on Egyptology?'

True to type, Giordino gave a worldly wise shrug. 'Oh I've picked it up here and there.'

Pitt was not fooled. Giordino had a sharp eye for detail. He seldom missed much, as proven by his observation of Egyptian art that went unnoticed by over 99 per cent of the tourists and was never mentioned by the guides.

Giordino finished a beer and rolled the cold bottle over his forehead. He pointed a finger at the shipwreck as the research boat passed over and the image began to slip off the screen. 'Hard to believe we've found ninety-four wrecks after surveying only 2 miles of river. Some stacked three deep.'

'Not so incredible when you consider how many thousands of years boats have been sailing the Nile,' Pitt lectured. 'Vessels of all civilizations were lucky to last twenty years before being lost by storm, fire, and collision. And those that survived usually rotted away from neglect. The Nile between the Delta and Khartoum has more sunken vessels per square kilometre than any other place on earth. Fortunately for archaeologists, the wrecks were covered over with silt and preserved. They could well last another four thousand years before they're excavated.'

'No sign of cargo,' said Giordino, peering over Pitt's shoulder at the vanishing ship. 'As you suggested, she probably outlived her usefulness and her owners let her deteriorate until she sank as a derelict.'

The pilot of the research boat, Gary Marx, kept one eye trained on the echo sounder while scanning the river ahead with the other. A tall blond with limpid blue eyes, he wore only shorts, sandals, and a rancher's straw hat. He quarter turned his head and spoke out of the side of his mouth. 'That finishes the down-stream run, Dirk.'

'Okay,' Pitt replied. 'Swing around and make another run as close as you can to the shoreline.'

'We're practically scraping bottom now,' Marx said flatly, without due concern. 'If we come any closer we'll have to tow the boat with a tractor.'

'No need for hysterics,' Pitt said dryly. 'Just bring us around, hug the riverbank, and mind we don't snag the sensor.'

Expertly, Marx turned the boat into the main channel, made a sweeping U-turn, and brought her parallel to the shore at a distance of no more than 5 or 6 metres. Almost immediately, the sensors picked up another wreck. The computer profiled this one as a nobleman's personal ship from the Middle Kingdom, 2040 to 1786 B.C.

The hull was slimmer than those of the cargo ships, and a cabin graced its afterdeck. They could see the remains of a guard rail running around the deck. The tops of the support posts looked to be carved with lions' heads. There was a wide gash in the port side, suggesting it sank after a collision with another ship.

Eight more ancient ships were discovered beneath the silt and duly recorded before the sensors struck the big casino.

Pitt straightened, his eyes set in concentration as an image, far larger than the previous contacts, sailed across his monitor. 'We have a royal barge!' he called out.

'Marking position,' Giordino acknowledged. 'You sure it has *pharaoh* written on it?'

'As pretty a picture as we'll ever see. Take a look.'

Giordino studied the growing image. 'Looking good. No sign of a mast. She's too large for anyone but royalty to own.'

The hull was long, with a delicate taper toward the ends. The stern stem was sculpted in the shape of a falcon's head, representing the Egyptian god Horus, but the forward section of the bow was missing. The high-resolution enhancement of the computer revealed the sides of the hull to be decorated with over a thousand carved hieroglyphics. There was a royal cabin that was also ornately carved. Banks of what remained of the oars still protruded from the hull. The rudder was a massive affair that looked like a huge canoe paddle and was braced to the side of the stern. The main attraction, though, was the great rectangular shape that sat on a deck platform amidships. It too bore carved sculptures.

Both men collectively held their breath as the computer hummed away. Then the profile swept across the screen.

'A stone sarcophagus,' blurted Giordino with uncharacteristic excitement. 'We've got a sarcophagus.' He rushed over to his console and checked the readings. 'The nonferrous scan shows large amounts of metal inside the cabin area and the sarcophagus.'

'Pharaoh Menkura's gold,' Pitt murmured softly.

'What do we have for a date?'

'Twenty-six hundred B.C. The time frame and configuration are right on the money,' Pitt said, smiling broadly. 'And the computer analysis shows charred wood forward, indicating the bow as burned away.'

'Then we have Menkura's missing funeral barge.'

'I wouldn't bet against it,' said Pitt, his expression set in absolute euphoria.

Marx anchored the research boat directly over the wreck site. Then for the next six hours, Pitt and Giordino subjected the funeral barge to a battery of electronic scans and probes, accumulating an extensive record of its condition and disposition for Egyptian authorities.

'God, how I wish we could get a camera inside the cabin and sarcophagus.' Giordino opened another beer but promptly forgot to drink it in the excitement.

'The inner coffins of the sarcophagus might be intact,' said Pitt. 'But the dampness has probably rotted away most of the mummy. As to the artifacts . . . who's to say? They might possibly equal the treasures of Tutankhamen.'

'Menkura was a far bigger nabob than King Tut. He must have carried a larger hoard with him for the afterlife.'

'Well we won't see any of it,' Pitt said, stretching his arms to the cabin ceiling. 'We'll be dead and buried ourselves before the Egyptians find the funding to raise and preserve the wreck for the Cairo museum.'

'Visitors,' Marx alerted them. 'An Egyptian river patrol boat approaching downriver.'

'Word travels fast around here,' said Giordino incredulously. 'Who could have tipped them off?'

'A routine patrol,' said Pitt. 'They'll pass by in midchannel.'

'They're coming straight toward us,' warned Marx.

'So much for a routine patrol,' grunted Giordino.

Pitt stood and removed a file folder from a cabinet. 'They're just being nosy and want to check us out. I'll meet them on deck with our permits from the antiquities office.'

He walked through the cabin door into the roasting air outside and stood on the open stern deck. The froth of the bow-wave died away to a series of ripples, the metallic hum of the twin diesels loping on idle as the dark grey patrol boat slipped alongside less than a metre away.

Pitt gripped a railing as the wash rocked the research vessel. He watched casually as two seamen, dressed in the uniform of the Egyptian navy, leaned over the sides and held the patrol boat at bay with padded boat hooks. He could see the captain inside the wheelhouse and was mildly surprised when a hand was raised in a friendly salute but no attempt was made to board. His surprise turned to astonishment when a wiry little man leaped over the gunwales and landed lightly on the deck almost on Pitt's feet.

Pitt gaped at him incredulously. 'Rudi! Where in hell did you drop from?'

Rudi Gunn, the Deputy Director of NUMA, smiled broadly and pumped Pitt's hand. 'Washington. Landed at the Cairo airport less than an hour ago.'

'What brings you to the Nile?'

'Admiral Sandecker sent me to pull you and Al off your project. I have a NUMA plane waiting to fly us to Port Harcourt. The Admiral will meet us there.'

'Where's Port Harcourt?' Pitt asked blankly.

'A seaport on the delta of the Niger River in Nigeria.'

'What's the big hurry? You could have instructed us by satellite communications. Why make the time and effort to tell us in person?'

Gunn made a negative gesture with his hands. 'I can't say. The Admiral didn't make me privy to the reason for secrecy or the mad rush.'

If Rudi Gunn didn't know what Sandecker had up his sleeve, no one did. He was slim, with narrow shoulders and matching hips. Extremely competent, a master of logistics, Gunn was a graduate of Annapolis and a former Commander in the Navy. He had come on board NUMA at the same time as Pitt and Giordino. Gunn stared at the world through thick horn-rimmed glasses and spoke past lips that were most always curled in a mischievous grin. Giordino likened him to an IRS agent about to make a kill.

'Your timing is ideal,' said Pitt. 'Come on inside. Let's get out of the heat. I've something I want to show you.'

Giordino had his back to the cabin door as Pitt and Gunn entered. 'What did the goochers want?' he asked irritably.

'For you to drop dead,' Gunn answered, laughing.

Giordino spun around, recognizing the little man, and

affecting great surprise. 'Oh for God's sake!' He came to his feet and shook Gunn's outstretched hand. 'What are you doing here?'

'To transfer you to another project.'

'Great timing.'

'My thoughts exactly,' Pitt grinned.

'Hi, Mr Gunn,' greeted Gary Marx, ducking into the electronics cabin. 'Good to have you on board.'

'Hello, Gary.'

'Am I being transferred too?'

Gunn shook his head. 'No, you have to stay here on the project. Dick White and Stan Shaw will be arriving tomorrow to replace Dirk and Al.'

'A waste of time,' said Marx. 'We're ready to wrap up.'

Gunn stared at Pitt questioningly for a moment, then understanding grew in concert with his widening eyes. 'The pharaoh's funeral barge,' he muttered. 'You found it?'

'A lucky hit,' Pitt revealed. 'And only the second day on the job.'

'Where?' Gunn blurted.

'You're standing on it, in a manner of speaking. She's resting 9 metres under our keel.'

Pitt displayed the digital isometric model of the wreck on the computer monitor. The hours spent in enhancing the coloured imagery paid off with a vivid, extremely detailed view of every square metre of the centuries-old ship.

'Indescribable,' muttered Gunn in awe.

'We've also recorded and positioned over a hundred other wrecks dating from 2800 B.C. to 1000 A.D.,' said Giordino.

'Congratulations to the three of you,' Gunn beamed warmly. 'You've pulled off an incredible accomplishment. One for the history books. The Egyptian government will pin medals on you.'

'And the Admiral?' Giordino asked succinctly. 'What will he pin on us?'

Gunn turned from the monitor and looked at them, his face suddenly turned dead serious. 'A dirty, rotten job, I suspect.'

'Didn't he drop a hint?' Pitt pressed.

'Nothing that made any sense.' Gunn stared at the ceiling, recalling. 'When I asked him why the urgency, he quoted a verse. I don't remember the exact words. Something about a ship's shadow and charmed water being red.'

Pitt quoted:

> *Her beams bemocked the sultry main,*
> *Like April hoarfrost spread;*
> *But where the ship's huge shadow lay,*
> *The charmèd water burnt alway,*
> *A still and awful red.*

'A verse from "The Rime of the Ancient Mariner" by Samuel Taylor Coleridge.'

Gunn looked at Pitt with new respect. 'I didn't know you could quote poetry.'

Pitt laughed. 'I memorized a few verses, that's all.'

'I wonder what Sandecker has on his evil mind?' said Giordino. 'Not like the old buzzard to get cryptic.'

'No,' Pitt said with uneasy trepidation, 'not like him at all.'

8

The pilot of the Massarde Enterprises helicopter flew north and eastward from the capital city of Bamako. For two and a half hours the vast desolation unrolled below like miniature scenery pasted on a scroll. After two hours, he spotted the sun's glint off steel rails in the distance. He banked and began following the tracks that seemingly travelled to nowhere.

The railroad, only completed the month before, ended at the immense solar waste detoxification project in the heart of the Malian desert. The facility was called Fort Foureau after a long-abandoned French Foreign Legion fort several miles away. From the project site the tracks ran 1600 kilometres in a nearly straight line across the border into Mauritania before finally terminating at the man-made port of Cape Tafarit on the Atlantic Ocean.

General Kazim peered from the lush comfort of the executive helicopter as the pilot caught and passed a long train of sealed, hazardous waste container cars pulled by two diesel locomotives. The train was outbound to Mauritania, having emptied its deadly cargo and turned around.

He smiled craftily as he turned his stare from the waste cars and nodded to the steward, who refreshed his glass of champagne and offered a tray of hors d'oeuvres.

The French, Kazim mused, they never seemed out of reach of champagne, truffles, and pâté. He considered them an insular race who only halfheartedly tried to build and maintain an empire. How the general citizenry must have sighed with collective relief, he thought, when they were forced to give up their outposts in Africa and the Far East. Deep down it angered him that the French had not disappeared entirely from Mali. Though they severed their colonial leash in 1960, the French had maintained their influence and a taut grip on the economy, exercising strong control over most all of the nation's mining, transportation, industrial and energy development. Many French businessmen saw investment opportunity and bought heavily into Malian ventures. But none had dug their money shovel deeper in the Sahara sands than Yves Massarde.

Once the wizard of France's overseas economic agency, Massarde had carved a profitable niche on the side, using his contacts and influence to take over and turn around ailing West African corporations. A tough and shrewd negotiator, his methods were cutthroat and it was rumoured that he was not above using strongarm tactics to consummate a deal. His wealth was estimated to be between two and three billion dollars, and the hazardous waste disposal project in the Sahara at Fort Foureau was the centrepiece of his empire.

The helicopter arrived over the sprawling complex, and the pilot swung around the perimeter to give Kazim a good view of the sprawling solar detoxification complex and its vast field of parabolic mirrors that collected solar energy and sent it to concentrating receivers, creating an incredible 60,000 suns with temperatures as high as 5000 degrees C. This superheated photon energy was then directed to photochemical reactors that destroyed the molecules of hazardous chemicals.

The General had seen it all several times, and he was more interested in selecting another bite of truffled goose pâté. He was just finishing his sixth glass of Veuve Clicquot Gold Label champagne when the helicopter slowly settled onto the flight pad in front of the project's engineering offices.

Kazim stepped to the ground and saluted Felix Verenne,

the personal aide of Massarde, who stood waiting in the sun. Kazim gloated at seeing the Frenchman suffering from the heat. 'Felix, how good of you to greet me,' he spoke in French, his teeth flashing beneath his moustache.

'Did you enjoy your journey?' Verenne asked patronizingly.

'The pâté was not up to your chef's usual standards.'

A slender, bald-headed man in his forties, Verenne forced a smile over his inner disgust for Kazim. 'I'll see that it meets with your approval on the return flight.'

'And how is Monsieur Massarde?

'He's waiting for you in his executive suite.'

Verenne led the way under an awning-covered walkway into a three-storey black solar glass building with rounded corners. Inside, they crossed a marble lobby that was totally deserted, except for one security guard, and entered an elevator. The doors opened onto a teak-panelled entry hall that led to the main salon that doubled as Massarde's living quarters and office. Verenne showed Kazim into a small but luxuriously decorated study and pointed to a Roche Bobois leather sofa.

'Please have a seat. Monsieur Massarde will be with you – '

'But Felix, I am here,' came a voice from the opposite doorway. Massarde stepped forward and embraced Kazim. 'Zateb, my friend, how good of you to come.'

Yves Massarde had blue eyes, black brows, and reddish hair. His nose was slender and his jaw square. The body was thin and the hips trim, but the stomach protruded. Nothing about him seemed to match. But it was not his physical impression that lingered in the memories of those he met. They only remembered the intensity that burst from within his being in a manner like that of static electricity.

He gave a knowing look to Verenne, who nodded and quietly left the room, closing the door behind.

101

'Now then, Zateb, my agents in Cairo inform me that your people made a fiasco of frightening the World Health Organization from coming to Mali.'

'A regrettable circumstance,' Kazim shrugged indifferently. 'The reasons are unclear.'

Massarde gave the general a hard stare. 'According to my sources of information, your assassins disappeared during a botched attempt to kill Dr Eva Rojas.'

'A penalty for their inefficient handling of the matter.'

'You executed them?

'I do not tolerate failure from my people,' Kazim lied. The failure of his men to kill Eva and their strange disappearance had baffled him. In frustration he had ordered the death of the officer who planned the murder, accusing him and the others of betraying his commands.

Massarde did not get where he was without being a shrewd judge of personalities. He knew Kazim well enough to suspect the general of laying a smoke screen. 'If we have outside enemies, it would be a grave mistake to ignore them.'

'It was nothing,' Kazim said, dismissing the subject. 'Our secret is safe.'

'You say that when a UN World Health team of contamination experts is landing at Gao within the hour? Do not treat this matter lightly, Zateb. If they trace the source here – '

'They won't find anything but sand and heat,' Kazim interrupted. 'You know better than I, Yves, whatever is causing the strange sickness near the Niger cannot be coming from here. I see no way your project can be responsible for pollution hundreds of kilometres to the east and south of here.'

'That's true,' Massarde said thoughtfully. 'Our monitoring systems show that the waste we burn for appearance sake is well within the stringent limits set by international policy standards.'

'So what's to worry,' shrugged Kazim.

'Nothing, so long as every avenue is covered.'

'Leave the UN research team to me.'

'Do not hinder them,' Massarde warned quickly.

'The desert takes care of intruders.'

'Kill them and Mali and Massarde Enterprises will be at great risk of exposure. Their leader, Dr Hopper, called a news conference in Cairo and played on the lack of cooperation from your government. He went on record as claiming his research team might encounter danger after their arrival. Scatter their bones around the desert, my friend, and we'll have an army of news reporters and UN investigators swarming over the project.'

'You weren't squeamish about having Dr Rojas removed.'

'Yes, but the attempt was not in our backyard where there could be suspicion of our involvement.'

'Nor were you disturbed when half of your engineers and their wives went for a picnic drive into the dunes and vanished.'

'Their disappearance was necessary to protect the second phase of our operation.'

'You were fortunate I was able to cover the situation without headlines in Paris newspapers or on-site investigations by French government agents.'

'You did well,' Massarde sighed. 'I could not do without your esteemed talents.' Like most of his desert countrymen, Kazim could not exist without perpetual compliments to his genius. Massarde loathed the General, but the clandestine operation could not exist without him. It was a contract made in hell by two evil men with Massarde getting the top end of the deal. He could afford to put up with the camel turd, as he called Kazim behind his back. After all, a payoff of fifty thousand American dollars a month was a pittance against the two million dollars a day Massarde was reaping from the waste disposal project.

Kazim walked over to a well-stocked bar and helped himself to a cognac. 'So how do you suggest we handle Dr Hopper and his staff?'

'You are the expert in these matters,' Massarde said with oily charm. 'I leave it to your skills.'

Kazim lifted a smug eyebrow. 'Elementary, my friend. I simply eliminate the problem they came to solve.'

Massarde seemed curious. 'How do you accomplish that?'

'I've already made a start,' answered Kazim. 'I sent my personal brigade to round up, shoot, and bury any victims of contamination sickness.'

'You'd slaughter your own people?' Massarde's voice was ironic.

'I'm only doing my patriotic duty to stamp out a national plague,' replied Kazim with more than a hint of indifference.

'Your methods are a bit extreme.' A worried crease appeared in Massarde's face. 'I caution you, Zateb, do not provoke an uproar. If the world accidentally discovers what we truly do here, an international tribunal will hang us both.'

'Not without evidence or witnesses, they won't.'

'What about those freakish devils who massacred the tourists at Asselar? Did you make them disappear too?'

Kazim gave a callous smile. 'No, they killed and ate themselves. But there are other villages suffering the same maladies. Should Dr Hopper and his party become overly annoying, perhaps I can see they witness a massacre firsthand.'

Massarde didn't need an illustrated explanation. He'd read Kazim's secret report of the slaughter at Asselar. His mind easily pictured disease-crazed nomads literally swallowing up the UN investigators as they had the tourist safari.

'A most efficient means of eliminating a threat,' he said to Kazim. 'It saves the expense of a burial party.'

'I agree.'

'But if one or two of them should survive and attempt to return to Cairo?'

Kazim shrugged, the thin bloodless lips under the moustache parted in an evil smile. 'Regardless of how they die, their bones will never leave the desert.'

9

Ten thousand years ago the sand-dry wadis of the Republic of Mali ran full to their banks with water while the barren flatlands were blanketed with forests filled with hundreds of varieties of plant life. The fertile plains and mountains were home to early man long before he rose out of the stone age and became a pastoral herdsman. For the next seven thousand years vast tribes hunted antelopes, elephants, and buffaloes as they herded their long-horned cattle from one grazing ground to another.

In time, overgrazing along with the decreasing rains caused the Sahara to dry out and become the barren desert it is today, ever expanding, ever creeping into the lusher, more tropical lands of the African continent. The great tribes gradually abandoned the region, leaving behind a desolate and nearly waterless area to the few nomadic bands who have lingered on.

By discovering the incredible endurance of the camel, the Romans were the first to conquer the desert wastes, utilizing the beast to carry slaves, gold, ivory, and many thousands of wild animals for shipment to the bloody arenas of Rome. For eight centuries their caravans plodded across the nothingness from the Mediterranean to the banks of the Niger. And when the glory of Rome faded, it was the camel that opened the Sahara frontier to the invading, light-skinned Berbers, who were followed by the Arabs and the Moors.

Mali represents the end of a line of powerful and long-vanished empires to rule black Africa. In the early Middle Ages the kingdom of Ghana expanded the great caravan routes between the Niger River, Algeria, and Morocco. In 1240 A.D., Ghana was destroyed by the Mandingos to the south who emerged as an even greater empire called Malinke, the basis of the name Mali. Great prosperity was achieved and the cities of Gao and Timbuktu became widely respected as the centres of Islamic learning and culture.

Legends were spun of the incredible wealth carried by the gold caravans, and the empire's fame spread through the Middle East. But two hundred years later, the empire had spiralled into decay as the Tuareg and Fulane nomads encroached from the north. The Songhai people to the east gradually took control and ruled until the Moroccan sultans pushed their armies to the Niger and devastated the kingdom in 1591. By the time the French launched their colonial flow southward in the early nineteenth century, the old empires of Mali were all but forgotten.

After the turn of the century, the French established the territories of West Africa into what became known as the French Sudan. In 1960, Mali declared its independence, drew up a constitution, and formed a government. The nation's first president was removed by a group of army officers led by Lieutenant Moussa Traore. In 1992, after a number of unsuccessful coup attempts, President (now General) Traore was overthrown by (then Major) Zateb Kazim.

Soon realizing he could not obtain foreign aid or loans as a military dictator, Kazim stepped down and installed the current President Tahir as a figurehead. A cunning manipulator, Kazim stacked the legislature with his cronies and kept his distance from the Soviet Union and the United States while maintaining close relations with France.

He soon set himself up as overseer of all trade, domestic and foreign, enriching a number of his secret bank accounts throughout the world. He dipped into development projects and despite installing strict customs controls, profited handsomely on the side from smuggling activities. French business payoffs for his cooperation, such as his association with Yves Massarde, made him a multimillionaire. Thanks to Kazim's absolute corruption and the greed of his officials, it was little wonder that Mali was one of the world's poorest nations.

The UN Boeing 737 banked so close to the ground Eva thought its wing tip would cut a groove through the mud and timber houses. Then the pilot levelled out on his approach to the primitive airport at the fabled city of Timbuktu and touched down with a firm thump. Gazing out her window, Eva found it difficult to imagine that the grubby town was once the great caravan market of the empires of Ghana, Malinke, and Songhai, and was inhabited by a hundred thousand people. Founded by Tuareg nomads as a seasonal camp in 1100 A.D., it became one of the largest trading centres in West Africa.

She found it difficult to envision a glorious past. But for three of the ancient mosques still standing, there were few sights of past grandeur. The town looked dead and abandoned, its narrow and crooked streets twisting around and seemingly going nowhere in particular. Its grip on life appeared tenuous and fruitless.

Hopper wasted no time. He was out the cabin door and on the ground before the whine of the jet engines died away. An officer, wearing the brief indigo headdress of Kazim's personal guard, walked up to him and saluted. He greeted the UN field researcher in English with a marked French accent.

'Dr Hopper, I presume.'

'And you must be Mr Stanley,' Hopper replied with his usual cutting humour.

There was no answering smile. The Malian officer gave Hopper an unfriendly look that was obviously coated with harboured suspicions. 'I am Captain Mohammed Batutta.

You will please accompany me to the airport terminal.'

Hopper stared at the terminal. It was little more than a metal shed with windows. 'Oh very well, if that's the best you can do,' he said dryly, refusing to kowtow.

They walked straight to the terminal and into a small, oven-hot office that was bare except for a shabby, wooden table and two chairs. Behind the table an officer, who was senior to Batutta and looked like he was going through a very unhappy phase, sat and studied Hopper for a moment with undisguised contempt.

'I am Colonel Nouhoum Mansa. May I see your passport please?'

Hopper had come prepared and handed over the six passports he'd collected from his team. Mansa flipped through the pages without interest, noting only the nationalities. Finally he asked, 'Why did you come to Mali?'

Hopper had travelled the world and had little use for ridiculous formality. 'I believe you know the purpose of our visit.'

'You will answer the question.'

'We're members of the United Nations World Health Organization on a mission to study reports of toxic illness among your people.'

'There is no such illness among my people,' the Colonel said firmly.

'Then you won't mind if we analyse water supplies and take air samples in a random selection of the towns and cities along the Niger.'

'We do not take kindly to foreigners seeking out deficiencies in our country.'

Hopper was not about to back down in the face of stupid authority. 'We're here to save lives. I thought General Kazim understood that.'

Mansa tensed. The fact that Hopper threw out Kazim's name instead of President Tahir caught him off guard.

'General Kazim . . . he's given orders authorizing your visit?'

'Why don't you ring him up and find out?' It was a bluff, but Hopper had nothing to lose.

Colonel Mansa rose and walked to the door. 'Wait here,' he ordered brusquely.

'Please tell the General,' said Hopper, 'that his neighbouring countries have invited United Nations scientists to help them locate the source of contamination, and if he refuses my team's entry into Mali, he will be scorned and lose face among the nations of the world.'

Mansa made no reply and left the stifling room.

While he waited, Hopper gave Captain Batutta his best intimidating stare. Batutta locked eyes for a few moments, but then turned away and began pacing the room.

After about five minutes, Mansa returned and sat down at the desk. Without a word, he precisely stamped each passport and then passed them to Hopper. 'You have been allowed to enter Mali to conduct your research. But please remember, Doctor, you and your people are guests here. No more. If you make unkind statements or take part in any action detrimental to security, you will be deported.'

'Thank you, Colonel. And please thank General Kazim for his kind permission.'

'You will be accompanied by Captain Batutta and ten of his men for your protection.'

'I'm honoured to have a bodyguard.'

'You will also report your findings directly to me. I expect your full cooperation in this matter.'

'How will I report from the hinterland?'

'The captain's unit will carry the necessary communications equipment.'

'We should get along handsomely,' Hopper said loftily to Batutta. He turned back to Mansa. 'My team and I will need a car, preferably a four-wheel-drive, for personnel and two lorries to transport our laboratory gear.'

Colonel Mansa's face reddened. 'I will arrange for military vehicles.'

Hopper was well aware that it was important for the colonel to save face and have the last word. 'Thank you, Colonel Mansa. You are a generous and honourable man. General Kazim must be very proud to have a true warrior of the desert at his side.'

Mansa leaned back, a growing look of triumph and satisfaction in his eyes. 'Yes, the General has often expressed gratitude for my loyalty and service.'

The interview was over, and Hopper returned to the aircraft and directed the unloading of the cargo. Mansa watched from the window of the terminal office, a faint smile on his lips.

'Shall I restrict their investigation to unclassified areas?' asked Batutta.

Mansa slowly shook his head without turning. 'No, allow them to go wherever they wish.'

'And if Dr Hopper finds signs of toxic sickness?'

'No matter. As long as I control communications with the outside world his reports will be altered to show our country to be clean of illness and hazardous wastes.'

'But when they return to the UN headquarters – '

'Won't the true findings be exposed?' Mansa finished. 'Yes, most certainly.' He swung around suddenly, his expression menacing. 'But not if their aircraft tragically meets with an accident during the return flight.'

10

Pitt dozed off and on during the plane ride from Egypt to Nigeria. He woke only when Rudi Gunn came down the aisle of the NUMA executive jet, three coffee mugs firmly gripped in both hands. Taking a cup, Pitt looked up at Gunn in weary resignation, his expression devoid of enthusiasm and any expectations for fun times.

'Where in Port Harcourt are we meeting the Admiral?' he asked without really caring.

'Not exactly in Port Harcourt,' Gunn hedged, handing Pitt a coffee.

'If not there, then where?'

'He's waiting on board one of our research ships 200 kilometres off the coast.'

Pitt fixed Gunn with the gaze of a hound staring at a cornered fox. 'You're holding out, Rudi.'

'Would Al like some coffee?'

Pitt glanced at Giordino who was snoring in sweet bliss. 'Save it. You couldn't wake him with a lighted firecracker in his ear.'

Gunn eased into a seat across the aisle from Pitt. 'I can't tell you what Admiral Sandecker has on his mind, because I honestly don't know. I do, however, suspect it has to do with a study NUMA marine biologists have conducted on coral reefs around the world.'

'I'm aware of the study,' said Pitt, 'but the results came in after Giordino and I left for Egypt.' Pitt was comfortable with the fact that Gunn would eventually level with him. He and Gunn had an easygoing relationship despite the obvious differences in their lifestyle. Gunn was an intellectual with degrees in chemistry, finance, and oceanography. He would be totally at home living in the basement of a library inundated by books, compiling reports and planning research projects.

Pitt, on the other hand, enjoyed working with his hands on things mechanical, especially on the old classic automobiles in his collection in Washington. Adventure was his narcotic. He was in paradise when flying antique aircraft or diving on historic shipwrecks. Pitt had a master's degree in engineering and took great pleasure in tackling the jobs others thought impossible. Unlike Gunn, he was seldom found at his desk in the NUMA headquarters building, preferring the excitement of probing the unknown depths of the sea.

'The bottom line is the reefs are in peril and dying off at an unheard-of rate,' Gunn answered. 'Right now, it's a hot topic among marine scientists.'

'What parts of the oceans show this trend?'

Gunn stared at his coffee. 'You name it. The Caribbean from the Florida Keys to Trinidad, the Pacific from Hawaii to Indonesia, the Red Sea, the coasts of Africa.'

'All with the same attrition rate?' asked Pitt.

Gunn shook his head. 'No, it varies by locale. The worst-case scenario appears to be along the West African coast.'

'I didn't think it uncommon for coral reefs to go through cycles where they stop reproducing and die before becoming healthy again.'

'That's correct,' Gunn nodded. 'When conditions return to normal the reef will recover. But we've never seen such widespread damage at such an alarming rate.'

'Any idea of the cause?'

'Two factors. One, the usual culprit, warm water. Periodic rises in water temperature, generally from changes in sea currents, cause the tiny coral polyps to eject, or vomit if you will, the algae they feed on.'

'The polyps being the little tubular devils that build the reefs with their skeletal remains.'

'Very good.'

'That about sums up my knowledge on coral,' Pitt admitted. 'The life-and-death struggle of coral polyps rarely makes the evening news.'

'A shame,' Gunn said briefly. Especially when you consider that changes in coral can be an accurate barometer of future trends in sea and weather conditions.'

'All right, so the polyps spit out the algae,' Pitt prodded. 'Then what?'

'Because algae is the nutrient that feeds the polyps and gives them vibrant colours,' Gunn went on, 'its loss starves the coral, leaving it white and lifeless, a phenomenon known as bleaching.'

'Which seldom occurs when the waters are cool.'

Gunn looked at Pitt. 'Why am I telling you this if you already know it all?'

'I'm waiting for you to get to the good part."

'Let me drink my coffee before it gets cold.'

There was a silence. Gunn wasn't really in the mood for coffee, but he sipped away until Pitt became impatient.

'Okay,' Pitt said. 'Coral reefs are dying around the world. So what's the second factor in their extinction?'

Gunn idly stirred his coffee with a plastic spoon. 'A new threat, and a critical one, is the sudden abundance of thick, green algae and seaweed that is blanketing the reefs like an out-of-control plague.'

'Hold on. You say the coral is starving because it's spitting out the algae even though it's smothered in the stuff?'

'The warmer water gives and takes. It acts to destroy the reefs while it aids in the growth of algae that can prevent nutrients and sunlight from reaching the coral. Somewhat like smothering it to death.'

Pitt ran a hand through his black hair. 'Hopefully the

114

situation will be corrected when the water turns cooler.'

'Hasn't happened,' said Gunn. 'Not in the Southern Hemisphere. Nor is a temperature drop in the water predicted in the next decade.'

'You think it's a natural phenomenon or fallout from the greenhouse effect?'

'A possibility, along with the usual indications of pollution.'

'But you have no solid evidence?' Pitt put to him.

'Neither I nor our NUMA ocean scientists have all the answers.'

'I never heard of a test tube junkie who didn't have a theory,' Pitt grinned.

Gunn smiled back. 'I've never looked at myself in that light.'

'Or those terms.'

'You love to stick it to people, don't you.'

'Only opinionated academics.'

'Well,' Gunn began, 'King Solomon, I ain't. But since you asked for it. My theory on the proliferation of the algae, as any school child can tell you, is that after generations of dumping untreated sewage, garbage, and toxic chemicals in the oceans, the saturation point has finally been reached. The delicate chemical balance of the seas is irretrievably lost. They're heating up, and we're all, particularly our grandchildren, going to pay a heavy price.'

Pitt had never seen Gunn so solemn.

'That bad.'

'I believe we've crossed the point of no return.'

'You're not optimistic for a turnaround?'

'No,' Gunn said sadly. 'The disastrous effects of bad water quality have been ignored too long.'

Pitt stared at Gunn, mildly surprised that the second-in-command of NUMA was prey to his own thoughts of doom and gloom. Gunn had painted a dire picture. Pitt did not share Gunn's total pessimism. The oceans might be sick, but they were far from terminal.

'Loosen up, Rudi,' Pitt said cheerfully. 'Whatever assignment the Admiral has up his sleeve, he's not about to expect the three of us to sally forth and save the seas of the world.'

Gunn looked at him and made a wan smile. 'I never second guess the Admiral.'

If either of them had known or even guessed how wrong they were, they'd have threatened the pilot with great bodily harm if he didn't turn the plane around and fly them directly back to Cairo.

Their ground time at an oil company airstrip outside of Port Harcourt was short and sweet. Within minutes they were airborne in a helicopter beating out over the Gulf of Guinea. Forty minutes later, the craft was hovering over the *Sounder*, a NUMA-owned research vessel Pitt and Giordino knew quite well, having directed survey projects aboard her on three different occasions. Built at a cost of eighty million dollars, the 120-metre ship was loaded with the most sophisticated seismic, sonar, and bathymetric systems afloat.

The pilot swung around the huge crane on the *Sounder*'s stern and settled onto the landing pad aft of the superstructure. Pitt was the first to step down to the deck, followed by Gunn. Giordino, moving like a zombie, brought up the rear, yawning every step of the way. Several crewmen and scientists, who were old friends, met and exchanged greetings with them as the rotor blades spun to a stop and the helicopter was tied down.

Pitt knew his way about and headed up a ladder to the hatch that led to one of the *Sounder*'s marine laboratories. He passed through the counters piled with chemical apparatus and into a conference and lecture room. For a working research ship, the room was pleasantly furnished like an executive board room with a long mahogany table and comfortably padded leather chairs.

A black man stood in front of a large, rear projection screen with his back to Pitt. He seemed engrossed in a graphic diagram that imaged on the screen. He was at least twenty years older than Pitt and much taller. Pitt guessed him at slightly over 2 metres tall with the loose-limbed movements of an ex-basketball player written all over him.

But what caught and locked the eye of Pitt and his two friends was neither the coloured graphics on the screen nor the incredibly tall presence of the stranger: It was the other figure in the conference room, a short, trim and yet commanding figure who leaned indifferently with one hand on the table while the other held a huge unlit cigar. The narrow face, the cold, authoritative blue eyes, the flaming but now greying red hair and precisely trimmed beard gave him the image of a retired naval admiral, which, as the blue blazer with the embroidered gold anchors on the breast pocket suggested, was exactly what he was.

Admiral James Sandecker, the driving force behind NUMA, straightened, smiled his barracuda smile, and stepped forward, his hand extended.

'Dirk! Al!' The greeting came as if he was surprised by their unexpected visit. 'Congratulations on discovering the pharaoh's funeral barge. A beautiful job. Well done.' He noticed Gunn and merely nodded. 'Rudi, I see you rounded them up without incident.'

'Like lambs to a slaughter,' Gunn said with a grim smile.

Pitt gave Gunn a hard look. then turned to Sandecker. 'You pulled us off the Nile in a hell of a hurry. Why?'

Sandecker feigned a hurt expression. 'No hello or glad to see you. No greeting at all for your poor old boss who had to cancel a dinner date with a ravishing, wealthy, Washington socialite and fly 6000 kilometres just to compliment your performance.'

'Why is it your highly dubious blessing fills me with anxiety?'

Giordino dropped moodily into a chair. 'Since we did so good, how about a nice fat raise, a bonus, a quick flight home, and a two-week vacation with pay?'

Sandecker said with forbearance, 'The ticker tape parade down Broadway comes later. After you've taken a leisurely cruise up the Niger River.'

'The Niger?' Giordino muttered moodily. 'Not another shipwreck search.'

'No shipwreck.'

'When?' asked Pitt.

'You start at first light,' answered Sandecker.

'What exactly do you want us to do?'

Sandecker turned to the towering man at the projection screen. 'First things first. Allow me to introduce Dr Darcy Chapman, chief ocean toxicologist at the Goodwin Marine Science Lab in Laguna Beach.'

'Gentlemen,' said Chapman in a deep voice that sounded like it rose out of a well. 'A sincere pleasure to meet you. Admiral Sandecker has filled me in on your exploits together. I'm truly impressed.'

'You used to play with the Denver Nuggets,' muttered Gunn, bending back at the waist to stare up into Chapman's eyes.

'Until the knees gave out,' Chapman grinned. 'Then it was back to school for my doctorate in environmental chemistry.'

Pitt and Gunn shook hands with Chapman. Giordino merely waved wearily from his chair. Sandecker picked up a phone and ordered breakfast from the galley.

'Might as well get comfortable,' he said briskly. 'We've got a lot of ground to cover before dawn.'

'You *do* have a rotten job for us,' Pitt said slowly.

'Of course it's a rotten job,' Sandecker said matter-of-factly. He nodded at Dr Chapman, who pressed a button on the screen's remote control. A coloured map showing the meandering course of a river appeared on the screen. 'The Niger River. Third longest in Africa behind the Nile and Congo. Oddly, it begins in the nation of Guinea, only 300 kilometres from the sea. But it flows northeast and then south for 4200 kilometres before emptying into the Atlantic at its delta on the coast of Nigeria. And somewhere along its course . . . somewhere a highly toxic poison is entering the current and being swept into the ocean. There, it's creating a catastrophic upheaval that is . . . well, incalculable in terms of a potential doomsday.'

11

Pitt stared at Sandecker, not sure if he heard right. 'Doomsday, Admiral? Did I understand you correctly?'

'I am not talking off the top of my head,' Sandecker replied. 'The sea off West Africa is dying, and the plague is spreading because of an unknown contaminant. The situation is rapidly developing into a chain reaction with the potential of destroying every single species of marine life.'

'That could lead to a permanent change in the earth's climate,' said Gunn.

'The least of our worries,' Sandecker remarked. 'The end result is extinction for all life forms on land, and that includes us.'

Gunn murmured accusingly. 'Aren't you overstating your case – '

'Overstating my case,' Sandecker interrupted acidly. 'The very words the cretin in Congress handed me when I began sounding the warning, when I pleaded for backing to isolate and solve the problem. They're more concerned with maintaining their precious power base and promising the moon to get re-elected. I'm sick to death of their endless, stupid committee hearings. Sick to death of their lack of guts in standing for unpopular issues, and spending the nation into bankruptcy. The two-party system has become a stagnant swamp of fraud and criminal promises. As with communism, the great experiment in democracy is withering from corruption. Who cares a damn if the oceans die? Well, by God, I do. And I'm going to the wall to save them.'

Sandecker's eyes blazed in bitterness, his lips stretched

tight by vehemence. Pitt was stunned by the depth of emotion. It was strangely out of character.

'Hazardous waste is dumped in nearly every river of the world,' Pitt said quietly, bringing the discussion back on track. 'What's so special about the Niger's pollution?'

'What's special is that it's creating a phenomenon commonly known as the red tide that is reproducing and spreading on a frightening scale.'

'*The charmèd water burnt alway, a still and awful red,*' Pitt quoted.

Sandecker flicked a glance at Gunn and then focused on Pitt. 'You got the message.'

'But not the connection,' Pitt admitted.

'You men are all divers,' said Chapman, 'so you probably know that red tide is caused by microscopic creatures called dinoflagellates, tiny organisms that contain a red pigment that gives the water a reddish-brown colour when they proliferate and float in mass.'

Chapman pressed a button on the remote control box and continued lecturing as an image of a strange-looking microorganism flashed on the viewing screen. 'Red tides have been recorded since ancient times. Moses supposedly turned the Nile to blood. Homer and Cicero also mentioned a red bloom in the sea, as did Darwin during the voyage in the *Beagle*. Outbreaks in modern times have occurred around the world. The most recent came off the west coast of Mexico after the water turned slimy and noxious. The resulting red tide caused the deaths of literally billions of fish, shellfish, and turtles. Even barnacles were wiped out. Beaches were closed for 200 miles and hundreds of natives and tourists died from eating fish that was contaminated by a species of deadly, toxin-containing dinoflagellates.'

'I've scuba dived in red tides,' said Pitt, 'and suffered no ill effects.'

'Fortunately you swam through one of the many

common, harmless varieties,' Chapman explained 'There is however, a newly discovered mutant species that produces the most lethal biological toxins we've ever known. No sea life lives that comes in the slightest contact with it. A few grams of it if evenly dished out could put every human on the face of the earth in a cemetery.'

'That potent.'

Chapman nodded. 'That potent.'

'And if the toxin isn't bad enough,' added Sandecker, 'the little critters consume themselves in an orgy of marine cannibalism that drastically decreases the oxygen in the water and causes any surviving fish and algae to suffocate.'

'It gets even worse,' Chapman carried on. 'Seventy per cent of all new oxygen is provided by diatoms, the tiny plant forms such as algae that live in the sea. The rest comes from vegetation on land. I see no need to enter into a lengthy discourse on how diatoms in the water or trees in the jungle manufacture oxygen through photosynthesis. You've all had that in elementary school. The smothering toxicity of the dinoflagellates as they cluster and bloom into a red tide kills the diatoms. No diatoms, no oxygen. The tragedy is we take oxygen for granted, never thinking that a slight imbalance of the amount created by plants and what we burn off in carbon dioxide could mean our last gasp.'

'Any possibility they'll eat themselves out of existence?' asked Giordino.

Chapman shook his head. 'They make up their losses at a ratio of ten births to one death.'

'Don't the tides eventually subside and disperse?' inquired Gunn. 'Or die out completely when cooler water currents come in contact with it?'

Sandecker nodded. 'Unfortunately, we're not looking at normal conditions. The mutant microorganism we're dealing with here seems immune to changing water temperatures.'

'So what you're saying is that there is no hope the red tide off Africa will fade and disappear?'

'Not if left on its own,' Chapman answered. 'Like trillions of cloning Frankensteins, the dinoflagellates are reproducing at an astronomical rate. Instead of several thousand in a gallon of water, they've mushroomed to nearly a billion per gallon. An increase never before recorded. At the moment they're unstoppable.'

'Any theory on where the mutant red tide evolved from?' asked Pitt.

'The instigator behind this new breed of prolific dinoflagellates is unknown. But we believe that a contaminant of some kind is spilling out of the Niger River and mutating the dinoflagellates that thrive in seawater and boosting their reproduction cycle.'

'Like an athlete taking steroids,' Giordino said dryly.

'Or aphrodisiacs,' Gunn grinned.

'Or fertility drugs,' threw in Pitt.

'If this red tide goes unchecked and expands without any deterrent throughout the oceans, covering the surface in one massive blanket of toxic dinoflagellates,' Chapman explained, 'the world's supply of oxygen will diminish to a level too low to support life.'

Gunn said, 'You've written a grim scenario, Dr Chapman.'

'Horror story might be a more apt description,' Pitt said quietly.

'Can't they be destroyed by chemical applications?' Giordino asked.

'A pesticide?' stated Chapman. 'Conceivably, it could make matters worse. Better to cut it off early at the head.'

'Do you have a time frame for this disaster?' Pitt asked Chapman.

'Unless the flow of contamination into the sea can be stopped dead within the next four months, it will be too late.

By then, the spread will be too enormous to control. It will also be self-sufficient, able to feed off itself, passing on the chemical poison it absorbed from the Niger to its offspring.' He paused to press a button on the remote control and a coloured graph appeared on-screen. 'Computer projections indicate millions will begin dying by slow suffocation within eight months, certainly not more than ten. Young children with small lung capacities will be the first to go, too starved for air to cry, their skin turning blue as they go into irreversible coma. It won't be a pretty picture for those few to die last.'

Giordino looked incredulous. 'Almost impossible to accept a dead world that ran out of oxygen.'

Pitt stood and moved closer to the screen, studying the cold numbers that indicated the time left for mankind. Then he turned and stared at Sandecker. 'So what this all boils down to is you want Al and Rudi and I to run a compact research vessel up the river and analyse water samples until we hunt down the source of the contamination that's forming the red tide. Then figure a way to turn off the spigot.'

Sandecker nodded. 'In the meantime we here at NUMA will work at developing a substance to neutralize the red tides.'

Pitt walked over and studied a map of the Niger River that was hung on a wall. 'And if we don't find the origin in Nigeria?'

'Then you keep heading upriver until you do.'

'Through the middle of Nigeria, northeast to where the river separates the nations of Benin and Niger and then into Mali.'

'If that's what it takes.' said Sandecker.

'What is the political situation in these countries?' asked Pitt.

'I have to admit it's slightly unstable.'

124

'What do you call "slightly unstable"?' Pitt asked sceptically.

'Nigeria,' Sandecker lectured, 'Africa's most populous nation at 120 million, is in the middle of an upheaval. The new democratic government was tossed out by the military last month, the eighth overthrow in only twenty years, not to mention countless unsuccessful bids. The inner countryside is torn by the usual ethnic wars and bad blood between Muslims and Christians. The opposition is assassinating government workers who are accused of corruption and mismanagement.'

'Sounds like a fun place,' muttered Giordino. 'I can't wait to smell the gunsmoke.'

Sandecker ignored him. 'The People's Republic of Benin is under a very tight dictatorship. President Ahmed Tougouri rules by terror. Across the river in Niger, the head of state is propped up by Libya's Muammar Qaddafi, who is after the country's uranium mines. The place is a festering crisis. Rebel guerrillas everywhere. I suggest you steer in the middle of the river when you pass between them.'

'And Mali,' Pitt probed.

'President Tahir is a decent man, but he's chained to General Zateb Kazim who runs a three-member Supreme Military Council that is bleeding the country dry. Kazim is a very nasty customer and quite unusual in that he's a virtual dictator who operates behind the front of an honest government.'

Pitt and Giordino exchanged cynical smiles and wearily shook their heads.

'Do you two have a problem?' inquired Sandecker.

' "A leisurely cruise up the Niger River," ' Pitt mildly repeated the Admiral's words. 'All we have to do is merrily sail 1000 kilometres of river that's crawling with bloodthirsty rebels hiding in ambush along the shore, dodge armed patrol boats, and refuel along the way without being arrested and executed as foreign spies. And this while casually collecting chemical samples of the water. No problem, Admiral, no problem at all, except it's damn well suicidal.'

'Yes,' Sandecker said imperturbably, 'it might look that way, but with a little luck you should come out of this without the least inconvenience.'

'Watching my head blown off seems more than an inconvenience.'

'Have you thought about using satellite sensors?' asked Gunn.

'Can't be done with enough accuracy,' answered Chapman.

'How about a low-flying jet aircraft?' tried Giordino.

Chapman shook his head. 'Same conclusion. Dragging sensors in the water at supersonic speeds won't work. I know. I was in on an experiment that tried it.'

'There are first-rate labs on board the *Sounder*,' said Pitt. 'Why not run her up the delta and at least pinpoint the type and class and level of contamination?'

'We tried,' replied Chapman, 'but a Nigerian gunboat warned us off before we could get within 110 kilometres of the river's mouth. Too far to make a precise analysis.'

'The project can only be done by a well-equipped small boat,' said Sandecker. 'One that can get through occasional rapids and shallow waters. There's no other way.'

'Has our State Department tried appealing to these governments to let a research team study the river on the grounds of saving billions of lives?' asked Gunn.

'The straightforward approach was tried. The Nigerians and the Malians turned the appeal down flat. Respected scientists came to West Africa to explain the situation. The African leaders didn't believe the pitch, even laughed at it. You can't really blame them. Their mentality is not exactly monumental. They can't conceive on a grand scale.'

'Don't they have a high death toll among their people

who drank from the contaminated river?' asked Gunn.

'Nothing widespread,' Sandecker shook his head. 'The Niger River has more than chemicals flowing in it. The cities and villages along its banks also dump human waste and sewage into its waters. The natives along its banks know better than to drink from it.'

Pitt saw the handwriting on the wall and didn't like it one bit. 'So you think a covert operation stands the only chance at tracking down the contamination?'

'I do,' Sandecker said doggedly.

'I hope you have a plan to overcome any and all obstacles.'

'Of course I have a plan.'

'Are we permitted to know just how we're supposed to find the contamination source and somehow stay alive?' asked Gunn quietly.

'No great secret,' Sandecker said in exasperation. 'Your arrival will be advertised as a working holiday by three wealthy French industrialists looking to invest in West Africa.'

Gunn looked stricken. Giordino dumbfounded. Pitt's face was clouded in growing anger.

'That's it,' demanded Pitt. 'That's your plan.'

'Yes, and a damned good one,' snapped Sandecker.

'It's crazy. I'm not going.'

'Me neither,' snorted Giordino. 'I look about as French as Al Capone.'

'Nor I,' added Gunn.

'Certainly not in a slow, unarmed research boat,' stated Pitt firmly.

Sandecker pretended not to notice the mutiny. 'That reminds me. I forgot the best part. The boat. When you see the boat, I guarantee you'll change your minds.'

12

If Pitt had dreamed of pursuing high performance, style, comfort, and enough firepower to take on the American sixth fleet, he found it in the boat Sandecker promised him. One look at her sleek, refined lines, the brute size of her engines, and incredible hidden armament, and Pitt was sold.

A masterpiece of aerodynamic balance in fibreglass and stainless steel, she was named *Calliope* after the muse of epic poetry. Designed by NUMA engineers and built under tight secrecy in a boat yard up a bayou in Louisiana, her 18-metre-length hull with its low centre of gravity and almost flat bottom drew only 1.5 metres of water, making her ideal for the shallow channels of the Niger River's upper course. She was powered by three V-12, turbo diesel engines that thrust her across the water at a top speed of 70 knots. Nothing was compromised in her construction. She was a one-of-a-kind build for a specific job.

Pitt stood at the helm and soaked up the unrivalled strength and ultrasmooth ride of the super sport yacht as she loafed along at 30 knots over the dull blue-grey water of the Niger Delta. His eyes ceaselessly scanned the waters ahead as the shoreline sped by, shifting occasionally to check the depths on a chart and the digital numbers on the depth-sounder. He'd passed one patrol boat, but the crew merely waved in blatant admiration at the sight of the yacht planing over the surface of the river. A military helicopter had circled curiously overhead, and a military jet, a French-built Mirage, Pitt judged, had dropped low to have a look at the boat and flown on, apparently satisfied. So far, so good. There had been no attempts to halt or detain them.

Down in the spacious interior, Rudi Gunn sat in the middle of a small but highly customized laboratory that was planned by a multidisciplinary team of scientists that included highly sophisticated, compact versions of instrumentation developed through NASA for space exploration. The lab was not only set up to analyse water samples but to telemeter the accumulated data via satellite to a team of NUMA scientists working with computer data bases to identify complex compounds.

Gunn, a scientist from toes to his thinning hairline, was oblivious to any danger outside the bulkheads of the elegant boat. He poured himself into his task with total commitment, trusting Pitt and Giordino to shield him from distraction or interruption.

The engines and weapon systems were Giordino's department. To muffle the roar of the engines he wore a headset that was plugged to a tape player and listened to Harry Connick, Jr., play the piano and sing old jazz favourites. He was sitting on a padded bench seat in the engine room, his hands busy unpacking several cases of portable rocket launchers and their missiles. The Rapier was a new all-purpose weapon designed to engage subsonic aircraft, seagoing vessels, tanks, and concrete bunkers. It could be fired from the shoulder or mounted in quad to a central firing system. Giordino was fitting the completed assemblies in housings that allowed the missile clusters to fire through the armoured ports of the domed turret above the engine room that looked to the casual eye like a skylight. The seemingly innocent superstructure protruded a good metre above the aft deck and could swivel on a 220-degree arc. After assembling the launcher and guidance units, and then inserting the missiles in their tubes, Giordino began concentrating on cleaning and loading a small arsenal of automatic rifles and handguns. Next, he unloaded a crate of incendiary concussion grenades and carefully loaded four of them in a bulky clip that hung from a stubby automatic grenade launcher.

They all went about their respective jobs with cold efficiency and an unerring sense of dedication that would ensure the success of their mission and their individual survival. Admiral Sandecker had handpicked the best. He couldn't have found a better crew to tackle the near impossible if he'd canvassed the entire country. His faith in them bordered on fanatical.

The kilometres flowed under the hull. The Cameroon Highlands and the Yoruba Hills bounding the southern part of the river rose in a haze flattened by dense humidity. Rain forests alternated with groves of acacias and mangroves along the shore. Villages and small towns appeared and slipped past as the bow of the *Calliope* cut the water in a great V of foam.

The traffic on the river consisted of every known vessel from dug out canoes to old chugging ferryboats dangerously overloaded with waving passengers to small cargo ships stained with rust that plodded from one port to the next, their funnel smoke fanned by a gentle northern breeze. It was a scene of peaceful contentment that Pitt knew couldn't last. Around each bend in the river, an unknown threat might be waiting to send them to meet the devil.

About noon they passed under the great 1404-metre bridge that spanned the river from the port and market city of Onitsha to the agricultural town of Asaba. Roman Catholic cathedrals stood sentinel over the bustling Onitsha streets that were bounded by industrial plants. Docks along the water were heavy with ships and boats that transported food and trade goods downstream and imported commodities upstream from the Niger Delta.

Pitt concentrated on skirting the river traffic, smiling to himself at the shaking fists and angry curses thrown at the *Calliope* as she roared perilously close to small boats that rolled wickedly from the wash of her churning wake. Once free of the port, he relaxed and released his hands from the wheel and flexed his fingers. He had been at the helm for nearly six hours, but suffered little stiffness or fatigue. His chair at the controls was as comfortable as any enjoyed by a corporate executive and the steering as light as that of an expensive, luxury automobile.

Giordino appeared with a bottle of Coors beer and a tuna sandwich. 'Thought you might need a little nutrition. You haven't eaten since we left the *Sounder*.'

'Thanks, I couldn't hear my stomach grumbling above the noise of the engines.' Pitt turned over the helm to his friend and nodded past the bow. 'Be wary of that tug towing those barges as you come abeam to pass. He's fishtailing all over the channel.'

'I'll keep a wide passage to port,' Giordino acknowledged.

'Are we in shape to repel boarders?' Pitt grinned.

'As ready as we'll ever be. Any suspicious characters lurking about?'

Pitt shook his head. 'A couple of flybys by the Nigerian air force, and friendly waves from passing patrol boats. Otherwise, a lazy, hazy day cruising up the river.'

'The local bureaucrats must have bought the Admiral's scam.'

'Let's hope the countries further upriver are as gullible.'

Giordino tossed a thumb at the French tricolour flapping on the stern. 'I'd feel a whole lot better if we had the Stars and Stripes, the State Department, Ralph Nader, the Denver Broncos, and a company of Marines behind us.'

'The battleship *Iowa* would be nice too.'

'Is the beer cold? I put a case in the galley fridge only an hour ago.'

'Cold enough,' Pitt answered between bites of the sandwich. 'Any startling revelations from Rudi?'

Giordino gave a negative dip of his head. 'He's wrapped

131

up in a chemical never, never land. I tried to make conversation but he waved me off.'

'I think I'll pay him a visit.'

Giordino yawned. 'Careful he doesn't bite your knee off.'

Pitt laughed and went down the stairway into Gunn's lab. The little NUMA scientist was studying a computer printout, his glasses pushed up on his forehead. Giordino had misread Gunn's disposition. He was actually in a good mood.

'Having any luck?' asked Pitt.

'This damn river has every pollutant in it known to man and then some,' replied Gunn. 'It's far more contaminated than the bad old days on the Hudson, the James, and the Cayuhoga.'

'Looks complicated,' said Pitt as he stepped around the cabin, studying the sophisticated equipment that was packed together from deck to ceiling. 'What function do these instruments serve?'

'Where did you get the brew?'

'Want one?'

'Sure.'

'Giordino's got a case crammed in the galley refrigerator. Hold on a minute.'

Pitt ducked through a cabin door to the galley and returned, handing Gunn a cold bottle of beer.

Gunn took several swallows and sighed. Then he said, 'Okay, to answer your question. There are three key elements to our search approach. The first requires an automated micro-incubator. I use this unit to expose a tiny sample of river water into vials containing red tide samples we obtained off the coast. The micro-incubator then optically monitors the growth of the dinoflagellates. After a few hours the computer gives me an indication of how potent the concoction and how rapid the growth of the little buggers. A little play with numbers and I have a reasonable estimate of how close we're coming to the source of our problem.'

'So the red tide stimulator isn't coming from Nigeria.'

'The numbers suggest the source is further up the river.'

Gunn moved around Pitt to a pair of square, box-like units about the size of small television sets but with doors where the screens would have been. 'These two instruments are for identifying the nasty glob, as I call it, or a combination of globs that's behind our problem. The first is a gas chromatograph/mass spectrometer. To put it concisely, I merely take vials of river water samples and place them inside. The system then automatically extracts and analyses the contents. The results are interpreted by our on-board computers.'

'What exactly does it tell you?' asked Pitt.

'It identifies synthetic organic pollutants, including solvents, pesticides, PCBs, dioxins, and a host of other drugs and chemical compounds. This baby, I hope, will home in on the chemistry of the compound that's mutating and stimulating the red tide.'

'What if the contaminant is a metal?'

'That's where the inductively coupled plasma/mass spectrometer comes in,' said Gunn, gesturing at the second instrument. 'Its purpose is to automatically identify all metals and other elements which might be present in the water.'

'Looks similar to the other one,' observed Pitt.

'Basically the same principle, but different technology. Again, I merely load the sample vials of water taken from the river, punch the start buttons, and check the performance every 2 kilometres.'

'What has it told you?'

Gunn paused to rub a pair of red-rimmed eyes. 'That the Niger River is carrying half the metals known to man, from copper to mercury to gold and silver, even uranium.

133

All in concentrations above their natural background levels.'

'Sifting through the scatter won't be easy,' murmured Pitt.

'Finally,' added Gunn, 'the data is telemetered to our researchers at NUMA who review my results in their own laboratories and look for something I might have missed.'

Pitt, for the life of him, couldn't see Gunn missing anything. It was plain that his friend for many years was more than just a competent scientist and analyst; he was a man who thought coldly, clearly, and as constructively as possible. He was a dedicated hard driver who didn't know the meaning of the word *quit*.

'Any hint yet of the toxic compound that might be our evil-doer?' Pitt asked.

Gunn finished off the beer and dropped it in a cardboard box filled with computer readout sheets. 'Toxic is only a relative term. In the world of chemistry there are no toxic compounds, only toxic levels.'

'Well?'

'I've identified a lot of different contaminants and naturally occurring compounds, both metal and organic. The systems are reading shocking levels of pesticides that are banned in the U.S. but are still widely used in the third world. But I haven't been able to isolate the synthetic chemical pollutants that cause the dinoflagellates to run crazy. At the moment, I don't even know what I'm tracking. All I can do is follow the bloodhounds.'

'The further we go, the hotter the swill,' mused Pitt. 'I was hoping you might have a handle on it by now. The deeper we get into Africa, the tougher the return trip to the open sea, especially if the local military decides to nose around.'

'Get used to the idea we might not find it,' Gunn said irritably. 'You don't realize how many chemicals are out there. The number comes to over seven million known man-made chemical compounds, and each week U.S. chemists alone create more than six thousand new ones.'

'But they can't all be toxic.'

'At some level most all of these chemicals will have some toxic properties. Anything is toxic if swallowed, inhaled, or injected in sufficient doses. Even water can be fatal if enough is consumed. Too much will flush out the necessary electrolytes from the body.'

Pitt looked at him. 'So there are no absolutes, no guarantees.'

'None,' Gunn shook his head. 'All I know for certain is we haven't passed the spot where our doomsday plague empties into the river. Since entering the delta and passing the main tributaries of the lower Niger, the Kaduna, and Benue Rivers, the water samples have driven the dinoflagellates into a frenzy. But I haven't a clue that points to the villain. The only good news is that I ruled out bacterial microorganisms as the cause.'

'How did you eliminate it?'

'By sterilizing the river water samples. The removal of bacteria didn't slow down the little buggers from proliferating one little bit.'

Pitt gave Gunn a light pat on the shoulder. 'If anyone can put a collar on it, Rudi, you can.'

'Oh I'll sift the stuff out.' Gunn pulled off his glasses and wiped the lenses. 'It may still be unknown, ungodly, and unnatural, but I'll sift it out. That's a promise.'

Their luck ran out the following afternoon, only an hour after they crossed the Nigerian border onto the stretch of river separating Benin and Niger. Pitt was gazing silently over the bow of the *Calliope* at the river walled by thick green jungle, a dank and forbidding jungle. Grey clouds had turned the water to a leaden colour. The river ahead curved slightly and seemed to beckon, like the bony finger of death.

Giordino was at the helm, the first faint edges of fatigue wrinkling the sides of his eyes. Pitt stood at his shoulder, attention shifting to a lone cormorant soaring delicately on an updraught above the water ahead. Suddenly, it flapped its wings and dipped into the trees along the bank.

Pitt lifted a pair of binoculars from the counter and glimpsed the bow of a vessel barely showing around a bend in the river. 'The locals are about to pay us a social call,' he announced.

'I see it.' Giordino raised out of the chair and shielded his eyes against the sun with one hand. 'Correction, them. There are two.'

'Heading straight toward us, guns tracking and looking for trouble.'

'What flag are they flying?'

'Benin,' Pitt answered. 'Russian-built, judging by their lines.' Pitt laid down the binoculars and spread out a recognition chart on West African air force and navy units. 'Riverine attack craft, armed with two twin, 30-millimetre guns with a rate of fire around five hundred rounds per minute.'

'Not good,' Giordino muttered briefly. He glanced down at the chart of the river. 'Another 40 kilometres and we'll be out of Benin territory and into Niger waters. With luck, and the engines pushed to the hilt, we could make the border by lunch.'

'Forget luck. These guys are not about to wave us a cheery bon voyage as we pass merrily on our way. This doesn't have the look of a routine inspection. Not with all their weapons aimed down our throats.'

Giordino looked back and pointed skyward over the stern. 'The plot thickens. They've called in a vulture.'

Pitt swung and spotted a helicopter angling around the last bend, no more than 10 metres above the water surface. 'All doubts of a friendly encounter have just evaporated.'

'Smells like a setup,' Giordino said calmly.

Pitt alerted Gunn, who came up out of his electronic cabin and was briefed on the situation.

'I half expected it,' was all he said.

'They've been waiting for us,' said Pitt. 'This is no chance encounter. If they only mean to lock us up and confiscate the boat, they'll damned well execute us as spies when they find out we're as French as a backup trio for Bruce Springsteen. We can't allow that. Whatever data we've accumulated since entering the river must get into the hands of Sandecker and Chapman. These guys are primed for trouble. No innocent, naive cooperation on our part. It's a case of they go under, or we do.'

'I might take out the helicopter, and if I'm lucky, the nearest boat,' said Giordino. 'But I can't take all three before one of them hammers us into scrap.'

'Okay, here's the drill,' Pitt spoke quietly, gazing at the approaching gunboats. He explained his game plan as Giordino and Gunn listened thoughtfully. When he concluded, he looked at them. 'Any remarks?'

'They speak French hereabout,' commented Gunn. 'How's your vocabulary?'

Pitt shrugged. 'I'll fake it.'

'Then let's do it,' Giordino said, his voice edged with icy anticipation.

His friends were head of the class, Pitt thought. Gunn and Giordino weren't professionally trained members of a Special Forces Team, perhaps, but brave and competent men to have standing at his side during a fight. He couldn't have felt more confident if he was commanding a missile destroyer manned by a crew of two hundred.

'Right,' he said with a grim smile. 'Wear your headsets and stay on the air. Good luck.'

Admiral Pierre Matabu stood on the bridge of the lead gunboat and peered through a pair of glasses at the sport yacht skimming up the river. He had the air about him of a con man eyeing an easy mark. Matabu was short, squat, in his mid-thirties, and dressed in an ostentatious, braid-embellished uniform of his own design. As Chief of the Benin navy, a position granted him by his brother, President Tougouri, he commanded a fleet consisting of four hundred men, two river gunboats, and three ocean-going patrol craft. His prior experience before achieving flag rank was three years as a deck hand on a river ferry.

Commander Behanzin Ketou, skipper of the vessel, stood slightly to his side and behind. It was wise of you to fly from the capital and take command, Admiral.'

'Yes,' beamed Matabu. 'My brother will be most happy when I present him with a fine, new pleasure craft.'

'The Frenchmen have arrived within the time you predicted.' Ketou was tall, slender, with proud bearing. 'Your foresight is truly inspiring.'

'Very considerate of then to do as my thought waves demand,' Matabu gloated. He did not mention that his paid agents had reported on the passage of the *Calliope* every two hours since it entered the delta in Nigeria. The happy fact that it cruised into Benin waters was a wish come true.

'They must be very important people to own such an expensive boat.'

'They are enemy agents.'

Ketou's face reflected a balance of uncertainty and scepticism. 'They appear somewhat conspicuous for enemy agents.'

Matabu dropped the binoculars and glared at Ketou. 'Do not question my information, Commander. Believe me when I say those white foreigners are part of a conspiracy to rape the natural wealth of our country.'

'Will they be arrested and tried in the capital?'

'No, you will shoot them after you board and discover evidence proving their guilt.'

'Sir?'

'I forgot to mention that you shall have the honour of leading the boarding party,' Matabu said pompously.

'Not an execution,' Ketou protested. 'The French will demand an investigation when they learn several of their influential citizens were murdered. Your brother may not condone – '

'You will throw the bodies in the river and not question my orders,' Matabu coldly interrupted.

Ketou caved in. 'As you wish, Admiral.'

Matabu stared through the binoculars again. The sport yacht was only 200 metres away and slowing. 'Position your men for boarding. I will personally hail the spies and order them to receive your party.'

Ketou spoke to his first officer, who repeated the commands over a bullhorn to the captain of the second gunboat. Then Ketou turned his attention back to the approaching yacht. 'Something funny about her,' he said to Matabu. 'No one is in sight except the man at the helm.'

'The European slime are probably lying drunk below. They suspect nothing.'

'Strange, they do not appear concerned at our presence nor do they show any reaction to our trained guns.'

'Shoot only if they try to escape,' Matabu cautioned him. 'I want that boat captured undamaged.'

Ketou focused his binoculars on Pitt. 'The helmsman is waving to us and smiling.'

'He won't be smiling for long,' Matabu said, his teeth showing ominously. 'In a few minutes he'll be dead.'

'Come into my parlour said the spider to the three flies,' Pitt muttered under his breath as he waved and flashed a wide, humourless smile.

'Did you say something?' asked Giordino inside the missile turret.

139

'Just mumbling to myself.'

'I can't see zilch from the bow ports,' Gunn spoke from the forward quarters. 'What's my line of fire?'

'Be ready to knock out the gunners on the boat off our starboard beam on my command,' said Pitt.

'Where's the helicopter?' asked Giordino, who was blind until he dropped the turret shield.

Pitt scanned the sky over the boat's wake. 'She's hovering 100 metres directly astern, about 50 metres above the surface of the river.'

There were no half measures in their preparations. No one doubted for an instant the Benin gunboats and helicopter were going to let them pass unchallenged. They all went silent, each man settled and resigned to fight to stay alive. Any fear was quickly passing as they approached the point of no return. There was a determination, a single-minded stubbornness against losing. They were not the kind to meekly submit and turn the other cheek. Three armed vessels against one, but surprise was on their side.

Pitt propped the launcher with the incendiary/concussion grenades under a niche beside his chair. Then he slipped the throttles to 'Idle' as his gaze swept back and forth between the two boats. He ignored the helicopter. In the opening stages of the battle, it would be Giordino's problem. He was close enough now to study the officers and quickly concluded that the fat African strutting the bridge of the gunboat in a Gilbert & Sullivan comic opera uniform was in command. His unblinking eyes also stared in hypnotic fascination into those of the Angel of Death, who stared back from the black muzzles of the guns, all aimed at him.

Pitt could not know the identity of the swaggering officer on the bridge who peered back at him through binoculars. Nor did he care. But he was thankful his opponent had made a tactical error by not stretching his two boats broadside across the river bow to stern, effectively blocking any

passage while every gun could be brought to bear on the
Calliope.

The wave carved by the bow fell away as the *Calliope*
slipped between the two gunboats that had already stopped
and were drifting with the river current. Pitt reduced speed
just enough to maintain a slight headway. The hulls of the
gunboats loomed over the *Calliope*, no more than 5 metres
off her sides. From his cockpit, Pitt could see most of the
crewmen standing in casual attitudes, each armed only with
holstered automatic pistols. None held automatic rifles.
They looked as if they were waiting their turn on a shooting
range. Pitt gazed innocently up at Matabu.

'*Bonjour!*'

Matabu leaned over the counter and shouted back for Pitt
to stop his boat and take on boarders.

Pitt didn't understand a word. He called back. '*Pouvez-
vous me recommander un bon restaurant?*'

'What did Dirk say?' Giordino asked Gunn.

'Good Lord!' Gunn moaned. 'He just asked the head
honcho to recommend a good restaurant.'

The gunboats were slowly drifting past on both sides as
Pitt kept the sport craft idling in gear against the current.
Matabu again ordered Pitt to stop and prepare to be
boarded.

Pitt stiffened and tried to look suave and disarming.
'*J'aimerais une bouteille de Martin Ray Chardonnay.*'

'Now what's he saying?' demanded Giordino.

Gunn sounded lost. 'I think he ordered a bottle of
California wine.'

'Next, he'll ask to borrow a jar of Grey Poupon Mustard,'
Giordino muttered.

'He must be trying to stall them until they drift past us.'

On board the gunboat, Matabu and Ketou's faces
registered a total lack of comprehension as Pitt called out,
this time in his native tongue.

'I do not understand Swahili. Can you try English?'

Matabu pounded on the bridge counter in exasperation and growing anger. He was not used to humoured indifference. He replied in broken English that Pitt could barely decipher.

'I am Admiral Pierre Matabu, Chief of the National Benin Navy,' he announced pompously. 'Stop your engines and heave-to for inspection. Heave-to or I will give the order to fire.'

Pitt nodded furiously and waved both hands in a gesture of compliance. 'Yes, yes, don't shoot. Please don't shoot.'

The cockpit of the *Calliope* was slowly coming even with the stern of Matabu's gunboat. Pitt kept just enough distance between the two boats to make it impossible for anyone but an Olympic broadjumper to leap across the gap. Two crewmen threw lines on Pitt's bow and stern decks, but he made no move toward them.

'Tie the lines,' Ketou ordered.

'Too far away,' Pitt shrugged. He held up a hand and made a half arc. 'Hold on. I'll come around.'

Not waiting for a reply, he eased the throttles forward and swung the helm so that the sport yacht slowly slipped into a 180 degree turn around the stern of the gunboat before straightening out and pulling up along the opposite side of the hull. Now both vessels were on a parallel course, bows pointed downriver. Pitt noted with no small amount of satisfaction that the 30-millimetre guns could not depress low enough to strike the *Calliope's* cockpit.

Matabu stared down at Pitt, eyes gloating, a smile of triumph beginning to spread across his thick jowls. Ketou didn't share his superior's wolfish expression. His face wore a very suspicious look indeed.

Calmly, still grinning, Pitt waited until Giordino's turret was directly in line with the gunboat's engine room. Keeping one hand on the wheel, he casually reached under the chair

142

and grasped the stock of the grenade launcher. Then he spoke softly into the microphone on his headset.

'Helicopter dead ahead. Gunboat to starboard. Okay, gentlemen, it's show time. Let's take 'em!'

As Pitt spoke, Giordino dropped the shield around his engine room turret and unleashed a rapier missile that ran straight and true into the helicopter's fuel tanks. Gunn popped up from the forward hatch, two modified M-16 automatic rifles clamped under each armpit, both hands gripping and squeezing the triggers, muzzles blazing, blowing away the men manning the 30-millimetre guns as though they were chaff spewed from a grain combine. Pitt aimed the muzzle of the grenade launcher into the air and fired the first of his incendiary/concussion grenades over Matabu's vessel onto the superstructure of the second. Unable to see the backup gunboat, he fired blindly, judging a trajectory that would drop on his target. The grenade bounced off a winch into the river, exploding with a thunderous boom underwater. The next lob missed the boat completely, bursting with the same result.

Matabu could never have been prepared for the horrific spectacle that exploded around him. It seemed to him as though the sky and air suddenly tore apart. His mind accepted only fleetingly in one stunned glimpse the total disintegration of the helicopter. It erupted in a giant fireball that was followed by a mushroom burst of shattered debris that rained down in a fiery torrent onto the river.

'The white bastards tricked us!' Ketou yelled in abrupt anger at having swallowed the bait. He rushed to the rail and furiously shook his fist at the *Calliope*. 'Depress guns and fire!' he screamed at his gun crews.

'Too late!' Matabu cried in terror. The admiral panicked and crouched there, frozen into immobility as he watched his crew crumple and die under the tearing slugs of Gunn's weapons. He stared petrified in disbelieving shock at the obscenely twisted corpses around the silent guns, all lying sprawled in foetal attitudes, their gore spreading across the deck. Matabu's mind simply could not accept a clandestine ship masquerading as an innocent yacht under a respected flag with the firepower to turn his comfortable little world into a horror. The stranger standing at the helm of the deadly boat had turned surprise into a tactical asset. Matabu's men were overwhelmed with shock they seemed unable to shake off. They milled about like cattle in a thunderstorm, caught off balance and struck with fear, falling without firing a shot in response. He realized then with blood-chilling certainty that he was going to die; he realized it when the turret above the stern of the sport yacht spun and unleashed another missile point blank against the gunboat that penetrated the wooden hull and struck a generator in the engine room before detonating.

At almost the same moment, Pitt's third toss struck home. Miraculously, the grenade impacted on a bulkhead and ricocheted into an open hatch of the second gunboat. In a concert of explosions, it exploded in a roar of flame, setting off the ammunition and cannon shells in the boat's magazine. Flying debris and swirling smoke shot up in an umbrella of splintered bulkheads, ventilators, pieces of lifeboats, and broken bodies. Shockingly, the gunboat ceased to exist. The shock wave came like a sledgehammer and drove Matabu's vessel hard against the sport yacht, knocking Pitt off his feet.

Giordino's missile blasted the gunboat's engine room into a holocaust of shredded metal and slashed timbers. Water gushed in through a massive hole ripped out of the bottom, and the gunboat began to sink quickly. Virtually the whole interior was a blazing bedlam with fiery tongues darting through the open ports. Veins of oily black smoke curled and billowed into the tropical air before drifting over the forested riverbank.

With no targets left standing at the guns or on the decks, Gunn fired his final rounds at the two figures on the bridge. Two slugs tore into Matabu's chest. He rose to his feet, stood there for several moments, hands in a death grip on the bridge railing, staring dumbly at the blood staining his immaculate uniform. Then he slowly sagged to the deck in a fat, inert lump.

For several seconds a desperate silence fell over the river, broken by the soft crackling of burning surface oil. Then abruptly, like a shriek from the very pits of hell, an agonized voice screamed out over the water.

13

'Western filth!' Ketou cried. 'You've murdered my crew.' He stood there against the grey sky, blood seeping from a wound in his shoulder, dazed by the sheer physical shock of the disaster around him.

Gunn stared up at him over the barrels of empty guns. Ketou glared back at him for a moment, and then he focused on Pitt who was pushing himself off the deck and reaching for the wheel.

'Western filth,' Ketou repeated.

'Fair is fair!' Pitt shouted back above the crackle of the flames. 'You lost the draw.' Then he added, 'Abandon your ship. We'll come around and pick you up – '

Fleetingly, almost like the blink of a camera shutter, Ketou leaped down the ladder and ran toward the stern. The gunboat had heeled sharply to port, her gunwales awash, as he struggled across the steeply angled deck.

'Get him, Rudi,' Pitt snapped into his mike. 'He's going for the stern gun.'

Gunn said nothing but cast aside his useless weapons, ducked into the forward compartment, and snatched a Remington TR870 automatic shotgun. Pitt shoved the throttles to their stops convulsively, spinning the wheel to port and skidding the *Calliope* around in a violent sheer that ended with the bow aimed upriver. The propellers bit and dug in, the water boiled under her stern, and the *Calliope* leaped like a race horse out of the gate.

There was only oil and floating debris drifting on the river now. Commander Ketou's gunboat was starting its final slide to the river bottom. The river flowed into the shattered hull and hissed in clouds of steam. Water was swirling around Ketou's knees when he reached the aft 30-millimetre guns, swung the muzzles toward the fleeing sport yacht, and pressed the fire control button.

'Al!' Pitt hailed.

His reply was the hissing blast of a missile that Giordino launched from his turret. A streak of orange flame and white smoke shot through the air toward the gunboat. But Pitt's abrupt turn of the wheel and the thrust of sudden acceleration had thrown off Giordino's aim. The missile swished over the sinking gunboat and exploded in the trees bordering the river.

Gunn appeared at Pitt's side in the cockpit, took careful aim, and began blasting away with the Remington over the stern at Ketou. Time seemed to slow as the shot splattered around the gun mount and into the African boat commander. They were too far away to see the hate and frustration in his shiny black features. Nor could they see that he died over the gun sight, his lifeless hand doggedly forcing down the fire control button.

A burst of fire shrieked after the *Calliope*. Pitt swiftly cut a sharp bend to starboard, but the irony of battle had yet to take its fair share. Ironic because a dead man had fought back through catastrophic defeat with a precision he could never know. Jets of water skipped white and straddled the speeding boat as shells ripped away the airfoil above and behind the cockpit that held the parabolic satellite dish antenna and communications antenna and navigation transponder, blasting the remains into the river. The windshield in front of the cockpit shattered and was carried away. Gunn threw himself prone on the deck, but Pitt could only hunch over the wheel and ride out the deadly storm. They could not hear the impact of the shells over the thunderous roar of the flatout turbo diesels. But they could see the bits and pieces of debris bursting all around them.

147

Then Giordino got in a clear shot and launched his last missile. The settling stern of the gunboat suddenly vanished in a puff of smoke and flame. And then the boat was gone, sliding under and leaving a large flutter of bubbles and a spreading slick of oil. The Commander-in-Chief of Benin's navy and his river fleet were no more.

Pitt forced himself to turn his back on the flotsam-filled river astern and look to his own boat and friends. Gunn was coming shakily to his feet, bleeding from a cut across his balding head. Giordino appeared from the engine room looking like a man who had just stepped off a handball court, sweating and weary, but ready for a new game.

He pointed up the river. We're in for it now,' he shouted the words in Pitt's ear.

'Maybe not.' Pitt shouted back. At this speed we'll cross into Niger in twenty minutes.'

'Hopefully, we didn't leave any witnesses.'

'Don't count on it. Even if there were no survivors, somebody must have caught the fight from shore.'

Gunn gripped Pitt's arm and yelled. 'As soon as we're in Niger, back off and we'll take up the survey again.'

'Affirmative,' Pitt agreed. He shot a quick look at the satellite dish and communications antenna. It was then he noticed they were gone along with the airfoil. 'So much for contacting the Admiral and giving him a full report.'

'Nor can the labs at NUMA receive my data transmission,' said Gunn sadly.

'Too bad we can't tell him the leisurely cruise up the river just turned into a bloody nightmare,' Giordino bellowed.

'We're dead meat unless we can figure another way out of here,' Pitt said grimly.

'I wish I could see the Admiral's face,' Giordino grinned at the thought, 'when he hears we broke his boat.'

'You will,' Gunn shouted through cupped hands as he descended into the electronic compartment. 'You will.'

What a stupid mess, Pitt thought. Only a day and a half into the project and they had killed at least thirty men, shot down a helicopter, and sunk two gunboats. All in the name of saving humanity, he mused sarcastically. There was no turning back now. They had to find the contaminant before the security forces of either Niger or Mali stopped them for good. Either way, their lives weren't worth the paper on a devalued dollar.

He glanced at the small radar dish behind the cockpit. There was a saving grace after all. The dish was undamaged and still turning. It would have been hell running the river at night or through fog without it. The loss of the satellite navigation unit meant they would have to position the contamination entry into the river by spotting nearby landmarks. But they were unhurt and the boat was still seaworthy and pounding over the river at close to 70 knots. Pitt's only worry now was striking a floating object or a submerged log. At this speed any collision would gouge out the bottom of the hull and send the boat cartwheeling and splintering into a shattered wreck.

Fortunately, the river flowed free of debris, and Pitt's calculations were only slightly off. They crossed into the Republic of Niger within eighteen minutes under skies and waters empty of security forces. Four hours later they were moored to the refuelling dock at the capital city of Niamey. After taking on fuel and enduring the traditional hassle from West African immigration officials, they were allowed to proceed on their way again.

As the buildings of Niamey and the bridge over the river named for John F Kennedy receded in the *Calliope's* wake, Giordino spoke in a brisk, cheerful voice.

'So far, so good. Things can't get worse than they already are.'

'*Not* good,' Pitt said at the wheel. 'And things can get a whole lot worse.'

149

Giordino looked at him. 'Why the gloom? The people in these parts don't seem to have a beef with us.'

'It went too easy,' said Pitt slowly. 'Things don't work that way in this part of the world. Certainly not in Africa, not after our little altercation with the Benin gunboats. Did you notice while we were showing our passports and ship's papers to the immigration officials there wasn't a policeman or armed military guard in sight?'

'Coincidence?' Giordino shrugged. 'Or maybe just lax procedure?'

'Neither,' Pitt shook his head solemnly. 'I've a hunch somebody is playing games with us.'

'You think the Niger authorities knew about our run-in with the Benin navy?'

'Word travels fast here, and I'm willing to bet it's travelled ahead of us. The Benin military most certainly alerted the Niger government.'

Giordino was not sold. 'Then why didn't the local bureaucrats arrest us?'

'I haven't a clue,' said Pitt pensively.

'Sandecker?' offered Giordino. 'Maybe he intervened.'

Pitt shook his head. 'The Admiral may be a big gun in Washington, but he has no sway here.'

'Then somebody wants something we've got.'

'Seems to be heading in that direction.'

'But what?' asked Giordino in exasperation. 'Our data on the contaminant?'

'Except for the three of us, Sandecker, and Chapman, no one knows the purpose of our project. Unless there's a leak, it has to be something else.'

'Like what?'

Pitt grinned. 'Would you believe our boat?'

'The *Calliope!*' Giordino was frankly disbelieving. 'You'll have to do better than that.'

'No,' stated Pitt flatly. 'Think about it. A highly

specialized craft, built in secrecy, capable of 70 knots, and with enough sting to take out a helicopter and two gunboats within three minutes. Any West African military leader would give his eyeteeth to get his hands on her.'

'Okay, I'll accept that,' Giordino said grudgingly. 'But answer me this. If the *Calliope* is so desirable, why wasn't she grabbed by Niger goons while we were standing around the refuelling dock in Niamey?'

'A shot in the dark? Okay, somebody cut a deal.'

'Who?'

'Don't know.'

'Why?'

'Can't say.'

'So when does the axe fall?'

'They've let us get this far, so the answer must lie in Mali.' Giordino looked at Pitt. 'So we're not returning the way we came.'

'We bought a one-way ticket when we sank the Benin navy.'

'I'm a firm believer of getting there is half the fun.'

'The fun is over, if you are morbid enough to call it that.' Pitt looked over the banks of the river. The green vegetation had given way to a barren landscape of scrub brush, gravel, and yellow dirt. 'Judging from the terrain, we may have to trade the boat for camels if we expect to see home again.'

'Oh God!' Giordino groaned. 'Can you picture *me* riding a freak of nature? A reasonable man who believes the only reason God put horses on earth is for background in western movies.'

'We'll survive,' said Pitt. 'The Admiral will move half of heaven and most of hell to get us out after we home in on the poison glop.'

Giordino turned and looked dolefully down the Niger. 'So this is it,' he said slowly.

'This is what?'

'The legendary creek people go up and lose their paddles.'

Pitt's lips curled in a crooked grin. 'If that's where we are, then pull down the French tricolour ensign, and by God we'll fly our own.'

'We're under orders to hide our nationality,' Giordino protested. 'We can't go about our sneaky business under the stars and stripes.'

'Who said anything about the stars and stripes?'

Giordino knew he was stepping into deep water. 'Okay, dare I ask what flag you intend to raise?'

'This one.' He reached into a drawer of the bridge counter and tossed Giordino a folded black ensign. 'I borrowed it at a costume party I attended a couple of months ago.'

Giordino made an expression of shocked dismay as he stared at the grinning skull in the centre of the rectangular cloth. 'The Jolly Roger, you intend to fly the Jolly Roger?'

'Why not?' Pitt's surprise at Giordino's anguish seemed genuine. 'I think it only fitting and proper we make a big splash under the appropriate banner.'

14

'Fine bunch of international contamination detectives we are,' grumbled Hopper as he watched the sunset over the lakes and marshlands of the upper Niger River. 'All we've come up with is typical third world indifference toward sanitation.'

Eva sat on a camp stool in front of a small oil stove to ward off the evening chill. 'I tested for most of the known toxins and failed to find a trace of any of them. Whatever our phantom malady is, it's proving very elusive.'

An older man sat beside her, tall, heavy, with iron-grey hair, light blue eyes, wise and thoughtful. A New Zealander, Dr Warren Grimes was the chief epidemiologist of the project. He contemplated a glass of club soda. 'Nothing on my end either. Every culture I've obtained within 500 kilometres showed free of disease-related microorganisms.'

'Is there anything we might have overlooked?' asked Hopper, dropping into a folding chair with padded cushions.

Grimes shrugged. 'Without victims, I can't conduct interviews or autopsies. Without victims I can't obtain tissue samples or analyse results. I have to have observational data to compare symptoms or do a case control study.'

'If anyone is dying from toxic contamination,' said Eva, 'they're not dying around here.'

Hopper turned from the fading orange light on the horizon and picked up a pot from the stove and poured a cup of tea. 'Can it be the evidence was false or exaggerated?'

'UN headquarters received only vague reports,' Grimes reminded him.

'Without hard data and exact locations to work with, it seems we jumped the gun.'

'I think it's a cover-up,' said Eva suddenly.

There was silence. Hopper looked from Eva to Grimes.

'If it is, it's a damned good one,' muttered Grimes finally.

'I'm not sure I'd disagree,' Hopper said, his curiosity aroused. 'The teams in Niger, Chad, and the Sudan are reportedly coming up dry too.'

'All that suggests is that the contamination is in Mali and not the other nations,' said Eva.

'You can bury victims,' observed Grimes. 'But you can't hide trace amounts of contamination. If it's around here, we would have found it. My personal opinion is that we've been on a wild goose chase.'

Eva looked at him steadily, her Dresden blue eyes large in the reflection of the flame from the camp stove. 'If they can hide victims, they can alter reports.'

'Aha,' Hopper nodded. 'Eva has something. I don't trust Kazim and his crew of snakes, haven't from the beginning. Suppose they did alter the reports to throw us off the playing field? Suppose the contamination isn't where we've been led to believe it is?'

'A possibility worth pursuing,' Grimes admitted. 'We've been concentrating in the dampest and most inhabited regions of the country because it follows suit they would carry the highest incidence of disease and contamination.'

'Where do we go from here?' asked Eva.

'Back to Timbuktu,' said Hopper firmly. 'Did you notice the look on people we interviewed before setting out to the south? They were nervous and worried. You could see it in their faces. It's just possible they were threatened to keep silent.'

'Especially the Tuaregs from the desert,' recalled Grimes.

'You mean especially their women and children,' Eva added. 'They refused to be examined.'

Hopper shook his head. 'I'm to blame. I made the

decision to turn our backs on the desert. It was a mistake. I know that now.'

'You're a scientist, not a psychic investigator,' Grimes consoled him.

'Yes,' Hopper agreed readily. 'I'm a scientist, but l hate being made the fool.'

'The tip-off we all missed.' said Eva, 'was the patronizing attitude of Captain Batutta.'

Grimes looked at her. 'That's right. Oh-ho. You've struck oil again, my girl. Now that you've brought it up, Batutta has been downright servile with cooperation.'

'True,' Hopper nodded. He's leaned over backward in allowing us to go our merry way, knowing we were hundreds of kilometres off the scent.'

Grimes finished off his soda water. 'Be interesting to see the look on his face when you tell him we're going out in the desert and start from scratch.'

'He'll be on the radio to Colonel Mansa before I get the words out of my mouth.'

'We could lie,' said Eva.

'Lie, for what reason?' asked Hopper.

'To throw him off, to throw them all off our trail.'

'I'm listening.'

'Tell Batutta the project is finished. Tell him we've found no sign of contamination and are returning to Timbuktu, folding up our tents and flying home.'

'You've missed me. Where is this leading?'

'For all appearances the team has quit, given up,' Eva explained. 'Batutta waves a relieved farewell as we take off. Only we don't fly to Cairo. We land in the desert and set up shop again on our own without a watchdog.'

The two men took a few seconds to absorb Eva's scheme. Hopper leaned forward, intently mulling it over. Grimes looked as if someone asked him to catch the next rocket to the moon.

'It's no good,' Grimes said at last, almost apologetically. 'You can't just land a jet aircraft in the middle of the desert. You need a runway at least 1000 metres long.'

'There are any number of areas in the Sahara where the ground is perfectly flat for hundreds of kilometres,' Eva argued.

'Too risky,' Grimes said stubbornly. 'If Kazim got wind of it, we'd pay dearly.'

Eva looked sharply at Grimes, then more slowly at Hopper. She detected the beginnings of a smile on Hopper's face. 'It *is* possible,' she said firmly.

'Anything is possible, but often not practical.'

Hopper smashed his fist down on the arm of his camp chair so hard he nearly broke it. 'By God, I think it's worth a go.'

Grimes stared at him. 'You can't be bloody serious?'

'Oh but I am. Our pilot and flight crew will have the final say, of course. But with the proper incentive, like a hefty bonus, I think they can be persuaded to risk it.'

'You're forgetting something,' said Grimes.

'Such as?'

'What do we use for transportation after we land?'

Eva tilted her head toward the small Mercedes four-wheel-drive car with an enclosed truckbed that had been provided by Colonel Mansa in Timbuktu. 'The little Mercedes should just fit through the cargo door.'

'That's 2 metres off the ground,' said Grimes. How are you going to lift it on board?'

'We'll use ramps and drive it on,' Hopper said jovially.

'You'll have to do it under Batutta's nose.'

'Not an insurmountable problem.'

'The vehicle belongs to the Malian military. How will you account for it gone missing?'

'A mere technicality,' Hopper shrugged. 'Colonel Mansa will be told a thieving nomad stole it.'

'This is crazy,' Grimes announced.

Hopper suddenly stood. 'Then it's settled. We'll launch our little charade first thing in the morning. Eva, I'll leave it to you to inform our fellow scientists of the plan. I'll hang out with Batutta and throw off suspicion by bemoaning our failure.'

'Speaking of our keeper,' said Eva glancing about the camp, 'where is he hiding?'

'In that fancy recreation vehicle with the communications equipment,' replied Grimes. 'He practically lives in there.'

'Strange that he conveniently, for us at any rate, wanders off whenever we're gathered in discussion.'

'Damned courteous of him, I say.' Grimes stood and stretched his arms over his head. He furtively stared at the communications vehicle, and not sighting Batutta, sat down again. 'No sign of him. He's probably sitting inside watching European music shows on the telly.'

'Or on the radio giving Colonel Mansa the latest gossip on our scientific circus,' said Eva.

'He can't have much to report,' laughed Hopper. He never hangs around long enough to see what mischief we're into.'

Captain Batutta was not reporting to his superior, not at the moment. He was sitting inside his truck listening through stereo headphones wired to an extremely sensitive electronic listening device. The amplifier was mounted on the roof of the truck and aimed toward the camp stove in the middle of the parked caravan. He leaned forward and adjusted the bionic booster, increasing the receiving surface.

Every word spoken by Eva and her two associates, every murmur and whisper, came through without the slightest distortion and was recorded. Batutta listened until the conversation ended and the trio split up, Eva to brief the rest of the team on the new plot, Hopper and Grimes to study maps of the desert.

Batutta picked up a phone uplink to a joint African nation communications satellite and dialled a number. A voice half a breath from a yawn answered.

'Security Headquarters, Gao District.'

'Captain Batutta for Colonel Mansa.'

'One moment, sir,' the voice said hastily.

It took almost five minutes before Mansa's voice came over the receiver. 'Yes, Captain.'

'The UN scientists are planning a diversion.'

'What kind of a diversion?'

'They are about to report they have turned up no trace of contamination or its victims – '

'General Kazim's brilliant plan to keep them out of the contaminated areas has been successful,' Mansa interrupted him.

'Until now,' said Batutta. 'But they have begun to see through the General's ploy. Dr Hopper intends to announce the closing down of the project, then lead his people back to Timbuktu where they will depart in their chartered aircraft for Cairo.'

'The General will be most pleased.'

'Not when he learns Hopper has no intention of leaving Mali.'

'What are you saying?' demanded Mansa.

'Their plan is to bribe the pilots to set the plane down in the desert and launch a new investigation into our nomadic villages for the contamination.'

Mansa's mouth suddenly felt as if it was filled with sand. 'This could prove to be disastrous. The General will be most angry when he hears of it.'

'Not our fault,' Batutta said quickly.

'You know his wrath. It falls on the innocent as well as the guilty.'

158

'We have done our duty,' Batutta replied resolutely.

'Keep me informed of Hopper's movements,' Mansa ordered. 'I'll make your report in person to the General.'

'He's in Timbuktu?'

'No, Gao. As luck would have it, he's on Yves Massarde's yacht, moored in the river just off the city. I'll take a military transport and be there in half an hour.'

'Good luck to you, Colonel.'

'Stay on Hopper every second. Inform me of any change in Hopper's plans.'

'As you order.'

Mansa hung up and stared at the phone, sorting out the complications of Batutta's intelligence revelation. If undetected, Hopper might have fooled them all and discovered victims of the contamination out in the Sahara where no one thought to search. That would have spelled calamity. Captain Batutta had saved him from a very messy situation, possibly even his execution under trumped-up charges of treason, Kazim's routine exercise for eliminating officers who displeased him. It was a near thing. By catching Kazim in the right mood, he might even wheedle a promotion to the general staff.

Mansa called to his aide in the office outside to fetch his dress uniform and ready an aircraft. He began to sense a creeping euphoria. Near catastrophe would turn into an opportunity to annihilate the foreign intruders.

A speedboat was waiting at the dock under a mosque when Mansa stepped from the military command car that carried him from the airport. A uniformed crewman whipped off the bow and stern lines and jumped down into the cockpit. He pressed the ignition switch and the big V-8 Citroen marine engine roared to life.

Massarde's yacht swung in the middle of the river on its bow anchor, lights reflecting in the rippling current. The yacht was actually a self-propelled houseboat three storeys high. Its flat bottom enabled it to easily cruise up and down the river during the seasons of high water.

Mansa had never been on board, but he'd heard stories of the glass-domed spiral staircase that ascended from the spacious master suite to the heliport. The ten sumptuous staterooms furnished in French antiques, the high-ceilinged dining room with murals from the time of Louis XIV taken from the walls of a Loire River château, the steam rooms, sauna, Jacuzzis, and cocktail bar in a revolving observation lounge, and the electronic communication systems linking Massarde to his worldwide empire, they all worked together to make the mansion on the water unlike anything ever built.

As the Colonel climbed from the boat onto the gangway and up the teak steps, he had hopes of seeing something of the luxurious craft, but his expectations turned sour when Kazim met him on the deck beside the gangway. He was holding a glass half filled with champagne. He made no effort to offer Mansa one.

'I hope your interruption of my business conference with Monsieur Massarde is as urgent as you implied in your message,' Kazim said coldly.

Mansa saluted smartly and began a hurried but precise briefing, embellishing the facts and polishing the details of Batutta's report on the United Nations World Health team, but never mentioning the captain by name.

Kazim listened with curious interest. His dark eyes deepened and stared unseeing into the glistening lights of the houseboat dancing on the water. A worried crease appeared in his face, but this was soon replaced with a tight smile across his lips.

When Mansa finished speaking, Kazim asked, 'When is Hopper and his caravan expected back in Timbuktu?'

'If they leave tomorrow morning, they should arrive by late afternoon.'

'More than enough time to circumvent the good doctor's plans.' He looked icily into Mansa's eyes. 'I trust you will appear disappointed and most solicitous when Hopper announces the failure of his investigation to you.'

'I will be at my diplomatic best,' Mansa assured him.

'Is his aircraft and its crew still on the ground in Timbuktu?'

Mansa nodded. 'The pilots are staying at the Hotel Azalai.'

'You say Hopper intends to pay them a bonus to land in the desert north of here?'

'Yes, that is what he told the others.'

'We must gain control of the aircraft.'

'You wish me to bribe the pilots above what Hopper offers them?'

'A waste of good money,' Kazim sneered. 'Kill them.'

Mansa half expected the order and did not react. 'Yes, sir.'

'And replace them with pilots from our own military who resemble their size and facial features.'

'A masterly plan, my General.'

'Also, inform Dr Hopper that I insist Captain Batutta accompany them to Cairo to act as my personal representative to the World Health Organization. He will oversee the operation.'

'What orders do you wish me to give our replacement officers?'

'Order them,' said Kazim with evil blackness in his eyes, 'to land Dr Hopper and his party at Asselar.'

'Asselar.' The name rolled off Mansa's tongue as if it was coated in acid. 'Hopper and his party will surely be murdered by the mutant savages of Asselar as were the members of the tourist safari.'

'That,' said Kazim coldly, 'is for Allah to decide.'

'And if for some unforeseen reason they should survive?' Mansa posed the question delicately.

An evil expression that sent a shiver through Mansa spread across Kazim's face. The General smiled cunningly, his dark eyes reflecting cold amusement. 'Then there is always Tebezza.'

PART TWO

Dead Ground

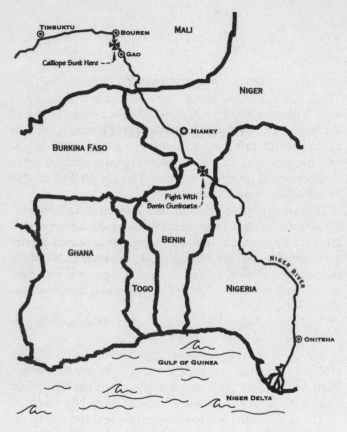

VOYAGE OF THE CALLIOPE UP THE NIGER RIVER

15

May 15, 1996
New York City

At Floyd Bennett Field on the shore of Jamaica Bay, New York, a man dressed like a sixties hippie leaned against a Jeep Wagoneer station wagon parked on a deserted end of the tarmac. He peered through a pair of granny glasses at a turquoise aircraft that taxied through a light morning mist and stopped only 10 metres away. He straightened when Sandecker and Chapman stepped from the NUMA jet and he moved forward to greet them.

The Admiral noted the car and nodded in satisfaction. He detested formal limousines, insisting on a four-wheel-drive for his personal transportation. He managed a brief smile at the Levi-jacketed, pony-tailed director of NUMA's vast computer data centre. Hiram Yaeger was the only person on Sandecker's top staff who ignored the dress code and got away with it.

'Thank you for picking us up, Hiram. Sorry to drag you away from Washington on short notice.'

Yaeger walked toward him with an outstretched hand. 'No problem, Admiral. I needed a break from my machines.' Then he tilted his head and stared up into the face of Dr Chapman. 'Darcy, how was the flight from Nigeria?'

'The cabin ceiling was too low and my seat too short,' the tall toxicologist complained. 'And to make matters worse, the Admiral beat me ten games to four at gin rummy.'

'Let me help you throw your luggage in the car, and we'll head into Manhattan.'

'Did you set an appointment with Hala Kamil?' asked Sandecker.

Yaeger nodded. 'I phoned the UN Headquarters as soon

as you radioed your time of arrival. Secretary General Kamil has rearranged her schedule to fit us in. Her aide was surprised she'd do that for you.'

Sandecker smiled. 'We go back aways.'

'She'll meet with us at ten-thirty.'

The Admiral glanced at his watch. 'An hour and a half. Time for a cup of coffee and some breakfast.'

'Sounds good,' said Chapman between yawns. 'I'm half starved.'

Yaeger took the parkway from the airport and turned off on Coney Island Avenue where he found a delicatessen. They settled into a booth and ordered from a waitress who openly stared at the towering figure of Dr Chapman.

'What'll it be gents?'

'Lox, cream cheese, and a bagel,' ordered Sandecker.

Chapman opted for a pastrami and salami omelette while Yaeger simply had a Danish. They were silent within their own thoughts until the waitress brought their coffee. Sandecker stirred an ice cube in his cup to cool the brew and then settled back against the booth's backrest.

'What do your electronic babies have to say about the red tides?' he asked Yaeger.

'The projections look pretty grim,' the computer expert said, toying with a fork. 'I've run a continuous update of the increasing dimensions from satellite photos. The growth rate boggles the mind. It's like the old adage of starting with a penny and doubling it every day until you're a billionaire by the end of the month. The red tide off West Africa is spreading and doubling its size every four days. At four o'clock this morning it covered an area measuring 240,000 square kilometres.'

'Or 100,000 square miles,' Sandecker translated into the old system of measurement.

'At that rate it will cover the entire South Atlantic in three to four weeks,' figured Chapman.

'Do you have a clue to the cause?' asked Yaeger.

'Only that it's probably an organometallic that's promoting a mutation of the dinoflagellates that make up the core of the red tide.'

'Organometallic?'

'A combination of a metal and an organic substance,' Chapman explained.

'Any particular compound that stands out?'

'Not yet. We identified dozens of contaminants, but none of them appear responsible. All we can guess at the moment is that a metallic element somehow got mixed with synthetic compounds or chemical by-products that were dumped in the Niger River.'

'Might even be waste from exotic biotech research,' suggested Yaeger.

'There are no exotic biotech experiments going on in West Africa,' Sandecker said firmly.

'Somehow this unidentified crap acts as an exciter,' Chapman continued, 'almost like a hormone as it creates a mutant red tide with a staggering growth rate and an incredible degree of toxicity as well.'

The conversation paused as the waitress served their breakfast off a tray. She left and returned with a pot of coffee and refilled their cups.

'Any chance we're looking at a bacterial reaction to a raw sewage spill?' asked Yaeger as he gazed sadly at a Danish that looked as if it had been stepped on by a greasy boot.

'Sewage can act as a nutrient for algae just as manure does with agricultural vegetation on land,' said Chapman. 'But not in this case. What we're dealing with is an ecological disaster that goes far beyond anything human waste can produce.'

Sandecker knifed the cream cheese on his bagel and laid on the salmon. 'So while we sit here and stuff our mouths, a red tide is forming that will make the '91 Iraqi oil spill look like a puddle in the Kansas prairie.'

'And we can do nothing to stop it,' admitted Chapman. 'Without the proper analysis of water samples, I can only theorize on the chemical compound. Until Rudi Gunn finds the needle in the haystack and who or what put it there, our hands are tied.'

'What's the latest word?' Yaeger asked.

'Word on what?' Sandecker mumbled between bites.

'Our three friends on the Niger,' Yaeger answered, irritated at Sandecker's seeming indifference. 'Transmission of their data telemetry suddenly stopped yesterday.'

The Admiral glanced around the delicatessen to make sure he wasn't heard. 'They became involved in a little altercation with two gunboats and a helicopter of the Benin navy.'

'A little altercation!' Yaeger blurted incredulously. 'How in hell did that happen? Were they injured?'

'We can only assume they survived in good shape,' Sandecker said guardedly. 'They were about to be boarded. To keep the project intact there was no choice but for them to go into a combat mode. During the fight their communications equipment must have been taken out.'

'That explains why their telemetry failed,' said Yaeger, calming down.

'Satellite photos from the National Security Agency,' continued Sandecker, 'show they blasted the hell out of both vessels and the copter and made it safely across the border into Mali.'

Yaeger sagged in his seat, suddenly not hungry. 'They'll never get out of Mali. They're sailing into a dead-end. I've run computer profiles on the Malian government. Their military leader has the worst record of human rights in West Africa. Pitt and the others will be caught and hung on the nearest date palm.'

'That's why we're meeting with the Secretary General of the UN,' said Sandecker.

'What good can she do?'

'The UN is our only hope to get our team and their data out safely.'

'Why am I beginning to get the idea our Niger River research was nonsanctioned?' Yaeger asked.

'We couldn't convince the politicians of the immediate urgency,' said Chapman in frustration. 'They kept insisting on setting up a special committee to look into the matter. Can you believe that? With the world on the brink of extinction, our illustrious elected officials want to strut their self-importance while bunched together in executive chairs and vocalize like an a cappella choir.'

'What Darcy is saying,' explained Sandecker, smiling at Chapman's choice of words, 'is that we explained the emergency to the President, the Secretary of State, and several Congressional leaders. They all refused our request to twist the arms of the West African nations to permit us to analyse the river water.'

Yaeger stared at him. 'So to get a head start you sent Pitt, Giordino, and Gunn in on the sly.'

'There was no other way. The clock is running down. We had to go around our own government. If this operation leaks out, my ass will be dipped in acid.'

'This is worse than I thought.'

'That's why we need the UN,' said Chapman. 'Without their cooperation there's too good a chance Pitt, Giordino, and Gunn will go into a Malian prison and never come out.'

'And the data we require so desperately,' said Sandecker, 'will disappear with them.'

Yaeger bore a look of sadness. 'You sacrificed them, Admiral. You willingly sacrificed our closest friends.'

Sandecker gave Yaeger a granite look. 'Do you think I didn't wrestle with the devil over my decision? Considering the stakes, who would you have trusted to get the job done? Who would you have sent up the Niger?'

Yaeger rubbed his temples for a moment before answering. Finally, he nodded. 'You're right, of course. They're the best. If anyone can accomplish the impossible, it's Pitt.'

'I'm delighted you agree,' Sandecker said gruffly. He looked at his watch again. 'We'd better pay up and get rolling. I don't want to keep Secretary General Kamil waiting. Not when I'm about to get down on my knees and beg like a lost soul.'

Hala Kamil, the Egyptian Secretary General of the United Nations, had the beauty and mystery of Nefertiti. Forty-seven years old, black eyes with a haunting quality, long ebony hair flowing slightly below her shoulders, delicate facial features enhanced by a flawless complexion, she kept her beauty and youthful look despite the heavy weight of her prestigious office. She was tall, and her shapely figure was apparent even under her conservative suit.

She rose and came from behind her desk as Sandecker and his friends were ushered into her office in the UN Headquarters Building. 'Admiral Sandecker, how nice to see you again.'

'My pleasure, Madam Secretary.' Sandecker fairly beamed when in the presence of a beautiful woman. He returned her firm handshake and made a slight bow. 'Thank you for seeing me.'

'You're amazing, Admiral. You haven't changed.'

'And you look even younger.'

She smiled a ravishing smile. 'Compliments aside. We've both added a wrinkle or two. It has been along time.'

'Almost five years.' Then he turned and introduced Chapman and Yaeger.

Hala took little notice of Chapman's size or Yaeger's

170

attire. She was too used to meeting multisized people from a hundred nations in a variety of dress. She held out a small hand in the direction of facing sofas. 'Please be seated.'

'I'll be brief,' Sandecker said without preamble. 'I need your help in an urgent matter concerning an environmental disaster in the making that is threatening the very existence of the human race.'

Her dark eyes stared at him sceptically. 'You've made a very weighty statement, Admiral. If this is another dire prediction of the greenhouse effect, I've become immune.'

'Something far worse,' Sandecker said seriously. 'By the end of the year most of the world's population will only be a memory.'

Hala looked at the faces of the men sitting across from her. Their faces were set and grim. She began to believe him. She didn't exactly know why she believed him. But she knew Sandecker well enough to feel confident he was not a man given to fancy, nor would he run around claiming the sky was falling unless he had absolute, scientific proof.

'Please go on,' she said briefly.

Sandecker turned the meeting over to Chapman and Yaeger, who reported their findings on the mushrooming red tide. After about twenty minutes, Hala excused herself and pressed a button on a desk intercom. 'Sarah, would you please call the ambassador of Peru and tell him an important matter has come up and ask him if it's convenient for him to postpone our meeting until this time tomorrow.'

'We deeply appreciate your time and interest,' said Sandecker, and he meant it.

'There is no doubt about the horror of this threat?' she put to Chapman.

'None. If the red tide spreads unhindered over the oceans, it will stifle the oxygen required to support global life.'

'And that doesn't take into consideration the toxicity,' added Yaeger, 'which is certain to cause mass death of all marine life and any human or animal that consumes it.'

She looked at Sandecker. 'What about your Congress, your scientists? Surely there must be concern by your government and the world environmental community.'

'There is concern,' replied Sandecker. 'We've presented our evidence to the President and members of Congress, but the gears of the bureaucracy grind slowly. Committees are studying the matter. No decisions are forthcoming. The scope of the horror is beyond them. They cannot conceive of the rapidly dwindling time element.'

'We have, of course, passed our preliminary findings along to ocean and contamination scientists,' said Chapman. 'But until we can isolate the exact cause of this plague on the seas, there is little any of us can do to create a solution.'

Hala was silent. It was difficult for her to come to grips with apocalypse, especially on such short notice. In a way she was powerless. Her position as Secretary General of the UN was more as an illusionary queen of a hollow kingdom. Her job was to watch over the diverse peacekeeping functions and the many trade and relief programmes. She could direct but not command.

She looked across a coffee table at Sandecker. 'Other than promise the cooperation of our United Nations Environment Program Organization, I don't see what else I can do.'

Sandecker's self-confidence took another step forward and his voice, low and tense, came slow and distinctly. 'I sent a boat with a team of men up the Niger River to analyse the water in an attempt to find the source behind the red tide explosion.'

Hala's dark eyes were cool and penetrating. 'Was that your boat that sank the Benin gunboats?' she asked.

'Your intelligence is very good.'

'I receive briefings from reports gathered around the world.'

172

'Yes, it was a NUMA vessel,' Sandecker admitted.

'You know, I assume, the Admiral who was Chief-of-Staff for the Benin navy and brother of the nation's president was killed in the battle.'

'I heard.'

'It was my understanding your boat was flying a French ensign. Doing your devious dirty work under a foreign flag could get your crew shot as enemy agents by the West Africans.'

'My men were aware of the danger and volunteered. They knew every hour counts if we are to stop the red tide before it expands beyond our technology to kill it.'

'Are they still alive?'

Sandecker nodded. 'As of a few hours ago they had traced the contamination across the Malian border and were approaching the town of Gao unmolested.'

'Who else in your government knows about this?'

Sandecker nodded at Chapman and Yaeger. 'Only the three of us and the men on the boat. No one outside of NUMA except you.'

'General Kazim, the Malian Chief of Security, is no fool. He'll learn about the battle with Benin's navy, and his intelligence will have warned him of your crew's entry into his country. He'll arrest them the minute they dock.'

'The very reason I came to you, Madam Secretary.'

This was it, Hala thought. 'What do you want from me, Admiral?'

'Your help in saving my men.'

'I thought it would come down to that.'

'It's vital they be rescued as soon as they discover the origin of the contamination.'

'We desperately need their analysis data,' said Chapman flatly.

'Then it's the findings you really want to rescue,' she said coldly.

'I'm not in the habit of abandoning brave men,' Sandecker said, his chin thrust forward.

Hala gave a negative shake of her head. 'Sorry, gentlemen, I can understand your desperation. But I cannot jeopardize the honour of this office by misusing my power to take part in an illegitimate international operation, regardless of how crucial.'

'Not even if the men you save are Dirk Pitt and Al Giordino and Rudi Gunn.'

Her eyes widened for a brief moment, and then she sagged back in her chair, her thoughts lost in the past for a brief instant. 'I begin to see the picture,' she said softly. 'You're using me just as you used them.'

'I'm not planning a celebrity tennis match,' said Sandecker flatly. 'I'm trying to prevent the loss of uncountable lives.'

'You really shoot for the heart, don't you.'

'When it's necessary.'

Chapman's eyebrows rose. 'I'm afraid I don't understand any of this.'

Hala stared off into space as she spoke. 'About five years ago, the three men you sent up the Niger saved my life from terrorist assassins, not once but twice. The first time was on a mountain in Breckenridge, Colorado; the other was at an abandoned mine near a glacier on the Straits of Magellan. Admiral Sandecker is playing on my conscience to repay the favour.'

'I seem to recall,' said Yaeger, nodding. 'It was during the hunt for the Alexandria Library treasure.'

Sandecker rose, came over, and sat down beside her. 'Will you help us, Madam Secretary?'

Hala sat motionless as a statue that slowly began to crack. Her breathing seemed faint and shallow. Finally, she turned slightly and faced Sandecker.

'All right,' she said softly. 'I promise to use every source

174

at my fingertips to get our friends out of West Africa. I can only hope we're not too late, and they're still alive.'

Sandecker turned away. He didn't want her to see the relief in his eyes. 'Thank you, Madam Secretary. I owe you. I owe you big.'

16

'No sign of life?' Grimes stared at the crumbling village of Asselar. 'Not even a dog or a goat.'

'Certainly looks dead,' said Eva, shielding her eyes against the sun.

'Deader than a flattened toad on a highway,' Hopper muttered as he peered through a pair of binoculars.

They stood on a small rise of rocky desert overlooking Asselar. The only evidence of humans were tyre tracks that led into the village from the northeast. Strangely, none appeared to indicate a departure. Eva had the impression of an abandoned city of ancient times as she stared through the heat waves at the ruins surrounding the central part of town. There was an eerie silence about the place that made her feel tense and uneasy.

Hopper turned to Batutta. 'Kind of you to cooperate with us, Captain, and allow us to land here, but it's obvious the village is a deserted ghost town.'

Batutta sat behind the wheel of the open Mercedes four-wheel-drive and shrugged innocently. 'A caravan from the salt mines at Taoudenni reported sickness in Asselar. What else can I tell you?'

'Won't hurt to have a look,' said Grimes.

Eva nodded in agreement. 'We should analyse the water from the well to be on the safe side.'

'If you please walk in from here,' said Batutta, 'I'll return to the aircraft and transport the rest of your people.'

'That's good of you, Captain,' acknowledged Hopper. 'You can ferry our equipment as well.'

Without a reply or a wave, Batutta spun away in a cloud

of dust and headed across a scrubby plain toward the parked aircraft that had landed on a long stretch of flat ground.

'Damned odd of him to suddenly become helpful,' muttered Grimes.

Eva nodded. 'Too helpful, if you ask me.'

'I don't much care for it,' said Grimes, gazing at the silent village. 'If this was an American western movie, I'd say we were walking into an ambush.'

'Ambush or not,' said Hopper, unconcerned, 'let's give a go at finding any inhabitants.' He set off down the slope in long strides, seemingly oblivious to the noonday sun and the heat radiating from the rock-strewn ground. Eva and Grimes hesitated a moment, and then set off after him.

Ten minutes later they entered the narrow, alley-like streets of Asselar. The narrow thoroughfares showed anything but a concern for neatness. They had to step over and around small mounds of trash and scattered rubbish that seemed to litter every square metre of ground. A light, hot breeze suddenly shifted, and the smell of decay and rotting meat struck their nostrils. The ugly odour grew more powerful with every step they took. It seemed to be drifting from inside the houses.

Hopper refrained from entering any buildings until they reached the marketplace. Here, an incredibly disgusting sight met their eyes. None of them in their wildest flights of nightmarish imagination could have envisioned the horror: scattered remains of human skeletons, skulls lined up as if displayed for sale, blackened and dried skin hanging from the tree in the market square that seemed alive under the attack of swarms of flies.

Eva's first thought was that she was gazing at the human debris of some massacre by an armed force. But that theory was quickly discarded in her mind as it didn't explain the positioning of the skull or the flayed skin. Something happened here that went far beyond atrocities committed by bloodthirsty soldiers or desert bandits. That much became apparent when she knelt down and picked up a bone, recognizing it as a humerus, the long bone of the upper arm. A chill coursed through her blood as she discovered that it was indented and chipped by what she correctly identified as human teeth marks.

'Cannibalism,' she whispered in shock.

For some reason the buzzing flies and the revelation uttered by Eva only served to heighten the deathly stillness of the village. Grimes gently took the bone from her hand and studied it.

'She's right,' he said to Hopper. 'Some bestial maniacs have eaten all these poor devils.'

'Judging from the stink,' said Hopper wrinkling his nose, 'there's still some who haven't turned to skeletons yet. You and Eva wait here. I'll check the houses and see if I can find a live one.'

'Doesn't look to me like they take to strangers,' Grimes resisted. 'I suggest we beat a hasty retreat back to the plane before we wind up on the local menu.'

'Nonsense,' Hopper scoffed. 'We're looking at an extreme case of abnormal behaviour. It might very well be caused by the toxic contaminant we're searching for, and I'm not about to run away until I get to the bottom of it.'

'I'll go with you,' Eva said resolutely.

Grimes shrugged. He was from the old school and not about to be out-braved by a woman. 'All right, we'll search together.'

Hopper slapped him on the back. 'Good show, Grimes. I'd be honoured to be an ingredient with you in the same soup du jour.'

The first house they entered, the walls little more than stacked rocks held together with dried mud, contained two bodies, a man and a woman, dead at least a week, the heat already having dried out their tissue and shrivelled and tightened their skin. Death had not been swift but agonizingly slow, Hopper determined after a cursory examination of the shocking remains. Theirs had not been the death of a fast-acting poison. It had been the death of people who suffered excruciating torment until they were released.

'Can't tell much without a pathological examination,' said Hopper.

Grimes looked down, his face calm and unperturbed. 'These people have been dead for some time. I'd stand a better chance of finding solid answers from a fresh victim.'

It sounded so cold and clinical to Eva. She shuddered, not from the cadavers but from recognizing a pile of small bones and skulls heaped in one corner of the darkened house. She could not help wondering if the couple had killed and eaten the flesh of their own children. The thought was too abhorrent to dwell on and she pushed it aside and struck out on her own, entering a house directly across the street.

She moved through a doorway that was more elaborate than the others. Beyond, there was an L-shaped courtyard that was clean and swept. Almost blasphemous as compared to the others that were filled with debris. The stench was particularly strong in this house. Eva dampened a small handkerchief with water from a canteen on her belt, then stepped cautiously from room to room. The walls were a chalky white and the ceilings high with exposed, rounded poles laid over a matting. There was plenty of light from numerous windows, all opening onto the courtyard.

It was one of the grander houses of the town, probably belonging to a merchant, Eva judged from the crafted chairs and tables that had somehow managed to remain upright in normal positions, unlike the furnishings in other houses that were tossed about and broken. She slowly edged around a doorway into a large rectangular room. She gasped and stood there, rooted in disgust at finding a grisly pile of rotting human limbs, neatly stacked in what was the kitchen.

Eva fought back the rising sickness, suddenly feeling drained and empty and frightened. She fled from the hideous sight and stumbled into a bedroom. Shock piled on top of shock. She froze and stared at a man lying on a bed as if relaxing, his eyes wide open. His head was propped up on a cushion and his hands were stretched at his side, palms up. He stared back at her through sightless eyes that might have been on loan from the devil. The whites of the eyes were a bright pinkish colour while the irises were a deep red. For a frightful instant she thought he was still alive. But there was no rise in his chest from breathing, and his satanic-coloured eyes never blinked.

Eva stood there, staring back for what seemed a long time. Finally, she mustered up her courage and walked over to the bed and touched the carotid artery in his neck with the tips of her fingers. There was no pulse. She leaned over and lifted his arm. Rigor mortis had barely stiffened his muscles. She straightened as she heard footsteps behind her. She whirled around and saw Hopper and Grimes.

They moved around her and looked down at the corpse. Then abruptly, Hopper laughed, the sound booming throughout the house. 'By God, Grimes. You wanted a fresh victim for an autopsy, and there it lies.'

After Batutta made the last trip into the village with the UN investigation team and their portable analysis equipment, he parked the Mercedes beside the aircraft. The inside of the cockpit and passenger cabin had quickly become an oven under the onslaught of the sun, and the crew was lounging in the shade under one wing. Though they had acted indifferent around the scientists when Batutta was present, they now came to attention and saluted him.

'Anyone left in the plane?' Batutta asked.

The chief pilot shook his head. 'You took the last of them to the village. The aircraft is empty.'

Batutta smiled at the pilot who wore an airline uniform with stripes on the sleeve. 'A fine piece of acting, Lieutenant Djemaa. Dr Hopper took the bait. You fooled him completely into thinking you were a substitute crew.'

'Thank you, Captain. And thank my South African mother for teaching me English.'

'I must use the radio to contact Colonel Mansa.'

'If you will come to the cockpit, l will set the frequency for you.'

Stepping into the aircraft cockpit was like stepping into a bucket of molten lead. Though Lieutenant Djemaa left the side windows open for ventilation, the heat still sucked the breath from Batutta. He sat and suffered while the disguised Malian air force pilot hailed Colonel Mansa's headquarters. Once contact was made Djemaa turned over the microphone to Batutta and thankfully left the steamy cockpit.

'This is Falcon-one. Over.'

'I'm here, Captain,' came the familiar voice of Mansa. 'You can dispense with the code. I doubt if enemy agents are listening in. What is your situation?'

'The natives of Asselar are all dead. The Westerners are operating freely in the village. I repeat, all the villagers are dead.'

'Those bloody cannibals killed themselves off, did they?'

'Yes, Colonel, down to the last woman and child. Dr Hopper and his people believe everyone was poisoned.'

'Do they have proof?'

'Not yet. They're analysing the water from the well and performing autopsies on the victims now.'

'No matter. Play along with them. As soon as they've finished with their little experiments, fly them to Tebezza. General Kazim has arranged a welcoming committee.'

Batutta could well imagine what the General had planned for Hopper. He detested the big Canadian; he detested them all. 'I shall see they arrive in sound shape.'

'Accomplish your mission, Captain, and I can safely promise you a promotion.'

'Thank you, Colonel. Over and out.'

Grimes set up shop in the house of the dead man Eva had discovered. It was the largest and cleanest of any building in the village. He performed pathology on the corpse found in the bedroom while Eva carried out blood tests. Hopper did chemical analysis of several wells that produced the town's meagre water supply. The other members of the team began analysing tissue and bone samples from a random selection of the dead. In one large storage house behind the market centre, they found the trashed Land Rovers from the safari whose members had been massacred. They put the vehicles into service shuttling supplies back and forth between the village and the aircraft while Captain Batutta wandered about, making himself generally useless.

The stench of the dead was too overpowering for sleep, so they worked through the night and into the next evening before taking a break. Camp was set up around the aircraft. After a brief sleep, dinner of packaged, condensed beef stew, the World Health team sat around an oil heater to ward off the 60-degree drop in temperature from the desert's daily high of 44 degrees C (111 degrees F). Batutta played congenial host and brewed them a pungent African tea, listening intently while everyone relaxed and compared notes.

Hopper puffed his pipe to life and nodded at Warren Grimes. 'Suppose you begin, Warren. And give us a report of your examination of the only decent body we found.'

Grimes took a clipboard from one of his assistants and studied it for a moment under the glare of a Coleman lantern. 'In all my years of experience, I've never seen so many complications in one human. Reddish discoloration of the eyes, both the iris and the whites. Skin tissue an extreme flushed, bronze colour. Greatly enlarged spleen. Blood clots in the vessels of the heart, the brain, and extremities. Kidneys damaged. Heavy scarring in the liver and pancreas. Very high haemoglobin. Degeneration of fatty tissue. No wonder these people ran amok and ate each other. Put all the disorders together and you could easily produce uncontrolled psychosis.'

'Uncontrolled?' asked Eva.

'The victim slowly went mad as the conditions increased, especially damage to the brain, and he eventually went berserk, as evidenced by the signs of cannibalism. In my humble estimation it's a miracle he lived as long as he did.'

'Your diagnostic conclusion?' Hopper probed.

'Death by massive polycythemia vera, a disease of unknown cause whose symptoms are increased numbers of red blood cells and haemoglobin in the circulation. In this case a massive infusion of red blood cells that produced irreparable damage to the victim's internal systems. And because blood clotting factors were not created in enough amounts for heart stoppage and stroke, haemorrhages occurred throughout the body, becoming especially visible in the skin and eyes. It is as though he was injected with massive doses of vitamin B-12, which as you all know is essential in the development of red blood cells.'

Hopper turned to Eva. 'You did the blood testing. What about the cells themselves? Did they maintain their normal flat, round shapes with depressed centres?'

Eva shook her head. 'No, they were formed like none I've ever seen before. Almost triangular with spore-like projections. As Dr Grimes stated, their number was incredibly high. There are roughly 5.2 million red cells per cubic millimetre of blood in the average adult human.

Our victim's blood carried three times that number.'

Grimes said, 'I might add that I also discovered evidence of arsenic poisoning, which would have also killed him sooner or later.'

Eva nodded. 'I confirmed Warren's diagnosis. Above normal concentrations of arsenic were found in the blood samples. Also, the cobalt level went off scale.'

'Cobalt?' Hopper straightened in his camp chair.

'Not surprising,' said Grimes. 'Vitamin B-12 contains almost 4.5 per cent cobalt.'

'Both of your findings pretty well back the results of my analysis of the community wells,' said Hopper. 'There was enough arsenic and cobalt in a common cup of water to choke a camel.'

'The underground water table,' said Eva, staring into the glow from the heater. 'The flow must have slowly worked itself through a geologic deposit of cobalt and arsenic.'

'If I recall my university geology class,' Hopper said, thinking back, 'a common arsenide is niccolite, a mineral often associated with cobalt.'

'Still only the tip of the iceberg,' cautioned Grimes. 'Both elements combined were not enough to cause this mess. Some other substance or compound acted as a catalyst with the cobalt and arsenic to push the level of toxicity beyond tolerant bounds and mushroomed the red cell count, one we missed.'

'And mutated them as well,' Eva added.

'Not to muddy the mystery any worse than it already is,' said Hopper. 'But something else turned up in my analysis. I found very high traces of radioactivity.'

'Interesting,' Grimes said lukewarmly. 'But if anything, long exposure to above normal radiation levels would have lowered the red cell count. I saw nothing during my examination to suggest chronic effects of radioactivity.'

'Suppose the radiation penetrated the well water only recently?' Eva offered.

'A distinct possibility,' admitted Grimes. 'But we're still left with the enigma of an unknown killer substance.'

'Our equipment is limited,' Hopper shrugged. 'If we're looking at a new strain of bacteria or some combinations of exotic chemicals, we may not be able to totally identify the causes here. We'll have to take samples back to our laboratory in Paris.'

'A synthetic by-product,' Eva murmured thoughtfully. Then she made a sweeping gesture around the desert. 'Where can it possibly come from? Certainly not from around here.'

'The hazardous waste disposal at Fort Foureau?' Grimes advanced.

Hopper studied the bowl of his pipe. 'Two hundred kilometres northwest. A bit far to carry a contaminant against prevailing winds and deposit it in the town wells. And that doesn't explain the high radiation levels. The Fort Foureau facility is not designed to accept radioactive waste. Besides, the hazardous materials are all burned, so there is no way they could penetrate an underground water supply and then be carried this far without having any deadly chemicals absorbed into the soil.'

'Okay,' said Eva. 'What's our next step?'

'Pack up and fly to Cairo and then on to Paris with our samples. We'll take our prime specimen also. Wrap him good and keep him cool and he should remain in decent shape until we get him bedded down in ice in Cairo.'

Eva nodded. 'I agree. The sooner we perform our research under proper conditions, the better.'

Hopper turned and stared at Batutta who had said nothing but sat listening, pretending indifference while a tape recorder under his shirt monitored every word.

'Captain Batutta.'

'Dr Hopper.'

'We have decided to push on to Egypt first thing in the morning. Is this agreeable with you?'

Batutta flashed a wide smile and twisted one end of his moustache. 'I regret I must stay behind and report to my superiors on the plight of the village. You are free to continue to Cairo.'

'We can't just leave you here.'

'There is plenty of gas in the vehicles. 1 will simply take one of the Land Rovers and drive back to Timbuktu.'

'That's a 400-kilometre trek. You know the way?'

'I was born and bred in the desert,' Batutta said. 1 will leave at sunrise and be in Timbuktu by nightfall.'

'Will our change of plan place you in any difficulty with Colonel Mansa?' asked Grimes.

'My orders were to serve you,' Batutta said patronizingly. 'Do not give it another thought. I am only sorry I cannot accompany you to Cairo.'

'That settles it,' said Hopper, rising from his chair. 'We'll load up our equipment first thing in the morning and take off for Egypt.'

As the meeting broke up and the scientists headed for their tents, Batutta lingered by the heater. He switched off the concealed tape recorder, and then raised a flashlight and blinked it twice at the cockpit window. A minute later the chief pilot climbed down the boarding ladder and approached Batutta.

'You signalled,' he said softly.

'The foreign pigs are leaving tomorrow,' replied Batutta. 'I must radio Tebezza and alert them of our arrival.'

'And remind them to give Dr Hopper and his people a proper greeting.'

The chief pilot winced knowingly. 'A disgusting place, Tebezza. Once the passengers are in custody, I don't plan to spend any more time on the ground than necessary.'

186

'Your orders are to fly back to the airport at Bamako,' said Batutta.

'Gladly,' the chief pilot made a brief bow of his head. 'Good night, Captain.'

Eva had taken a short walk to enjoy the clear air and the carpet of stars across the sky. She returned in time to see the pilot walk toward the aircraft, leaving Batutta alone by the heater.

Too compliant and far too eager to please, she mused. There's going to be trouble. She shook her head as if to cast off the thought. There you go again with your suspicious female nature. What can he do to stop them? Once in the air there would be no turning back. They would be free of the horror and on their way to a more friendly and open society. She took satisfaction in knowing she would never return. And yet something deep inside, her intuition perhaps, cautioned her not to feel too secure.

17

'How long have they been on our tail?' Giordino asked, rubbing three hours of sleep from his eyes and focusing on the image emanating within the radar screen.

'I spotted them about 75 kilometres back, just after we passed into Malian territory,' answered Pitt. He stood to one side of the wheel, casually steering with his right hand.

'You get a look at their armament?'

'No, the boat was concealed 10 metres up a branch of the river. I caught a hard reflection on the surface radar that looked suspicious. Soon as we passed out of sight around a bend, they pulled into the channel and began chasing our wake.'

'Might be only a routine patrol.'

'Routine patrols don't hide under camouflaged netting.'

Giordino studied the distance scale on the radar. 'They're making no attempt to narrow the gap.'

'Just biding their time.'

'Poor old gunboat,' Giordino said sorrowfully. 'It doesn't know it's about to go to that great scrap yard in the sky.'

'Sad to say, there are complications,' said Pitt slowly. 'The gunboat isn't the only bloodhound on the scent.'

'They have friends?'

'The Malian military has thrown out the steel welcome mat.' Pitt twisted his body and looked up at the flawless blue, afternoon sky that was barren of clouds. 'A flight of Malian fighter jets is circling the sky to the east of us.'

Giordino caught sight of them at once. The blazing sun glinted off their cockpit canopies. 'French Mirage fighters, the newer modified model, I reckon. Six — no, seven of them — less than 6 kilometres away.'

Pitt twisted again and pointed across the river to the west. 'And that dust cloud beyond that range of hills running along the shoreline. That belongs to a convoy of armoured cars.'

'How many?' Giordino asked as he mentally inventoried his remaining missiles.

'I counted four when they raced across a stretch of open ground.'

'No tanks?'

'Our speed is 30 knots. Tanks couldn't keep up with us.'

'We won't be surprising anyone this time,' said Giordino matter-of-factly. 'Word of our bite has preceded us.'

'An obvious deduction judging by their reluctance to come within our effective range.'

'The question that comes to mind is when will old what's-his-name — '

'Zateb Kazim?'

'Whoever,' Giordino shrugged indifferently. 'When will he sound the charge?'

'If he's smarter than that comic strip Admiral of the Benin navy, and he wants to confiscate the *Calliope* for his own pleasure, all he has to do is wait us out. Eventually, we'll run out of river.'

'And fuel.'

'That too.' Pitt went silent and gazed at the wide, lazy Niger wandering through the sandy plain. The yellow-gold sun was creeping toward the horizon as blue and white storks winged the hot afternoon air or strolled the shallows on long stick-like legs. A school of Nile perch leaped in the air and sparkled like miniature fireworks as the *Calliope* chased them over the placid water. A pinnace glided past on its way downriver, hull stained black with colourful painted designs on its double-ender bow and stern, its sail barely filled under

189

a whisper of wind. A few of the crew slept on a cargo of rice sacks under a frayed awning while others poled with the current. All was serene and picturesque. Pitt found it hard to believe death and destruction skirted their course up the river.

Giordino broke Pitt's revery. 'Didn't you mention that woman you met in Egypt was going to Mali?'

Pitt nodded. 'She's connected with the UN team from the World Health Organization. They were flying to Mali to investigate a strange epidemic that had broken out among the desert villages.'

'Too bad you can't rendezvous with her,' said Giordino, smiling. 'You could sit under a desert moon with your arm around her, whisper of your exploits in her ear, and sift sand.'

'If that's your idea of a hot date, no wonder you bat zero.'

'How else can you entertain a geologist?'

'Biochemist,' Pitt corrected him.

Giordino's expression suddenly turned serious. 'Did it ever occur to you that she and her scientist buddies might be looking for the same toxin we are?'

'The thought crossed my mind.'

At that moment Rudi Gunn hustled up from his lab below, his face haggard but broken by a wide grin. 'Got it,' he announced triumphantly.

Giordino looked at him, not comprehending.

'Got what?'

Gunn didn't answer. He just smiled and smiled.

Pitt knew almost immediately. 'You found it?'

'The glop that's exciting the red tides?' Giordino muttered.

Gunn nodded.

Pitt pumped his hand. 'Congratulations, Rudi.'

'I was almost ready to give up,' said Gunn. 'But my negligence opened the door. I've been putting hundreds of water samples through the gas chromatograph, and haven't been checking on the inner workings as often as I should. When I finally took a look at the results, I found a coating of cobalt inside the instrument's test column. I was shocked to see a metal was being extracted with synthetic organic pollutants and finding its way into the gas chromatograph. After frantic hours of experiments, modifications, and tests, I identified an exotic organometallic compound that's a combination of an altered synthetic amino acid and cobalt.'

'Sounds Greek to me,' shrugged Giordino. 'What's an amino acid?'

'The stuff proteins are made of.'

'How can it get in the river?' asked Pitt.

'Can't say,' replied Gunn. 'My guess is the synthetic amino acid came from a genetic engineering biotechnology laboratory whose wastes are being dumped along with chemical and nuclear wastes at the source area. For it to naturally mix into the vicious pollutant that's causing the red tides after reaching the sea seems remote. I believe it's forming at a common location.'

'Could it be a dump site with nuclear waste too?'

Gunn nodded. 'I'm finding fairly high readings of radiation in the water. It's only another portion of the overall pollution and has no relation to our contaminant's qualities, but there is a definite connection.'

Pitt didn't reply but looked again into the radar screen at the image of the gunboat, still out of eyesight astern. If anything, it had dropped farther back. He turned and scanned the sky for the fighterjets. They were still lazily clawing at the sky, conserving their fuel while keeping a distant watch over the *Calliope*. The river had widened to several kilometres and he lost sight of the armoured cars.

'Our job is only half done,' he said. 'The next exercise is to target where the toxin enters the Niger. The Malians don't seem in any hurry to harass us. So we'll continue our survey upstream and attempt to wrap this thing up before they slam the door.'

'With our data transmission system kaput, how do we get the results to Chapman and Sandecker?' asked Giordino.

'I'll figure something.'

Gunn placed his trust in Pitt without hesitation. He nodded without speaking and returned to his cabin lab.

Pitt thankfully turned over the helm to Giordino while he stretched out on a deck mat under the cockpit canopy and caught up on his lost sleep.

When he woke up, the sun's orange ball was a third down over the horizon, and yet the air felt 10 degrees warmer. A quick check of the radar showed the gunboat was still dogging their stern, but the watchdog fighter jets were on a course back to their base to refuel. They were getting cocky, Pitt surmised. The Malians must have thought their quarry was in the bag. Why else would the fighters depart without being relieved by another flight. As he rose to his feet and stretched his arms and shoulders, Giordino handed him a mug of coffee.

'Here, this should wake you up. Good Egyptian coffee with mud on the bottom of the cup.'

'How long was I in dreamland?'

'You were dead to the world for a little over two hours.'

'Have we passed Gao?'

'Cruised past the city about 50 kilometres back. You missed seeing a floating villa with a bevy of bikini-clad beauties throwing kisses to me from the railings.'

'You're putting me on.'

Giordino held up three fingers. 'Scout's honour. It was the fanciest houseboat I've ever laid eyes on.'

'Is Rudi still reading strong toxin levels?'

Giordino nodded. 'He says the concentration gets hotter with each passing kilometre.'

'We must be close.'

'He thinks we're almost on top of the stuff.'

Just for an instant something flickered deep in Pitt's eyes, a sudden gleam, almost as if something was created, something imagined that reflected from inside his brain. Giordino always knew when Pitt departed reality and travelled to some unknown destination. With a blink of his opaline eyes all recognition was gone, replaced with a view of another scene.

Giordino stared at him curiously. 'I don't like that look.'

Pitt came back down to earth. 'Just thinking of a way to keep the *Calliope* from a despotic backwater jerk who wants it for his drunken orgies.'

'And how do you expect to erase the possessive gleam in Kazim's eye?'

Pitt smiled like a reincarnated Fagin. 'By conjuring up a dirty scheme to defeat his expectations.'

Shortly before sunset, Gunn called from below. 'We've crossed into clean water. The contamination just disappeared off my instruments.'

Pitt and Giordino immediately turned their heads and scouted the shores. The river at this point ran on a slight angle from west of north to east of south. There were no villages or bordering roads to be seen. Only desolation met the eyes, level and barren without disruption all the way to the four horizons.

'Empty,' muttered Giordino. 'Empty as a shaven armpit.'

Gunn emerged, staring back over the stern. 'See anything?'

'Look for yourself,' Giordino swung an arm like a compass. 'The cupboard's bare. Nothing but sand.'

'We have a break in the geology to the east,' said Pitt, motioning at a wide ravine dividing the shore. 'Looks as though it once carried water.'

'Not in our lifetime,' said Gunn. 'Appears to have been

a tributary into the main channel during wetter centuries.'

Giordino studied the ancient streambed solemnly. 'Rudi must have tuned in a video game. There's no contamination entering the river here.'

'Swing around and make another run so I can recheck my data,' said Gunn.

Pitt complied and ran several lanes back and forth as if mowing a lawn, beginning close to the shore and working out into the channel toward the opposite bank until his props churned silt on the rising bottom. The radar showed the tailing gunboat had stopped, the captain and his officers probably wondering what the crew of the *Calliope* was up to.

Gunn popped his head through the hatch after the final run. 'Swear to God, the highest concentration of toxin comes from the mouth of that big wash on the east bank.'

They all stared dubiously at the centuries-old dry riverbed. The rock-strewn bottom curled northward toward a range of low dunes in the desert wasteland. No one spoke as Pitt set the throttles on idle and let the yacht drift with the current.

'No evidence of toxic residue beyond this point?' questioned Pitt.

'None,' Gunn answered flatly. 'The concentration goes off scale just below the old wash and then disappears upstream.'

'Maybe it's a natural by-product of the soil,' offered Giordino.

'This ungodly compound can't be produced by nature,' muttered Gunn. 'I promise you that.'

'How about an underground drainage pipe running from a chemical plant beyond the dunes,' Pitt speculated.

Gunn shrugged. 'Can't tell without further investigation. This is as far as we can go. We've kept our end of the bargain. Now it's up to contamination specialists to pick up the rest of the pieces.'

Pitt gazed over the stern at the gunboat that had crept into view. 'Our hounds are getting nosy. Not bright of us to show them what devilment we're about. We'd best continue on course as though we're still taking in the scenery.'

'Some scenery,' grunted Giordino. 'Death Valley is a garden spot compared to this.'

Pitt pushed the throttles forward, and the *Calliope* lifted her bow and surged ahead with a mellow roar from her exhaust. In less than two minutes the Malian gunboat was left far in the yacht's spreading wake. Now, he thought, comes the fun part.

18

General Kazim sat in a leather executive chair at the end of a conference table flanked by two of Mali's cabinet ministers and his military Chief-of-Staff. At first glance the modern paintings on the silk-covered walls and the thick carpet gave the meeting room the look of a posh office in a modern building. The only giveaway was the curved ceiling and the muffled sound of the jet engines.

The elegantly furnished Airbus Industrie A300 was only one of several gifts Yves Massarde had presented to Kazim in return for allowing the Frenchman industrialist to conduct his vast operations in Mali without wasting time on such trifling details as government laws and restrictions. Whatever Massarde wanted, Kazim gave, so long as the general's foreign bank accounts became fat and he was kept in expensive toys.

Besides acting as a private means of transportation for the General and his cronies, the Airbus was electronically fitted out as a military communications command centre, mostly to divert any accusations of corruption from the small but vocal opposition party members of President Tahir's parliament.

Kazim listened silently while his Chief-of-Staff, Colonel Sghir Cheik, explained in detail the reports of the destruction of the Benin gunboats and helicopter. He then passed Kazim two photographs taken of the super yacht on her passage up the river from the sea. 'In the first photo,' Cheik pointed out, 'the yacht is flying the French tricolour. But since entering our country, she is sailing under a pirate flag.'

'What nonsense is this?' demanded Kazim.

'We don't know,' Cheik confessed. 'The French ambassador swears the boat is unknown to his government and is not documented under French ownership. As to the pirate flag, it is an enigma.'

'You must know where the boat came from.'

'Our intelligence sources have been unable to trace its manufacturer or the country of origin. Its lines and style are unfamiliar to the major boat yards in America and Europe.'

'Japanese or Chinese perhaps,' suggested Mali's Foreign Minister, Messaoud Djerma.

Cheik pulled the hairs of his wedge-shaped beard and adjusted his tinted, designer glasses. 'Our agents have also canvassed boat builders in Japan, Hong Kong, and Taiwan who design premier yachts with speeds exceeding 50 kilometres an hour. None had any record or knowledge of such a boat.'

'You have no information about this intrusion at all?' Kazim asked unbelievingly.

'Nothing.' Cheik held up his hands. 'It's as though Allah dropped her from the heavens.'

'An innocent-looking yacht that changes flags like a woman changes dresses sails up the Niger River,' Kazim snarled coldly, 'destroys half the Benin navy and its commanding Admiral, calmly enters our water without bothering to stop for customs and immigration inspection, and you sit there and tell me my intelligence network can't identify the nationality of the builder or the owner.'

'I'm sorry, my General,' said Cheik nervously. His myopic eyes avoided Kazim's icy stare. 'Perhaps if I had been permitted to send an agent on board at the dock in Niamey . . .'

'It cost enough as it was to bribe Niger officials to look the other way when the boat docked for refuelling. The last thing I needed was a bumbling agent causing an incident.'

'Have they replied to radio contact?' asked Djerma.

Cheik shook his head. 'Our warnings have gone unanswered. They have ignored all communications.'

'What in Allah's sacred name do they want?' questioned Seyni Gashi. The Chief of Kazim's Military Council looked far more like a camel trader than a soldier. 'What is their mission?'

'It seems the mystery is beyond my intelligence people's mentality to solve,' said Kazim irritably.

'Now that it's entered our territory,' said Foreign Minister Djerma, 'why not merely board and take possession?'

'Admiral Matabu tried it, and now he lies at the bottom of the river.'

'The boat is armed with missile launchers,' Cheik pointed out. 'Highly effective judging from the results.'

'Surely, we have the necessary firepower – '

'The crew and their boat are trapped on the Niger with nowhere to go,' interrupted Kazim. 'There is no turning back and running 1000 kilometres to the sea. They must realize any attempt to flee will be cause for our fighter aircraft and land artillery to destroy them. We wait and watch. And when they run out of fuel, their only hope of survival will be to surrender. Then our questions will be answered.'

'Can we safely assume the crew will be persuaded to reveal their mission?' inquired Djerma.

'Yes, yes,' Cheik quickly answered. 'And much more.'

The copilot stepped from the cockpit and snapped to attention. 'We have the boat in visual sight, sir.'

'So at last we can see this enigma for ourselves,' said Kazim. 'Tell the pilot to give us a good view.'

The weariness of the punishing grind and the disappointment of not pinpointing the actual source of the toxin had dulled Pitt's vigilance. His usually sharp powers of perception

198

lagged and his mind sidetracked any vision of the steel pincers that were slowly snapping shut on the *Calliope*. It was Giordino who heard the distant whine of jet engines, looked up, and saw it first — an aircraft flying less than 200 metres above the river, running lights blinking in the blue dusk. It visibly swelled into a large passenger jet with Malian national colours striped along the side of its fuselage. Two or three fighters as escorts would have been enough. This plane was surrounded by twenty. It seemed at first the pilot intended to fly straight down the river and buzz the *Calliope*, but 2 kilometres away it banked and began to circle, drawing closer in a slow spiral. The fighter escort spun off upward and launched into a series of figure eights overhead.

When the jet — Pitt by now had spotted the huge radar dome on the nose and recognized it as command centre aircraft — came within 100 metres, faces could be distinguished through the ports staring down, taking in every detail of the super yacht.

Pitt exhaled a long, silent sigh and waved. Then he made a theatrical bow. 'Step right up, folks, and see the pirate ship with its merry band of river rats. Enjoy the show, but do not damage the merchandise. You could get hurt.'

'Ain't it the truth.' Crouched on the ladder to the engine room, poised to leap at his missile launcher, Giordino stared warily at the circling plane. 'If he so much as waggles his wings I'll divide, demolish, and disperse him.'

Gunn leisurely sat in a deck chair and doffed his cap at the aerial spectators. 'Unless you have a method for making us invisible, I suggest we humour them. It's one thing to be an underdog, but it's quite another to be easy pickings.'

'We're overmatched all right,' Pitt said, shaking off any trace of weariness. 'Nothing we do will make any difference. They've got enough firepower to blow the *Calliope* into toothpicks.'

Gunn scanned the low banks of the river and the barren

landscapes beyond. 'No use in grounding on shore and making a run for it. The countryside is wide open. We wouldn't get 50 metres.'

'So what do we do?' asked Giordino.

'Surrender and take our chances,' Gunn offered lamely.

'Even chased rats slash and run,' said Pitt. 'I'm for the last defiant gesture, a wasted gesture maybe, but what the hell. We give them a nasty sign with our fists, shove the throttles to the wall, and run like hell. If they get downright belligerent, we make cemetery fodder out of them.'

'More likely they'll do it to us,' complained Giordino.

'You really mean that?' Gunn demanded incredulously.

'Not on your life,' Pitt said emphatically. 'Mrs Pitt's boy has no death wish. I'm gambling Kazim wants this boat so bad, he paid off Niger officials to let it pass into Mali so he could grab it. If I win, he won't want even the slightest scratch or dent in the hull.'

'You're putting all your eggs in the wrong basket,' argued Gunn. 'Shoot down one plane and you'll stir up a hornet's nest. Kazim will send everything he's got after us.'

'I certainly hope so.'

'You're talking like a crazy man,' said Giordino suspiciously.

'The contamination data,' Pitt said patiently. 'That's why we're here. Remember?'

'We don't have to be reminded,' said Gunn, beginning to see a slip of light in Pitt's seeming loss of reality. 'So what's boiling in your evil cauldron of a brain?'

'As much as I hate to ruin a beautiful and perfectly good boat, a diversion may be the only way one of us can escape and carry the results of our operation out of Africa and into the hands of Sandecker and Chapman.'

'There's method to his madness after all,' Giordino admitted. 'Keep talking.'

'Nothing complicated,' explained Pitt. 'In another hour

it will be dark. We reverse course and get as close to Gao as we can before Kazim gets tired of the game. Rudi goes over the side and swims for shore. Then you and I start the fireworks show and take off downriver like a vestal virgin chased by barbarian hordes.'

'That gunboat might have something to say about that, don't you think?' Gunn reminded him.

'A mere trifle. If my timing is on key, we'll flash past the Malian navy before they know we've come and gone.'

Giordino peered over his sunglasses. 'Sounds remotely possible. Once the good times roll, the Malian's attention won't be focused on a body in the water.'

'Why me?' Gunn demanded. 'Why not one of you?'

'Because you're the best qualified,' Pitt justified. 'You're sly, cunning, and slippery. If anyone can grease their way into the airport at Gao and onto an airplane out of the country, it's you. You're also the only bona fide chemist among us. That alone entitles you to lay bare the toxic substance and its entry point into the river.'

'We could make a run for our embassy in the capital city of Bamako.'

'Fat chance. Bamako is 600 kilometres away.'

'Dirk makes good sense,' Giordino agreed. 'His grey matter and mine put together couldn't give you the formula for bathroom soap.'

'I'll not run out and allow the two of you to sacrifice your lives for me,' Gunn insisted.

'Don't talk stupid,' Giordino said stonily. 'You know damn well Dirk and I don't have a mutual suicide pact.' He turned to Pitt. 'Do we?'

'Perish the thought,' Pitt said loftily. 'After we cover Rudi's getaway, we fix the *Calliope* so Kazim never enjoys its luxury. After that, we abandon ship ourselves and then mount a safari across the desert to discover the true source of the toxin.'

'We what?' Giordino looked aghast. 'A safari . . .'

'You have an incredible knack for simplicity,' said Gunn.

'Across the desert,' Giordino mumbled.

'A little hike never hurt anybody,' Pitt said with a jovial air.

'I was wrong,' Giordino moaned. 'He wants us to self-destruct.'

'Self-destruct?' Pitt repeated. 'My friend, you just said the magic words.'

19

Pitt took one final look at the aircraft overhead. They still circled aimlessly. They had shown no inclination to attack and obviously had no intention of making any now. Once the *Calliope* began her dash downriver Pitt could not afford the time to keep them under observation. Running wide open over a strange waterway in the black of night at 70 knots would take every shred of his concentration.

He shifted his gaze from the aircraft to the huge flag he'd run up the mast that supported the shattered satellite antenna. He had removed the small Jolly Roger from the stern jackstaff after finding a United States ensign folded away in a flag locker. It was large, stretching almost 2 metres, but with no breeze to lift it in the dry night air, it hung curled and flaccid around the antenna.

He glanced at the dome on the stern. The shutters were closed. Giordino was not preparing to launch the remaining six rockets. He was attaching them around the fuel tanks before wiring them to a timer/detonator. Gunn, Pitt knew, was below, stuffing the analysis data tapes and water sample records in a plastic cover that he tightly bound and stuffed in a small backpack along with food and survival gear.

Pitt turned his attention to the radar, fixing the position of the Malian gunboat in his mind. He found it surprisingly easy to shake off the tentacles of fatigue. His adrenaline was pumping now that their course was irrevocably set.

He took a deep breath and jammed the triple throttles wide open and crammed the wheel to the starboard stop.

To the men watching from the command aircraft it was as though the *Calliope* had suddenly leaped from the water and twisted around in midair. She carved a sharp arc in the centre of the river, and hurtled downriver under full power, sheeted in a great curtain of foam and spray. Her bow came out of the water like an uplifted sword as her stern plunged deep under a great rooster tail that exploded in the air behind her transom.

The stars and stripes jerked taut and streamed out under the sudden onslaught of wind. Pitt well knew he was going against all government policy, defiantly flying the national emblem on foreign soil during an illegal intrusion. The State Department would scream bloody murder when the enraged Malians beat their breasts and lodged a flaming protest. God only knew the hell that would erupt inside the White House. But he flat didn't give a damn.

The dice were rolling. The black ribbon of water beckoned. Only the dim light of the stars reflected on the smooth surface, and Pitt did not trust his night vision to keep him in the deep part of the channel. If he ran the boat aground at its maximum speed it would disintegrate. His eyes constantly darted from the radar screen to the depth sounder to the dark watercourse ahead before repeating the routine.

He did not waste a glance at the speedometer as the needle hung at the 70-knot mark and then quivered beyond it. Nor did he have to look at the tachometers to know they were creeping past their red lines. The *Calliope* was giving it everything she had for her final voyage, like a thoroughbred running a race beyond her limits. It was almost as if she knew she would never make home port.

When the Malian gunboat moved almost to the centre of the radar screen, Pitt squinted into the darkness. He just discerned the low silhouette of the vessel turning broadside to the channel in an effort to block his passage. It ran no lights, but he didn't doubt for an instant that the crew had their guns aimed down his throat.

He decided to feint to starboard and then cut port to throw off the gunners before skirting the shallows and charging under the gunboat's bow. The Malians had the initiative, but Pitt was banking on Kazim's unwillingness to ruin one of the world's finest speed yachts. The General would be in no hurry. He still had a comfortable margin of several hundred kilometres of river to stop the fleeing boat.

Pitt planted his feet squarely on the deck and positioned his hands on the wheel in preparation for the fast turns. For some unearthly reason the roar from the flat-out turbo diesels and the crescendo of wind pounding in his ears reminded him of the last act of Wagner's *Twilight of the Gods*. All that was missing was the thunder and lightning.

And then that struck too.

The gunboat let loose, and a whole mass of shrieking fire burst through the night, ear-piercing, nightmare bedlam of shells that found and slammed into the *Calliope*.

Aboard the command plane, Kazim stared in shock at the unexpected attack. Then he flew into a rage.

'Who told the Captain of that gunboat to open fire?' he demanded.

Cheik looked stunned. 'He must have taken it upon himself.'

'Order him to cease fire, immediately. I want that boat intact and undamaged.'

'Yes, sir,' Cheik acknowledged, jumping from his chair and rushing to the communications cabin of the aircraft.

'Idiot!' Kazim snapped, his face twisted in anger. 'My orders were explicit. No battle unless I so ordered. I want the Captain and his ship's officers executed for disobeying my command.'

Foreign Minister Messaoud Djerma stared at Kazim in disapproval. 'Those are harsh measures –'

Kazim cut Djerma off with a withering stare. 'Not for those who are disloyal.'

Djerma shrank from the murderous gaze of his superior. No man with a wife and family dared face up to Kazim. Those who questioned the General's demands disappeared as though they never existed.

Very slowly Kazim's eyes turned from Djerma and refocused on the action taking place on the river.

The vicious tracers, glowing weirdly in the desert blackness, streaked across the water, at first swinging wildly to the port of the *Calliope*. It sounded as if a dozen guns were blazing at once. Waterspouts thrashed the water like hail. Then the aim of the gunners steadied and became deadly as the fiery shells walked across the river and began thudding into the now defenceless boat at almost point-blank range. Jagged holes appeared in the bow and foredeck; the shells would have travelled the interior length of the unarmoured boat if they hadn't been absorbed by spare coils of nylon line and deflected by the anchor chain in the forecastle.

There was no time to avoid the initial barrage, barely time to react. Caught totally off balance, Pitt instinctively crouched and in the same movement desperately spun the wheel to avert the devastating fire. The *Calliope* responded and shot clear for a few moments until the gunners corrected and the orange, searing flashes skipped across the river and found the high-speed craft again, ripping the steel hull and shattering the fibreglass superstructure. The thud of the impacts sounded like the tyre of a speeding car thumping over highway centreline reflectors.

Smoke and flame leaped from the holes torn in the forecastle where the tracers had fired the coils of line. The instrument panel shattered and exploded around Pitt. Miraculously, he wasn't hit by the shell, but he faintly felt a trickle of liquid down his cheek. He cursed his stupidity in thinking the Malians wouldn't destroy the *Calliope*. He deeply regretted having Giordino remove the missiles from their launchers and secure them to the fuel tanks. One shell into the engine room and they would all be blown into unidentifiable morsels for the fish.

He was so close to the gunboat now, if he had looked, he could have read the orange dial of his old Doxa dive watch from the muzzle flashes.

He cranked the wheel savagely, swerving the riddled yacht around the gunboat's bow with less than 2 metres to spare. And then he was past, the avalanching slab of water from the sport yacht's wash pitching the gunboat into a rolling motion that threw off the aim of the gunners and sent their shells whistling harmlessly into the night.

And then, quite suddenly, the continuous blast from the gunboat's cannon stopped. Pitt did not bother to fathom the reason for the reprieve. He maintained a zigzag course until the gunboat was left far behind in the darkness. Only when he was sure they were in the clear and the still functioning radar unit showed no indication of attacking aircraft did he relax and exhale his breath in welcome relief.

Giordino appeared beside him, concern on his face. 'You okay?'

'Mad at myself for playing a sucker. How about you and Rudi?'

'A few bruises from being thrown around by your lousy driving. Rudi received a nasty knock on his head when he was knocked flat during a hard turn, but it hasn't stopped him from fighting the fire in the bow.'

'He's a tough little guy.'

Giordino raised a flashlight and shined it on Pitt's face. 'Did you know you have a piece of glass sticking out of your ugly mug?'

Pitt raised one hand from the wheel and tenderly touched a small piece of glass from a gauge that was embedded in his cheek. 'You can see it better than I can. Pull it out.'

Giordino slipped the butt end of the flashlight between his teeth, pointed the beam at Pitt's wound, and gently took hold of the glass shard between his forefinger and thumb. Then with a quick jerk, he yanked it free. Bigger than I thought,' he commented offhandedly. He threw the glass overboard and retrieved a first aid kit from a cockpit cabinet. Three stitches and a bandage later, while Pitt kept his eyes on the instruments and the river, Giordino stood back and admired his handiwork. 'There you go. Another brilliant operation in the continuing saga of Dr Albert Giordino, desert surgeon.'

'What's your next great moment in medicine?' Pitt asked as he spied a dim yellow glow from a lantern and slewed the *Calliope* into a wide arc, just missing a pinnace sailing in the dark.

'Why, presenting the bill, of course.'

'I'll mail you a check.'

Gunn appeared from below, holding a cube of ice against a blossoming bump on the back of his head. 'It's going to break the Admiral's heart when he hears what we did to his boat.'

'Down deep, I don't think he ever expected to see her again,' Giordino prophesied.

'Fire out?' Pitt asked Gunn.

'Still smouldering, but I'll give it another shot from an extinguisher after I breathe the smoke out of my lungs.'

'Any leaks below?'

Gunn shook his head. 'Most of the hits we took were topside. None below the waterline. The bilge is dry.'

'Are the aircraft still in the neighbourhood? The radar only shows one.'

Giordino tilted his head at the sky. 'The big one is still giving us the eye,' he confirmed. 'Too dark to make out the fighters, and they're out of earshot, but my old bones tell me they're hanging around.'

'How far to Gao?' asked Gunn.

'About 75 or 80 kilometres,' Pitt estimated. Even at this speed we won't see the city's lights for another hour or more.'

'Providing those characters up there leave us alone,' Giordino said, his voice raised two octaves to overcome the wind and exhaust.

Gunn pointed to the portable radio that rested on a counter shelf. 'Might help if we strung them along.'

Pitt smiled in the darkness. 'Yes, I think it's time we take calls.'

'Why not?' Giordino went along. 'I'm curious to hear what they have to say.'

'Talking to them might buy us the time we need to reach Gao,' advised Gunn. 'We've a fair way to go.'

Pitt turned the helm over to Giordino, tuned up the volume on the portable radio's speaker so they could all hear above the roar, and spoke into the mouthpiece. 'Good evening,' he answered pleasantly. 'How may I help you?'

There was a short pause. Then a voice replied in French.

'I hate this,' muttered Giordino.

Pitt stared up at the plane as he spoke. *'Non parley vous francais.'*

Gunn wrinkled his brows. 'Do you know what you said?'

Pitt looked at him innocently. 'I informed him I can't speak French.'

'Vous is you,' Gunn lectured him. 'You just told him, *he* can't speak French.'

'Whoever he is will get the drift.'

The voice crackled through the speaker again. 'I understand English.'

'That's helpful,' Pitt replied. 'Go ahead.'

'Identify yourself.'

'You first.'

'Very well, I am General Zateb Kazim, Chief of the Mali Supreme Military Council.'

At the reply Pitt turned and looked at Giordino and Gunn. 'The big man himself.'

'I've always wanted to be recognized by a celebrity,' Giordino said with heavy sarcasm. 'Never thought it would happen in the middle of nowhere.'

'Identify yourself,' Kazim repeated. 'Are you commanding an American vessel?'

'Edward Teach, Captain of the *Queen Anne's Revenge*.'

'I attended university at Princeton,' Kazim replied dryly. 'I am quite familiar with Blackbeard the pirate. Please cease with the satire and surrender your ship.'

'And if I have other plans?'

'You and your crew will be destroyed by Malian Air Force fighter-bombers.'

'If they don't shoot any better than your navy gunboats,' Pitt needled Kazim, 'we haven't a care in the world.'

'Do not toy with me,' Kazim said, his tone suddenly viperous. 'Who are you, and what are you doing in my country?'

'You might say we're down-home folks on a little fishing trip.'

'Stop and surrender your vessel immediately!' Kazim spat.

'No, I don't think I will,' Pitt answered cavalierly.

'You and your crew will surely die if you do not.'

'Then you will lose a boat like no other in the world. A one of a kind. I assume you have an idea of what she's capable of.'

There was a long silence, and Pitt knew that his long shot had struck home.

'I've read the reports of your little altercation with my late friend, Admiral Matabu. I am fully versed on your boat's firepower.'

'Then you know we could have blasted your gunboat to the bottom of the river.'

'I regret that they fired on you against my orders.'

'We can also knock your lumbering command plane out of the sky,' Pitt bluffed.

Kazim was not mentally deficient. He had already considered that event. 'I die, you die. What is the percentage in that?'

'Give me some time to think that over, say until we reach Gao.'

'I'm a generous man,' Kazim said with unaccustomed patience. 'But at Gao you will cease headway and bring your boat alongside the city's ferry dock. If you persist in your foolish attempt to escape, my air force will put you in infidel hell.'

'I understand, General. You make our choice crystal clear.' Pitt flicked off the radio transmit switch and grinned from ear to ear. 'I just love it when I make a good deal.'

The lights of Gao bloomed in the darkness, less than 5 kilometres ahead. Pitt took the wheel from Giordino and motioned at Gunn. 'Get set to hit the water, Rudi.'

Gunn peered hesitantly at the white water swirling past at nearly 75 knots. 'Not at this speed, I won't.'

'Not to worry.' Pitt eased his mind. 'I'll make a sudden cut down to 10 knots. You slip over the side opposite the aircraft. Soon as you're away, I'll crank her up again.' Then to Giordino, 'Sweet talk Kazim. Keep him occupied.'

Giordino lifted the radio and spoke in a muffled tone. 'Could you repeat your terms, General?'

'Stop your senseless attempt at escape, turn over your vessel at Gao, and you live. Those are the terms.'

As Kazim talked, Pitt edged the *Calliope* closer to the shore of the river that held the town. The tension in the cockpit and his anxiety increased, a tension that spread to his three friends. He reasoned that Gunn had to go in before the lights of Gao revealed him in the black water by their reflection. And he had cause to be anxious. The game was to keep the Malians from becoming suspicious by his deceptive manoeuvre. The depth-sounder showed the bottom was coming up fast. He yanked the throttles back, lurching the *Calliope*'s bow deep into the water. The speed fell off so quickly that he was thrown forward against the cockpit counter.

'Now!' Pitt yelled at Gunn. 'Go for it and good luck.'

Without a word of farewell, the little scientist from NUMA tightly clutched the straps to his backpack and rolled over the railing out of sight. Almost instantly, Pitt shoved the throttles to their stops again.

Giordino stared out over the stern, but Gunn was completely lost in the black river. Satisfied his friend was safely swimming across the 50 metres of water separating the bank from the boat, he turned back and calmly continued his conversation with General Kazim.

'If you promise us safe passage out of your country, the boat is yours, or what's left of it after your gunboat mangled it.'

Kazim indicated no suspicion of the brief pause in the *Calliope*'s velocity through the water. 'I accept,' he purred, fooling nobody.

'We have no wish to die in a hail of gunfire in a polluted river.'

'A wise choice,' replied Kazim. The words came formal and civil, but the hostility, the triumph were apparent in his tone. 'Indeed there are no options for you to do anything else.'

Pitt had a sinking feeling he had overplayed his hand. There was little doubt in his mind, or in Giordino's mind too, that Kazim meant to kill them and throw their bodies to the vultures. They had one shot at diverting the Malians from Gunn, one shot at staying alive, but the odds were slim, so low in fact that no selfrespecting gambler would waste a cheap bet on them.

His plan, if it could subtly be called that, would buy them a few hours' time, nothing more. He began to curse his folly for thinking they might get away with it.

But a moment later, salvation, unexpected and unimagined, appeared through the night.

20

Giordino tapped Pitt's shoulder and pointed down the river. 'That blaze of lights off the starboard bow, that's the jazzy houseboat I told you about. The one we passed earlier. It's decked out like a billionaire's yacht, complete with helicopter and a bevy of friendly women.'

'Think it might carry a satellite communications system we could borrow to contact Washington?'

'I wouldn't be surprised if it had telex.' Pitt turned and smiled down at Giordino. 'Since we have no pressing engagements, why not drop in?'

Giordino laughed and clapped him on the back. 'I'll set the detonator.'

'Thirty seconds should do it.'

'Done.'

Giordino handed the radio back to Pitt and dropped down the ladder to the engine room. He reappeared almost immediately while Pitt was in the act of programming the course into a computer and engaging the automatic pilot. Luckily the river was wide and straight, allowing the *Calliope* to cruise on her own for a considerable distance after they abandoned her.

He nodded at Giordino. 'Ready?'

'Say the word.'

'Speaking of words.' Pitt raised the portable radio to his mouth, 'General Kazim.'

'Yes?'

'I've changed my mind. You can't have the boat after all. Have a nice day.'

Giordino grinned. 'I like your style.'

Pitt casually tossed the radio overboard and stood poised until the *Calliope* was even with the houseboat. Then he pulled back the throttles.

As soon as the speed fell off to 20 knots he shouted, 'Now!'

Giordino needed no coaxing. He ran across the rear deck and launched himself over the stern. He struck the water in the centre of the churning wake, his splash lost in a spray of seething froth. Pitt hesitated only long enough to cram the throttles forward before leaping over the side, curling himself in a ball. The sudden impact came with a jolt that nearly knocked the wind out of him. Thankfully, the water was lukewarm and smothered him like a thick blanket. He took great care not to swallow any of the contaminated river. Their predicament was dire enough without becoming deathly sick.

He rolled over on his back just in time to see the *Calliope* rushing into the darkness with the speed and roar of an express train, a boat lifeless and abandoned with only moments to live. Pitt floated and stared and waited for the missiles and the fuel tanks to explode. He did not wait long. Even at over a kilometre the blast was deafening, and the shock wave that travelled through the water came like an invisible blow to his body. Flame belched through the blackness in a huge orange ball as the faithful *Calliope* blew herself into a thousand pieces. Within half a minute the flames were swallowed by the night and all trace of the beautiful sport yacht was gone.

There was also a strange hush now that the roar of the yacht's engines and the explosion faded across the desert beyond the shore. The only sounds came from the drone of Kazim's command plane and the soft strains of a piano playing on the houseboat.

Giordino sidestroked past. 'Swimming? I thought you'd be walking.'

'Only on special occasions.'

Giordino lifted a hand skyward. 'Think we conned them?'

'Temporarily, but they'll figure it out soon enough.'

'Shall we crash the party?'

Pitt rolled over and began an easy breaststroke. 'By all means.'

As he swam he studied the houseboat. It was the perfect craft to navigate a river. The draft couldn't have been more than 4 feet. The design and shape reminded Pitt of an old Mississippi side paddle steamer, like the famed *Robert E. Lee*, except there were no paddle wheels and the superstructure was far more modern. One true similarity was the pilothouse perched on the forward part of the upper deck. If built for the open sea with an oceangoing hull it would have fallen in the elegant class of a mega-yacht. He studied the sleek helicopter perched on the middle stern deck, the glass-enclosed three-level atrium filled with tropical plants, the space-age electronics that sprouted from behind the wheelhouse. The incredible houseboat was a fantasy turned real.

They were within 2 metres of the houseboat gangway when the Malian gunboat came forging downriver at full speed. Pitt could see the shadowy figures of the boat's officers on the bridge. They were all peering intently toward the explosion and paid no attention to the water off their beams. He also saw a group of crewmen on the bow and didn't have to be told they were scanning the dark river for survivors while clutching automatic weapons with the safety catches in the *off* position.

In a quick glance before he ducked under the swirling wave chopped out by the gunboat's twin props, Pitt saw a crowd of passengers suddenly appearing on the houseboat's promenade deck. They were talking excitedly among themselves and gesturing in the direction of the *Calliope's* final resting place. The entire boat and water surrounding it were brightly illuminated by floodlights mounted on the upper deck. Pitt resurfaced and paused, treading water in the dark, slightly beyond the outer limits of the lighted perimeter.

'This is as far as we can go without being spotted,' he said quietly to Giordino, who was calmly floating on his back a metre away.

'No grand entrance?' Giordino queried.

'Discretion tells me we'd be better off to advise Admiral Sandecker of our situation *before* we crash the party.'

'You're right as usual, O great one,' Giordino acquiesced. 'The owner might take us for thieves in the night, which we are, and clap us in irons, which he will no doubt do anyway.'

'I judge it about 20 metres. How's your wind?'

'I can hold my breath as long as you can.'

Pitt took several deep breaths, hyperventilating to purge the carbon dioxide from his lungs, and then inhaled until every cubic millimetre was filled with oxygen before slipping under the water.

Knowing that Giordino was following his lead, he dived deep and angled against the unseen current. He stayed deep, almost 3 metres down, stroking for the side of the houseboat. He could tell when he was getting close by the increasing light on the surface. When a shadow slipped over him he knew he had passed under the curve of the hull. Extending a hand over his head so he wouldn't strike his head, he slowly ascended until his fingers touched the slime that had formed on the boat's bottom. Then he slightly veered so his head broke the water alongside the aluminium side.

He sucked in the night air and looked up. Except for several hands draped on the railing only 2 metres above his head, he could not see the passengers, nor could they see him, unless one of them leaned over and stared straight

217

down. It was impossible to board the ship on the gangway without being seen. Giordino surfaced and immediately read the predicament.

Silently, Pitt motioned under the hull. He held apart his hands, indicating the depth of the boat's draft. Giordino nodded in understanding as they both filled their lungs again. Then they quietly rolled forward out of sight, levelled off, and swam under the bottom of the hull. The beam was so wide it took them nearly a minute before they resurfaced on the other side.

The port decks were empty and lifeless. Everyone was around the starboard side, attracted by the destruction of the *Calliope*. A rubber bumper hung along the hull and Pitt and Giordino used it to pull themselves on board. Pitt hesitated all of two seconds to figure a rough layout of the boat. They were standing on the deck that held the guest suites. They would have to go up. Trailed by Giordino he cautiously moved up a stairway to the next deck. One quick peek through a large port at a dining salon with the size and elegance of a deluxe hotel restaurant and they continued upward to the deck just below the pilothouse.

He cracked open a door and peered into what was a lavishly furnished lounge. All glass, delicately curved metalwork, and leather in golds and yellows. An ornate, fully stocked bar graced one wall.

The bartender was gone, probably gawking with the others outside, but a blond-haired woman with long bare legs, narrow waistline, and bronze-tanned skin sat at a baby grand piano that was covered in gleaming brass. She wore a seductively tight, black sequined mini dress. She was playing a moody rendition of 'The Last Time I Saw Paris,' and was playing it badly while singing the words in a throaty voice. Four empty martini glasses sat in a row above the keyboard. She looked as if she had spent the entire day since sunup drowning in gin, the obvious cause behind her sour performance. She stopped in mid-chorus, staring in hazy curiosity at Pitt and Giordino through velvet green eyes, bleary and barely half open.

'What cat dragged you guys in here?' she slurred.

Pitt, catching a glimpse of himself and Giordino in the mirror behind the bar, a glimpse of a pair of men in soaked T-shirts and shorts, of men whose hair was plastered down on their heads and who hadn't bothered to shave in over a week, thought wryly to himself that he couldn't blame her for looking at them like they were drowned rats. He held a finger to his lips for silence, took one of her hands and kissed it, then flitted past her through a doorway into a hall.

Giordino paused and gave her a wistful look and winked a brown eye. 'My name is Al,' he whispered in her ear. 'I love you and shall return.'

And then he too was gone.

The hallway seemed to stretch into infinity. Side passages ran in every direction, an intimidating labyrinth to those suddenly thrust in its midst. If the houseboat looked large from the outside, it seemed downright enormous on the inside.

'We could use a couple of motorcycles and a road map,' Giordino muttered.

'If I owned this boat,' said Pitt, 'I'd put my office and communications centre up forward to enjoy the view over the bow.'

'I think I want to marry the piano player.'

'Not now,' Pitt murmured wearily. 'Let's head forward and check the doors as we go.'

Identifying the compartments turned easy. The doors were labelled with fancy scrolled brass plates. As Pitt guessed, the one at the end of the hallway bore the title of *Mr Massarde's Private Office*.

'Must be the guy who owns this floating palace,' said Giordino.

Pitt didn't answer but eased open the door. Any corporate executive officer of one of the larger companies of the Western world would have turned green with envy at seeing the office suite of the houseboat anchored in the desert wilderness. The centrepiece was a Spanish antique conference table with ten chairs upholstered in dyed wool designs by master weavers on the Navajo reservation. Incredibly, the decor and artifacts on the walls and pedestals were American Southwest territorial. Life-size Hopi Kachina sculptures carved entirely from the huge roots of cottonwood trees stood in tall niches set within the bulkheads. The ceiling was covered by *latillas*, small branches placed across *vigas*, poles that acted as a roof support; the windows were covered by willow-twig shutters. For a moment Pitt couldn't believe he was on a boat.

Collections of fine ceremonial pottery and coil-woven baskets sat comfortably on long shelves behind a huge desk built from sun-bleached wood. A complete communications system was mounted in a nineteenth-century *trastero*, or cabinet.

The room was vacant, and Pitt lost no time. He crossed hurriedly to the phone console, sat down, and studied the complex array of buttons and dials for a few moments. Then he began punching numbers. When he completed the country and city codes, he added Sandecker's private number and sat back. The speaker on the console emitted a series of clicks and clacks. Then came ten full seconds of silence. At last the peculiar buzz sound of an American telephone being rung echoed from the speaker.

After ten full rings, there was no reply. 'For God's sake, why doesn't he answer,' Pitt said in frustration.

'Washington is five hours behind Mali. It's midnight there. He's probably in bed.'

Pitt shook his head. 'Not Sandecker. He never sleeps during a project crisis.'

'He'd better get on the horn quick,' Giordino implored. 'The posse is following our water tracks up the hallway.'

'Keep them at bay,' Pitt said.

'What if they have guns?'

'Worry about it when the time comes.'

Giordino glanced around the room at the Indian art. 'Keep them at bay, he says,' Giordino grunted. 'Custer having fun in Montana, that's me.'

At last a woman's voice came over the speaker. 'Admiral Sandecker's office.'

Pitt snatched the receiver out of its cradle. 'Julie?'

Sandecker's private secretary, Julie Wolff, sucked in her breath. 'Oh Mr Pitt, is that you?'

'Yes, I didn't expect you to be in the office this time of night.'

'Nobody has slept since we lost communications with you. Thank God, you're alive. Everyone at NUMA has been worried sick. Is Mr Giordino and Mr Gunn all right?'

'They're fine. Is the Admiral nearby?'

'He's meeting with a UN tactical team about how to smuggle you out of Mali. I'll get him right away.'

Less than a minute later, Sandecker's voice came on in combination with a loud pounding on the door. 'Dirk?'

'I don't have time for a lengthy situation report, Admiral. Please switch on your recorder.'

'It's on.'

'Rudi isolated the chemical villain. He has the recorded data and is headed for the Gao airport where he hopes to stow away on a flight out of the country. We pinpointed the location where the compound enters the Niger. The exact position is in Rudi's records. The rub is that the true source lies at an unknown location in the desert to the north. Al and I are remaining behind in an attempt to track it down. By the way, we destroyed the *Calliope* — '

'The natives are getting testy,' Giordino shouted across

the office. He was putting his considerable muscle against the door as it was being kicked in from the other side.

'Where are you?' questioned Sandecker.

'Ever hear of some rich guy named Massarde?'

'Yves Massarde, the French tycoon, I've heard of him.'

Before Pitt could answer, the door burst in around Giordino and six burly crewmen rushed him like the forward wall of a rugby team. Giordino decked the first three before he was buried under a pile of thrashing bodies.

'We're uninvited guests on Massarde's houseboat,' Pitt rushed the words. 'Sorry, Admiral. I have to go now.' Pitt calmly hung up the receiver, turned in the chair, and looked across the office at a man who entered the room behind the mêlée.

Yves Massarde was immaculately dressed in a white dinner jacket with a yellow rose in the lapel. One hand was stylishly slipped into the side pocket of his jacket, the elbow bent outward. He impassively stepped around the bruised and bloodied crewmen who were fighting to restrain Giordino as if they were derelicts on the street. Then he paused and stared through a haze of blue smoke from a Gauloise Bleu cigarette that dangled from one corner of his mouth. What he saw was a cold-eyed individual who sat behind his personal desk, arms folded in icy indifference, and benignly smiling back with bemused interest. Massarde was a keen judge of men. This one he immediately sensed was cunning and dangerous.

'Good evening,' Pitt said politely.

'American or English?' inquired Massarde.

'American.'

'What are you doing on my boat?' he demanded.

The firm lips fixed in a slight grin. 'It was urgent that I borrow your telephone. I hope my friend and I haven't put you out. I'll be more than happy to reimburse you for the call and any damage to your door.'

'You might have asked to come aboard my boat and used the phone like gentlemen.' Massarde's tone clearly indicated he thought of Americans as primitive cowboys.

'Looking like we do, would you have invited perfect strangers who suddenly appeared out of the night into your private office?'

Massarde considered that, and then smiled thoughtfully. 'No, probably not. You're quite right.'

Pitt took a pen from an antique inkwell and scribbled on a note pad, then tore off the top paper, stepped from behind the desk, and handed it to Massarde. 'You can send the bill to this address. Nice talking with you, but we have to be on our way.'

Massarde's hand came out of his jacket with a small automatic pistol. He lined up the muzzle with Pitt's forehead. 'I must insist you stay and enjoy my hospitality before I turn you over to Malian security forces.'

Giordino had been roughly manhandled to his feet. One eye was already swelling and a small trickle of blood dropped from one nostril. 'Are you going to clap us in irons?' he asked Massarde.

The Frenchman studied Giordino as if he was a bear in a zoo. 'Yes, I think restraint is in order.'

Giordino looked at Pitt. 'See,' he muttered sullenly. 'I told you so.'

21

Sandecker returned to the conference room in the NUMA headquarters building and sat down with a look of optimism that wasn't there ten minutes before. 'They're alive,' he stated tersely.

Two men were seated at the table whose surface was covered with a large map of the western Sahara and intelligence reports on the Malian military and security police forces. They stared at Sandecker and nodded approvingly.

'Then we continue with the rescue operation as planned,' said the senior of the two, a man with brushed-back grey hair and hard-jewelled eyes with the gleam of blue topaz set in a large round face.

General Hugo Bock was a far-seeing man who planned accordingly. A soldier who possessed a remarkable variety of skills, he was a born killer. Bock was senior commander of a little-known security force called UNICRATT, the abbreviation for United Nations International Critical Response and Tactical Team. Highly trained and extremely capable fighters, the team was composed of men from nine countries who performed undercover missions for the United Nations that were never publicized. Bock had led a distinguished career in the German army, constantly on the move as an advisor to third world countries whose governments requested his services during revolutionary wars or conflicts over border disputes.

His second-in-command was Colonel Marcel Levant, a highly decorated veteran of the French Foreign Legion. There was an old-fashioned aristocratic quality about him. A graduate of Saint Cyr, France's foremost military college, he had served around the world and was a hero of the short desert war against Iraq in 1991. His face was intelligent, even handsome. Although he was almost thirty-six years old, his slim build, long brown hair, a large but neatly clipped moustache, and large grey eyes made him appear only recently emerged from a university graduation ceremony.

'Do you have their location?' Levant asked Sandecker.

'I do,' answered Sandecker. 'One is attempting to smuggle himself on board a plane at the Gao airport. The other two are on a houseboat in the Niger River belonging to Yves Massarde.'

Levant's eyes widened at hearing the name. 'Ah yes, the Scorpion.'

'You know him?' asked Bock.

'Only by reputation. Yves Massarde is an international entrepreneur who amassed a fortune estimated to be around two billion American dollars. He's called the Scorpion because a number of his competitors and business partners mysteriously disappeared, leaving him the sole proprietor of several large and very profitable corporations. He's considered quite ruthless, not to mention an embarrassment to the French government. Your friends couldn't have picked worse company.'

'Does he carry out criminal activities?' asked Sandecker.

'Most definitely, but he leaves no evidence that would convict him in a court of law. Friends in Interpol tell me they have a file on him a metre thick.'

'Of all the people in the Sahara,' murmured Bock, 'how did your people run into him?'

'If you knew Dirk Pitt and Al Giordino,' Sandecker shrugged wearily, 'you'd understand.'

'I'm still at a loss why Secretary General Kamil approved an operation to smuggle your NUMA people out of Mali,' said Bock. 'Missions by our UN Critical Response and Tactical Team are usually undertaken in deep secrecy during times of international crisis. I fail to see why saving the lives of three NUMA researchers is so crucial.'

Sandecker looked Bock straight in the eye. 'Believe me, General, you'll never have a mission more important than this one. The scientific data these men have gathered in West Africa must be brought to our labs in Washington at the first opportunity. Our government, for stupid reasons known only to God, refuses to become involved. Hala Kamil, thankfully, saw the urgency of the situation and sanctioned your mission.'

'May I ask what sort of data?' Levant queried Sandecker.

The Admiral shook his head. 'I can't tell you.'

'Is this a classified matter concerning only the United States?'

'No, it concerns every man, woman, and child who walks the earth.'

Bock and Levant exchanged quizzical glances.

After a moment Bock turned back to Sandecker. You stated that your men have split up. This factor makes a successful operation extremely difficult. We run a high risk by dividing our force.'

'Are you telling me you can't get all my men out?' asked Sandecker incredulously.

'What General Bock is saying,' explained Levant, 'is that we double the risk by attempting two missions simultaneously. The element of surprise is cut in half. As an example, we stand a far greater chance of success by concentrating our force on removing the two men off Massarde's houseboat because we don't expect it to be secured by heavily armed military guards. And, we can determine the exact location. The airport is a different story. We have no idea where your man . . .'

'Rudi Gunn,' Sandecker offered. 'His name is Rudi Gunn.'

'Where Gunn is hiding,' Levant continued. 'Our team

226

would have to waste precious time searching him out. Also, the field is used by the Malian air force as well as commercial airliners. Military security runs around the clock. Anyone attempting to escape the country from the Gao airport would have to be extraordinarily fortunate to make it out in one piece.'

'You want me to make a choice?'

'To plan for unforeseen difficulties,' said Levant, 'we must designate which rescue mission is a top priority and which one is our secondary.'

Bock looked at Sandecker. It's your call, Admiral.'

Sandecker looked down at the map of Mali spread out across the table, focusing his eyes on the red line in the Niger River that marked the course of the *Calliope*. There was really little doubt in his mind as to a decision. The chemical analysis was all that mattered. Pitt's final words about remaining behind and continuing the search for the contamination origin came back to haunt him. He took out one of his custom-rolled cigars from a leather case and slowly lit it. He stared at the marking that indicated Gao for a long, meaningful moment before looking up at Bock and Levant again.

'Gunn must be your priority rescue,' Sandecker said flatly. Bock nodded. 'So be it.'

'But how can we be sure Gunn hasn't already managed to board a plane departing the country?'

Levant gave a knowledgeable shrug. 'My staff has already checked the flight schedules. The next flight by an Air Mali aircraft, or any other aircraft for that matter, scheduled to depart Gao for a destination outside the country is four days from now, providing it isn't cancelled, which is by no means a rare event.'

'Four days,' Sandecker repeated, his expectations suddenly dashed. 'No way Gunn can hide out for four days. Twenty-four hours maybe. After that, Malian security forces are bound to ferret him out.'

'Unless he speaks Arabic or French and looks like a native,' said Levant.

'No chance of that,' said Sandecker.

Bock tapped the map of Mali with his finger. 'Colonel Levant and a tactical team of forty men can be on the ground at Gao inside of twelve hours.'

'We could, but we won't,' cautioned Levant. 'Twelve hours from now would put us there just after sunup, Mali time.'

'My mistake,' Bock corrected himself. 'No way I can risk our force in daylight.'

'The longer we wait,' said Sandecker acidly, 'the better Gunn's chances for being caught and shot.'

'I promise you my men and I will do our best to get your man out,' Levant said solemnly. 'But not at great risk to others.'

'Do not fail.' Sandecker looked at Levant steadily. 'He's carrying information that is critical for the survival of us all.'

Bock's face wore a sceptical expression as he weighed Sandecker's words. Then his eyes turned hard. 'Fair warning, Admiral, sanctioned or not by the Secretary General of the UN, if a score of my men die on a wild goose chase to save just one of yours, there better be urgent justification, or by God somebody is going to deal with me personally.'

The inference of who *somebody* was came through clearly. Sandecker didn't even bat an eyelid. He had called in a debt from an old friend with an intelligence agency who passed him file copies of the UNICRATT force. They were called unicrazies by other special forces, tough men who lived and fought on the edge. Unafraid to die, totally fearless in combat, and incapable of mercy, there were few better at the craft of killing. And each acted as agents of their own nation, passing on information concerning undercover UN activities as a matter of course. He'd read a psychological profile on General Bock and knew squarely where he stood.

Sandecker leaned across the table and gazed at Bock through eyes that seemed to spark like knives on a grindstone. 'Now hear this, you big Luger head. I don't give a damn about how many men you lose spiriting Gunn out of Mali. Just get him out. Screw up and your ass is mine.'

Bock didn't hit him. He just sat there, staring at Sandecker from under great shrubs of grey eyebrows, and the bemused look in the eyes was that of a grizzly bear tucking in his napkin before dining on a rancher's calf. The Admiral was less than half Bock's size and any fight would have been over in the blink of an eye. Then the big German relaxed with a laugh.

'Now that you and I understand each other. why don't we get on with it and hatch a foolproof plan.'

Sandecker smiled and slowly relaxed in his chair. He offered Bock one of his mammoth cigars. 'A pleasure doing business with you, General. Let us hope the association will prove profitable.'

Hala Kamil stood on the steps of the Waldorf Astoria Hotel waiting for her limousine after leaving a formal dinner given in her honour by the UN Ambassador from India. There was a light rain and the streets reflected the lights of the city on the wet pavement. As the long black Lincoln pulled to the curb she stepped under an umbrella held by the doorman, gathered up the long skirt of her dress, and gracefully slipped into the rear seat.

Ismail Yerli was already seated inside. He took her hand and kissed it. 'I'm sorry to meet you like this,' he apologized, 'but it's too risky for us to be seen together.'

'It's been a long time, Ismail,' said Hala, her large eyes soft and radiant. 'You've avoided me.'

He glanced toward the chauffeur's compartment, making sure the divider window was raised. 'I felt it best for you if I simply faded away. You've come too far and worked too hard to lose it all because of scandal.'

'We could have been discreet,' Hala said in a low voice.

Yerli shook his head. 'Love affairs of men in power are largely ignored. But a woman in your position; the news media and gossip mongers would savage you in every nation of the world.'

'I still have great affection for you, Ismail.'

He put his hand over hers. 'And I for you, but you are the best thing that ever happened to the United Nations. I won't be the cause of your downfall.'

'So you walked out,' she said, a hurt look growing in her eyes. 'How very noble of you.'

'Yes,' he said without hesitation. 'To avoid headlines reading, "Secretary General of the UN revealed as mistress to French intelligence agent working undercover in the World Health organization." My superiors at the Second Division of the National Defense Staff wouldn't exactly be overjoyed at my exposure either.'

'We've kept our relationship secret until now,' she protested. 'Why not continue?'

'Impossible.'

'You're well known as a Turkish national. Who could possibly discover the French recruited you when you were a student at Istanbul University?'

'If someone digs deep enough they'll strike secrets. The first rule of a good agent is to operate in the shadows without being too furtive and too visible. I compromised my cover at the UN when I fell in love with you. If either British, Soviet, or American intelligence get even a whiff of our relationship, their investigation teams would never stop until they filled a file with sordid details which they would then use to extort favours from your high office.'

'They haven't yet,' she said hopefully.

'No, and they're not going to,' he said firmly. 'That's why

we must not see each other outside the UN building.'

Hala turned away and stared through the rain-streaked window. 'Then why are you here?'

Yerli took a deep breath. 'I need a favour.'

'Something concerning the UN or your French bosses?'

'Both.'

She felt as if she were being turned inside out. 'You only use me, Ismail. You twist my emotions so that you can play your petty little spy games. You are an unscrupulous rat.'

He didn't speak.

She gave in as she knew she would. 'What do you want me to do?'

'There is an epidemiology team from the WHO,' he spelled out, his voice suddenly businesslike, 'which is investigating reports of strange diseases in the Malian desert.'

'I recall the project. It was mentioned during my daily briefing several days ago. Dr Frank Hopper is directing the research.'

'That is correct.'

Hala nodded. 'Hopper is a well-respected scientist. What is your involvement with his mission?'

'My job is to coordinate their travel and see to their logistics, food, transportation, lab equipment, that sort of thing.'

'You still haven't made clear what you want from me.'

'I'd like you to recall Dr Hopper and his investigators immediately.'

She turned and looked at him in surprise. 'Why would you ask that?'

'Because they're in great danger. I have it on good authority they are to be murdered by West African terrorists.'

'I don't believe you.'

'It's true,' he said seriously. 'A bomb will be placed on their plane, set to explode over the desert.'

'What kind of monsters do you work for?' she snapped, her voice shocked. 'Why come to me? Why haven't you warned Dr Hopper?'

'I've tried to alert Hopper. but he has ignored all communications.'

'Can't you persuade the Malian authorities to relay the threat and offer protection?'

Yerli shrugged. 'General Kazim looks upon them as intruding foreigners and cares less about their safety.'

'I'd be a fool if I didn't think there was more intrigue here than a simple bomb threat.'

He looked into her face. 'Trust me, Hala. My only thought is to save Dr Hopper and his people.'

Hala wanted desperately to believe him, but deep inside her heart she knew he was lying. 'It seems everybody is searching for contamination in Mali these days. And they all urgently require salvation and evacuation.'

Yerli looked puzzled but said nothing, waiting for her to explain.

'Admiral Sandecker of the United States National Underwater and Marine Agency came to me and requested approval for the use of our Critical Response and Tactical Team to rescue three of his people from Malian security forces.'

'The Americans were searching for contamination in Mali?'

'Yes, apparently it was an undercover operation, but the Malian military intercepted them.'

'They were caught?'

'Not as of four hours ago.'

'Where exactly were they searching?'

Yerli seemed upset, and Hala detected the strained urgency in his tone. 'The Niger River.'

Yerli clutched her arm and his eyes turned deadly. 'I want to know more about this.'

For the first time she felt a chill run through her. 'They were hunting for the source of a chemical compound that is causing the giant red tide off the coast of Africa.'

'I've read about it in the newspapers. Go on.'

'I was told they used a boat with chemical analysis equipment to track the chemical to where it emptied into the river.'

'Did they find it?' he demanded.

'According to Admiral Sandecker, they had traced it as far as Gao in Mali.'

Yerli didn't look convinced. 'Disinformation, that has to be the answer. This thing must be a cover-up for something else.'

She shook her head. 'Unlike you, the Admiral does not lie for a living.'

'You say NUMA was behind the operation?'

Hala nodded.

'Not the CIA or another American intelligence agency?'

She shook her arm free and smiled smugly. 'You mean your devious intelligence sources in West Africa had no idea the Americans were operating under their noses?'

'Don't be absurd. What spectacular secrets could an impoverished nation like Mali possibly have that would attract American interests?'

'There must be something. Why don't you tell me what it is?'

Yerli seemed distracted and did not immediately answer her. 'Nothing . . . nothing of course.' He rapped on the glass to get the driver's attention. Then he motioned to the kerb.

The chauffeur braked and pulled to a stop in front of a large office building. 'You're tearing yourself away from me?' Her voice was thick with contempt.

He turned and looked at her. 'I am truly sorry. Can you forgive me?'

Something inside her ached. She shook her head. 'No,

Ismail. I won't forgive you. We will never meet again. I expect your resignation letter on my desk by noon tomorrow. If not, I will have you expelled from the UN.'

'Aren't you being a bit harsh?'

Hala's path was set. 'Your concerns are not with the World Health Organization. Nor, if they only knew it, are you even 50 percent loyal to the French. If anything, you're working for your own financial ends.' She leaned over him and pushed open the door. 'Now get out!'

Silently, Yerli climbed from the car and stood on the kerb. Hala, with tears forming in her eyes, pulled the door shut and never looked back as the driver shifted the limousine into gear and merged into the one-way traffic.

Yerli wished he could feel remorse or sadness, but he was too professional. She was right, he had used her. His affection toward her was an act. His only attraction for her was sexual. She had simply been another assignment. But like too many women who are drawn to aloof men who treat them indifferently, she could not help herself from falling in love with him. And she was only now beginning to learn the cost.

He walked into the cocktail lounge of the Algonquin Hotel, ordered a drink, and then used the pay phone. He dialled a number and waited for someone to answer on the other end.

'Yes?'

He lowered his voice and talked in a confidential tone. 'I have information vital to Mr Massarde.'

'Where do you come from?'

'The ruins of Pergamon.'

'Turkey?'

'Yes,' Yerli cut in quickly. He never trusted telephones and hated what he thought were childish codes. 'I am in the bar of the Hotel Algonquin. When can I expect you?'

'One A.M. too late?'

'No. I'll have a late dinner.'

Yerli hung up the phone thoughtfully. What did the Americans know about Massarde's desert operation at Fort Foureau, he wondered? Did their intelligence services have a hint of the true activities at the waste disposal plant and were they snooping around? If so, the consequences could be disastrous, and the fall of the current French government would be the least of the backlash.

22

Behind him was black darkness, ahead the sparsely scattered street lights of Gao. Gunn still had 10 metres to swim when one of his kicking feet dug into the soft riverbed. Slowly, very cautiously, he reached down and grabbed the silt with his hands, pulling himself through the shallows until he was lying at the waterline. He waited, listening and squinting into the darkness shrouding the bank of the river.

The beach sloped at an angle of 10 degrees, ending at a low rock wall that bordered a road. He crawled across the sand, enjoying its heat against the wet skin of his bare arms and legs. He stopped and rolled onto his side, resting for a few minutes, reasonably secure that he was only an indistinct blur in the night. He had a cramp in his right leg and his arms felt numb and heavy.

He reached back and felt the backpack. For a brief instant, after he had struck the rushing water like a cannonball, he thought that it might have been torn from his back. But its straps still clung tightly to his shoulders.

He rose to his feet and sprinted in a crouching position to the wall, dropping to his knees behind it. He warily peered over the top and scanned the road. It was empty. But a badly paved street that ran diagonally into town had a fair amount of foot traffic. Out of the upper edge of one eye he caught a dim flare and looked up on the roof of a nearby house in time to see a man light a cigarette. There were others: dim figures of people, some illuminated by lanterns, happily chatting with their neighbours on adjoining roofs. They must come up like moles, Gunn surmised, to enjoy the cool of the evening.

He studied the stream of the pedestrians on the street, trying to absorb a rhythm to their movements. They seemed to glide up and down the street in their loose, flowing garments on silent feet like wraiths. He unstrapped the backpack, opened it, and removed a blue bed sheet. He tore part of it in a crude body pattern and then draped it around himself in the style of a djellaba, a long skirted garment with full sleeves and a hood. He wouldn't win a local fashion award, he thought, but felt reasonably satisfied it would pass unnoticed in the dimly lit streets. He considered removing his glasses, but decided against the idea, positioning the hood to cover the rims. Gunn was nearsighted and couldn't see a moving bus 20 metres away.

He slipped the backpack under the robe and strapped it around his front as if it was simply a protruding stomach. He then sat on the wall and swung his legs over to the far side. He casually stepped across the road and up the narrow street, joining the citizens of Gao who were out for their evening stroll. After two blocks he reached a main intersection. The only vehicles prowling the streets were a few dilapidated taxis, one or two run-down buses, and a few scattered motorbikes and a bevy of bicycles.

It would be nice to simply hail a cab for the airport, he thought wistfully, but that was inviting attention. Before abandoning the boat he had studied the map of the area and knew the airport was a few kilometres south of town. He considered stealing a bicycle, but quickly eliminated the idea. The theft would have probably been noticed and reported, and he wanted no trace of his presence known. If the police or security forces did not have reason to think there was an illegal alien wandering in their midst, they would have no cause to search for him.

Gunn leisurely walked through the main section of town, past the market square, the decrepit Hotel Atlantide, and the merchants hawking their wares from stalls under arches across from the hotel. The smells were anything but exotic. Gunn welcomed the breeze that fanned most of the town's odours into the desert. Signposts were nonexistent but he navigated down the sandy streets by occasionally glancing up at the north star.

The people dressed in a blaze of green and blues and a smattering of yellow. The men were dressed in some form of djellaba or caftan. A number wore western pants and tunics. Few were bare-headed. Most male heads and faces were heavily swathed in blue cloth. Many of the women were covered in elegant cloaks, others long, flowered dresses. Most all were unveiled.

They all chattered constantly in strange low tones. Children ran everywhere, no two dressed alike. Gunn found it hard to imagine such social activity and congeniality in the middle of great poverty. It was as though nobody informed the Malians they were poor.

Keeping his head down and face covered by the hood so the white skin of his face wouldn't show, Gunn merged with the crowd and made his way out of the busy part of town. No one stopped him and asked awkward questions. If for some unexpected reason he was apprehended and interrogated he would claim to be a tourist on a hiking trip along the Niger. He did not dwell on that possibility for long. The danger of being stopped by someone who was looking specifically for an illegal American was nil.

He passed a road sign with a pointing arrow and a drawing of an airplane. He was making his way toward the airport easier than he expected. His luck hadn't skipped out on him yet.

He walked through the more affluent merchant-owned neighbourhoods and into the surrounding slums. From the time he left the river, Gao had given him the impression of a town where, with the coming of darkness, some unseen horror crawls up through the sandy streets. It seemed to him a town drenched in the blood and violence of centuries. His imagination began to work overtime as he walked the dark and nearly deserted streets, beginning for the first time to see curious and hostile looks from people sitting in front of their crumbling houses.

He ducked into a narrow alley that looked to be empty and paused to take a revolver from the backpack, an old, snub-nosed Smith & Wesson 38-calibre Bodyguard model that had belonged to his father. His instinct told him that this was a place you didn't walk at night if you expected to see the dawn.

A truck rumbled past, stirring up the fine sand, its flatbed piled with bricks. A quick realization that it was going in his direction, and Gunn threw caution to the desert winds. He took a running leap and scrambled up the back of the truck. He came to rest flat on his stomach on top of the bricks facing forward and looking down on the roof of the cab.

The smell of the exhaust from the diesel engine came as a relief after the aroma of the town. From his vantage view atop the truck's cargo, Gunn picked out a pair of red lights blinking a few kilometres ahead and to his left. As the truck bounced closer, he could see a few floodlights mounted on a terminal building and two hangars across a darkened field.

'Some airport,' he muttered to himself dryly. 'They turn out all the runway lights when it's not in use.'

A dip in the road showed in the truck's headlights, and the driver slowed. Gunn took advantage of the decreased speed and hit the ground running. The truck rolled on into the darkness, sand streaming from its tyres, the driver blissfully unaware he'd carried a passenger. Gunn followed the truck's taillights until he came to an asphalt side road and a wooden sign painted in three languages that advertised the Gao International Airport.

'International,' Gunn read aloud. 'Oh how I hope so.'

He walked along the side of the entry road, keeping off to one side in the remote chance a vehicle might happen by. There was little need for caution. The airport terminal was dark and the parking lot totally empty. His hopes took a downturn at a closeup view of the terminal building. He'd seen better-looking condemned warehouses than the wooden structure with a rusting metal roof. It took a brave man to climb and work in the nearby control tower sitting precariously on support girders that were almost eroded through. He walked around the buildings onto the dead and darkened tarmac. Across the field, illuminated by floodlights, sat eight Malian jet fighters and a transport plane.

He stood motionless as he spied two armed guards sitting outside a security shack. One was dozing in a chair, the other was leaning against the shack smoking a cigarette. Great, he thought, just great. Now he had to contend with the military.

Gunn held up his Chronosport dive watch and peered at the dial. It read twenty past eleven. He suddenly felt tired. He'd made it this far only to find a deserted airport that looked as if it hadn't seen an arriving or departing airliner in weeks. If that wasn't bad enough, the field was guarded by Malian air force security. No predicting how long he could sit it out before being discovered or expiring from lack of food and water.

He resigned himself for a long wait. Not good to hang around during daylight. He moved 100 metres into the desert before stumbling onto a small pit half filled with debris from some long forgotten shed. He scooped out a depression in the dry sand, climbed in, and pulled several rotting boards over him. The hole could have been filled with ants or scorpions for all he knew, but he was too tired to care.

He was asleep within thirty seconds.

*

Roughly manhandled by Massarde's crewmen, Pitt and Giordino's wrists were cuffed, and they were forced in a kneeling position by short chains that wound around a steam pipe. They were helplessly confined in the bilge area below heavy steel plating that served as a deck of the engine and power-generating room above. Overhead, a guard armed with an automatic machine pistol slowly paced back and forth, his shoes clicking on the steel floor. They knelt in the dank bilge of the houseboat, their wrists chafing in the tight handcuffs, bare knees below their shorts only a few degrees from being burned by the hot metal flooring.

Escape was impossible. It was only a matter of time before they were turned over to General Kazim's security police, and their existence would end with a virtual death sentence.

The atmosphere in the bilge was stifling and nearly unbreathable. Sweat streamed out their pores from the damp heat that radiated from the steam pipe. The torment increased with each passing moment. Giordino felt badly weakened and debilitated, his strength almost totally sapped away after two hours of confinement in that hellhole. The humidity was worse than any steam bath he had ever sat in. And the loss of body liquids was driving him half mad from thirst.

Giordino looked across at Pitt to see how his self-determined friend was taking this torturous confinement. As far as he could tell, Pitt showed no reaction at all. His face, soaked in perspiration, looked thoughtful and complacent. He was studying a row of wrenches that hung neatly in a row on the aft bulkhead. He could not reach them because the chain on his cuffs was stopped from slipping along the pipe by an overhanging brace. He thoughtfully measured the distance that stretched beyond his touch. Every so often he turned his attention to the grating and the guard, then back to the wrenches.

'Another fine mess you've gotten us into, Stanley,' said

Giordino, echoing a line from Laurel and Hardy comedies.

'Sorry, Ollie, all in the name of humanity,' Pitt said with a grin.

'Think Rudi made it?'

'If he stayed in the shadows and kept his cool, there's no reason for him to wind up like us.'

'What do you think old French moneybags expects to gain by making us sweat?' Giordino mused, wiping the sweat from his face with his arm.

'I have no idea,' answered Pitt. 'But I suspect we'll know why he stuck us in this hot box instead of turning us over to the gendarmes before too long.'

'He has to be a real sorehead if he's mad over us using his telephone.'

'My fault,' said Pitt, his eyes reflecting mirth. 'I should have made a collect call.'

'Oh well, you couldn't know the guy is a cheap screw.

Pitt looked at Giordino in long, slow admiration, He marvelled that the stocky Italian could still summon up a sense of humour despite being on the brink of passing out.

In the long, agonizing minutes that followed, their oven-hot cell in the bilge, their ominous predicament, was pushed aside in Pitt's mind as he focused his thoughts on escape. At the moment any optimism was futile. There was not nearly enough muscle between them to break their chains, and neither he nor Giordino had the means to pick the locks on their handcuffs.

His mind conjured up a dozen contingencies, each ready to be cancelled in favour of another. None were workable unless certain situations fell into place. The main hitch was the chains. Somehow or other they would have to come off the steam pipe. If not, Pitt's best-laid plans evaporated before they could get off the ground.

He broke off his mental gymnastics as the guard pulled up one of the floor plates and swung it back on its hinges.

He took a key from his belt and opened the cuffs attached to their chains. Four crewmen were standing in the engine room. They leaned down and lifted Pitt and Giordino to their feet, dragged them through the engine room, up a stairway, and into a lush-carpeted hallway of the houseboat. One knocked on a teak door, then pushed the door wide and shoved the two prisoners into the room.

Yves Massarde sat in the middle of a long, leather couch smoking a thin cigar and swirling a goblet of cognac. A dark-skinned man in an officer's military uniform sat in a facing chair, drinking champagne. Neither man rose as Pitt and Giordino stood before them barefoot dressed only in shorts and T-shirts, dripping with sweat and moisture.

'These are the pitiful specimens you fished from the river?' asked the officer, regarding them curiously through black, cold, and empty eyes.

'Actually, they came aboard without an invitation,' replied Massarde. 'I caught them in the act of using my communications equipment.'

'You think they got a message through?'

Massarde nodded. 'I was too late to stop them.'

The officer sat his glass on an end table, rose from his chair, and walked across the room until he was standing directly in front of Pitt. He was taller than Giordino, but a good 6 inches shorter than Pitt.

'Which of you was in contact with me on the river?' he asked.

Pitt's expression cleared. 'You must be General Kazim.'

'I am.'

'Just goes to show you can't judge a person by their voice. I pictured you as looking more like Rudolph Valentino than Willie the Weasel — '

Pitt crouched and turned sideways as Kazim, his face abruptly flushed with hate, his teeth clenched in sudden rage, lashed out at Pitt's groin with his booted foot. The thrust

243

was vicious and carried most of Kazim's weight behind it. His expression of wrath suddenly turned to one of shock as Pitt, in a lightning move, caught the flailing foot with his hands in mid-flight and gripped it like a vice.

Pitt did not move, did not cast Kazim's leg aside. He merely stood there holding it between his hands, keeping the General balancing on one leg. Then very slowly he pushed the maddened Kazim backward until he dropped into his chair.

There was a stunned silence in the room. Kazim was in shock. As a virtual dictator for over a decade, his mind refused to accept insubordinate and contemptuous treatment. He was so used to people quivering before him, he did not know how to immediately react at being physically subdued. His breathing came quickly, his mouth a taut white line, his dark face crimson with anger. Only the eyes remained black and cold and empty.

Slowly, deliberately, he eased a gun from a holster at his side. An older automatic, Pitt observed with remote detachment, a 9-millimetre Beretta NATO model 92SB. Unhurriedly Kazim thumbed down one side of the ambidextrous safety and aimed the muzzle at Pitt. An icy smile curled beneath the heavy moustache.

Pitt flicked a side glance at Giordino and noted that his friend was tensed to leap at Kazim. Then his gaze locked on Kazim's grip on the automatic, waiting for the slightest tightening of the hand, the tiniest flexing of the trigger finger, bracing his knees to dodge to his right. This could have been an opportunity for an escape attempt, but Pitt knew he had lost any advantage by pushing Kazim too far. His death would be slow and deliberate. It stood to reason Kazim was a good shot, and he would not miss at that close range. Pitt knew he might move fast enough to duck the first shot, but Kazim would quickly adjust his aim and shoot to maim, first one knee cap, then the next. The General's evil eyes did not reflect a quick kill.

Then, half an instant away from when the room would explode in gunfire and convulsive bodies, Massarde made a flourish in the air with his hand and spoke in a commanding voice.

'If you please, General, conduct your execution elsewhere, certainly not in my party room.'

'This tall one is going to die,' Kazim hissed, the black eyes gazing at Pitt.

'All in due time, my good comrade,' said Massarde while casually pouring himself anther cognac. 'Do me the courtesy of refraining from bloodying up my rare Nazlini Navajo rug.'

'I'll buy you a new one,' Kazim growled.

'Did you consider the fact he might want a fast and easy way out? It's obvious he baited you, choosing a fast death rather than suffering the agony of long, drawn-out torture.'

Very slowly the pistol dropped, and Kazim's deathly smile turned wolfish. 'You read him. You knew exactly what he was about.'

Massarde gave a Gallic shrug. 'The Americans call it street smarts. These men have something to hide, something vital. We both might benefit if they could be persuaded to talk.'

Kazim pushed himself from the chair, approached Giordino, and raised the automatic again, this time shoving the Beretta's barrel against Giordino's right ear.

'Let's see if you are more talkative than you were on your boat.'

Giordino didn't flinch. 'What boat?' he asked, his tone as innocent as a priest at confession.

'The one you abandoned minutes before it blew up.'

'Oh, *that* boat.'

'What was your mission? Why did you come up the Niger to Mali?'

'We were researching the migratory habits of the fuzzwort

245

fish by following a school of the slimy little devils upriver to their spawning grounds.'

'And the weapons aboard your boat?'

'Weapons, weapons?' Giordino made a downward turn of his lips and raised his shoulders in ignorance. 'We ain't got no weapons.'

'Have you forgotten your run-in with the Benin naval patrol boats?'

Giordino shook his head. 'Sorry, it doesn't ring a bell.'

'A few hours in the interrogation chambers of my headquarters in Bamako might jog your memory.'

'Not a healthy climate for uncooperative foreigners I assure you,' said Massarde.

'Stop conning the man,' said Pitt, looking at Giordino. 'Tell him the truth.'

Giordino turned and stared blankly at Pitt. 'Are you crazy!'

'Maybe you can stand torture. I can't. The thought of pain makes me ill. If you won't tell General Kazim what he wants to know, I will.'

'Your friend is a sensible man,' said Kazim. You would be wise to listen to him.'

Just for a second Giordino's blank look slipped, then it was back again, only this time it was beaming with anger. 'You dirty scum. You traitor – '

Giordino's verbal abuse was abruptly cut off as Kazim pistol-whipped him across the face, opening a bloody gash on his chin. Giordino staggered two steps backward, then stopped and lurched forward like a maddened bull. Kazim lifted the automatic and aimed it between Giordino's eyes.

Here it comes, Pitt thought coldly, thrown off track by Giordino's bursting temper. Pitt rapidly stepped in front of Kazim and grabbed Giordino's arms, pinning them behind his partner's back. 'Steady, for God's sake!'

Unnoticed, Massarde pressed a button on a small console

by the couch. Before anyone spoke or made another move a small army of crewmen surged into the room, their combined mass and weight driving Pitt and Giordino to the floor. Pitt barely had a fleeting glimpse of the avalanche before he tensed for the crush. He went down without fighting back, knowing it was useless, determined to save his strength. Not Giordino, he thrashed like a crazy man, filling the room with curses.

'Take that one back to the bilge,' shouted Massarde, coming to his feet and pointing at Giordino.

Pitt felt the pressure fall away as the guards concentrated on wrestling Giordino into submission. One of the guards swung a short snapper cosh, a weight on the end of a flexible cable, and cracked Giordino on the neck just below and behind the ear. A grunt of pain and all fight went out of Giordino. He went limp as the guards grabbed him under the arms and dragged him from the room.

Kazim pointed the automatic at Pitt, who was still lying on the floor. 'Now then, since you prefer cordial conversation to agony, why don't you begin by giving me your correct name.'

Pitt twisted to his side and sat up. 'Pitt, Dirk Pitt.'

'Should I believe you?'

'It's as good a name as any.'

Kazim turned to Massarde. 'Did you have them searched?'

Massarde nodded. 'They carried no credentials or papers of any kind.'

Kazim stared at Pitt, his face a mask of repugnance. 'Perhaps you can enlighten me on why you've entered Mali without a passport?'

'No problem, General,' Pitt let the words rush out. 'My partner and I are archaeologists. We were given a contract by a French foundation to search the Niger River for ancient shipwrecks. Our passports were lost when our boat was fired on by one of your patrol vessels and destroyed.'

247

'Honest archaeologists would be begging like simpering children after being chained in a steam compartment for two hours. You men are too hardened, unafraid, and arrogant to be anything but trained enemy agents – '

'What foundation?' Massarde broke in.

'The Society of French Historical Exploration,' Pitt answered.

'I've never heard of it.'

Pitt made a helpless gesture with his hands. 'What can I say?'

'Since when do archaeologists explore for artifacts in a super yacht equipped with rocket launchers and automatic weapons?' asked Kazim sarcastically.

'It never hurts to be prepared for pirates or terrorists,' Pitt smiled stupidly.

At that moment there was a knock on the door. One of Massarde's crewmen entered and handed him a message. 'A reply, sir?'

Massarde scanned the contents and nodded. 'Express my compliments and say he is to continue his investigation.'

After the crewman left, Kazim asked, 'Good news?'

'Most enlightening,' Massarde purred. 'From my agent with the United Nations. It seems these men are from the National Underwater and Marine Agency in Washington. Their mission was to hunt down a source of chemical contamination that originates in the Niger and causes a rapid growth in red tides after it enters the sea.'

'A facade,' sneered Kazim, 'nothing more. They were sniffing around for something far more significant than pollution. My guess is oil.'

'The very thoughts of my agent in New York. He suggested it might be a cover, and yet his source of information didn't think so.'

Kazim looked at Massarde suspiciously. 'Not a leak from Fort Foureau, I hope?'

'No, not at all,' Massarde answered without hesitation. 'My project is too distant to impact the Niger. No, it can only be another one of your many clandestine ventures you haven't seen fit to reveal.'

Kazim's face went rigid and lifeless. 'If anyone is responsible for spilling contamination in Mali, old friend, it must be you.'

'Not possible,' Massarde said flatly. He stared at Pitt. 'You find this conversation interesting, Mr Pitt?'

'I don't know what you're talking about.'

'You and your partner must be very valuable men.'

'Not really. At the moment we're just your everyday, garden-variety prisoners.'

'What do you mean by valuable?' inquired Kazim.

'My agent also reports the UN is sending a special tactical team to rescue them.'

Just for a second Kazim looked shocked. Then he quickly came back on balance. 'A special force is coming here?'

'Probably already on its way, now that Mr Pitt was able to contact his superior.' Massarde glanced at the message again. 'According to my agent, his name is Admiral James Sandecker.'

'It would appear there is no fooling you.' The elegant room on the houseboat was cooled by air conditioning, and Pitt shivered uncontrollably after suffering the steamed heat in the bilge, but he was more conscious of a nameless chill. It came as a shock that Massarde was privy to the entire mission. He tried to imagine who might have betrayed them, but no one came immediately to mind.

'Well, well, well, we are not so clever and indifferent now that our cover is blown, are we my friend?' Kazim poured himself another glass of Massarde's excellent champagne. Then he looked up abruptly from his glass. 'Where were you planning to rendezvous with the UN force, Mr Pitt?

Pitt was trying to give his impression of a man with

amnesia. This was a dead-end street. The Gao airport was too obvious a pickup point. He dared not compromise Gunn, but he took a long shot in hopes that Kazim was as dumb as he looked.

'The Gao airport, they're flying in at dawn. We were to wait at the west end of the airstrip.'

Kazim stared at Pitt for a brief moment, then suddenly he struck Pitt across the forehead with the barrel of his Beretta. 'Liar!' he snapped.

Pitt ducked his head and covered his face with his arms. 'It's the truth, I swear.'

'Liar,' Kazim repeated. 'The airstrip at Gao runs north and south. There is no west end.'

Pitt exhaled his breath in a long silent sigh, and shook his head very slowly. 'I guess it would be useless to hold out. You'll get it out of me sooner or later.'

'Unfortunately for you, I have methods for doing just that.'

'Very well,' Pitt said. 'Admiral Sandecker's instructions after we destroyed the boat were to head due south of Gao about 20 kilometres to a wide, shallow ravine. A helicopter is to be flown in from Niger.'

'What is the signal for a safe pickup?'

'There is no need for a signal. The surrounding countryside is deserted. I was told the helicopter will scout the area with its landing lights until they spot us.'

'What time?'

'Four A.M.'

Kazim looked at him long and pensively, then said caustically, 'If you have lied to me again, you will deeply regret it.'

Kazim put his Beretta back in its holster and turned to Massarde. 'No time to waste. I have to prepare a welcoming ceremony.'

'You would be smart, Zateb, to keep the UN at arm's

length. I strongly advise against interfering with their tactical team. When they do not find Pitt and his friend, they will fly back to Nigeria. Shooting down the helicopter and killing every man on board will only open a hornet's nest.'

'They are invading my country.'

'A trivial point,' Massarde waved his hand. 'National pride does not become you. The loss of aid and funding for your, shall we say, nefarious programmes, would not be worth satisfying a blood lust. Let them go unmolested.'

Kazim gave a twisted smile, and a dry, humourless laugh. 'Yves, you take all the pleasure from my life.'

'While putting millions of francs in your pockets.'

'And that too,' Kazim acquiesced.

Massarde nodded at Pitt. 'Besides, you can still have your fun with this one and his friend. I'm sure they will tell you what you wish to learn.'

'They will talk before noon.'

'I'm quite sure they will.'

'Thank you for softening them up in your engine room sweat box.'

'My pleasure.' Massarde walked to a side door.'Now if you will excuse me, I must see to my guests. I've ignored them far too long.'

'A favour,' said Kazim.

'You have but to name it.'

'Keep Mr Pitt and Mr Giordino in your steam room for a while longer. I would like any remaining spirit and hostility melted away before I have them transported to my headquarters in Bamako.'

'As you wish,' Massarde agreed.'I'll instruct my crew to return Mr Pitt to the bilge.'

'Thank you, Yves, my friend, for capturing and turning them over to me. I'm grateful.'

Massarde bowed his head.'My pleasure.'

Before the door closed behind Massarde, Kazim refocused

his attention on Pitt. His black eyes blazed with fiendishness. Pitt could only remember once before seeing such concentrated malevolence in a human face.

'Enjoy your stay in the sweat bilge, Mr Pitt. Afterward, you will suffer, suffer beyond your wildest nightmares.'

If Kazim expected Pitt to tremble with fear, it didn't happen. If anything, Pitt looked incredibly calm. He wore the beaming expression of a man who just hit a jackpot on a slot machine. Inwardly, Pitt was rejoicing because the General had unwittingly unravelled the hitch in his escape plans. The gate had cracked open, and Pitt was going to slip through.

23

Too wound up to sleep, Eva was the first of the dozing scientists to notice the descent of the aircraft. Though the pilots feathered the controls as gently as possible, Eva sensed the slight drop in engine power and knew the plane had lost altitude when her ears suddenly popped.

She looked out the window, but all she saw was total blackness. There were no lights to be seen on the empty desert floor. A glance at her watch told her it was ten past midnight, only one and a half short hours since they loaded the last of the equipment and contamination samples on board and took off from the graveyard that was Asselar.

She sat quietly and relaxed, thinking that perhaps the pilots were simply turning on a new course and changing altitude. But the sinking sensation in her stomach told her the plane was still dropping.

Eva rose into the aisle and walked to the rear of the cabin where Hopper exiled himself so he could smoke his pipe. She approached his seat and gently shook him awake. 'Frank, something's wrong.'

Hopper was a light sleeper and almost instantly focused his eyes and looked up at her questioningly. 'What did you say?'

'The plane is descending. I think we're landing.'

'Nonsense,' he snorted. 'Cairo is five hours away.'

'No, I heard the engines slack off.'

'The pilots have probably throttled back to conserve fuel.'

'We're losing altitude. I'm sure of it.'

Hopper reacted to the seriousness of her tone and sat up and tilted his head, listening to the engines. Then he leaned over his armrest and peered down the aisle toward the forward bulkhead of the passenger cabin. 'I believe you're right. The nose seems angled down slightly.'

Eva nodded toward the cockpit. 'The pilots have always kept the door open during flight. It's closed now.'

'Does appear odd, but I'm sure we're overreacting.' He threw off the blanket covering his large frame and stiffly rose to a standing position. 'However, it won't hurt to have look.'

Eva followed him up the aisle to the cockpit door. Hopper turned the knob and his face suddenly clouded with concern. 'The damn thing's locked.' He pounded on the door, but after a few moments there was no response. If anything, the aircraft's angle of descent increased. 'Something mighty queer is going on. You better wake the others.'

Eva hurried back down the aisle and prodded the other members of the team out of their weary sleep. Grimes was the first to reach Hopper.

'Why are we landing?' he asked Hopper.

'I haven't the vaguest idea. The pilots aren't of a mind to communicate.'

'Perhaps they're making an emergency landing.'

'If they are, they're keeping it to themselves.'

Eva leaned over a seat and peered into the darkness through a window. A small cluster of dim, yellow lights pierced the night several kilometres beyond the nose of the aircraft. 'Lights ahead,' she announced.

'We could kick the door in,' Grimes suggested.

'For what purpose?' demanded Hopper. 'If the pilots mean to land, there's no way we can stop them. None of us can take control of a jetliner.'

'Then there is little we can do but return to our seats and fasten our seatbelts,' said Eva.

The words had not left her mouth when the landing lights flashed on, illuminating a faceless desert. The landing gear dropped and the pilot made a tight bank as he lined up on the as yet unseen airfield. By the time they had all strapped themselves in, the tyres thumped into hard-packed sand and the engines roared as the pilot engaged the air brakes. The soft surface of the unpaved runway produced enough drag to slow the plane down without the pilots standing on the brakes. The plane taxied toward a row of floodlights that stood beside the airstrip and rolled to a halt.

'I wonder where this is?' murmured Eva.

'We'll find out soon enough,' said Hopper, moving toward the cockpit door, determined this time to kick it in. But it swung open before he reached it, and the pilot stepped into the cabin. 'What is the meaning of this stopover?' Hopper demanded. 'Is there a mechanical problem?'

'This is where you get off,' the pilot said slowly.

'What are you talking about? You're supposed to fly us to Cairo.'

'My orders are to set you down at Tebezza.'

'This is a UN chartered aircraft. You were hired to take us to whatever destination we require, and Tebezza, or whatever you call it, is not one of them.'

'Consider it an unscheduled stop,' the pilot said doggedly.

'You simply can't throw us out in the middle of the desert. How do we get out of here and continue to Cairo?'

'Arrangements have been made.'

'What about our equipment?'

'It will be guarded.'

'Our samples must get to the World Health laboratory in Paris as soon as possible.'

'That is not my concern. Now if you will please collect your personal items and disembark.'

'We'll do no such thing,' Hopper said indignantly. The pilot brushed past Hopper and walked swiftly down the aisle to the rear exit. He undogged the shaft locks and pushed a large switch. The hydraulic pumps whirred as the aft floor slowly dropped and became a stairway leading to the ground. Then the pilot raised a large-calibre revolver he'd been holding behind his back and waved it at the startled scientists.

'Get off the aircraft, now!' he ordered gruffly.

Hopper moved until he was standing almost toe to toe with the pilot, completely ignoring the gun barrel touching his stomach. 'Who are you? Why are you doing this?'

'I am Lieutenant Abubakar Babanandi of the Malian air force, and I am acting under orders from my superiors.'

'And just who might they be?'

'The Malian Supreme Military Council.'

'You mean General Kazim. He calls the shots around here – '

Hopper grunted in agony as Lieutenant Babanandi rammed the muzzle of his revolver sharply into the scientist's upper groin. 'Please do not cause trouble, Doctor. Depart the plane or I will shoot you where you stand.'

Eva clutched Hopper by the arm. 'Do what he says, Frank. Don't let your pride kill you.'

Hopper swayed on his feet, hands instinctively pressed against his groin. Babanandi seemed hard and cold, but Eva detected more fear in his eyes than hostility. Without another word, Babanandi crudely pushed Hopper onto the first step.

'I warn you. Do not linger.'

Twenty seconds later, half supported by Eva, Hopper stepped to the ground and looked around.

A half dozen men, their heads and faces hidden in the indigo-tinted, heavily wrapped veil of the Tuaregs, walked over and stood in a semicircle around Hopper. They were all quite tall and menacing. They wore long flowing black robes, and were armed with broadswords that hung in sashes tied around their waists. They held automatic rifles, whose muzzles were collectively pointing at Hopper's chest.

Two other figures approached. One was a towering man,

thin with light-skinned hands, the only part of him that showed except for eyes barely visible through the slit in his *litham*. His robe was dyed a deep purple but his veil was white. The top of Hopper's head just came level with the stranger's shoulders.

His companion was a woman who was built like a gravel truck whose bed was fully loaded. She was dressed in a dirty, loose-fitting dress that stopped short of the knees, revealing legs that were as thick as telephone poles. Unlike the others, her head was uncovered. Though she was as dark as the southern Africans and her hair was woolly, she had high cheekbones, a rounded chin, and sharp nose. Her eyes were small and beady, and her mouth stretched nearly the full width of her face. There was a cold and sadistic look about her, enhanced by a broken nose and a scarred forehead. It was a face that had once been brutalized. She held a thick leather thong in one hand that had a small knot on one end. She eyed Hopper as if she was a torturer of the Inquisition measuring her next victim for the iron maiden.

'What is this place?' Hopper demanded without introduction.

'Tebezza,' answered the tall man.

'I've already been told that. But just where is Tebezza?'

The answer came in English accented in what Hopper guessed was a northern Irish. 'Tebezza is where the desert ends and hell begins. Here gold is mined by convicted prisoners and slaves.'

'Something on the order of the salt mines at Taoudenni,' said Hopper, staring at the rifles aimed at him as he spoke. 'Do you mind not sticking those guns in my face?'

'They are a necessity, Dr Hopper.'

'Not to worry. We haven't come to steal your — ' Hopper broke off in midsentence. His eyes turned blank as the colour ebbed from his face, and he spoke in an astonished whisper. 'You know my name?'

'Yes, we have been expecting you.'

'Who are you?'

'My name is Selig O'Bannion. I am Chief Engineer of the mining operation.' O'Bannion turned and nodded at the big woman. 'My straw boss is Melika, which means queen. You and your people will take your orders from her.'

Perhaps ten seconds passed in silence broken only by the slowly turning turbines of the aircraft. Then Hopper blurted, 'Orders, what the hell are you talking about?'

'You were sent here, courtesy of General Zateb Kazim. It is his express wish that you work in the mines.'

'This is kidnapping!' Hopper gasped.

O'Bannion shook his head patiently. 'Hardly kidnapping, Dr Hopper. You and your UN team of scientists will not be ransomed or held as hostages. You have been condemned to labour in the mines of Tebezza, excavating gold for the national treasury of Mali.'

'You're madder than a cockroach – ' Hopper began, then staggered back against the steps as Melika slashed him across the face with her heavy thong. He stiffened from the shocking blow and touched the welt that was rising on his cheek.

'Your first lesson as a slave, you putrid pig,' the mountainous woman spat. 'Beginning now, you do not speak unless ordered.'

She raised her thong to strike Hopper again, but O'Bannion grabbed her arm. 'Easy, woman. Give him time to get used to the idea.' He looked up at the other scientists who had descended the steps and formed around Hopper, shock spread across their faces, the beginnings of terror in their eyes. 'I want them in good condition for their first day's work.'

Reluctantly, Melika lowered the thong. 'I fear you are shedding your thick skin, Selig. They are not made of porcelain.'

'You're an American,' said Eva.

Melika grinned. 'That's right, honey. Ten years as Chief of Guards at the Women's Institution in Corona, California. Take it from one who knows, they don't come any tougher than there.'

'Melika takes special care of the female workers,' said O'Bannion. I'm sure she'll see to it you're considered one of the family.'

'You make women work in the mines?' Hopper said disbelievingly.

'Yes, a number of them, including their children,' O'Bannion answered matter-of-factly.

'You're flagrantly committing human rights violations,' said Eva angrily.

Melika looked at O'Bannion, a fiendish expression on her face. 'May I?'

He nodded. 'You may.'

The big woman shoved the end of the thong into Eva's stomach, doubling her over. Then she brought it down on the back of Eva's neck. Eva folded like a wet blanket and would have struck the ground if Hopper hadn't grabbed her around the waist.

'You'll soon learn that even verbal resistance is futile,' said O'Bannion. 'Better you cooperate and make your remaining time on earth as painless as possible.'

Hopper's lips parted in incredulity. 'We're respected scientists of the World Health Organization. You can't just execute any of us on a whim.'

'Execute you, good doctor?' O'Bannion said casually. 'Nothing of the sort. I intend to work you to death.'

24

The scheme went exactly as Pitt hoped. After the guard shoved him back into the steamy bilge with Giordino. he appeared subservient and cooperative by raising his hands so the guard could lock his cuff chain around the steam pipe. Only this time Pitt held his hands up on the opposite side of the pipe bracket. Satisfied Pitt was solidly rechained, the guard silently let the steel trapdoor drop with a loud clang on his prisoners in the stifling atmosphere of the confined compartment.

Giordino sat uncaringly in a pool of moisture and massaged the back of his head. In the dense mist Pitt could hardly see him. 'How'd it go?' Giordino asked.

'Massarde and Kazim are thick as thieves. They're partners in some kind of shady operation. Massarde pays off the General for favours. That much was obvious. Beyond that, I didn't learn much.'

'Next question.'

'Shoot.'

'How do we get out of this teapot?'

Pitt lifted his hands and grinned. 'With a mere twist of the wrist.'

Now bound to the opposite side of the bracket, he slid his chain along the pipe until he reached the aft bulkhead that held the rack that contained several different-sized wrenches. He took one and tried it around the fitting mounted on the bulkhead to support the passage of the steam pipe. It was too large, but the next wrench was a perfect fit. He laid hold of the handle and pulled. The fitting was frozen with rust and failed to budge. Pitt rested a moment, then planted his feet against a steel beam, grasped the wrench with both hands, and heaved with all his strength. The fitting's threads begrudgingly broke their hold, and it moved. The first quarter turn took every muscle in Pitt's arms. With each twist the fitting began to rotate more easily. When it was finally free and attached by only two threads. Pitt paused and turned to Giordino.

'Okay, she's ready to be disconnected. We're lucky it's fed by low-pressure steam for heating the staterooms above or we'll know how a poor lobster feels in the pot when she drops loose. As it is, we'll be drenched with enough steam to smother us if we don't get out of here in one hell of a hurry.'

Giordino rose to his feet, knees flexed, head bent low as his soaked curly black hair met the deck plating above. 'Put the guard within my reach, and I'll take care of the rest.'

Pitt nodded wordlessly and gave the fitting a series of fast rotations until it slipped free. Then he used the chain on his cuffs to hang on the pipe, using his weight to pull it free. A cloud of steam erupted and burst into the small confines of the bilge. Within seconds it was so thick Pitt and Giordino became completely lost to each other. In one swift movement, Pitt slipped his chain free over the end of the flowing pipe, scalding the backs of his hands.

In harmony he and Giordino began shouting and pounding on the bottom of the deck plate. Startled by the sudden hiss of escaping steam and seeing it billow from between the seams in the deck, the guard reacted as per Pitt's script and yanked open the plating. A billow of steam engulfed him while Pitt's unseen hands reached up from below and yanked him into the mist-filled bilge. The guard dropped headfirst and struck his jaw against a steel beam. He went out instantly.

One second later Pitt had torn the automatic rifle from the stunned guard's hands. Another five seconds later

Giordino had blindly rummaged the man's pockets until his fingers touched the key to the locks of their handcuffs. Then as Giordino freed his wrists, Pitt leaped catlike onto the upper deck and crouched, swinging the barrel of the automatic rifle. The engine room was empty. No other crewmen had been on duty except the guard.

Pitt turned and knelt down, wiping the moisture falling from his brow, squinting into the rolling steam. 'You coming?'

'Take the guard,' an invisible Giordino grunted through the mist. 'No reason to let the poor bastard die down here.'

Pitt groped downward, feeling a pair of arms, and clutched them. He dragged the unconscious guard into the engine room and laid him on the deck. Next, he caught Giordino's wrist and pulled him from the hellhole, wincing from the pain that suddenly burst from his hands.

'Your hands look like boiled shrimp,' said Giordino.

'I must have roasted them when I slipped my chain over the end of the pipe.'

'We should wrap them with something.'

'No time.' He lifted his manacled hands. Mind doing me the honour?'

Giordino quickly unlocked Pitt's chain and cuffs. He held up the key before dropping it in his pocket. 'A keepsake. You never know when we'll get arrested again.'

'Judging from the mess we're in, it won't take long,' muttered Pitt. 'Massarde's passengers will soon be complaining about the lack of heat, especially any women wearing bare-shouldered dresses. A crewman will be sent to repair the problem and discover us gone.'

'Then it's time to exit stage left with style and discretion.'

'With discretion anyway.' Pitt moved to a hatch, eased it open, and peered onto an outside deck that ran aft to the stern of the houseboat. He moved out to the railing and gazed upward. People could be seen through large view windows in the lounge, drinking and conversing in evening dress, oblivious to the punishment that Pitt and Giordino had suffered almost directly below in the engine room.

He motioned for Giordino to follow, and they moved stealthily along the deck, ducking under portholes that opened into the crew's compartments until they came to a stairway. They pressed back in the shadows beneath the steps and stared through the upper opening. Sharply defined under bright overhanging lights, as if in full daylight, burgundy and white paint etched against the black sky, they could clearly see Massarde's private helicopter moored to the roof deck over the main salon. It sat deserted without a crewman around.

'Our chariot awaits,' said Pitt.

'Beats swimming,' Giordino agreed. 'If Frenchy had known he was entertaining a pair of old air force pilots, he'd have never left it unattended.'

'His oversight, our fortune,' Pitt said mildly. He climbed to the top of the stairs and scanned the deck and peered through nearby ports for signs of life. What few heads he spotted in the cabins were uninterested in events outside and were turned away. He moved quietly across the deck, opened the door to the copter, and climbed in. Giordino pulled out the wheel chocks and removed the tie-down ropes before following Pitt, closing the door and settling in the right seat.

'What have we got here?' Giordino murmured as he studied the instrument panel.

'A late model, French-built, twin turbine Ecureuil, by the look of her,' Pitt answered. 'I can't tell what model, but we have no time to translate all the bells and whistles. We'll have to forgo a checklist, stoke her up, and go.'

A precious two minutes were lost in start-up, but no alarm had been sounded as Pitt released the brake and the rotor blades began slowly turning, accelerating until they reached lift-off rotation. The centrifugal force fluttered the helicopter on its wheels. Like most pilots, Pitt didn't have to translate the French labels on the gauges, instrument and switches spread across the panel. He knew what they indicated. The controls were universal and caused him no problem.

A crewman appeared and stared curiously through the spacious windshield. Giordino waved at him and smiled broadly as the crewman stood there, indecision etched on his face.

'This guy can't figure out who we are,' said Giordino.

'He got a gun?'

'No, but his buddies who are charging up the stairs look none too friendly.'

'Time to be gone.'

'All gauges read green,' Giordino said reassuringly.

Pitt didn't hesitate any longer. He held a deep breath and lifted the helicopter into a brief hover over the deck before dipping the nose and applying the throttles, forcing the machine into forward flight. The houseboat dropped behind, a blaze of light against the black of the water. Once clear, Pitt levelled at barely 10 metres and swung the craft on a course downriver.

'Where we headed?' asked Giordino.

'To the spot where Rudi found the contamination spilling into the river.'

'Aren't we heading in the wrong direction? We found the toxin entry a good 100 kilometres in the other direction.'

'Merely a feint to throw off the hounds. As soon as we're a safe distance away from Gao, I'll swing south and we'll backtrack across the desert and pick up the river again 30 kilometres upstream.'

'Why not drop in at the airport, pick up Rudi, and get the hell out of the country?'

'Any number of reasons,' explained Pitt, nodding at the fuel gauges. 'One, we don't have enough fuel to fly more than 200 kilometres. Two, once Massarde and his buddy Kazim spread the alarm, Malian jet fighters will hunt us down with their radar and either force us to land or blow us out of the sky. I give that little scenario about fifteen minutes. And three, Kazim thinks there were only two of us. The more distance we can put between Rudi and us gives him that much better chance to escape with the samples.'

'Does all this just strike you out of the blue?' Giordino complained. 'Or do you come from a long line of soothsayers?'

'Consider me your friendly, neighbourhood plot diviner,' Pitt said condescendingly.

'You should audition for a carnival fortune-teller,' Giordino said dryly.

'I got us out of the steam bath and off the boat, didn't I?'

'And now we're going to fly across the middle of the Sahara Desert until we run out of fuel. Then walk across the world's largest desert looking for a toxic we-know-not-what till we expire or get captured by the Malian military as fodder for their torture dungeons.'

'You certainly have a talent for painting bleak pictures,' Pitt said sardonically.

'Then set me straight.'

'Fair enough,' Pitt nodded. 'Soon as we reach the location where the contamination seeps into the river, we ditch the helicopter.'

Giordino looked at him. 'In the river?'

'Now you're getting the hang of it.'

'Not another swim in this stinking river — not again.' He shook his head in conviction. 'You're nuttier than Woody Woodpecker.'

'Every word a virtue, every move sublime,' Pitt said airily, then, suddenly serious, added: 'Every aircraft the Malians can put in the air will be searching for this bird. With it buried under the river, they won't have a starting place to track us down. As it is, the last place Kazim would expect us to run is north into the desert wastes to look for toxic contamination.'

'Sneaky,' said Giordino. 'That's the word for you.'

Pitt reached down and pulled a chart out of a holder attached to his seat. 'Take the controls while I lay out a course.'

'I have her,' Giordino acknowledged as he took hold of the collective control lever beside his seat and the cyclic-pitch control column.

'Take us up to 100 metres, maintain course over the river for five minutes, and then bring us about on a heading of two-six-oh degrees.'

Giordino followed Pitt's instructions and levelled off at 100 metres before looking down. He could just discern the surface of the river. 'Good thing the stars reflect on the water or I couldn't see where the hell I was going.'

'Just watch for dark shadows on the horizon after you make your turn. We don't want to spread ourselves over a protruding rock formation.'

Only twenty minutes passed during their wide swing around Gao before they approached their destination. Massarde's fast helicopter flitted through the night sky like a phantom, invisible without navigation lights, with Giordino deftly handling the controls while Pitt navigated. The desert floor below was faceless and flat, with few shadows thrown by rocks or small elevations. It almost came as a relief when the black waters of the Niger River came into view again.

'What are those lights off to starboard?' asked Giordino.

Pitt did not look up, but kept his eyes on the chart. 'Which side of the river?'

'North.'

'Should be Bourem, a small town we passed in the boat shortly before we moved out of the polluted water. Stay well clear of her.'

'Where do you want to ditch'

'Upriver, just out of earshot of any residents with acute hearing.'

'Any particular reason for this spot?' asked Giordino suspiciously.

'It's Saturday night. Why not go into town and check out the action?'

Giordino parted his lips to make some appropriate comeback, gave up, and refocused his concentration on flying the helicopter. He tensed as he scanned the engine and flight gauges on the instrument panel. Approaching the centre of the river, he eased back on the throttles as he delicately pushed the collective and tapped right rudder, turning the craft with its nose upriver while in a hover.

'Got your rubber ducky life vest?' asked Giordino.

'Never go anywhere without it,' Pitt nodded. 'Lower away.'

Two metres above the water, Giordino shut down the engines as Pitt closed all the fuel switches and electrical bars. Yves Massarde's beautiful aircraft fluttered like a wounded butterfly, and then fell into the water with a quiet splash. It bobbed long enough for Pitt and Giordino to step out the doors and leap as far away as they could get, before diving into the river with arms and legs furiously stroking to escape the reach of the dying but still slowly spinning rotor blades. When the water reached the open doors and flooded the interior, the craft slipped beneath the smooth black water with a great sigh as the air was expelled from the passenger cabin.

No one heard it come down, no one from shore saw it sink. It was gone with the *Calliope*, settling into the soft silt of the river that would someday completely cover her airframe and become her burial shroud.

25

It wasn't exactly the Polo Lounge of the Beverly Hills Hotel, but to someone who had been thrown in a river twice, parboiled in a steam bath, and was footsore from stumbling around the desert in the dark for two hours, no watering hole could have offered greater sanctuary. He had never, Pitt thought, seen a dingier dive that looked so good.

They had the feeling of entering a cave. The rough mud walls met a well-trodden dirt floor. A long board propped on concrete bricks that served as the bar sagged in the middle, so much so it seemed that any glass set on its surface would immediately slide to the centre. Behind the decrepit bar, a shelf that appeared wedged into the mud brick wall held a weird assortment of pots and valves that brewed coffee and tea. Next to it were five bottles of obscurely labelled liquor in various levels of consumption. They must have been stocked for the rare tourist who ventured in the place, Pitt surmised, since Muslims weren't supposed to touch the stuff.

Against one wall a small stove was throwing out a comforting degree of heat along with a pungent aroma that neither Pitt nor Giordino as yet identified as camel dung. The chairs looked like rejects from both the Goodwill and Salvation Army stores. None of them matched. The tables weren't much better, darkened by smoke, surfaces burned by countless cigarettes and carved with graffiti going back to the French colonial days. What little illumination there was in the closet-size room came from two bare light bulbs hanging from a single wire held up by nails in a roof beam.

They glowed dimly, their limited power coming from the town's overworked diesel generator.

Trailed by Giordino, Pitt sat down at an empty table and shifted his attention from the furnishings to the clientele. He was relieved to find that none wore uniforms. The room held a composite of locals, Niger boatmen and fishermen, villagers, and a sprinkling of men whom Pitt took for farmers. No women were in attendance. A few were drinking beer but most sipped at small cups of sweet coffee or tea. After a cursory glance at the newcomers, they all went back to their conversations or refocused their concentration on a game similar to dominos.

Giordino leaned across the table and murmured, 'Is this your idea of a night on the town?'

'Any port in a storm,' said Pitt.

The obvious proprietor, a swarthy man with a massive thicket of black hair and an immense moustache, ambled from behind the makeshift bar and approached the table. He stood and looked down at them without a word, waiting for them to speak first.

Pitt held up two fingers and said, 'Beer.'

The proprietor nodded and walked back to the bar. Giordino watched as he pulled two bottles of German beer from a badly dented metal icebox, then turned and stared at Pitt dubiously.

'Mind telling me how you intend to pay?' asked Giordino.

Pitt smiled, leaned under the table, and slipped off his left Nike and removed something from the sole. Then with a cool, watchful expression his eyes travelled around the room. None of the other patrons showed the slightest interest in either himself or Giordino. He cautiously opened his hands so only Giordino could see. Between his palms lay a neat stack of Malian currency.

'Confederation of French African francs,' he said quietly. 'The Admiral didn't miss a trick.'

'Sandecker thought of everything all right,' Giordino admitted. 'How come he trusted you and not me with a bankroll?'

'I have bigger feet.'

The proprietor returned and set, more like dropped, the bottles of beer on the table. '*Dix francs*,' he grunted.

Pitt handed him a bill. The proprietor held it up to one of the light bulbs and peered at it, then rubbed his greasy thumb over the printing. Seeing no smear, he nodded and walked away.

'He asked for ten francs,' Giordino said. 'You gave him twenty. If he thinks you're a big spender we'll probably be mugged by half the town when we leave.'

'That's the idea,' said Pitt. 'Only a matter of time before the village con artist smells blood and circles his victims.'

'Are we buying or selling?'

'Mostly buying. We need a means of transportation.'

'A hearty meal should take priority. I'm hungry as a bear out of hibernation.'

'You can try the food here, if you like,' said Pitt. 'Me, I'd rather starve.'

They were on their third beer when a young man no more than eighteen entered the bar. He stood tall and slender with a slight hunch to his shoulders. He had a gentle oval face with wide sad-looking eyes. His complexion was almost black and his hair thick and wiry. He wore a yellow T-shirt and khaki pants under an open, white cotton sheet-like garment. He made a quick study of the customers and settled his gaze on Pitt and Giordino.

'Patience, the beggar's virtue,' Pitt murmured. 'Salvation is on the way.'

The young man stopped at the table and nodded his head. 'Bonsoir.'

'Good evening,' Pitt replied.

The melancholy eyes widened slightly. 'You are English?'

270

'New Zealanders,' Pitt lied.

'I am Mohammed Digna. Perhaps I can assist you gentlemen in changing your money.'

'We have local currency,' Pitt shrugged.

'Do you need a guide, someone to lead you through any problems with customs, police, or government officials?'

'No, I don't think so.' Pitt held out his hand at an empty chair. 'Will you join us for a drink?'

'Yes, thank you.' Digna said a few words in French to the proprietor-bartender and sat down.

'You speak English real well,' said Giordino.

'I went to primary school in Gao and college in the capital of Bamako where I finished first in my class,' he said proudly. 'I can speak four languages including my native Bambara tongue, French, English, and German.'

'You're smarter than me,' said Giordino. 'I only know enough English to scrape by on.'

'What is your occupation?' asked Pitt.

'My father is chief of a nearby village. I manage his business properties and export business.'

'And yet you frequent bars and offer your services to tourists,' Giordino murmured suspiciously.

'I enjoy meeting foreigners so I can practise my languages,' Digna said without hesitation.

The proprietor came and set small cup of tea in front of Digna.

'How does your father transport his goods?' asked Pitt.

'He has a small fleet of Renault trucks.'

'Any chance of renting one?' Pitt put to him.

'You wish to haul merchandise?'

'No, my friend and I would like to take a short drive north and see the great desert before we return home to New Zealand.'

Digna gave a brief shake of his head. 'Not possible. My father's trucks have left for Mopti this afternoon loaded with textiles and produce. Besides, no foreigner from outside the country can travel in the desert without special passes.'

Pitt turned to Giordino, an expression of sadness and disappointment on his face. 'What a shame. And to think we flew halfway around the world to see desert nomads astride their camels.'

'I'll never be able to face ny little old white-haired mother,' Giordino moaned. 'She gave up her life's savings so I could experience life in the Sahara.'

Pitt slapped the table with his hand and stood up. 'Well it's back to our hotel at Timbuktu.'

'Do you gentlemen have a car?' asked Digna.

'No.'

'How did you get here from Timbuktu?'

'By bus,' replied Giordino hesitantly, almost as if asking a question.

'You mean a truck carrying passengers.'

'That's it,' Giordino said happily.

'You won't find any transportation travelling to Timbuktu before noon tomorrow,' said Digna.

'There must be a good vehicle of some kind in Bourem that we can rent,' said Pitt.

'Bourem is a poor town. Most of the townspeople walk or ride motorbikes. Few families can afford to own autos that are not in constant need of repair. The only vehicle of sound mechanical condition currently in Bourem is General Zateb Kazim's private auto.'

Digna might as well have prodded a pair of harnessed bulls with a pitchfork. Pitt and Giordino's minds worked on the same wavelength. They both stiffened but immediately relaxed. Their eyes locked and their lips twisted into subtle grins.

'What is his car doing here?' Giordino asked innocently. 'We saw him only yesterday at Gao.'

'The General flies most everywhere by helicopter or

272

military jet,' answered Digna. 'But he likes his own personal chauffeur and auto to transport him through the towns and cities. His chauffeur was transporting the auto on the new highway from Bamako to Gao when it broke down a few kilometres outside of Bourem. It was towed here for repairs.'

'And was it repaired?' Pitt inquired, taking sip of beer to appear indifferent.

'The town mechanic finished late this evening. A rock had punctured the radiator.'

'Has the chauffeur left for Gao?' Giordino wondered idly.

Digna shook his head. 'The road from here to Gao is still under construction. Driving on it at night can be hazardous. He didn't want to risk damaging General Kazim's car again. He plans to leave with the morning light.'

Pitt looked at him. 'How do you know all this?'

Digna beamed. 'My father owns the auto repair garage, and I oversee its operation. The chauffeur and I had dinner together.'

'Where is the chauffeur now?'

'A guest at my father's house.'

Pitt changed the drift of the conversation to local industry. 'Any chemical companies around here?' he asked.

Digna laughed. 'Bourem is too poor to manufacture anything but handicrafts and woven goods.'

'How about a hazardous waste site?'

'Fort Foureau, but that's hundreds of kilometres to the north.'

There was a short lull in the conversation, then Digna asked suddenly, 'How much money do you carry?'

'I don't know,' Pitt answered honestly. 'I never counted it.'

Pitt saw Giordino look strangely at him and then flick his eyes at four men seated at a table in the corner. He glanced at them and caught them abruptly turning away. This had to be a setup, he concluded. He stared at the proprietor who was leaning over the bar reading a newspaper and rejected him as one of the muggers. A quick look at the other customers was enough to satisfy him that they were only interested in conversing between themselves. The odds were five against two. Not half bad at all, Pitt thought.

Pitt finished his beer and came to his feet. 'Time to go.'

'Give my regards to the Chief,' said Giordino, pumping Digna's hand.

The young Malian's smile never left his face, but his eyes became hard. 'You cannot leave.'

'Don't worry about us,' Giordino waved. 'We'll sleep by the road.'

'Give me your money,' Digna said softly.

'The son of a chief begging for money,' Pitt said dryly. 'You must be a great source of embarrassment for your old man.'

'Do not offend me,' Digna said coldly. 'Give me all your money or your blood will soak the floor.'

Giordino acted as if he was ignoring the confrontation and edged toward one corner of the bar. The four men had risen from the table and seemed to be waiting for a signal from Digna. The signal never came. The Malians seemed confused by the utter lack of fear shown by their potential victims.

Pitt leaned across the table until his face was level with Digna's. 'Do you know what my friend and I do to sewer slime like you?'

'You cannot insult Mohammed Digna and live,' he snarled contemptuously.

'What we do,' Pitt calmly continued, 'is bury them with a slice of ham in their mouth.'

The ultimate abhorrence to a devout Muslim is any contact with a pig. They consider them the most unclean of creatures and the mere thought of spending eternity in the grave with so much as a sliver of bacon is enough to cause their worst nightmares. Pitt knew the threat was as good as a wooden stake pressed against a vampire's chest.

For a full five seconds Digna sat immobile, making sounds from his throat as if he was being strangled. The muscles of his face tautened and his teeth bared in uncontrolled rage. Then he leaped to his feet and pulled a long knife from under his robe.

He was two seconds slow and one second too late.

Pitt rammed his fist into Digna's jaw like a piston. The Malian lurched backward, crashing into the table surrounded by men playing dominos and spilling the game pieces before sprawling to the floor in a twisted heap, out for the count. Digna's henchmen all launched themselves against Pitt, circling him warily, three of them drawing nasty-looking curved knives while the fourth came at him with a raised axe.

Pitt grabbed his chair and swung down on his lead attacker, breaking the man's right arm and shoulder. A shout of pain went up as the room erupted in confusion. The stunned customers crushed against each other in their panic to escape through the narrow door to safety outside the bar. Anther exclamation of agony exploded from the assailant with the axe as a well-aimed bottle of whisky thrown by Giordino smashed with a sickening thud into the side of the man's face.

Pitt lifted the table above his head, his hand gripping two of its legs. In the same instant came the sound of shattered glass and Giordino was standing beside him, his hand thrust forward, clutching the jagged neck of a bottle.

The attackers stopped dead in their tracks, the odds now even. They stared dumbly at their two friends, one swaying on his knees, moaning and holding a badly skewed arm, the other sitting cross-legged with hands covering his face, blood streaming through his fingers. Another downward glance at their unconscious leader, and they began backing toward the door. In the blink of an eye they were gone.

'Not much of an exercise,' Giordino muttered. 'These

275

guys wouldn't last five minutes on the streets of New York.'

'Watch the door,' said Pitt. He turned to the proprietor who stood completely unperturbed and unconcerned, turning the pages of his newspaper as if he regarded fights on his premises as regular nightly entertainment. 'Le garage?' Pitt asked.

The proprietor raised his head, tugged at his moustache, and wordlessly jerked his thumb in a vague direction beyond the south wall of the bar.

Pitt threw several francs on the sagging bar to pay for the damage and said, 'Merci.'

'This place kind of grows on you,' said Giordino. 'I almost hate to part with it.'

'Picture it in your mind always,' Pitt checked his watch. 'Only four hours before daylight. Off we go before an alarm is turned in.'

They exited the dingy bar and skirted the rear of the buildings, hugging the shadows and peering furtively around corners. Their precaution, Pitt realized, was largely an overkill: The almost total lack of street lights and the darkened houses with their sleeping inhabitants voided any chance of suspicion.

They came to one of the more substantial mud brick buildings in town, a large warehouse-like affair with a wide metal gate in the front and double doors at the rear. The chain-link fenced yard in back looked like an automotive junkyard. Nearly thirty old cars were parked in rows, stripped bare with little left of them but body shells and frames. Wheels and grimy engines were stacked in one corner of the yard near several oil drums. Transmissions and differentials leaned against the building, the ground around soaked from years of leaking oil.

They found a gate in the fence that was tied shut by a rope. Giordino picked up a sharp stone and cut through the rope, swinging open the gate. They moved carefully toward the doors, listening for any sound of a guard dog and peering through the darkness for signs of a security system. There must have been little need for theft prevention, Pitt decided. With so few cars in town, anyone stealing a part to repair a private vehicle would have immediately been suspect.

The double doors were latched and sealed with a rusty padlock. Giordino gripped it in his massive hands and gave it a heavy tug. The shackle popped free. He looked at Pitt and smiled.

'Nothing to it really. The tumblers were old and worn.'

'If I thought there was the least hope we'd ever get out of this place,' Pitt said tartly, 'I'd put you in for a medal.'

He gently pulled one door open far enough for them to enter. One end of the garage was an open pit for mechanics to work under cars. There was a small office and a room filled with tools and machinery. The rest of the floor space held three cars and a pair of trucks in various stages of disassembly. But it was the car that sat in the open centre of the garage that drew Pitt. He reached through one of the windows of a truck and pulled the light switch, illuminating an old pre-World War II automobile with elegant lines and a bright rose-magenta colour scheme.

'My God,' Pitt muttered in awe. 'An Avions Voisin.'

'A what?'

'A Voisin. Built from 1919 until 1939 in France by Gabriel Voisin. She's a very rare car.'

Giordino walked from bumper to bumper, studying the styling of the quite unique and different car. He noted the unusual door handles, the three wipers mounted on the glass of the windshield, the chrome struts that stretched between the front fenders and radiator, and the tall, winged mascot atop the radiator shell. 'Looks weird to me.'

'Don't knock it. This classy set of wheels is our ticket out of here.'

Pitt climbed behind the steering wheel, which was set on

the right side, and sat in the art deco-designed upholstery of the front seat. A single key was in the ignition. He switched it on and stared at the fuel gauge needle as it climbed to the full line. Next he pressed the button that turned over the electrical motor that extended through the bottom of the radiator, and served as both the starter and the generator. There was utterly no sound of the engine being cranked over. The only indication that it was suddenly running was an almost inaudible cough and a slight puff of vapour out the exhaust pipe.

'A quiet old bird,' observed Giordino, impressed.

'Unlike most modern engines with poppet valves,' said Pitt, 'this one is powered by a Knight sleeve-valve engine that was quite popular in its day for silent operation.'

Giordino gazed at the old classic car with great scepticism. 'You actually intend to drive this old relic across the Sahara Desert?'

'We've got a full tank of gas, and it beats riding a camel. Find some clean containers and fill them with water, and see if you can scrounge anything to eat.'

'I doubt seriously,' Giordino said, morosely staring around the run-down garage, 'this establishment has a soft drink and candy machine.'

'Do what you can.'

Pitt opened the rear doors of the building and pushed out the yard gate far enough to allow the car to pass through. Then he checked over the car to ensure the oil and water were filled to capacity and there was air in the tyres, particularly the spare. Giordino came up with half a case of locally produced soft drink and several plastic bottles of water. 'We won't go thirsty for a few days, but the best I could do in the culinary department is two cans of sardines I found in a desk and some gooey stuff that looks like boiled candy.'

'No sense in hanging around. Throw your cache in the backseat and let's hit the road.'

Giordino obliged and climbed in the passenger's seat as Pitt pushed the gear lever on the Cotal gearbox, actually a switch on an arm that protruded from the steering column, into low gear, pressed the accelerator pedal, and eased out the clutch. The sixty-year-old Voisin moved forward smoothly and quietly.

Pitt slowly picked his way between the junked cars and passed out the gate, cautiously driving down an alley until he reached a narrow dirt road leading to the west on a parallel course with the Niger River. He turned and followed the faint tracks, creeping along no faster than 25 kilometres an hour until he was out of sight of the town. Only then did he turn on the headlights and pick up speed.

'Might help if we had a road map,' said Giordino.

'A map of camel tracks might be more practical. We can't risk taking the main highway.'

'We're okay so long as this cow path runs along the river.'

'Soon as we strike the ravine where Gunn's instruments detected the contamination, we'll turn and follow it north.'

'I'd hate to be around when the chauffeur notifies Kazim that his pride and joy has been stolen.'

'The General and Massarde will think we headed for the nearest border, which is Niger,' said Pitt confidently. 'The last place they'd expect us to cut and run is the middle of the desert.'

'I must say,' Giordino grumbled, 'I'm not looking forward to the trip.'

Neither was Pitt. It was a mad attempt with practically no chance of living to a ripe old age. The headlights showed the land was flat with patches of small, brown-stained rock. The beams caught haunting shadows cast from an occasional manna tree that seemed to flit and dart across the landscape like wraiths.

It was, thought Pitt, a very lonely place to die.

26

The sun rose hot, and by ten o'clock it was already
32 degrees C (90 degrees F). A wind began to blow from
the south, and offered a small but mixed blessing for Rudi
Gunn. The breeze felt refreshing to his sweating skin, but
it swirled sand into his nose and ears. He wrapped his head
cloth more tightly to keep out the grit and pressed his dark
glasses against his face to protect his eyes. He took a small
plastic bottle of water from his backpack and drained half
of it. No need to ration, he thought, after spying a dripping
tap beside the terminal.

The airport looked as dead as the night before. On the
military side, there had been a changing of the guards, but
the hangars and flight line were still void of activity. At the
commercial air terminal he watched a man ride up on a
motorbike and climb to the control tower. Gunn saw that
as a good omen. No one with half a brain would willingly
suffer in an elevated, glass-enclosed hot box under a blazing
sun unless a plane was scheduled to arrive.

A falcon circled above Gunn's nest in the sand. He gazed
at it for a while before cautiously rigging a few weather-
worn boards over his body for shade. Then he surveyed the
airfield once again. A truck had arrived on the tarmac in
front of the terminal. Two men got out and unloaded a set
of wooden chocks, which they set on the tarmac to block
the aircraft's tyres after landing. Gunn stiffened and began
mentally preparing his best strategic approach to where the
aircraft would park. He fixed the route in his mind, picking
the shallow ravines and scattered growth for cover.

Then he lay back, settled in to endure the increasing heat,

and stared up at the sky. The falcon had homed in on a plover that was streaking and dodging toward the river. A few cotton puff clouds drifted across the vast blue expanse. He wondered how they could survive much less exist in the searing atmosphere. So intent was he on watching the clouds that he did not at first hear the low hum in the distance that signalled the approach of a jet aircraft. Then a glint caught his eye, and he sat up. The sun had flashed on a tiny speck in the sky. He waited, staring until the glint came again, only this time it was lower against the barren horizon. It was an aircraft on approach for landing but still too far away to be recognized. It had to be commercial, he surmised, or it wouldn't be expected to stop at the civilian side of the airfield.

He pushed off the boards shielding the sun, pulled on the backpack, and crouched in readiness for his furtive approach. He squinted into the glaring sky until the plane was only a kilometre away, his heart beginning to pound with anxiety. The seconds dragged past until at last he could distinguish the type and markings; a civilian French airbus carrying the light and dark green stripes of Air Afrique.

The pilot flared out just past the end of the runway, touched down, and braked. Then he taxied to the front of the terminal and rolled the big airbus to a halt. The engines were not shut down but kept turning as the two ground crewmen shoved the chocks under the wheels and then rolled a boarding stairway to the main exit door.

They stood and waited at the bottom of the stairway expectantly for passengers to disembark, but the exit door did not immediately open. Gunn began to make his move, scurrying toward the edge of the runway. After covering 50 metres, he paused behind the shelter of a small acacia tree and studied the airliner again.

The forward passenger door was finally sliding to one side, and a female flight attendant came down the boarding steps. She walked past the two Malian ground crewmen without looking at them and set a course for the control tower. The Malians turned their attention from the aircraft and stared at her with rapt curiosity. When she reached the base of the tower, she extracted a small pair of wire cutters from a bag slung over her shoulder and calmly severed the power and communication cables running from the controller's equipment to the terminal. Then she waved a signal at the plane's cockpit.

A ramp abruptly dropped from the rear of the fuselage accompanied by the high but muffled revolutions of an automobile engine. Suddenly, what looked to Gunn like an off-road dune buggy flew out of the cavern of the aircraft and down the ramp. The driver threw it into a sideway skid and aimed it toward the guard shack on the military side of the airfield.

Gunn had once been a member of the pit crew for Pitt and Giordino when they had entered a cross-country race in Arizona, but he had never seen an all-terrain vehicle like this one. There was no common body or chassis. The construction was a maze of tubular supports welded together and powered by a supercharged V-8 Rodeck, 541-cubic-inch engine used by American drag racers. The driver sat within a small cockpit at the front of the vehicle, just ahead of the mid-mounted engine. A gunner sat slightly above the driver, manning a wicked-looking six-barrel, lightweight Vulcan-type machine gun. Another gunner sat over the rear axle and faced backward with a 5.56-millimetre Stoner 63 machine gun. This type of vehicle, Gunn recalled, had been most effective during the desert war when used by American special forces teams behind the Iraqi lines.

It was followed down the ramp by a platoon of heavily armed men in unfamiliar uniforms who quickly rounded up the stunned Malian ground crew and secured the terminal building.

The two Malian air force guards on the military side of the airfield watched in fascination as the strange vehicle raced toward them. Only when it was within 100 metres did they recover and recognize it as a threat. They raised their guns to fire but were cut down with a quick burst from the forward gunner and his Vulcan.

Then the driver swung a sharp turn and the gunners began concentrating their fire on the eight Malian jet fighters parked on the tarmac. Unthreatened by a wartime emergency, the aircraft were not dispersed, but lined up in two neat rows as if awaiting inspection. The heavily armed vehicle bored in, lashing out with short, devastating bursts from its automatic weapons. In quick succession, aircraft after aircraft went up in fiery explosions and black storms of smoke as rivers of shells sledgehammered into their fuel tanks. One moment a sleek fighter jet was there, the next it was gone, a burning mass of wreckage. Gunn observed the drama in genuine astonishment. He cringed behind the acacia as if its slim trunk was one wide concrete shield. The whole operation had taken no more than six minutes. The armed all-terrain vehicle sped back toward the jetliner, taking up a position at the entrance of the terminal. Then a man in an officer's uniform stepped from the boarding steps, holding what looked to Gunn like a bullhorn.

The officer held the speaker to his lips and spoke, his voice carrying over the flaming destruction on the other side of the airfield. 'Mr Gunn! Will you please step forward. We don't have much time.'

Gunn was stunned. He hesitated, not knowing whether it was some sort of complex trap. He quickly shook the thought off as stupid. General Kazim would hardly destroy his air force just to capture one man. Yet, he still was reluctant to rush into view of so much firepower.

'Mr Gunn!' the officer boomed again. 'If you are within

sound of my voice, I implore you to hurry or I will be forced to leave without you.'

That was all the urging Gunn needed. He leaped from behind the acacia tree and ran over the uneven ground toward the jetliner, waving his hands and shouting like a madman.

'Hold on! I'm coming!'

The unknown officer who had hailed him paced the tarmac like an impatient passenger, irritated at a flight delay. When Gunn jogged up and stopped, he studied the NUMA scientist as one might look at a street beggar. 'Good morning. Are you Rudi Gunn?'

'I am,' answered Gunn, panting from exertion and the heat. 'Who are you?'

'Colonel Marcel Levant.'

Gunn gazed with admiration at the elite force efficiently guarding the perimeter around the aircraft. They had the appearance of a tough group of men with no qualms about killing. 'What group is this?'

'A United Nations tactical team,' replied Levant.

'How did you know my name and where to find me?'

'Admiral James Sandecker received a communication from someone called Dirk Pitt saying you were hiding near the airport, and that it was urgent you be evacuated.'

'The Admiral sent you?'

'With the approval of the Secretary General,' replied Levant. 'How do I know you're Rudi Gunn?'

Gunn gestured around the desolation in the surrounding countryside. 'How in hell many Rudi Gunns do you think just happened to be roaming around this part of the desert waiting for your beck and call?'

'You have no papers, no proof of identity?'

'My personal documents are probably on the bottom of the Niger River. You'll just have to trust me.'

Levant passed the bullhorn to an aide and nodded toward

the aircraft. 'Recall and board,' he ordered tersely. He turned back to Gunn and regarded him with a marked lack of cordiality. 'Step into the plane, Mr Gunn. We have no more time to waste in idle conversation.'

'Where are you taking me?'

Levant threw a glance of irritation at the sky and said, 'To Paris. From there you will be flown to Washington by Concorde where a number of very important people are anxiously waiting to debrief you. That is all you're required to know. Now please move along. Time is crucial.'

'What's the rush?' Gunn demanded. 'You've obviously destroyed their air force.'

'Only one squadron I fear. There are three others based around the capital city at Bamako. Once alerted they can still intercept us before we escape Malian air space.'

The armed dune buggy had already driven on board and was quickly followed by the ground forces. The flight attendant who had bravely cut the control tower cables took Gunn by the arm and hustled him up the boarding ramp.

'We don't have a first-class cabin with gourmet meals and champagne, Mr Gunn,' she said brightly. 'But we do have cold beer and bologna sandwiches.'

'You don't know how good that sounds,' Gunn smiled.

He should have felt a great surge of relief as he climbed the boarding stairs, but suddenly he was swept by a wave of anguish. Thanks to Pitt and Giordino he was safely escaping to freedom. They had sacrificed to save him. How on heaven's earth did they ever manage to find a radio and contact Sandecker, he wondered.

They were mad to stay behind in that scorched land, he thought. Their commitment to finding the contamination was madness. Kazim would unleash his entire security force to hunt them down. If the desert didn't devour them, the Malians would.

He hesitated before entering the aircraft, turned, and

gazed out over the ugly vastness of sand and rock. From his elevated position he could clearly see the Niger River, little more than a kilometre to the west.

Where were they now? What was their situation?

He tore himself from the sight and entered the cabin, the air-conditioned air striking his sweating body like a breaking wave. His eyes were smarting as the aircraft lifted off the runway past the flaming jet fighters.

Colonel Levant sat in the seat next to Gunn and studied the sorrowful expression. He searched Gunn's eyes for understanding, but found none. 'You don't seem happy to be getting out of this mess.'

Gunn stared out the window. 'Just thinking of the men I left behind.'

'Pitt and Giordino, they were good friends?'

'For many years.'

'Why didn't they come with you?' asked Levant.

'They had a job to finish.'

Levant shook his head, uncomprehending. 'They are either very brave men or very stupid.'

'Not stupid,' said Gunn. 'Not stupid at all.'

'They will surely end up in hell.'

'You don't know them.' Only then did Gunn force a grin. 'If anyone can enter hell and walk out again carrying a glass of tequila over ice,' he said with renewed confidence, 'it's Dirk Pitt.'

27

Six elite soldiers of General Kazim's personal bodyguard force snapped to attention as Massarde stepped from his launch to the dock. A Major stepped forward and saluted. 'Monsieur Massarde?'

'What is it?'

'General Kazim has asked that I escort you to him immediately.'

'Did he know my presence is required at Fort Foureau and I do not wish to have my schedule interrupted?'

Politely the Major bowed. 'I believe his request for a meeting with you is quite urgent.'

Massarde gave a Gallic shrug of annoyance and motioned for the Major to lead. 'After you.'

The Major nodded and gave a curt order to a sergeant. Then he walked over the worn and bleached dock planking toward a large warehouse that bordered the dock. Massarde duly followed in the Major's footsteps, surrounded by the security guard.

'Please, this way,' the Major said, gesturing around the corner of the warehouse while stepping into a small side alley.

There, under heavy security by armed guards, stood a Mercedes-Benz truck and trailer that was General Kazim's private mobile command and living quarters. Massarde was ushered up steps and through a door that immediately closed behind him.

'General Kazim is in his office,' said the Major, opening another door and standing aside. The interior of the office felt like an Arctic ice floe after the heat outside. Kazim must have kept the air conditioning running at full blast, Massarde surmised. Curtains were drawn over bullet-proof windows and he stood motionless for a moment waiting for his eyes to adjust after the bright sunlight.

'Come in, Yves, sit down,' Kazim called from a desk as he replaced the receiver from one of four telephones.

Massarde smiled and remained standing. 'Why so many guards? Do you expect an assassination?'

Kazim smiled back. 'In light of the events of the past few hours, extra security seems a valid precaution.'

'Have you found my helicopter?' Massarde asked directly.

'Not yet.'

'How can you lose a helicopter in the desert? It only had enough fuel for half an hour's flight.'

'It appears the two Americans you allowed to escape — '

'My houseboat is not equipped to contain prisoners,' Massarde snapped. 'You should have taken them off my hands when you had the chance.'

Kazim stared directly at him. 'Be that as it may, my friend, mistakes were made. It appears that after the NUMA agents stole your helicopter, they flew to Bourem where I have reason to believe they sank it in the river, walked to the village, and then stole my car.'

'Your old Voisin?' Massarde pronounced it *Vahsaan*.

'Yes,' Kazim acknowledged through taut lips. 'The American scum made off with my rare, classic car.'

'And you haven't found it or apprehended them yet?'

'No.'

Massarde finally sat down, anger at losing his aircraft mixed with delight over the theft of Kazim's precious automobile. 'What of their rendezvous with a helicopter south of Gao?'

'Much to my regret, I fell for their lie. The force I positioned in ambush 20 kilometres to the south waited in vain, and my radar field units detected no sign of aircraft. They came instead to the Gao airport in a commercial airliner.'

'Why weren't you alerted?'

'It did not appear to be a security matter,' Kazim answered. 'Only an hour before sunrise, Air Afrique officials in Gao were notified that one of their aircraft was making an unscheduled landing so a group of tourists could visit the city and take a short cruise on the river.'

'The airline officials believed it?' asked Massarde incredulously.

'And why not. They routinely asked for confirmation from company headquarters in Algiers and received it.'

'Then what happened?'

'According to the airport controller and the ground crew, the aircraft, flying the markings of Air Afrique, supplied the proper identification on approach. But after it set down and taxied to the terminal, an armed force along with a weapons vehicle shot from the plane's interior and gunned down the security guards on the military side of the field before they could resist. Then the weapons vehicle destroyed an entire squadron of eight of my jet fighters.'

'Yes, the explosions woke everyone on the houseboat,' said Massarde. 'We saw the smoke rise in the direction of the airport and thought a plane had crashed.'

Kazim grunted. 'Nothing that ordinary.'

'Did the ground crew or controller identify the assault force?'

'The attackers wore unfamiliar uniforms with no badges or insignia.'

'How many of your people were killed?'

'Fortunately, only two security guards. The rest of the base personnel, maintenance crew, and pilots were on leave for a religious festival.'

Massarde's face grew serious. 'This is no mere intrusion

289

to find contamination. This sounds more like a raid by your rebel opposition. They're smarter and more powerful than you give them credit for.'

Kazim waved his hand in a gesture of dismissal. 'A few dissident Tuaregs fighting on camels with swords. Hardly what you'd call highly trained special forces with modern firepower.'

'Maybe they've hired mercenaries.'

'With what funds?' Kazim shook his head. 'No, this was a well-conceived plan carried off by a professional force. The destruction of the fighters was purely to eliminate any means of counterattack or interception during their escape after picking up one of the NUMA agents.'

Massarde gave Kazim a bitter look. 'Forgot to tell me about that little item, didn't you?'

'The ground crewmen reported that the leader of the attackers called for a man named Gunn, who appeared out of the desert where he'd been hiding. After Gunn boarded the aircraft, it took off on a northwesterly course and flew toward Algeria.'

'Sounds like the plot for a second-rate motion picture.'

'Do not be facetious, Yves.' Kazim's tone was smooth but with a sharp edge. 'The evidence points toward a conspiracy that goes far beyond a search for oil. I strongly believe both our interests are threatened by outside forces.'

Massarde was hesitant to completely buy Kazim's theory. Their minimal trust was built on respect for each other's shrewd mind and a healthy fear of their respective powers. Massarde was very leery of the game that Kazim was playing. A game that could only end with the General on the receiving end. He looked into the eyes of a jackal while Kazim gazed into the eyes of a fox.

'What brought you to that descriptive conclusion?' asked Massarde sarcastically.

'We know now there were three men on the boat that blew

up on the river. I suspect they set the explosives as a diversion. Two came aboard your houseboat while the third, who must have been the man called Gunn, swam to shore and made his way to the airport.'

'The raid and evacuation seem incredibly well conceived and timed to coincide with the pickup of this Gunn fellow.'

'It developed quickly because it was planned and carried out by first-rate professionals,' Kazim replied slowly. 'The assault force was alerted to the time and place of Gunn's location, most certainly by the agent who called himself Dirk Pitt.'

'How can you know that?'

Kazim shrugged. 'A calculated guess.' He looked at Massarde. 'Are you forgetting that Pitt used your satellite communications system to contact his superior, Admiral James Sandecker. That's why he and Giordino came on board your boat.'

'But that doesn't explain why Pitt and Giordino didn't make any attempt to escape with Gunn.'

'Obviously you caught them before they could swim across the river and join him at the airport.'

'Then why didn't they flee after stealing my helicopter? The Nigerian border is only 150 kilometres away. They could have almost made it with the fuel remaining in the helicopter's tanks. Makes little sense to fly deeper into the interior of the country, then ditch the craft and steal an old car. There are no bridges across the river in the area so they can't drive south to the border. Where can they possibly go?'

Kazim's ferret eyes looked at him steadily. 'Perhaps where no one expected.'

Massarde's brows pinched together. 'North, into the desert?'

'Where else?'

'Absurd.'

'I'm open to a better theory.'

Massarde shook his head sceptically. 'For what possible reason would two men steal a sixty-year-old car and strike out across the most desolate desert in the world? They'd be committing suicide.'

'Until now their actions have defied explanation,' Kazim admitted. 'They were on some sort of covert mission. That much is certain. We still aren't certain what it is they were after.'

'Secrets?' Massarde offered simply.

Kazim shook his head. 'Any classified material on my military programme is no doubt on file at the CIA. Mali has no secret projects that would interest a foreign nation, even those of our bordering nations.'

'There are two you've forgotten.'

Kazim looked at Massarde curiously. 'What are you suggesting?'

'Fort Foureau and Tebezza.'

Was it possible, Kazim thought, that the waste disposal project and the gold mines might be connected to the intruders. His mind tried to sift for answers, but there were none. 'If those were their objectives, why are they mucking around over 300 kilometres to the south?'

'I can't answer you. But as my agent at the United Nations insisted, they were searching for a source of chemical contamination that originated in the Niger and caused an expansive growth of red tides after entering the sea.'

'I find that utter rot. Most likely a red herring to hide their real mission.'

'Which might well be the penetration of Fort Foureau and a human rights exposé of Tebezza,' Massarde threw out seriously.

Kazim was silent, his expression reflecting doubt.

Massarde continued. 'Suppose Gunn already had vital information on him when he was evacuated. Why else would such a complex operation be mounted to rescue him while Pitt and Giordino headed north toward our joint projects?'

'We'll find the answers when I capture them,' said Kazim, his voice becoming tense with anger. 'Every available military and police unit has already closed all roads and camel trails leading out of the country. I've also ordered my air force to conduct aerial reconnaissance over the northern desert. I intend to cover every option.'

'A wise decision,' said Massarde.

'Without supplies they won't last two days in the heat of the desert.'

'I trust your methods, Zateb. I have no doubt you will have Pitt and Giordino in one of your interrogation cells by this time tomorrow.'

'Sooner, I should think.'

'That's most reassuring,' Massarde said, smiling.

But somehow he knew Pitt and Giordino would not be easy game to run down.

Captain Batutta came to attention and saluted as he stood in front of Colonel Mansa who merely returned the salute with an indifferent wave.

'The UN scientists are imprisoned at Tebezza,' Batutta reported.

A slight smile touched Mansa's lips. 'I imagine O'Bannion and Melika were happy to obtain new workers for the mines.'

Batutta flashed an expression of disgust. 'She's one cruel witch, that Melika. I don't envy any man who feels the sting of her quirt.'

'Or woman,' added Mansa. 'She makes no distinction when she metes out punishment. I give Dr Hopper and his party four months before the last of them lies buried in the sand.'

'General Kazim will be the last to shed a tear over their demise.'

The door opened, and Lieutenant Djemaa, the Malian air force pilot of the UN scientists' plane, walked in and saluted. Mansa looked up at him. 'Did everything go off all right?'

Djemaa smiled. 'Yes sir, we flew back to Asselar, dug up the required number of corpses, and loaded them on the plane. Then returned north where my copilot and I bailed out over the designated area of the Tanezrouft Desert, a good 100 kilometres from the nearest camel track.'

'The plane burned after it crashed?' asked Mansa.

'Yes sir.'

'Did you inspect the wreckage?'

Djemaa nodded. 'After the driver of the desert vehicle you stationed to pick us up arrived, we drove to the crash site. l had set the controls so it went down in a vertical dive. It exploded on impact, blasting a crater almost 10 metres deep. Except for the engines there wasn't a piece of wreckage larger than a shoe box.'

Mansa's face broadened with a smile of satisfaction. 'General Kazim will be pleased. Both you men can expect promotions.'

He looked at Djemaa. 'And you, Lieutenant, will be in command of the search operation to find Hopper's plane.'

'But why would I direct a search,' asked Djemaa in confusion, 'when I already know where it is?'

'Why else would you fill it with dead bodies?'

'Captain Batutta did not inform me of the plan.'

'We play our benevolent role in discovering the wreckage,' Mansa explained. 'And then turn it over to international flight accident investigators, who will not have enough human remains to identify or evidence to provide the cause of the crash.' He gave a hard stare at Djemaa. 'Providing the Lieutenant has done a complete job.'

'I personally removed the flight recorder,' Djemaa assured him.

'Good, now we can begin displaying our country's concern over the disappearance of the UN scientists' flight to the international news media and express our deep regret for their loss.'

28

The afternoon heat was suffocating as it reflected off the sunbaked surface. Without proper dark glasses, the immense plain of rock and sand, dazzled by the fiery sun, blinded Pitt's eyes as he sat on the gravelled bottom of a narrow gorge under the shade of the Avions Voisin. Except for the supplies they had scrounged from the garage in Bourem, they only possessed the clothes on their backs.

Giordino was in the midst of using the tools he'd found in the trunk of the car to remove the exhaust pipe and muffler to give the car more ground clearance. They had already reduced the tyre pressure for better traction in the sand. So far the old Voisin moved through the inhospitable landscape like an ageing beauty queen walking through the Bronx in New York, stylish but sadly misplaced.

They travelled during the cool of night beneath the light of the stars, groping over the barren expanse at no more than 10 kilometres an hour, stopping every hour to raise the hood and let the engine cool. There was no thought of using the headlights. The beams could have been caught by a keen observer from an aircraft far out of earshot. Quite often the passenger had to walk ahead to examine the ground. Once they almost drove into a steep ravine and twice they had to dig and scoop their way out of patches of soft sand.

Without a compass or a map, they relied on celestial navigation to record their location and trail as they followed the ancient riverbed from the Niger River north ever deeper into the Sahara. By day they hid in gulleys and ravines where they covered the car with a thin coating of sand and scrub brush so it would blend in with the desert floor and appear from the air as a small dune sprouting a few pieces of sparse growth.

'Would you care for a cold, sparkling glass of Sahara spring water or the refreshing fizz of a Malian soft drink?' Giordino grinned, holding out a bottle of the local pop and a cup of the warm, sulphur-tasting liquid from the water tap he'd found in the village garage.

'I can't stand the taste,' said Pitt, taking the cup of water and wrinkling his nose, 'but it's best we drink at least three quarts every twenty-four hours.'

'You don't think we should ration it?'

'Not while we have an ample supply. Dehydration will only come on that much quicker if we hoard and sip it a little at a time. Better to drink as much as we need to quench our thirst and worry when it's gone.'

'How about a gourmet sardine for dinner?'

'Sounds jazzy.'

'The only thing missing is a Caesar salad.'

'You're thinking of anchovies.'

'I never could tell the difference.'

After savouring his sardine, Giordino licked his fingers. 'I feel like an idiot sitting here in the middle of the desert eating fish.'

Pitt smiled. 'Be thankful you've got them.' Then he tilted his head listening.

'Hear something?' asked Giordino.

'Aircraft.' Pitt cupped his hands behind his ears. 'A low-flying jet judging by the sound.'

He crawled up the side of the ravine on his stomach until he reached the upper edge and moved behind a small tamarisk shrub so his head and face merged with its broken shadow. Then he began a slow, deliberate observation of the sky.

The throaty roar of a jet turbine exhaust came very clearly now as he peered ahead of the trailing sound waves. He squinted into the blazing blue sky but failed to see anything at first. He dropped his gaze lower, and then spotted a sudden movement against the empty desert terrain about 3 kilometres away. Pitt recognized it as an old American-built Phantom, sporting Malian air force insignia, about 6 kilometres to the south, flying less than 100 metres off the ground. It was like some great vulture, camouflage-brown against the yellow-grey of the landscape. and flying in great lazy arcs as if a sixth sense was telling it there was prey in the neighbourhood.

'See it?' asked Giordino.

'An F-4 Phantom,' answered Pitt.

'What direction?'

'Circling in from the south.'

'Think he's onto us?'

Pitt turned and looked down at the palm fronds tied to the bumpers behind the rear wheels that were dragged along to cover the tyre tracks. The parallel indentations in the sand that trailed off down the middle of the ravine were almost completely obliterated. 'A search crew in a hovering helicopter might spot our trail but not the pilot of a jet fighter. He has no vision directly below his aircraft and has to bank if he wants to see anything. And he's flying too fast, too close to the ground to detect a vague pair of tyre tracks.'

The jet roared toward the ravine, close enough now so that its desert camouflage markings stained the pure blue of the sky. Giordino wiggled under the car as Pitt pulled the tamarisk shrub's branches over his head and shoulders. He watched as the pilot of the Phantom made a soaring turn, scanning the seemingly blank and empty world of the Sahara below.

Pitt tensed and held his breath. The aircraft's swing was bringing it directly over their gorge. Then it tore overhead, the air rushing past its wings like a wave cut by a ship's bow, the thrust of its turbine swirling the sand. Pitt felt the heat of its fiery exhaust sweep over him. It seemed almost as if the aircraft had materialized right over the gorge, so low Pitt swore he could have thrown a rock into its intake scoops. And then it was gone.

He feared the worst as he watched it roaring away. But it continued on its slow, circling search as though the pilot had seen nothing of interest. Pitt watched it until the plane was out of sight over the horizon. He kept watching for a few more minutes, wary that the pilot might have spied something suspicious and entertained the notion of a wide sweep before whipping over the gorge in hope of catching his quarry by surprise.

But the sound of the jet exhaust finally faded away in the distance, leaving the desert dead and silent once again.

Pitt slid back down the slope of the gorge and regained the shade of the ancient Voisin as Giordino crawled from beneath its chassis.

'A near thing,' said Giordino, flicking a small platoon of ants from one arm.

Pitt doodled in the sand with a small, withered stick. 'Either we didn't fool Kazim by heading north or he isn't taking any chances.'

'Must blow his mind that a car painted a colour as loud as this one can't be found in a wasteland against a flat and colourless background.'

'He can't be jumping for joy,' Pitt agreed.

'I bet he went nuclear when he found out it was stolen, and figured we were the culprits,' Giordino laughed.

Pitt held a hand up to shield his eyes and gazed at the sun dipping into the west. 'Be dark in another hour, and we can be on our way.'

'How does the ground ahead look?'

'Once we pass out of this gorge and back into the riverbed it continues as flat sand and gravel with a few scattered boulders. Good for driving if we keep a sharp eye and avoid jagged stones that can slice open a tyre.'

'How far do you figure we've gone since leaving Bourem?'

'According to the odometer, 116 kilometres, but as the crow flies, I'd judge about 90.'

'And still no sign or trace of a chemical production or waste facility.'

'Not even an empty container drum.'

'I can't see much sense in going on,' said Giordino. 'No way a chemical spill could flow 90 kilometres over a dry riverbed into the Niger.'

'It does seem a lost cause,' Pitt admitted.

'We can still make a try for the Algerian border.'

Pitt shook his head. 'Not enough gas. We'd have to walk the last 200 kilometres to the Trans-Saharan Motor Track to even catch a ride to civilization. We'd die of exposure before making it halfway.'

'So what are our options?'

'We push on.'

'How far?'

'Until we find what we're looking for, even if it means doubling back.'

'And litter the landscape with our bones in either case.'

'Then at least we accomplish something by eliminating this section of the desert as a source for the contamination.' Pitt spoke without emotion, staring into the sand at his feet as if trying to see a vision.

Giordino looked at him. 'We've been through a lot together over the years. Be a damn shame for it to end in the armpit of the world.'

Pitt grinned at him. 'The old guy with the scythe hasn't put in an appearance just yet.'

'This will be most embarrassing when we make the obituary columns,' Giordino persisted pessimistically.

'What will?'

'Two directors of the National Underwater and Marine Agency lost and feared dead in the middle of the Sahara Desert. Who in their right mind will believe it? . . . Did you just hear something?'

Pitt stood up. 'I heard.'

'A voice singing in English. God, maybe we are already dead.'

They stood side-by-side as the sun began disappearing over the horizon, listening to a voice singing what they recognized as the old camp song, 'My Darling Clementine.' The words became distinct as the off-key singing became very close.

'You are lost and gone forever, dreadful sorry Clementine.'

'He's coming up the gorge,' Giordino murmured, clutching a lug wrench.

Pitt picked up several rocks as weapons. They took up positions silently on opposite ends of the sand-covered car, crouching in readiness to attack, waiting for whoever was approaching to appear around a nearby bend in the gorge.

'In a cavern, in a canyon, excavating for a mine. . .' The figure of a man shadowed by the wall of the gorge walked around the bend leading an animal. 'Lived a miner forty-niner and his daughter Clementine . . .'

The voice trailed off as he spied the car blanketed by sand. He came to a halt at the unexpected sight of the camouflaged vehicle and studied it not so much from surprise as simple curiosity. He moved closer, pulling the stubborn-acting animal behind him on a tether. Then he stopped beside the car, reached out, and brushed the sand from the roof.

Pitt and Giordino slowly rose and confronted the stranger, staring at the man as if he was an alien from another planet. This was no Tuareg leading a camel through the wilderness of his native land. This apparition was totally inconsistent with the Sahara, completely in the wrong place and time.

'Maybe he doesn't carry a scythe anymore,' muttered Giordino.

The man was dressed like an old American western desert prospector. Battered old Stetson hat, denim pants held up by suspenders and tucked into scrapped and faded leather boots. A red bandanna was tied around his neck and covered the lower part of his face, giving him the appearance of an early bandit.

The animal behind him was not a camel, but a burro, its back loaded with a pack almost as large as he was, containing goods and supplies including several round water canteens, blankets, tins of food, a pick and shovel, and a lever-action Winchester rifle.

'I knew it,' Giordino whispered in awe. 'We've expired and gone to Disneyland.'

The stranger pulled down the bandanna, revealing a white moustache and beard. His eyes were green, almost as green as Pitt's. His brows matched the beard but the hair that leaked from under the Stetson was still greying with streaks of dark brown. He stood tall, about the same height as Pitt and was more heavy than thin. His lips broadened into a friendly smile.

'I sure hope you fellas speak my language,' he said warmly. 'Because I could sure use the company.'

29

Pitt and Giordino looked at each other blankly, and then back at the old desert rat, certain their eyes and their minds had run amuck.

'Where did *you* come from?' Giordino blurted.

'I might ask you the same thing,' replied the stranger. He gazed at the coating of sand on the Voisin. 'You the fellas that airplane was lookin' for?'

'Why do you want to know?' asked Pitt.

'If you two gents want to play question and answer games, I'll be on my way.'

The intruder hardly wore the image of a nomad, and since he talked and looked like a fellow countryman, Pitt quickly decided to trust him. 'My name is Dirk Pitt and my friend here is Al Giordino, and yes the Malians are looking for us.'

The old man shrugged. 'Not surprised. They don't take kindly to foreigners around here.' He gazed in wonder at the Voisin. 'How in heaven's name did you drive a car this far without a road?'

'It wasn't easy, mister . . .'

The stranger moved closer and stuck out a calloused hand. 'Everybody just calls me the Kid.'

Pitt smiled and shook hands. 'How did a man your age come to be called that?'

'Long time ago after, after I'd return from a prospecting trip, I'd always head for my favourite waterin' hole in Jerome, Arizona. When I'd belly up to the bar, my old saloon pals used to greet me with, "Hey, the Kid's back in town." The name just sort of stuck.'

Giordino was staring at the Kid's companion. 'A mule

seems out of place in this part of the world. Wouldn't a camel be more practical?'

'To begin with,' the Kid said with noticeable indignation, 'Mr Periwinkle ain't no mule, he's a burro. And a real tough one. Camels can go further and longer without water, but the burro was bred for the desert too. Found Mr Periwinkle roamin' free in Nevada eight years ago, tamed him, and when I came to the Sahara I shipped him over. He's not half as rotten as a camel, eats less, and can carry as much weight. Besides, standin' lower to the ground like he does, he's a helluva lot easier to pack.'

'A fine animal,' Giordino retreated.

'You look like you're fixin' to move on. I was hopin' we might sit and talk a spell. I haven't met up with another soul except an Arab takin' a couple of camels to sell in Timbuktu. And that was three weeks ago. I never figured in a thousand years I'd run on to other Americans out here.'

Giordino looked at Pitt. 'Might be smart to hang around and pump information from someone who knows the territory.'

Pitt nodded in agreement, opened the rear door of the Voisin, and gestured inside. 'Would you care to take a load off your feet?'

The Kid stared at the leather seats of the car as if they were upholstered in gold. 'I can't remember when I sat in a soft chair. I'm much obliged.' He ducked into the car, sank into the rear seat, and sighed with pleasure.

'We only have a can of sardines, but we'd be happy to share it with you,' offered Giordino with a gracious generosity seldom witnessed by Pitt.

'Nope, dinner's on me. I've got plenty of concentrated food packs. Be more than pleased to split them with you. How's beef stew sound?'

Pitt smiled. 'You don't know how happy we are to be

304

your guests. Sardines aren't exactly our idea of a taste treat in the wild.'

'We can down the stew with our soft drinks,' Giordino suggested.

'You got soda pop? How you fellas fixed for water?'

'Enough for a few days,' answered Giordino.

'If you're running short I can point you toward a well about 10 miles to the north.'

'We're thankful for any help,' said Pitt.

'More than you know,' added Giordino.

The sun had fallen below the horizon and twilight still lit the sky. With the approach of evening the air became breathable again. After hobbling Mr Periwinkle, who found and began happily chomping on several clumps of coarse grass growing out of a small dune, the Kid added water to the concentrated beef stew and, to the relief of Pitt, cooked it over a small Coleman stove along with biscuits. If Kazim had sent aircraft to hunt them by night, a small fire, no matter how shielded by the walls of the gorge, would have been a dead giveaway. The old prospector also provided tin plates and eating utensils.

As Pitt soaked the final remains of his stew with a biscuit, he pronounced it as the most magnificent meal he'd ever eaten. He thought it amazing how a small measure of food could rejuvenate his optimism again. After they finished, the Kid produced a half-full bottle of Old Overholt straight rye whisky and passed it around.

'Well now, if you've a mind to, why don't you boys tell me why you're drivin' around the worst part of the Sahara in a car that looks as old as I am.'

'We're searching for a source of toxic contamination that's polluting the Niger and being carried down to the sea,' answered Pitt directly.

'That's a new one. Where's the stuff supposed to come from?'

'Either a chemical plant or a waste disposal facility.'

The Kid shook his head. 'Ain't nothin' like that in these parts.'

'Any heavy construction around this section of the Sahara?' asked Giordino.

'Can't think of any, except maybe Fort Foureau a ways to the northwest.'

'The solar detoxification plant run by the French?'

The Kid nodded. 'A real big spread. Mr Periwinkle and me tramped past it about six months ago. Got chased off. Guards everywhere. You'd have thought they were secretly buildin' nuclear bombs.'

Pitt took a swallow of the rye, taking pleasure as it burned all the way down his throat to his stomach. He passed the bottle to Giordino. 'Fort Foureau is too far from the Niger to pollute its water.'

The Kid sat silent a moment. Finally, he stared at Pitt with a curious twinkle in his eyes. 'It might if the plant sat over the Oued Zarit.'

Pitt leaned forward and repeated, 'Oued Zarit?'

'A legendary river that ran through Mali until a hundred and thirty years ago when it began sinkin' into the sands. The local nomads, myself included, think the Oued Zarit still flows underground and empties into the Niger.'

'Like an aquifer.'

'A what?'

'A geological stratum that allows water to penetrate through pores and openings,' Pitt answered. 'Usually through porous gravel or limestone caverns.'

'All I know is that if you dig deep enough, you'll strike water in the old river channel.'

'I never heard of a river disappearing yet continuing its course deep in the earth,' said Giordino.

'Nothin's unusual in that,' explained the Kid. 'Most of the flow of the Mojave River runs under the Mojave Desert

306

of California before emptyin' in a lake. There's one tale of a prospector finding a cave leading hundreds of feet down to the underground stream. So his story goes, he found tons of placer gold along the water.'

Pitt turned and looked steadily at Giordino. 'What do you think?'

'Sounds to me like Fort Foureau might be the only game in town,' Giordino replied soberly.

'A long shot. But an underground stream running from the toxic waste plant to the Niger could be our contamination carrier.'

The Kid waved a hand up the gorge. 'I guess you boys know this gulch runs into the old riverbed.'

'We know,' Pitt assured him. 'We've been following it from the bank of the Niger most of last night. We holed up in this ravine during the heat of the day to keep from being seen by Malian search parties.'

'Looks like you fooled them so far.'

'What's your story?' Giordino asked the Kid, handing him the rye bottle. 'You prospecting for gold?'

The Kid studied the label on the bottle for a moment as if trying to make up his mind to reveal the reason behind his presence. Then he shrugged and shook his head. 'Lookin' for gold, yes. Prospectin', no, I guess it won't hurt me none to tell you boys. The truth is I'm lookin' for a shipwreck.'

Pitt studied him with bleak suspicion. 'A shipwreck . . . a shipwreck here in the middle of the Sahara Desert?'

'A Confederate ironclad to be exact.'

Pitt and Giordino sat there in dazed incomprehension with the growing tentative wish there was a straitjacket in the Voisin's tool box. They both stared at the Kid in a very peculiar way. It was almost dark now, but they could still see the earnest expression in his eyes.

'Without the risk of sounding stupid,' said Pitt sceptically, 'would you mind telling us how a warship from the war between the states got here?'

The Kid took a long swallow from the rye bottle and wiped his mouth. Then he unrolled a blanket on the sand and stretched out, propping the back of his head with his hands. 'It was back in April of 1865, the week before Lee surrendered to Grant. A few miles below Richmond, Virginia, the Confederate ironclad *Texas* was loaded with the records of the dyin' Confederate government. At leastways they said it was documents and records, but it was really gold.'

'Are you sure it wasn't a myth like so many other treasure tales?' said Pitt.

'President Jefferson Davis himself, before he died, claimed the gold from the Confederate States treasury was loaded in the dead of night on board the *Texas*. He and his cabinet hoped to smuggle it through the Union navy blockade into another country so they could form a new government in exile and continue fightin' the war.'

'But Davis was captured and imprisoned,' Pitt said.

The Kid nodded. 'The Confederacy died, never to be reborn.'

'And the *Texas*?'

'The ship fought one hell of a battle as it steamed down the James River past half the Union navy and the forts at Hampton Roads before gainin' Chesapeake Bay and escapin' into the Atlantic. The last anybody saw the ship and any of its crew on this side of the ocean was when it vanished in a fog bank.'

'And you think the *Texas* sailed across the sea and entered the Niger River?' Pitt ventured.

'I do,' the Kid replied firmly. 'I've traced contemporary sightin's by French colonials and natives who passed down stories of the monster without sails that floated by their villages on the river. Descriptions of the warship and the dates it was observed satisfy me that it was the *Texas*.'

'How could a warship the size and tonnage of an ironclad steam this far into the Sahara without stranding?' asked Giordino.

'That was in the days before the century of drought. This part of the desert had rain then, and the Niger ran much deeper than it does now. One of its tributaries was the Oued Zarit. At that time the Oued Zarit flowed from the Ahaggar Mountains northeast of here 600 miles to the Niger. Journals of French explorers and military expeditions say it was deep enough to afford passage for large boats. My guess is the *Texas* turned up the Oued Zarit from the Niger then grounded and became trapped when the water level began to drop with the approach of the summer heat.'

'Even with a fair depth of water it seems impossible for a heavy vessel like an ironclad to sail this far from the sea.'

'The *Texas* was built for military operations on the James River. She had a flat bottom and shallow draft. Navigatin' the tricky turns and depths of a river was no problem for her and her crew. The miracle was that she crossed an open ocean without sinkin' in rough water and heavy weather like the *Monitor*.'

'A ship could have reached any number of unpopulated regions during the 1860s up and down the North and Central American shores,' Pitt said. 'Why risk losing the gold hoard by sailing over dangerous seas and crossing uncharted country?'

The Kid took a cigar stub from his shirt pocket and lit it with a wooden match. 'You have to admit, the Union navy never would have thought to search for the *Texas* a thousand miles up a river in Africa.'

'Probably not, but it certainly seems like an extreme.'

'I'm with you,' said Giordino. 'Why the desperation? They couldn't rebuild another government in the middle of a desert wasteland.'

Pitt looked at the Kid thoughtfully. 'There had to be more to the hazardous voyage than smuggling gold.'

'There was a rumour.' The subtle change in tone could hardly be called evasive, but it was unmistakable. 'Lincoln was on board the Texas when she left Richmond.'

'Not Abraham Lincoln,' Giordino scoffed.

The Kid silently nodded.

'Who dreamed up that piece of fiction?' Pitt waved off another offer of the rye.

'A Confederate cavalry captain by the name of Neville Brown made a deathbed statement to a doctor in Charleston, South Carolina, when he died in 1908. He claimed his troop captured Lincoln and delivered him on board the *Texas*.'

'The ravings of a dying man,' murmured Giordino in absolute disbelief. 'Lincoln must have caught the Concorde to arrive in time to be shot by John Wilkes Booth at Ford's Theatre.'

'I don't know the whole story,' admitted the Kid.

'A fantastic but intriguing tale,' said Pitt. 'But tough to take seriously.'

'I can't guarantee the Lincoln legend,' the Kid said adamantly, 'but I'll bet Mr Periwinkle and the remains of my grubstake, the *Texas* and the bones of her crew, along with the gold, lie here in the sand somewhere. I've been roamin' the desert for five years searchin' for her remains and by God I'm gonna find her or die tryin'.'

Pitt gazed at the shadowed form of the old prospector in sympathy and respect. He rarely saw such dedication and determination. There was a burning confidence in the Kid that reminded Pitt of the old miner in *The Treasure of the Sierra Madre*.

'If she's buried under a dune, how do you intend on discovering her?' asked Giordino.

'I got a good metal detector, a Fisher 1265X.'

Pitt could think of nothing more of consequence to say

except, 'I hope good luck leads you to the *Texas*, and she's all you imagined.'

The Kid lay there on his blanket without speaking for several seconds, seemingly lost in his thoughts. Finally, Giordino broke the silence. 'It's time we were on our way if we want to make any distance by dawn.'

Twenty minutes later the engine of the Voisin was quietly idling as Pitt and Giordino said their goodbyes to the Kid and Mr Periwinkle. The old prospector had insisted they take several packages of concentrated food from his stock. He had also drawn them a rough map of the ancient riverbed, marking in landmarks and the only well near the trail leading to the waste facility at Fort Foureau.

'How far?' asked Pitt.

The Kid shrugged. 'About 110 miles.'

'A hundred and seventy-seven kilometres on the odometer,' translated Giordino.

'Hope you fellas find what you're lookin' for.'

Pitt shook hands and smiled. 'You too.' He climbed in the Voisin and settled behind the wheel, almost sad to leave the old man.

Giordino lingered a moment as he bid a farewell. 'Thank you for your hospitality.'

'Glad to be of help.'

'I've been wanting to say this, but you look vaguely familiar.'

'Can't imagine why. I don't recall meetin' up with you fellas before.'

'Would I offend you if I asked you your real name?'

'Not at all, I don't take offence easily. It's an odd name. Never used it much.'

Giordino waited patiently without interrupting.

'It's Clive Cussler.'

Giordino smiled. 'You're right, it is an odd name.'

Then he turned and settled in the front seat beside Pitt.

311

He turned to wave as Pitt eased out the clutch and the Voisin began rolling over the flat bed of the gully. But the old man and his faithful burro were quickly lost in the dark of evening.

PART THREE

Desert Secrets

30

May 18, 1996
Washington, D.C.

The Air France Concorde touched down at Dulles Airport and taxied up to an unmarked U.S. government hangar near the cargo terminals. The sky was overcast, but the runway was dry and showed no sign of rain. Still clutching his backpack as if it was part of him, Gunn exited the sleek aircraft almost immediately and hurried down the mobile stairway to a waiting black Ford sedan driven by uniformed capital police. With flashing lights and screaming siren, he was whisked toward the NUMA headquarters building in the nation's capital.

Gunn felt like a captured felon, riding in the backseat of the speeding police car. He noticed that the Potomac River looked unusually green and leaden as they shot over the Rochambeau Memorial Bridge. The blur of pedestrians was too immune to revolving lights and sirens to bother looking up as the Ford shot past.

The driver did not pull up at the main entrance but swung around the west corner of the NUMA building, tyres squealing, and flew down a ramp leading to a garage beneath the lobby floor. The Ford came to an abrupt stop in front of an elevator. Two security guards stepped forward, opened the door, and escorted Gunn into the elevator and up to the agency's fourth floor. A short distance down the hallway they stood back and opened the door to the NUMA's vast conference room with its sophisticated visual displays.

Several men and women were seated around a long mahogany table, their attention focused on Dr Chapman, who was lecturing in front of a screen that depicted the middle Atlantic Ocean along the equator off West Africa.

The room abruptly hushed as Gunn walked in. Admiral Sandecker rose out of his chair, rushed forward, and greeted Gunn like a brother who had survived a liver transplant.

'Thank God, you got through,' he said with unaccustomed emotion. 'How was your flight from Paris?'

'Felt like an outcast sitting in a Concorde all by myself.'

'No military planes were immediately available. Chartering a Concorde was the only expedient means of getting you here fast.'

'Nice, so long as the taxpayers don't find out.'

'If they knew their very existence was at stake, I doubt if they'd complain.'

Sandecker introduced Gunn around the conference table. 'With three exceptions I think you know most everyone here.'

Dr Chapman and Hiram Yaeger came over and shook hands, showing their obvious pleasure at seeing him. He was introduced to Dr Muriel Hoag, NUMA's director of marine biology, and Dr Evan Holland, the agency's environmental expert.

Muriel Hoag was quite tall and built like a starving fashion model. Her jet-black hair was brushed back in a neat bun and her brown eyes peered through round spectacles. She wore no makeup, which was just as well, Gunn thought. A complete makeover by Beverly Hills' top beauty salon would have been a wasted effort.

Evan Holland was an environmental chemist and looked like a basset hound contemplating a frog in his dish. His ears were two sizes too large for his head, and he had a long nose that rounded at the tip. His eyes stared at the world as if they were soaked in melancholy. Holland's appearance was deceiving. He was one of the most astute pollution investigators in the business.

The other two men, Chip Webster, satellite analyst for

NUMA, and Keith Hodge, the agency's chief oceanographer, Gunn already knew.

He turned to Sandecker. 'Someone went to a lot of trouble to evacuate me out of Mali.'

'Hala Kamil personally gave her authorization to use a UN tactical team.'

'The officer in charge of the operation, a Colonel Levant, acted none too happy to greet me.'

'General Bock, his superior, and Colonel Levant both took a bit of persuading,' Sandecker admitted. 'But when they realized the urgency of your data they gave their full cooperation.'

'They masterminded a very smooth operation,' Gunn said. 'Incredible they could plan and carry it through overnight.'

If Gunn thought Sandecker would fill him in on the details, he was to be disappointed. Impatience was etched in every crease in the Admiral's face. There was a tray with coffee and sweet rolls, but he didn't offer Gunn any. He grabbed him by one arm and hustled him to a chair at one end of the long conference table.

'Let's get to it,' the Admiral said brusquely. 'Everyone is anxious to hear about your discovery of the compound causing the red tide explosion.'

Gunn sat down at the table, opened his knapsack, and began retrieving the contents. Very carefully, he unwrapped the glass vials of water samples and laid them on a cloth. Next he unpacked the data disks and set them to one side. Then he looked up.

'Here are the water samples and results as interpreted by my on-board instruments and computers. Through a bit of luck I was able to identify the stimulator of the red tide as a most unusual organometallic compound, a combination of a synthetic amino acid and cobalt. I also found traces of radiation in the water, but I do not believe it has any direct relation to the contaminant's impact on the red tide.'

'Considering the hardships and obstacles thrown in your path by the West Africans,' said Chapman, 'it's a miracle you were able to get a grip on the cause.'

'Fortunately, none of my instruments were damaged after our run-in with the Benin navy.'

'I received an inquiry from the CIA,' said Sandecker with a tight smile, 'asking if we knew anything about a maverick operation in Mali after you destroyed half the Benin navy and a helicopter.'

'What did you tell them?'

'I lied. Please go on.'

'Fire from one Benin gunboat did, however, manage to destroy our data transmission system,' Gunn continued, 'making it impossible to telemeter my results to Hiram Yaeger's computer network.'

'I'd like to retest your water samples while Hiram verifies your analysis data,' said Chapman.

Yaeger stepped next to Gunn and tenderly picked up the computer disks. 'Not much I can contribute to this meeting, so I'll get to work.'

As soon as the computer wizard had left the room, Gunn stared at Chapman. 'I double- and triple-checked my results. I'm confident your lab and Hiram will confirm my findings.'

Chapman sensed the tension in Gunn's tone. 'Believe me when I say I don't question your procedures or data for a minute. You, Pitt, and Giordino did one hell of a job. Thanks to your efforts we now know what we're dealing with. Now the President can use his clout to lean on Mali to shut off the contaminant at the source. This will buy us time to formulate ways to neutralize its effects and stop further expansion of the red tides.'

'Don't break out the cake and ice cream just yet,' Gunn

warned seriously. 'Though we tracked the compound to its entry point into the river and identified its properties, we were unable to discover the location of its source.'

Sandecker drummed his fingers on the table. 'Pitt gave me the bad news before he was cut off. I apologize for not passing along the information, but I was counting on a satellite survey to fill in the missing piece.'

Muriel Hoag looked directly into Gunn's eyes. 'I don't understand how you successfully pursued the compound through 1000 kilometres of water and then lost it on land.'

'It was easy,' Gunn shrugged wearily. 'After we sailed beyond the point of highest concentration, our contaminant readings dropped off and the instruments began showing water with commonly known pollutants. We made several runs back and forth to confirm. We also took visual sightings in every direction. No hazardous waste dump site, no chemical storage or manufacturing facilities were visible along the river or inland. No buildings or construction, nothing. Only barren desert.'

'Could a dump site have been buried over at some time in the past?' suggested Holland.

'We observed no evidence of excavation,' replied Gunn.

'Any chance the toxin was brewed by mother nature?' asked Chip Webster.

Muriel Hoag smiled. 'If tests bear out Mr Gunn's analysis of a synthetic amino acid, it must have been produced by a biotech laboratory. Not mother nature. And somewhere, somehow, it was discarded along with chemicals containing cobalt. Not the first time accidental integration of chemicals produced a previously unknown compound.'

'How in God's name could such an exotic compound suddenly appear in the middle of the Sahara?' wondered Chip Webster.

'And reach the ocean where it acts as steroids to dinoflagellates,' added Holland.

Sandecker looked at Keith Hodge. 'What's the latest report on the spread of the red tide?'

The oceanographer was in his sixties. Unblinking dark brown eyes gazed from a continually fixed expression on a lean, high-cheekboned face. With the correctly dated clothing he could have stepped from an eighteenth-century portrait.

'The spread has increased 3 per cent in the past four days. I fear the growth rate is exceeding our most dire projections.'

'But if Dr Chapman can develop a compound to neutralize the contamination, and we find and cut it off at the source, can't we then control the tide's expansion?'

'Better make it soon,' answered Hodge. 'At the rate it's proliferating, another month and we should see the first evidence of it beginning to feed off itself without stimulation flowing from the Niger.'

'That's three months early!' Muriel Hoag said sharply.

Hodge gave a helpless shrug. 'When you're dealing with an unknown the only sure commodity is uncertainty.'

Sandecker swung sideways in his chair and gazed at the blown-up satellite photo of Mali projected on one wall. 'Where does the compound enter the river?' he asked Gunn.

Gunn stood and walked over to the enlarged photo. He picked up a grease pencil and circled a small area of the Niger River above Gao on the white backdrop reflecting the projection. 'Right about here, off an old riverbed that once flowed into the Niger.'

Chip Webster pressed the buttons of a small console sitting on the table, and enlarged the area around Gunn's marking. 'No structures visible. No indication of population. Nor do I make out any sign of excavated dirt or a mound that would have to be in evidence if any type of trench was dug to bury hazardous materials.'

'This is an enigma, all right,' muttered Chapman. 'Where in the devil can the rotten stuff come from?'

'Pitt and Giordino are still out there searching for it,' Gunn reminded them.

'Any late word of their condition or whereabouts?' asked Hodge.

'Nothing since Pitt's call aboard Yves Massarde's boat,' replied Sandecker.

Hodge looked up from his notepad. 'Yves Massarde? God, not that pond slime.'

'You know him?'

Hodge nodded. 'I crossed paths with him after a bad chemical spill in the Med off Spain four years ago. One of his ships that was carrying waste carcinogenic chemicals known as PCBs for disposal in Algeria broke up and sank in a storm. I personally think the ship was scuttled in a combination insurance scam and illegal dump. As it turned out, Algerian officials never had any intention of accepting the waste for disposal. Then Massarde lied and cheated and pulled every legal dodge on the books to evade responsibility for cleaning up the mess. You shake hands with that guy and you better count your fingers when you walk away.'

Gunn turned to Webster. 'Intelligence-gathering satellites can read newspapers from space. Why can't we orbit one over the desert north of Gao in search of Pitt and Giordino?'

Webster shook his head. 'Negative. My contacts at the National Security Agency have their best eyes in the sky keeping tabs on the new Chinese rocket firings, the civil war going on in the Ukraine, and the border clashes with Syria and Iraq. They're not about to spare us time from their intelligence scans to find civilians in the Sahara Desert. I can go with the latest-model GeoSat. But it's questionable whether it can distinguish human forms against the uneven terrain of a desert like the Sahara.'

'Wouldn't they show up against a sand dune?' asked Chapman.

Webster shook his head. 'No one travelling the Sahara

in their right mind would walk across the soft sand of dunes. Even the nomads skirt around them. Wandering in a sea of dunes means certain death. Pitt and Giordino are smart enough to avoid them like the plague.'

'But you *will* do a search and survey,' Sandecker insisted.

Webster nodded. He was quite bald with little indication of a neck. A round belly hung over his belt, and he might have posed as a 'before' on a weight-loss commercial. 'I've a good friend who's a top analyst over at the Pentagon and an expert on satellite desert reconnaissance. I think I can sweet-talk him into examining our GeoSat photos with his state-of-the-art enhancing computers.'

'I'm grateful for your backup,' Sandecker said sincerely.

'If they're out there, he can locate them if anyone can,' Webster promised him.

'Has your satellite seen any sign of the plane carrying that team of disease investigators?' asked Muriel.

'Not yet I'm afraid. Nothing showed on our last pass across Mali except a small smudge of smoke faintly drifting in from one side of our camera path. Hopefully on the next orbit we can obtain a more detailed picture. It may prove to be nothing but a nomad bonfire.'

'There isn't enough wood in that part of the Sahara for a bonfire,' Sandecker said solemnly.

Gunn looked lost. 'What disease investigation team are you talking about?'

'A group of scientists from the World Health Organization on a mission to Mali,' explained Muriel. 'They were searching for the cause behind an outbreak of strange afflictions reported in nomadic desert villages. Their plane disappeared somewhere between Mali and Cairo.'

'Was there a woman on the team? A biochemist?'

'A Dr Eva Rojas was the team biochemist,' replied Muriel. 'I once worked with her on a project in Haiti.'

'Did you know her?' asked Sandecker of Gunn.

'Not me, but Pitt. He dated her in Cairo.'

'Maybe it's just as well he doesn't know,' Sandecker said. 'He must have enough problems just staying alive without bad news to fog his mind.'

'There's no confirmation of a crash yet,' said Holland hopefully.

'Maybe they made a forced landing in the desert and survived,' Muriel said hopefully.

Webster shook his head. 'Wishful thinking I'm afraid. I fear General Zateb Kazim has his dirty hands in this business.'

Gunn recalled, 'Pitt and Giordino had a conversation with the General on our boat's radio shortly before I hit the river. I got the impression he's a nasty customer.'

'As ruthless as any Middle East dictator,' said Sandecker. 'And twice as hard to deal with. He won't even meet or speak with our State Department diplomats unless they hand him a fat foreign aid cheque.'

Added Muriel, 'He ignores the United Nations and refuses any outside relief supplies to his people.'

Webster nodded. 'Any human rights activist dumb enough to enter Mali and protest, simply vanishes.'

'He and Massarde are thick as thieves,' said Hodge. 'Between the two of them they've raped the country into total poverty.'

Sandecker's face hardened. 'Not our concern. There won't be a Mali, a West Africa, or anywhere else on earth if we don't stop the red tide. Right now, nothing else matters.'

Chapman spoke up. 'Now that we have data we can sink our teeth into, we can all focus our skills and work together to formulate a solution.'

'Make it quick,' said Sandecker, his eyes narrowing. 'If you've failed thirty days from now, none of us will get a second chance.'

31

A brisk breeze was quivering the leaves along the Palisades above the Hudson River as Ismail Yerli peered through binoculars at a small bluish-grey bird perched on a tree trunk upside down. He acted as if his full attention was on the little bird and failed to notice the appearance of a man behind him. Actually, he had been aware of the approaching intruder for nearly two minutes.

'A white-breasted nuthatch,' said the tall, rather handsome stranger who wore an expensive burgundy leather jacket. He sat down on a flat rock next to Yerli. His sandy hair was neatly slicked down with a razor-edge part on the left side. He stared indifferently at the bird through pale blue eyes.

'The duller black on the back of the head suggests a female,' said Yerli without lowering his glasses.

'The male is probably nearby. Perhaps tending the nest.'

'Good call, Bordeaux,' said Yerli, using the other man's code name. 'I didn't know you were a bird watcher.'

'I'm not. What can I do for you, Pergamon?'

'It was you who requested this meeting.'

'But not in the boondocks under a bone-chilling wind.'

'Meeting in gourmet restaurants is not my idea of working undercover.'

'I never took to the idea of operating in the shadows and living in slums,' Bordeaux said dryly.

'Not wise to act flamboyant.'

'My job is to protect the interests of a man who, I might add, pays me extremely well. The FBI isn't about to put me under surveillance unless they suspect me of espionage. And since our job — at least my job — is not to steal classified American secrets, I fail to see why I have to melt into the foul-smelling masses.'

Bordeaux's contemptuous outlook toward intelligence did not sit well with Yerli. Although they had known each other and often worked together over the years on behalf of Yves Massarde, strangely neither man knew the other's real name and never made an effort to learn it. Bordeaux was head of Massarde Enterprises' commercial intelligence operations in the United States. Yerli, only known to him as Pergamon, often passed along information vital to Massarde's international projects. For this he was paid handsomely up and above his salary as a French intelligence agent. A situation tolerated by his superiors because of Massarde's strong connections with many of France's cabinet members.

'You're getting careless, my friend.'

Bordeaux shrugged. 'I am getting bored dealing with uncouth Americans. New York is a cesspool. The country is divided by racial and ethnic diversity and is disintegrating. Someday, the United States will repeat the economic and regional strife going on in Russia and the Commonwealth States today. I long to return to France, the only truly civilized nation in the world.'

'I hear one of the NUMA people escaped from Mali,' Yerli said, abruptly changing the subject.

'That idiot Kazim let him slip through his fingers,' replied Bordeaux.

'Didn't you pass on my warning to Mr Massarde?'

'Of course I warned him. And he in turn alerted General Kazim. Two other men were captured by Mr Massarde on his houseboat, but Kazim, in all his dazzling brilliance, was too stupid to search for the third agent who escaped and was evacuated by the UN tactical team.'

'What are Mr Massarde's thoughts on the situation?'

325

'He's not happy, knowing there is a serious risk of an international investigation into his project at Fort Foureau.'

'Not good, any threat to expose and close down Fort Foureau is a threat to our French nuclear programme.'

'Mr Massarde is quite aware of the problem,' said Bordeaux acidly.

'What of the World Health scientists? The morning newspapers said their plane is reported overdue and presumed missing.'

'One of Kazim's better ideas,' answered Bordeaux. 'He faked the plane crash in an uninhabited part of the desert.'

'Faked? I forewarned Hala Kamil of what I had conceived as a genuine bomb plot to destroy the aircraft and Hopper and his team.'

'A slight change in your plan to frighten off any future inspections by World Health scientists,' said Bordeaux. 'The plane crashed all right, but the bodies on board were not those of Dr Hopper and the rest.'

'They're still alive?'

'They're as good as dead. Kazim sent them to Tebezza.'

Yerli nodded. 'Better they should have died quickly than in the mines of Tebezza as overworked and starved slaves.' Yerli paused thoughtfully, then said, 'I think Kazim has made a mistake.'

'The secret of their true situation is safe,' said Bordeaux indifferently. 'No one escapes from Tebezza. They go into the mines and never come out.'

Yerli took a Kleenex out of his coat pocket and began wiping the lenses of his binoculars. 'Did Hopper discover any evidence that might prove damaging to Fort Foureau?'

'Enough to cause renewed interest and promote a deeper investigation if his report had been made public.'

'What is known about the NUMA agent who escaped?'

'His name is Gunn, and he's the Deputy Director of the National Underwater and Marine Agency.'

'An influential man.'

'Indeed.'

'Where is he now?'

'We traced the aircraft that evacuated him to Paris, where he boarded a Concorde for Washington. From there, he was taken directly to NUMA headquarters. My sources say he was still inside the building as of forty minutes ago.'

'Is it known if he smuggled vital information out of Mali?'

'Whatever information he obtained, if any, from the Niger River is a mystery to us. But Mr Massarde feels confident nothing was discovered that could jeopardize the Fort Foureau operation.'

'Kazim should have an easy time making the other two Americans talk.'

'I received word just as I left to meet you. Unfortunately, they escaped too.'

Yerli stared at Bordeaux in sudden irritation. 'Who bungled?'

Bordeaux shrugged. 'Makes no difference who's to blame. Frankly, it's not our concern. What's important is that they are still inside the country. There is little hope of them escaping over the border. It's only a matter of hours before Kazim's search operation hunts them down.'

'I should fly down to Washington and penetrate NUMA. With the right moves I might discover if there was more behind this than a cut-and-dried pollution investigation.'

'Let that go for now,' said Bordeaux coolly. 'Mr Massarde has other work for you.'

'Did he clear it with my superiors at the National Defense Staff?'

'Your official release for outside duty will be conveyed to you within the hour.'

Yerli said nothing but resumed peering through his glasses at the little nuthatch that was still perched bottom-side-up, pecking away at the bark of the tree trunk. 'What does Massarde have in mind?'

'He wants you in Mali to act as liaison to General Kazim.'

Yerli showed no reaction. He kept the glasses trained on the bird as he spoke. 'I was assigned for eight months in the Sudan some years ago. A dreadful place. The people were quite friendly though.'

'One of Massarde Enterprises' jets will be waiting at La Guardia Airport. You're to board at six o'clock this evening.'

'So I'm to play nursemaid to Kazim to prevent him from making any further blunders.'

Bordeaux nodded. 'The stakes are too high to allow the madman to run amok.'

Yerli reinserted his binoculars in their case and slung it over his shoulder. 'I once dreamed I died in the desert,' he said quietly. 'I pray to Allah that it was just that . . . a dream.'

In a typical windowless room somewhere in a little-travelled part of the Pentagon building, Air Force Major Tom Greenwald put down the phone after notifying his wife he would be late for dinner. He relaxed for a long minute as he turned his thoughts from the satellite photo analysis of the fighting going on between Chinese army units and democratic rebel forces to the job at hand.

The film from the GeoSat cameras sent by courier from Chip Webster at NUMA was processed and loaded in the military's sophisticated display and enhancing equipment. When all was ready, Greenwald settled himself in a comfortable chair with a console installed in one arm. He opened a can of Diet Pepsi and began turning the dials and knobs on the console as he stared up at a television monitor the size of a small movie theatre screen.

The GeoSat photos reminded him of the old spy-in-the-sky images of thirty years ago. Granted, the Geosat was designed purely for space geological and water current survey, but it came nowhere close to the incredible imagery detail received by the latest intelligence-gathering Pyramider and Houdini satellites sent up by the space shuttles. Yet it was a vast improvement over the old LandSat that mapped the earth for over twenty years. The new model had cameras that could penetrate darkness and cloud cover, and even smoke.

Greenwald made adjustments and corrections with his console as each photo, showing different sections of the Malian northern desert, crossed the viewing screen and was computer-enhanced. He soon began to pick out tiny specks that were flying aircraft and a camel train winding across the desert floor from the salt mines of Taoudenni south to Timbuktu.

As the photo trail moved north from the Niger into the Azaouad, a barren region of dunes and nothingness that made up but one of the many areas of the Sahara, Greenwald found fewer and fewer signs of human presence. He could discern bones of animals, camels most likely, scattered around isolated wells, but a standing human was very difficult to detect, even for his exotic electronics systems.

After nearly an hour, Greenwald rubbed his tired eyes and massaged his temples. He had found nothing that indicated the slightest trace of the two men he had been asked to look for. The photos of the extreme northerly search grid that Webster thought they might have reached on foot were examined unsuccessfully and set aside.

Greenwald had done his bit for the cause and was about to call it a day and go home to his wife, but he decided to give it one final try. Years of experience had taught him that a target was never where he expected to find it. He sifted out the satellite photos revealing the deeper regions of the desolate Azaouad and gave them a fast scan.

The stark void appeared as empty as the Dead Sea.

He almost missed it, he would have missed it but for an indescribable feeling that a tiny object on the landscape did not fit its surroundings. It might have passed as a rock or a small dune, but the shape was not irregular like geology produced by nature. The lines were straight and well defined. His hand moved over a row of knobs, magnifying and enhancing the object.

Greenwald knew he was on to something. He was too much the expert to be fooled. During the war with Iraq, he became something of a legend for his uncanny knack at detecting the Iraqi army's hidden bunkers, tank and artillery emplacements.

'A car,' he muttered aloud to himself. 'A car covered over with sand to hide its presence.'

After tighter study, he could distinguish two tiny specks alongside the car. Greenwald wished he was looking at images received from a military satellite. He could have read the time on the target's wristwatches. But the GeoSat was not built for fine detail. Even with careful tuning he could just make them out as two humans.

Greenwald took a moment to sit back and savour his discovery. Then he walked over to a nearby desk and dialled a phone. He waited patiently, hoping that a taped voice wouldn't come on with an announcement to leave a message. On the fifth ring, a man answered who sounded as if he was out of breath.

'Hello.'

'Chip?'

'Yes. This Tom?'

'You been jogging?'

'The wife and I were out in the backyard talking to neighbours,' explained Webster. 'I ran like hell when I heard the phone ringing.'

'I found something I think you'll be interested in.'

'My two men, you pulled them from the GeoSat photos?'

'They're over 100 kilometres further north than you reckoned,' said Greenwald.

There was a pause. 'Sure you're not looking at a pair of nomads?' asked Webster. 'No way my people could have walked that far across a burning desert in forty-eight hours.'

'Not walked but drove.'

'Like drove a car?' asked Webster in surprise.

'Difficult to make out details. Looks to me as though they cover it with sand during the day as camouflage from searching aircraft and drive by night. It has to be your two guys. Who else can be playing fugitive games where the grass don't grow.'

'Can you tell if they're trying for the border?'

'Not unless they have a lousy sense of direction. They're smack in the centre of northern Mali. The nearest border to another country is a good 350 kilometres.'

Webster took a long moment to reply. 'It must be Pitt and Giordino. But where in hell did they find a car?'

'Looks to me like they're resourceful men.'

'They should have given up searching for the contamination source long ago. What madness has overtaken them?'

It was a question Greenwald could not answer. 'Maybe they'll give you a call from Fort Foureau,' he suggested, half serious, half in jest.

'They're heading for the French solar waste project?'

'They've only another 50 kilometres to go. And it's the only slice of Western civilization around.'

'Thank you, Tom,' said Webster sincerely. 'The next favour is mine. How about me taking you and our wives to dinner?'

'Sounds good. Pick any restaurant and call me with day and time.'

331

Greenwald dropped the receiver in its cradle and refocused his attention on the fuzzy object and the two tiny figures next to it.

'You guys have to be crazy,' he said to the empty room. Then he closed down the system and went home.

32

The dawn sun came up and cast a wave of heat across the desert like an oven door thrown open. The cool of the night vanished as quickly as the passing of a cloud. A pair of ravens flew across the oppressive sky, spied something that did not belong on the empty landscape, and began circling in hopes of finding a meal. On closer inspection they saw that a live human offered nothing of taste, and they slowly winged off to the north.

Pitt lay stretched out on the upper slope of a low dune, almost buried in the sand, and stared up at the birds for a few moments. Then he turned his attention back to the immense sprawl of the Fort Foureau solar detoxification project. It was an unreal place. Not simply a man-made edifice to technology but a thriving, productive facility surrounded by a land that had long since died under the onslaught of drought and heat.

Pitt twisted slightly as he heard the soft movement of sand behind him and saw Giordino approaching on his stomach, wiggling up the dune like a lizard.

'Enjoying the scenery?' asked Giordino.

'Come take a look. I guarantee you'll be impressed.'

'The only thing that would impress me right now is a beach with nice cool surf.'

'Don't let your curly locks show,' said Pitt. 'A black tuft of hair against the yellow-white sand stands out like a skunk on a fence post.'

Giordino grinned like the village idiot as he poured a handful of sand into his hair. He moved alongside Pitt, peering over the summit of the dune. 'My, my,' he murmured in awe. 'If I didn't know better, I'd say I was looking at a city on the moon.'

'The sterile landscape is there,' Pitt admitted, 'but there's no glass dome over the top.'

'This place is almost as big as Disney World.'

'I'd estimate 20 square kilometres.'

'We have incoming freight,' said Giordino, pointing to a long train of railroad cars drawn by four diesel engines. 'Business must be booming.'

'Massarde's toxic gravy train,' Pitt mused. 'I estimate about a hundred and twenty cars filled with poisonous garbage.'

Giordino nodded toward a vast field covered with long trough-like basins with concave surfaces that bounced the sun's rays like a sea of mirrors. 'Those look like solar reflectors.'

'Concentrators,' said Pitt. 'They collect solar radiation and concentrate it into tremendous heat and proton intensities. The radiant energy is then focused inside a chemical reactor that completely destroys the hazardous waste.'

'Aren't we the bright one,' said Giordino. 'When did you become an expert on sunlight?'

'I used to date a lady who was an engineer with the Solar Energy Institute. She took me on a guided tour of their research facilities. That was several years ago when they were still in the test stages of developing solar thermal technology for eliminating industrial toxic wastes. It appears Massarde has mastered the techniques.'

'I've missed something,' said Giordino.

'Like what?'

'This whole setup. Why go to the added expense and effort to erect this cathedral to sanitation in the middle of the world's biggest sandbox. Me, I'd have built it closer to a major industrial centre. Must cost a bundle just to transport the stuff across half an ocean and 1600 kilometres of desert.'

'A most astute consideration,' Pitt admitted. 'I'm curious too. If Fort Foureau is such a masterpiece of toxic waste destruction, and is judged by hazardous waste experts to be a safe, blue-ribbon operation, it doesn't make sense not to set it in a more convenient location.'

'You still think it's responsible for the contamination leak into the Niger?' Giordino asked.

'We found no other source.'

'That old prospector's story about an underground river may well be the solution.'

'Except there's a flaw,' said Pitt.

'You never were the trusting type,' Giordino muttered.

'Nothing wrong with the underground theory. What I don't buy is leaking contamination.'

'I'm with you,' Giordino nodded. 'What's to leak if they're supposed to be incinerating the crap?'

'Exactly.'

'Then Fort Foureau isn't what it's advertised?'

'Not to my way of thinking.'

Giordino turned and looked at him suspiciously. 'I hope you're not thinking of strolling around down there as if we were a couple of visiting firemen.'

'I had cat burglars more in mind.'

'How do you propose we get in? Drive up to the gate and ask for a visitor's pass?'

Pitt nodded at the line of freight cars rolling over a siding that paralleled a long loading dock inside the facility. 'We hop the train.'

'And for a getaway?' Giordino asked suspiciously.

'With the Voisin's fuel gauge knocking on empty, bidding a fond farewell to Mali and driving off into the sunset was the last thing on my agenda. We catch the outward bound express for Mauritania.'

Giordino made a glum face. 'You expect me to ride first class in freight cars that have carried tons of toxic chemicals? I'm too young to melt into sludge.'

Pitt shrugged and smiled. 'You'll just have to be careful not to touch anything.'

Giordino shook his head in exasperation. 'Did you consider the obstacles involved?'

'Obstacles are made to be hurdled,' Pitt answered pontifically.

'Like the electrified fence, the guards with Doberman pinschers, the patrol cars bristling with automatic cannon, the overhead lamps that light up the place like a baseball stadium?'

'Yes, now that you had to go and remind me.'

'Mighty strange,' Giordino reflected,' 'that a toxic waste incinerator has to be guarded like a nuclear bomb arsenal.'

'All the more reason to inspect the premises,' said Pitt calmly.

'You won't change your mind and head for home while we're still a team.'

'Seek and ye shall find.'

Giordino threw up his hands. 'You're crazier than that old prospector and his cockamamy story of a Confederate ironclad with Abe Lincoln at the helm that's buried in the desert.'

'We do have much in common,' Pitt said easily. He rolled on his side and gestured toward a structure about 6 kilometres to the east, a short walk from the railroad tracks. 'See that old abandoned fort?'

Giordino nodded. 'The one with *Beau Geste*, Gary Cooper, and the French Foreign Legion written all over it. Yes, I see it.'

'Where Fort Foureau got its name,' said Pitt. 'No more than 100 metres separates its walls from the railroad. As soon as it's dark we'll use it for cover until we can hop an incoming train.'

336

'I've already noticed they whip over the rails too fast for even a professional hobo to board.'

'Prudence and patience,' said Pitt. 'The locomotives begin to slow just before they reach the old fort. Then they come to a crawl when they pull into what looks like a security station.'

Giordino studied the station the train had to pass through to enter the heart of the project. 'A dime to a dollar an army of guards checks out every freight car.'

'They can't be too overzealous. Examining over a hundred freight cars filled with drums of toxic waste is not exactly a job a sane man would throw his heart and soul into. Besides, who would be dumb enough to stow away in one?'

'You're the only one who comes to mind,' Giordino said dryly.

'I'm always open to more practical suggestions for sneaking past your electrified fence, Dobermans, floodlights, and patrol cars.'

Giordino was in the middle of giving Pitt a long solemn look of exasperation when he tensed and twisted his head at the sky in the direction of the oncoming thump of an approaching helicopter.

Pitt looked up too. It was coming from the south and heading directly over them. It was not a military craft but a beautifully streamlined civilian version that was easily identified by the Massarde Enterprises name along the fuselage.

'Damn!' cursed Giordino. He looked back at the mound of sand they had thrown over the Voisin. 'Any lower and he'll blow the sand right off the car.'

'Only if he passes directly over it,' Pitt said. 'Burrow down and don't move.'

An alert eye might have caught them, noticed the suspicious sand dune with its strange shape, but the pilot was concentrating on the landing pad near the project's main office building and did not glance down at the disturbed sands or the forms hugging the dune. The helicopter's sole passenger was occupied with studying a financial report and did not glance out a window.

It swept right over them, banked slightly, sank down toward the pad, hovered for a few moments, and then settled to the concrete. A few seconds later the rotor stopped, the passenger door opened, and a man climbed down to the pad. Even at half a kilometre without binoculars, Pitt correctly guessed the identity of the figure who vigorously strode toward the office complex.

'I think our friend has returned to haunt us,' he said.

Giordino cupped his hands round his eyes and squinted. 'Too far to tell for sure, but I do believe you're right. A shame he didn't bring the piano player from the houseboat.'

'Can't you get her out of your mind?'

Giordino looked at Pitt with a hurt expression. 'Why would I want to?'

'You don't even know her name.'

'Love will conquer all,' Giordino said moodily.

'Then conquer your amorous thoughts and let's rest up until nightfall. Then we've got a train to catch.'

They had bypassed the well described by the old prospector when the Oued Zarit's former riverbed meandered in a different direction. The soft drinks were gone and their supply of water was down to 2 litres, slightly more than 2 quarts. But they divided and drank it all to avoid dehydration, trusting in finding a source near the project.

They parked the Voisin in a small ravine a kilometre south of the abandoned fort that sat beside the railroad, then burrowed into the sand under the car, achieving a small measure of shelter from the sweltering heat. Giordino dropped off quickly, but Pitt's mind was too restless for sleep.

338

The night sweeps across the desert quickly. The dusk is short before the darkness. There was a strange stillness, the only sound coming from the faint tick of the Voisin's engine as it cooled. The dry desert air became cleansed from the heat and blowing sand of the day and magnified the great storm of stars that gleamed in an obsidian sky. They were so sharp and distinct Pitt could actually separate the red stars from the blue and green. He had never seen such a cosmic display, even on the open sea.

They covered the car in the gulch for the last time and hiked under the stars to the fort, careful to sweep their tracks with a palm frond as they proceeded. They passed by the old Legion graveyard and scouted around the 10-metre-high walls until they came to the main gate. The giant wooden doors, solid and bleached white by the sun, stood slightly ajar. They entered and found themselves on the dark and deserted parade ground.

It took little for their imaginations to see a ghostly formation of French Foreign Legion footsloggers standing at attention in their blue tunics, baggy white trousers, and white kepi caps, before marching out onto the burning sands to fight a horde of Tuaregs.

The actual size of the former outpost was small by most Foreign Legion standards. The walls, each 30 metres in length, were formed in a perfect square. They were a good 3 metres thick at the base with staggered bastions at the top to protect the defenders. The entire structure could have easily been manned by no more than fifty men.

The interior showed the usual signs of neglect. Debris left by the departing French troops and bits of trash left by desert wanderers who took advantage of the fort's walls during sandstorms lay scattered on the ground and in the barracks' quarters. Materials left over by construction workers during the building of the railroad were stacked against one wall: concrete railroad ties, various tools, several drums of diesel oil, and a forklift that looked in surprisingly good condition.

'How'd you like to be stationed in this place for a year?' muttered Giordino.

'Not for a week,' said Pitt, surveying the fort.

While they waited for a train, time dragged by with tormenting slowness. The odds were good to excellent that the chemical compound Gunn had discovered as the cause of the exploding red tide was filtering out of the solar detoxification plant. After their run-in with Massarde, Pitt knew that a knock on the door and a cheery request to inspect the property would not be met with open arms and a hearty handshake. They had to worm their way in and find positive evidence.

There was something far more sinister going on at Fort Foureau. To all appearances it was contributing to the battle against the world's millions of tons of toxic waste. But scratch the surface, Pitt thought, and we shall see what we shall see.

He was calculating their chances of passing through the security station and getting out again as extremely bleak, when his ears picked out a sound in the distance. Giordino came out of a light sleep and heard it too.

They looked at each other wordlessly and came to their feet.

'An inbound train,' said Giordino.

Pitt held up his Doxa dive watch and studied the luminous hands. 'Eleven-twenty. Plenty of time to do our inspection act and get out before daylight.'

'Providing there's a scheduled outbound,' Giordino cautioned.

'So far they've been tooting by like clockwork every three hours. Like Mussolini, Massarde keeps them running on time.' Pitt stood and brushed off the sand. 'Off we go. I don't want to be left standing on an empty track.'

'I wouldn't mind.'

'Keep low,' Pitt warned. 'The desert reflects starlight, and the ground is open between the fort and the tracks.'

'I'll flit through the night like a bat,' Giordino assured him. 'But if a drooling dog with big fangs or beady-eyed guard with an automatic weapon has other ideas?'

'We prove our suspicions that Fort Foureau is a facade.' Pitt said firmly, 'One of us has to escape and alert Sandecker, even if it means sacrificing one for the other.'

A thoughtful expression crossed Giordino's face and he stared at Pitt without saying anything. Then the air horn on the lead diesel locomotive sounded to announce its impending arrival at the security station. He nodded at the tracks. 'We'd better hurry.'

Pitt nodded silently. Then they stepped through the fort's big gate and ran toward the tracks.

33

An abandoned Renault truck sat forlornly about halfway between the fort and the railroad tracks. Everything that could be stripped from the body and chassis was long gone. Tyres and wheels, engine, transmission and differential, even the windshield and doors were removed for parts or sold for scrap, hauled off by camel to Gao or Timbuktu by an enterprising merchant.

To Pitt and Giordino, as they huddled behind the truck to avoid being caught in the glare of the light on the forward diesel engine, the deserted loneliness of an object used by man and then forgotten and discarded was overwhelming. But it made for the perfect cover as the long freight train approached.

The revolving light above the engine swept across the desert and illuminated every rock and every blade of sparse grass for almost a kilometre. They crouched out of the beam until the engines thundered past at what Pitt estimated as nearly 50 kilometres an hour. The engineers were braking now as they prepared to enter the security station. Pitt waited patiently as the train's speed tapered off. By the time the last cars in line reached the abandoned truck, he estimated, the train's momentum would be down to about 15 kilometres, a speed slow enough for them to run alongside and board.

They left the safety of the scrapped truck and dashed the final few metres to the roadbed, hunching down and observing the flatbed cars that carried huge removable cargo containers as they rumbled toward Fort Foureau. The end car was in sight now, not an ordinary-type caboose for the train crew, but an armoured car with turreted heavy machine guns manned by corporate security guards. Massarde ran a tight operation, Pitt thought. The escorts were probably professional mercenaries hired out at above average wages.

Why the ironbound security? Most governments looked upon chemical waste as a nuisance. Sabotage or an accidental spill in the middle of the desert would go almost unnoticed in the international media or environmentalist circles. Who were they guarding it from? Certainly not the occasional bandit or terrorist.

If Pitt had formed any character analysis of Yves Massarde, he'd have predicted the French tycoon played both sides against the middle, paying off the Malian rebels at the same time he pumped cash to Kazim.

'Let's go for the second cargo container forward of the armoured car,' he said to Giordino. 'Boarding the first might be cutting it too fine if an alert guard was looking down along the track.'

Giordino nodded. 'I'm with you. The cars closest to the guards won't be as thoroughly searched as the ones further forward.'

They rose swiftly to their feet and began sprinting along the roadbed. Pitt had misjudged the speed. The train was moving nearly twice as fast as either of them could run. There was no thought of stopping or dropping out. If they veered away, the guards would likely spot them under the lights that flashed from the rear of the armoured car, spilling in a semicircle around the wheels and gleaming on the rails.

They gave it everything they had. Pitt was taller and had longer arms. He caught a ladder rung, was jerked forward and, using the momentum, swung aboard.

Giordino reached out and missed the rear ladder of the car by only a few centimetres. The roadbed was gravel and difficult to run on. He turned his head for a backward glance. After missing his intended ride, his only hope now was to risk boarding the car directly in front of the one carrying the guards.

The ladder that extended from the flatbed railroad car to the top of the cargo container was approaching at what seemed to Giordino as Mach speed. He glanced down at the steel wheels rolling over the tracks uncomfortably close. This would be his last chance. Miss and fall under the wheels or be shot by the guards. Neither prospect excited him.

He grabbed one rung of the ladder with both hands as it rushed by and was pulled off his feet by the forward motion of the train. He held on desperately, his legs flailing as they struggled to catch up. Releasing his left hand, Giordino used it to grab the next rung. Then his right hand joined it, and he could bend his knees and lift his feet in the air and find them a hold on the lower rung.

Pitt had paused a few seconds to catch his breath before clambering to the top of the cargo container. Not until he turned around did he realize that Giordino wasn't where he should have been — climbing the ladder of the same car. He looked down, saw the dark form clinging to the side of the car behind his, and the white blur of Giordino's grim and determined face.

Pitt watched in helpless frustration as Giordino hung there motionless for several seconds, clutching the ladder of the container as the flatbed car rattled and swayed. He twisted his head and stared down the length of the train. The lead engine was only a kilometre from the security station. Then a tingling sixth sense made Pitt look sharply backward and he froze.

A guard was standing on a small platform that extended out from the rear of the armoured car. He was standing with his hands spread on the railing, staring down over the desert flashing past below his feet. He looked to Pitt to be lost in thought, perhaps thinking of something faraway or maybe a girl somewhere. He had only to turn and gaze down the length of the train and Giordino was finished.

The guard straightened, then turned and walked back into the cool comfort of his car.

Giordino wasted no more time and scrambled up the ladder to the top of the container where he lay down and pressed his body against the roof. He lay there breathing heavily. The air was still hot and mixed with the exhaust from the diesel engines. He wiped the sweat from his forehead and looked onto the next car for Pitt.

'Come on across,' Pitt shouted above the noise of the moving freight train.

Cautiously crawling on his hands and knees, Giordino peered down at the blur of concrete ties and rails as they rushed under the cars below. He waited a moment to build courage, and then he stood, took a short run, and then leaped forward. His feet touched down with half a metre to spare before he landed arms outstretched on the roof. When he looked around for a helping hand, there was none.

With utter confidence in his friend's athletic ability, Pitt was calmly studying an air conditioner installed on the top of the cargo container to keep highly combustible chemical waste from igniting under the extreme heat conditions during its journey across the desert. A heavy-duty model especially designed to combat scorching temperatures, its compressor was turned over by a small gas engine whose exhaust popped quietly through a silenced muffler.

As the lights of the security station loomed ahead, Pitt had turned his thoughts to evading detection. He didn't think it likely guards would walk the train in the manner of railroad police carrying clubs, who searched the yards and trains for hobos and bindle stiffs riding the rails during the 1930s depression. Nor would Massarde's security people rely on dogs. No way a hound with a sensitive nose could sniff out a man from the overpowering aroma of chemicals and diesel fumes.

TV cameras, Pitt determined. The train simply passed through and under an array of cameras that were monitored inside the building. No question that Yves Massarde would have relied on modern security technology.

'Have you something to turn screws?' he asked without acknowledging Giordino's approach.

'You're asking me for a screwdriver?' Giordino queried incredulously.

'I want to pull the screws out of this big panel on the side of the air conditioner.'

Giordino reached into his pocket, mostly emptied after the search by Massarde's crewman on board the houseboat. But he found a nickel and a dime. He passed them to Pitt. 'This is the best I can do on the spur of the moment.'

Quickly running his hands over a large side panel on the air conditioner, Pitt found the screw heads that held it in place. There were ten of them, thankfully slotted and not Phillips heads. He wasn't at all sure he could unscrew them in time. The nickel was too large but the dime fitted perfectly. He feverishly began removing the screws as fast as his fingers could turn the dime.

'You picked a strange time to repair an air conditioner,' said Giordino curiously.

'I'm banking on the guards using TV cameras to inspect the train for transients like us. They'll spot us up here for sure. Our only chance to ride through without getting caught is to hide behind this panel. It's big enough to cover us both.'

The train was down to a crawl now and half the container cars had passed into the project rail yard beyond the security station.

'You'd better hurry,' Giordino said anxiously.

The sweat trickled into Pitt's eyes, but he shook the drops off while he twisted the dime. Their car moved relentlessly closer to the TV cameras. Three quarters of the train was cleared when Pitt still had three screws to go.

He was down to two, then one. The next car was passing into the station. Out of sheer desperation he gripped the big panel with both hands and tore it from its slot, ripping the last screw from its threads.

'Quick, sit with your back against the air conditioner,' he ordered Giordino.

They both shoved their backs as far into the air-conditioning housing as possible and then thrust the panel up in front of them like a shield.

'You think this will fool anybody?' Giordino asked dubiously.

'TV monitors are two-dimensional. So long as they're pointing at us head on, we'll present an illusion to any viewer.'

The container car rolled slowly into a sterile white tunnel with TV cameras positioned to view the undercarriage, sides, and roof. Pitt gripped the panel with his fingertips rather than extending them around the edges where they might be seen by the security guard monitoring the train. The makeshift facade may not have reeked with finesse, but the best he could hope for was a guard bored with the monotony of staring at a seemingly endless line of cargo containers on an array of television monitors. Like being forced to watch a hundred reruns of the same programme on ten different screens, the mind would soon go into a drugged state and begin to wander.

They huddled there, waiting for the bells and sirens, but no alarm was given. The container car rolled out under the night sky again and was pulled onto a siding next to a long concrete loading dock with large overhead derricks that moved on parallel tracks.

'Oh brother,' Giordino mopped his brow again. 'I don't look forward to that little scam again.'

Pitt grinned, gave Giordino a friendly punch on the shoulder, and turned to the rear of the train. 'Don't get carried away just yet. Our friends are still with us.'

They remained motionless there on the roof of the container, holding the air-conditioning panel as the guard's armoured car was uncoupled and pulled away by a small electric switch engine. The four diesels' locomotives also dropped their rear coupling and chugged off toward a siding where a long row of empty cars was waiting to be hauled back to the port in Mauritania.

Safe for the moment, Pit and Giordino stayed where they were and calmly waited for something to happen. The dock was lit with big overhead arc lamps and appeared deserted of life. A long line of strange-looking vehicles sat like squat bugs on the loading dock. They each had four wheels with no tyres, flat, level cargo beds, and little else except a small box-like unit that extended from the front and contained lights and bug-eyed lenses aimed forward.

Pitt was about to reattach the air-conditioner panel when he caught a movement above his head. Fortunately, he saw the TV camera mounted on a pole by the dock before it swung through its full arc and found them. A quick look around the dock, and he spotted four more cameras.

'Stay put,' he alerted Giordino. 'They've got remote sensing equipment everywhere.'

They ducked back behind the panel and were figuring the next move when the lights on the derricks suddenly flashed on and their electric motors began to hum. None had a cabin for an operator. They were all operated by remote control from a command centre somewhere within the project. They moved along the train and dropped horizontal metal shafts that slid into slots on the top edges of the containers. Then a short blast from a horn sounded and the derricks hoisted the big containers from their rail cars, swung over the dock, and lowered them onto one of the flatbed trucks. The lifting shafts were removed and the derricks went on to the next container.

For the next few minutes they remained behind the panel, not moving as the nearest derrick poised directly above them, eased in the shafts, and picked up their container. Pitt was impressed the entire operation went so smoothly without human presence. Once the container was firmly settled on the truck, there was a buzz and it began to silently roll along the dock and then down a long ramp that led into an open shaft that corkscrewed underground.

'Who's driving?' Giordino murmured.

'A robotic transporter,' answered Pitt. 'Controlled from a command centre somewhere in the project.'

They quickly replaced the panel and tightened it with just a couple of screws. Next they crawled to the forward edge of the container and studied the scene unfolding around them.

'I've got to admit,' said Giordino softly, 'I've never seen efficiency like this anywhere.'

Pitt had to agree, it was an intriguing sight. The curving ramp, a marvel of engineering, went deep, deep into the bowels of the desert. Already, he reasoned, the transporter and its cargo had travelled over 100 metres straight down, passing four different levels that travelled beyond view into the earth.

Pitt studied the large signs above the passages. They were identified with symbols as well as terminology in French. The upper levels were designated for biological waste, the lower levels for chemical waste. Pitt began to wonder what the container they were riding on carried inside.

He found the mystery intensifying. Why would a reactor that burned waste be buried so deep underground? To his way of thinking it should have been above the surface near the solar concentrators.

At last the ramp straightened out into an immense cavern that seemed to stretch on forever. The ceiling was a good four storeys high with rock-hewn side tunnels spreading in all directions like spokes on a wheel. It looked to Pitt that a work of nature had been expanded by an enormous excavation project.

Pitt's senses were probing ahead for him like antennae. He was continually surprised to still see no people, no workers or machine operators. Every movement in what he perceived to be a storage cavern was controlled by automation. The electrically powered transporter, like a drone ant, followed the one ahead and turned into one of the side tunnels that was marked by a red sign with a black diagonal slash that hung from the ceiling. Up ahead came various sounds and echoes.

'A land office business,' said Giordino, pointing to a number of transporters moving in the opposite direction, the doors of their cargo containers open and revealing empty interiors.

After moving almost a full kilometre the truck began to slow as the noises grew louder. Around a bend it moved into a vast chamber, filled and stacked floor to roof with thousands of box-shaped containers built from concrete, all painted yellow with black markings. A robotic machine was off-loading the barrels from the cargo containers and stacking them with a sea of other containers that rose toward the roof of the cavern.

Pitt's teeth ground softly together. He stared in growing shock and suddenly wished he was somewhere else, any place but in that underground chamber of deadly horror.

The barrels were marked with the symbol for radioactivity. He and Giordino had stumbled on Fort Foureau's secret, an underground dumping ground for nuclear waste on an unheard-of colossal scale.

Massarde took one long comprehensive look at the TV monitor and shook his head in wonderment. Then he turned to his aide, Felix Verenne.

'Those men are incredible,' he murmured.

'How did they get through security?' mused Verenne.

'By the same method they escaped my houseboat, stole General Kazim's car, and drove halfway across the Sahara. Cunning and dogged persistence.'

'Should we prevent their escape from the storage chamber?' asked Verenne. 'Keep them trapped in there until they die of radiation sickness?'

Massarde thought for a moment, and then shook his head. 'No, send security to apprehend them. Give them a good scrubbing to remove any contamination and bring them here. I'd like to talk with Mr Pitt again before I have him disposed of.'

34

Massarde's security guards captured them twenty minutes later, after they rode inside an empty container car up to the surface from the waste storage cavern. They had dropped from the roof of the container and into the emptied interior. A concealed TV camera had caught them in an unguarded moment before they could slip inside.

The door was thrown open moments before the container was to be lifted onto a railroad car. They had no chance of putting up any fight or making an attempt to escape. The surprise was well coordinated and complete.

Ten, Pitt counted them, ten men standing with menacing steadiness, pointing machine guns at the two unarmed men inside the cargo container. Pitt felt the stinging bitterness of failure cut through him like a knife. He could taste the bitterness of defeat on his tongue. To be trapped and caught once by Massarde was a miscalculation. To be caught twice was damned stupid. He stared at the guards feeling no fear, only anger for getting snared. He cursed himself for not being more alert.

They could do nothing now but bide their time and hope they weren't executed before another chance at escape, no matter how slim, appeared. Pitt and Giordino slowly raised their hands and clasped them behind their heads.

'I hope you'll forgive the intrusion,' Pitt said quietly. 'But we were looking for a bathroom.'

'You wouldn't want us to have an accident,' Giordino added.

'Still! Both of you!' A voice erupted from a security officer in a smartly creased uniform, a red pillbox cap of the French military perched on his head. The tone was harsh and cold in English with almost no trace of French. 'I'm told you are dangerous men. Push all thoughts of escape from your minds. My men are not trained to wound resisting captives.'

'What's the big deal?' asked Giordino with an innocent look. 'You act like we stole a drum of used dioxin.'

The officer ignored Giordino's remark. 'Identify yourselves.'

Pitt stared at him. 'I'm Rocky and my friend is — '

'Bullwinkle,' Giordino finished.

A tight smile curled the officer's lips. 'No doubt more appropriate than Dirk Pitt and Albert Giordino.'

'So if you know, why ask?' said Pitt.

'Mr Massarde was expecting you.'

'The last place they'd expect us to cut and run is the middle of the desert,' said Giordino, mimicking Pitt's words in Bourem. 'Kind of misguessed, didn't we?'

Pitt lightly shrugged his shoulders. 'I read the wrong script.'

'How did you men penetrate our security?' asked the officer. 'We took the train,' answered Pitt easily, making no attempt to hide the truth.

'The doors to the cargo containers are locked with combinations after loading. You could not have forced your way inside while the train was moving.'

'You should tell whoever monitors your television cameras to study the air conditioners on the roofs. A simple matter to remove a panel and use it as a screen.'

'Indeed?' Captain Brunone was highly interested. 'Most clever. I'll see that your means of entry is added to our security manual.'

'I'm deeply flattered,' Pitt grinned.

The officer's eyes narrowed. 'You won't be for long, rest assured.' He paused and spoke into a portable radio. 'Mr Massarde?'

'I'm here,' Massarde's voice rasped through the speaker.

'Captain Charles Brunone, sir, Chief of Security.'

'Pitt and Giordino?'

'In my hands.'

'Did they resist?'

'No, sir, they gave up quietly.'

'Please bring them to my office, Captain.'

'Yes, sir, as soon as they've been decontaminated.'

Pitt said to Brunone, 'Would it help if we said we were sorry?'

'It seems American humour never stops,' said Brunone coldly. 'You can offer your apologies to Mr Massarde in person, but since you destroyed his helicopter, I wouldn't expect any pity if I were you.'

Yves Massarde didn't smile often, but he was smiling now as Pitt and Giordino were escorted into his vast office, leaning back in his expensive leather executive's chair, elbows parked on the armrests, fingers entwined under his chin, he smiled benignly like a mortician after a typhoid epidemic.

Felix Verenne stood by a window overlooking the facility. His eyes stared expressionless, like camera apertures, the lines in his face grim, his mouth tight in contempt. A marked contrast to his superior's bemused stare.

'Splendid work, Captain Brunone,' Massarde purred. 'You collected them uninjured and unmarked.' He gazed speculatively at the two men standing before him in clean, white coveralls, at their tanned faces and excellent physical condition, took note of their seemingly unconcerned expressions, and remembered encountering the same indifference on his houseboat. 'So they proved cooperative.'

'Like schoolchildren beckoned to class,' Brunone said formally. 'They did as they were ordered.'

'Very wise of them,' Massarde murmured approvingly.

He pushed back his chair and came around the desk and faced Pitt. 'I compliment you on your passage across the desert. General Kazim doubted you would last two days. A remarkable accomplishment to have come so far over hostile ground so fast.'

'General Kazim is the last man I'd rely on for a prediction,' said Pitt pleasantly.

'You stole my helicopter and crashed it in the river, Mr Pitt. That will cost you dearly.'

'You treated us shabbily aboard your houseboat, so we repaid you in kind.'

'And General Kazim's valuable old car?'

'The engine seized up so we burned it,' Pitt lied.

'You seemed to have developed a nasty habit for destroying other people's expensive possessions.'

'I broke all my toys when I was a kid,' Pitt said casually. 'Drove my Dad up the walls.'

'I can always purchase another helicopter, but General Kazim cannot replace his Avions Voisin. Enjoy what time you have left before his sadists work you over in his torture chamber.'

'Lucky for me I'm a masochist,' Giordino said, unruffled.

Just for a second Massarde looked amused, then his face turned curious. 'What did you find that was so interesting that you drove halfway across the Sahara to Fort Foureau?' he demanded.

'We enjoyed your company so much on your houseboat, we thought we'd pay you another social visit — '

Massarde's hand lashed out as he viciously backhanded Pitt across the face, a large diamond ring cutting a path through the right cheek. Pitt's head twisted from the blow, but his feet remained firmly rooted to the carpet. 'Does this mean you're challenging me to a duel?' he muttered through a taut grin.

'No, it means I am going to have you slowly lowered in a drum of nitric acid until you talk.'

Pitt looked at Giordino, then back to Massarde, and shrugged. 'All right, Massarde, you've got a leak.'

Massarde frowned. 'Be specific.'

'Your hazardous waste, the chemicals you're supposed to be burning, are seeping into groundwater that flows under an ancient riverbed and is polluting every well between here and the Niger. From there it flows to the Atlantic where it's causing a catastrophic disaster that will eventually destroy all sea life. And that's just for starters. We followed the old riverbed and discovered it once flowed directly beneath Fort Foureau.'

'We are almost 400 kilometres from the Niger,' said Verenne. 'Impossible for water to flow that far under the desert's surface.'

'How do you know?' asked Pitt. 'Fort Foureau is the only project or plant within Mali that receives chemical and biological waste. The compound responsible for the problem can only come from here, the only possible source. There's no question in my mind now that I know that you're hiding waste instead of burning it.'

Irritation flickered at the edge of Massarde's mouth. 'You're not entirely correct, Mr Pitt. We do burn waste at Fort Foureau. A considerable amount as a matter of fact. Come into the next room, and I'll show you.'

Captain Brunone stood back and gestured for Pitt and Giordino to follow Massarde.

He led them across a hall into a room whose centre was filled by a three-dimensional scale, cutaway model of the Fort Foureau hazardous waste disposal project. The layout was elaborate, the detail so meticulous it was like looking at the real thing from a helicopter.

'Is this mock-up true to life or a fantasyland?' asked Pitt.

'What you see is an exact representation,' Massarde assured him.

356

'And you're about to give us a no-frills, fact-filled lecture on its operation.'

'A lecture you can take with you to the grave,' Massarde said reproachfully. He picked up a long ivory pointer and aimed its tip at a large field on the south side of the project covered with huge flat modules slanted toward the sun. 'We are completely energy sufficient,' Massarde began. 'We produce our own electricity with this photovoltaic grid system of flat-plate solar cell modules made from polycrystalline silicon that covers 4 square kilometres. Are you familiar with photovoltaics?'

'I know that it's rapidly becoming the world's most economical energy source,' answered Pitt. 'As I understand it, photovoltaics is a solar technology that converts the sun's power into direct current electrical energy.'

'Quite right,' said Massarde. 'When sunlight, or what scientists refer to as solar photon energy, strikes the surface of these cells after its 115-million-kilometre journey from the sun, a flow of electricity is produced, enough to operate a project three times this size should we wish to expand.' He paused and aimed the pointer at a structure near the array of modules. 'This building houses the generators powered by the energy converted from the modular field and the battery subsystem where the energy is stored for nighttime use or for days when the sun does not shine, which is a rarity in this part of the Sahara.'

'Efficient,' said Pitt. 'An efficient power system. But your array of solar concentrators, they do not operate with the same degree of effectiveness?'

Massarde looked thoughtfully at Pitt. He wondered why this man always seemed a step ahead of him. He swung the pointer toward a field next to the solar cells that held the array of parabolic trough collectors Pitt had observed the day before.

'They do,' he replied icily. 'My solar thermal technology

for the destruction of hazardous wastes is the most advanced programme of any industrial nation. This field of superconcentrators delivers solar concentrations higher than the normal light of eighty thousand suns. This high-intensity sunlight, or photon energy, is then focused into the first of two quartz reactors.' Massarde paused to touch the pointer against a miniature building. 'The first breaks the toxic waste down into harmless chemicals at a temperature of 950 degrees Celsius. The second reactor, at temperatures around 1200 degrees Celsius, incinerates any remaining infinitesimal residue. The destruction of every known man-made toxic chemical is total and complete.'

Pitt looked at Massarde with respect mixed with doubt. 'This all sounds very thorough and final. But if your detoxification operation is a state-of-the-art wonder of utility, why are you hiding millions of tons of waste underground?'

'Very few people are aware of the staggering number of chemicals that are spread around the globe. There are over seven million known man-made chemical compounds. And each week chemists create ten thousand new ones. At current rates, over two billion tons of waste are accumulating around the world every year. Three hundred million alone in the United States. Twice that in Europe and Russia. More than double that amount when you throw in South America, Africa, Japan, and China. Some is burned by incinerators; most is illegally dumped in landfills or discharged in water supplies. There is no place for it to go. Here in the Sahara, far from the crowded cities and farmlands, I have provided a safe place for international industries to send their toxic waste. At the moment Fort Foureau can destroy over four hundred million tons of hazardous waste a year. But I cannot destroy it all, not until my solar thermal detoxification projects in the Gobi Desert and Australia are completed to handle

358

waste from China and nations of the Far East. For your interest, I also have a facility only two weeks away from start-up in the United States.'

'Very commendable, but that doesn't excuse you from burying what you can't destroy and charging for it.'

Massarde nodded. 'Cost efficiency, Mr Pitt. It's cheaper to hide toxic waste than destroy it.'

'And you follow the same line of logic for nuclear waste,' said Pitt accusingly.

'Waste is waste. As far as humans are concerned, the only basic difference between nuclear and toxic is that one kills with radioactivity and the other with poison.'

'Dump and forget it, and to hell with the consequences.'

Massarde gave an indifferent shrug. 'It has to go somewhere. My country has the largest nuclear energy programme in the world second only to the United States in number of reactors in operation to generate electricity. Two radioactive waste repositories are already in operation. One at Soulaines, the other at La Manche. Unfortunately, neither was designed to dispose of longlife or high-level nuclear waste. Plutonium 239, for example, has a half-life of twenty-four thousand years. There are other radioactive nuclides that have half-lives a hundred times longer. No containment system will last more than ten or twenty years. As you have discovered on your uninvited expedition into our storage cavern, we receive and dispose of the high-level waste here.'

'Then despite your holier-than-thou speech on hazardous waste management, your solar detoxification project is a front.'

Massarde smiled thinly. 'In sense, yes. But as I've explained, we actually destroy a high amount of waste.'

'Mostly for appearance's sake,' Pitt said, his voice cold and compelling. 'I give you credit, Massarde, building this phoney project without international intelligence agencies getting wind of it. How did you fool spy satellites while you excavated your storage caverns?'

'Nothing really,' Massarde said arrogantly. 'After I built the railroad to bring in construction workers and materials, the excavation began under the first building erected. The soil was secretly removed and loaded in the empty railroad containers returning to Mauritania and used for a landfill in the nation's port city, a profitable ongoing project I might add.'

'Very shrewd. You get paid for the waste coming in and for the sand and rock going out.'

'I never stop at seeking merely one advantage,' Massarde said philosophically.

'No one is the wiser, and no one complains,' said Pitt. 'No environmental protection agencies threatening to close you down, no international uproar over polluting underground water systems. No one questions your methods of operation, particularly the corporations that produce the waste, and who are only too glad to get rid of it for a price.'

Verenne's expressionless gaze rested on Pitt. 'There are few saints who practice what they preach when it comes to saving the environment,' he said coldly. 'Everyone is guilty, Mr Pitt. Everyone who enjoys the benefits of chemical compounds from gasoline to plastics to water purification and food preservatives. It is a case of the jury secretly agreeing with the guilty. No one man or organization can control and destroy the monster. It is a self-propagating Frankenstein that is too late to kill.'

'So you make it worse by feeding on it in the name of profit. Instead of a solution, you've created a hoax.'

'Hoax?'

'Yes, by reneging on the expense of building long-lasting waste canisters and excavating deep deposit chambers several kilometres underground, in geologically stable rock formations far beneath existing water tables.' Pitt turned from Verenne to Massarde. 'You're nothing more than a shyster contractor who charges exorbitant prices for inferior construction that endangers lives.'

Massarde's face went red, but he was a master at controlling anger. 'The threat of waste leakage fifty or a hundred years from now killing off a few sand beggars matters little.'

'That's easy for you to say,' said Pitt, his face hardened in scorn. 'But the leakage is occurring today, and desert nomads are dying as we talk. And lest we forget that, what you've caused here could affect every living life form on earth.'

The threat of guilt for killing off the world made no impression. But the reference to dying nomads triggered something in Massarde's mind. 'Are you working in concert with Dr Frank Hopper and his World Health inspection team?'

'No, Giordino and I are strictly on our own.'

'But you are aware of them.'

Pitt nodded. 'I'm acquainted with his biochemist if that makes you happy.'

'Dr Eva Rojas,' said Massarde slowly, watching for the effect.

Pitt saw the trap, but with nothing to lose he decided to string along. 'Good guess.'

Massarde didn't become brilliantly successful by winning a lottery. He was a master of deception and intrigue, but his greatest asset was insight. 'I'll make another guess. You were the man who saved her from General Kazim's assassins outside of Cairo.'

'I happened to be in the neighbourhood, yes. You're in the wrong business, Massarde. You missed your calling by not becoming a palm reader.'

To Massarde the novelty of the confrontation was wearing off. He was not used to being talked down to. For a man who controlled a vast financial empire on a day-to-day basis, wasting time with a pair of unwelcome interlopers was merely an annoyance to be pushed aside and handled by employees.

He nodded at Verenne. 'Our little talk has ended. Please arrange for General Kazim to take these men into custody.'

Verenne's statue face finally broke into a python grin. 'With pleasure.'

Captain Brunone did not come from the same mould as Massarde or Verenne. A product of the French military establishment, he may have resigned for triple wages but he still retained a level of honour. 'Begging your pardon, Mr Massarde. I wouldn't turn a rabid dog over to General Kazim. These men may be guilty of trespassing, but they certainly don't deserve to be tortured to death by ignorant barbarians.'

Massarde considered Brunone's comment for a moment. 'Quite right, quite right,' he said, strangely agreeable. 'We can't lower ourselves to the level of the General and his butchers.' A gleam came to his eyes as he stared at Pitt and Giordino. 'Transport them to the gold mine at Tebezza. He and Dr Rojas can enjoy each other's company while they dig in the pits.'

'What about Kazim?' asked Verenne. 'Won't he feel cheated out of making them pay for destroying his car?'

'No matter,' Massarde said with utter unconcern. 'By the time he discovers their whereabouts they'll be dead.'

35

The President looked across his desk in the oval office at Sandecker. 'Why wasn't I briefed on this earlier?'

'I was informed that it was a low-priority item that did not warrant interrupting your busy schedule of appointments.'

The President shifted his gaze toward the White House Chief of Staff, Earl Willover. 'Is this true?'

A balding, bespectacled man about fifty with a large red moustache shifted in his chair, leaned forward, and glared at Sandecker. 'I ran the red tide theory by our national science board. They didn't agree that it was a worldwide threat.'

'Then how do they explain the incredible growth that's sweeping the middle Atlantic Ocean?'

Willover returned the President's gaze impassively. 'Respected ocean scientists believe the growth is temporary and the tide will soon begin to dissipate as it has in the past.'

Willover ran the Executive Branch like Horatius standing against the entire Etruscan army defending the bridge to Rome. Few got across to the oval office, and few escaped Willover's wrath if they overstayed their visit or had the audacity to disagree with the President and argue over policy. It went without saying, almost every member of Congress hated his intestines.

The President looked down at the satellite photos of the Atlantic spread on his desk. 'It seems pretty obvious to me this is not a phenomenon to ignore.'

'Left to its own resources the red tide would normally fade away,' explained Sandecker. 'But off the west coast of

363

Africa it is being nursed by a synthetic amino acid and cobalt that stimulate the tide's growth to incredible proportion.'

The President, a former senator from Montana, looked more at home in the saddle than behind a desk. He was long and lean, spoke in a soft drawl, and stared through bright blue eyes. He addressed every man as sir and every woman as ma'am. Whenever he escaped from Washington, he headed for his ranch located not far from the Custer battlefield on the Yellowstone River. 'If this threat is as serious as you say, the whole world is at risk.'

'If anything, we've probably underestimated the potential danger,' said Sandecker. 'Our computer experts have updated the rate of expansion. Unless we stop the spread, all life as we know it on earth will die from lack of oxygen in the atmosphere by late next year, probably sooner. The oceans will be dead before spring.'

'That's ridiculous,' Willover scoffed. 'I'm sorry, Admiral, but this is a classic case of Chicken Little claiming the sky is falling.'

Sandecker gave Willover a look equal to a jab with a spear.

'I am not Chicken Little, and the coming annihilation is very real. We're not talking about the potential risks of ozone depletion and its effects on skin cancer two centuries from now. No geological upheavals or unknown plague, no nuclear Armageddon with ensuing darkness, no meteor striking the planet in a raging cataclysm. Unless the scourge of the red tide is stopped, and stopped quickly, it will suck up the oxygen from the atmosphere, causing the total destruction of every living thing on the face of the earth.'

'You paint a grim picture, sir,' said the President. 'This is all but impossible for me to visualize.'

'Let me put it this way, Mr President. If you are reelected, the odds are you won't be around at the end of your term.

364

Nor will you have a successor because there will be no one left to vote for him.'

Willover wasn't buying any of it. 'Come now. Admiral, why don't you put on a sheet and walk around holding a sign saying the world ends at midnight? To think we'll see complete extinction of mankind by this time next year because of oversexed behaviour by some microscopic organisms is too farfetched.'

'The facts speak for themselves,' said Sandecker patiently.

'Your deadline sounds like nothing more than a scare tactic,' replied Willover. 'Even if you're correct, our scientists still have ample time to invent a solution.'

'Time we don't have. Let me give you a little illustration in simplified terms. Imagine that the red tide could double itself in size every week. If allowed to spread unhindered, it would cover every square kilometre of the earth's oceans in one hundred weeks. If history repeats itself, world governments will decide to shove aside the problem until the oceans are half covered. Only then do they institute a crash programme to eliminate the red tide. My question to you, Mr President, and you too, Mr Willover, is what week will the oceans be covered by the tide, and how much time until the world can prevent disaster?'

The President exchanged confused looks with Willover. 'I have no idea.'

'Nor I,' said Willover.

'The answer is the oceans will be half covered in ninety-nine weeks, and you would have only one week to act.'

The President recognized the horrendous possibility with renewed respect. 'I think we both get your point, Admiral.'

'The red tide shows no sign of dying,' Sandecker continued. 'We now know the cause. That's a step in the right direction. The next problem is to cut off the contamination at the source, and then seek out another compound that will either stop or at least hinder the growth.'

365

'Excuse me, Mr President, but we must cut this short. You're supposed to have lunch with the Senate majority and minority leaders.'

'Let them wait,' the President said irritably. 'Do you have a handle on where this stuff is coming from, Admiral?'

Sandecker shook his head. 'Not yet, but we suspect it flows through an underground stream to the Niger River from the French solar detoxification project in the Sahara.'

'How can we be certain?'

'My Special Projects Director and his right arm are inside Fort Foureau now.'

'You are in contact with them?'

Sandecker hesitated. 'No, not exactly.'

'Then how do you know this?' Willover pushed him.

'Intelligence satellite photos identified them penetrating the facility on board an incoming trail of hazardous material.'

'Your Special Projects Director,' mused the President. 'Would that be Dirk Pitt?'

'Yes, and Al Giordino.'

The President stared across the room, unseeing for a moment as he remembered. Then he smiled. 'Pitt was the man who saved us from the Kaiten nuclear car bomb menace.'

'One and the same.'

'Is he by chance responsible for that debacle with the Benin navy on the Niger River?' asked Willover.

'Yes, but the blame is mine,' said Sandecker. 'Since my warnings went unheard, and I could get no cooperation from your staff or the Pentagon, I sent Pitt and two of NUMA's best men up the Niger to track the source of the compound.'

'You ordered an unauthorized operation without permission into a foreign nation,' Willover exploded furiously.

'I also persuaded Hala Kamil to lend me a UN tactical

366

team to go into Mali and get my chief scientist and his data safely out of the country.'

'You could have jeopardized our entire African policy.'

'I didn't know you had one,' Sandecker tossed back, completely unafraid of Willover, his eyes blazing with animosity.

'You're stepping over your bounds, Admiral. This could have serious repercussions on your career.'

Sandecker was not one to shrink from a fight. 'My duty is to my God, my country, and my President, Willover. You and my career come about eighty-sixth on my list.'

'Gentlemen,' interrupted the President, 'gentlemen.' The frown on his face was more for theatrics than a show of anger. Secretly, he enjoyed seeing his aides and cabinet members slug it out with words. 'I don't want to see any further friction between you. I'm convinced we're faced with a grim reality, and we'd better damn well work together for a solution.'

Willover let out a sigh of exasperation. 'I will, of course, follow your instructions.'

'As long as I'm no longer shouting to be heard in a hurricane,' said Sandecker calmly, 'and can obtain the backup to stop the scourge, you won't have any problems with me.'

'What do you advise we do?' asked the President.

'My NUMA scientists are already working round the clock on a counteractive chemical that will either neutralize or kill the red tide without upsetting the balance of marine ecology. If Pitt proves the contamination is indeed originating from Fort Foureau, I leave it up to you, Mr President, to use whatever means in your power to shut the site down.'

There was a pause, then Willover said slowly. 'Despite the awesome prospects, assuming for a moment the Admiral is on the beam, it won't be a simple matter to unilaterally close a multi-million-dollar installation owned by French business interests in a sovereign nation such as Mali.'

'We'd have some hard explaining to do,' the President acknowledged, 'if I ordered in the air force to level the project.'

'Tread cautiously, Mr President,' said Willover, 'I see nothing but quicksand in this for our administration.'

The President looked at Sandecker. 'What about scientists in other countries? Are they aware of the problem too?'

'Not to its full extent,' answered the Admiral, 'not yet.'

'What showed you the trail?'

'Only twelve days ago, one of NUMA's ocean current experts noticed the unusually large area of the red tide in photos taken by our SeaSat cameras and began plotting its growth. Stunned by the incredible speed by which it multiplied, he quickly brought it to my attention. After careful study I made the decision not to go public until we can bring this thing under control.'

'You had no right to take matters into your own hands,' snapped Willover.

Sandecker shrugged idly. 'Official Washington turned a deaf ear to my warnings. I felt I had no option but to act on my own.'

'What steps do you propose for immediate action?' asked the President.

'For the moment, we can do little but continue collecting data. Secretary General Hala Kamil has consented to call a special closed-door meeting of leading world oceanographers at UN headquarters in New York. She's invited me to reveal the situation and set up an international committee of marine scientists to coordinate efforts and share data while searching for a solution.'

'I'm giving you a free hand, Admiral. Please update me on all new developments any time of the day or night.' Then the President turned his attention to Willover. 'You'd better alert Doug Oates over at the State Department and my National Security Council. If Fort Foureau proves to be the culprit, and if no cooperation is forthcoming from concerned nations, we'll have to go in and take the place out ourselves.'

Willover came to his feet. 'Mr President, I strongly advise we exercise patience. I'm convinced this sea plague, or whatever it is you want to call it, will blow over, as do scientists whose opinions I respect.'

'I trust Admiral Sandecker's counsel,' said the President, his eyes locked on Willover. 'In all my years in Washington, I've never known him to make a bad call.'

'Thank you, Mr President,' said Sandecker. 'There is one other matter that requires our attention.'

'Yes.'

'As I mentioned, Pitt and his backup, Al Giordino, have penetrated Fort Foureau. Should they be seized by the Malians or French security, it will be essential that they be rescued for any information they might have obtained.'

'Please, Mr President,' Willover persisted. 'There can be a nasty political backlash by risking Army Special Forces or a Delta Team in a desert rescue mission if it fails and word leaks to the news media.'

The President nodded thoughtfully. 'I agree with Earl on this one. I'm sorry, Admiral, but we'll have to think of another option to save your people.'

'You say a UN force rescued your man who accumulated the data on the Niger River contamination?' asked Willover.

'Hala Kamil was most helpful by ordering the UN Critical Response and Tactical Team to carry out the mission.'

'Then you'll have to prevail upon her to use them again if Pitt and Giordino are caught.'

'God knows I'll be crucified,' said the President, 'if I send in American men to strew the desert with French nationals.'

Sandecker's face reflected disappointment. 'I doubt if I can convince her to send them back in a second time.'

'I'll make the request myself,' the President promised.

Willover was curt. 'You can't have it all your way, Admiral.'

Sandecker gave a tired sigh. The horrible consequences of the mushrooming red tide had not totally sunk in. His mission was becoming more gruelling, oppressive, and frustrating with every passing hour. He stood up and looked down on the President and Willover. His voice came like the arctic cold.

'Be prepared for the very worst, because if we can't stop the red tide before it reaches the North Atlantic and spreads into the Pacific and Indian Oceans, our extinction will surely come.'

Then Sandecker turned and quietly left the room.

Tom Greenwald sat in his office and computer enhanced the images received by a Pyramider spy satellite. Through ground command he had shifted its orbit slightly to pass over the section of the Sahara where he discerned the car and figures of Pitt and Giordino on the old GeoSat photos. No one above him had given him permission, but so long as he could send the satellite back over the Ukrainian civil war in another couple of passes, nobody would be the wiser. Besides, the fighting had fizzled to a few rebel ambushes and only the Vice-President seemed to find the intelligence images interesting. The President's National Security Council had their minds focused elsewhere, like the secret nuclear arms build-up of Japan.

Greenwald flew against orders purely out of curiosity. He wanted to examine sharper pictures of the two men he had discovered earlier as they boarded the train to enter the project. Using the Pyramider he could now make a positive identification. Now his analysis revealed a tragic reversal of events.

The images of the two men being led under guard to a helicopter were little short of astounding. Greenwald could easily compare them to identification photos given him by Chip Webster from NUMA files. The images taken from hundreds of kilometres out in space clearly showed the capture of Pitt and Giordino.

He moved from the viewing monitor to his desk and dialled the phone. After two rings, Chip Webster over at NUMA answered.

'Hello.'

'Chip? This is Tom Greenwald.'

'What have you got for me, Tom?'

'Bad news. Your men were captured.'

'Not what I wanted to hear,' Webster said. 'Damn!'

'I have excellent images of them being loaded into a helicopter, in chains, and surrounded by a dozen armed security guards.'

'Determine a heading for the copter?' asked Webster.

'My satellite had passed out of view only a minute after it lifted off. My guess is that it was heading to the northeast.'

'Further into the desert?'

'Looks that way,' answered Greenwald. 'The pilot might have made a wide swing in a different direction, but I have no way of knowing.'

'Admiral Sandecker isn't going to like this turn.'

'I'll stay on it,' said Greenwald. 'If I turn up anything new, I'll call immediately.'

'Thank you, Tom. I owe you a big favour for this one.'

Greenwald hung up and stared at the image on the monitor. 'Poor bastards,' he muttered to himself. 'I wouldn't want to be in their shoes.'

36

The welcoming committee at Tebezza stayed home. Pitt and Giordino clearly didn't rate a reception by the local dignitaries. Two Tuaregs greeted them silently from behind automatic rifles as a third locked iron shackles around their hands and ankles. The worn condition of the chains and cuffs gave the impression they had passed through several owners.

Pitt and Giordino were shoved roughly into the back of a small Renault truck. One Tuareg drove while the other two climbed in the back, held their rifles across their thighs, and kept wary eyes on the prisoners through the slit in their indigo litham headdresses.

Pitt paid the guards only the slightest attention as the engine was started and the truck moved away from the landing field. The helicopter that had flown them from Fort Foureau quickly lifted into the furnace-baked air for its return flight. Already Pitt was weighing chances for escape. His eyes were studying the surrounding landscape. No fences stretched anywhere, no guard houses rising from the sand. Any attempt to cross 400 kilometres of open desert while restrained by manacles made security obstacles entirely unnecessary. Successful escape seemed impossible, but he quickly thrust aside thoughts of total hopelessness. Prospects of escape were dim, but not totally gone.

This was pure desert with not a growing thing in sight. Low brown dunes rose like warts as far as Pitt could see, separated by small valleys of brilliant white sand. Only toward the west did a high plateau of rock rise above the desert floor. It was treacherous country, and yet there was a beauty about it that was difficult to describe. It reminded Pitt of the background scenery in the old motion picture, *Song of the Desert*.

Sitting with his back against the side of the truck bed, he tilted his head and peered forward around the cab. The road, if it could be called that, was only tyre tracks leading toward the plateau. No structures stood on the barren land no equipment or vehicles were in evidence. No sign of ore tailings. He began to wonder if mining operations at Tebezza were a myth.

Within twenty minutes the truck slowed, then turned into a narrow ravine cut into the plateau. So soft was the sand that had drifted into the deep-walled crack that prisoners and guards together had to get out and help push the truck to firmer ground. After nearly a kilometre the driver swung into a cave just large enough for the truck to pass through. Then it entered a long gallery excavated in the rock.

The driver braked the truck in front of a brightly lighted tunnel. The guards jumped out to the ground, obeying the silent gestures of the gun muzzles, Pitt and Giordino awkwardly climbed down in their restricting shackles. The guards motioned them into the tunnel and they shuffled off, thankful to be out of the sun and in a cool underground atmosphere.

The gallery became a corridor with fluted walls and a tile-glazed floor. They were marched past a series of arched openings cut into the rock and fitted with antique carved doors. The guards stopped at a large double door at the end of the corridor, opened it, and pushed them inside. Both men were surprised to find themselves standing on thick blue carpet in a reception room as luxurious as any inside a New York, Fifth Avenue corporate executive's office. The walls were painted in a light blue to match the carpet and were decorated with photographs of breathtaking desert sunrises and sunsets. The lighting came from tall chrome lamps with soft grey shades.

Directly in the centre was an acacia desk with matching sofa and chairs in grey leather. In the rear corners, as though guarding a door to the sanctum sanctorum, stood two bronze sculptures of a Tuareg man and woman in proud poses. The air in the room was cool but not dank smelling. Pitt was sure he detected a slight aroma of orange blossom.

A woman sat behind the desk, quite beautiful with glowing purple-grey eyes and long black hair that fell to her buttocks behind the backrest of her chair. Her facial features were Mediterranean, of exactly what national origin, Pitt was unable to tell. She looked up and studied the two men for a moment as nonchalantly as if she was classifying salesmen. Then she rose from a chair, revealing an hourglass body wrapped in a garment draped like an Indian sari, opened the door between the sculptures, and silently held out her hand for them to enter.

They stepped into a large chamber with high-domed ceiling, lined on all four sides with bookshelves that were niched into solid rock. The entire room was one giant sculpture, chiselled as it was excavated. A huge, horseshoe-shaped desk rose from the rock as if it was part of the floor, its top strewn with engineering diagrams and papers. The desk faced two long stone benches separated by an intricately sculpted coffee table. Besides the books and desk litter, the only object not cut from rock was a wooden scale model of a mine gallery shored up with timbers that stood off to one side of the unusual room.

An extremely tall man was standing in the far corner, absorbed in a book he had pulled from a shelf. He stood in a purple robe of the nomads with a white litham bound around his head. Beneath his robe, a pair of snake-skin cowboy boots protruded incongruously. Pitt and Giordino stood there several moments before he turned and acknowledged their presence with a scant glance. Then his eyes flicked back to the pages of the book as if his visitors had turned around and departed.

'Nice place you've got here,' Giordino opened loudly, his voice echoing off the stone. 'Must have cost you a bundle.'

'Could use some windows,' Pitt said, surveying the bookcases. Then he looked up. 'A stained-glass skylight might help brighten up things a bit.'

O'Bannion casually inserted the book between two volumes and stared at them with bemused curiosity. 'You'd have to drill 120 metres through solid rock to reach the surface and sunlight. Not exactly worth the expense. I have more practical projects for my workers.'

'Don't you mean slaves,' said Pitt.

O'Bannion gave a slight lift to his shoulders. 'Slaves, labourers, prisoners, they're all the same at Tebezza.' He slid the book back on its shelf and approached them.

Pitt had never stood that close to someone who stood almost two heads above him. He had to tilt his head sharply backward to stare up into his captor's eyes.

'And we're the latest edition to your army of drones.'

'As Mr Massarde no doubt informed you, digging in the mines is a less painful option than being tortured by General Kazim's thugs. You should consider yourselves thankful.'

'I don't suppose there's any chance for parole, Mr . . .'

'My name is Selig O'Bannion. I manage the operation of the mine. And no, there is no parole. Once you go down into the pits, you will not come out.'

'Even for burial?' asked Giordino without a hint of fear.

'We have an underground vault for those who succumb,' answered O'Bannion.

'You're as murderous as Kazim,' said Pitt. 'Maybe worse.'

'I've read of your undersea exploits, Mr Pitt,' O'Bannion said, brushing off Pitt's insult. 'It will be most enjoyable having another party whose intellect is on a level with mine. I found your reports on deep-sea mining of particular interest. You must dine with me from time to time and tell me of your underwater engineering operations.'

Pitt's face turned to ice. 'Privileges so soon after incarceration? No thanks. I'd rather eat with a camel.'

O'Bannion's lips bent minutely downward. 'Suit yourself, Mr Pitt. Perhaps you'll change your mind after a few days of working under Melika.'

'Who?'

'My overseer. She has an uncommon cruel streak. You two are in good physical condition. So I'd estimate that when we next meet, she will have turned you into a pair of subdued vermin.'

'A woman?' asked Giordino curiously.

'Like no woman you'll ever meet again.'

Pitt said nothing. The world knew of the notorious salt mines of the Sahara. They had become a byword for blue-and white-collar workers everywhere as a job description. But a gold mine manned by slaves that was virtually unknown was a new twist. General Kazim no doubt had his hands in the profits, but the operation smelled like another venture of Yves Massarde. The quasi-solar detoxification project and the gold mine, and God only knew what else. This was a big game, a game that stretched in all directions like octopus tentacles, an international game that spelled more than just money, but inconceivable power.

O'Bannion stepped over to his desk and pressed a button on a small console. The door opened and the two guards walked into the room and stood behind Pitt and Giordino. Giordino glanced at Pitt, searching for a sign, a nod or movement of the eyes signalling a coordinated attack on the guards. Giordino would have charged an oncoming rhino without hesitation if Pitt had given the word. But Pitt stood there stiffly as if the feel of the manacles on his ankles and wrists had dulled his sense of survival. Somehow, above all else, he had to focus his wits on getting the secret of Fort Foureau into Sandecker's hands or die trying.

'I'd like to know who I'm working for,' Pitt said.

'Didn't you know?' asked O'Bannion dryly.

'Massarde and his pal, Kazim?'

'Two out of three. Not bad.'

'Who's the third?'

'Why me, of course,' O'Bannion answered patiently. 'A most satisfactory arrangement. Massarde Enterprises provides the equipment and arranges for the sale of the gold. Kazim provides the labour, and I direct the mining and ore extraction operation, which is only fair since it was I who discovered the vein of gold.'

'What percentage do the Malin people receive?'

'Why none,' O'Bannion said impassively. 'What would a nation of beggars do with riches if they were dropped in their laps? Squander or be fleeced out of them by shrewd foreign businessmen who know every angle for taking advantage of impoverished peoples? No, Mr Pitt, the poor are better off poor.'

'Have you notified them of your philosophy?'

O'Bannion's expression was one of pure boredom. 'What a dull world this would be if we all were rich.'

Pitt plunged on. 'How many men die here in a year?'

'It varies. Sometimes two hundred, sometimes three, depending on disease epidemic or mine accidents. I really don't keep count.'

'Amazing the workers don't strike,' said Giordino idly.

'No work, no food,' O'Bannion shrugged. 'And then Melika usually gets them moving by whipping the skin off the ringleaders.'

'I'm lousy with a pick and shovel,' Giordino volunteered.

'You'll quickly become expert. If not, or you cause

trouble, you'll be transferred to the extraction section.'
O'Bannion paused to check his watch. 'Still time for you
to work a fifteen-hour shift.'

'We haven't eaten since yesterday,' complained Pitt.

'Nor will you eat today,' O'Bannion nodded at the guards
as he turned back to his bookshelves. 'Take them.'

The guards prodded them out. Apart from the receptionist
and two men wearing tan coveralls and hard hats with
miners' lamps, speaking in French and examining a piece
of ore under a magnifying glass, there were no other people
to be seen until they reached an office-type elevator with
carpeted floor and chrome walls. The doors opened and the
operator, a Tuareg, motioned them inside. The doors rattled
shut and the hum of machinery reverberated off the walls
of the shaft as they descended.

The elevator dropped quickly, the ride seemingly never-
ending. Black caverns flashed past, their circular openings
marking the entrance to upper galleries. Pitt judged they
had dropped well over a kilometre when the elevator began
to slow and finally stopped. The operator opened the door,
revealing a narrow, horizontal shaft leading off into the
rock. The two guards escorted them to a heavy iron door.
One of them took a key ring from his robe, selected a key.
and turned the lock. Pitt and Giordino were pushed against
the door so that it swung open. Inside was a much larger
shaft with narrow rails laid on its floor. The guards closed
the door and left them standing there.

As a matter of routine, Giordino checked the door. It was
a good 2 inches thick and there was no handle on the inside,
only a keyhole. 'We won't be using this exit unless we can
steal a key.'

'Not to be used by the hired help,' said Pitt. 'For
O'Bannion and his cronies only.'

'Then we'll have to find another way. They obviously
remove the ore through a different vertical shaft.'

Pitt stared at the door thoughtfully. 'No, I can't accept that. It's the executive elevator or nothing.'

Before Giordino could reply, the whirring of an electric motor and the clanking sound of steel wheels against the rails came from one end of the shaft. A small generator-driven locomotive pulling a long train of empty ore cars appeared and slowed to a stop. A black woman climbed down from the driver's seat and confronted the two men.

Pitt had never laid eyes on a woman with a body that was almost as wide as it was tall. She was, he decided, the ugliest woman he had ever laid eyes on. She'd have made a fitting gargoyle, he thought, on the eaves of a medieval cathedral. A heavy leather thong extended from her hand as if it had grown there. Without a word she stepped up to Pitt.

'I am Melika, foreman of the mines. I am to be obeyed and never questioned. Do you understand?'

Pitt smiled. 'A new experience, taking orders from someone who resembles a toad with a weight problem.'

He saw the thong whipping through the air, but too late to duck or ward off the blow. It caught him high on the side of the face, and he saw stars in front of his eyes as he staggered back against a shoring timber. The blow struck with such force he came within a speck of blacking out.

'Seems as though everyone is hitting on me today,' Pitt said thickly through the agony.

'A short lesson on discipline,' she snapped. Then in a lightning movement, incredibly swift for someone of her heavy build, she swung the thong backhanded toward Giordino's head. But she wasn't fast enough. Unlike Pitt, he had warning. He grasped her wrist in an iron grip, stopping the thong in midair. Slowly, as if in a test of wills, the two arms trembled as their muscles exerted every pressure at their command.

Melika had the strength of an ox. She had never imagined that any man could have been capable of gripping her so hard. Surprise showed in her widened eyes, then disbelief, then anger. With his other hand, Giordino tore the thong from her grasp as one would snatch a stick from a snarling dog, and hurled it into an ore car.

'You dirty scum,' she hissed. 'You'll suffer for this.'

Giordino puckered up his lips and blew her a kiss. 'Love-hate relationships are the best.'

His cockiness cost him. He missed the sudden shift of the eyes, the foot lifting off the ground as the knee bent and thrust into his groin. Giordino released his grip on her wrist, dropped to his knees, and fell to his side, writhing in silent agony.

Melika smiled satanically. 'You fools have condemned yourselves to a hell you can't imagine.' She wasted no more time with talk. She retrieved the thong and waved it toward an empty ore car and said the single word: 'In.'

Five minutes later the train of ore cars stopped and then backed into a shaft. Lights strung along the timber trailed into the dark shadows. It looked to be a new working. Men's voices travelled over the noise of the train and a moment later the gleam of their lamps flickered around a bend. They were herded along by Tuareg guards with whips and guns, chanting in tired, hoarse voices. All were Africans, some southern tribesmen, some desert people. Zombies in old horror movies looked in better health than these poor dregs. They moved slowly, dragging their feet. Most were dressed only in ragged shorts. Sweat covered their bodies that were also heavily coated with rock dust. The glazed look in their eyes and the ribs showing through their chests told of a starvation diet. All were scarred by lash marks and a number of them were missing fingers; a few had dirty bandages around the stumps that once were attached to hands. Their weak chanting faded as the light from their lamps was lost around the next bend.

The tracks ended at a pile of rock that had been blasted

by the explosive crew they had passed in the shaft. Melika unhitched the locomotive. 'Out!' she ordered.

Pitt helped Giordino climb over the bucket edge of the car and half supported him as they stood staring ferociously at the barrel-shaped slave driver.

Her huge lips spread in a Novocain grin. 'You'll soon look like those scum.'

'You should pass out vitamins and steel gloves,' said Giordino, suddenly straightening, his face pale with pain.

Melika raised her thong and slashed him across the chest. Giordino did not blink or flinch. These men weren't yet cowed, she thought. It was only a question of days before she reduced them to animals. 'The blasting crew has accidents,' she said matter-of-factly. 'Lost limbs go with the job.'

'Remind me not to volunteer,' muttered Pitt.

'Load this rock into the cars. When you've finished, you can eat and sleep. A guard will make his rounds at unannounced times. He finds you sleeping, you work extra shifts.'

Pitt hesitated. A question was on the tip of his tongue. But it stuck in his throat. It was time to lay low. He and Giordino stared at the tons of ore piled at the end of the shaft and then at each other. It seemed a hopeless, backbreaking task for two men to accomplish in less than forty-eight hours while hampered by shackles.

Melika climbed onto the electric locomotive and nodded at a TV camera mounted on a cross beam. 'Don't waste your time thinking of escape. You're under constant surveillance. Only two men made it out of the mines. Their bones were found by nomads.'

She gave off a witch's cackle and rode off down the mine shaft. They watched until she had disappeared and all sounds faded. Then Giordino raised his hands and let them drop to his sides. 'I think we've been had,' he muttered as he sadly counted up to thirty-five empty ore cars.

Pitt lifted the chain attached between his hand and ankle manacles and hobbled over to a large stack of beams, waiting to shore up the tunnel as it was excavated. He paced off one beam and did the same with an ore car. Then he nodded.

'We should be able to wrap this up in six hours.'

Giordino gave him a very sour look indeed. 'If you believe that, you'd better sign up for a course in elementary physics.'

'A little trick I learned picking raspberries one summer in high school,' said Pitt curtly.

'I hope it fools the surveillance camera,' Giordino groaned.

Pitt grinned, insidiously. 'Watch and learn.'

37

The guards came and went with irregularity as Melika promised. They seldom stayed but a minute, satisfying themselves that the two prisoners were feverishly loading ore cars as if attempting to set some kind of record. In six and a half hours all thirty-five cars appeared brimming over with ore.

Giordino eased to a sitting position with his back against a timber. 'You load 16 tons and what do you get?' he said, quoting the song.

'Another day older and deeper in debt,' Pitt finished.

'So that's how you picked raspberries.'

Pitt settled next to Giordino and smiled. 'During a trip around the states with a school buddy one summer, we stopped at a farm in Oregon that advertised for berry pickers. We thought it would be easy gas money and applied. They paid fifty cents a lug, which if I remember correctly, held about eight small boxes. What we didn't know is that raspberries are much smaller and softer than strawberries. Picking as fast as we could go it seemed forever to fill up a lug.'

'So you loaded the bottoms with dirt and layered the tops with berries.'

Pitt laughed. 'At that, we only averaged thirty-six cents an hour.'

'What do you think will happen when the old bitch finds out we laid timbers as false floors in the ore cars and only piled a few rocks on top to make them look fully loaded?'

'She won't be happy.'

'Throwing a handful of dust on the lens of the camera

to blur our images was a nice touch. The guards never caught on.'

'At least our little con job bought us some time without exhausting our reserves.'

'I'm so thirsty I could drink dust.'

'If we don't get water soon, we'll be in no shape to make a break.'

Giordino eyed the chains on his manacles and then the rails under the ore cars. 'I wonder if we can cut our chains by laying them on the rails and running a car over them.'

'I thought about that five hours ago,' said Pitt. 'The chains are too thick. Nothing less than a full-size Union pacific diesel locomotive could crush these links.'

'I hate a spoilsport,' Giordino grumbled.

Pitt idly picked up a piece of ore and studied it under the string of overhead lights. 'I'm no geologist, but I'd say this is gold bearing quartz. Judging from the grains and flakes in the rock, it comes from a fairly rich vein.'

'Massarde's share must go toward expanding his sordid empire.'

Pitt shook his head in dissent. 'No, he wouldn't spread it around and incur tax problems. I bet he skips converting it into cash and hoards the ingots somewhere. Since he's French, my guess is one of the Society Islands.'

'Tahiti?'

'Or Bora Bora or Moora. Only Massarde or his flunky, Verenne, knows for sure.'

'Maybe when we get out of here we can go on a treasure hunt to the South Seas — '

Suddenly Pitt sat up and held a finger to his mouth for silence. 'Another guard coming,' he announced.

Giordino cocked an ear and gazed down the shaft. But the guard was not in sight yet. 'Pretty clever of you to scatter gravel around the other side of the bend. You can hear the crunch of their footsteps before they appear.'

'Let's look busy.'

They both leaped to their feet and made a show of busily stacking ore on the heaps already topping the cars. A Tuareg guard walked around the bend and watched them for a minute. As he turned to leave and continue his rounds, Pitt shouted at him.

'Hey, pal, we're finished. See, all loaded. Time to knock off.'

'Get food and water,' Giordino jumped in.

The eyes of the guard darted from Pitt down along the line of ore cars. Suspiciously, he walked the train from end to end and back again. He looked at the large pile of ore remaining on the floor of the shaft and scratched his head through his litham. Then he shrugged and gestured with his automatic weapon for Pitt and Giordino to begin moving toward the entrance of the shaft.

'They're not big on small talk around here,' grunted Giordino.

'Makes it tough to bribe them.'

Once into the main tunnel, they followed the narrow set of rails up a long sloping grade cut in the bowels of the plateau. An ore train with a guard driving the locomotive rumbled into view, and they had to press their backs against the side of the hewn wall to allow it to pass. A short distance later they reached a hollowed-out cavern where the rails from other cross shafts congregated at a large elevator that could hold four ore cars at one time.

'Where are they taking the ore?' asked Giordino.

'Must go to an upper level where it's crushed to powder and the gold is recovered and refined.'

The guards led them to a massive iron gate mounted on equally massive hinges and weighing close to half a ton. It was designed to keep more than chickens cooped up. Two other Tuaregs waited on the other side. They nodded and exerted every muscle in pulling open the gate, then silently motioned for Pitt and Giordino to move inside. One guard handed them dirty tin cups half filled with brackish water.

Pitt gazed into the cup, then at the guard. 'How creative, water garnished with bat's vomit.'

The guard couldn't understand the words but he easily read the savage look in Pitt's eyes. He snatched back the cup and threw the water in the dirt and kicked Pitt into the chamber.

'That'll teach you to look a gift horse in the mouth,' Giordino said, smiling broadly as he emptied his cup on the ground too.

Their new home was 10 metres wide by 30 long and lit by four tiny light bulbs. Four-tiered wooden bunks were arranged the length of both walls. The dungeon, for that's what it was, had no ventilation and the stench of crowded living conditions was ghastly. The only sanitary conveniences were several holes sunk in the rock along the rear wall. In the centre were two long eating tables with crude wooden benches. There had to be, Pitt guessed, more than three hundred human beings crammed in the nauseating area.

The bodies slumped in the nearest bunks looked to Pitt as if they were comatose. Their faces looked as expressionless as cabbages. Twenty men were huddled around the table using their hands to eat out of a community pot like starving maggots. None of the faces looked frightened or worried; they were far beyond showing ordinary emotion; they were drawn and haggard from lack of food and exhaustion. They moved mechanically like living cadavers, staring through eyes dead with defeat and submission. None of them gave Pitt and Giordino so much as a glance as they made their way through the sea of human misery.

'Not exactly a carnival atmosphere,' muttered Giordino.

'Humanitarian principles don't count for much around here,' Pitt said in disgust. 'It's worse than I ever imagined.'

'Much worse,' agreed Giordino, cupping a hand over his nose in a futile effort to ward off the smell. 'The Black Hole of Calcutta had nothing on this dump.'

'Feel like eating?'

Giordino winced as he stared at the remains of the slop clinging to the sides of the pot. 'My appetite just filed for bankruptcy.'

The newly unbreathable air and lack of ventilation in the dungeon-like cave raised the heat and humidity from the packed bodies to unbearable levels. But Pitt suddenly felt himself turn as cold as if he'd stepped onto an iceberg. For a moment all the defiance and anger left him and the horror and suffering seemed to dissolve and fade as he recognized a figure bending over a bunk in a lower tier against the right wall of the cave. He rushed over and knelt beside a woman who was tending a sick child.

'Eva,' he said gently.

She was bone weary from forced labour and lack of food, and her face was pale and marked by welts and bruises, but she turned and stared at him through eyes that gleamed with courage.

'What do you want?'

'Eva, it's Dirk.'

It didn't sink in. 'Leave me alone,' she muttered. 'This little girl is terribly sick.'

He took her hand between his and leaned closer. 'Look at me. I'm Dirk Pitt.'

Then her eyes widened in recognition. 'Oh Dirk, is it really you?'

He kissed her and gently touched the bruises on her face. 'If I'm not, someone is playing a cruel trick on us both.'

Giordino appeared at Pitt's shoulder. 'A friend of yours?'

Pitt nodded. 'Dr Eva Rojas, the lady I met in Cairo.'

'How did she get here?' he asked in surprise.

'How did you?' Pitt asked her.

'General Kazim hijacked our plane and sent us here to work in the mines.'

'But why?' queried Pitt. 'What threat were you to him?'

'Our UN health team, under the supervision of Dr Frank Hopper, was close to identifying a toxic contaminant that was killing villagers all over the desert. We were on our way back to Cairo with biological samples for analysis.'

Pitt looked up at Giordino. 'Massarde asked us if we were working with Dr Hopper and his group.'

Giordino nodded. 'I recall. He must have known Kazim had already imprisoned them here.'

She dabbed a wet handkerchief on the little girl's forehead and suddenly leaned her head against Pitt's chest and sobbed. 'Why did you come to Mali? Now you're going to die like the rest of us.'

'We have a date, remember?'

Pitt was concentrating his attention on Eva and didn't see the three men cautiously moving in between the bunks and surrounding them. The leader was a big man with a red face and bushy beard. The other two looked haggard and worn out. They all bore lash marks on their naked backs and chests. The menacing expressions on their faces brought a grin from Giordino as he turned and faced them. Their physical conditions were so pathetic he was confident he could have laid out all three without breathing hard.

'These men bothering you?' the red-faced man said to Eva protectively.

'No, no, not at all,' Eva murmured. 'This is Dirk Pitt, the man who saved my life in Egypt.'

'The man from NUMA?'

'The same,' Pitt replied. He turned to Giordino. 'This is my friend, Al Giordino.'

'By God, a real pleasure. I'm Frank Hopper and this shabby fellow on my left is Warren Grimes.'

'Eva told me a great deal about you in Cairo.'

'Damned sorry we have to meet under such grim circumstances.' Hopper stared at the deep cuts on both of Pitt's cheeks and touched the long scab that ran across his own face. 'It seems we've both angered Melika.'

'Only on the left side. The right one came from another source.'

The third man stepped forward and held out his hand. 'Major Ian Fairweather,' he introduced himself.

Pitt shook the outstretched hand. 'British?'

Fairweather nodded. 'Liverpool.'

'Why were you brought here?'

'I led tourist safaris across the Sahara until one was massacred by plague-crazed villagers. I barely escaped with my life, and after struggling across the desert, was rescued and hospitalized in Gao. General Zateb Kazim arrested me so I couldn't reveal what I'd seen and sent me here to Tebezza.'

'We did pathology studies on the villagers Major Fairweather is referring to,' explained Hopper. 'All died from a mysterious chemical compound.'

'Synthetic amino acid and cobalt,' said Pitt.

Hopper and Grimes looked peculiarly stunned. 'What, what did you say?' demanded Grimes.

'The toxic contamination causing death and sickness throughout Mali is an organometallic compound that's a combination of an altered synthetic amino acid and cobalt.'

'How could you possibly know that?' asked Hopper.

'While your team was searching in the desert, mine was tracking it up the Niger River.'

'And you identified the stuff,' Hopper said with a look of optimism that wasn't there before. Pitt briefly told of the red tide explosion, his expedition up the river, and the presumed flight by Rudi Gunn with their data.

'Thank God, you got your results out,' muttered Hopper.

'The source,' pressed Grimes. 'Where is the source?'

'Fort Foureau,' Giordino answered him.

'Not a chance — ' Grimes stared dumbly. 'Fort Foureau and the contamination sites are hundreds of kilometres apart.'

'It's carried by underground water movement,' Pitt clarified. 'Al and I had a look around inside the project before we were captured. High-level nuclear waste, as well as ten times the hazardous waste that's being burned, is being buried in underground caves where it leaks into the groundwater.'

'The world environmental regulation organizations must be told of this,' exclaimed Grimes. 'The damage a toxic dump the size of Fort Foureau can produce is inestimable.'

'Enough talk,' said Hopper. 'Time is precious. We have to move forward on the escape plan for these men.'

'What about the rest of you?'

'We're in no shape to cross the desert. Our strength has been sapped and our bodies racked from slaving in the mines, too little sleep, and almost no food or water. No way we can make it. So we did the next best thing. Hoarded supplies and prayed for someone like you to arrive in good physical condition.'

Pitt looked down at Eva. 'I can't leave her.'

'Then stay and die with the rest of us,' Grimes said abruptly. 'You're the only hope for everyone in this hellhole.'

Eva clutched Pitt's hand. 'You must go, and go quickly,' she pleaded. 'Before it's too late.'

'She's right, you know,' added Fairweather. 'Forty-eight hours in the shafts and they break you. Look at us. We're washed out. None of us could cross 5 kilometres of desert before dropping.'

Pitt stared at the dirt floor. 'How far do you think Al and I'd get without water? Twenty, maybe 30 kilometres farther than you?'

'We've only hoarded enough for one man,' said Hopper. 'We'll leave it to you to decide who makes the attempt and who stays.'

Pitt shook his head. 'Al and I go together.'

'Two will never get far enough for rescue.'

'What kind of distance are we talking about?' asked Giordino.

'The Trans-Saharan Motor Track is close to 400 kilometres due east of here, across the border in Algeria,' replied Fairweather.'After 300, you'll have to trust to luck to get you the rest of the way. Once you reach the track, you should be able to flag down a passing vehicle.'

Pitt tilted his head as if he didn't hear Fairweather right. 'Maybe I missed something. You neglected to explain how we breeze past the first 300 kilometres?'

'You steal one of O'Bannion's trucks once you reach the surface. It should carry you that far.'

'A little optimistic, aren't we,' said Pitt. 'What if its fuel tank is empty?'

'No one ever keeps an empty petrol tank in the desert,' Fairweather said firmly.

'Just walk out of here, punch an elevator button, ride to the surface, steal a truck, and roll merrily on our way,' Giordino scowled. 'Sure we will.'

Hopper smiled. 'Do you have a better plan?'

'To be honest,' Pitt laughed, 'we don't even have an outline.'

'We'd hurry things up a bit,' warned Fairweather. 'Melika will be dragging everyone back to the mines within the hour.'

Pitt looked around the prisoner's cave. 'Do you all blast and load ore?'

'The political prisoners, which includes us,' answered Grimes, 'dig and load the ore after it's blasted from the rock. The criminal prisoners labour in the rock crusher and recovery levels. They also make up the blasting crew. Poor devils, none of them last long. If they don't blow themselves to bits with explosives they die from the mercury and cyanide used in the amalgamation and refining of the gold.'

'How many foreign nationals are you?'

'There are five of us left from the original team of six. One was murdered by Melika, who beat her to death.'

'A woman?'

Hopper nodded. 'Dr Marie Victor, a vivacious lady and one of the finest physiologists in Europe.' Hopper's jovial expression had vanished. 'She was the third since we arrived. Two of the wives of the French engineers from Fort Foureau were murdered by Melika too.' He paused to look sadly at the wasted little girl in the bunk. 'Their children suffer the worst, and there is nothing we can do.'

Fairweather pointed to a group of people clustered around three of the tiered bunks. Four were women, eight were men. One of the women was holding a little boy about three against her body.

'My God!' Pitt whispered. 'Of course, of course! Massarde couldn't allow the engineers who constructed his project to return to France and spill the truth.'

'How many women and children all told are down here?' Giordino asked with an expression clouded with wrath.

'The current count is nine women with four small children,' Fairweather answered.

'Don't you see,' Eva said softly. 'The sooner you get free and bring help, the more people you'll save.'

Pitt didn't need any further convincing. He turned back to face Hopper and Fairweather. 'Okay, let's hear your plan.'

38

It was a plan shot full of holes, the scheme of desperate men with little or no resources, incredibly oversimplified, but just crazy enough to work.

An hour later, Melika and her guards walked through the cave dungeon and forced the slave labourers into the main chamber where they were assembled in work gangs before moving toward their assigned stations in the mines. It seemed to Pitt as if she took devious delight in wielding her thong right and left against the sea of unprotected flesh, cursing and beating men and women alike who looked as if they belonged in coffins.

'The witch never tires of adding scars to the helpless,' Hopper seethed.

'Melika means queen, a name she gave herself,' Grimes said to Pitt and Giordino. 'But we call her the wicked witch of the west because she was a matron in a women's prison in the United States.'

'You think she's rotten now,' Pitt muttered. 'Wait until she finds the ore cars Al and I covered with a facade of rock.'

Giordino and Hopper hovered beside Pitt as he circled his arm around Eva's waist and guided her outside. Melika spied Pitt and moved toward him, stopped, and then stared at Eva menacingly. She grinned, knowing she could enrage Pitt not by striking him but laying the thong on Eva.

She swung but Giordino stepped between them and the thong made a sickening slapping sound as it met and bounced off his flexed biceps.

Except for an angry red welt that formed and began to

ooze blood, Giordino showed no ill effects from a blow that would have left any normal man clutching his arm and groaning in agony. Without so much as a tic, he gave her a cold stare and said, 'Is that the best you can do?'

The mob went dead still. They all halted in mid-stride, holding their breath for the storm that would surely come. Five seconds passed as if time was frozen in ice. Melika stood numb from the unexpected show of boldness, and then she quickly turned crimson with crazed anger. She reacted as though she couldn't cope with ridicule, snarling like a wounded bear and lashing out at Giordino with the thong.

'Restrain yourself!' came a commanding voice at the gate. Melika spun around. Selig O'Bannion was standing just outside the dungeon, a giant amid munchkins. She held the thong poised in mid-air for a few moments before lowering it, glaring at O'Bannion in humiliation, her eyes coals of bitter resentment, like a neighbourhood bully chastised in front of her victims by the cop on the beat.

'Do not injure Pitt and Giordino,' ordered O'Bannion. 'I want them to live the longest so they can carry the others into the burial chamber.'

'Where's the sport in that?' said Pitt.

O'Bannion laughed softly and nodded at Melika. 'Breaking Pitt physically will give me little enjoyment. Breaking his mind into quivering mush will be a happy experience for both of us. See that they have a light work load for the next ten shifts.'

Melika begrudgingly nodded her head in compliance as O'Bannion mounted a locomotive and rode into one of the shafts for an inspection tour. 'Out, you stinking scum,' she growled, waving the blood-stained thong above her grotesque head and barrel-like body.

Eva stumbled, barely able to keep on her feet, as Pitt helped her to where the labourers assembled. 'Al and I will get through,' he promised her. 'But you've got to hang on until we return with an armed force to rescue you and these other poor souls.'

'Now l have a reason for living,' she said softly. 'I'll be waiting.'

He kissed her on the lips and the bruises on her face lightly. Then he turned to Hopper, Grimes, and Fairweather, who were standing around them in a protective ring. 'Take care of her.'

'We will,' Hopper nodded in assurance.

'I wish you wouldn't deviate from our original plan,' said Fairweather. 'Hiding you in one of the ore cars going up to the crusher is safer than your idea.'

Pitt shook his head. 'We'd still have to move through the ore crushing level, then the refining and recovery areas before reaching the surface. I don't like the odds. Taking the direct route up the executive elevator and through the engineering offices has more appeal.'

'If there's a choice between sneaking out the back door or strutting out the front,' said Giordino plaintively, 'he'll go for style every time.'

'Do you have a rough guess as to the number of armed guards?' Pitt directed his question to Fairweather because the safari leader had endured the mines longer than Hopper and his people.

'A rough guess?' Fairweather thought a moment. 'Somewhere between twenty and twenty-five. The engineers are armed too. I've counted about six of them besides O'Bannion.'

Grimes passed two small canisters to Giordino who hid them under his tattered shirt. 'All the water we've been hoarding. Everyone contributed out of their ration. A little less than 2 litres is all we managed. I'm sorry there isn't more.'

Giordino placed his hands on Grimes' shoulders, unusually touched by the sacrifice. 'I'm aware of the cost, thank you.'

'The dynamite?' Pitt queried Fairweather.

'I have it,' answered Hopper, slipping Pitt a small stick of explosives with a detonation cap. 'One of the blasting crew smuggled it out in his shoe.'

'Two final items,' said Fairweather. 'A file to cut through your chains, stolen out of a locomotive toolbox by Grimes. And a diagram of the shafts that also shows the surveillance cameras. On the back, I've drawn a crude map of the country you have to cross before reaching the Trans-Saharan Track.'

'If anybody knows the desert, Ian does,' affirmed Hopper.

'I'm grateful,' said Pitt. Uncharacteristically, his eyes began to water. 'We'll do our best to return with help.'

Hopper put a great bear-like arm around Pitt. 'Our prayers and hearts go with you.'

Fairweather shook his hand. 'Remember to skirt the dunes. Don't attempt to cross them. You'll only get bogged down and die.'

'Good luck,' Grimes said simply.

A guard came over and prodded Pitt and Giordino away from the others with his gun butt. Pitt disregarded him, leaned down, and gave Eva a final light kiss.

'Don't forget,' he said. 'You and I and the bay of Monterey.'

'I'll wear my most revealing dress,' she smiled gamely.

Before he could say more, the guard shoved him away. As he reached the exit tunnel, he turned to wave a farewell, but she and the others were lost to view amid the milling mass of labourers and guards.

The guard led Pitt into the shaft where they'd loaded ore a few hours earlier and then left them. Another empty ore train was sitting on the track alongside a fresh pile of excavated rock.

'I'll make a show of competing for employee of the month while you work on your chains out of camera range,' said Pitt. He began tossing rocks in the ore cars as Giordino attacked his shackles with the file Grimes had provided.

Fortunately, the iron was old and of poor quality. The file bit through the links quickly and Giordino pulled the broken chain through the loops in his manacles, freeing his hands and feet of restricted movement. 'Your turn,' he said.

Pitt draped his chain over the edge of an ore car for support and sliced through a link in less than ten minutes. 'We'll have to work on the cuffs later, but at least now we can dance and jab.'

Giordino casually swung his chain like an aircraft propeller. 'Who takes the guard, you or me?'

'You,' answered Pitt candidly as he reinserted the split chain through his manacles. 'I'll fake him out.'

A half an hour later, as the crunch of gravel announced the guard's approach, Pitt yanked the power supply cord from the TV camera. This time two guards appeared around the bend. Two Tuaregs moving on opposite sides of the ore train rails, guns levelled in an ever-constant firing position. Their unblinking eyes, barely visible through the slit in their lithams, seemed frozen in cold implacability.

'Two coming to visit,' whispered Giordino. 'And they don't look in the mood for a friendly social call.'

The guard on the right approached and poked the muzzle of his gun in Pitt's ribs to hurt and harass him. A slightly raised eyebrow was all that indicated a surprised flinch. Pitt backed away and smiled disarmingly.

'Nice that you could drop by.'

It was essential to make a lightning move before the guards realized they were about to be attacked. The words had hardly left his lips when Pitt snatched the gun with his left hand, twisted it away, and hurled a boulder with unerring aim. A strikeout pitch, the rock thudded against the guard's forehead. The guard arched over backward like a tightly strung bow and dropped flat across the rails.

For two seconds, though it seemed much longer, the second guard stared unbelievingly down at his fallen companion. No guard at Tebezza had ever been attacked by the slave labour, and the realization that it was happening momentarily stunned him. Then the awareness of possible death struck him and he shook off the spell. He lifted his weapon to shoot.

Pitt pivoted away from the gun muzzle, and threw himself to one side, grabbing desperately for the fallen guard's weapon. He had a fleeting glimpse of a chain being flipped over the Tuareg's head like a child's jump rope, and then of Giordino pulling and twisting the ends like a garrote. Giordino's great strength lifted the guard off the ground, feet kicking wildly in the air. The machine gun clattered onto the rails as the guard's hands released their grip and grabbed frantically at the chain biting into his throat.

When the thrashing settled to a feeble twitch, Giordino loosened the chain and allowed the guard to fall to the ground next to his unconscious partner only two gasps away from death. Then he swept up the gun and cradled it in his arms, the sights aiming down the mine shaft.

'How benevolent of us not to kill them,' Giordino muttered.

'Only a temporary reprieve,' said Pitt. 'When Melika gets through with them for allowing us to escape, they'll find themselves working alongside the people they've beaten and tormented.'

'Can't leave these guys laying around where they'll be found.'

'Dump them in one of the ore cars and cover them with rock. They won't wake up for at least two hours. More than enough time for us to be well on our way across the desert.'

'Providing a repairman doesn't rush to repair the camera.'

As Giordino went to work disposing of the guards, Pitt consulted Fairweather's diagram of the mine shafts. There was no way he could retrace his steps to the engineer's private elevator by memory, not with a maze of mine shafts honeycombing in every direction, and without a compass, picking the correct course was all but impossible.

Giordino finished his chore and picked up the automatic rifles and studied them. 'All plastic and fibreglass five-five-six-millimetre French-manufacture general military issue. Nice little piece.'

'No shooting if we can help it,' said Pitt. 'We have to be discreet before Melika realizes we're missing.'

Once outside their work shaft they went straight across the main tunnel into the opening directly opposite. Fifty metres later, carefully ducking the TV cameras marked on Fairweather's map, they had reached another cavern without seeing anyone. No one challenged them, no one attacked them. They were alone for the first part of their escape.

They followed the railroad track that had carried them into the mines from the elevator, stopping at cross tracks for Pitt to recheck the map. Those precious seconds wasted seemed like years.

'Got any idea where we are?' asked Giordino quietly.

'I wished I sprinkled bread crumbs when we came in,' Pitt murmured, holding up the map to a light bulb coated with dust. Suddenly, the approaching metal scraping against metal sounds of an ore train reverberated some distance behind in the tunnel.

'Freight coming,' said Giordino.

Pitt pointed to a natural fissure in the rock just 10 metres away on the far side of the tracks. 'In there till it passes.'

They darted into the fissure and stopped suddenly. A terrible sickly stench came through the crack in the rock, a putrid stench of nauseating vileness. Carefully, with great

399

apprehension they moved through the fissure until it opened into a larger chamber. Pitt felt as if he was entering a dank catacomb. The chamber was pitch black, but the groping hand he ran along the wall touched an electrical switch. He pressed the switch upward and a vast cave was illuminated in a ghostly light.

It *was* a catacomb, a subterranean cemetery for the dead. They had stumbled into the burial cave where O'Bannion and Melika stored the bodies of the labourers who were beaten and starved and overworked until death cane as a welcome parole. The dead showed little sign of decomposition in the dry atmosphere. No ceremony here. The stiffened bodies were stacked crudely like timbers, nearly thirty to a pile. It was a ghastly, unnatural, and sorrowful sight.

'My God,' Giordino gasped. 'There must be over a thousand stiffs in here.'

'Most convenient,' Pitt said as a white flame of anger burnt within him. 'O'Bannion and Melika don't have to bother with digging graves.'

A chilling vision passed before Pitt's eyes, a vision of Eva, Dr Hopper, and the rest heaped like all the other corpses, their sightless eyes staring at the rock ceiling. He closed his eyes, but the scene remained.

Only when the ore train clattered by the entrance to the crypt did he shake off the terrible image in his mind. When he spoke his voice came in a rasping whisper he scarcely recognized as his.

'Let's get to the surface.'

The sound of the ore train faded into the distance as they paused and peered from the fissure leading to the catacomb, checking to see that there were no guards patrolling close by. The tunnel was clear and they ran into a side shaft that Fairweather's map indicated as a shortcut to the engineer's elevator. Then came an incredible piece of luck. This shaft was dripping damp and floored with duckboard.

Pitt tore up one of the duckboards and stared almost joyously at the puddle of water underneath. 'Happy hour,' he said. 'Drink your gut full so we can save the canisters Hopper gave us.'

'I don't have to be told,' said Giordino, dropping to his knees and downing the cool water from cupped hands.

They had just taken their fill and were dropping the duckboard back in place when they heard the sound of voices at the rear end of the passage followed almost at once by the clank of chains.

'A work crew coming up behind us,' Giordino murmured softly.

They hurried on, refreshed and with building optimism. Another minute and they reached the iron door leading to the elevator. They paused as Giordino shoved the small stick of dynamite in the keyhole and connected the cap. Then he moved back as Pitt picked up a rock and hurled it at the cap. He missed.

'Just pretend you're trying to drop a pretty girl into a water tank at a carnival,' suggested Giordino wryly.

'Let's just hope the bang doesn't arouse the guards or alert the elevator operator,' said Pitt, picking up another rock.

'They'll think it's only an echo from the blasting crew.'

This time Pitt's throw was true and the cap burst, detonating the dynamite. The resulting detonation came as a sharp thud as the lock was blown apart. They rushed forward and pulled the iron door open, quickly entering the short passage to the elevator.

'What if there is a code for calling down the elevator?' asked Giordino.

'A little late to think of that now,' Pitt grunted. 'We'll just have to use our own code.'

He stepped up to the elevator, thought for a moment, and

then pressed the button beside the door once, twice, then three times, paused and pressed twice more. Through the doors they could hear the switches click and the electric motor hummed to life as the elevator began its descent from a level above.

'You must have struck a chord,' said Giordino, smiling.

'I trusted to luck that any combination might work just so long as it wasn't one long buzz.'

In a half minute the hum stopped and the doors opened. The operator guard looked out and didn't see anyone. Curious, he stepped over the threshold and was knocked out by a quick thrust of Pitt's gun butt against the nape of his neck. Giordino quickly dragged the operator inside as Pitt closed the doors.

'All aboard for a nonstop run to the executive offices,' said Pitt, pressing the upper button of the panel.

'No tours of the crusher or cyanide recovery floors?'

'Only if you insist.'

'I'll pass,' Giordino grunted as the elevator began rising. They stood side-by-side in the small enclosure, watching the lights blink on the indicator above the switch panel, wondering if they'd be greeted by an army of Tuareg guards ready to shoot them full of holes. The hum ceased and the elevator eased to a stop so smoothly it was hardly sensed.

Pitt readied his gun and nodded to Giordino. 'Get set.'

The door opened and nobody pumped bullets into them. There was an engineer and a guard walking together in the corridor, it was true, but they were absorbed in conversation and walking away, their backs to the elevator.

'It's almost as if they want us to leave,' Giordino mumbled.

'Don't tempt the gods,' Pitt said curtly. 'We're not out of here yet.'

There was nowhere to hide the elevator operator, so Pitt pushed the button to the lowest level and sent him on his way. They tagged behind the guard and engineer, keeping out of sight, until O'Bannion's men turned and entered an office behind one of the antique carved doors.

The fluted wall corridor was as deserted as when the guards marched them through less than twenty-four hours previously. Guns poised and aimed ahead, they each ran along one wall of the corridor until it met the tunnel leading to the Gallery where the trucks were parked. A Tuareg, seated on a camp stool, guarded the entrance. Not expecting trouble from the engineering offices and living quarters behind him, he was sitting and smoking a pipe while reading the Koran.

They stopped to take a breath and looked back the way they had come. No one had appeared behind them. They turned their attention to the final hurdle. It was open ground for a good 50 metres with no visible sign of surveillance cameras.

'I can run faster than you,' Pitt whispered as he handed his gun to Giordino. 'If he comes on to me before I reach him, take him out with a quick shot.'

'Just don't get in my line of fire,' Giordino warned him.

Pitt removed his shoes, then took a sprinter's start position, firmly gripped his feet on the rock floor, tensed, and then sprang forward, accelerating to a fast pace. He was, Pitt knew with sickening certainty, terribly exposed. Though his stocking feet were muffled, the acoustics in the rock-hewn tunnel were too acute. He had covered almost 40 metres before the guard, curious at the sound of thumping feet behind him, turned and stared dumbly at the slave labourer hurtling toward him. But Pitt's saving grace was the guard's slow reaction time. The machine gun's barrel was just beginning to rise as Pitt leaped and smashed into the guard.

Shock it was that showed in the guard's eyes, then quick, flashing pain as his head struck the rock wall and the eyes rolling into the head as he went limp under Pitt's weight. Pitt rolled off the guard, sucking in air to catch his breath. He lay on his back panting as Giordino approached and looked down.

'Not bad speed for an old man crowding forty,' he said, extending his hand and helping Pitt to his feet.

'I'm not going to try that again. Not ever,' Pitt shook his head in finality. On his feet again his gaze took in the long underground gallery. Two Renault trucks were parked side-by-side just next to the narrow tunnel leading out into the ravine. Then he stared at the crumpled form of the Tuareg. 'You're a big strong boy,' he said to Giordino. 'Carry him over to the nearest truck and dump him in the bed. We'll take him with us. If anyone wanders by, they might think he got bored, left his post, and went for a joyride.'

Giordino easily shouldered the guard and hoisted him over the tailgate of the first truck as Pitt stepped into the cab and checked the dashboard instruments. There was no ignition key but the switch turned off and on without one. As Fairweather had promised, the fuel gauge read 'Full.' He flipped on the switch and pressed the starter button. The engine kicked over and started right up.

'Is there a clock on the dash?' inquired Giordino.

A quick scan and Pitt shook his head. 'This is a cheap model with no options. Why do you want to know?'

'Those dirty Tuaregs took my watch. I've lost all track of time.'

Pitt slipped off one boot and retrieved his Doxa dive watch where he'd hidden it under his sole. He slipped it back on his wrist and held it up in front of Giordino. 'One-twenty in the morning.'

'Nothing like an early start.'

Pitt shifted into first gear and eased out the clutch, steering the truck into the exit tunnel, moving only slightly faster than idle so the sound of the exhaust wouldn't travel up the tunnel to suspicious ears.

The walls were so close they nearly touched the sides of the truck. Pitt cared little about scratching the paint. His main concern was scraping noises that might have drawn attention, but once they broke into the open and entered the narrow ravine, he shifted up, mashed the accelerator to the floor, and switched on the headlights. The Renault plunged through the tight ravine, bouncing crazily and trailing a swirling cloud of dust.

Pitt mentally recalled where the soft spots in the sand were located during the trip through the canyon. He had surveyed the nearby landmarks when he was required to push the truck to firmer ground. Now he threw the truck through the tight crack of the rocky plateau with reckless abandon, hurtling across the yielding sand patches that grabbed at the tyres but failed to bog them down because of the truck's rapid momentum.

He took no notice of the smell of freedom, the cold night air of the desert, nor did he waste a quick look at the stars above. Each kilometre they put between them and pursuit was golden, every minute precious. He drove like a demon, pushing the truck to its limits.

Giordino made no complaints, no appeals to slow down. He put his implicit faith in Pitt, propped his feet against the dashboard, and gripped the bottom of his seat, teeth clenched against the jarring ride, eyes fixed on the barely distinct tyre tracks looming in the darkness under the steep walls of the canyon.

Abruptly the headlights showed empty flatlands ahead as they sped out into flat desert. Only then did Pitt look up at the sky, pick out the north star, and aim the radiator cap of the truck toward the east.

They had crossed the point of no return in a suicidal attempt with odds so high that failure seemed inevitable.

But Pitt wouldn't have had it any other way. There could be no stopping until they reached water or rescue.

Ahead lay 400 kilometres of desert, inviting, ominous, and deadly. The race for survival was on.

39

For the five hours of remaining darkness, Pitt spun the truck's wheels through the awesome wilderness of sand where time had little meaning. This was truly a land of no compromise that chilled with its cold mornings, choked with its fine sand, and baked with a sun that seemed magnified by a crystal atmosphere. He felt as if he had entered a world not of his universe.

They were moving through a section of the Sahara called the Tanezrouft, huge sprawling badlands with almost 200,000 square kilometres of bleak, grotesque wasteland broken only by a few rugged escarpments and an occasional sea of sand dunes that relentlessly moved across the flats like ghostly armies of veiled phantoms.

This was the desert primeval without a weed in sight.

And yet, there was life. Moths fluttered about the headlights. A pair of ravens, the desert's scavenging, cleaning service, disturbed by the approach of the truck took wing and squawked in annoyance. Large black scarabs scampered over the sand to escape the tyres as did an occasional scorpion and tiny green lizard.

Pitt found it easy to become intimidated by the surrounding void, by the hundreds of kilometres they had yet to travel, the almost certain hunger, thirst, and privations that remained to be endured. His only solace was the steady roar of the Renault's engine. It hadn't skipped a beat since leaving the mines, and the four-wheel-drive performed flawlessly, surging through soft spots Pitt was sure would bog them down. On four occasions he was forced to drive into deep, narrow dry washes with sloping soft gravel banks, barely making it up and over the opposite edge in low gear. Often he found no way to dodge sudden drop-offs or boulders and having to risk going over seeming impossible barriers, but somehow the sturdy Renault pulled them through.

They took no time to stop, get out, and stretch their legs. They would get enough of walking later when they abandoned the truck. They even took calls of nature on the fly without braking.

'How far have we travelled?' asked Giordino.

Pitt glanced at the odometer. 'A hundred and two kilometres.'

Giordino looked at him. 'You take the wrong short cut or are we going in circles? We should have covered almost 200 kilometres by now. Are we lost?'

'We're on course,' said Pitt confidently. 'Blame it on Fairweather's directions. He gave distances as the crow flies. No crow with half a brain would be flying around the desert if he could be attacking a scarecrow in an Iowa cornfield. Impossible to maintain a straight line when we've already had to detour 40 kilometres to avoid two deep ravines and a herd of sand dunes.'

Giordino stirred uncomfortably. 'Why do I get a sinking feeling we're about to hike a lot further than 100 kilometres across no-man's-land.'

'*Not* a cheery thought,' Pitt agreed.

'Be light soon. We'll lose the stars to navigate by.'

'Don't need them. I finally remembered how to build a do-it-yourself compass straight out of the *Army Field Manual*.'

'Glad to hear it,' Giordino yawned. 'What does the fuel gauge read?'

'Slightly over half a tank left.'

Giordino turned and looked back at the Tuareg they had tied up in the truck bed. 'Our friend looks about as happy as a shanghaied sailor.'

'He doesn't know it yet, but he's our ticket to evade pursuit,' answered Pitt.

'The devious mind again. It never stops churning.'

Pitt briefly stared up at the sickle moon. He would have preferred a full phase, but he was thankful for what little light it sent down as he drove the truck across a terrain equal to a lunar landscape. He shifted gears and strained his eyes on the uneven ground revealed by the headlights. Then suddenly the desert smoothed out and began to sparkle like fireworks.

The Renault rolled onto a huge dry lake with crystal deposits that reflected the twin beams from the headlights like prisms in rainbow colours. Pitt opened the Renault up in high gear and felt exhilarated to be speeding over a firm, flat surface at nearly 90 kilometres an hour. The desert floor seemed to reach into infinity, the early morning stars falling below the horizon line as if the great brink of a flat world abruptly fell away into space. The sky looked as if it was closing in all around them like the four walls and ceiling of a small room. An unnerving sense of disorientation gripped Pitt. Yet he was following nearly the same parallel as Havana, Cuba, so the big dipper was still above the horizon. He continually used Polaris as a base point to line up a star to the east and then steered toward it.

Hour passed upon monotonous hour as the crystal lake gave way to low, boulder-strewn hills. Pitt could not recall having experienced such a heavy shroud of monotony. His only respite was a small peak off his left to the north that rose like an island in the middle of a vast and sterile sea.

Giordino took over the driving chore as the sun burst from the horizon as if shot from a cannon. There it seemed to hang without moving throughout the day until suddenly falling like a rock shortly before sunset. Shadows stretched far into the distance or did not exist. There was no in-between.

An hour after daylight, Pitt stopped the truck and searched around the cargo bed until he found a loose pipe about a metre in length. Then he stepped to the ground and pushed the pipe into the sand until it stood vertical and cast a shadow. Picking up two small stones, he placed one at the tip of the shadow.

'Is this your poor man's compass?' asked Giordino, studying Pitt's actions from the shade of the truck.

'Observe the master at work.' He joined Giordino and waited approximately twelve minutes before marking the distance the shadow had travelled with another stone. Next he drew a straight line from the first stone to the second and extended it about half a metre beyond. He then stood with the toe of his left foot at the first rock and toe of his right where the line ended. Lifting his left arm and pointing straight ahead, he said, 'That's north.' Then he extended his right arm to the side. 'East to the Trans-Saharan Track.'

Giordino sighted down Pitt's outstretched right arm and hand. 'I see a dune in that direction we can use as a reference point.'

They moved on, repeating the process every hour. At about nine o'clock the wind began to blow from the southeast, swirling the sand in clouds that cut visibility to less than 200 metres. By ten, the heated wind had increased and was seeping into the cab of the truck despite the rolled-up windows. Swept up in small gusts, the sand rose and twisted like whirling dervishes.

The mercury jumped and fell like a pogo stick. This day the temperature rose from 15 degrees C (60 degrees F) to 35 degrees C (95 degrees F) in three hours, topping off during the hottest part of the afternoon at 46 degrees C (114 degrees F). Pitt and Giordino felt as if they were driving into a furnace, the air hot and dry in their nostrils as they breathed in and exhaled. Their only relief came from the breeze generated by their speed over the stripped and barren land.

The needle on the temperature gauge wavered and hung a millimetre off the red boiling mark, but the radiator showed no sign of leaking steam. They stopped every half hour now, as Pitt sighted direction from what little sun shone through the dust cloud and allowed the pipe to cast a faint shadow. He opened one of the canisters of water and offered it to Giordino. 'Liquid refreshment time.'

'How much?' asked Giordino.

'We'll split it. That will give us half a litre each with one in reserve for tomorrow.'

Giordino steered with his knees as he gauged his share of the water and then drank. He passed the canister back to Pitt. 'O'Bannion must have set his dogs on the trail by now.'

'Driving the same make and model truck, they won't close the gap unless they've got a Formula One, Grand Prix champion driver at the wheel. Their only advantage is having extra fuel on to continue the chase after we've run dry.'

'Why didn't we think of loading on reserves?'

'There were no gas storage drums around the truck parking area. I looked. They must have stored them elsewhere, and we didn't have time to spare for a search.'

'O'Bannion just might whistle up a whirlybird,' Giordino said as he down-shifted to crawl over a low dune.

'Fort Foureau and the Malian military are his only sources for a helicopter. And my guess is the last people he'll call on for help are Kazim and Massarde. He knows damn well they wouldn't look kindly on his losing public enemies one and two only a few hours after we were placed in his tender and loving care.'

'You don't think O'Bannion's posse can hunt us down before we cross into Algeria?'

'They can't follow us through a sandstorm any more than a Mountie can track his man through a blizzard.' Pitt tilted a thumb over his shoulder out the rear window. 'No tracks.'

Giordino looked into a sideview mirror and saw the wind

411

sweep the sand over the tyre tracks as if the truck was a small boat on a vast sea that closed over its wake. He relaxed and slouched in his seat. 'You don't know what a pleasure it is to travel with a Pollyanna.'

'Don't write off O'Bannion just yet. If they reach the Trans-Saharan Track first and patrol back and forth until we appear, the show is over.'

Pitt finished off the canister and tossed it in the back with the Tuareg guard who had become conscious and was sitting with his back against the tailgate of the truck, glaring at the men inside the cab.

'How's the gas?' Pitt asked.

'Almost on fumes.'

'Time to throw out a red herring. Bring the truck around on a reverse heading toward the west. Then come to a stop.' Giordino dutifully did what he was ordered, twisted the wheel, and braked to a halt. 'Now we walk?'

'Now we walk. But first, bring the guard up front and check the truck for any item that might prove useful, like cloth to wrap our heads to prevent sunstroke.'

A strange combination of fear and menace burned in the guard's eyes as they propped him in the front seat, cut strips from his robe and headdress, and then bound him tightly so his hands and feet could not touch the steering wheel or floor pedals.

They foraged through the truck, finding a few oily rags and two wash towels that they fashioned into turbans. The guns were left behind, buried in the sand. Then Pitt tied the steering wheel so it couldn't turn and shifted the truck into second gear and jumped from the cab. The faithful Renault lurched forward carrying its trussed-up passenger and bounced back toward Tebezza until it became lost in the blowing sand.

'You're giving him a better chance to live than he'd have given us,' Giordino protested.

'Maybe, maybe not,' Pitt said mildly.

'How far do you figure we have to hike?'

'About 180 kilometres,' Pitt answered as if it was a short jaunt.

'That's almost 112 miles on one litre of water that wouldn't grow cactus,' Giordino complained. He stared critically into the turbulent wind-blown sand. 'I just know my poor old tired bones are going to bleach in the sand.'

'Look on the bright side,' said Pitt, tucking in his crude turban. 'You can breathe the pure, open air, bask in the silence, commune with nature. No smog, no traffic, no crowds. What can be more invigorating for the soul?'

'A bottle of cold beer, a hamburger, and a bath,' Giordino sighed.

Pitt held up four fingers. 'Four days, and you'll get your wish.'

'How are you at desert survival?' Giordino asked hopefully.

'I went on a weekend camping trip with the Boy Scouts in the Mojave Desert when I was twelve.'

Giordino shook his head sadly. 'That certainly eases all thoughts of anxiety.'

Pitt took another direction reading. Then using his compass pipe for a staff, he bent his head against the wind and sand and began walking toward what he determined was east. Giordino hooked a hand in Pitt's belt so they wouldn't lose each other in a sudden, blinding wall of sand and trudged along behind.

40

The closed-door meeting at the UN headquarters began at ten o'clock in the morning and lasted well past midnight. Twenty-five of the world's leading ocean and atmospheric scientists along with another thirty biologists, toxicologists, and contamination experts sat in rapt attention as Hala Kamil made a short opening address before turning over the secret conference to Admiral Sandecker who kicked off the proceedings by revealing the scope of the ecological disaster.

Sandecker then introduced Dr Darcy Chapman who lectured the assembly on the chemistry of the prolific red tides. He was followed by Rudi Gunn with an update on the contamination data. Hiram Yaeger rounded out the briefing by displaying satellite photos of the spreading tide and providing statistics on its projected growth.

The information session lasted until two o'clock in the afternoon. When Yaeger sat down and Sandecker returned to the podium, there was a strange silence in place of the normal protests by scientists who seldom agreed with each other's theories and revelations. Fortunately, twelve of those in attendance were already aware of the extraordinary growth of the tide and had launched studies of their own. They elected a spokesperson who announced findings that supported the results accumulated by the men from NUMA. Those few who had refused to accept a catastrophic disaster in the making now came around and endorsed Sandecker's dire warning.

The final programme on the agenda was to form committees and research teams to commit their resources and cooperation in sharing information toward the goal of halting and reversing the threat of human extinction.

Though she knew it was a futile plea, Hala Kamil returned to the podium and begged the scientists to not speak to members of the news media until the situation had attained a measure of control. The last thing they needed, she implored, was worldwide panic.

Kamil closed the meeting with an announcement of the time for the next conference to assimilate new information and report on progress toward a solution. There was no polite applause. The scientists filed up the aisles in groups, talking in unusually quiet voices and motioning with their hands as they exchanged viewpoints in their respective areas of expertise.

Sandecker sank wearily in a chair on the rostrum. His face was lined and tired but splendidly etched with strength of will and determination. He felt at last that he had turned the corner and was no longer pleading a case before deaf and hostile ears.

'It was a magnificent presentation,' said Hala Kamil.

Sandecker half rose from his chair as she sat down beside him. 'I hope it did the job.'

Hala nodded and smiled. 'You've inspired the top minds in the ocean and environmental sciences to discover a solution before it's too late.'

'Informed maybe, but hardly inspired.'

She shook her head. 'You're wrong, Admiral. They all grasped the urgency. The enthusiasm to tackle the threat was written in their faces.'

'None of this would have happened if not for you. It took a woman's foresight to recognize the danger.'

'What looked obvious to me, seemed absurd to others,' she said quietly. 'I feel better now that the debate and controversy are over and we can concentrate our efforts to stop this thing.'

'The next problem we face is keeping it a secret. The story will most certainly go public within forty-eight hours.'

'An invasion by an army of reporters is almost inevitable,' Sandecker nodded. 'Scientists aren't exactly noted for keeping a tight lip.'

Hala stared out over the now empty auditorium. The spirit of cooperation was far above anything she'd seen in the General Assembly. Maybe there was hope after all for a world divided by so many ethnic cultures and languages.

'What are your plans now?' she asked.

Sandecker shrugged. 'Get Pitt and Giordino out of Mali.'

'How long has it been since they were arrested at the solar waste project?'

'Four days.'

'Any word of their fate?'

'None I'm afraid. Our intelligence is weak in that part of the world, and we have no idea where they were taken.'

'If they've fallen into Kazim's hands I fear the worst.'

Sandecker could not bring himself to accept Pitt and Giordino's loss. He changed the subject. 'Have investigators found any sign of foul play in the deaths of your World Health inspection team?'

For a moment she did not answer. 'They're still probing through the wreckage of the plane,' she finally said. 'But preliminary reports say there is no evidence the crash was caused by a bomb. So far it's a mystery.'

'There were no survivors?'

'No, Dr Hopper and his entire team were killed along with the flight crew.'

'Hard to believe Kazim wasn't behind it.'

'He is an evil man,' Hala said, her face sombre and thoughtful. 'I too think he was responsible. Dr Hopper must have discovered something about the plague that is sweeping Mali, something Kazim could not allow to be revealed, especially among foreign governments that provide him with aid.'

'Hopefully, Pitt and Giordino will have the answers.'

She looked at Sandecker, an expression of sympathy in her eyes. 'You must face the very real possibility that they are already dead, executed on Kazim's orders.'

The weariness seemed to fall off Sandecker like a discarded overcoat as a grim smile touched his lips. 'No,' he said slowly, 'I'll never accept Pitt's death, not until I make a positive identification myself. He's come back from the dead on any number of occasions with uncanny regularity.'

Hala took Sandecker's hand in hers. 'Let us pray that he can do it again.'

Felix Verenne was waiting at the Gao airport when Ismail Yerli came down the boarding stairs. 'Welcome back to Mali,' he said, extending a hand. 'I hear you spent time here some years ago.'

Yerli did not smile as he took the offered hand. 'Sorry for arriving late, but the Massarde Enterprises plane you sent to pick me up in Paris had mechanical problems.'

'So I heard. I would have ordered another plane, but you had already departed on an Air Afrique flight.'

'I was under the impression Mr Massarde wanted me here as soon as possible.'

Verenne nodded. 'You were informed by Bordeaux as to your assignment?'

'I'm well aware, of course, of the unfortunate investigations by the United Nations and the National Underwater and Marine Agency, but Bordeaux only insinuated that my job was to become chummy with General Kazim and prevent him from interfering with Mr Massarde's operations.'

'The idiot has blundered this whole contamination inspection thing. It's a wonder the world news media hasn't gotten wind of it.'

'Are Hopper and his team dead?'

'Might as well be. They're labouring as slaves in a secret gold mining operation of Mr Massarde's in the deepest part of the Sahara.'

'And the NUMA intruders?'

'They were also captured and sent to the mines.'

'Then you and Mr Massarde have everything under control.'

'The reason Mr Massarde sent for you. To prevent any more fiascos by Kazim.'

'Where do I go from here?' asked Yerli.

'To Fort Foureau for instructions from Massarde himself. He'll arrange an introduction with Kazim, glorifying the horrifying little man with your intelligence accomplishments. Kazim has a fetish for spy novels. He'll leap at the opportunity to use your services, unknowing you will be reporting his every movement and action to Mr Massarde.'

'How far is Fort Foureau?'

'A two-hour flight by helicopter. Come along, we'll pick up your luggage and be on our way.'

Like the Japanese who conducted their business without buying products manufactured by the nations they hustled, Massarde only hired French engineers and construction workers as well as using French-manufactured equipment and transportation. The French-built Ecureuil helicopter was a mate to the one Pitt crashed in the Niger River. Verenne had the copilot collect Yerli's bags and deposit them on board.

As he and the expressionless Turk settled in comfortable leather chairs, a steward served hors d'oeuvres and champagne.

'A bit fancy aren't we?' asked Yerli. 'Do you always throw out the red carpet for ordinary visitors?'

'Mr Massarde's orders,' replied Verenne stiffly. 'He abhors the American practice of offering soft drinks, beer, and nuts. He insists that as Frenchmen we demonstrate refined taste in keeping with French culture, regardless of the status of our visitors.'

Yerli held up his glass of champagne. 'To Yves Massarde, may he never cease being generous.'

'To our boss,' said Verenne. 'May he never stop his generosity to those who are loyal.'

Yerli downed his glass with an indifferent shrug of his shoulders and held it out for a refill. 'Any feedback on your operations at Fort Foureau from environmentalist groups?'

'Not really. They're in a bit of a quandary. They applaud our self-sufficient solar energy design, but they're scared to death of what burning toxic wastes will do to the desert air.'

Ycrli studied the bubbles in his champagne glass. 'You are certain the secret of Fort Foureau is still safe? What if European and American governments get wind of the real operation?'

Verenne laughed. 'Are you joking? Most of the governments of the industrialized world are only too happy to go along with secretly getting rid of their hazardous garbage without public knowledge. Privately, bureaucratic officials and business executives of nuclear and chemical plants around the world have given us their blessing.'

'They know?' Yerli asked in surprise.

Verenne looked at him with a bemused smile. 'Who do you think are Massarde's clients?'

41

After leaving the truck, Pitt and Giordino walked through the heat of the afternoon and under the cold of the night, wanting to travel as far as possible while they were still reasonably fresh. When they finally stopped and rested, it was the following dawn. By burrowing in the sand and covering their bodies during the heat of the day, they shielded themselves from the blazing sun and reduced their water loss. The gentle pressure from the sand also gave some relief to their tired muscles.

They made 48 kilometres (30 miles) toward their goal the first trek. They actually walked further, meandering across the hard floor valleys between sand dunes. The second night they set out before sunset so Pitt could position the stake and set their course until the stars came out. By sunup the next morning the Trans-Saharan Track was another 42 kilometres closer. Before digging under their daily blanket of sand, they drained the last drops of water from the canister. From now on, until they found a new supply of water, their bodies would begin to wither and die.

The third night of their trek, they had to cross a barrier of dunes that stretched out of sight to the right and left. The dunes, though menacing, were things of beauty. Their delicate, smooth surfaces were sculptured into fragile, ever-moving ripples by the restless wind. Pitt quickly learned their secrets. After a gentle slope, the dune usually dropped sharply on the other side. They travelled when practical on the razor-edged crests of the dunes to prevent slogging up and down the soft, giving sand. If this proved difficult, they meandered through the hollows where the sand was firmer beneath their feet.

On the fourth day the dunes gradually became lower and finally fell away onto a wide sandy plain, dreary and waterless. During the hottest part of the day the sun beat down on the parched flatland like a blacksmith's hammer against red hot iron. Though thankful to be crossing a level surface, they found the walking difficult. Two kinds of ripples covered the sandy ground. The first being small, shallow ridges, which presented no problem. But the other, large ripples spaced farther apart, crested at exactly the length of their strides, creating a tiring effect much like walking the ties of a railroad.

Their hiking time became shorter and the rest stops longer and more frequent. They plodded on, their heads down, silent. Talking only made their mouths drier. They were prisoners of the sand, held captive by a cage measured only by distance. There were few distinct landmarks except for the jagged peaks of a low range of rock that reminded Pitt of the vertebra of a dead monster. It was a land where each kilometre looked exactly like the last and time ran without meaning as if turning on a treadmill.

After 20 kilometres, the plains met a plateau. The new sun was about to rise when they put it to a vote and decided to climb the steep escarpment to the top before resting for the day. Four hours later, when they finally struggled over the edge, the sun had risen well above the horizon. The effort had taken what little reserves they had left. Their hearts pounded madly after the torturous strain of the strenuous ascent, leg muscles fiery with pain, chests heaving as starving lungs demanded more air.

Pitt was exhausted and afraid to sit down for fear he could never regain his feet again. He stood weakly, swaying on the ledge, and gazed around as if he was a captain on the bridge of a ship. If the plain below was a featureless wasteland, the surface of the plateau was a sun-blasted, grotesque nightmare. A sea of confused, twisted tumbles of scorched red and black rock, interspersed with rusting obelisk-like outcroppings of iron ore spread out to the east directly in their path. It was like staring at a city destroyed centuries ago by a nuclear explosion.

'What part of Hades is this?' Giordino rasped.

Pitt pulled out Fairweather's map, now badly wrinkled and beginning to split apart, and flattened it across his knee. 'He shows it on the map, but didn't write in a name.'

'Then from this moment on, it shall be known as Giordino's hump.'

Pitt's parched lips cracked into a smile. 'If you want to register the name, all you have to do is apply with the International Geological Institute.'

Giordino collapsed on the rocky ground and stared vacantly across the plateau. 'How far have we come?'

'About 120 kilometres.'

'Still 60 to go to the Trans-Saharan Track.'

'Except that we ran up against a manifestation of Pitt's law.'

'What law is that?'

'He who follows another man's map comes up 20 kilometres short.'

'You sure we didn't take a wrong turn back there?'

Pitt shook his head. 'We haven't travelled in a straight line.'

'So how much farther?'

'I reckon another 80 kilometres.'

Giordino looked at Pitt through sunken eyes that were reddened from fatigue and spoke through lips cracked and swollen. 'That's another 50 miles. We've already come the last 70 without a drop of water.'

'Seems more like a thousand,' Pitt said hoarsely.

'Well,' Giordino muttered. 'I have to say the issue is in doubt. I don't think I can make it.'

Pitt looked up from the map. 'I never thought I'd hear that from you.'

'I've never experienced total agonizing thirst before. I can remember when it was a daily sensation. Now it's become more of an obsession than a craving.'

'Two more nights and we'll dance on the track.'

Giordino slowly shook his head. 'Wishful thinking. We don't have the stamina to walk another 50 miles without water in this heat, not as dehydrated as we are.'

Pitt was haunted by the constant vision of Eva slaving in the mines, being beaten by Melika. 'They'll all die if we don't get through.'

'You can't squeeze blood out of a turnip,' said Giordino. 'It's a miracle we made it this far — ' He sat up and shaded his eyes. Then he pointed excitedly toward a jumbled mass of huge rocks. 'There, between those rocks, doesn't that look like the small entrance to a cave?'

Pitt's eyes followed his pointing hand. There was indeed a black opening amid the rocks. He took Giordino's hand and pulled him to his feet. 'See, our luck's changing for the better already. Nothing like a nice, cool cave to while away the hottest time of the day.'

Already the heat was suffocating as it reflected off the red-brown rocks and iron outcroppings. They felt as if they were walking through the cinders of a barbecue. Without sunglasses they screwed their eyes up and covered them with the cloth of their makeshift turbans, peering down through tiny slits, seeing only the ground a few metres in front of them.

They had to climb a pile of loose boulders to the entrance of the cave, careful not to touch the rock with their bare hands or they would be sorely burnt. A small wall of sand had drifted across the floor of the entrance and they knelt and scooped it away with their hands. Pitt had to duck under the overhanging rock to enter the cave while Giordino waded through the sand while standing fully erect.

They did not have to wait for their eyes to get used to the dim light. There was no dark zone. The cavern had not been carved by wind or water eroding their way through limestone. A huge mass of rocks had been stacked upon one another during a great Palaeozoic upheaval of the earth, forming a hollow cavern. The centre was lit by the sun's rays that passed through openings in the rocks above.

As Pitt moved deeper into the interior, two large human figures loomed over him in the shadows. Instinctively, he stepped back, colliding with Giordino.

'You just stepped on my foot,' grunted Giordino.

'Sorry,' Pitt gestured up at a smooth wall where a figure was about to throw a spear at a buffalo. 'I didn't expect company.'

Giordino looked over Pitt's shoulder at the spear thrower, stunned to face rock artwork in the most barren part of the world. He slowly peered round at a massive gallery of prehistoric and ancient art that displayed centuries of artistic styles of successive cultures.

'Is this real?' he muttered.

Pitt moved closer to the mysterious rock paintings and examined a 3-metre-high figure with a mask that sprouted flowers from its head and shoulders. The thirst and fatigue dropped away as he stared in awe. 'The art is genuine all right. I wish I was an archaeologist and could interpret the various styles and cultures. The earliest paintings seem to begin at the back of the cave, and then the overlapping cultures work chronologically forward to more recent times.'

'How can you tell?'

'Ten to twelve thousand years ago the Sahara had a moist and tropical climate. Plant life blossomed. It was far more livable than it is now.' He nodded at a group of figures surrounding and thrusting spears at a giant, wounded buffalo with enormous horns. 'This must be the earliest painting because it shows hunters killing a buffalo almost the size of an elephant that's been long extinct.'

Pitt moved to another piece of artwork that covered several square metres. 'Here you can see herders with cattle,' he said, gesturing at the images with his hands. 'The pastoral era began about 5000 B.C. This later-style art shows more creative composition and an eye for detail.'

'A hippopotamus,' said Giordino, staring at a colossal drawing that covered one entire side of a flattened rock. 'This part of the Sahara can't have seen one of these for a while.'

'Not in three thousand years anyway. Hard to visualize this area once was a vast grassland that supported life from ostrich to antelope to giraffe.'

As they moved on, and the passage of time in the Sahara unrolled across the rock, Giordino observed, 'About here it looks like the local artists stopped drawing cattle and the vegetation.'

'Eventually the rains died away and the land began to dry out,' lectured Pitt, recalling a long forgotten course in ancient history. 'After four thousand years of uncontrolled grazing the vegetation was gone and the desert began to take over.'

Giordino moved from the inner recesses of the cavern toward the entrance, stopping in front of another painting. 'This one shows a chariot race.'

'People from the Mediterranean introduced horses and chariots sometime before 1000 B.C.,' explained Pitt. 'But I had no idea they penetrated this deep into the desert.'

'What comes next, teacher?'

'The camel period,' answered Pitt, standing in front of a long painting of a caravan depicting nearly sixty camels strung out in an S shape. 'They were brought into Egypt after the Persian conquest of 525 B.C. Using camels, the Roman caravans pushed clear across the desert from the coast to Timbuktu. Camels have been here ever since because of their incredible endurance.'

In a more recent period in time the paintings with camels became more crude and rudimentary than earlier art styles. Pitt paused in front of another series of paintings in the rich gallery of ancient art, studying a finely drawn battle that was engraved into the rock and then painted in a magnificent red ochre colour. Bearded warriors with square beards, lifting spears and shields in the air, rode in two-wheel chariots pulled by four horses, attacking an army of black archers whose arrows rained from the sky.

'Okay, Mr smart guy,' said Giordino, 'explain this one.'

Pitt stepped over, his eyes following Giordino's gaze. For a few seconds Pitt stared at the drawing on the rock, mystified. The image was drawn in linear, child-like style. A boat rode on a river bounding with fish and crocodiles. It was hard to imagine the hell outside the cave was once a fertile region where crocodiles once swam in what were now dry riverbeds.

He moved closer, disbelief reflected in his eyes. It was not the crocodiles or the fish that gripped his concentration; it was the vessel floating in swirls that indicated the current of a river. The craft should have been a depiction of an Egyptian-style boat, but it was a totally different design, far more modern. The shape above the water was a truncated pyramid, a pyramid with the top chopped off and parallel to the base. Round tubes protruded from the sides. A number of small figures stood in various poses around the deck under what appeared to be large flag stiffened by a breeze. The ship stretched nearly 4 metres across the coarse surface of the rock wall.

'An ironclad,' Pitt said incredulously. 'A Confederate States Navy ironclad.'

'It can't be, not here,' said Giordino, completely off balance.

'It can and it is,' Pitt said flatly. 'It must be the one the old prospector told us about.'

'Then it isn't a myth.'

'The local artists couldn't have painted something they'd never seen. It's even flying the correct Confederate battle ensign that was adopted near the end of the Civil War.'

'Maybe a former rebel naval officer wandering the desert after the war painted it.'

'He wouldn't have copied local art style,' Pitt said thoughtfully. 'There is nothing in this painting that reflects Western influence.'

'What do you make of the two figures standing on the casemate?' asked Giordino.

'One obviously is a ship's officer. Probably the captain.'

'And the other,' Giordino whispered, his face set in disbelief.

Pitt examined the figure next to the captain from head to toe. 'Who do you think it is?'

'I don't trust my sunburned eyes. I was hoping you'd tell me.'

Pitt's mind struggled to adjust to a set of circumstances that was completely foreign to him. 'Whoever the artist,' Pitt murmured in bewildered fascination, 'he certainly painted a remarkable likeness of Abraham Lincoln.'

427

42

Resting all day in the cool of the cave rejuvenated Pitt and Giordino to the point that they felt physically able to attempt a go for broke, nonstop crossing of the naked and hostile land to the Trans-Saharan Track. All thoughts and conjectures over the legendary ironclad in the desert were shelved temporarily in the recesses of their minds as they mentally prepared themselves for the almost impossible ordeal.

Late in the afternoon Pitt stepped outside the cave into the unremitting fire from the sun to set up his pipe for another compass reading. Only a few minutes in that open oven and he felt as if he was melting like a wax candle. He picked out a large rock that protruded from the horizon about 5 kilometres due east as a goal for the first hour of walking.

When he returned to the cool comfort of the cave of murals he did not have to feel the exhaustion and suffering or realize how weak he had become. His misery was all reflected in Giordino's hollow eyes, the filthy clothes, and grizzled hair, but especially in the look of a man who had come to the end of his rope.

They had endured countless dangers together, but Pitt had never seen Giordino with the look of defeat before. The psychological stress was winning over physical toughness. Giordino was pragmatic to the core. He met setbacks and hard knocks with characteristic stubbornness, assaulting them head-on. Unlike Pitt, he could not use the power of his imagination to banish the torture of thirst and the screaming pain of a body beginning to wind down from lack of food and water. He could not bring himself to sink into a dream world where torment and despair were substituted with swimming pools, tall tropical drinks, and endless buffet tables piled high with appetizing delicacies.

Pitt could see that tonight was the last. If they were to beat the desert at its deadly game, they would have to redouble their determination to survive. Another twenty-four hours without water would finish them off. No strength would be left to go on. He was grimly afraid that the Trans-Saharan Track was a good 50 kilometres too far.

He gave Giordino another hour of rest before prodding him out of a dead sleep. 'We have to leave now if we want to make any distance before the next sun.'

Giordino opened his eyes into mere slits and struggled to a sitting position. 'Why not stay in here another day and just take it easy?'

'Too many men, women, and children are counting on us to save ourselves so we can return and save them. Every hour counts.'

The fleeting thought of the suffering women and frightened children down in the Tebezza gold mines was enough to wake Giordino from the heavy fog of sleep and bring him dazedly to his feet. Then at Pitt's urging, they feebly managed a few minutes of stretching exercises to loosen their aching muscles and stiff joints. One last look at the astounding rock paintings, their eyes lingering on the image of the rebel ironclad, and they set out across the great, sloping plateau, Pitt leading off toward the rock he'd pinpointed to the east.

This was it. Except for short rest stops, they had to forge on until they reached the track and were found by a passing motorist, hopefully one with a hefty supply of water. Whatever happened, searing heat, sand driven by the wind that blasted skin, difficult terrain, they had to keep going until they dropped or found rescue.

After having done its damage for the day, the sun slipped away and a swollen half moon took its place. Not a breath of air stirred the sand and the desert went profoundly still and silent. The desolate landscape seemed to reach into infinity, and the rocks protruding from the plateau like dinosaur bones still gave off shimmering waves from the day's heat. Nothing moved except the shadows that crept and lengthened behind the rocks like wraiths coming to life in the evening's fading light.

They walked on for seven hours. The rock used as a compass point came and went as the night wore on and became colder. Dreadfully weak and wasted, they began to shiver uncontrollably. The extreme ups and downs in temperature made Pitt feel as if he was experiencing seasonal changes, with the heat of day as summer, the evening as fall, midnight as winter, morning as spring.

The change in terrain came so gradually, he didn't realize the rocks and iron outcroppings had grown smaller and vanished completely. Only when he stopped to glance up at the stars for a heading and then looked ahead did he see they had come off the gradual slope of the plateau onto a flat plain cut by a series of wadis, or dry streams, carved out by long dead water flows or forgotten flash floods.

Their progress slowed with fatigue and tapered to a plodding stumble. The weariness, the sheer exhaustion, were like weights they were forced to carry on their shoulders. They walked and kept on walking, their misery deepening. Yet they made slow and even progress toward the east on what little strength they could spare. They were so weak that after the rest stops they could hardly rise to their feet and take up the struggle again.

Pitt kept himself going with images of how O'Bannion and Melika were treating the women and children in that hell pit of a mine. He had visions of Melika's thong viciously striking helpless victims and slaves, sick from deprivation and overwork. How many had died in the days since he had escaped? Had Eva been carried to the chamber of corpses? He might have pushed aside such dire thoughts, but he let them linger since they only served to spur him to become a man beside himself, ignoring the suffering and continuing with the cold fortitude of a machine.

Pitt found it odd that he couldn't remember when he last spit. Though he sucked on small pebbles to relieve the relentless thirst, he could not even recall when he felt saliva in his mouth. His tongue had swelled like a dry sponge and felt as if it was dusted with alum, and yet he found he could still swallow.

They had lessened the loss of perspiration by walking in the cool of night and keeping their shirts on during the day to help control sweat evaporation without missing some of its cooling effects. But he realized that their bodies were badly desalinated, which contributed to their weakened condition.

Pitt tried every trick he could dredge up from his memory on desert survival, including breathing through his nose to prevent water loss and talking very little, and only then when they took a rest.

They came to a narrow river of sand that ran through a valley of boulder-strewn hills. They followed the riverbed until it turned ·north, and then climbed its bank and continued on their course. Another day was breaking, and Pitt paused to check Fairweather's map, holding up the tattered paper away from the brightening sky in the east. The rough drawing indicated a vast dry lake that stretched nearly unbroken to the Trans-Saharan Track. Though the level ground made for easier walking, Pitt saw a murderous environment, an open holocaust where shade did not exist.

There could be no resting during the fiery heat of the day. The ground was too gravelly firm to burrow under its surface. They would have to keep going and endure heat with the ferocity of an open flame. Already the sun was bursting into the sky and signalling another day of hideous torture.

The agony wore on and a few clouds appeared, hiding the sun, giving the men nearly two hours of grateful relief. And then the clouds drifted on and dissipated and the sun returned, hotter than ever. By noon Pitt and Giordino were barely clinging to life. If the heat of the day didn't conquer their agonized bodies the long night of intense cold surely would.

Then abruptly, they came to a deep ravine with steeply sloping banks that dropped 7 metres below the surface of the dry lake, slicing across it almost like a man-made canal. Because he was staring down at the ground Pitt nearly walked off the edge. He staggered to a halt, gazing despairingly at the unexpected barrier. There was simply not enough left in him to climb down into the bottom of the ravine and struggle up the other side. Giordino stumbled up beside him and collapsed, his body sagging limply before sinking to the ground, his head and arms hanging over the rim of the ravine.

As Pitt gazed across the crack in the dry lake at the vast nothingness ahead, he knew their epic struggle of endurance had come to an end. They had covered only 30 kilometres and there were another 50 to go.

Giordino slowly turned and looked up at Pitt, who was still on his feet, but swaying unsteadily, gazing at the eastern horizon as if seeing the goal that was tantalizingly near but impossible to reach.

Pitt, spent and played out as he was, appeared magnificent. His rugged, severe face, his full stature, his incisive piercing opaline eyes, his nose thrust forward like a bird of prey, his head enveloped by a dusty white towel through which straggled the strands of his wavy black hair — none gave him the appearance of a man suffering defeat and facing certain death.

His gaze swept the bottom of the ravine in both directions and stopped, a puzzled expression forming in the eyes that peered through the narrow opening in his towelled turban. 'My sanity is gone,' he whispered.

Giordino lifted his head. 'I lost mine about 20 kilometres back on the trail.'

'I swear I see . . .' Pitt shook his head slowly and rubbed his eyes. 'It must be a mirage.'

Giordino stared across the great empty furnace. Sheets of water shimmered in the distance under the heat waves. The imagined sight of what he so desperately craved was more than Giordino could bear. He turned away.

'Do you see it?' Pitt asked.

'With my eyes closed,' Giordino rasped faintly. 'I can see a saloon with dancing girls beckoning with huge mugs of ice cold beer.'

'I'm serious.'

'So am I, but if you mean that phoney lake out there on the flats, forget it.'

'No,' Pitt said briefly. 'I mean that airplane down there in the gully.'

At first, Giordino thought his friend had lost it, but then he slowly rolled back on his stomach and stared downward in the direction Pitt was facing.

Nothing manufactured by man disintegrates or rots in the desert. The worst that can occur is the pitting of metal by the driving sand. There, resting against one bank of the sterile streambed like an alien aberration, scoured and rustless, with almost no erosion or coating of dust, sat a wrecked airplane. It appeared to be an old high-wing monoplane that had lain in crippled solitude for several decades.

'Do you see it?' Pitt repeated. 'Or have I gone mad?'

'Not if I've gone mad too,' said Giordino in abject astonishment. 'It looks like a plane all right.'

'Then it must be real.'

Pitt helped Giordino to his feet, and they stumbled along the brink of the ravine until they were standing directly over the wreck. The fabric on the fuselage and wings was amazingly still intact, and they could plainly read the identification numbers. The aluminium propeller had shattered when it came in contact with the bank, and the radial engine with its exposed cylinders was partially shoved back into the cockpit and tilted upward in broken mountings. But for that, and the collapsed landing gear, the plane seemed little damaged. They saw, too, the indentations on the ground, made when the plane made contact before running off the edge into the bottom of the dry wash.

'How long do you think it's been here?' croaked Giordino.

'At least fifty, maybe sixty years,' Pitt replied.

'The pilot must have survived and walked out.'

'He didn't survive,' said Pitt. 'Under the port wing. The legs of a body are showing.'

Giordino's stare moved beneath the left wing. One old-fashioned lace-up leather boot and a section of tattered khaki pants protruded from under the shadow of the wing. 'Think he'll mind if we join him? He's got the only shade in town.'

'My thoughts precisely,' said Pitt, stepping off the edge and sliding down the steep bank on his back, raising his knees and using his feet as brakes.

Giordino was right beside him, and together they dropped into the dry streambed in a shower of loose gravel and dust. As in their initial excitement during their discovery of the cave of the paintings, all cravings of thirst were temporarily deprived of stimulation as they staggered to their feet and approached the long-dead pilot.

Sand had drifted over the lower part of the figure that lay with its back resting against the fuselage of the airplane.

A crude crutch fashioned from a wing strut lay near one exposed foot that was missing a boot. The aircraft's compass lay nearby, half embedded in the sand.

The pilot was amazingly well preserved. The fiery heat and the frigid cold had worked together to mummify the body so that any skin that showed was darkened and smoothly textured like tanned leather. There was a recognizable expression of tranquillity and contentment on the face, and the hands, rigid from over sixty years of inertness, were clasped peacefully across the stomach. An early flier's leather helmet with goggles lay draped over one leg. Black hair, matted and stiff and filled with dust after weathering the elements for so long, fell below the shoulders.

'My God,' muttered Giordino dazedly. 'It's a woman.'

'In her early thirties,' observed Pitt. 'She must have been very pretty.'

'I wonder who she was,' Giordino panted curiously.

Pitt stepped around the body and untied a packet wrapped in oilskin that was attached to the cockpit door handle. He carefully pulled open the oilskin, which revealed a pilot's log book. He opened the cover and read the first page.

'Kitty Mannock,' Pitt read the name aloud.

'Kitty who?'

'Mannock, a famous lady flier, Australian as I recall. Her disappearance became one of aviation's greatest mysteries, second only to that of Amelia Earhart.'

'How did she come to be here?' asked Giordino, unable to take his eyes off her body.

'She was trying for a record-breaking flight from London to Cape Town. After she vanished, the French military forces in the Sahara made a systematic search but found no trace of her or her plane.'

'Too bad she came down in the only ravine within 100 kilometres. She'd have easily been spotted from the air if she'd landed on the dry lake's surface.'

Pitt thumbed through the pages in the log book until they went blank. 'She crashed on October 10, 1931. Her last entry was written on October 20.'

'She survived ten days,' Giordino murmured in admiration. 'Kitty Mannock must have been one tough lady.' He stretched out under the shade of the wing and sighed wearily through his cracked and swollen lips. 'After all this time she's finally going to have company.'

Pitt wasn't listening. His attention was focused on a wild thought. He slipped the log book into his pants pocket and began examining the remains of the aircraft. He paid no regard to the engine, checking out the landing gear instead. Though the struts were flattened out from the impact, the wheels were undamaged and the tyres showed little sign of rot. The small tail wheel was also in good condition.

Next he studied the wings. The port wing had suffered minor damage and it appeared that Kitty had cut a large piece of fabric from it, but the right was still in surprisingly good shape. The fabric covering the spars and ribbing was hard and brittle with thousands of cracks, but had not split under the extremes of heat and cold. Lost in thought, he laid a hand on an exposed metal panel in front of the cockpit and jerked his hand back in pain. The metal was as hot as a well-flamed frying pan. Inside the fuselage he found a small toolbox that also included a small hack saw and a tyre repair kit with hand pump.

He stood there in contemplation, seemingly untouched by the sun's blasting heat. His face was gaunt, his body parched and wasted. He should have been immobilized in a hospital bed being pumped full of fluids. The old guy with the hood and scythe was centimetres away from laying a bony finger on his shoulder. But Pitt's mind still smoothly turned, balancing the pros and cons.

He decided then and there he wasn't going to die.

He moved round the tip of the right wing and approached Giordino. 'You ever read *The Flight of the Phoenix* by Elleston Trevor?' he asked.

Giordino squinted up at him. 'No, but I saw the movie with Jimmy Stewart. Why? Your tyres need rotting if you think you can make this wreck fly again.'

'Not fly.' Pitt replied quietly. 'I've checked out the plane, and I think we can cannibalize enough parts to build a land yacht.'

'Build a land yacht,' Giordino echoed in exasperation. 'Sure, and we can stock a bar and a dining room − '

'Like an ice boat, only it sails on wheels,' Pitt continued, deaf to Giordino's sarcasm.

'What do you intend to use for a sail?'

'One wing of the aircraft. It's basically an elliptical airfoil. Stand it on end with the wing tip up and you've got a sail.'

'We haven't enough left in us,' Giordino protested. 'A make-over like you're suggesting would take days.'

'No, hours. The starboard wing is in good shape, the fabric still intact. We can use the centre section of the fuselage between the cockpit and the tail for a hull. Using struts and spars, we can fabricate extended runners. With the two landing gear wheels and small tail wheel, we can work out a tricycle gear system. And we have more than enough control cable for rigging and a tiller setup.'

'What about tools?'

'There's a tool kit in the cockpit. Not the best, but it should serve the purpose.'

Giordino shook his head slowly, wonderingly, from side to side. It would have been the easiest thing in the world to cross Pitt's idea off to a hallucination, lie back on the ground, and let death peacefully carry him off to oblivion. The temptation was overwhelming. But deep inside him beat a heart that wouldn't quit and a brain that could not die without a fight. With the effort of a sick man lifting a heavy weight, he heaved himself to his feet and spoke, his words slurred from fatigue and overexposure to the heat.

'No sense in laying around here feeling sorry for ourselves. You remove the wing mounts and I'll disassemble the wheels.'

43

In the shade of one wing Pitt outlined his concept for building a land yacht, using bits and pieces from the old aircraft. Incredibly simple in scope, it was a plan born in a desert crypt by men who were dead but refused to accept it. To construct the craft they would have to reach even deeper within themselves to find the strength they thought was long gone.

Land sailing was nothing new. The Chinese used it two thousand years ago. So did the Dutch who raised sails on lumbering wagons to move small armies. American railroaders often built small carts with sails to breeze along tracks across the prairies. The Europeans turned it into a sport on their resort beaches in the early 1900s, and then it was only a matter of time before Southern California hot-rodders, racing their souped-up cars across the Mojave Desert's dry lakes, picked up on the idea, eventually holding organized racing events that drew participants from around the world who attained speeds close to 145 kilometres or 90 miles an hour.

Using the tools Pitt found in the cockpit, he and Giordino tackled the easiest jobs during the broiling afternoon and took on the heavier tasks in the cool of the evening. For men whose favourite pastimes were restoring old classic cars and airplanes the work went smoothly and efficiently with little wasted motion to conserve what little energy they had left.

They remembered little about their efforts as they worked fervently toward a finality, driving themselves without rest, talking little because their swollen tongues and dust-dry mouths made it difficult. The moon lit their activities, casting their animated shadows against the bank of the ravine.

They reverently left Kitty Mannock's body untouched, working around her without any display of emotion, sometimes addressing her as if she was alive as their thirst-crazed minds wandered in and out of limbo.

Giordino removed the two large landing wheels and small tail wheel, cleaned the grit from the bearings, and relubricated them with sludge from the engine's oil filter. The old rubber tyres were cracked and sun-hardened. They still retained their shape, but there was no hope of them holding air, so Giordino removed the brittle innertubes, filled the tyre casings with sand, and remounted them on the wheels.

Next he constructed runner extensions for the wheels from ribs he disassembled from the damaged wing. When finished, he cut the longitudinal spars attaching the centre fuselage to the bulkhead just behind the cockpit with the hack saw. Then he did the same with the tail section. After the midsection came free he began fastening the wider cockpit end to the fabricated wing extensions to support the two main landing wheels. The wheels now stretched 2.5 metres from the bottom side of the fuselage at its largest end. The opposite end that had tapered to the tail section was now the front of the land yacht, giving it a primitive aerodynamic appearance. The final touch to what now became the hull of the craft was the building of a runner bolted to the small tail wheel that extended 3 metres out in front. The nearly completed product resembled, to anyone old enough to remember the *Our Gang and the Little Rascals* comedies, a 1930s backyard soapbox racer.

While Giordino was knocking together the hull, Pitt concentrated on the sail. Once the wing had been detached from the plane's fuselage, he stiffened the ailerons and flaps and extended the heavier spar inside the leading edge so that it formed a mast. Together, he and Giordino lifted the wing into a vertical position, stepped the mast into the centre of the hull and mounted it, a job made easy by the lightness of the desert-dried wooden spars and fabric covering of the old airfoil. What they had created was a pivoting wind sail. Next Pitt used the aircraft's control cables to attach guy wires from Giordino's side runners, and the bow to the mast as supports. He then fashioned a tiller steering apparatus from the interior of the hull to the front runner and wheel with the aircraft's control cables. Finally, he fitted out a rigging system for the wind sail.

The finishing touches were the removal of the pilot's seats and their placement in the land yacht's cockpit, installing them in tandem. Pitt also unscrewed the aircraft compass from its instrument panel and mounted it beside the tiller. The tube he had used as a compass to guide their path this far, he tied to the mast for a good luck souvenir.

They completed the job at three in the morning and then dropped like dead men in the sand. They lay there shivering in the bitter cold, staring at their masterpiece.

'It'll never fly,' Giordino muttered, totally spent.

'She only has to move us across the flats.'

'Have you figured out how we're going to get it out of the gulch?'

'About 50 metres down the valley, the incline of the east bank becomes gradual enough to pull it onto the surface of the dry lake.'

'We'll be lucky to walk that far much less drag this thing up a slope. And at that, there's no guarantee it'll work.'

'All we need is a light wind,' said Pitt, scarcely audible. 'And if the last six days are any indication, we don't have to worry on that score.'

'Nothing like pursuing the impossible dream.'

'She'll go,' Pitt said resolutely.

'What do you think she weighs?'

'About 160 kilograms or 350 pounds.'

'What are we going to call her?' asked Giordino.

'Call her?'

'A name, she's got to have a name.'

Pitt nodded toward Kitty. 'If we make it out of this pressure cooker, we'll owe it to her. How about the *Kitty Mannock*?'

'Good choice.'

They babbled vaguely and sporadically, whispered voices in a great void of dead space, until they drifted off into a welcome sleep.

The bleaching sun was probing the bottom of the ravine when they finally awoke. Just rising to their feet was a monumental task of will. They bid a silent goodbye to Kitty and then staggered to the front of their improvised hope of survival. Pitt tied two lengths of cable to the front of the land yacht and handed one to Giordino.

'You feel up to it?'

'Hell no,' Giordino spat out of a shrivelled mouth.

Pitt grinned despite the pain from his cracked and bleeding lips. His eyes raked Giordino's, searching for the glow that would see them through. It was there, but very dim. 'Race you to the top.'

Giordino swayed as though like a drunk in a wind storm, but he winked and gamely said, 'Eat my dust, sucker.' And then he slung the cable over his shoulder, leaned forward to take up the strain, and promptly fell on his face.

The land yacht rolled as easily as a shopping cart across the tile floor of a supermarket and almost ran over him.

He looked up at Pitt through red eyes, surprise on his sunburned face. 'By God she moves light as a feather.'

'Of course, she had a pair of first-rate mechanics.'

With no more talk they pulled their hand-built land yacht down the middle of the wash until they came to a slope that angled 30 degrees up to the surface of the dry lake.

The climb was only 7 metres, but to men who were staring in the grave only eighteen hours before, the top edge of the slope looked like the summit of Mount Everest. They had not expected to live through another night, and yet here they were confronting what they were certain was the final obstacle between rescue or death.

Pitt made the attempt first while Giordino rested. He clasped one of the tow cables around his waist and began crawling up the incline like a drunken ant, edging upward a few centimetres at a time. His body was but a terribly worn-out machine serving the demands of a mind that had only the thinnest grip on reality. His aching muscles protested with shooting agony. His arms and legs gave out early in the climb, but he forced them to carry on. His bloodshot eyes were almost closed from fatigue, his face deeply etched in suffering, lungs sucking in air with painful gasps, heart beating like a jackhammer under the inhuman strain.

Pitt could not let himself stop. If he and Giordino died, all the poor souls slaving their lives away at Tebezza would die too, their true fate unknown to the outside world. He could not give up, collapse, and expire, not now, not this close to beating the old guy with the scythe. He ground his teeth together in a rage of tenacity and kept climbing.

Giordino tried to shout words of encouragement, but all he could rasp out was an inaudible whisper.

And then mercifully, Pitt's hands groped over the edge and he summoned the will to pull his battered body onto the dry lake. He lay there a faint shadow away from unconsciousness, aware of only his hoarse gasping breathing and a heart that felt as if it was going to pound its way through his rib cage.

He wasn't sure how long he lay fully exposed under the baking sun until his breathing and heart slowed to something close to a regular pace. Finally, he pushed to his hands and knees and peered down the slope. Giordino was sitting comfortably in the shade of the wing sail, and managed a weak wave.

'Ready to come up?' Pitt asked.

Giordino wearily nodded, took hold of the tow cable, and pressed his body against the slope, feebly working his way upward. Pitt slung his end of the cable over his shoulder and used the leverage of his weight by leaning forward without exerting energy. Four minutes later, half crawling, half dragged by Pitt, Giordino rolled limply onto flat ground like a fish that had been reeled in after a long struggle against hook and line.

'Now comes the fun part,' Pitt uttered weakly.

'I'm not up to it,' Giordino gasped.

Pitt looked down at him. Giordino already looked dead. His eyes were closed, his face and ten-day beard powdered with white dust. If he could not help Pitt pull the land yacht out of the ravine both of them would die this day.

Pitt knelt down and struck him sharply across the face. 'Don't quit on me now,' he muttered harshly. 'How do you expect to score with Massarde's gorgeous piano player if you don't get off your butt and pitch in.'

Giordino's eyes fluttered open and he rubbed a hand across his dust-coated cheek. With a supreme effort of will, he hauled himself to his feet and tottered drunkenly. He stared at Pitt without any malice at all, and despite his misery, he managed a grin. 'I hate myself for being so predictable.'

'Good thing too.'

Like a team of emaciated mules in harness, they took up the tow cables and pitched forward, their bodies too weak to do much more than take a few plodding steps as their combined weight slowly but immeasurably pulled the land yacht up the slope. Their heads were bowed, backs hunched

444

over, minds lost in the delirium of thirst. Progress was heartbreakingly slow.

Soon they dropped to their knees and pitifully crawled forward. Giordino noticed that blood was dripping from Pitt's hands where the cable had burned into his palms, but he was entirely oblivious to it. Then suddenly the cables slackened and the improvised land yacht was over the top and had bumped into them. Fortunately Pitt had the foresight to tie down the rigging of the wind sail so its trailing edge was now pointing directly into a light wind and did not generate any driving force.

After unclasping the tow cables, Pitt helped Giordino into the fuselage until he dropped like a sack of potatoes in the forward seat. Then Pitt looked up at the thin strip of tell-tale cloth he'd tied in the rigging and threw a handful of sand in the air to pinpoint the wind direction. It was blowing out of the northwest.

The moment of truth had arrived. He looked down at Giordino who made a listless forward gesture with one hand and spoke in a weak, husky whisper.

'Move it out.'

Pitt leaned on the rear of the fuselage and pushed the craft from a standstill until it was moving slowly across the sand. After a few stumbling steps he fell limply into the rear seat. The wind was to the leeward behind his left shoulder, and he let out the sheet line and eased over the tiller so that he was carried on a downwind tack. He took in a little on the sheet line as the wind built up on the wing sail and the *Kitty Mannock* began to move on her own. Her speed picked up rapidly as Pitt took in a little more line.

He glanced down at the aircraft compass, took a reading, and set his course, exhaustion and exhilaration flooding through his seemingly dusty arteries at the same time. He trimmed the wing sail as it flexed under the wind and soon the land yacht was whipping across the dry lake, her wheels kicking up trails of dust, in glorious silence at nearly 60 kilometres an hour.

The thrill quickly reversed to near panic as Pitt overcorrected and suddenly there was daylight under the windward wheel. Higher it lifted in a condition known among land sailors as *hiking*. He had moved the sail too far into the wind, increasing power. Now he had to take corrective action to prevent the hike from capsizing the land yacht, a disaster in the making because neither he nor Giordino had the strength to right it again.

He was almost at the point of no return when he eased the sheet lines and gently swung the tiller, sending the craft luffing to windward. He held his course and the hike settled and shallowed until the wheel was barely touching the ground.

Pitt had sailed small boats when he was a boy growing up in Newport Beach, California, but certainly never at this speed. As he headed off the wind on a broad reach angle of 45 degrees, he began fine-trimming his huge wing sail with the sheet lines and small steering corrections. A quick check of his compass heading told him it was time to tack on a new zigzag course eastward.

As he began to feel more confident, he had to restrain himself from pushing and challenging the outside edge, the high speed line that divides control from an accident. He wasn't about to back off now, but discretion reminded him that the *Kitty Mannock* was not the most stable of land yachts, and she was held together with little more than sixty-year-old wire, cable, and spit.

He settled back and kept a wary eye on the dust devils that swirled across the desolate lake. A sudden puff or gust out of nowhere and over they'd go, never to continue. Pitt well knew they were riding on luck. Another ravine, unseen until it was too late, or a rock that could tear off a runner, any one of a dozen catastrophes could leap at them from the merciless desert.

She skidded and she yawed but the *Kitty Mannock* sped across the dry lake at speeds Pitt had not imagined the oddball craft was capable of. The head wind began driving sand into his face like buckshot. With a steadily increasing wind at his back he guessed they were reaching 85 kilometres an hour. After plodding across the desert wastes for days, it seemed as though they were skimming over the ground in a jet. He hoped against hope the *Kitty Mannock* would hang together.

After half an hour, his stinging eyes swept the unvaried landscape ahead in search of an object to rest upon. Pitt's new worry was passing over the Trans-Saharan Track without recognizing it. An easy proposition since it was only a vague trail in the sand that ran from north to south. Miss it and they would virtually head out into the miraged immensity of the desert and beyond until it was too late to return.

He saw no sign of vehicles, and the terrain became warted again with rolling dunes. Had they crossed over the border into Algeria, he wondered. There was no way to tell. Any sign of the great caravans that had marched between the once lush Niger Valley and the Mediterranean with their cargos of gold, ivory, and slaves had long ago vanished into history without leaving debris of their passing. In their place, a few cars with tourists, trucks carrying parts and supplies, and the occasional army vehicle on patrol were all that sometimes rolled through the barren wilderness that God ignored.

If Pitt had known that in reality the neat red line indicating the track on maps did not exist as such, and was a figment of cartographers' imaginations, he would have been extremely frustrated. The only true indications, if he were lucky enough to spot them, were scattered bones of animals, a solitary stripped vehicle, tyre tracks that had not been covered by wind-blown sand, and a string of old oil drums spaced 4 kilometres apart, providing the latter hadn't been borrowed by passing nomads for reuse or resale in Gao.

Then, near the horizon on his right, he saw a man-made object, a dark speck in a shimmering heat wave. Giordino saw it too and pointed toward it, the first sign of life from him since the land yacht was launched. The air was clear and transparent as glass. They had sailed off the dry lake, and no dust reared from the ground or swirled in the air. They distinguished the object now as the forsaken remains of a Volkswagen bus, stripped of every conceivable part that wasn't part of the body and frame. Only the shell was left, an ironic slogan sprayed on the side with a can of paint that read in English, 'Where is Lawrence of Arabia when you need him?'

Satisfied they had reached the track, Pitt gybed on a new course and swung north, beating to windward. The terrain had turned sandy with stretches of gravel. Occasionally they struck a soft patch, but the land yacht was too light to sink in and gracefully skimmed right over with only a slight drop in momentum.

After ten minutes, Pitt spied an oil drum standing starkly on the horizon. Now he was positive they were speeding along the track, and he began a series of 2-kilometre tacks northward into Algeria.

There was no further movement from Giordino. Pitt reached forward and shook his shoulder, but the head slowly leaned to one side before dropping forward, chin on chest. Giordino had finally lost his grip on consciousness and was drifting away. Pitt tried to shout, roughly shake his friend, but he couldn't find the strength. He could see the blackness growing around the edge of his own vision and knew he was only minutes away from blacking out.

He heard what he thought was an engine off in the distance but saw nothing ahead and crossed it off to delirium. The sound grew louder and he vaguely recognized it as a diesel engine accompanied by the loud rumble of exhaust. Still there was no sign of the source. He was certain now oblivion was about to wash over him.

Then came the great blast from an air horn, and Pitt turned his head weakly to one side. A big British-built Bedford truck and trailer was pulling alongside, the Arab driver staring down on the two figures in the land yacht with curious eyes and a wide toothy smile. Unknown to Pitt, the truck had overhauled them from the rear.

The driver leaned out his window, cupped one hand to his mouth, and shouted, 'Do you need help?'

Pitt could only nod faintly.

He had made no provisions for braking the boat to a stop. He made a languid attempt to pull the sheet line and bring the sail into the wind, but he only succeeded in turning the boat in a half circle. His senses weren't functioning properly and he badly misjudged a sudden gust. He let the sheet go but was too late. Wind and gravity took the craft away from him and it flipped over, tearing off runners and wind sail and throwing Pitt and Giordino's bodies out across the sand like limp, stuffed dolls in a cloud of dust and debris.

The Arab driver veered next to them and stopped his truck. He leaped down from the cab and rushed over to the mess and stooped over the unconscious men. He immediately recognized their signs of dehydration and hurried back to the truck, returning with four plastic bottles of water.

Pitt climbed from the hole of blackness almost immediately as he sensed liquid being splashed on his face and trickled through his half open mouth. The transformation was like a miracle. One minute he was dying and then after downing almost two gallons of water he became a reasonably fit, functioning human being again.

Giordino's bone-dry body had returned to life too. It

seemed incredible they could bounce back from sure death so quickly after soaking up a healthy supply of liquid.

The Arab driver also offered them salt tablets and some dried dates. He had a dark and intelligent face and wore an unmarked baseball cap on his head. He sat on his haunches and watched the rejuvenation with great interest.

'You sail your machine from Goa?' he asked

Pitt shook his head. 'Fort Foureau,' he lied. He still was not positive they were in Algeria. Nor could he trust the truck driver not to turn them into the nearest security police if he knew they had escaped from Tebezza. 'Where exactly are we?'

'In the middle of the Tanezrouft wasteland.'

'What country?'

'Why Algeria, of course. Where did you think you were?'

'Anywhere so long as it wasn't Mali.'

The Arab made a sour expression. 'Bad people live in Mali. Bad government. They kill many people.'

'How far to the nearest telephone?' asked Pitt.

'Adrar is 350 kilometres north. They have communications.'

'Is it a small village?'

'No, Adrar is a large town, much progress. They have an airfield with regular passenger service to Algiers.'

'Are you heading in that direction?'

'Yes, I drove a load of canned goods to Goa, and now I'm deadheading back to Algiers.'

'Can you give us a lift to Adrar?'

'I would be honoured.'

Pitt looked at the driver and smiled. 'What is your name, my friend?'

'Ben Hadi.'

Pitt shook the driver's hand warmly. 'Ben Hadi,' he said softly, 'you don't know it, but by saving our lives you also saved the lives of a hundred others.'

PART FOUR

Echoes of the Alamo

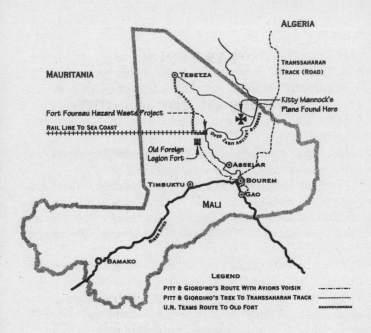

ALGERIA

MAURITANIA

○ TEBEZZA

TRANSSAHARAN
TRACK (ROAD)

Fort Foureau Hazard Waste Project

Kitty Mannock's
Plane Found Here

RAIL LINE TO SEA COAST

OUED ZARIT ANCIENT RIVERBED

Old Foreign
Legion Fort

○ ASSELAR

○ BOUREM

TIMBUKTU ○

○ GAO

MALI

NIGER RIVER

○ BAMAKO

LEGEND

PITT & GIORDINO'S ROUTE WITH AVIONS VOISIN ————
PITT & GIORDINO'S TREK TO TRANSSAHARAN TRACK ....
U.N. TEAMS ROUTE TO OLD FORT xxxxxxxxxxx

THE MALIAN SAHARA

44

May 26, 1996
Washington, D.C.

'They're out!' Hiram Yaeger shouted as he burst into Sandecker's office with Rudi Gunn at his heels.

Sandecker, his mind lost on the budget of an undersea project, looked up blankly. 'Out?'

'Dirk and Al, they've crossed over the border into Algeria.'

Sandecker suddenly looked like a kid who was told Santa Claus was coming. 'How do you know?'

'They phoned from the airport near a desert town called Adrar,' answered Gunn. 'The connection was bad, but we understood them to say they were catching a commercial flight to Algiers. Once there, they would reestablish contact from our embassy.'

'Was there anything else?' Gunn glanced at Yaeger and nodded. 'You were on the line with Dirk before I came on.'

'Pitt's voice kept fading,' said Yaeger. 'Algeria's desert phone system is only two steps above tin cans tied to waxed string. If l heard him correctly, he insisted that you request a Special Forces Team to return with him to Mali.'

'Did he explain?' Sandecker asked curiously.

'His voice was too indistinct. Interference broke up our conversation. What little I could make out sounded crazy.'

'Crazy, in what manner?' Sandecker demanded.

'He said something about rescuing women and children in a gold mine. His voice sounded strangely urgent.'

'That makes no sense at all,' said Gunn.

Sandecker stared at Yaeger. 'Did Dirk reveal how they escaped from Mali?'

Yaeger looked like a man who was lost in maze. 'Don't

quote me, Admiral, but I'd swear he said they sailed across the desert in a yacht with some woman named Kitty Manning or Manncock.'

Sandecker sat back in his chair and smiled resignedly. 'Knowing Pitt and Giordino as I do, I wouldn't put it past them.' Then abruptly his eyes narrowed and his expression turned quizzical. 'Could the name have been Kitty Mannock?'

'The name was garbled, but yes, I think that was it.'

'Kitty Mannock was a famous aviator back in the twenties,' explained Sandecker. 'She broke long-distance speed records over half the globe before vanishing in the Sahara. I believe it was back in 1931.'

'What could she possibly have to do with Pitt and Giordino?' Yaeger wondered aloud.

'I have no idea,' said Sandecker.

Gunn studied his watch. 'I checked the air distance between Adrar and Algiers. It's only a little over 1200 kilometres. If they're in the air now, we should be hearing from them in approximately an hour and a half.'

'Instruct our communications department to open a direct line to our Algerian embassy,' ordered the Admiral. 'And tell them to make sure it's secure. If Pitt and Giordino stumbled onto any vital data concerning the red tide contamination, I don't want it leaked to the news media.'

When Pitt's call came through to NUMA's worldwide communications network, Sandecker and the others, including Dr Chapman, were gathered around a phone console that recorded the conversation and amplified Pitt's voice through a speaker system so they could all converse without microphones or telephone receivers.

Most of the questions that had mounted over the past ninety minutes were answered in Pitt's precise, hour-long report. Everyone sat listening intently and making notes as he related the harrowing events and epic struggles he and Giordino endured after parting with Gunn on the Niger River. He described in detail their discovery of the fraudulent operation at Fort Foureau. He shocked them with his revelation that Dr Hopper and the World Health Organization scientists were alive and suffering as slaves in the mines of Tebezza along with Massarde's French engineers, their wives and children, plus a score of other kidnapped foreigners and political prisoners of General Kazim. He ended his report on the accidental and fortunate finding of Kitty Mannock and her long-lost aircraft as they trekked across the desert. His audience could not help smiling among themselves as he recounted the construction of the land yacht.

The men seated around the console now understood why Pitt demanded to return to Mali with an armed force. The exposure of the gold mines of Tebezza and the hideous, inhuman conditions appalled them. But they were even more stunned to hear of the secret nuclear and toxic waste underground storage at Fort Foureau. Learning that the state-of-the-art solar disposal operation was a fraud brought worried expressions on their faces as they each began to wonder how many other Massarde Enterprises hazardous waste projects around the world were cover-ups.

Pitt followed by setting them straight on the criminal relationship between Yves Massarde and Zateb Kazim. He repeated in detail what he heard during his conversations with Massarde and O'Bannion.

Then the questions came, launched by Chapman. 'You've concluded that Fort Foureau is the source of the red tide contamination?' asked Dr Chapman.

'Giordino and I are no experts on groundwater hydrology,' replied Pitt, 'but there is little doubt in our minds the toxic waste that is not burned but hidden below the desert is leaking and migrating directly into the groundwater. From there it flows beneath an old riverbed southward until it empties into the Niger.'

'How could large excavations be conducted below-ground without international environmental inspectors catching on?' asked Yaeger.

'Or discovery by satellite photos?' Gunn added.

'The key is the railroad and the cargo containers,' Pitt answered. 'The excavation did not begin during construction of the solar reactor, photovoltaic, and concentrator arrays. Only after a large building was erected to shield the operation did trains hauling in nuclear and toxic waste begin returning to Mauritania with rock and dirt from the excavation for a landfill. From what Al and I were able to examine, Massarde took advantage of already existing limestone caverns.'

Everyone was silent for a moment, then Chapman said, 'When this thing gets out, the scandal and investigations will never end.'

'Do you have documented proof?' Gunn asked Pitt.

'We can only tell you what we saw on the site and heard from Massarde. I'm sorry we can't offer you more.'

'You've done an incredible job,' said Chapman. 'Thanks to you the contaminant's source is no longer unknown, and plans can be formed to cut off its leakage into the groundwater.'

'Easier said than done,' Sandecker reminded him. 'Dirk and Al have handed us a gigantic can of worms.'

'The Admiral's right,' said Gunn. 'We can't simply walk into Fort Foureau and close it down. Yves Massarde is a powerful and wealthy man with inside connections to General Kazim and the upper levels of the French government — '

'And a lot of other powerful men in business and government,' Gunn added.

'Massarde is a secondary consideration,' Pitt cut in. 'Our

most urgent priority is to save those poor people at Tebezza before they're all killed.'

'Are any of them Americans?' asked Sandecker.

'Dr Eva Rojas is a U.S. citizen.'

'She is the only one?'

'As far as I know.'

'If no President has ever kicked ass in Lebanon to free our hostages, there's no way our current President will send in a Special Force Team to save one American.'

'Won't hurt to ask,' proposed Pitt.

'He already turned me down when I made the request to rescue you and Al.'

'Hala Kamil offered the UN Critical Response and Tactical Team before,' said Gunn. 'Surely she'll authorize a rescue mission to save her own scientists.'

'Hala Kamil is a lady with high principles,' said Sandecker with conviction. 'More idealistic than most men I know. I think we can safely rely on her to have General Bock send Colonel Levant and his men back into Mali.'

'People are dying in the mines like rats,' said Pitt, the bitterness of his tone obvious to the men listening. 'God only knows how many were murdered since Al and I escaped. Every hour counts.'

'I'll contact the Secretary General and brief her,' promised Sandecker. 'If Levant moves as fast as he did to save Rudi, I suspect you'll be explaining the situation face-to-face with him before breakfast in your time zone.'

Ninety minutes after Sandecker's call to Hala Kamil and General Bock, Colonel Levant and his men and equipment were in the air and winging over the Atlantic toward a French air force base outside of Algiers.

General Hugo Bock arranged the maps and satellite photos on his desk and picked up an antique magnifying glass that had been given to him by his grandfather when he collected stamps as a young boy. The glass was highly polished without a flaw, and when adjusted to his eyes, enlarged the image it was trained upon without distortion around the circular edges. The piece had travelled with Bock all during his army career as a kind of good luck charm.

He took a sip of coffee and began examining the area inside the small circles he'd marked on the maps and photographs that indicated the approximate location of Tebezza. Though Pitt's description of the mine site, relayed to Bock from Sandecker by fax, was a rough estimate, the general's eye soon zeroed in on the landing strip and the vague road that led off through the narrow canyon splitting the high, rooky plateau.

This fellow Pitt, he thought, was most observant.

The man must have memorized what few landmarks he had seen during his epic trek across the desert into Algeria and back-tracked them in his mind's eye to the mine.

Bock began to study the terrain of the surrounding desert and did not like what he saw. The mission to rescue Gunn from the Gao airport had been relatively simple. Launched from an Egyptian military base near Cairo, the UN force had only to swoop in and seize the Gao airport, retrieve Gunn, and be on their way. Tebezza was a much tougher nut to crack. Levant's team would have to land at the desert airstrip, travel nearly 20 kilometres to the mine entrance, assault and secure a maze of tunnels and caverns, transport God knows how many prisoners back to the airstrip, load everyone on board, and take off.

The critical problem was too much time on the ground. The transport was a sitting duck and invited attack by Kazim's air force. The time involved in a round trip of 40 kilometres over a primitive desert road considerably raised the odds of failure.

The attack could not rely purely on split-timing. There

458

were too many unknown variables. Preventing any outside communication was critical. Bock could not see how the operation could be accomplished in less than one and a half hours minimum. Two could spell disaster.

His fist cracked the desk. 'Damn!' he uttered harshly to himself. 'No time for preparation, no time for planning. An emergency mission to save lives. Hell, we'll probably lose more than we save.'

After looking at the operation from every angle, Bock sighed and dialled his desk phone. Hala Kamil's secretarial aide put him right through.

'Yes, General,' she said. 'I did not expect to hear from you so soon. Is there a problem with the rescue mission?'

'A number of them, I'm afraid, Madam Secretary. We're stretched far too thin on this one. Colonel Levant is going to need backup.'

'I'll authorize whatever additional UN forces you require.'

'We have none to spare,' explained Bock. 'My remaining forces are on security duty at the Syrian-Israeli border or performing civilian rescue operations during the unrest and rioting inside India. Colonel Levant's backup will have to come from outside the UN.'

There was a moment of silence as Hala assembled her thoughts. 'This is most difficult,' she said finally. 'I'm not sure who I can turn to.'

'What about the Americans?'

'Unlike his predecessors, their new President is most reluctant to interfere in the problems of third world nations. As a point of fact, it was he who requested that I authorize you to save the two men from NUMA.'

'Why was I not informed?' Bock asked.

'Admiral Sandecker could provide us with no intelligence as to their exact whereabouts. While waiting for leads, they escaped on their own, making any rescue attempt unnecessary.'

'Tebezza will not be a swift and sure operation,' Bock said grimly.

'Can you guarantee me success?' asked Hala.

'I'm confident in the ability of my men, Madam Secretary, but I cannot make any guarantees. If anything, I fear the cost in casualties will be high.'

'We cannot sit back and do nothing,' Hala said solemnly. 'Dr Hopper and his team of scientists are members of the UN. It is our duty to save our own people.'

'I quite agree,' said Bock. 'But I'd feel more secure if we could count on a backup force should Colonel Levant become trapped by Malian military forces.'

'Perhaps the British or the French will be more willing — '

'The Americans can mount a more rapid response,' Bock interrupted. 'If I had my way, I would demand their Delta Force.'

Hala went quiet, reluctant to give a concession, knowing the Chief Executive of the United States would prove stubborn and noncommittal. 'I will talk with the President and present our case,' Hala said resignedly. 'I can do no more.'

'Then I shall inform Colonel Levant there is no room for misjudgment or error, and that he can expect no help.'

'Perhaps he will benefit from luck.'

Bock breathed deeply. He could feel a cold chill of apprehension down his spine. 'Whenever I banked on luck, Madam Secretary, something always went terribly wrong.'

St Julien Perlmutter was sitting in his immense library that housed thousands of books, most neatly arranged on varnished mahogany shelves. At least two hundred, however, were haphazardly stacked and scattered loosely around the Persian carpet or piled on a badly worn rolltop desk. He sat with slippered feet propped on the untidy desktop reading a seventeenth-century manuscript while

460

dressed in his uniform of the day, silk pyjamas under a paisley robe.

Perlmutter was a legendary expert on maritime history. His collection of historical records and literature on ships and the sea was considered the finest in the world. Museum curators around the nation would have happily given any limb he requested or a blank cheque to obtain his massive library. But money mattered little to a man with a fifty-million-dollar inheritance, except to purchase additional rare books about the sea he didn't already own.

Love of women didn't come close to his love of research. If any man or woman could passionately give an hour lecture on any shipwreck ever recorded, it was St Julien Perlmutter. Every salvager and treasure hunter in Europe and America sooner or later showed up on his doorstep for guidance.

A monster of a man, he weighed nearly 181 kilograms, or 400 pounds. He was a product of gourmet food and drink and little or no exercise beyond picking up a book and opening its pages. He had merry sky-blue eyes and a red face buried under a huge grey beard.

His phone rang, and he pushed aside several opened books to reach it. 'Perlmutter here.'

'Julien, it's Dirk Pitt.'

'Dirk, my boy,' he fairly shouted. 'A long time since I've heard your voice.'

'Can't be more than three weeks.'

'Who counts the hours when one is on the track of a shipwreck,' he laughed.

'Certainly not you or I.'

'Why don't you hop over for a bite of my famous Crepes Perlmutter?'

'I'm afraid they'd get cold by the time I arrived,' Pitt replied.

'Where are you?'

'Algiers.'

Perlmutter snorted. 'What are you doing in that dreadful place?'

'Among other things, I'm interested in a shipwreck.'

'In the Med off North Africa?'

'No, in the Sahara Desert.'

Perlmutter knew Pitt too well to know he was joking. 'I'm familiar with the legend of a ship in the California desert above the Sea of Cortez, but I'm not aware of one in the Sahara.'

'I've run across three different references to it,' Pitt explained. 'One source was an old American desert rat who was looking for a Confederate ironclad called the *Texas*. He swore it steamed up a now dry river and became lost in the sand. Supposedly it was carrying gold from the Confederate treasury.'

'Where do you find them?' Perlmutter laughed. 'What sort of desert weed was this fellow smoking?'

'He also claimed that Lincoln was on board.'

'Now you've gone from the ridiculous to pure humbug.'

'Strange as it sounds, I believed him. And then I found two other sources for the legend. One was an old rock painting in a cave that showed what had to be a Confederate design warship. The other was a reference to a sighting in a log book I found in Kitty Mannock's airplane.'

'Hold on a minute,' Perlmutter said sceptically. 'Whose airplane?'

'Kitty Mannock.'

'You found her! My God, she vanished over sixty years ago. You really discovered her crash site?'

'Al Giordino and I stumbled on her body and the wreck of the plane in a hidden ravine while we were crossing the desert.'

'Congratulations!' Perlmutter boomed. 'You've just cleared up one of aviation's most famous mysteries.'

'Pure luck on our part,' Pitt admitted.

'Who's paying for this call?'

'The U.S. embassy in Algiers.'

'In that case, hold the line. I'll be right back.' Perlmutter hefted his bulk from the desk chair, ambled over to a bookshelf, and scanned its contents for a few seconds. Finding the book he was looking for, he pulled it out, returned to the desk, and thumbed through the pages. Then he retrieved the phone. 'You did say the name of the ship was the *Texas*?'

'Yes, that's it.'

'An ironclad ram,' Perlmutter recited. 'She was built at the Rocketts naval yard in Richmond and launched in March of 1865, just a month before the war ended, 190 foot length with a 40-foot beam. Twin engines, twin screws, drawing 11 feet of water, 6-inch armour. Her battery consisted of two 100-pound Blakelys and two 9-inch, 64-pounders. Speed, 14 knots.' Perlmutter paused. 'You get all that?'

'She sounds like a pretty powerful ship for her day.'

'Yes indeed, and about twice as fast as any other armoured vessel in both the Union and Confederate navies.'

'What was her history?'

'Pretty short,' answered Perlmutter. 'Her one and only appearance in combat was an epic running fight down the James River through an entire Union navy fleet and past the forts in Hampton Roads. Badly damaged, she escaped into the Atlantic and was never seen again.'

'Then her disappearance was a reality,' said Pitt.

'Yes, but hardly an unnatural phenomenon. Since none of the Confederate ironclads were built for other than river and harbour duty, they were unsafe for ocean passage. It was generally thought she floundered in rough water and sank.'

'You think it possible she could have crossed the ocean to West Africa and steamed up the Niger River?'

'The *Atlanta* is the only other Confederate ironclad I

recall that tried to cross open water. She was captured during a fight with two Union monitors on Wassaw Sound in Georgia. About a year after the war she was sold to the King of Haiti for his navy. She left Chesapeake Bay for the Caribbean and vanished. Crews that served on her claimed she took on water even in mild weather.'

'And yet the old prospector swore French colonists and natives handed down stories of an iron monster without sails going up the Niger.'

'Do you want me to check it out?'

'Could you?'

'I'm hooked already,' said Perlmutter. 'I see another little enigma that makes the *Texas* so interesting.'

'What's that?' asked Pitt.

'I'm looking at the bible of Civil War navies,' replied Perlmutter slowly. 'They all list several or more references for additional research. The poor *Texas* has no references at all. It's almost as if someone meant for her to be forgotten.'

45

Pitt and Giordino discreetly left the American embassy through the lobby of the passport office, stepped out onto the street, and hailed a taxi. Pitt gave the driver directions written down in French by an embassy aide and settled back as the taxi wove through the main square past the city's picturesque mosques with their towering minarets. Their luck of the draw was a hyper driver who constantly honked and cursed the crowds of pedestrians and heavy auto traffic that flowed blissfully through stop lights and past policemen who showed little interest in controlling the mess.

At the main thoroughfare that paralleled the busy waterfront, the driver swung south and drove to the city's outskirts where he stopped in a winding alley as instructed. Pitt paid him off and waited until the taxi turned out of sight. In less than a minute, a French air force staff car pulled up, a 605 Peugeot diesel sedan. They climbed into the back seat without any acknowledgment from the uniformed driver, who accelerated down the alley before Giordino closed the rear door.

Ten kilometres later, the car stopped at the main gate of a military airfield flying the tricolor over the sentry house. The security guard took one look at the Peugeot and nodded it through as he threw a sharp French salute with the palm facing outward. At the entrance to the tarmac the driver stopped and inserted the staff of a chequered flag into a socket mounted on the left front fender.

'Don't tell me,' said Giordino, I'm keen to guess. We're the grand marshals in a parade.'

Pitt laughed. 'Have you forgotten your air force days?

Any vehicle that drives across the flight line has to fly an authorization flag.'

The Peugeot rolled by a long row of Mirage 2000 delta wing fighters being serviced by their ground crews. One end of the flight line held a squadron of AS-332 Super Puma helicopters that looked as if they were designed by a myopic Buck Rogers. Built to carry air-to-surface missiles, they did not have the killer look of most other attack helicopters.

The driver continued to the deserted end of a secondary runway and parked. They sat there waiting, Giordino promptly dozing off under the comfort of the staff cars air conditioning, while Pitt casually read an embassy copy of the *Wall Street Journal*.

Fifteen minutes later a big airbus silently banked out of the west and touched down. Neither Pitt nor Giordino was aware of the aircraft's approach until they heard the screech of its tyres hitting the concrete runway. Giordino came awake and Pitt folded up his paper as the plane braked and then slowly turned on one wheel until it had rotated 180 degrees. As soon as the huge tyres rolled to a stop, the driver of the Peugeot shifted in gear and drove up within 5 metres of the rear of the aircraft.

Pitt observed that the entire airbus was painted a light desert tan, and he noted the indistinguishable markings on its surfaces that had been painted over. A woman wearing desert combat fatigues with a patch on one sleeve, signifying the UN world symbol with a sword through it, dropped from a hatch in the aircraft's belly between the huge landing gear. She double-timed over to the staffcar and opened the rear door.

'Please to follow me,' she said in English heavily coated with Spanish. As the car drove away, the UN tactical team member led them under the bulbous fuselage and gestured for them to climb inside. They entered the lower cargo bay of the airbus and stepped toward a narrow stairwell that rose to the main cabin.

Giordino paused and glanced at three armoured personnel carriers that sat in a row, squat and low, topping out at less than 2 metres. Then he stared in rapt fascination at the heavily armoured dune buggy used in the rescue of Gunn at Gao.

'Enter an off-road race with this thing,' he said admiringly, 'and no competitor would dare pass you.'

'It does look pretty intimidating,' Pitt agreed.

An officer was waiting for them when they surfaced in the main cabin. 'Captain Pembroke-Smythe,' he introduced himself. 'Jolly good of you to come. Colonel Levant is waiting for you in the planning room.'

'You're obviously English,' said Giordino.

'Yes, you'll find us a rather mixed lot,' Pembroke-Smythe said cheerfully as he swung the end of a swagger stick around the cabin at three dozen men and three women engaged in various stages of cleaning and assembling weapons and equipment. 'Some creative soul thought the UN should have its own tactical unit to go where international governments fear to tread, so to speak. Secret warriors we're sometimes called. Each highly trained by his own country's special forces. All volunteers. Some are permanent, a few of us are simply attached on a year's tour of duty.'

They were as tough and rugged a group as Pitt had ever seen. Bodies hardened through exercise and brutal training, they were quiet, purposeful professionals with all the skills and intelligence demanded by covert actions. There wasn't one that Pitt cared to meet in a dark alley, including the women.

Pembroke-Smythe ushered them into a compartment that was the command centre of the aircraft. The area was spacious and filled with an array of electronic systems. One operator monitored communications equipment while another was in the act of programming data for the approaching mission to Tebezza into a computer.

Colonel Levant graciously came from behind a desk and greeted Pitt and Giordino at the door. He wasn't sure what to expect. He had read extensive dossiers on both men, supplied by the United Nations International Intelligence Service, and could not help but be impressed with their accomplishments. He also read a brief report of their trials in the desert after escaping Tebezza and had to admire their tenacity.

Levant had previously expressed deep reservations about taking Pitt and Giordino along but quickly realized that without their guidance into the mines the operation could be in deep jeopardy. They appeared gaunt and showed the results of long exposure to the sun, but seemed in amazingly good condition as he shook their hands.

'After studying your exploits, gentlemen, I've looked forward to meeting you. I am Colonel Marcel Levant.'

'Dirk Pitt, and my nasty little friend here is Al Giordino.'

'After reading a report of your ordeal I expected you to be carried on board on stretchers, but I'm pleased to see you look quite fit.'

'Liquids, vitamins, and plenty of exercise,' said Pitt, smiling, 'have their benefits.'

'Don't forget fun in the sun,' muttered Giordino.

Levant did not respond to the humour but stared past them at Pembroke-Smythe. 'Captain, please alert the men and order the chief pilot to prepare for immediate takeoff.' Then he turned his attention back to the men standing before him. 'If what you say is correct, time is measured in lives. We can run over details for the mission while we're in the air.'

Pitt nodded in total accord. 'I applaud your expediency.'

Levant checked his watch. 'Flying time is slightly more than four hours. Our time window is very narrow. We can't

468

delay if we intend to make our assault during the prisoners' rest period. Too soon or too late and they will be scattered throughout the mine shafts on work crews and we'd never find and round them up before our scheduled withdrawal.'

'Four hours will put us over Tebezza at night.'

'Twenty hundred hours give or take five minutes.'

'You're going in with landing lights?' asked Pitt incredulously. 'You might as well add fireworks to let them know we're coming.'

Levant twisted one end of his moustache, a gesture Pitt was to see often in the next ten hours. 'We land in the dark. And before I explain, I think you should sit down and fasten your seat belts.'

His words were enforced with the strangely muted roar of the engines as the pilot advanced the throttles. The big airbus began accelerating down the runway with only the slightest rumble of thrust from its engines.

Giordino found Levant a bit too stuffy and arrogant for his taste and acted with polite indifference. Pitt, on the other hand, recognized a savvy and street-smart operator when he saw one. He also sensed a subtle undercurrent of respect from the Colonel that Giordino missed.

During lift-off, Pitt remarked about the unusual silence of the engines. The typical roar was not evident for an aircraft under full power.

'Specially modified silencers for the turbine exhaust,' explained Levant.

'They work well,' said Pitt admiringly. 'When you landed, I didn't hear anything until the tyres touched down.'

'You might call it a stealth factor for covert landings in places we're not welcome.'

'Do you also sneak in without lights?'

Levant nodded. 'Without lights.'

'Is your pilot equipped with fancy, high-tech night vision equipment?'

'No, Mr Pitt, nothing fancy. Four of my men drop by parachute on the Tebezza airstrip, secure it, and then place a series of infrared lights to guide our pilot onto the runway.'

'Once down,' said Pitt, 'covering the ground between the airstrip and mine entrance in the black of night won't be an easy chore.'

'That,' said Levant grimly, 'is the least of our problems.'

The plane was in a gradual climb and banking to the south when he unfastened his seat belt and stepped to a table with an enlarged satellite photo of the plateau above the mines. He picked up a pencil and tapped on the photo.

'Landing helicopters onto the plateau and rappelling down the canyon walls to the mine entrance would have greatly simplified our problem and given us a higher level of surprise. Unfortunately, there were other considerations.'

'I understand your dilemma,' said Pitt. 'A round-trip to Tebezza is beyond helicopter range. Setting up fuel depots across the desert would have cost additional delay.'

'Thirty-two hours according to our estimates. We considered leapfrogging our small copter squadron, one carrying fuel while the other carried men and supplies, but we ran into complications with that plan too.'

'Too complicated and too slow,' said Giordino.

'The speed factor also favoured the use of this aircraft,' said Levant. 'Another important factor of using an airliner over a fleet of helicopters is that we can carry our own transportation. We also have space for on-board medical facilities to tend the large number of people you stated in your report that are in dire need of attention.'

'How many make up your assault team?' asked Pitt.

'Thirty-eight fighters and two medics,' Levant answered. 'After we land, four will remain to guard the plane. The medical team will accompany the main force to care for the captives.'

'That doesn't leave much room in your personnel carriers to transport everyone.'

'If some of my people ride on the roofs and hang onto the sides, we can evacuate forty prisoners.'

'There may not be that many left alive,' Pitt said solemnly.

'We'll do our best for those who are,' Levant assured him.

'And the Malians,' Pitt asked, 'the political dissenters and enemies of General Kazim. What about them?'

'They will have to remain,' Levant shrugged. 'All food stores in the mines will be opened to them, and they'll be armed with the guard's weapons. Beyond that, there is little we can do for them. They will be on their own.'

'Kazim is sadistic enough to demand their mass execution after he's learned his prize slaves have flown the coop.'

'I have my orders,' Levant stated simply. 'And they don't include saving local criminals.'

Pitt stared down at the blowup of the desert surrounding the Tebezza plateau. 'So you intend to land the airbus in the dead of night on a desert airstrip, drive over a road that's tough to trace in daylight, assault the mine, carry off all foreign prisoners, and then rush back to the strip and take off for the lights of Algiers. We may be biting off more than we can chew with the limited resources at your command.'

Levant saw no disapproval in Pitt's expression, nor did he sense sarcastic criticism. 'As you say where you come from, Mr Pitt, what you see is what you get.'

'I'm not doubting the fighting quality of your people, Colonel. But I had expected a larger, better equipped force.'

'I regret the UN does not lavishly fund our Response and Tactical Team with expansive manpower and ultrasophisticated equipment like most special operations forces. But our budget is tight and we must work within our limits.'

'Why a UNICRATT team?' asked Pitt curiously. 'Why

not a British or French Foreign Legion commando unit or one from American Special Forces?'

'Because no other nation, including yours, wished to risk dirtying their hands on this mission,' explained Levant wearily. 'We were volunteered by Secretary General Kamil.'

The name brought back a fond memory in Pitt's mind of an interlude spent with Hala Kamil on board a ship in the Straits of Magellan. Two years ago, he recalled, during the search for the Alexandria Library treasures.

Levant caught the faraway look and Giordino knowingly smiled. Pitt saw their expressions and refocused his attention to the satellite map. 'There is a catch.'

'There are several,' said Levant evenly. 'But they can all be overcome.'

'Except two.'

'And they are . . .?'

'We don't know where O'Bannion's communications centre and security monitoring rooms are located. If he sends out an alert to Kazim's security forces before you can stop him, we won't stand a bishop's chance in hell of making it back to this aircraft and getting a good headstart to Algeria before one of his fighter squadrons shows up and nails us to the nearest barn door.'

'In that case, we have to get in and out of the mine within forty minutes,' said Levant. 'Not impossible if most of the captives can make it above ground without help. If many of them have to be carried, we will lose valuable time we cannot spare.'

At that moment Captain Pembroke-Smythe appeared with a tray of coffee and sandwiches from the aircraft's galley. 'Our fare is filling if not gourmet,' he said cheerfully. 'You have a choice between chicken salad and tuna fish.'

Pitt looked at Levant and grinned. 'You weren't kidding when you said you ran on a tight budget.'

*

As the airbus soared over the desert as black as the sea, Pitt and Giordino sketched large diagrams of the mine levels as they remembered them. Levant was amazed at their recollections. Neither professed to photographic memories, but they recalled an enormous amount of detail for the short time they were held prisoner in the mine.

Levant and two other officers interrogated the NUMA men in depth, often repeating questions three or four times in hopes of obtaining details observed but overlooked. The track to the canyon, the layout of the mine, the weapons of the guards, it was all covered over and over.

The data was voice recorded on computer and the sketches of the mine programmed into three dimensions. Nothing was overlooked. The weather forecast for the next several hours. the flight time of Kazim's jet fighters from Gao, alternate escape plans and routes should the airbus be destroyed on the ground. Every possible contingency was given a plan.

An hour before touchdown at Tebezza, Levant assembled his small force of men and women in the main cabin. Pitt led off the briefing by describing the guards, their numbers and arms, and observations of their indolent attitude from living and working beneath the desert.

He was followed by Giordino who gave them a tour of the mine levels with the oversized sketches pinned to a standing easel.

Pembroke-Smythe divided up the UN tactical team that was to execute the assault into four units and passed out individual maps of the underground tunnels printed from the computer. Levant capped the briefing by instructing the teams on their missions.

'I apologize for our lack of intelligence,' he began. 'We've never attempted such a dangerous mission with so little data. The charts you've been given of the mine show probably less than 20 percent of the existing tunnels and shafts. We have to strike hard and fast by securing the offices and

473

guards' quarters. Once we've eliminated resistance, we will round up the prisoners and begin our withdrawal. Final rendezvous will be at the entrance cavern exactly forty minutes from the time we go in. Any questions so far?'

A hand went up and a man near the front spoke up with a Slavic accent. 'Why forty minutes, Colonel?'

'Any more, Corporal Wadilinski, and a Malian fighter pilot at the nearest air force base can close and shoot us down before we're safely back into Algeria. I'm hoping that most of the captives can make it to our transports without help. If many of them have to be carried, we will be delayed.'

Another hand. 'What if we get lost in the mine and cannot find our way back to the rendezvous in time for the withdrawal?'

'Then you will be left behind,' Levant answered conversationally. 'Anyone else?'

'Do we get to keep any gold we find?'

The query came from a muscle-bound character in the back, followed by a round of laughter.

'You will all be strip searched at the end of the mission,' replied Pembroke-Smythe jovially. 'And any gold found will be turned over to my personal account in Switzerland.'

'The ladies too?' This from one of the women.

He threw her a wily smile. 'Especially the ladies.'

Though it did not crack his serious expression, Levant was thankful for the show of humour to relax the tense atmosphere. 'Now that we know where the booty goes,' he said, 'let us wrap this up. I will lead the first unit with Mr Pitt as our guide. We will clear the offices on the upper level before descending into the mine and releasing the captives from their hellhole. Unit two, under the command of Captain Pembroke-Smythe and led by Mr Giordino, will drop down the elevator and secure the guards' quarters. Lieutenant Steinholm will be in charge of unit three and will follow as backup and take up defensive positions at the side

474

shafts off the main tunnel to prevent flanking movements. Unit four under Lieutenant Morrison will secure the gold ore recovery levels. Except for the medical team, the rest of you will remain to guard the airstrip. Any further questions shall be directed to your unit commanders.'

Levant paused and stared around the interior of the cabin at the faces of his men. 'I regret we've had so little time to prepare for this operation, but it should not prove beyond the capabilities of a team that has successfully accomplished its last six missions without the loss of a single man or woman. If you should confront the unexpected, improvise. We have to get in, free the captives, and get out fast before we are pursued by the Malian air force. End of speech. Good luck to all of you.' Then Levant turned and walked into his command compartment.

46

The data from satellite positioning systems was downlinked to the navigational computer which fed the course into the automatic pilot and put the UN airbus precisely over the plateau of Tebezza. A slight correction toward a new grid coordinate and the pilot was soon circling the airstrip that showed as a barren strip across the desert on the monitor of the sonar/radar system.

The rear cargo doors swung outward and four of Levant's commandos lined up at the edge of the black void. Twenty seconds later a buzzer sounded and they leaped forward and swiftly dropped into the night. The doors closed and the pilot circled to the north for twelve minutes before banking around on his landing approach.

The pilot peered through night-vision goggles as his copilot scanned the desert below through specially tinted bifocal glasses that enabled him to detect the infrared lights set up by the parachutists while glancing at the instrument readings.

'I have clear ground,' announced the pilot. The copilot shook his head as he detected four lights blinking in unison on the starboard side. 'You're picking up a short field for light planes. The main strip is half a kilometre to starboard.'

'Okay, I have it. Gear down.'

The copilot pulled the lever and the wheels clumped down into position. 'Landing gear down and locked.'

'How do those Apache helicopter pilots keep from smacking into the ground?' muttered the pilot. This is like looking through twin toilet paper tubes with green fog inside.'

The copilot had no time to smile or reply. He was too busy reading off airspeed, altitude, and course corrections. The big wheels struck the sand and gravel, throwing up a cloud of dust that obliterated the stars behind the speeding aircraft. The reverse thrusters were amazingly quiet as the plane hurtled down the airstrip. Then the brakes were firmly applied and the airbus settled to a stop less than 10 metres from the end of the strip.

The dust was still billowing in the aircraft's wake when the rear ramp swung down and the vehicles drove out and parked in a convoy, the attack dune buggy at the front. The six-man security team that was to remain behind came next and dispersed around the aircraft. The main force followed and swiftly boarded the personnel carriers. The leader of the parachute team ran up to Colonel Levant as he stepped to the ground and saluted.

'The area is deserted, sir. No sign of guards or electronic security.'

'Any facilities?' asked Levant.

'Only a small brick building containing tools and drums of automobile diesel and aircraft jet fuel. Shall we destroy it?'

'Wait until we've returned from the mine.' He gestured to a shadowy figure next to him. 'Mr Pitt?'

'Colonel.'

'Mr Giordino told me you have raced off-road vehicles.'

'Yes sir, that is correct.'

Levant motioned him into the driver's seat of the attack vehicle and handed him a pair of night-vision goggles. 'You know the way to the mine. Please take the wheel and lead us in.' He turned and faced another figure who appeared in the dark. 'Captain Pembroke-Smythe.'

'Sir.'

'We're moving out. Ride in the last carrier and keep a watch to our rear, especially the sky. I don't want an aircraft sneaking up on the column.'

'I'll keep a tight eye,' Pembroke-Smythe assured him.

If the UNICRATT team operated on a shoestring, Pitt couldn't help wondering how incredibly exotic the equipment must be for U.S. Special Forces with unlimited funding. All of Levant's men and women, including Pitt and Giordino, wore night camouflage-grey and black flame-resistant combat suits with bulletproof assault vests, protective night goggles, and helmets containing miniature radio communications gear, and carried Heckler & Koch MP5 submachine guns.

Pitt threw a wave to Giordino, who was climbing beside the driver of the rear personnel carrier, and settled into a cramped seat, his head tucked beneath the six-barrel, Vulcan machine gun. He slipped on the goggles and adjusted his eyes to the sudden light magnification that made the desert for 200 metres in front of the dune buggy look like the green surface of an alien planet. He pointed toward the northwest. 'The track to the mine begins about 30 metres ahead and to our right.'

Levant nodded, then turned and confirmed that his tactical team was all loaded and ready to roll. He made a forward gesture with his hand and slapped Pitt on the shoulder. 'Time is passing, Mr Pitt. Please go.'

Pitt accelerated rapidly as he shifted the dune buggy's five-speed gear box. The vehicle leaped ahead, tailed by the three personnel carriers. The ground soon blurred beneath the widetrack tyres. Fine sand particles burst and exploded in its trail, forcing the personnel carriers to drive in a staggered V-formation to escape the blinding dust clouds. It did not take long before the vehicles and their passengers were all caked in a layer of fine brown-grey dust.

'How fast will she go?' Pitt asked Levant.

'On a level surface, 210 kilometres.'

'That's around 130 miles an hour,' said Pitt. 'Not bad considering her lack of aerodynamics and heavy weight.'

'Your Navy SEALs came up with the idea of using them during the desert war with Iraq.'

Pitt nudged Levant. 'Tell your drivers we're going to bear left 30 degrees and then continue straight and steady for about 8 kilometres.'

Levant issued the directions over his radio communication system, and a moment later the personnel carriers swung around in formation and followed the dune buggy's lead.

Landmarks were scarce on the faint track running from the airstrip to the canyon carved in the plateau. Pitt relied half on his memory and half on eyesight. Plunging across the desert in the dead of night was nerve-racking enough, even with night-vision goggles. There was no way of seeing or knowing for certain what was behind the next hump in the road, or whether he had strayed off course and was leading the convoy off a cliff into a bottomless pit. Only an occasional stretch of tyre track that hadn't been covered by wind-blown sand told him he was dead on the trail.

He stole a quick glance at Levant. The Colonel sat relaxed and incredibly composed. If he felt any fear of Pitt's wild drive over dark ground, he gave not the slightest indication. His only expression of concern came when he turned and checked to see that all three personnel carriers were following behind.

The plateau loomed ahead, its towering mass shutting off the lower curtain of stars to the west. Four minutes later a wave of relief swept Pitt. He had hit the slot right on the money. The opening into the twisting canyon split the plateau's black walls like the blow from an axe. He slowed and stopped.

'The entrance cave that leads into the equipment parking cavern is only a kilometre from here,' he said to Levant. 'Do you wish to send a scouting party ahead on foot?'

Levant shook his head. 'Continue on slowly, if you please, Mr Pitt. At the risk of giving away our approach, we'll go in with the vehicles and save time. Make sense to you?'

'Why not? No one is expecting us. If O'Bannion's guards detect our approach, they'll probably assume we're a new batch of prisoners sent by Kazim and Massarde.'

Pitt eased the dune buggy forward. The personnel carriers fell behind the dune buggy in a column. He feathered the accelerator only when he began to lose traction in the sand. He travelled in third gear with the engine turning over at little more than idling speed. The column crawled around the base of the steep walls that were defined in crisp black shadows. The specially modified mufflers on the vehicles could not completely stifle the sound of the exhaust, and the beat of the engines drummed softly across the hard surfaces of the rock like the distant drone of a piston engine aircraft. The night air was cool and there was only a whisper of wind, but the canyon walls still radiated with the memory of the day's heat.

The cave entrance suddenly yawned out of the darkness, and Pitt drove the dune buggy through the tight rock walls and into the main gallery as though it was the most natural thing to do. The interior was lit only by the lights that flooded from the office tunnel and stood empty except for one Renault truck and the expected security guard.

The heavily robed and turbaned Tuareg casually stared at the approaching vehicles more out of curiosity than wariness. Only when the dune buggy had pulled within a few metres did his eyes begin to widen in suspicion. He unslung his machine pistol from around his shoulder and was bringing it level when Levant shot him between the eyes with a silenced Beretta automatic.

'Nice shot,' Pitt commented dryly as he braked the attack vehicle to a stop.

Levant checked his watch. 'Thank you, Mr Pitt. You put us here twelve minutes ahead of schedule.'

'I aim to please.'

The Colonel swung from the dune buggy and made a series of hand signals. Quickly, silently the UN tactical team members jumped to the ground, immediately formed into their respective units, and began moving into the tunnel. Once into the corridor with the fluted walls and tiled floor, Levant's men began quietly entering the arched openings and rounding up O'Bannion's startled engineering crew as Giordino led the other three tactical units toward the main freight elevator indicated on Fairweather's map that dropped to the lower levels.

Four of O'Bannion's rogue mining engineers were taken as they were seated around a table playing poker. Before the surprised card players could react to the sudden appearance of armed men in camouflaged combat gear, who surrounded them with gun muzzles aimed at their heads, they were bound and gagged and thrown in a storeroom.

Silently, with only the slightest of pressure, Levant eased open the door marked as security monitoring centre. The room inside was lit only by the light coming from an array of television monitors displaying different locations throughout the mines. A European male sat in a swivel chair with his back to the door. He was wearing a designer shirt and Bermuda shorts. He smoked a thin cigar in leisurely unconcern as he scanned the monitors whose video cameras were sweeping the mine shafts.

It was the reflection in one monitor with a dead screen that betrayed them. Alerted by the images of men entering the room behind him, the man shifted slightly to his left as his fingers casually crawled toward a small console containing a row of red switches. Too late Levant leapt at the man, swinging his Heckler & Koch in a vicious chop downward. The security guard went limp in his chair, then slumped unconscious over the console. But not before an alarm system began whooping like an ambulance siren throughout the entire mine.

'Damn the luck!' Levant cursed bitterly. 'All surprise is gone.' He shoved the guard aside and squeezed off ten rounds into the console. Electrical sparks and smoke erupted from the shattered switches and the whooping abruptly went silent.

Pitt ran down the corridor, throwing open doors until he kicked in the one to the communications room. The operator, a pretty Moorish-featured woman, was not intimidated by the abrupt intrusion and did not even look up from her radio equipment at Pitt's approach. Alerted by the siren, she was shouting rapid French into the microphone of the headset perched on her flowing black hair. He quickly stepped forward and clubbed her with his fist on the back of the neck. But like Levant with the security monitor, he was too late. Before he cut her off and she crumpled to the stone floor, the alarm had been transmitted to General Kazim's security forces.

'Not in time,' said Pitt as Levant rushed into the room. 'She got off a message before I could stop her.'

Levant took in the situation with one quick glance. Then he turned and shouted a command. 'Sergeant Chauvel!'

'Sir!' It was almost impossible to tell the Sergeant was a woman under her heavy combat suit.

'Get on the radio,' Levant ordered in French, 'and tell the Malians that the alarm was a short circuit. Relieve any suggestion of an emergency. And for God's sake talk them out of taking any responsive action.'

'Yes sir,' Chauvel snapped purposefully before kicking the former radio operator out of the way and sitting down at the radio.

'O'Bannion's office is at the end of the corridor,' said Pitt, pushing by Levant and running down the corridor. He didn't stop until he put his shoulder down and collided with the door. It was unlocked and he barrelled into the reception chamber like a defensive tackle blitzing a quarterback.

The receptionist with the purple-grey eyes and buttocks-length hair sat calmly at her desk, gripping a wicked-looking automatic pistol in both hands. Pitt's momentum carried him across the room and over the top of the desk, crashing into the woman and taking them both to the blue-carpeted floor in a tangled heap. But not before she ripped off two shots into Pitt's bulletproof assault vest.

Pitt's chest felt as though someone had struck it twice with a hammer. The blows had temporarily knocked the wind out of him but in no way slowed him down. The receptionist tried to extricate herself while shouting what Pitt was certain were obscenities in a language unknown to him. She fired off another shot that went over his shoulder, ricocheting off the rock ceiling into a painting, before he snatched the gun from her hand. Then he jerked her to her feet and flung her onto a couch.

He turned away and stepped between the two bronze sculptures of the Tuaregs and tried the handle to the door of O'Bannion's office. It was locked. He lifted the gun taken from the receptionist, placed it against the lock, and pulled the trigger three times. The gunfire was deafening in the rock room, but there was no longer any need for stealth. He stood around the wall and shoved the door open with his toe.

O'Bannion was leaning with his back against the desk, hands outstretched on the surface. He looked as though he was expecting to greet the corporate executive of a rival company. The eyes that showed through his litham bore a haughty expression without a trace of fear. But they quickly turned to astonishment when Pitt walked into the room and pulled off his helmet.

'I hope I'm not late for dinner, O'Bannion. As I recall, you expressed a wish to dine with me.'

'You!' O'Bannion hissed, the colour ebbing from the skin showing around his eyes.

'Back to haunt you,' Pitt said with a half smile. 'And I

brought a few friends who don't take kindly to sadists who enslave and murder women and children.'

'You should be dead. No one could have crossed the desert without water and lived.'

'Neither Giordino nor I died.'

'One of General Kazim's search aircraft found the truck overturned in a wadi far to the west of the Trans-Saharan Track. You couldn't have reached the track on foot.'

'And the guard we left tied at the wheel.'

'Alive, but he was soon shot for allowing you to escape.'

'Life is certainly cheap in these parts.'

The shock was slowly fading from O'Bannion's eyes, but there was still no fear. 'Have you come to rescue your people? Or to steal gold?'

Pitt stared at him. 'Right on the first, wrong on the second. We also intend to put you and your scum out of business, permanently.'

'Your force has invaded a sovereign nation. You have no rights in Mali or jurisdiction over me and the mine.'

'My God! You're lecturing me on jurisdiction? What about the rights of all the people you enslaved and murdered?'

O'Bannion shrugged. 'General Kazim would have executed most of them anyway.'

'What stopped you from providing them with humane treatment?' Pitt demanded.

'Tebezza is not a resort or a spa. We are here to mine gold.'

'For the profit of you, Massarde, and Kazim.'

'Yes,' O'Bannion nodded. 'Our aims are mercenary. So what?'

O'Bannion's cold and ruthless character threw open a floodgate of anger in Pitt, released a series of mental pictures of the suffering endured by countless men, women, and children, pictures of the corpses stacked in the underground crypt, memories of Melika beating the helpless labourers with her bloodstained thong, the conviction that three men sick with greed were responsible for untold slaughter. He walked over to O'Bannion and smashed the shoulder stock of his machine gun into the part of the indigo litham covering O'Bannion's mouth.

For a long moment Pitt stared down at the nomad-robed Irish mining engineer who now lay stretched on the carpet, blood spreading through the cloth of his headdress, swore in maddened fury, and then slung the unconscious man over his shoulder. He met Levant in the corridor.

'O'Bannion?' asked the Colonel.

Pitt nodded. 'He had an accident.'

'So it would seem.'

'How do we stand?'

'Unit four has secured the ore recovery levels. Units two and three are meeting little resistance from the guards. It appears they're better suited for beating helpless people than fighting hardened professionals.'

'The VIP elevator to the mine levels is this way,' said Pitt, setting off down a side corridor. The carpeted and chromed-wall elevator had been abandoned by its operator as Pitt, Levant, and the members of unit one who were not guarding O'Bannion's engineers and office workers dropped down to the main level. They exited and approached the iron door that was hanging askew on its hinges and whose lock was still shattered from the blast of dynamite.

'Someone beat us to it,' mused Levant.

'Giordino and I blew it when we escaped,' explained Pitt.

'Looks like they never got around to repairing it.'

The shaft reverberated with the sharp explosions of gunfire from somewhere within the bowels of the mine. Pitt hoisted O'Bannion's still limp body onto the shoulder of a big, muscular commando and set off at a run down the shaft in the direction of the cavern holding the prisoners.

They reached the central chamber without meeting resistance and met up with members of unit two that were in the act of disarming a group of O'Bannion's guards who stood fearfully with hands clutched behind their necks. Giordino and two of the tactical team had shot off the lock and were leaning against the great iron gate to the slave labourers' dungeon cavern. Pembroke-Smythe spotted Levant, hurried over, and reported.

'Sixteen guards have been rounded up, Colonel. One or two escaped into the mine shafts. Seven made the mistake of resisting and are dead. We only have two men wounded, neither seriously.'

'We have to speed things up a bit,' said Levant. 'I fear they transmitted an alert before we could cut off communications.'

Pitt stepped beside Giordino and added his muscle into heaving open the gate. Giordino turned and looked at him.

'Well, it's about time you made an appearance.'

'I paused for a brief chat with O'Bannion.'

'Does he need a doctor or a mortician?'

'A dentist actually,' Pitt answered.

'Have you seen Melika?'

'No sign of her in the engineering offices.'

'I'll find her,' said Giordino, a biting fierceness in his voice. 'She's mine.'

The gate was manhandled against its stops, and the tactical team stepped into the cavern. Through firsthand experience Pitt and Giordino knew what to expect, but they were still sickened at the sight. The commandos froze, their faces gone white at the overpowering stench and the incredible degree of suffering before their eyes. Even Levant and Pembroke-Smythe stood shocked before mustering up the effort to enter.

'Good lord,' Smythe mumbled, 'this looks as bad as Auschwitz and Dachau.'

Pitt rushed through the mass of packed captives who were numbed beyond desperation by the monotonous existence and starved into barely walking skeletons. He found Dr Hopper sitting on a bunk staring blankly through dazed eyes, his filthy clothes hanging loosely on a body decimated by overwork and lack of food. He broke into a broad smile, lifted himself weakly to his feet, and embraced Pitt.

'Thank God, you and Al made it. It's a miracle.'

'I'm sorry we took so long,' said Pitt.

'Eva never gave up on you,' said Hopper, his voice choking. 'She knew you'd come through.'

Pitt looked around. 'Where is she?' Hopper nodded toward a bunk. 'You didn't get here a minute too soon. She's in a bad way.'

Pitt walked over and knelt beside a statue-like form in a lower bunk. Sadness showed in every line of his face. He couldn't believe how wasted she had become in a week's time. He gently took hold of her shoulders and gave her a light shake. 'Eva, I've come back for you.'

Slowly she stirred, her eyes fluttered open, and she vaguely stared up at him. 'Please let me sleep little longer,' she murmured.

'You're safe now. I'm taking you out of this place.'

She recognized him then and her vision became blurred with tears. 'I knew you would come for me . . . for us all.'

'We came within a hair of not making it.'

She looked into his eyes and smiled gamely. 'I never doubted for a moment.'

Then he kissed her, long, soft, and tenderly.

Levant's medical team went to work immediately, treating the captives while the combat units began evacuating those who could walk to the upper level where they were loaded aboard the personnel carriers. Initial fears proved true as the operation went slowly because many were too weak to move on their own and had to be carried out.

After seeing that Eva and the other women and children were cared for and on their way to the surface, Pitt borrowed a satchel of plastic explosives from Levant's demolition expert and then returned to a now conscious O'Bannion who sat beside an ore car under the watchful eye of a tough lady commando.

'Come along, O'Bannion,' Pitt ordered. 'We're going for a stroll.'

O'Bannion's litham had unravelled and fallen away and now revealed a face heavily scarred and disfigured from a premature dynamite explosion during his younger mining days in Brazil. His ugly features were heightened by a mouth leaking blood and the lack of two front teeth, knocked out by the blow from Pitt's gun butt.

'Where?' he asked abruptly through swollen lips.

'To pay our respects to the dead.'

The guard stood aside as Pitt roughly pulled O'Bannion to his feet and prodded him along the ore car tracks toward the burial crypt. Neither man spoke as they walked through the mine, occasionally stepping around the body of a Tuareg guard who had made the mistake of resisting Levant's assault force. When they came to the cavern of the dead, O'Bannion hesitated, but Pitt coldly pushed him inside.

O'Bannion turned and faced Pitt, his eyes still contemptuous. 'Why did you bring me here, to lecture me on cruelty to my fellow man before you execute me?'

'Not at all,' Pitt replied quietly. 'The lesson is obvious without a lecture, and no, I'm not going to execute you. That would be too quick, too clean. A quick flash of pain and then darkness. No, I think you deserve a more appropriate end.'

For the first time a flicker of fear danced in O'Bannion's eyes. 'What do you have in mind?'

Pitt swung the muzzle of his weapon around the stacks of cadavers. 'I'm going to give you time to contemplate your brutality and greed.'

O'Bannion looked confused. 'Why? You're badly mistaken if you expect me to cry for forgiveness and beg for leniency.'

Pitt looked over at a pile of bodies, at the frail, starved frame and open unstaring eyes of a girl no more than ten years old. Anger flamed and seethed within him and he fought desperately to control his emotions.

'You're going to die, O'Bannion, but very slowly, suffering the agony of thirst and hunger you imposed on these pitiful dead around you. By the time your friends Kazim and Massarde find you, providing they even bother to search, you'll have joined the rest of your victims.'

'Shoot me, kill me now!' O'Bannion savagely demanded.

Pitt smiled a smile as cold as dry ice and said nothing. He jabbed his gun at O'Bannion, forcing him to retreat to the end of the cave. Then Pitt stepped into the entrance tunnel, placed the plastic explosives at different intervals, and set the timers on the igniters. He gave O'Bannion one final callous wave and ran out into the shaft, crouching behind a train of ore cars.

Four loud, booming detonations, each fractionally following the other, hurled dust and splintered support timbers from the crypt's entrance tunnel into the main shaft. The explosions echoed through the mines for several moments before an eerie silence took over. Pitt wondered in dumb anger if he had placed the explosives in the wrong positions. But then he heard a faint reverberating sound that amplified into a great rumble as the roof of the tunnel collapsed under hundreds of tons of rock and sealed the entrance to the burial chamber.

Pitt waited until the dust began to settle before he casually shouldered his gun and began walking back to the evacuation area, along the ore car rails, whistling *'I've been working on the railroad.'*

Giordino heard a sound and then saw a movement in a crosscut shaft to his left. He stepped along the train rails until he came to a solitary, empty ore car. Silently edging along the wall, careful his boots did not strike any loose rock, he crept closer. Quick as a cat, he leaped over the rails and rammed the muzzle into the ore car.

'Throw out your gun,' he said sharply.

Caught by surprise, the Tuareg guard slowly rose from the empty bucket of the ore car, his machine gun held high over his head. He could not speak English and did not fully comprehend Giordino's command, but he quickly recognized a lost cause. His eyes followed Giordino's gun as it jabbed at him and moved off to the side. He caught the message and dropped his weapon over the edge of the ore car.

'Melika!' Giordino snapped.

The guard shook his head, but Giordino read the look of abject fear in the eyes. He pressed his gun muzzle against the guard's lips and pushed it into his mouth while flexing his finger on the trigger.

'Melika!' the guard mumbled around the steel barrel jammed halfway down his throat, frantically nodding through the pain.

Giordino pulled back the gun. 'Where's Melika?' he demanded in a threatening tone.

The guard appeared as frightened of Melika as he did of Giordino. With widened eyes he silently nodded his head into the depths of the shaft. Giordino motioned for him to move out of the crosscut and into the central shaft. Then he pointed.

'Go back to the main cavern. You understand?' The Tuareg bowed with his hands over his head and backed out of the crosscut, stumbling and falling across the ore car rails in his haste to comply. Giordino turned and cautiously continued into the dark tunnel that stretched ahead of him, expecting a burst of gunfire with each step.

It was deathly quiet save for the light step of his boots over the rail ties. Twice he paused, every sense of his body warning him of danger. He came to a sharp bend in the shaft and stopped. There was a glimmer of light coming around from the other side. There was also a shadow and the sound of rock against rock. He slipped a tiny signal mirror from one of the many pockets in his combat suit and eased it slowly around a support timber.

Melika was working feverishly stacking ore rocks at the end of the shaft, raising a false wall to hide behind. Her back was to Giordino, but she was still a good 10 metres away, and a gun was propped against the tunnel wall within easy reach. She took no precautions as she worked, having placed her trust in the guard Giordino had already disarmed to warn her. Giordino could have stepped into the centre of the shaft and shot her before she sensed his presence. But a quick kill was not in his mind.

Giordino stealthily moved round the bend in the shaft toward Melika, stepping quietly, any sounds of his approach covered by the crunch of the rock as her hiding place was rushed to completion. When he came close enough, he snatched her weapon and threw it over his shoulder into the shaft behind him.

She spun around, took in the situation within two seconds, and rushed Giordino, the deadly thong already in one hand whistling over her shoulder. Unfortunately for her the element of surprise did not exist. Giordino did not flinch. His face was a mask of cold implacability as he calmly pulled the trigger and shot away her kneecaps.

Revenge dominated all of Giordino's emotions. Melika was as mad and vicious as a rabid pit bull. She had maimed and murdered for the pure enjoyment of it. Even now, as she lay twisted across the loose rock, legs grotesquely bent, she stared up at him with bared teeth and pure malignity glaring out of her black eyes. Her crazed sadism welled up from within and overcame the searing pain. She snarled at Giordino like a wounded beast and struggled to lash out at him with the thong while shouting the vilest of obscenities.

Giordino easily stepped back and bemusedly observed her futile assault. 'It's a violent, unrelenting world,' he said slowly, 'but less so now that you're leaving it.'

'You sawed-off little bastard,' she snarled. 'What do you know about a violent world? You've never lived amid filth and suffered the torment and rottenness I have.'

Giordino's expression was as hard as the rock in the mine shaft. 'That didn't give you a licence to inflict agony on others. As judge and executioner, I'm not interested in your life's problems. Maybe you have your reasons for becoming what you are. If you ask me, you were born sick. You've left a long road littered with innocent victims. There is no excuse for you to live.'

Melika did not beg. The black hatred and venomous malevolence poured out of her mouth in curses. With calculated efficiency, Giordino shot her in the stomach twice. The blazing eyes took their last look, seeing only Giordino's indifferent expression, and then went vacant as her massive body seemed to shrivel into the rock floor of the shaft.

Giordino looked down at her for several moments before he finally spoke to an unhearing corpse.

'Ding dong,' he muttered, 'the witch is dead.'

47

'Total count is twenty-five,' Pembroke-Smythe reported to Levant. 'Fourteen men, eight women, and three children. All half dead from attrition.'

'That's one woman and one child less than when Giordino and I left here,' said Pitt in solemn anger.

Levant stared at the personnel vehicles that were being loaded with the freed captives and then glanced at his watch. 'We're sixteen minutes over our deadline,' he said impatiently. 'Hurry things along, will you Captain. We must be on our way.'

'Ready to go in a jiff,' Pembroke-Smythe said cheerfully as he rushed around the vehicles, urging the tactical team members to speed up the loading effort.

'Where is your friend, Giordino?' Levant asked Pitt. 'If he doesn't show soon, he'll be left behind.'

'He had a chore to do.'

'He'll be lucky to make his way through the rioting on the lower levels. After the prisoners broke into the food stores and water supply, they began wreaking their vengeance on the guards. The last team to withdraw from the lower levels reported a massacre in progress.'

'They can hardly be blamed after the hell they've endured,' said Pitt thoughtfully.

'I feel bad having to abandon them,' admitted Levant. 'But if we don't leave soon they'll come surging up the elevators, and we'll have a devil of a time fighting them off our vehicles.'

Giordino came trotting out of the office corridor past a six-man commando team guarding the entrance to the equipment cavern. A very smug expression was settled on his face. He grinned at Pitt and Levant. 'Glad to see you held up the show just for little old me.'

Levant was not amused. 'You're hardly the reason behind our delay.'

'Melika?' Pitt asked.

Giordino held up the thong he'd taken as a souvenir. 'Signing the guest register in hell. And O'Bannion?'

'Managing the mortuary.'

'Ready to push off,' Smythe shouted from a personnel vehicle.

Levant nodded. 'Mr Pitt, if you will kindly lead us back to the airstrip.'

Pitt made a quick check on Eva, amazed at her rapid revival after drinking nearly a gallon of water and ravenously downing a quick meal provided by the UN medical team. Hopper, Grimes, and Fairweather also looked as if they had been resurrected. Then he ran to the armed dune buggy and swung into the driver's seat.

With only seconds to spare, the rear guard ran toward the last departing vehicle and was pulled aboard as the prisoners flooded out of the mines and rushed through the offices into the equipment cavern. They arrived too late and could only watch in cruel disappointment as the special force that had saved them from a brutal death sped off into the night, leaving them to an uncertain fate.

Pitt saw no need for caution as he accelerated through the canyon. He turned on the narrow-beamed headlights of the desert assault vehicle and kept his foot flat on the floorboard. At Colonel Levant's urging he had left the personnel vehicles far in his wake as they rushed ahead to oversee the preparations for a hasty boarding and fast takeoff. Giordino was driving the lead carrier now and easily tracked the several sets of tyre indentations once

Pitt and his trailing dust cloud had pulled out of sight.

Levant was edgy on the return trip. Doggedly he checked his watch every few minutes with dire foreboding, disturbed that they were now a tardy twenty-two minutes behind his timetable. With only 5 kilometres to go, he began to feel more at ease. The sky was clear and there was no indication of aircraft. He began to feel a tinge of optimism. Perhaps Kazim's security forces were lulled by Sergeant Chauvel's deceptive excuse for the alert signal after all.

Disillusionment came quickly. Above the hum of the dune buggy's muted exhaust, they suddenly heard the unmistakable sound of jet engines and caught sight of aircraft navigation lights streaking across the dark sky. Levant was instantly giving orders over his helmet radio for the flight crew and security unit to scramble away from the airbus and take cover.

Pitt slammed on the brakes and threw the assault vehicle into a four-wheel drift sideways, an act that was as automatic as it was immediate, stopping in a swirl of dust behind a small sand dune. He relaxed his grip on the wheel and stared up at the intruding aircraft. 'I think we've just attracted a whole lot of unwelcome attention.'

'Kazim must have sent a single reconnaissance plane as insurance to check any possibility that the alert was a genuine attack.' Levant's voice was hard, but his expression reflected deep apprehension.

'The pilot may not suspect a problem, or he wouldn't soar in here as nice as you please with his wing lights flashing.'

Levant stared grimly at the outline of the jet fighter as it circled the airbus on the end of the airstrip. 'I fear he's reporting an unidentified aircraft and requesting instructions to attack.'

They weren't kept in suspense for long. The fighter, now recognized by Levant as a French Mirage, suddenly banked and swooped toward the airstrip, lining up its laser sights on the airbus that sat as helpless as a sleeping cow in front of a cannon.

'He's beginning his run!' Pitt snapped.

'Open fire!' Levant shouted to the man sitting behind them who was hunched over the Vulcan multi-barrelled machine gun. 'Bring him down!'

The gunner visually tracked the Malian fighter over the lead-computing gun sight, and the instant he established the lead angle and distance he actuated the firing system. Like the Gatling guns of the nineteenth century, the six barrels on the Vulcan spun in a rotational blur as thousands of 20-millimetre rounds sliced the black sky. The shells homed in and began shredding the Mirage fighter at the exact moment in time that the pilot unleashed two missiles at the helpless airbus on the ground.

The desert became a cauldron of noise and flame as both aircraft exploded into simultaneous eruptions of fire. The jet fighter, now a bright orange ball, continued its descending attack angle in a straight line as if pulled by a string until it plunged into the ground, throwing fiery pieces of debris in a great fan across the uncaring desert. The airbus was no longer a plane, just a great mass of flame that licked toward an oily smoke cloud that rose in a huge column into the sky, effectively shutting out the stars.

Mesmerized, Pitt watched what only seconds ago were two solid, intact aircraft. Now he saw only fire and destruction. He and Levant climbed out of the assault vehicle and were riveted where they stood. In the blazing glow of the fiery devastation, Pitt saw the bitter expression of defeat in Levant's face.

'Dammit!' Levant cursed. 'This was exactly what I was afraid would happen. Now we're trapped without a chance of rescue.'

'Kazim will soon suspect a foreign force has reinvaded his territory,' Pitt added severely. 'He'll order his entire air force to Tebezza. Then your backup helicopters will be shot to pieces before they can rendezvous.'

'There's no alternative but to make a run for the border,' Levant conceded.

'We'd never see it. Even if Kazim's planes failed to use us for target practice or his security forces missed dropping across our path and attacking us every step of the way, your vehicles will run out of gas long before we reach a relief force. A few of your toughest commandos might get through, but those poor souls you rescued from death in the mines will surely die in the desert. I know, I've been that route.'

'You were forced to go east toward the Trans-Saharan Track,' Levant reminded Pitt. 'That was close to 400 kilometres. If we head due north, we only have to travel 240 kilometres before crossing into Algeria and meeting up with a relief force from Algiers. Our fuel is ample for the distance.'

'You're forgetting Kazim and Massarde have high stakes in the Tebezza mines,' said Pitt, looking directly at Levant. 'They'll do whatever is necessary to keep the secret of their atrocities from discovery.'

'You think they would strike us in Algeria – '

'Your rescue operation has forced them to become desperate men,' Pitt interrupted. 'A little thing like a national border won't stop them from ordering air strikes into a desolate section of Algeria. Once your force is softened up and the rescue craft is destroyed or driven away, they'll follow up by dropping in their elite security forces to ensure our total annihilation. They can't afford even one survivor to escape and unveil their inhuman activities.'

Levant turned from the destruction, his face glowing orange from the fire, and stared at Pitt. 'You don't sanction my contingency plans?'

'I have an aversion to pursuing the expected.'

'Are you being cryptic, Mr Pitt, or merely modest?'

'Practical,' Pitt answered briefly. 'I have every reason to believe Kazim won't pull back at the border.'

'What do you propose?' Levant asked patiently.

'Head south until we intersect with the railroad out of Fort Foureau,' Pitt answered briefly. 'Then hijack a train to Mauritania. If we play our cards right, Kazim won't catch on until we reach Port Etienne and the sea.'

'Into the lion's den,' Levant muttered sceptically. 'You make it sound absurdly simple.'

'The ground between here and the Fort Foureau hazardous waste project is mostly flat desert with occasional sand dunes. If we maintain an average speed of 50 kilometres an hour, we can reach the railroad before sunup with fuel to spare.'

'Then what? We'd be exposed from every side.'

'We hide out in an old Foreign Legion fort until dark before stopping and hiding everyone on an outward-bound train.'

'The original Fort Foureau. It was abandoned just after World War II. I visited it once.'

'The same.'

'We'd be tempting suicide without a guide to lead us through the dunes,' Levant argued.

'One of the rescued captives is a professional tourist guide. He knows the Malian desert like a nomad.'

Levant turned his attention back on the burning airbus for several moments, his mind considering the pros and cons of Pitt's proposal. If he could trade places with General Kazim, he would expect his quarry to run north for the nearest border crossing too. And he would also commit all his mobile fighting forces in an attempt to block them off. Pitt was right, he concluded. There was absolutely no hope of escaping north into Algeria. Kazim would never call off the pursuit until they were all dead. Striking out in the opposite direction just might fool the General and Massarde into a wild goose chase long enough for the tactical team to steal into the clear.

'I didn't tell you, did I, Mr Pitt? I spent eight years in the desert when I was a member of the Foreign Legion.'

'No, Colonel, you didn't.'

'The nomads have a fable about a lion with a hunter's spear in his side that walked north from the jungle and swam across the Niger River so he could die in the warm sand of the desert.'

'Is there a lesson in it somewhere?' asked Pitt vaguely.

'Not really.'

'So what's the meaning?'

Levant turned as the personnel vehicles approached and stopped beside the dune buggy. Then he looked back at Pitt and slowly smiled. 'What it means is that I'm going to trust your judgment and push south to the railroad.'

48

Kazim entered Massarde's office at eleven o'clock in the evening. He helped himself to a gin on the rocks and sat down in a chair before Massarde bothered to look up and acknowledge the General's presence.

'I was informed of your unexpected arrival, Zateb,' said Massarde. 'What brings you to Fort Foureau this time of night?'

Kazim studied his drink as he swirled the ice cubes. 'I thought it best I tell you in person.'

'Tell me what?' Massarde inquired impatiently.

'Tebezza has been raided.'

Massarde frowned. 'What are you talking about?'

'About nine o'clock, my communications section received an emergency alert from the mine's security system,' explained Kazim. 'A few minutes later, the Tebezza radio operator announced an all-clear, saying the alarm went off due to a faulty electrical circuit.'

'Sounds innocent enough.'

'Only on the surface. I do not trust seemingly innocent situations. I ordered one of my air force fighters to make a reconnaissance flight over the area. The pilot radioed that an unidentified jet transport plane was sitting on Tebezza's airstrip. The same type of French airbus, I might add, that snatched the American from the Gao airport.'

Massarde's face turned sober with sudden concern. 'Your pilot was positive of this?'

Kazim nodded. 'Since no aircraft can land at Tebezza without my authority, I ordered my pilot to destroy it. He acknowledged and launched his attack. He reported a hit on the target in almost the same instant his radio went dead.'

'Good God, man, it could have been a commercial airliner that simply made an emergency landing.'

'Commercial airliners do not fly the skies without markings.'

'I think you're overreacting.'

'Then explain why my pilot did not return to his base.'

'Mechanical malfunction?' Massarde shrugged. 'He could have suffered any number of problems.'

'I prefer to believe he was shot down by the force that raided the mines.'

'You don't know that.'

'Nonetheless, I've ordered a fighter squadron over the area and sent in an elite security force by helicopter to check out the situation.'

'What of O'Bannion?' asked Massarde. 'Hasn't he contacted you?'

'No response, nothing. Forty minutes after they denied an emergency, all communication with Tebezza went silent.'

Massarde mulled over Kazim's report, but was lost for answers. 'Why raid the mines?' he asked finally. 'For what purpose?'

'Most likely the gold,' Kazim replied.

'Stupid to steal ore. We remove all pure gold to our South Pacific depository as soon as it's processed. The last shipment was two days ago. A band of thieves with half a brain between them would attempt to hijack it during transport.'

'For the moment, I have no theories,' Kazim confessed. He held up his watch. 'My forces should be landing on the plateau above the mines about now. We'll have answers within the hour.'

'If what you say is true, something strange is happening,' Massarde murmured.

'We have to consider the possibility that the same United

501

Nations commando team that struck my air force base in Gao is responsible for the raid on Tebezza.'

'Gao was a different operation. Why return and strike Tebezza? Under whose orders?'

Kazim finished off his gin and poured another. 'Hala Kamil? Perhaps word leaked out about the abduction of Dr Hopper and his party. So she sent in her tactical team to rescue them.'

'Impossible,' said Massarde, shaking his head. 'Unless your men talked.'

'My men know they would die if they betrayed my trust.' Kazim said coldly. 'If there was a leak, it came from your end.'

Massarde gave Kazim a benign stare. 'Stupid of us to argue. We can't alter the past, but we *can* control the future.'

'In what way?'

'You said your pilot claimed hit on the airliner.'

'His final words.'

'Then we can assume the raiding party's only means of escape from Mali has been eliminated.'

'Providing damage to their aircraft was severe enough.'

Massarde rose and turned to face a large plaster contour map of the Sahara that stretched on the wall behind his desk. 'If you were in command of the raiders and your plane was destroyed, how would you see your situation?'

'All but hopeless.'

'What are your options?'

Kazim came over and tapped his glass against the plaster map. 'There are no options but one. Cut and run for the Algerian border.'

'Can they make it?' asked Massarde.

'Assuming their vehicles are intact and fuelled, they should be able to cross over into Algeria sometime around dawn.'

Massarde looked at him. 'Can you catch and destroy them before they reach the border?'

'Our night fighting systems are limited. I might shave them down a bit, but to wipe them out I would need daylight.'

'Then you will be too late.'

Kazim took a cigar from a ceramic humidor, lit it, and sipped from his gin. 'Let us be practical. We're looking at the Tanezrouft, the most desolate and remote part of the Sahara. The Algerian military rarely sends a patrol into the uninhabited region along the border. And why should they. They have no quarrel with Mali, and we have none with them. My security forces can easily strike 10 miles inside our northern neighbour without detection.'

Massarde looked sharply at Kazim. 'Should it turn out to be a rescue mission by the UN forces, none of Hopper's people or my engineers and their families can be allowed to escape. If only one gets through to expose Fort Foureau or Tebezza, you and I are finished as business partners.'

The beginnings of a smile widened across the General's face. 'Not to worry yourself, Yves my friend. We have too good a thing going to allow a few prying samaritans to pull the rug from under us. I promise you that by tomorrow at noon they will all be carrion for the vultures, every last one of them.'

After Kazim had left, Massarde spoke briefly into his intercom. A few seconds later Ismail Yerli entered the room.

'You heard and observed on the monitor?' asked Massarde.

Yerli nodded. 'Amazing the man can be so cunning and yet so stupid at the same time.'

'You read Kazim quite accurately. You can see you won't have an easy time keeping a leash on him.'

'When does he expect me to join his entourage?'

'I'll introduce you this evening at a dinner party I'm hosting in honour of President Tahir.'

503

'With the situation at Tebezza in a critical stage, isn't Kazim too occupied to show?'

Massarde smiled. 'The great lion of Mali is never too busy to attend an elegant dinner put on by a Frenchman.'

Sitting in his small command centre office in the UN building in New York, General Bock read the report relayed by a United Nations communications satellite by Colonel Levant. There was a grave expression on his ageing face as he picked up a secure phone and called Admiral Sandecker's private number. The Admiral's answering machine beeped and Bock left a terse message. Sandecker was back to him within eight minutes.

'I've just received an unpleasant report from Colonel Levant,' Bock announced.

'What's the situation?' Sandecker asked flatly.

'Aircraft of the Malian air force destroyed their transport plane on the ground. They are cut off and trapped.'

'What of the rescue operation at the mine?'

'It went off as planned. All foreign nationals still alive were placed under medical care and evacuated. Levant reported his casualties as light.'

'Are they currently under attack?'

'Not as yet. But it is only a matter of hours before forces of General Kazim close in.'

'Do they have an optional escape route?'

'The Colonel was quite clear in stating their only hope lay in reaching the Algerian border before daylight.'

'Not much of a choice,' Sandecker said grimly.

'I suspect it was red herring.'

'Why do you say that?'

'He sent his report over an open frequency. Kazim's communications operators were sure to pick it up.'

Sandecker paused to take notes. 'You think Colonel Levant is heading on a different tack than he advertised?'

'I was hoping you'd tell me,' said Bock.

'Clairvoyance is not one of my strong points.'

'There was a message to you in Levant's report from your man, Pitt.'

'Dirk.' There was sudden warmth in Sandecker's voice and a touch of reverence. Leave it to Pitt to come up with an unthinkable scheme. 'What is the message?'

'It reads, "Tell the Admiral that when I return to Washington, I'll take him to see Harvey's girlfriend Judy sing at the AT&S saloon." Is this a crude joke, or what?'

'Dirk is not known for crude jokes,' Sandecker said definitely. 'He's trying to tell us something with some sort of riddle.'

'Do you know this Harvey?' asked Bock blankly.

'The name isn't familiar,' murmured Sandecker. 'I've never heard Dirk mention anyone called Harvey.'

'Is there such a place in Washington as the AT&S saloon with a singer by the name of Judy?' Bock inquired.

'Not that I've ever been in,' Sandecker answered, searching for a clue in the recesses of his mind. 'And the only singer I ever knew named Judy was – '

The answer struck Sandecker with all the suddenness of a slap in the face. The ingenious simplicity, the elementary code was obvious to anyone who was an old motion picture buff like the Admiral. He might have known, he might have guessed Pitt would have played on that knowledge. He laughed.

'I fail to see the humour,' Bock said sternly.

'They're not running for the border into Algeria,' Sandecker stated triumphantly.

'What did you say?'

'Colonel Levant's force is heading south toward the railroad running between the sea and Fort Foureau.'

'May I ask what brought you to that conclusion?' Bock asked suspiciously.

'Dirk's thrown us a conundrum, a common riddle that Kazim is unlikely to solve. Judy the singer is Judy Garland and Harvey represents a movie she starred in called *The Harvey Girls*.'

'How does the AT&S saloon fit in the picture?'

'Not a saloon, but a song. The hit song Judy Garland sang in the movie. It was called *The Atchison, Topeka and the Santa Fe*. The name of a railroad.'

Bock said slowly, 'That explains why Levant sent a report that Kazim's communications people could easily intercept. He misled them into believing he was heading north into Algeria.'

'When in fact they're travelling in the opposite direction,' Sandecker finished.

'Levant has rightly assumed that crossing the Mali/Algeria border did not guarantee safety. Men as ruthless as Kazim have no qualms about ignoring international law. He will pursue our force until they are all slaughtered.'

'The next question is what do they do after reaching the railroad?'

'Perhaps steal a train,' suggested Bock.

'Makes sense, but in broad daylight?'

'There is more to the message from your man, Pitt.'

'Please go on.'

'The next part reads, "Also inform the Admiral that Gary, Ray, and Bob are going over to Brian's house for fun and games." Can you interpret this?'

Sandecker thought a moment. 'If Pitt is still coding in movies then Gary must be Gary Cooper. And I'll guess that he means Ray Milland.'

'Do you recall a picture they starred in together'

'I do indeed,' Sandecker fairly beamed over the telephone. 'Dirk might just as well have hung out a neon sign. They starred with Robert Preston and Brian Donlevy in a 1939 epic called *Beau Geste*.'

'I saw it when I was a boy,' said Bock. 'The story was about three brothers who served in the French Foreign Legion.'

'The reference to Brian's house suggests a fort.'

'Certainly not the Fort Foureau hazardous waste facility. That would be the last place Levant would go.'

'Is there another fort in the area?'

Bock paused to consult his maps. 'Yes, an old Legion outpost several kilometres west of the waste project. The very one, in fact, Massarde named his project after.'

'Sounds like they intend to hole up there until dark.'

'I would do the same if I was in Colonel Levant's place.'

'They're going to need help,' said Sandecker.

'Precisely the reason for my call to you,' said Bock. becoming brisk and businesslike. 'You must persuade the President to send an American special forces group to assist in bringing Levant and the freed captives out of General Kazim's territory.'

'Did you discuss this with Secretary General Kamil? She carries more weight with the President than I do.'

'Unfortunately, she was suddenly called away to an emergency conference in Moscow. You are the only one I can turn to on rush notice.'

'How much time have we got?'

'Virtually none. Daylight will come in their part of the desert within two hours.'

'I'll do what I can,' promised Sandecker. 'I only hope the President hasn't gone to bed yet, or I'll pay hell getting his aides to wake him.'

49

'You must be out of your mind, demanding to see the President this time of night,' Earl Willover said angrily.

Sandecker looked at the President's Chief of Staff who was neatly attired in a dark double-breasted wool pin stripe that showed only the slightest sign of creases in the pants. Sandecker wondered if the man ever left his office and slept standing up. 'Take my word for it, Earl, I wouldn't be here if it wasn't urgent.'

'I won't wake the President unless faced with an international crisis that endangers the security of the nation.'

So far Sandecker had held his temper in check, but it began to slip away. 'All right, tell him there's a taxpaying voter downstairs in the White House office who's mad as hell.'

'You *are* mad.'

'Mad enough to charge up to his bedroom and wake him myself.'

Willover looked like he was on the verge of a boiling fit. 'You try it, and I'll have the Secret Service take you in custody.'

'A lot of innocent people, including women and children, are going to die if the President doesn't act.'

'I hear that old story every day of the week,' Willover sneered.

'And make jokes about the victims, right?'

Willover finally lost it. 'You've got an answer for everything, you arrogant anchor-clanker. I can break you any time I want to. You understand?'

Sandecker moved close enough to Willover to smell the man's minty breath. 'Listen up, Earl. One day the

President's term of office will be over and you'll only be another one of the great unwashed public again. Then I will ring your doorbell and tear out your liver.'

'I bet you would too,' came a familiar voice.

Sandecker and Willover both turned and faced the President who was standing in a doorway in his pyjamas and bathrobe. He was nibbling from a plate of canapés he held in one hand.

'I sneaked down for a late snack from the kitchen refrigerator and overheard heated voices.' He stared at Sandecker. 'Now suppose you tell me what this is all about, Admiral.'

Willover stepped in front of Sandecker. 'Please sir, it's a matter of little consequence.'

'Why don't you let me be the judge of that, Earl. Okay, Admiral, speak your piece.'

'First let me ask you, Mr President, have you been briefed on the latest developments on the Fort Foureau operation?'

The President looked at Willover. 'I was told that your men, Pitt and Giordino, had managed to escape into Algeria and that they provided vital information regarding Yves Massarde's corrupt and unscrupulous hazardous waste operations.'

'May I ask what your response is?'

'We're calling for an international environmental tribunal of European and North African legal representatives to meet and discuss a plan of action,' answered Willover.

'Then you don't plan to . . . I believe you said, Mr President . . . "go in and take the place out ourselves." '

'Cooler heads have prevailed,' said the President, nodding at Willover.

'Even now, with proof that chemicals leaking from Fort Foureau are causing the expanding red tide, all anyone is going to do is sit down and talk about it?' Sandecker said, controlling his exasperation.

'We'll discuss this another time,' said the President, turning to return to his bedroom upstairs in the White House. 'Earl will set up an appointment.'

'Did Earl also brief you on the Tebezza gold mines?' asked Sandecker suddenly.

The President hesitated and shook his head. 'No, I'm not familiar with the name.'

'After Pitt and Giordino were captured at Fort Foureau,' Sandecker went on, 'they were taken to another one of General Kazim and Yves Massarde's sinister enterprises, a little-known gold mine where opposition and dissident prisoners are enslaved and worked to death under the most barbaric and inhumane conditions. A number of them were French engineers and their families Massarde imprisoned so they couldn't return home and expose Fort Foureau. My men also found the missing World Health Team that was supposedly killed in a plane crash, all horribly starved and exhausted from overwork and little food.'

The President gave Willover a cold stare. 'It seems I'm kept in the dark on a number of matters.'

'I try to do my job fielding priorities,' Willover offered hastily.

'So where is this leading?' the President asked Sandecker.

'Knowing it was useless to ask you for a special force,' Sandecker continued, 'Hala Kamil again came to the rescue and volunteered the United Nations critical response team. With Pitt and Giordino to guide them, Colonel Levant and his force landed in the desert near the mines, conducted a successful raid, and rescued twenty-five foreign national men, women, and children — '

'Children were forced to work the mines?' the President interrupted.

Sandecker nodded. 'They belonged to the French engineers and their wives. There was also an American, Dr Eva Rojas, who was a member of the World Health Team.'

'If the raid was successful, what is the urgent problem?' demanded Willover.

'Their transport, the aircraft they flew from Algeria, was destroyed on the ground at the Tebezza airstrip by fighters of the Malian air force. The entire force along with the rescued captives are trapped in the middle of Mali. It's only a matter of hours before Kazim's military finds and attacks them.'

'You paint a bleak picture,' said the President seriously. 'Is there no way they can safely reach the Algerian border?'

'It would matter little if they did,' explained Sandecker. 'Kazim won't hesitate to run the risk of a confrontation with the Algerian government to stop the captives from exposing the atrocities at Tebezza and dangers of Fort Foureau. He'll send his military deep into Algeria to destroy them and guarantee their silence.'

The President went silent, studying the canapés without biting into one. The implications of what Sandecker had told him were not to be brushed aside as he knew Willover was about to advise. But he could not stand by and do nothing while a backwater despot murdered innocent foreign citizens.

'Kazim is as bad as Saddam Hussein,' muttered the President. He turned to Willover. 'I'm not going to hide under the covers on this one, Earl. Too many lives are at stake including those of three Americans. We've got to lend a hand.'

'But Mr President,' Willover protested.

'Contact General Halverson at Special Forces Command in Tampa. Alert him for an immediate operation.' The President stared at Sandecker. 'Who do you suggest to coordinate this thing, Admiral?'

'General Bock, commander of the UN Critical Response and Tactical Team. He's in contact with Colonel Levant and can provide General Halverson with constant updates on the situation.'

The President set the canapés aside on a credenza and

placed his hands on Willover's shoulders. 'I value your advice, Earl, but I've got to act on this one. We can kill two birds with one stone and take half the flak if the operation goes sour. I want our Special Forces to secretly infiltrate Mali, rescue the UN tactical team and the captives. Then get the hell out before Kazim and Massarde know what hit them. Afterward, perhaps we can figure a way to neutralize the Fort Foureau waste project.'

'You get my endorsement,' Sandecker smiled broadly.

'I guess nothing I can say will change your mind,' Willover said to the President.

'No, Earl,' said the President, retrieving his canapés tray, 'we're going to close our eyes and bet the bankroll on an inside straight.'

'And if we lose?'

'We can't lose.'

Willover looked at him curiously. 'Why not, sir?'

The President matched Sandecker's smile. 'Because I'm dealing the hand, and I have the greatest confidence in our Special Operations Forces to kick slime like Kazim and Massarde into the bog where they belong.'

Several miles west of Washington, D.C., in the Maryland countryside, a large hill rises above the flat surrounding farmland. Passing motorists who take the time to notice the anomaly think of it as merely a geological trick of nature. Almost none know that it was secretly man-made from soil that was excavated for a command centre and shelter for the capital city's politicians and military leaders in World War II.

During the cold war, work never stopped, and the subterranean spread was enlarged into a vast storeroom for the nation's records and artifacts dating back to the first pioneers who settled the eastern coastline in the 1600s. The interior space is so expansive it is not measured in metres or acres but in square miles or kilometres. To those few who are aware of its existence it is known as ASD (Archival Safekeeping Depository).

Thousands of secrets are buried away in the seemingly unending archival storage bins of the depository. For some strange reason, known only to certain very few bureaucrats, entire sections of the depository hold classified material and objects that will never be revealed to the public. The bones of Amelia Earhart and Fred Noonan and Japanese records of their execution on Saipan, the secret conspiracy files of both Kennedy assassinations, the intelligence of Soviet sabotage behind American space rocket and shuttle accidents and the retaliation at Chernobyl, staged films of the Apollo moon landing hoax, and much, much more — it was all filed and stored away, never to see the light of day.

Since St Julien Perlmutter didn't drive, he took a cab to the small Maryland town of Forestville. After waiting on a bus stop bench for nearly half an hour, he was finally picked up by a Dodge van.

'Mr Perlmutter,' asked the driver, a government security agent wearing regulation mirrored sunglasses.

'I am him.'

'Please get in.'

Perlmutter did as he was told, thinking to himself that all this subterfuge was a childish game. 'Don't you want to see my driver's licence,' he said acidly.

The driver, a dark brown-skinned African-American, shook his head. 'No need. You're the only one in this town who fits the description.'

'Do you have a name?'

'Ernie Nelson.'

'What agency you with? National Security Federal Bureau? Special Secrets?'

'I'm not at liberty to say,' answered Nelson officially.

'Aren't you going to blindfold me?'

Nelson gave a quick shake of his head. 'No need. Since your

request to search through historical files was approved by the President, and you once held a Beta-Q clearance, I think you can be trusted not to reveal what you see today.'

'If you had dug deeper into my file, you'd have seen that this is my fourth research trip to ASD.'

The agent did not respond and remained silent for the rest of the trip. He turned off the main highway and drove down a paved road to a security gate, showed his credentials, and entered. They passed through two more guard stations before the road led into a small barn-like structure in the middle of a farm complete with pigs and chickens and wash hanging on a line. Once inside the barn they rolled down a wide concrete ramp that dropped deep underground. They finally arrived at a security station where the agent parked the car.

Perlmutter knew the routine. He exited the car and walked over to a waiting electric vehicle that looked similar to a golf cart. An archivist/curator wearing a white lab coat shook Perlmutter's hand.

'Frank Moore,' he introduced himself. 'Good to see you again.'

'A pleasure, Frank. How long has it been?'

'Three years since you were last here. You were doing research on the *Sakito Maru*.'

'The Japanese passenger-cargo ship that was sunk by the U.S. submarine *Trout*.'

'As I recall, she was carrying German V-2 rockets to Japan.'

'You have a good memory.'

'I refreshed it while digging out the records of your previous visits,' Moore admitted. 'What can I do for you this trip?'

'Civil War,' answered Perlmutter. 'I'd like to study any records that might throw some light on the mysterious loss of a Confederate ironclad.'

'Sounds interesting.' Moore motioned to a seat in the

electric car. 'Our Civil War records and artifacts are housed in buildings about 2 kilometres from here.'

After a final security check and a brief meeting with the Curator-in-Charge, Perlmutter signed an affidavit stating that he would not publish or make public any of his findings without government approval. Then he and Moore moved off in the electric auto, passing a small crew of men who were unloading mementos and keepsakes people had left at the Vietnam Veterans Memorial. Photographs, old army boots and uniforms, buttons, watches and wedding rings, dog tags, dolls, each object was catalogued, tagged, and placed in plastic wrappers on endless shelves.

The government threw nothing away.

Though he had seen part of the subterranean expanse on his previous visits, Perlmutter could not help but be astounded by the incredible size of the place and the tier upon tier of storage bins full of records and old artifacts, a great many of them from foreign countries. The Nazi section alone covered the size of four football fields.

The Civil War memorabilia was housed in four three-storey buildings – the concrete ceilings of the depository were 15 metres high. Placed in neat rows in front of the structures, different types of cannon from the Civil War stood as pristine and immaculate as when they were sent to fields of battle. They were mounted on their carriages and hitched to limbers that still held shot and shell. Immense naval cannon from such famous ships as the *Hartford*, the *Kearsage*, the *Carondelet*, and the *Merrimack* were also on display as if for inspection.

'The records are kept in Building A,' explained Moore. 'Buildings B, C, and D hold weapons, uniforms, medical relics, and furniture once belonging to Lincoln, Jefferson Davis, Lee, Grant, and other famous people from the war between the states.'

They stepped from the vehicle and entered Building A.

The ground floor was one vast sea of filing cabinets. 'Any papers pertaining to the Confederacy are on the ground floor,' Moore said, sweeping his hands around the cavernous room. 'All Union records are filed on the second and third. Where would you like to begin?'

'Anything you have on the *Texas*.'

Moore paused to thumb through several pages of a directory he had carried in from the vehicle. 'Confederate naval records are kept in the blue files along the far wall.'

Despite the fact that no one had been through the files in years, and in many cases never since storage, there was surprisingly little dust. Moore helped Perlmutter zero in on a packet containing the known history on the ill-fated ironclad.

Moore pointed to a table and chair. 'Make yourself comfortable. You're familiar with the regulations regarding the care of records and know that I'm required to remain close by to monitor your research.'

'I'm fully aware of the rules,' Perlmutter acknowledged.

Moore held up his watch. 'Your permit to conduct research at ASD ends after eight hours. Then we must return to the curator's office where you will be driven back to Forestville. Do you understand?'

Perlmutter nodded. 'Then I had best get started.'

'Go ahead,' said Moore, 'and good luck.'

Within the first hour, he had cleaned out two grey metal file cabinets before he found an ancient yellow file folder containing records of the Confederate steamship *Texas*. The papers inside revealed little historic information that wasn't already known and published. Specifications of the warship's construction, eyewitness reports of her appearance, one sketch by her chief engineer, and a list of her officers and crew. There were also several contemporary accounts of her running battle with Union warships during her historic dash into open seas. One of the articles, written by a northern reporter on board a Union monitor that took hits from the *Texas*, had two lines cut out. Why the censorship, wondered Perlmutter curiously. It was the first time in all his years of researching on Civil War shipwrecks that he had come across a display of censor's scissors.

Then he found a brittle news clipping and carefully unfolded it on the table. It was a deathbed statement given by a man named Clarence Beecher to a British reporter in a small hospital outside of York. Beecher claimed he was the only survivor of the mysterious disappearance of the *C.S.S. Texas*. Beecher's dying words described the voyage across the Atlantic and up a large African river. The ship steamed comfortably past hundreds of miles of lush shorelines before entering the outskirts of a great desert. Because the pilot was unfamiliar with the uncharted river, he mistakenly turned off the main channel into a tributary. They steamed on another two days and nights before the captain realized the mistake. When coming about to return downriver, the ironclad grounded, and no amount of effort could set her free.

The officers conferred and decided to wait out the summer until the fall rains raised the river again. There was a limited supply of food on board but the river would provide the necessary water. The captain also bought goods from passing tribes of Tuaregs, paying with gold. On two occasions large bands of desert bandits made the mistake of attempting to attack and loot the grounded warship of its seemingly inexhaustible gold supply.

By August, typhoid, malaria, and a starvation diet had ravaged the crew, decimating their numbers until there were only two officers, the president, and ten seamen who could still walk.

Perlmutter stopped and gazed off into space, his curiosity snagged. Who was the *president* Beecher referred to? He found it most intriguing.

Beecher went on to say that he and four other armed men were selected to row down the river in one of the ironclad's boats to try and find help from the outside world. Only Beecher barely survived to reach the mouth of the Niger River. Nursed back to health by merchants at a British trading outpost, he was given free passage to England, where he eventually married and became a farmer in Yorkshire. Beecher said he never returned to his native state of Georgia because he was certain to be hung for the terrible crime committed by the *Texas*, and he had been too frightened to speak about it until now.

After he breathed his last, the doctor and Beecher's wife shrugged off his final statement as the demented ravings of a dying man. It appeared that the reporter's editor had only printed the story because of a slow news day and a lack of editorial to fill up that day's paper.

Perlmutter reread the article a second time. He would have liked to accept it at face value despite the scepticism of the wife and doctor, but a quick check of the crew showed there was no Clarence Beecher present during muster immediately before the *Texas* left the navy yard at Richmond, Virginia. He sighed and closed the file.

'I have all I'm going to find here,' he said to Moore. 'Now I'd like to hunt through Union navy records.'

Moore helpfully returned the files to their respective cabinets and guided him up a steel stairway to the second floor. 'What month and year are you interested in?' he asked.

'April 1865.'

They threaded their way through narrow aisles stacked to the roof with cabinets on top of cabinets. Moore produced a ladder in case Perlmutter wanted to probe files in the upper stratosphere and directed him to the proper cabinet.

Methodically, Perlmutter began expanding his search from April 2, 1865, the date the *Texas* cast off from the pier below Richmond. He had his own system for research investigations and there were few who were better at scratching out leads than him. He used dogged persistence along with instinctive reasoning to narrow down the deadwood from the consequential.

He started with official reports of the battle. When he exhausted those, he went on to eye-witness accounts by civilians who watched along the banks of the James River and crewmen on the Union warships. Within two hours, he had scanned the pertinent contents of nearly sixty letters and fifteen diaries. He transcribed notes on a large legal pad, all the while under the watchful gaze of Frank Moore, who trusted Perlmutter but had caught too many certified researchers trying to steal historical papers and letters not to be conscientious.

Once Perlmutter found the thread, he began to unravel it as one offhand description, one seemingly insignificant bit of information led to revelation after revelation of a story that seemed too incredible to believe. Finally, when he could go no further, he motioned to Moore.

'How much time do I have?'

'Two hours and ten minutes.'

'I'm ready to move on.'

'Where do you wish to look?'

'Any private correspondence or documents you might have of Edwin McMasters Stanton.'

Moore nodded. 'Lincoln's crusty old Secretary of War. I've no idea what we have on him. His papers have never been fully catalogued. But it would be upstairs on the U.S. government documents floor.'

The Stanton files were voluminous, ten file cabinets full. Perlmutter worked steadily, stopping only once to go to the nearest bathroom. He waded through the documents as swiftly as he could, finding surprisingly little on Stanton's relationship with Lincoln near the end of the war. It was a well-known bit of history that the Secretary of War did not like his President and had destroyed a number of pages from the diary of Lincoln's assassin, John Wilkes Booth, including a number of papers relating to Booth's co-conspirators. To the frustration of historians Stanton had purposely left many unanswered questions swirling around the assassination at Ford's Theater.

Then, with only forty minutes left on his deadline, Perlmutter struck pay dirt.

Hidden in the extreme back of a cabinet, Perlmutter found a packet yellowed with age that still had an unbroken wax seal on it. He stared at the brown inked writing that gave the date as July 9, 1865, two days after Booth's fellow conspirators, Mary Surratt, Lewis Paine, David Herold, and George Atzerodt, were hanged in the Washington Arsenal's prison yard. Under the date were the words 'Not to be opened until one hundred years after my death.' It was signed Edwin M. Stanton.

Perlmutter sat down at a study table, broke the seal, opened the packet, and began reading the papers inside with thirty-one years leeway on Stanton's instructions.

As he read he felt as if he was transported back in time. Despite the coolness of the underground facility, beads of sweat glistened on his forehead. When he finished forty minutes later and set the final paper aside, his hands were trembling. He exhaled his breath in a long silent sigh, and shook his head very slowly.

'My God,' Perlmutter whispered.

Moore looked across the table at him. 'Find something interesting?'

Perlmutter did not answer. He simply stared at the pile of old papers and muttered, 'My God,' over and over.

50

They lay together behind the crest of a dune, staring at the empty tracks that stretched across the sand like ghost rails to oblivion. The only signs of life to pierce the predawn darkness were the distant lights of the Fort Foureau hazardous waste site. Across the tracks, less than a kilometre west, the black shadow of the abandoned Foreign Legion fort rose against an ivory black sky like a gloomy castle out of a horror movie.

The mad race across the desert had gone smoothly without detection or mechanical problems. The captives had suffered from the hard springs of the trucks but were too happy to be free to complain. Fairweather accurately guided them over the ancient camel trail that travelled between the old salt mines at Taoudenni south to Timbuktu. He had laid the convoy on the railroad within sight of the fort using only his knowledge of the terrain and a borrowed compass.

Once during their journey, Pitt and Levant had stopped, listening as they detected the engine sounds of an unseen helicopter task force escorted by jet fighters. The aircraft were flying north toward Tebezza and the Algerian border. As Pitt had predicted, the Malian air force pilots flew over the convoy, blissfully unaware their quarry was sitting directly below them.

'Fine work, Mr Fairweather,' complimented Levant. 'As good a job of navigating as I've ever seen. You put us right on target.'

'Instinct,' Fairweather smiled. 'Pure instinct mixed with a bleedin' bit of luck.'

'Better move out across the tracks and into the fort,' said

Pitt. 'We have less than an hour before daylight to hide the vehicles.'

Like strange creatures of the night, the dune buggy and personnel carriers drove on the track bed, bouncing over the concrete ties, until they came even with the fort. Pitt turned past the wreck of the Renault truck, the same one he and Giordino used for cover when they hopped the train to Fort Foureau, and came to a stop at the gate. The high wooden doors were still slightly ajar just as they had left them over a week before. Levant called up a squad of men who pushed them open wide enough to allow the convoy to enter the parade ground.

'If I may suggest, Colonel,' Pitt said tactfully, 'there's just enough time for a detail of your people to brush away our tyre tracks leading from the railroad to the fort. To an inquiring mind it should look like a convoy of Malian military vehicles rolled out of the desert and then continued along the track bed into the waste disposal project.'

'Sound idea,' said Levant. 'Make them think it was one of their own patrols.'

Pembroke-Smythe, tailed by Giordino and Levant's other officers, gathered around their commander for orders.

'Our first priority is to camouflage the tracks and find some sort of shelter for the women and children,' said Levant. 'Then prepare the fort for attack should the Malians decide they're chasing ghosts and look for any sign of our tracks the wind hasn't covered.'

'When do you plan to withdraw from here, sir?' asked an officer with a Swedish accent.

Levant turned to Pitt. 'How say you, Mr Pitt?'

'We stop the first outward-bound train that passes by here after dark,' Pitt answered, 'and borrow it.'

'Trains have communication systems,' said Pembroke-Smythe. 'The engineer will scream bloody murder if you attempt to abscond with his train.'

'Once alerted, the Malians will block the track down the line,' finished the Swedish officer.

'Don't give it another thought,' Pitt said reproachfully. 'Just leave it to old Jesse James Pitt and Butch Cassidy Giordino. We've been practising the old-fashioned art of silent train hijacking for at least . . . he looked at Giordino. 'Al?'

'At least a week from last Thursday,' Giordino responded.

Pembroke-Smythe looked at Levant forlornly. 'One might be advised to increase our insurance premiums.'

'Too late for that now,' said Levant, surveying the darkened interior of the fort. 'These walls were never built to stand up against air-to-ground missiles or heavy artillery. Kazim's forces can reduce this place to rubble in half an hour. So to prevent problems, we have to maintain its abandoned look.'

'The Malians won't be going up against helpless civilians this time,' Pembroke-Smythe said resolutely. 'The ground is level as a cricket field for 2 kilometres in every direction. No cover for attacking forces. Those of us who survive any air assault will make Kazim pay a heavy price in blood before he takes this place.'

'You better hope he hasn't any tanks in the area,' Giordino reminded him.

'Post lookouts on the ramparts,' Levant ordered. 'Then search for an opening leading below-ground. As I recall during my visit there was an arsenal to store shells and ammunition.'

As Levant suggested, steps leading underground were quickly found beneath a floor in the barracks. The two small rooms below were empty except for a few open metal boxes that once held clips of rifle cartridges. The captives of Tebezza were quickly unloaded and assisted below, thankful to be out of the personnel vehicles and on firm earth again. The medical team made them as comfortable as possible and tended to those in serious condition.

The tactical team's vehicles were soon hidden and covered over to look like piles of debris. By the time the sun threw its heat against the walls, the old Foreign Legion fort had regained its abandoned appearance. The two overriding dilemmas facing Levant were discovery before nightfall and the vulnerability to air attack. He felt little sense of security. Once caught, there was no place to run. Already, the guards on the ramparts wistfully watched a train leave the waste project for the Mauritania coast, grimly longing to be on it.

Pitt surveyed what had been a mctor pool with a collapsed roof. He inspected a dozen steel drums of diesel fuel half buried under a pile of old trash. He tapped the metal containers and found six of them nearly full. He was in the act of unscrewing the spout caps as Giordino strolled under the shelter.

'Planning on making a fire?' he asked.

'Might not be a bad idea if we're hit by armoured vehicles,' said Pitt. 'The UN troops lost their anti-tank missile launchers when their aircraft blew up.'

'Diesel fuel,' mused Giordino, 'must have been stored here by the construction crew that laid the railroad.'

Pitt probed a finger through the spout opening and then held it up. 'As pure as the day it came out of the refinery.'

'What good is it except for Molotov cocktails?' Giordino asked with a dubious expression. 'Unless you want to boil it and play knights of old by pouring it on the enemy when they scale the walls?'

'You're getting warm.'

Giordino grimaced at the pun. 'Five men and a small boy couldn't lift one of those drums and carry it to the walls, not when it's full to the gills.'

'Ever see a torsion spring bow?'

'Not in my lifetime,' Giordino grunted. 'Will I sound stupid if ask you to draw a picture?'

To Giordino's surprise Pitt did just that. He hunched down, pulled a double-edged commando knife from a leg sheath, and began sketching a diagram in the dust on the floor. The design was rough, but Giordino recognized what Pitt was attempting to project. When Pitt was finished, he looked up.

'Think we can build one?'

'Don't see why not,' said Giordino. 'Plenty of beams in the fort to choose from, and the personnel vehicles carry lengths of nylon line for rock climbing and emergency towing. The catch, as I see it, is we'll need something to provide torsion.'

'The leaf springs on the rear axles?'

Giordino pondered a moment, then nodded. 'They might work. Yes by God, they should work perfectly.'

'Probably a waste of time,' said Pitt, studying his drawing. 'No reason to think one of Kazim's patrols will stumble in here and blow the whistle before train time.'

'Eleven hours until dark. It will give us something to keep us occupied.'

Pitt began moving toward the door. 'You start assembling the parts. I've got an errand to run. I'll catch up to you later.'

Pitt walked past a group of men who were strengthening the doors of the main gate and made his way around the walls of the fort, careful to cover his footprints. He dropped down into a narrow ravine and walked until he came to a mound rising beside a steep slope.

The Avions Voisin sat in undisturbed solitude.

Most of the sand he and Giordino had hastily thrown over the roof and hood had blown away but enough was left to have kept it difficult to spot by Kazim's air patrols. He opened the door, sat behind the wheel, and pressed the starter button. Almost at once the engine settled into a quiet idle.

Pitt sat there for a few minutes, admiring the workmanship of the old auto. Then he turned off the ignition switch, stepped out, and recovered the body with sand.

Pitt climbed down the stairs into the arsenal. He saw immediately that Eva was on the mend. Although she was still haggard and pale, and her clothing tattered and filthy, she was helping to feed a young boy who was cradled in his mother's arms. She looked up at Pitt with an expression that reflected renewed strength and determination.

'How is he doing?' he asked.

'He'll be playing soccer in no time after he's eaten some solid food and a healthy supply of vitamins.'

'I play football,' the boy whispered.

'In France?' Eva asked curiously.

'We call it soccer,' said Pitt, smiling. 'In every country but ours it's known as football.'

The father of the boy, one of the French engineers who had constructed the Fort Foureau project, came over and shook Pitt's hand. He looked like a scarecrow. He wore crude leather sandals, his shirt was torn and stained, and his pants were held up by a knotted rope. His face was half hidden under a black beard and one side of his head was heavily bandaged.

'I am Louis Monteux.'

'Dirk Pitt.'

'On behalf of my wife and boy,' Monteux said weakly, 'I can't thank you enough for saving our lives.'

'We're not out of Mali yet,' said Pitt.

'Better a quick death than Tebezza.'

'By this time tomorrow we'll be beyond General Kazim's reach,' Pitt assured him.

'Kazim and Yves Massarde,' Monteux spat. 'Murdering criminals of the first magnitude.'

'The reason Massarde sent you and your family to

Tebezza,' Pitt questioned him, 'it was to keep you from exposing the fraudulent operation at Fort Foureau?'

'Yes, the team of scientists and engineers who originally designed and constructed the project discovered upon completion that Massarde planned to bring in far more toxic waste than the operation was capable of disposing.'

'What was your job?'

'To design and oversee the construction of the thermal reactor for the destruction of the waste.'

'And it's working.'

Monteux nodded proudly. 'Yes indeed. Extremely well. It happens to be the largest and most efficient detoxification system operating anywhere in the world today. The solar energy technology of Fort Foureau is the finest in its field.'

'So where did Massarde go wrong? Why spend hundreds of millions of dollars for state-of-the-art equipment only to use it as a facade to secretly bury nuclear and excessive train loads of toxic waste?'

'Germany, Russia, China, the United States, half the world is awash in high-level nuclear waste, the violently radioactive sludge that remains from reprocessed reactor fuel rods and the fissionable material from the production of nuclear bombs. Though it only represents less than one percent of all leftover nuclear material, there are still millions of gallons of it sitting around with nowhere to go. Massarde offered to dispose of it all.'

'But some governments have built disposal repositories.'

'Too little, too late,' Monteux shrugged. 'France's new burial site at Soulaines was almost filled when completed. Then there is the Hanford Reservation waste facility at Richland, Washington, in your country. The tanks that were designed to contain high-level liquid waste for half a century began leaking after twenty years. Close to a million gallons of highly radioactive waste have escaped into the ground to contaminate the groundwater.'

'A neat setup,' said Pitt thoughtfully. 'Massarde makes under-the-table deals with governments and corporations desperate to get rid of their toxic waste. Because Fort Foureau in the western Sahara seemed an ideal dumping ground, he goes into partnership with Zateb Kazim as a buffer against domestic or foreign protest. Then he charges exorbitant fees and smuggles the waste into the middle of the world's most useless piece of real estate and buries it under the guise of a thermal detoxification centre.'

'A simple but reasonably accurate description. But how do you know all this?'

'My friend and I penetrated the underground storage chamber and saw the nuclear waste containers.'

'Dr Hopper told us you were captured at the project.'

'In your opinion, Mr Monteux, could Massarde have built a beneficial and reliable project at Fort Foureau to dispose of all the waste that comes in?'

'Absolutely,' Monteux said decisively. 'If Massarde had excavated waste storage chambers 2 kilometres deep in stable rock formations immune to seismic activity, he would have been raised to sainthood. But he is a miserly, ruthless businessman interested only in profit and gain. Massarde is a sick man, addicted to power and money that he siphons to a secret hoard somewhere.'

'Did you know that it was chemical waste that leaked into the underground water?' Pitt asked.

'A chemical?'

'My understanding is that the compound responsible for thousands of deaths throughout this section of the desert is made up from a synthetic amino acid and cobalt.'

'We heard nothing after we arrived at Tebezza,' said Monteux. He visibly shuddered. 'God, it's already become more horrible than I ever imagined. But the worst has yet to come. Massarde has used inferior canisters to store the nuclear and toxic wastes. It is only a question of time before

528

the whole storage chamber and the land for miles around is swimming in liquid death.'

'Something else you don't know,' said Pitt. 'The compound is seeping through underground streams to the Niger River where it is carried downstream into the ocean. There, it is causing an explosion of the red tides that is consuming all life and oxygen in the water.'

Monteux rubbed his face with his hands in saddened shock at the news. 'What have we done? If we'd only known that Massarde was out to build a cheap and dangerous operation, none of us would have allowed it.'

Pitt looked at Monteux. 'You must have figured Massarde's scheme early in the construction.'

Monteux shook his head. 'Those of us imprisoned in Tebezza were all outside consultants and contractors. We were only involved in the design and construction of the photovoltaic array and thermal reactor. We paid little attention to the excavation. That was an altogether separate project under Massarde Enterprises.'

'When did your suspicions become aroused?'

'Not at first. If anyone questioned Massarde's workers out of simple curiosity, they were told that the excavation was for temporary storage of incoming waste before detoxification. No one was allowed near the area except the underground construction crew. Only near completion of the project did we begin to see through the lie.'

'What finally gave Massarde away?' asked Pitt.

'We all assumed the underground storage chamber was fully completed about the time the thermal reactor was successfully tested for full operation. At that point the toxic materials began arriving on the railroad Massarde had built with cheap labour provided by General Kazim. One evening an engineer, who had been assembling the parabolic solar collectors, slipped into the storage chamber by stealing an entry badge. He discovered the digging had never ceased and was an ongoing project after he saw excavated dirt being secretly shipped out in the cargo containers that carried in the toxic waste. He also found caverns holding canisters filled with nuclear waste.'

Pitt nodded. 'My friend and I stumbled on those secrets too, unaware we were on Massarde's security video show.'

'The engineer escaped back to our living quarters and spread the word before he could be stopped,' Monteux explained. 'Shortly after, all of us who were non-Massarde Enterprises consultants and our families were forcibly rounded up and sent to Tebezza to keep the secret from getting back to France.'

'How did he cover up your sudden disappearance?'

'A phoney story about a disaster at the project, a fire that killed us all. The French government insisted on a full inquiry, but Kazim refused to allow foreign inspectors into Mali, claiming his government would conduct the investigation. Of course, none took place and our supposed cremated bodies were reported as scattered over the desert after a proper ceremony.'

The green in Pitt's eyes deepened. 'Massarde is a thorough man. But he made a series of mistakes.'

'Mistakes?' Monteux said curiously.

'He let too many people live.'

'When you were captured, did you meet him?'

Pitt raised his hand and touched one of the scabs that cut across his cheeks. 'He also has a nasty disposition.'

Monteux smiled. 'Consider yourself lucky that is your only gift from him. When we were assembled and given our death sentence as slave labour in the mines, one woman resisted and spat in Massarde's face. He calmly shot her between the eyes right in front of her husband and ten-year-old daughter.'

'The more I hear about the man,' Pitt said, his tone cold, 'the less he endears himself to me.'

'The commandos say we will attempt to capture a train, and then escape into Mauritania tonight.'

Pitt nodded. That's the plan if we're not discovered by Malian military forces before dark.'

'We have talked between ourselves,' said Monteux solemnly. 'None will go back to Tebezza. All would rather die. We have made a pact to kill our wives and children rather than allow them to suffer in the mines again.'

Pitt stared at Monteux and then to the women and children resting on the stone floor of the arsenal. His craggy and weathered face took on a look of sorrow tinged with anger. Then he said softly, 'Let's hope it doesn't come to that.'

Eva was too tired to sleep. She looked up into Pitt's eyes. 'A walk under the morning sun with me?'

'No one is allowed to wander in the open. The fort has to appear abandoned to passing trains and any aircraft that might fly over.'

'We travelled all last night and I've been locked up underground for nearly two weeks. Isn't there some way I can see the sun?' she implored him.

He said nothing but gave her his best buccaneer grin as he swept her in his arms and carried her up the stairs onto the parade ground. Not stopping, he climbed to the platform that stretched around the fort's ramparts before lightly setting her on her feet.

The sun blinded Eva for a few moments, and she didn't see the approach of a female commando who was on duty as a lookout. 'You must stay below out of sight,' the guard ordered. 'Colonel Levant's orders.'

'A couple of minutes,' Pitt pleaded. 'The lady hasn't seen blue sky for quite a while.'

The tactical team fighter may have looked tough as nails in her combat suit, bristling with ammo and weapons, but she possessed twice the compassion and understanding of any man. One look at the wasted woman leaning against Pitt, and her expression softened. 'Two minutes,' she smiled ever so slightly. 'Then you'll have to get back undercover.'

'Thank you,' said Eva. 'I'm very grateful to you.'

The scorching temperatures were still an hour away as Pitt and Eva looked out from their vantage point across the nearby railroad tracks toward the endless, unbroken terrain to the north. Strangely, it was Pitt and not the woman who saw a magnificence in the parched and hostile landscape, despite the fact that it had almost killed him.

'I can't wait to see the ocean again,' she said.

'Do you dive?' he asked.

'I've always loved water, but never got beyond the snorkel stage.'

'Varied sea life abounds around Monterey. Beautiful fish among the kelp forests, and incredible rock formations, especially down the coast past Carmel toward Big Sur. When we get there, I'll give you scuba lessons and take you diving.'

'I'll look forward to it.'

She closed her eyes, tilted back her head, and soaked in the sun, her cheeks glowing from the rising heat of the day. He gazed down at her, taking in every lovely detail that had not been affected by her long ordeal. The lookouts stationed around the ramparts faded into the bright sunlight. He wanted to wrap her in his arms, forget the dangers, forget everything but this moment and kiss her.

And he did.

For a long moment she gripped him tightly around the neck and kissed back. He squeezed her around the waist and pulled her to her toes. How long they clung together, neither could remember.

Finally she pushed back and looked up into his opaline green eyes, and felt weakness, excitement, and love wrapped up in one swirling emotion. She whispered, 'I knew from that dinner together in Cairo I'd never be able to resist you.'

He said softly, 'And I thought I'd never see you again.'

'Will you be going back to Washington after we escape?' She spoke the words as if reaching safety was a certainty.

He shrugged without letting her go. 'I'm sure they'll want me to return and work on stopping the red tides. And you, after a good rest, where will it be? Another mission of mercy to an underdeveloped country to fight disease?'

'It's my job,' she murmured. 'Helping to save lives is all I've ever wanted to do since I was a little girl.'

'Doesn't leave much time for romance, does it?'

'We're both prisoners of our occupations.'

The lookout came over then. 'You'll have to get down below out of sight now,' she said as if embarrassed. 'We can't be too careful now, can we?'

Eva pulled Pitt's beard-stubbly face down to hers and whispered again in his ear. 'Would you think me wanton if I said I want you?'

He smiled. 'I'm an easy mark for wanton girls.'

She made a small gesture at brushing back her hair and straightening out her dirty and tattered clothing. 'But certainly not one who hasn't bathed in two weeks and is as skinny as an underfed alley cat.'

'Oh I don't know. Unwashed skinny women have been known to bring out the animal in me.'

Without another word, Pitt led her down to the parade ground and into a small storeroom off of what was once the kitchen and mess hall. It was empty except for a wooden keg of iron spikes. No one was in sight. He left her for a minute and returned with two blankets. Then he laid the blankets on the dusty floor of the empty storeroom and locked the door.

They could barely see each other from the light that crept under the door as he squeezed her with his arms again. 'Sorry I can't offer you champagne and a king-size bed.'

Eva daintily straightened the blankets and knelt down, looking up at his dim, rugged-looking face. 'I'll just close my eyes and imagine I'm with my handsome lover in the most luxurious suite in the finest hotel in San Francisco.'

Pitt kissed her and laughed softly. 'Lady, you've got one fantastic imagination.'

51

Massarde's chief aide, Felix Verenne, stepped into his boss's office. 'A call from Ismail Yerli at Kazim's headquarters.'

Massarde nodded and picked up the phone. 'Yes, Ismail, I hope this is good news.'

'I regret to tell you, Mr Massarde, the news is anything but good.'

'Did Kazim catch the UN combat unit?'

'No, he has yet to find them. Their plane was destroyed as we thought, but they vanished in the desert.'

'Why can't his patrols follow their tracks?' Massarde demanded angrily.

'The desert wind has blown sand over them,' Yerli answered calmly. 'All trace of their trail has been obliterated.'

'What is the situation at the mine?'

'The prisoners have rioted, killed the guards, and destroyed the equipment and ravaged the offices. Your engineers are dead too. It will take six months to put the mine back in full operation.'

'What of O'Bannion?'

'Disappeared. No sign of his body. My men did find his sadistic overseer, however.'

'The American he called Melika?'

'The prisoners mutilated her body with a vengeance, almost beyond recognition.'

'The raiders must have taken O'Bannion as informant against us,' suggested Massarde.

'Too soon to tell,' Yerli replied. 'Kazim's officers have just begun interrogating the prisoners. Another bit of news

I can pass along that won't sit well with you is that the Americans, Pitt and Giordino, were recognized by one surviving guard. They somehow fled the mines over a week ago, crossed into Algeria, and returned with the UN raiders.'

Massarde was thunderstruck. 'Good God, that means they reached Algiers and made outside contact.'

'My thoughts also.'

'Why weren't we informed by O'Bannion they had escaped?'

'Fear of how you and Kazim would react, obviously. How they travelled over 400 kilometres of desert without food and water is a mystery.'

'If they exposed our operation of the mine with captive labour to their superiors in Washington, they must have also revealed the secret of Fort Foureau.'

'They have no documented proof,' Yerli reminded him. 'Two foreigners who illegally crossed sovereign borders and committed criminal acts against the Malian government will not be taken seriously in any international court of law.'

'Except that my project will be besieged with news correspondents and world environmental investigators.'

'Not to worry. I will advise Kazim to close the borders to all outsiders, and have them expelled if they do.'

'You're forgetting,' said Massarde, trying to remain calm, 'the French engineers and scientists I contracted to build the project and threw into Tebezza. Once they reach safety, they will spread the word of their abduction and imprisonment. Even more damaging, they will expose our illegal waste dumping operation. Massarde Enterprises will be attacked on all fronts, and I will face criminal charges in every country I have an office or project.'

'None will live to give evidence,' Yerli said as if it was a foregone conclusion.

'What is the next step?' Massarde asked.

'Kazim's aerial reconnaissance and motor patrols can find

no indication of their crossing into Algeria. That means they're still in Mali, staying undercover and awaiting rescue.'

'Which Kazim's forces will stop.'

'Of course.'

'Could they have headed west for Mauritania?'

Yerli shook his head to himself. 'Not with over 1000 kilometres between them and the first village with water. Also, they couldn't possibly have carried enough fuel for that distance.'

'They must be stopped, Ismail,' said Massarde without concealing a note of desperation. 'They must be exterminated.'

'And they shall be,' Yerli promised. 'I vow to you, they will not get out of Mali. Every last one of them will be hunted down. They may fool Kazim, but they won't fool me.'

El Haj Ali sat in the sand under the shade of his camel and waited for a train to pass by. He had walked and ridden over 200 kilometres from his village of Araouane to see the wonder of a railroad, described to him by a passing Britisher who was leading a group of tourists across the desert.

Just past his fourteenth birthday, Ali's father had given him permission to take one of the family's two camels, a superb white animal, and travel north to the shining rails and witness the great steel monster with his own eyes. Though he had seen automobiles and distant aircraft in the sky, other wonders such as cameras, radios, and television sets were a mystery to him. But to actually see and perhaps touch a locomotive would make him the envy of every boy and girl in his village.

He drank tea and sucked on boiled sweets as he waited. After three hours and no sign of an approaching train, he mounted his camel and set off along the tracks toward the Fort Foureau project so he could tell his family about the immense buildings that rose out of the desert.

As he passed the long-abandoned Foreign Legion fort, surrounded by high walls, isolated and lonely, he turned off the rails and approached the gate out of curiosity. The big, sun-bleached doors were shut tight. He jumped from his camel and led it around the fort's walls looking for another opening to gain entrance inside, but finding only solid mud and stone, he gave up and walked back toward the railroad.

He looked to the west, intrigued with the way the silver rails strung out far into the distance and curled under the heat waves rising from the sun-baked sands. His eye caught something as he stood on the ties and stared. A speck appeared and floated through the heat waves. It enlarged and came toward him. The great steel monster, he thought with excitement.

But as the object drew closer, he could see it was too small for a locomotive. Then he discerned two men riding on it as if it was an open automobile driving on the rails. Ali moved off the track bed and stood next to his camel as the motor cart carrying two section hands who were inspecting the track rolled to a stop in front of him.

One was a white foreigner, the other, a dark-skinned Moor, greeted him. '*Sallam al laikum.*'

'*Al laikum el sallam,*' Ali replied.

'Where do you come from, boy?' asked the Moor in the Berber language of the Tuareg.

'From Araouane to see the steel monster.'

'You've come a long way.'

'The trip was easy,' Ali boasted.

'You have a fine camel.'

'My father loaned me his best.'

The Moor looked at a gold wristwatch. 'You don't have long to wait. The train from Mauritania is due in about forty-five minutes.'

'Thank you. I will wait,' said Ali.

'See anything interesting inside the old fort?'

538

Ali shook his head. 'I could not enter. The gates are locked.'

The two section men exchanged quizzical glances and conversed in French for a few moments.

Then the Moor asked, 'Are you certain? The fort is always open. That is where we keep ties and equipment to repair the track bed.'

'I do not lie. See for yourself.'

The Moor stepped down from the motor cart and walked up to the front of the fort. He returned a few minutes later and spoke to the white man in French.

'The boy is right. The doors to the main gate are locked from within.'

The face of the French track surveyor turned serious. 'We must continue into the waste project and report this.'

The Moor nodded and climbed back on the motor cart. He threw Ali a wave. 'Do not stand too close to the tracks when the train comes, and keep a tight grip on your camel.'

The engine's exhaust popped and the motor cart rolled down the rails in the direction of the hazardous waste project, leaving Ali staring after it while his camel gazed stoically at the horizon and spat on the track.

Colonel Marcel Levant realized he could not prevent the nomad boy and the railroad section hand from inspecting the exterior of the fort. Silently, menacingly, a dozen unseen machine guns had been trained on the curious intruders. They could have easily been shot and dragged into the fort, but Levant did not have the stomach for killing innocent civilians so they were spared.

'What do you think?' Pembroke-Smythe asked as the motor cart sped down the track toward the waste site's security station.

Levant studied the boy and his camel, his eyes squinting like those of a sniper. They were still resting beside the tracks waiting for the next passing train. If those two on the cart tell Massarde's security guards the fort is sealed up we can expect an armed patrol to investigate.'

Pembroke-Smythe checked the time. 'A good seven hours before dark. Let's hope they're slow in responding.'

'Any late word from General Bock?' asked Levant.

'We've lost contact. The radio was knocked about during the journey from Tebezza and the circuitry became damaged. We can no longer transmit and reception is quite weak. The General's last message came through too garbled to decode properly. The best the operator could make of it was something abut an American special operation force team that was going to hook up with us in Mauritania.'

Levant stared incredulously at Pembroke-Smythe. 'The Americans are coming, but only as far as Mauritania? Good God, that's over 3 kilometres from here. What in hell good will they do us in Mauritania if we're attacked before we can escape over the border?'

'The message was unclear, sir,' Pembroke-Smythe shrugged helplessly. 'Our radio operator did his best. Perhaps he misunderstood.'

'Can he somehow rig the radio to our combat communications gear?'

Pembroke-Smythe shook his head. 'He already thought of that angle. The systems are not compatible.'

'We don't even know if Admiral Sandecker deciphered Pitt's code correctly,' Levant said wearily. 'For all Bock knows we may be wandering around the desert in circles or fleeing for Algeria.'

'I like to think positive, sir.'

Levant sank down heavily and leaned against a rampart. 'No chance of making a run for it. Not nearly enough fuel. Getting caught in the open by the Malians is almost a certainty. No contact with the outside world. I'm afraid many of us are going to die in this rat hole, Pembroke-Smythe.'

'Look on the bright side, Colonel. Perhaps the Americans will come charging in here like General Custer's seventh cavalry.'

'Oh God!' Levant moaned despairingly. 'Why did you have to go and mention *him?*'

Giordino lay stretched out on his back under a personnel carrier removing a chassis spring when he saw Pitt's boots and legs step into his limited view. 'Where've you been?' he grunted while twisting a nut from a shackle bolt.

'Tending to the weak and infirm,' answered Pitt cheerfully.

'Then tend to the framework of your oddball whatchacallit. You can use the beams from the ceilings in the officers' quarters. They're dry but sound.'

'You've been busy.'

'A pity you can't say the same,' Giordino said complainingly. 'You'd better start figuring out how you're going to attach it all together.'

Pitt lowered a small wooden keg to the ground in Giordino's line of sight. 'Problem solved. I found half a keg of spikes in the mess hall.'

'The mess hall.'

'Exposed in a storeroom in the mess hall,' Pitt corrected himself.

Giordino pushed himself from under the vehicle and examined Pitt, his eyes travelling from the unlaced boots to the half-opened combat suit to the dishevelled hair. When he finally spoke, it was in a voice heavy with sarcasm.

'I bet that keg wasn't the only thing you exposed in the storeroom.'

52

When the report from the railroad section hands came into Kazim's security headquarters from Fort Foureau, it was given a quick read and set aside by Major Sid Ahmed Gowan, Kazim's personal intelligence officer. He saw nothing of value in it, and certainly no reason to pass it on to that Turkish interloper, Ismail Yerli.

Gowan failed to spot a connection between an abandoned fort and an elusive prey 400 kilometres to the north. The railroad workers who insisted the fort was locked from the inside were haughtily brushed off as a pair of dubious informants attempting to ingratiate themselves with their superiors.

But as the hours dragged by without any sighting of the UN force, Major Gowan took another look at the account and his suspicions began to grow. He was a thoughtful man, young and highly intelligent, the only officer in General Kazim's security forces who was educated in France and had graduated from Saint Cyr, France's foremost military college. He began to see a possibility of pulling off a coup to please his leader and make Yerli appear an amateur intelligence specialist.

He picked up the phone and called the commander of the Malian air forces, requesting an aerial reconnaissance of the desert south of Tebezza with special emphasis on vehicle tracks in the sand. As a backup precaution he also advised Fort Foureau to stop all trains from leaving or entering the project. If ,the UN force had indeed crossed the desert southward without being observed, Gowan speculated, perhaps they had holed up in the old Foreign Legion fort during daylight hours. With their vehicles certain to be low on fuel, they would probably await darkness before attempting to capture an outbound train headed for the Mauritanian border.

All Gowan needed to confirm his hunch was an aerial sighting of fresh vehicle tracks travelling from Tebezza to the railroad. Positive that he was now on the right trail, he rang Kazim and explained his new analysis of the search operation.

Inside the fort the hardest ingredient of suffering was time. Everyone counted the minutes until darkness. Each hour that passed without sign of an attack was considered a gift. But by four o'clock in the afternoon. Levant knew something was terribly wrong.

He was standing on a rampart studying the hazardous waste project through binoculars when Pembroke-Smythe approached with Pitt in tow.

'You sent for me, Colonel?' asked Pitt.

Levant replied without dropping the glasses. 'When you and Mr Giordino penetrated the grounds of the waste project, did you by chance time the passing trains?'

'Yes, the inbound and outbound trains alternated, one entering three hours after one exited.'

Levant put down the glasses and stared at Pitt. 'Then what do you make of the fact that no train has appeared for four and a half hours?'

'A problem with the track, a derailment, breakdown of equipment. There could be any number of reasons for a slowdown in the schedule.'

'Is that what you believe?'

'Not for an instant.'

'What is your best guess?' Levant persisted.

Pitt stared at the empty rails running in front of the old fort. 'If I was betting a year's wages, I'd have to say they're on to us.'

'You think the trains were halted to prevent us from escaping?'

Pitt nodded. 'It stands to reason that once Kazim wises up to our end run, and his search patrols spot our wheel tracks travelling south to the railroad, he'll realize our objective was to hijack a train.'

'The Malians are smarter than I gave them credit for,' Levant admitted. 'Now we're trapped with no means of communicating our situation to General Bock.'

Pembroke-Smythe cleared his throat. 'If I may suggest, sir. I would like to volunteer to make a dash toward the border to meet up with the American Special Forces team and lead them back.'

Levant looked at him sternly for a moment. 'A suicide mission at best.'

'It may well be our only chance at getting anyone out of here. By taking the fast attack vehicle, I can be over the border inside of six hours.'

'You're optimistic, Captain,' Pitt corrected him. 'I've driven over this part of the desert. Just when you're travelling at speed across what looks like a flat dry plain, you drop 50 feet off a slope into a ravine. And there is no travelling through sand dunes if you expect to make time. I'd say you'll be lucky to hit Mauritania by late tomorrow morning.'

'I intend to travel as the crow flies by driving on the railroad.'

'A dead giveaway. Kazim's patrols will be all over you before you've covered 50 kilometres, if they haven't already set up blockades across the tracks.'

'Aren't you forgetting our lack of fuel?' added Levant. 'There isn't enough gas to carry you a third of the way.'

'We can drain what's left from the tanks of the personnel carriers,' Pembroke-Smythe said without a sign of retreat.

'You'll be cutting it a mite thin,' said Pitt.

Pembroke-Smythe shrugged. 'A dull ride without some risk.'

'You can't go it alone,' said Levant.

'A night crossing of the desert at high speed can be a risky business,' cautioned Pitt. 'You'll need a co-driver and a navigator.'

'I have no intention of attempting it alone,' Pembroke-Smythe informed them.

'Who have you selected?' asked Levant.

Smythe looked and smiled at the tall man from NUMA. 'Either Mr Pitt or his friend Giordino, since they've already had a crash course in desert survival.'

'A civilian won't be of much help in a running fight with Kazim's patrols,' warned Levant.

'I plan to lighten the assault vehicle by removing all armour and weapons. We'll carry a spare tyre and tools, enough water for the next twenty-four hours, and handguns only.'

Levant thought out Pembroke-Smythe's mad plan carefully in his methodical way. Then he added. 'All right, Captain. Get to work on the vehicle.'

'Yes sir.'

'There is, however, one other thing.'

'Sir?'

'Sorry to put a crimp in your escapade, but as second in command, I require your services here. You'll have to send someone in your place. I suggest Lieutenant Steinholm. If I remember correctly, he once drove in the Monte Carlo Rally.'

Pembroke-Smythe did not attempt to conceal the expression of disappointment on his face. He began to say something, but saluted and hurried down the ladder to the parade field without a word of protest.

Levant looked at Pitt. 'You'll have to volunteer, Mr Pitt. I do not have the authority to order you to go.'

'Colonel,' Pitt said with the barest of grins, 'I've been chased all over the Sahara in the past week, came within a millimetre of dying of thirst, been shot at, steamed like a lobster, and cuffed in the face by every unsavoury scum I met. This is the last stop for Mrs Pitt's boy. I'm getting off the train and staying put. Al Giordino will go out with Lieutenant Steinholm.'

Levant smiled. 'You're a fraud, Mr Pitt, a sterling, gilt-edged fraud. You know as well as I it's sure death to remain here. Giving your friend a chance of escape in your place is a noble gesture. You have my deepest respect.'

'Noble gestures are not part of my act. I have a thing about leaving jobs unfinished.'

Levant looked down at the strange machine taking shape under the protection of one wall. 'You mean your catapult.'

'Actually, it's sort of a spring bow.'

'Do you actually think it will work against armoured vehicles?'

'Oh, she'll do the job,' said Pitt in a tone of utter confidence. 'The only unknown is how well.'

Shortly after sunset, the hurriedly filled sandbags and makeshift obstructions were removed from the main gate and the massive doors opened. Lieutenant Steinholm, a big, blond, handsome Austrian, strapped himself behind the wheel and received his final instructions from Pembroke-Smythe.

Giordino stood beside the stripped-down dune buggy and quietly made his farewells to Pitt and Eva. 'So long, old buddy,' he said to Pitt, forcing a tight smile. 'Not fair me going instead of you.'

Pitt gave Giordino a quick bear hug. 'Mind the pot holes.'

'Steinholm and I'll be back with beer and pizza by lunchtime.'

The words were empty of meaning. Neither man doubted

546

for a second that by noon the following day the fort and everybody in it would be only a memory.

'I'll keep a light in the window,' said Pitt.

Eva gave Giordino a light kiss on the cheek and handed him a small package wrapped in plastic. 'A little something to eat on the road.'

'Thank you.' Giordino turned away so they couldn't see his watering eyes and climbed in the attack vehicle, his smile suddenly gone, his face taut with sadness. 'Put your foot on it,' he said to Steinholm.

The Lieutenant nodded, shifted gears, and rammed his foot on the accelerator. The dune buggy leaped forward and shot through the open gate, roaring into the fading orange of the western sky as its rear wheels kicked up twin rooster tails of dust.

Giordino twisted in his seat and looked back. Pitt stood just outside the gate, one arm around Eva's waist. He lifted a hand in a gesture of farewell. Giordino could still see the flash of Pitt's devilish smile before the trailing dust closed off all view.

For a long minute the entire combat team watched the dune buggy speed across the desert. Their reactions ranged all the way from a weary kind of sorrow to resigned acceptance as the vehicle became a faint speck in the gloom of dusk. Every hope they had of surviving went with Giordino and Steinholm. Then Levant gave a quiet command and the commandos pushed the doors closed and barricaded the gate for the final time.

Major Gowan received the report he was expecting from a helicopter patrol that followed the tyre tracks of Levant's convoy to the railroad where they disappeared. Further reconnaissance was called off because of darkness. The few aircraft of the Malian air force equipped with night vision equipment were grounded for mechanical repairs. But

Gowan did not require additional search and recon missions. He knew where his quarry was hiding. He contacted Kazim and confirmed his assessment of the situation. His delighted superior promoted him to Colonel on the spot and promised a decoration for meritorious service.

Gowan's part in the operation was over. He lit a cigar, propped his feet on his desk, and poured a glass of expensive Remy Martin cognac he kept in his desk for special occasions, and this was indeed a special occasion.

Unfortunately for his Commander-in-Chief, General Kazim, Gowan's canny perception and powers of deduction were turned off for the remainder of the operation. Just when Kazim needed his intelligence chief most, the newly promoted Colonel had gone home to his villa beside the Niger for a holiday with his French mistress, oblivious to the storm brewing across the desert to the west.

Massarde was on the phone listening to an up-to-date report by Yerli on the progress of the search. 'What's the latest word?' he asked anxiously.

'We have them,' Yerli announced triumphantly, taking credit for Major Gowan's farsighted intuition. 'They thought they could outfox us by reversing their escape route and heading into the Malian interior, but I was not to be fooled. They are trapped in the abandoned Legion fort not far from you.'

'I'm very glad to hear it,' sighed Massarde, letting out a deep sigh. 'What are Kazim's plans?'

'Demand their surrender for openers.'

'And if they comply?'

'Put the commandos and their officers on trial for invading his country. After conviction, they'll be held as hostages in exchange for economic demands from the United Nations. The Tebezza prisoners will be taken to his interrogation chambers, where they will be properly dealt with.'

'No,' Massarde said. 'Not the solution I want. The only solution is to destroy them all, and quickly. None must be left alive to talk. We cannot afford any more complications. I must insist you talk Kazim into ending this matter immediately.'

His demand came so forcibly, so abruptly, that Yerli was stunned into temporary silence. 'All right . . .' Yerli finally said slowly. 'I'll do my best to persuade Kazim to launch the attack at first light with his fighter jets followed by helicopter assault units. Fortunately, he has four heavy tanks and three infantry companies in the vicinity on military manoeuvres.'

'Can he attack the fort tonight?'

'He will need time to assemble his forces and coordinate an attack. This can't be done before early morning.'

'Just see that Kazim does whatever is necessary to prevent Pitt and Giordino from escaping again.'

'The very reason I took the precaution of halting all trains in and out of Mauritania,' Yerli lied.

'Where are you now?'

'In Gao, about to board the command aircraft that you so generously provided Kazim as a gift. He plans to personally oversee the assault.'

'Remember, Yerli,' said Massarde as patiently as he could, 'no prisoners.'

53

They came just after six o'clock in the morning. The UN tactical team members were bone-tired after digging deep entrenchments beneath the base of the walls, but they were all alert and primed to resist. Most were now holed up like moles in their dugouts for the expected air attack. Deep in the underground arsenal the team medics set up a field hospital while the French engineers and their families huddled on the floor under old wooden tables and furniture to ward off rock and debris that might fall from the ceiling. Only Levant and Pembroke-Smythe, along with the crew manning the Vulcan that had been removed from the assault vehicle, remained on the fort's wall, protected only by the parapets and hastily piled sandbags.

The incoming jet aircraft were heard before they were seen and the alarm was given.

Pitt did not seek cover, but fussed over his spring bow, making frantic last-minute adjustments. The truck springs, mounted vertically within a maze of wooden beams, were bent almost double by the hydraulic lifting gear on the old forklift found stored with the railroad supplies. Attached to the stressed springs, a half-filled drum of diesel oil with perforated holes on the upper side lay on a grooved board that angled sharply toward the sky. After helping Pitt assemble the Rube Goldberg contraption, Levant's men moved away, doubtful the drum of fuel oil could be tossed over the top of the wall without bursting inside the fort and burning everyone on the parade ground.

Levant knelt behind the parapet, his back protected by a pile of sandbags, and peered into a cloudless sky. He spotted the aircraft and studied them through his binoculars as they began circling at no more than 500 metres above the desert only 3 kilometres south of the fort. He noted their apparent unconcern toward surface-to-air missiles. They seemed confident the fort had nothing to offer in the way of air defence.

As with many third world military leaders who preferred glitz over practicality, Kazim had purchased fast Mirage fighters from the French more for show than actual combat. With little to fear from the weaker military forces of his neighbouring countries, Kazim's air and ground security forces were created to inspire respect for his ego and instill fear in the minds of any revolutionaries.

The Malian attack force was backed up by a small fleet of lightly armed helicopters whose sole mission was to conduct search patrols and transport assault troops. Only the fighters were capable of unleashing missiles that could knock out armoured tanks or fortifications. But unlike the newer laser-guided bombs, the Malian pilots had to manually sight and guide their old-type tactical missiles to the target.

Levant spoke into the microphone on his helmet. 'Captain Pembroke-Smythe, stand by the Vulcan crew.'

'Standing by Madeleine and ready to fire,' Pembroke-Smythe acknowledged from the gun emplacement on the opposite rampart.

'Madeleine?'

'The crew have formed an endearing attachment to the gun, sir, and named it after a girl whose favours they enjoyed in Algeria.'

'Just see that Madeleine doesn't get fickle and jam.'

'Yes sir.'

'Let the first plane make its firing run,' Levant instructed. 'Then blast it from the rear as it banks away. If your timing is right, you should be able to swing back and strike the

551

second plane in line before it can launch its missiles.'

'Jolly good, sir.'

Almost as Pembroke-Smythe replied, the lead Mirage broke from formation and dropped down to 75 metres, boring in without any attempt at jinking back and forth to avoid ground fire. The pilot was hardly a top jet driver. He came slow and fired his two missiles a trifle late.

Powered by single-stage solid-propellant rocket motor, the first missile soared over the fort, its high explosive warhead bursting harmlessly in the sand beyond. The second struck against the north parapet and exploded, tearing a 2-metre gouge in the top of the wall and hurling shattered stone in a shower across the parade ground.

The Vulcan's crew tracked the low-flying jet, and the instant it passed over the fort they opened fire. The revolving six-barrel Gatling gun, set to fire a thousand rounds a minute instead of its two thousand maximum to conserve supply, spat a hail of 20-millimetre shells at the fleeing aircraft as it banked into a vulnerable position. One wing broke away as cleanly as if it had been cut by a surgeon's scalpel, and the Mirage violently twisted over on its back and crashed into the ground.

Almost before the impact, Madeleine was swung 180 degrees and cut loose again, her stream of shells walking into the path of the second jet and smashing it head on. There was a black puff and the fighter exploded in a fiery ball and disintegrated, pieces of it splattering into the fort's outer wall.

The next fighter in line launched its missiles far too soon in panic and banked away. Levant watched with a bemused expression as twin explosions dug craters a good 200 metres in front of the fort. Now leaderless, the squadron broke off the attack and began circling aimlessly far out of range.

'Nice shooting,' Levant complimented the Vulcan crew.

'Now they know we can bite, they'll launch their missiles at a greater distance with less accuracy.'

'Only about six hundred rounds left,' reported Pembroke-Smythe.

'Conserve it for now and have the men take cover. We'll let them pound us for a while. Sooner or later one will get careless and come in close again.'

Kazim had listened to his pilots excitedly calling to one another over their radios, and he watched the opening débâcle from the video telephoto system through the command centre monitors. Their confidence badly shaken during their first actual combat with an enemy who shot back at them, the pilots were babbling over the airwaves like frightened children and begging for instructions.

His face flushed with anger, Kazim stepped into the communications cabin and began shouting over the radio. 'Cowards! This is General Kazim. You airmen are my right arm, my executioners. Attack, attack. Any man who does not show courage will be shot when he lands and his family sent to prison.'

Undertrained, over confident until now, the Malian air force pilots were more adept at swaggering through their streets and pursuing pretty girls than fighting an opponent out to kill them. The French had made a diligent attempt at modernizing and schooling the desert nomads in air-fighting tactics, but traditional ways and cultural thinking were too firmly entrenched in their minds to make them an efficient fighting force.

Stung by Kazim's words and more fearful of his wrath than the shot and shell that had blasted their flight leader and his wingman from the sky, they very reluctantly resumed the attack and dived in single file at the still stalwart walls of the old Foreign Legion fort.

*

As if he thought himself 'unkillable,' Levant stood and observed the attack from between the ramparts with the calmness of a spectator at a tennis match. The first two fighters fired their missiles and banked sharply away before coming anywhere near the fort. All their rockets went high and burst on the other side of the railroad.

They came from all sides in wild, unpredictable manoeuvres. Their assaults should have been basic and organized, concentrating on levelling one wall instead of haphazardly attacking the fort from whatever direction suited them. Experiencing no more return fire, they became more accurate. The fort began to take devastating hits now. Gaping holes appeared in the old masonry as the walls began to crumble.

Then, as Levant predicted, the Malian pilots became overconfident and bolder, pressing ever closer before launching their missiles. He rose from behind his small command post and brushed away the dust on his combat suit.

'Captain Pembroke-Smythe, any casualties?'

'None reported, Colonel.'

'It's time for Madeleine and her friends to earn their money again.'

'Manning the gun now, sir.'

'If you plan well, you'll have enough shells left to down two more of the devils.'

The job was made easier when two aircraft raced across the open desert wing tip to wing tip. The Vulcan swung around to engage and open fire. At first it looked as though the gun crew had missed. Then there was a burst of flame and black smoke erupted from the starboard Mirage. The plane didn't explode nor did the pilot seem to lose control. The nose simply fell on a slight angle downward and the fighter descended until it crashed into the sand.

Madeleine was shifted to the port fighter and opened up

like a screeching banshee. Seconds later, the last of the rounds left the revolving barrels and she abruptly went silent. But not before her short spurt of fire made the second fighter appear as if it had run into a junkyard scrap grinder. Pieces of the plane split off including the canopy.

Oddly there was no sign of smoke or fire. The Mirage settled onto the desert, bounced once, and then smashed into the east wall, exploding with a deafening roar and hurling stone and flaming debris throughout the parade ground and collapsing the officers' quarters. To those inside it felt as though the tired old fort was lifted clear of the ground by a rippling detonation.

Pitt was whirled around and thrown violently to the ground as the sky tore apart. He felt as if the detonation was almost directly above him when in fact it came on the opposite side of the fort. His breath came as though he was sucking air in a vacuum as the concussion reverberated all round him in a bedlam of compressed air.

He pushed himself to his knees, coughing from the dust that blanketed the interior of the fort. His first concern was the spring bow. It still stood undamaged amid the dust cloud. Then he noticed a body lying near him on the ground.

'My . . . God!' the man uttered in a halting croak.

It was then Pitt recognized Pembroke-Smythe who had been blown off the ramparts by the force of the explosion. He crawled over and peered down into a pair of closed eyes. Only the throbbing pulse in the side of the Lieutenant's neck gave any indication of life.

'How badly are you hurt?' Pitt asked, not thinking of anything else to say.

'Bloody well knocked the wind out of me and ruined my back,' Pembroke-Smythe gasped between clenched teeth.

Pitt glanced up at the section of the parapet that had collapsed. 'You had quite a fall. I don't see any blood and no bones look broken. Can you move your legs?'

Pembroke-Smythe managed to raise his knees and swivel his booted feet. 'At least my spine is still connected.' Then he lifted a hand and pointed behind Pitt across the parade ground. The dust had begun to settle, and his face glowered helplessly as he glimpsed the great mound of rubble that had buried several of his men. 'Dig the poor beggars out!' he implored. 'For God's sake, dig them out!'

Pitt turned suddenly, focusing on the shattered and fallen wall. What had been a massive bulwark of mortar and stone was now a great heap of rubble. No one who was buried under the collapsed wall could have survived without being crushed to death. And those who might miraculously still be alive while trapped inside their dugouts would not last long before succumbing to suffocation. Pitt felt the prickle of horror in the nape of his neck as he realized that nothing less than heavy construction equipment could dig them out in time.

Before he could react, another salvo of missiles bore into the fort, bursting and creating a shambles of the mess hall. The roof support beams were soon ablaze, sending a column of smoke into the climbing heat of the morning. The walls now looked as though a giant had worked them over with a sledgehammer. The north wall had suffered the least; incredibly the main gate remained unscarred. But the other three were severely damaged and their crests breached in several places.

With four of their planes lost, their missiles expended, and low on fuel, the remaining fighters regrouped and set a course back to their base in the south. The surviving UN commandos rose from their underground shelters like dead from the grave and frantically began tearing at the debris for their comrades. In spite of their desperate efforts there was no chance any of those buried under the wall could be rescued with mere human hands.

Levant came down from the parapet and began giving

commands. Wounded were sent or carried down to the safety of the arsenal where the medical personnel were ready to receive them, assisted by Eva and the other women who acted as nurses.

The faces on the men and women of the tactical team were filled with anguish as Levant ordered them to cease digging under the wall and tackle the job of filling in the worst breaches. Levant shared their sorrow, but his responsibility was for the living. There was nothing to be done for the dead.

Grinning and bearing the agony radiating from his back, the irrepressible Pembroke-Smythe hobbled around the fort, taking casualty reports and giving words of encouragement. Despite the death and the horror that was engulfing them, he tried to instill a sense of humour to combat their ordeal.

The count came to six dead and three seriously wounded with bones broken from flying stone. Seven others returned to their posts after having assorted cuts and bruises sanitized and bandaged. It could have been worse, Colonel Levant told himself as he surveyed his situation. But he knew the air attacks were only the opening act. After a brief intermission. the second act began as a missile burst under the lee of the south wall, fired from one of four tanks 2000 metres to the south. Then three more line-of-sight wire-guided battlefield missiles slammed into the fort in quick succession.

Levant quickly climbed onto the rubble that had once been a wall and lined up his glasses on the tanks. 'French AMX-30-type tanks firing SS-11 battlefield missiles,' he calmly announced to Pitt and Pembroke-Smythe. 'They'll soften us up for a bit before coming on with their infantry.'

Pitt stared around the battered fortress.'Not much left to soften,' he muttered laconically.

Levant lowered the glasses and turned to Pembroke-Smythe who was standing beside them, hunched over like a man of ninety-five.

557

'Order everyone into the arsenal. Except for a lookout, we'll weather the storm down there.'

'And when those tanks come knocking at our door?' asked Pitt.

'Then it's up to your catapult isn't it,' said Pembroke-Smythe pessimistically. 'That's all we'll have against those bloody tanks.'

Pitt smiled grimly. 'It looks as though I have to make a believer out of you, Captain.'

Pitt was proud of his acting. He nicely concealed the apprehension that was swamping him in great trembling waves. He hadn't the slightest clue whether his medieval anti-tank weapon stood a ghost of a chance of actually working or not.

54

Four hundred kilometres to the west the dawn broke absolutely still; no whisper of wind rustled the air over the empty, shapeless and desolate sands. The only sound came from the muffled tone of the fast attack vehicle's exhaust as it scurried across the desert like a black ant on a beach.

Giordino was studying the vehicle's on-board computer that subtracted the distance travelled in a straight line from the deviations that had forced them to detour around impassable ravines and a great sea of dunes. On two occasions they had to backtrack nearly 20 kilometres before continuing on their course again.

According to the digital numbers that flashed on a small screen, it had taken Giordino and Steinholm nearly twelve hours to cover the 400 kilometres between Fort Foureau and the Mauritanian border. Staying well clear of the railroad had cost them dearly in time lost. But too much was riding on them to risk encountering armed troops patrolling the tracks or being detected and blown to shreds by roving Malian fighter jets.

The last third of the journey was over hard ground, peppered with rocks that had been polished smooth by tiny grit blown by the wind. The rocks varied in size from marbles to footballs and made driving a horror, but they never gave thought to reducing their speed. They bounced over the uneven ground at a constant rate of 90 kilometres an hour, enduring the choppy, bone-jarring ride with stoic determination.

Exhaustion and suffering were overcome by thinking of what must be happening to the men and women they left behind. Giordino and Steinholm well knew, that if there was any hope for them at all, the American Special Operations Forces must be found, and found quickly if a rescue mission was to reach the fort before Kazim massacred everyone inside. Giordino's promise to return by noon came back to haunt him. The prospect looked dim indeed.

'How far to the border?' asked Steinholm in English with an Arnold Schwarzenegger accent.

'No way of telling,' Giordino answered. 'They don't erect welcome signs in empty desert. For all I know, we've already crossed it.'

'At least now it's light enough to see where we're going.'

'Makes it easier for the Malians to pick us off too.'

'I vote we head north toward the railroad,' said Steinholm. 'The fuel gauge is touching on empty. Another 30 kilometres and we'll have to walk.'

'Okay, you sold me.' Giordino checked the computer once more and pointed toward the compass mounted above the instrument panel. 'Turn on a heading of 50 degrees northwest and run a diagonal course until we bisect the track bed. That will give us a few more kilometres in case we haven't passed into Mauritania yet.'

'The moment of truth,' Steinholm said, smiling. He jammed the pedal to the floor, spinning the wheels in the rock and sand, showering the air with pebbles and dust. In unison he twisted the wheel and sent the military version of the dune buggy tearing over the desert toward Massarde's railroad.

The fighters returned at eleven o'clock and resumed devastating the already wrecked fort with their missiles. When they finished their bomb runs, the four tanks took up the bombardment as the desert echoed with the constant rumble of explosives. To the defenders the thunder and devastation never seemed to end as Kazim's ground forces moved to within 300 metres and blasted away at the ruins with mortars and sniper fire.

The concentration of firepower was unlike anything the French Foreign Legion had ever experienced fighting the Tuaregs during their hundred-year occupation of West Africa. Shell after shell rained down, the detonations merging in a never-ending clap of thunder. The remnants of the walls continued to be pulverized from the constant explosions that hurled stone, mortar, and sand high into the air until little of the old fort bore any resemblance to its original shape. It now looked like a ruin from antiquity.

General Kazim's command aircraft had landed at a nearby dry lake. Accompanied by his Chief-of-Staff, Colonel Sghir Cheik, and Ismail Yerli, he was met by Captain Mohammed Batutta. The Captain led them to a four-wheel-drive staff car and drove them to the hastily set up headquarters of his Field Commander, Colonel Nouhoum Mansa, who stepped forward to greet them.

'You have them completely hemmed in?' Kazim demanded.

'Yes, General,' Mansa quickly answered. 'My plan is to gradually compress our lines around the fort until the final assault.'

'Have you attempted to persuade the UN team to surrender?'

'On four different occasions. Each time I was flatly rejected by their leader, a Colonel Levant.'

Kazim smiled cynically. 'Since they insist on dying, we'll help them along.'

'There cannot be many of them left,' observed Yerli as he peered through a telescope mounted on a tripod. 'The place looks like a pulverized sieve. They must all be buried under the stone from the fallen walls.'

'My men are anxious to fight,' said Mansa. 'They wish to put on a good show for their beloved leader.'

Kazim looked pleased. 'And they shall have their opportunity. Give the order to charge the fort in one hour.'

There was no pause from the incessant hammering. Down in the arsenal, now crammed with nearly sixty commandos and civilians, the stones supporting the arched roof, their mortar crumbling, began falling on the huddled mass of people below.

Eva was crouched near the stairway, bandaging a female fighter whose shoulder was punctured in several places by small shrapnel, when a mortar shell burst at the head of the upper entrance. Her body shielded the woman she was tending as the blast mauled her with flying rock. She lost consciousness and awoke later to find herself laid out on the floor with the other wounded.

One of the medics was at work on her as Pitt sat and held her hand, his face tired, streaked with sweat, and wearing a stubble of beard turned nearly white with billowing dust, lit up with a loving smile.

'Welcome back,' he said. 'You gave us quite a scare when the stairway caved in.'

'Are we trapped?' she murmured.

'No, we can break out when the time comes.'

'It seems so dark.'

'Captain Pembroke-Smythe and his team cleared an exit only big enough for us to breathe. It doesn't let in much light, but keeps out the shrapnel.'

'I feel numb all over. How strange there is no pain.'

The medic, a young red-headed Scotsman, grinned at her. 'I've heavily sedated you. I couldn't have you waking up on me while I set your lovely bones.'

'How bad am I?'

'Except for a broken right arm and shoulder, one or more

cracked ribs — I can't tell without X-rays — fractured left tibia and ankle, plus a sea of bruises and possible internal injuries, you're quite all right.'

'You're very honest,' said Eva, gamely forcing a thin smile at the medic's battlefield whimsy.

The medic patted her good arm. 'Forgive my bleak bedside manner, but I think it best you know the cold truth.'

'I appreciate that,' she said weakly.

'Two months' rest and you'll be ready to swim the channel.'

'I'll stick to heated swimming pools, thank you.'

Pembroke-Smythe, indefatigable as ever, moved about the crowded arsenal keeping everyone's spirits up. He came over and knelt by Eva. 'Well, well, you're one iron lady, Dr Rojas.'

'I'm told I'll survive.'

'She won't be engaging in wild and crazy sex for a while,' teased Pitt.

Pembroke-Smythe made a comic leer. 'What I wouldn't give to be around when she recovers.'

Eva missed the Captain's sly innuendo. Almost before he finished his remark she had slipped back into unconsciousness.

Pitt and Pembroke-Smythe stared over her into each other's eyes, the faces suddenly devoid of humour. The Captain nodded at the automatic pistol slung under Pitt's left arm.

'In the end,' he said quietly, 'will you do her the honour?'

Pitt nodded solemnly. 'I'll take care of her.'

Levant came up, looking grimy and tired. He knew his men and women could not endure this punishment much longer. The added burden of watching the suffering of women and children wrenched at his tough, professional spirit. He hated to see them and his beloved tactical team being mercilessly subjected to such torment. His coldest fear was being overrun when the bombardment stopped, and then watching helplessly as the Malians ran amok in butchery and rape.

His best guess of the force against them was between one thousand and fifteen hundred. The number of his men and women still capable of fighting was down to twenty-nine, including Pitt. And then there were the four tanks to contend with. He had no idea how long they could hold out before being overrun. An hour, maybe two, more likely less. They would make a fight of it, that much was certain. The bombardment had oddly worked in their favour. Most of the rubble from the walls had fallen outward, making it difficult for assaulting troops to climb over it.

'Corporal Wadilinski reports the Malians are beginning to form up and move in,' he said to Pembroke-Smythe. 'The assault is imminent. Widen the entrance to the stairs and have your people ready to move out the instant the firing stops.'

'Right away, Colonel.'

Levant turned to Pitt. 'Well, Mr Pitt. I believe the time has arrived to test your invention.'

Pitt stood and stretched. 'A wonder it hasn't been blown to splinters.'

'When I gave a quick look above ground a few minutes ago it was still sitting in one piece under a section of one wall that was still standing.'

'Now that's enough to get me to quit drinking tequila.'

'Nothing so drastic as that I hope.'

Pitt looked into Levant's eyes. 'Mind if I ask what your answer was to Kazim's surrender demands?'

'The same reply we French gave at Waterloo and Camerone, *merde*.'

'In other words, *crap*,' Pembroke-Smythe translated.

Levant smiled. 'A polite way of putting it.'

Pitt sighed. 'I never thought Mrs Pitt's boy would end up like Davy Crockett and Jim Bowie at the Alamo.'

'Taking into account our small number and the enemy's firepower,' said Levant, 'I'd have to say our odds of surviving are no better and probably worse.'

A silence fell so abruptly that it seemed a great blanket was thrown over the underground arsenal. Everyone froze and looked up at the ceiling as if they could see through 3 metres of rock and sand.

Holed up and pounded for six hours, the members of the tactical team who could still stand and fight threw aside the rubble that sealed the entrance, poured into the heat and scorching sun, and spread out through the ruins. They found the fort almost unrecognizable. It looked like a warehouse after a demolition crew had finished with it. Black smoke spewed up from the burning personnel carriers and all buildings had been almost completely flattened. Bullets were whining and ricocheting through the heaps of jumbled stone like crazed hornets.

The UN team was sweating from the Saharan heat, dirty, hungry, and dead tired, but they were totally devoid of fear and madder than hell at having taken everything the Malians had thrown at them without responding. Short on everything, but not fighting guts, they took up their defensive positions, coldly swearing to make their attackers pay a heavy price before the last of them fell.

'On my command maintain a clear, steady fire,' ordered Levant over his helmet radio.

Kazim's battle plan was ridiculously simple, calling for the tanks to break through the battered main gate on the north wall while the assault troops charged from all sides. Every man at his command was to be thrown into battle, all 1470 of them. None would be kept in reserve.

'I expect all-out victory with no quarter,' Kazim told his officers. 'Shoot down any of the UN commandos who attempt to escape.'

'No prisoners?' Colonel Cheik asked in surprise. 'Do you think that wise, my General?'

'You see a problem, old friend?'

'When the international community finds out we executed an entire United Nations force, there could be serious countermeasures taken against us.'

Kazim drew himself up. 'I have no intention of allowing hostile incursion across our borders to go unpunished. The world will soon learn that the people of Mali are not to be treated like desert vermin.'

'I agree with the General,' said Yerli on cue. 'The enemy of your people must be destroyed.'

The excitement within Kazim was more than he could contain. He had never led troops into battle before. His rapid advancement and power had come from devious manipulations. He did little more than order others to kill those who presented opposition. Now he pictured himself as a great warrior about to charge foreign infidels.

'Order the advance,' he ordered. 'This is a historic moment. We engage the enemy.'

The assault troops ran across the desert in the classic infantry textbook attack, dropping to provide covering fire for other advancing members of the force, then rising and coming on again. The first wave of elite troops began shouting boldly after they reached within 200 metres of the fort without receiving enemy fire. Ahead of them, the tanks had failed to fan out properly and came on in a staggered formation.

Pitt decided to try for the one bringing up the rear. With the help of five commandos, he pulled the debris off the spring bow and dragged it to an open area. On the ancient siege engines the tension would have been taken up by a windlass and tackle. But on Pitt's model the forklift was tipped over so that its twin lifting prongs could pull the springs of the bow back on a horizontal line. As one perforated drum of diesel fuel was loaded on the spring bow, five more, consisting of Pitt's entire supply of missiles, were lined up alongside.

'Come on baby,' he muttered as the starter kicked over the forklift's balky engine. 'Now is not the time to get finicky.' Then came a coughing through the carburettor and the exhaust popped and settled in a steady roar.

Earlier, during the predawn darkness, Levant had left the fort and set stakes in the sand around its perimeter for a firing mark. To have waited until the defenders saw the whites of the attackers' eyes would have meant certain death. The odds were simply too overwhelming to allow closed-in fighting. Levant set the stakes at 75 metres.

Now, as the tactical team waited to open up, every eye was on Pitt. If the tanks could not be stopped, the Malian assault troops would have little to do but mop up.

Pitt took a knife and cut an elevation mark on the spot where the ends of the bent springs met the launch plank as an indicator to judge tension for distance. Then he climbed on one of the support beams and stared at the tanks again.

'Which one are you aiming for?' asked Levant.

Pitt pointed to the lagging tank on the left end of the line. 'My idea is to start at the rear and work forward.'

'So the tanks in front don't know what's happening behind,' mused Levant. 'Let's hope it works.'

The blazing heat from the sun radiated on the armoured contours of the tanks. Supremely confident they would find nothing but already dead bodies, the tank commanders and their drivers rolled forward with open hatches, their guns throwing shells against the few remaining ramparts of the fort.

When Pitt could almost make out the individual features of the lead tank's driver, he lit a torch and pressed the flaming end against the leaking oil on top of the punctured drum. Flame burst immediately. Then Pitt jammed the torch

567

in the sand and yanked on the line that released the trigger catch he had built from a door latch. The taut nylon line and cable holding the springs whipped free and the truck springs snapped straight.

The flaming drum of diesel oil flew over the ravaged wall like a fiery meteor and sailed high over the rear tank, striking the ground a considerable distance to its rear before exploding.

Pitt stood amazed. 'This thing does the job better than I ever imagined,' he muttered.

'Down 50 metres and 10 to the right,' observed Pembroke-Smythe as nonchalantly as if he was relating a soccer score.

As Levant's men helped hoist another barrel in place, Pitt cut a new mark on the launch plank to adjust for the distance. Next, he engaged the forklift's hydraulics, bending back the spring bow again. The torch was applied, the trigger mechanism was unleashed, and the second oil drum was on its way.

This one struck a few metres in front of the rear tank, bounced, and then rolled underneath and between the treads before exploding. The tank was instantly enveloped in flames. The crew, in their desperation to abandon the vehicle, fought each other to be first to escape through the hatches. Only two out of four made it out alive.

Pitt lost no time in setting up the spring bow again. Another oil drum was manhandled into place and flung at the advancing tanks. Pitt scored a direct hit this time. The drum flew in an arc over the wall and dropped squarely on the next tank's turret where it exploded and turned the vehicle into a blazing incinerator.

'It's working, it's really working,' Pitt muttered jubilantly as he readied the spring bow for the next shot.

'Jolly good show!' shouted the normally reserved Pembroke-Smythe. 'You hit the bleeding wogs where it hurts most.'

Pitt and the commandos who struggled to hoist the next oil drum on the launch plank didn't need any urging. Levant climbed to the only undamaged parapet and surveyed the battlefield. The unexpected destruction of two of Kazim's tanks had temporarily halted the advance. Levant was highly pleased with the initial success of Pitt's machine, but if only one tank survived to reach the fort, it was enough to spell disaster for the defenders.

Pitt triggered the release mechanism for the fourth drum. It flew true but the tank commander was aware of the fiery onslaught from the fort, ordered his driver to zigzag. His caution paid off as the drum's trajectory carried it 4 metres behind the left rear tread. The drum burst, but only a portion of the blazing liquid splashed on the armoured tail of the tank, and the monster relentlessly pressed on toward the fort.

To the fighters crouched amid the rubble, the approaching horde of Malians looked like an army of migrating ants. There were so many, so bunched together it would be nearly impossible to miss. The Malians, shouting their individual war cries, came on firing steadily.

The first wave was only a few metres from Levant's firing stakes, but he held off giving the order to fire, guardedly hopeful that Pitt could take out the two remaining tanks. His wish was answered as Pitt, anticipating the tank commander's next change in course, adjusted his spring bow accordingly and laid his fifth flaming missile almost into the driver's front hatch.

A sheet of fire covered the front of the tank. And then incredibly, it blew up. The entire advance halted as they all stared in astonishment at the tank's turret that was thrown whirling high into the desert sky before falling and embedding itself in the sand like a leaden kite.

Pitt was down to his last drum of diesel oil. He was so exhausted now with the physical effort in the body-sapping heat, he could hardly stand. His breath came in great heaves and his heart was pounding from the continuous strain of helping manhandle the heavy drums onto the launching plank, and then straining to shift the spring bow and its supports for aiming.

The huge 60-ton tank loomed through the dust and smoke like an immense steel gargoyle searching for victims to consume. The tank's commander could be seen giving orders to his driver and directing his gunner as his machine gun opened up at point blank range.

Everyone in the fort tensed and held their breath as Pitt lined up the spring bow. Many thought the end had come. This was his final shot, the last of the oil-filled containers.

No football place kicker ever had more riding on a field goal in overtime play to win a game. If Pitt misjudged, a lot of people were going to die, including himself and those children down in the arsenal.

The tank came straight on, its commander making no attempt to dodge. It was so close that Pitt had to elevate the rear of the spring bow to depress the launch plank. He kicked the trigger and hoped for the best.

The tank's gunner fired at the same moment. In a fantastic freak of coincidence the heavy shell and the flaming drum met in midair.

In his excitement, the gunner inside the tank had loaded an armour-piercing shell that bored right through the drum, causing a great sheet of fiery oil to spray all over the tank. The steel monster immediately became lost in a curtain of fire. In panic, the driver threw the tank in reverse in a vain attempt to escape the holocaust, colliding with the burning tank behind. Locked together, the great armoured vehicles quickly became a raging conflagration, punctuated by the roar of their exploding shells and fuel tanks.

The commando's cheers rose above the sound of the incoming gunfire. Their worst fears eliminated by Pitt's scratch-built spring bow, their morale at a fever pitch, they became more determined than ever to make a fight of it. Fear did not exist in battered old Fort Foureau this day.

'Pick your targets and commence firing,' Levant ordered in a formal tone. 'Now it's our turn to make *them* suffer.'

55

One minute Giordino could make out a long line of four trains stopped dead on the tracks; the next, everything was blanked out by a sudden current of swirling air that whipped up a sandstorm. Visibility went from 20 kilometres to 5 metres.

'What do you think?' asked Steinholm as he idled the dune buggy in third gear, trying to nurse the last precious few drops of fuel. 'Are we in Mauritania?'

'I wish I knew,' Giordino conceded. 'Looks like Massarde stopped all incoming trains but I can't tell which side of the border they're on.'

'What does the navigational computer have to say?'

'The numbers suggest we crossed the border 10 kilometres back.'

'Then we might as well approach the track bed and take our chances.'

As he spoke, Steinholm threaded the vehicle between two large rocks and drove up the crest of a small hill, then braked to a sudden halt. Both men heard it at the same instant. The sound was unmistakable through the blowing of the wind. It was faint, but there was no mistaking the strange thump. Each second it became clearer, and then seemed to be on top of them.

Steinholm hurriedly twisted the wheel, shoved the accelerator to the fire wall, and swung the fast attack vehicle in a wheel-spinning broadside until it had snapped around on a reverse course. Then abruptly, the engine sputtered and died, starved from lack of gas. The two men sat helplessly as the vehicle rolled to a stop.

'Looks to me as if we just bought the farm,' grunted Giordino bleakly.

'They must have picked us up on their radar and are coming straight at us,' Steinholm lamented as he angrily pounded the steering wheel.

Slowly through the brown curtain of sand and dust, like some huge beastly insect from an alien planet, a helicopter materialized and hovered 2 metres off the ground. Staring into a 31-millimetre Chain gun, two pods of thirty-eight 2.75-inch rockets, and eight laser-guided anti-tank missiles was an unnerving experience. Giordino and Steinholm sat rigid in the dune buggy, braced for the worst.

But instead of a fiery blast and then oblivion, a figure dropped from a hatch in the belly. As he approached they could see he was wearing a desert combat suit laden with high-tech gizmos. The head was covered by a camouflaged cloth-covered helmet and the face with a mask and goggles. He carried a levelled submachine gun as though it was an appendage of his hands.

He stopped beside the dune buggy and looked down at Giordino and Steinholm for a long moment. Then he pulled aside his mask and said, 'Where in hell did you guys come from?'

Finished with the spring bow, Pitt grabbed a pair of submachine guns from two badly wounded tactical team fighters and took up a position in a one-man stronghold he'd fashioned from fallen stone. He was impressed with the uniformed nomads from the desert. They were big men who ran and dodged with imposing agility as they swept toward the fort. The closer they got without encountering opposition, the braver they became.

Outnumbered fifty to one, the UN tactical team could not hope to hold out long enough for rescue. This was one time the underdog had no chance of pulling off an upset. Pitt quickly realized how the defenders of the Alamo must have felt. He sighted the incoming horde and pressed the trigger at Levant's command to fire.

The first wave of the Malian security force was met with a withering blast of gunfire that ripped into their advance. They made easy targets over ground totally denuded of cover. Hunched down in the rubble, the UN fighters took their time and fired with deadly aim. Like weeds before a scythe, the attackers fell in heaps almost before they knew what hit them. Within twenty minutes, more than two hundred and seventy-five lay dead and wounded around the perimeters of the fort.

The second wave stumbled over the bodies of the first, hesitated as their ranks were devastated, and fell back. None, even their officers, had expected anything resembling hardcore resistance. Kazim's hastily planned attack unravelled in chaos. His force began to panic, many in the rear firing blindly into their own men in front.

As the Malians fell back in confusion, most running like animals before a brush fire, a brave few walked slowly backward, continuing to shoot at anything that remotely looked like the head of a fort defender. Thirty of the attackers tried to take cover behind the burning tanks, but Pembroke-Smythe had expected that tactic and directed an accurate fire that cut them down.

Only one hour after the assault had begun, the crack of gunfire faded and the barren sand around the fort became filled with the cries of the wounded and the moans of the dying. The UN team was stunned and angered to see that no effort was made by the Malians to retrieve their own men. They did not know that an enraged Kazim had given orders to leave the injured to suffer under the blistering Sahara sun.

Amid the debris of the fort, the commandos slowly rose from their rifle pits and began to take count. One dead and three wounded, two seriously, Pembroke-Smythe reported to Levant. 'I'd say we gave them a good drubbing,' he said jauntily.

'They'll be back,' Levant reminded him.

'At least we cut the odds a bit.'

'So did they,' said Pitt, offering the Colonel a drink from his water container. 'We have four less able-bodied men to repel the next attack while Kazim can call in reinforcements.'

'Mr Pitt is right,' agreed Levant. 'I observed helicopters bringing in two more companies of men.'

'How soon do you reckon they'll try again?' Pitt asked Levant.

The Colonel held up a hand to shield his eyes and squinted at the sun. 'The hottest time of the day, I should think. His men are better acclimated to the heat than we are. Kazim will let us fry for a few hours before ordering another assault.'

'They've been blooded now,' said Pitt. 'Next time there will be no stopping them.'

'No,' said Levant, his face haggard with fatigue. 'I don't guess there will.'

'What do you mean,' Giordino demanded in white hot anger, 'you won't go in there and bring them out?'

Colonel Gus Hargrove was not used to being challenged, especially by a cocky civilian who was a good head shorter than he was. Commander of an Army Ranger covert-attack helicopter task force, Hargrove was a hardened professional soldier, having flown and directed helicopter assaults in Vietnam, Grenada, Panama, and Iraq. He was tough and shrewd, respected by his subordinates and superiors alike. His helmet came down and met a pair of blue eyes that blazed with the hardness of tempered steel. A cigar was stuffed in one side of his mouth, which was occasionally removed so he could spit.

'You don't seem to get it, Mr Giordano.'

'Giordino.'

'Whatever,' Hargrove muttered indifferently. 'There was an information leak, probably through the United Nations. The Malians were waiting for us to cross into their air space. Half their air force is patrolling just beyond the border as we speak. In case you don't know it, the Apache helicopter is a great missile platform but no match for Mirage jet fighters. Certainly not in daylight hours. Without a squadron of Stealth fighters to fly protective cover, we can't go in until after dark. Only then can we take advantage of low terrain and desert gulches to fly under their radar screen. Do you get the picture?'

'Men, women, and children are going to die if you don't reach Fort Foureau within the next few hours.'

'Rushing my unit over here with advance notice to the other side, without backup, and in the middle of the day was bad timing and ill advised,' Hargrove stated firmly. 'We attempt to go into Mali from Mauritania now, and my four choppers will be blasted out of the sky 50 kilometres inside the border. You tell me, *sir*, just what good would that do your people inside the fort?'

Properly pinned against the wall, Giordino shrugged. 'I stand rebuked. My apologies, Colonel. I wasn't aware of your situation.'

Hargrove softened. 'I understand your concern, but now that we've been compromised and the Malians are chafing at the bit to ambush us, I'm afraid chances of saving your people are out of the question.'

Giordino felt as if his stomach was squeezed by a vice. He turned away from Hargrove and stared across the desert. The sandstorm had passed and he could see the trains standing on the track in the distance.

He turned back. 'How many men under your command?'

'Not counting the chopper crews, I have a fighting force of eighty men.'

576

Giordino's eyes widened. 'Eighty men to take on half the Malian security force?'

'Yes,' Hargrove grinned as he removed the cigar butt and spat. 'But we have enough firepower to level half of western Africa.'

'Suppose you could cross the desert to Fort Foureau without detection?'

'I'm always open to a good plan.'

'The inbound trains for the Fort Foureau hazardous waste project, have any been allowed through?'

Hargrove shook his head. 'I sent a team leader to check out the situation. He reported that the train crews were instructed by radio to halt at the Mauritania/Mali border. The engineer for the first train said he was told to sit idle until ordered to proceed by the superintendent of the project's rail yard.'

'How strong is the Malian check point on the border?'

'Ten guards, maybe twelve.'

'Could you take them out before they gave an alarm?'

Mechanically, Hargrove's eyes travelled over the train's cargo cars, lingered on the five flatbed cars and the canvas covers that protected new freight vehicles bound for Fort Foureau, and then moved briefly to the Malian border guard house sitting beside the track before returning to Giordino. 'Could John Wayne ride a horse?'

'We can be there in two and a half hours,' said Giordino. 'Three on the outside.'

Hargrove removed the cigar from his mouth and seemed to be contemplating it. 'I think I've got your slant now. General Kazim would never expect my force to come charging into his playground on a train.'

'Load the men inside the cargo container cars. Your choppers can ride on the flatbed cars undercover. Get to the objective before Kazim sees through the facade, and we have a good chance at evacuating Colonel Levant's people

577

and the civilians and beating it back to Mauritania before the Malians know what hit them.'

Giordino's plan appealed to Hargrove, but he had doubts.

'Suppose one of Kazim's hotshot pilots sees a train ignoring instructions and decides to blow it off the tracks?'

'Kazim, himself, wouldn't dare destroy one of Yves Massarde's hazardous waste trains without absolute proof it had been hijacked.'

Hargrove paced up and down. The daring of the scheme sounded outlandish to him. Speed was essential. He decided to lay his career on the line and go for it.

'All right,' he said briefly. 'Let's get the Wabash Cannonball rolling.'

Zateb Kazim raved like a madman in frustration at failing to bludgeon Levant and his small team from the old Foreign Legion fort. He cursed and ranted at his officers almost in hysteria, like a child who had his toys taken away from him. He dementedly slapped two of them in the face and ordered them all shot on two different occasions before his Chief of Staff, Colonel Cheik, soothingly talked him out of it. Barely under control, Kazim stared at his retreating troops scathingly and demanded they reform immediately for a second assault.

Despairing of Kazim's wrath, Colonel Mansa drove through his retreating force, shouting and berating his officers, accusing them of shame that sixteen hundred attackers could not overrun a pitiful handful of defenders. He harangued them into regrouping their companies for another try. To drive home the message there would be no more failure, Mansa had ten men who were caught trying to desert the battlefield shot on the spot.

Instead of attacking the fort with encircling waves, Kazim massed his forces into one massive column. The reinforcements were formed in the rear and ordered to shoot any man in front of them who broke and ran. The only command from Kazim that was passed down the lines from company to company was 'fight or die.'

By two o'clock in the afternoon, the Malian security forces were reformed and ready for the signal. One look at his sullen and fearful troops and any good commander would have aborted the attack. Kazim was not a leader his men loved enough to die for. But as they looked out over the body-littered ground around the fort, anger slowly began to replace their fear of death.

This time, they silently vowed between them, the defenders of Fort Foureau were going to their graves.

56

With an incredible display of casual indifference to sniper bullets, Pembroke-Smythe sat under the torrid sun on a shooting stick, a spiked cane that opens into a seat, and observed the Malian formations as they lined up for the assault.

'I do believe the beggars are about to make another go,' he informed Levant and Pitt.

A series of flares were shot in the air to signal the advance. There was no dodging with covering fire like the previous assault. The Malian force raced over the flat ground at a dead run. Shouts erupted and echoed over the desert from nearly two thousand throats.

Pitt felt like an actor on a stage in a theatre-in-the-round surrounded by a hostile audience. 'Not exactly what you'd call tactical imagination,' he said, standing beside Levant and Pembroke-Smythe while staring at the massed column. 'But it just may do the trick.'

Pembroke-Smythe nodded. 'Kazim is using his men like a steamroller.'

'Good luck, gentlemen,' said Levant with a grim smile. 'Perhaps we'll all meet in hell.'

'Couldn't be hotter than here,' Pitt grinned back.

The Colonel looked at Pembroke-Smythe. 'Reposition our units to repulse a single frontal assault. Then tell them to fire at will.'

Pembroke-Smythe shook hands with Pitt and began moving from man to man. Levant took his place atop the remaining parapet as Pitt returned to the little fort he had dug from the rubble. Already bullets were splattering the fortress and ricocheting off the broken stone.

The forward wall of the attacking force stretched 50 metres wide. With the reinforcements they numbered almost eighteen hundred. Kazim threw them against the side of the fort that had suffered the worst during the later aerial attacks and mortar bombardments. This was the north wall with the shattered main gate.

The men in the rear ranks were cheered by the certainty that they would be alive to drive inside the fort. The men in the forward wall had different ideas. None expected to cross that open space of death and survive. They knew there was to be no mercy from the defenders ahead or their own forces behind.

Already gaps began to appear in the first rank as the pitifully few men in the fort laid down an appalling fire. But the Malians pushed forward in their headlong onslaught, leaping over the bodies of those who fell in the first assault. There was no stopping them this time; they could smell the bloody scent of victory.

Pitt aimed and fired off short bursts at the approaching mass as a man in a dream. Aim and fire, aim and fire, then eject and reload. The routine, it seemed to him, continued endlessly when in fact only ten minutes had passed since the signal for the assault.

A mortar shell burst somewhere behind him. Kazim had directed the bombardment be kept up until his leading ranks entered the fort. Pitt felt the shrapnel whistle past his head, felt the tiny breeze of its passing. The Malians were so close now they filled up the sights of his machine gun.

Mortar shell after mortar shell rained down in a maelstrom of fire. Then the barrage ceased as elements of the first rank reached the fallen rubble and began scrambling over the jagged stone. Here they were most vulnerable. The forward ranks melted away as they were raked by the desperate fire of the defenders. There was no place for them to take cover, and they could not climb over the rubble and shoot at the same time at targets that didn't show themselves.

The defenders, on the other hand, couldn't miss. The Malians stumbled and crawled over the broken masonry into a swarm of bullets. The first rank had been swept away at 100 metres, the second by the time it reached the shadow of the fort. Then the rank behind that. All along the north wall, the attackers and their officers cried out and fell. Their massed fire, however, no matter how wild, could not help but strike some of the defenders.

There were simply too many for the UN team to stop and their fire began to slacken as one by one they were killed or wounded.

Levant knew disaster was only moments away. 'Blast them!' he roared over the helmet radios. 'Blast them back off the wall.'

It seemed impossible but the hail of bullets from the UN team suddenly increased. The head of the Malian column was shot to a standstill. Pitt was out of ammunition but was throwing grenades as fast as he could activate them. The explosions caused havoc in the struggling crowd. The Malians began to fall back. They were stunned and disbelieving that anyone could fight with such fury and wrath. Only with determined courage did they rally and surge through the splintered remains of the main gate.

The UN team rose from their dugouts, firing from the hip as they retired across the parade ground and around their smouldering personnel carriers, forming a new line of defence within the ruins of the former Legion barracks and officers' quarters. Dust, debris, and smoke cut visibility to less than 5 metres. The constant blast of guns had deafened the fighters to the cries of the wounded.

The horrible casualties inflicted on the Malians were enough to shatter the morale of any attacking force, but they kept coming and poured into the fort in a human flood.

Temporarily exposed on the parade ground, the first company of men through the wall were shredded as they milled around in confusion at not finding a pathetic few survivors caught in the open.

Pembroke-Smythe took a head count inside the collapsed barracks and officers' quarters as the few wounded they were able to save were carried down into the arsenal. Only Pitt and twelve of the UN Tactical Team were still capable of fighting. Colonel Levant was missing. He was last seen firing from the parapet when the attacking horde broke through the remains of the north gate.

At recognizing Pitt, Pembroke-Smythe flashed a smile. 'You look positively awful, old man,' he said, nodding at the red stains in Pitt's combat suit that were spreading on the left arm and shoulder. Blood also trickled down the side of one cheek from a cut caused by a shard of flying stone.

'You're no picture of health yourself,' Pitt replied, pointing at the nasty wound in Pembroke-Smythe's hip.

'How's your ammo?'

Pitt held up his remaining submachine gun and let it drop to the ground. 'Gone. I'm down to two grenades.'

Pembroke-Smythe handed him an enemy machine gun. 'You'd better get down in the arsenal. What's left of us will hold them off until you can . . .' He couldn't bring himself to finish and he stared down at the ground.

'We hurt them badly,' Pitt said steadily as he ejected the clip and counted the bullets inside. 'They're like mad dogs drooling for revenge. They'll make it hard on whoever of us they find still living.'

'The women and children cannot fall into Kazim's hands again.'

'They won't suffer,' Pitt promised.

Pembroke-Smythe stared up at him, seeing the agony of grief in Pitt's eyes. 'Goodbye, Mr Pitt. It has indeed been an honour to know you.'

Pitt shook the Captain's hand as a storm of gunfire burst around them. 'Likewise, Captain.'

Pitt turned away and scrambled down through the debris choking the stairway into the arsenal. Hopper and Fairweather saw him at the same time and approached.

'Who's winning?' Hopper asked.

Pitt shook his head. 'Not our side.'

'No sense in waiting for death,' said Fairweather. 'Better to make a fight of it. You wouldn't happen to have a spare gun on you?'

'I could use one too,' added Hopper.

Pitt handed Fairweather the machine gun. 'Sorry, except for my automatic, it's all I have. There are plenty of weapons topside, but you'll have to snatch one off a dead Malian.'

'Sounds like good sport,' boomed Hopper. He gave Pitt a mighty slap on the back. 'Good luck, my boy. Take care of Eva.'

'That's a promise.'

Fairweather nodded. 'Nice to have known you, old chap.'

As they went up the stairway together into the fight above, a female medic rose from a wounded man and waved for Pitt's attention.

'How does it look?' she asked.

'Prepare for the worst,' Pitt answered quietly.

'How long?'

'Captain Pembroke-Smythe and what's left of your team are making a last stand. The end can't be more than ten or fifteen minutes away.'

'What about these poor devils?' The medic indicated the wounded strewn on the floor of the arsenal.

'The Malians won't be showing any compassion,' Pitt answered her heavily.

Her eyes widened slightly. 'They're not taking prisoners?'

He shook his head. 'It doesn't look that way.'

'And the women and children?'

He didn't answer, but the pained look of sorrow written on his face told her the worst.

She made a brave effort to smile. 'Then I guess those of us who can still pull a trigger will go out with a bang.'

Pitt gripped her by the shoulders for a moment, then released her. She smiled bravely and turned to pass on the dire news to her fellow medic. Before Pitt could step over to where Eva was lying, he was approached by the French engineer, Louis Monteux.

'Mr Pitt.'

'Mr Monteux.'

'Has the time come?'

'Yes, I'm afraid it has.'

'Your gun. How many shells does it carry?'

'Ten, but I have another clip with four.'

'We only need eleven for the women and children,' Monteux whispered as he held out his hand for the weapon.

'You may have it after I've taken care of Dr Rojas,' Pitt said with quiet firmness.

Monteux looked up as the sounds of the fighting above came closer and echoed down the stairway. 'Do not take too long.'

Pitt moved away and sat on the stone floor beside Eva. She was awake and looked up at him with an unmistakable expression of affection and concern. 'You're bleeding, you're wounded.'

He shrugged. 'I forgot to duck when the grenade went off.'

'I'm so glad you're here. I was beginning to wonder if I was ever going to see you again.'

'I hope you have a dress all picked out for our date,' he said as he put his arm around her shoulders and gently moved her until her head rested in his lap. Out of sight behind her view, he eased the automatic from his belt and held the muzzle a centimetre behind her right temple.

'I have a restaurant all picked out . . .' She hesitated and tilted her head as if listening. 'Did you hear it?'

'Hear what?'

'I'm not sure. It sounded like a whistle.'

Pitt was certain the sedatives had caused her mind to wander. There was no way a strange sound could be heard above the din of the fighting. His finger began to tighten on the trigger.

'I don't hear anything,' he said.

'No . . . no, there it is again.'

He hesitated as her eyes came alive and reflected a vague sort of anticipation. But he willed himself to go through with it. He leaned down to kiss her lips and distract her as he began to squeeze the trigger again.

She tried to lift her head. 'You must hear it?'

'Goodbye, love.'

'A train whistle,' she said excitedly. 'It's Al, he's come back.'

Pitt released the pressure on the trigger and cocked his head toward the upper entrance to the stairway. Then he heard it over the sporadic gunfire. Not a whistle, but the faint blare of a diesel locomotive air horn.

Giordino stood beside the engineer and pulled the air horn cord like a crazy man as the train thundered over the rails toward the fighting. He stared and stared at the fort, hardly recognizing the ravaged structure as it grew larger through the windshield of the locomotive cab. The utter devastation, the pall of black smoke rising in the sky, made him sick at heart. From all appearances the relief force was too late.

Hargrove gazed, fascinated. He couldn't believe that anyone could live through such destruction. Most all the parapets were shot away, the ramparts in unbelievable shambles. The front wall where the main gate once stood was nothing but a small mountain of tangled stone. He was astounded at the number of bodies strewn around the perimeter of the fort and the four burned-out tanks.

'God but they put up a hell of a fight,' Hargrove muttered in awe.

Giordino pressed the muzzle of a pistol against the engineer's temple. 'Lay on the brakes and stop this thing. Now!'

The engineer, a Frenchman, who had been pirated away from operating the superfast TVG train between Paris and Lyons by double the salary from Massarde Enterprises, applied the brakes, stopping the train directly between the fort and Kazim's field headquarters.

With clock-like precision, Hargrove's special operations warriors poured off the train in both directions simultaneously and hit the ground running. One unit launched an immediate attack on the Malian field headquarters, catching Kazim and his staff by complete surprise. The rest of the force began assaulting the Malian army from the rear. The covers were quickly thrown off the Apache helicopters that were tied down on the flatbed cars. Within two minutes they were lifting into the air, swinging into position to fire their hellfire missiles.

In the sudden panic and confusion, Kazim stood rooted at the realization that the American Special Forces had sneaked across the border under the noses of his air screen. He was sick to his stomach in shock and made no effort to direct a defence or run for cover.

Colonels Mansa and Cheik each grabbed Kazim by an arm and hustled him out of his headquarters' tent into a staff car as Captain Batutta quickly jumped behind the wheel. Ismail Yerli shared their love of self-preservation and climbed in the seat beside Batutta.

'Get out of here!' Mansa shouted at Batutta as he and Cheik climbed in the backseat on each side of Kazim. 'In the name of Allah, move before we're all killed.'

Batutta had no more wish to die than his superiors. Leaving their men to fight out of the trap on their own, the officers had no second thoughts about fleeing the battlefield to save their own skins. Frightened beyond logical thinking, Batutta raced the engine and threw the staff car in gear. Though the vehicle was a four-wheel-drive, he dug the tyres deeply in the soft sand, cutting twin trenches without achieving traction. In panic, Batutta kept his foot jammed on the accelerator. The engine shrieked in protest at the excessive revolutions as he stupidly made matters worse by driving the wheels into the ground up to their axle hubs.

Mouthing soundless words, Kazim abruptly returned to reality, and his face twisted in terror. 'Save me!' he screamed. 'I order you to save me!'

'You fool!' Mansa yelled at Batutta. 'Let off the gas or we'll never get away.'

'I'm trying!' Batutta snapped back, sweat bursting from his forehead.

Only Yerli sat calmly and accepted his fate. He stared out the side window silently as he watched death approaching in the shape of a big, purposeful-looking man in American desert combat gear.

Master Sergeant Jason Rasmussen of Paradise Valley, Arizona, had led his team off the train and straight at Kazim's headquarters' tents. Their job was to capture the communications section and prevent the Malians from spreading an alarm that would bring on an attack by Kazim's air force. In and out faster than a vampire pisses blood, as Colonel Hargrove had expressed it so picturesquely during the briefing, or else they were all dead meat if the Malian jet fighters caught them before their helicopters could recross the Mauritanian border.

After his team members had swept aside weak resistance from the stunned Malian soldiers and achieved their goal of cutting off all communications, Rasmussen noticed the staff car out of the corner of his eyes and began running after it. From the rear he could make out three heads in the backseat and two in the front. His first thought, when he saw that the car appeared stuck in the sand, was to take the men inside as prisoners. But then the vehicle suddenly leaped forward and bounced onto firm ground. The driver cautiously increased speed and the car began to pull away.

Rasmussen opened up with his machine gun. His fire peppered the doors and windows. Glass shattered and sparkled in the bright sun as bullets stitched across the car doors. After he emptied two clips, the heavily riddled car slowed and rolled to a halt. As he cautiously approached, Rasmussen saw that the driver had slumped lifeless over the wheel. The body of a senior Malian officer was leaning halfway out one window while another officer had fallen from an open door to his back on the ground and stared vacantly into the sky. A third man sat in the middle of the backseat, eyes wide open as if he was peering at some distant object while under hypnosis. The man in the passenger's seat in front, though, had a strange peaceful look in sightless eyes.

To Rasmussen, the officer in the middle looked like some kind of cartoon field marshal. The coat of his uniform was covered in a maze of gold braid, sashes, ribbons, and medals. Rasmussen could not bring himself to believe this character was the leader of the Malian force. He leaned through the open door and gave the high-ranking officer a nudge with his gun butt. The body sagged sideways on the seat, revealing two neat bullet holes through the spinal cord at the base of the neck.

Sergeant first-class Rasmussen checked to see if the others were beyond medical help. All had suffered fatal wounds. Rasmussen had no idea that he had accomplished his mission far away and above expectations. Without direct orders from Kazim or his immediate staff, there were no subordinate officers willing to call an air strike on their own. Singlehandedly the sergeant from Arizona had changed the face of a West African nation. In the wake of Kazim's death a new political party supporting democratic reform would sweep out the old leaders of Mali and launch a new government. One that was unfavourable toward the manipulations of scavengers like Yves Massarde.

Unaware he had altered history, Rasmussen reloaded his weapon, dismissed the carnage from his mind, and trotted back to help in mopping up the area.

Nearly ten days would pass before General Kazim was buried in the desert beside his final defeat, unmourned, his grave forever unmarked.

57

Pitt ran up the steps of the arsenal and joined the surviving members of the tactical team who were making their final stand within a small pocket around the underground entrance. They had thrown up hasty barricades and were raking the parade ground with a steady fire. In the sea of devastation and death they still hung on, fighting with an almost insane ferocity to prevent the enemy from entering the arsenal and slaughtering the civilians and wounded before Giordino and the Special Forces could intervene.

Bewildered by a stubborn defence that refused to die, the decimated flood of Malian attackers crested and stalled as Pitt, Pembroke-Smythe, Hopper, Fairweather, and twelve UN fighters moved not back, but leaped forward. Fourteen men charging nearly a thousand. They rushed at the stunned mass, yelling like underworld demons and shooting at everything that stood in front of them.

The wall of Malians parted like the Red Sea before Moses and fell back before the horrific onslaught that punched into their ranks. They scattered in every direction. But not all had been invaded by crippling paralysis. A few of the braver ones knelt and fired into the flying wedge. Four of the UN fighters fell, but the momentum carried the rest forward and the fighting became hand-to-hand.

The report from Pitt's automatic slammed deafening in his ears as a group of five Malians melted away in front of him. There was no retreating or covering up as long as the Malian security forces held their ground.

Face to face with a wall of men, Pitt emptied his pistol

and then threw it before he was hit in the thigh and fell to the ground.

At the same moment, Colonel Gus Hargrove's Rangers came pouring into the fort, laying down a murderous fire that took the late General Zateb Kazim's unsuspecting forces by complete surprise. Resistance in front of Pitt and the others seemed to melt away as the stunned aliens became aware of the assault on their rear. All courage and rationality dissolved. On a flat battlefield it would have been a complete rout, but within the fort there was no place to run. As if obeying an unspoken command they began throwing down their weapons and clasping their hands behind their heads.

The intense firing quickly became sporadic and finally died away altogether. A strange silence settled over the fort as Hargrove's men began rounding up the Malians and disarming them. It seemed an eerie, disquieting moment for the sudden end of the battle.

'Good Gawd!' one of the American Rangers uttered at seeing the unbelievable amount of carnage. From the time they had burst from the train and charged across the desert separating the fort from the track, they had jumped over and dodged around a vast carpet of dead and wounded, often so many they could not step between them. Now inside the demolished fortress, the bodies were piled three and four deep in some areas of the rubble. None had ever seen so many dead in one place before.

Pitt painfully lifted himself up and hopped on one leg. He tore off a sleeve and wrapped it around the hole in his thigh to stem the flow of blood. Then he looked at Pembroke-Smythe who stood stiffly, grey-faced, and obviously in great pain from several wounds.

'You look even worse than the last time I saw you,' said Pitt.

The Captain stared Pitt up and down and casually brushed a thick layer of dust from his shoulder insignia. 'They'll never let you in the Savoy Hotel looking as shabby as you do either.'

As if resurrected from the grave, Colonel Levant rose from the incredible devastation and limped toward Pitt and Pembroke-Smythe, using a grenade launcher as a crutch. Levant's helmet was gone and his left arm hung limply at his side. He was bleeding from a gash across his scalp and a badly wounded ankle.

Neither man had expected to find him alive. They both solemnly shook hands with him.

'I'm happy to see you, Colonel,' said Pembroke-Smythe cheerfully. 'I thought you were buried under the wall.'

'I was for a time.' Levant nodded at Pitt and smiled. 'I see you're still with us, Mr Pitt.'

'The proverbial bad penny.'

Levant's face took on a saddened look as he saw the pitifully few men of his force that moved forward to surround and greet him. 'They whittled us down somewhat.'

'We whittled them down too,' Pitt muttered grimly.

Levant saw Hargrove and his aides approaching, accompanied by Giordino and Steinholm. He stiffened and turned to Pembroke-Smythe. 'Form up the men, Captain.'

Pembroke-Smythe found it difficult to keep a steady voice as he assembled the remnant of the UN Tactical Team. 'All right, lads . . .' He hesitated, seeing there was one female corporal helping to hold up a big sergeant. 'And ladies. Straighten up the line.'

Hargrove stopped in front of Levant and the two colonels exchanged salutes. The American was stunned at seeing the meagre number that had fought so many. The international fighting team stood proud, none unscathed, everyone a walking wounded. They looked like statues, they were covered with so much dust. Their eyes were deep-sunk and red, and the faces haggard by their ordeal. The men all wore stubbled beards. Their combat suits were torn and filthy.

Some wore crude bandages that were soaked through with blood. And yet they stood undefeated.

'Colonel Jason Hargrove,' he introduced himself. 'United States Army Rangers.'

'Colonel Marcel Levant, United Nations Critical Response Team.'

'I deeply regret,' said Hargrove, 'we couldn't arrive sooner.'

Levant shrugged. 'It is a miracle you are here at all.'

'A magnificent stand, Colonel.' Hargrove glanced around the destruction. Then he stared past Levant at the battle-weary fighters lined up behind, an incredulous look on his face. 'Is this all of you?'

'Yes, all that's left of my fighting force.'

'How many under your command?'

'About forty at the beginning.'

As if in a trance, Hargrove again saluted Levant. 'My compliments on a glorious defence. I've never seen anything like it.'

'We have wounded in the fort's underground arsenal.' Levant informed Hargrove.

'I was told you also were originally convoying women and children.'

'They are below with my wounded.'

Hargrove abruptly turned and shouted to his officers. 'Get our medics up here and take care of these people. Bring up those from below and evacuate them onto the transport choppers, double quick. The Malian air force can show up any second.'

Giordino walked up to Pitt who was standing off to one side and embraced him. 'I thought this time, old friend, you weren't going to make it.'

Pitt still tried a grin despite the waves of fatigue and the gnawing pain from the bullet hole in the fleshy part of his thigh. 'The devil and I couldn't agree on terms.'

'I'm sorry I couldn't have put the show on the road two hours sooner,' Giordino lamented.

'No one expected you by train.'

'Hargrove couldn't risk flying his choppers through Kazim's fighter defence screen in daylight.'

Pitt looked up as an Apache warbird circled the fort, its sophisticated electronics probing over the horizons for intruders. 'You made it through without detection,' he said. 'That's what counts.'

Giordino looked into Pitt's eyes guardedly. 'Eva?'

'Alive but badly injured. Thanks to you and your air horn, she missed dying by two seconds.'

'She came that close to being shot by Kazim's mob?' Giordino asked curiously.

'No, shot by me.' Before Giordino could reply, Pitt gestured toward the entrance to the arsenal. 'Come along. She'll be happy to see your Quasimodo face.'

Giordino's face grew sober at the sight of all the wounded with their bloody bandages and splints lying jammed on the floor of the cramped area. He was surprised by the damage caused by falling stones from the ceiling. But what stunned him most was the incredible silence. None of the wounded uttered a sound, no moan escaped their lips. No one in that crumbling arsenal cellar spoke. The children merely stared at him, totally subdued after hours of fright.

Then, as if on cue, they all broke into weak cheers and applause at recognizing Giordino as the one who brought reinforcements and saved their lives. Pitt was amused by it all. He had never seen Giordino display so much modesty and embarrassment as the men reached out to shake his hand and the women kissed him like a long-lost lover.

Then Giordino spotted Eva as she raised her head and flashed a wide smile. 'Al . . . oh Al, I knew you'd come back.'

He crouched beside her, careful not to make contact with

her injuries, and awkwardly patted her hand. 'You don't know how glad I am to see you and Dirk still breathing.'

'We had quite a party,' she said bravely. 'Too bad you missed it.'

'They sent me out for ice.'

She glanced around at the others suffering around her. 'Can't something be done for them?'

'The medics from the Special Forces are on their way,' Pitt explained. 'Everyone will be evacuated as soon as possible.'

Another few moments of small talk and the big, tough-looking Rangers appeared and began tenderly carrying the children and helping their mothers outside to a waiting transport helicopter that had set down on the parade ground. The Ranger medics, assisted by the exhausted UN medical team, then directed the evacuation of the wounded.

Giordino obtained a stretcher, and with Pitt hobbling on one end, gently carried Eva into the bright afternoon sun.

'I never thought I'd hear myself say the desert heat feels good,' she murmured.

Two Rangers reached through the open cargo door of the helicopter. 'We'll take her from here,' said one.

'Put her in first class,' Pitt smiled at the men. 'She's a very special lady.'

'Eva!' a voice thundered from inside the helicopter. Dr Hopper sat up on a stretcher, a bandage covering half his bare chest and another across one side of his face. 'Let us hope this flight has a more enjoyable destination than the last one.'

'Congratulations Doc,' said Pitt. 'I'm glad to see you came through.'

'Got four of the beggars before one downed me with a hand grenade.'

'Fairweather?' asked Pitt, not seeing the Britisher.

Hopper shook his head sadly. 'He didn't make it.'

Pitt and Giordino helped the Rangers tie down Eva's stretcher next to Hopper's. Then Pitt brushed her hair back with his hands. 'You're in good company with the Doc.'

She looked up at Pitt, wishing with all her heart that he could sweep her into his arms. 'You're not coming?'

'Not this trip.'

'But you need medical care,' she protested.

'I have some unfinished business.'

'You can't stay in Mali,' she implored him. 'You mustn't, not after all that's happened.'

'Al and I came to West Africa to do a job. It isn't finished yet.'

'Is this the end of us then?' she asked in a choking voice.

'No, nothing so final.'

'When will I see you again?'

'Soon, if all goes well,' he said sincerely.

She lifted her head, her eyes gleaming in the sunlight with unshed tears. Then she kissed him lightly on the mouth. 'Please hurry.'

Pitt and Giordino stepped back as the helicopter's pilot increased the rpms and the craft lifted off the ground, throwing up a maelstrom of dust inside the fort. They watched the chopper as it rose above the crumpled walls and swung toward the west.

Then Giordino turned to Pitt and nodded at his injuries. 'We'd better get you patched up if you're about to do what I think you want to do.'

Pitt insisted on waiting until all of the more seriously wounded were treated before he allowed a medic to remove the shrapnel from his left arm and shoulder, stitch them up along with the bullet hole in the flesh of his thigh, give him two shots for infection and one for pain, before padding him with bandages. Afterward, he and Giordino bid their goodbyes to Levant and Pembroke-Smythe before the UN

597

officers were airlifted out with the surviving members of the UN team.

'You're not joining us?' asked Levant.

'The one who lies behind all this senseless slaughter cannot be allowed to walk away,' Pitt answered cryptically.

'Yves Massarde?'

Pitt nodded silently.

'I wish you luck.' He shook their hands. 'Gentlemen, I can think of little more to say except to thank you for your services.'

'A pleasure, Colonel,' said Giordino with a cocky smile. 'Call on us anytime.'

'I hope they give you a medal,' said Pitt, 'and promote you to General. No man deserves it more.'

Levant surveyed the devastation as if searching for something, perhaps envisioning the men of his command who were still buried under the rubble. 'I hope the sacrifices endured by both sides were worth the terrible price in lives.'

Pitt shrugged heavily. 'Death is paid for by grief and measured only by the depth of the grave.'

Pembroke-Smythe, head high, glorious disdain engraved on his handsome face, was the last to board. 'Bloody good sport,' he said. 'We must all get together and do it again some time.'

'We can hold a reunion,' muttered Giordino sarcastically.

'If we ever meet in London,' said Pembroke-Smythe, unperturbed, 'the Dom Perignon is on me. In fact, I'll introduce you to some marvellous girls who oddly find Americans appealing.'

'Will we get a ride in your Bentley?' asked Pitt.

'How did you know I drove a Bentley?' replied Pembroke-Smythe in mild surprise.

Pitt grinned. 'Somehow it fitted.'

They turned away without a backward look as the helicopter carrying the last of the UN Tactical Team soared across the desert toward Mauritania and safety. A young black lieutenant trotted across their path and waved them to a stop.

'Pardon me, Mr Pitt, Mr Giordino?'

Pitt nodded. 'That's us.'

'Colonel Hargrove wants you over at the Malian headquarters across the railroad track.'

Giordino knew better than to offer Pitt a shoulder as his friend limped across the sand, teeth gritted against the pain shooting from his thigh. The opaline eyes never ceased to gleam with determination from a gaunt face partly covered by a bandage.

The tents making up Kazim's former field headquarters bore desert camouflage markings but were shaped more like stage settings from a production of *Kismet*. Colonel Hargrove was in the main tent leaning over a table, studying Kazim's military communication codes when they walked inside. A stub of a cigar was pushed between his lips.

Without greeting, he asked, 'Do either of you by chance know what Zateb Kazim looks like?'

'We've met him,' answered Pitt.

'Could you identify him?'

'Probably.'

Levant straightened and moved through the tent's opening. 'Out here.' He led them across a short stretch of level ground to a bullet-riddled car. He removed the cigar and spat in the sand. 'Recognize any of these clowns?'

Pitt leaned into the interior of the car. Already hordes of flies were swarming on the blood-coated bodies. He glanced at Giordino who was peering in from the other side. Giordino simply nodded.

Pitt turned to Hargrove. 'The one in the middle is the late General Zateb Kazim.'

'You're sure,' Hargrove demanded.

'Positive,' Pitt said firmly.

'And the others must be high-ranking members of his staff,' added Giordino.

'Congratulations, Colonel. Now all you have to do is inform the Malian government that you have the General in your custody and are holding him as hostage to ensure the safe return of your force to Mauritania.'

Hargrove stared at Pitt. 'But the man is a corpse.'

'So who's to know? Certainly not his subordinates in the Malian security forces.'

Hargrove dropped his cigar and ground it into the sand. He looked at the several hundred survivors of Kazim's assault force that were now massed in a large circle and guarded by his American Rangers. 'I see no reason why it won't work. I'll have my intelligence officer open communications while we wind up the evacuations.'

'Since you're no longer in a big rush to dash out of here, there is one other thing.'

'That is?' asked Hargrove.

'A favour.'

'What exactly is it I can do for you?'

Pitt smiled down at Hargrove who was half a head shorter. 'One of your helicopters, Colonel. I'd like to borrow it and several of your best men.'

58

After he communicated with high-level Malian officials and threw them the lie he was holding Kazim hostage, Hargrove was convinced no military action would be taken against his evacuating force. He was no longer filled with trepidation and was highly relieved now that the pressure was off the final stage of his rescue mission. He was also quite amused when the puppet president of Mali begged him to execute General Kazim.

But Hargrove had no intention of loaning his personal Sikorsky H-76 Eagle helicopter, its crew, and six of his Rangers to a pair of smart-ass bureaucrats, certainly not in a combat area. His only concession to Pitt's request was to pass it along to Special Operations Command in Florida over Kazim's captured communications systems, positive his superiors would have a good laugh out of it.

He was dumbstruck when the request came back almost immediately. Not only was it granted, but it was approved by presidential order.

Hargrove said acidly to Pitt, 'You must have friends in high places.'

'I'm not out for a joyride,' Pitt replied, failing to hide the satisfaction in his voice. 'You weren't told, but there was far more at stake here than a covert rescue mission.'

'Probably just as well,' Hargrove sighed heavily. 'How long do you require my men and chopper?'

'Two hours.'

'And then?'

'If all goes according to my plan, it will be returned to you, along with your men and crew, in pristine condition.'

'And you and Giordino?'

'We remain behind.'

'I won't bother asking why,' said Hargrove, shaking his head. 'This whole operation has been a mystery to me.'

'Ever heard of a military operation that wasn't?' said Pitt seriously. 'What you accomplished here today has a ripple effect beyond anything you can imagine.'

Hargrove's eyebrows lifted questioningly. 'Think I'll ever know what it is you're talking about?'

'To use the time-honoured method of finding out government secrets,' Pitt said slyly, 'you read about them in tomorrow's newspaper.'

After a 20-kilometre detour to an abandoned village where they took contaminated water samples from a well in the marketplace, Pitt directed the Eagle's pilot to fly a leisurely scouting pattern around the Fort Foureau hazardous waste project.

'Let the security guards get a good look at your armament,' Pitt said to the pilot. 'But stay alert for ground fire.'

'Massarde's executive helicopter is sitting on the landing pad with its rotor blades turning,' observed Giordino. 'He must be planning a hasty departure.'

'With Kazim dead, he can't have received word yet on the final outcome of the fight,' said Pitt, 'but he's canny enough to know something went wrong.'

'A shame we have to cancel his flight,' Giordino said fiendishly.

'No sign of ground fire, sir,' the pilot notified Pitt.

'Okay, let us off on the landing pad.'

'You don't want us to go in with you?' asked a rugged-looking sergeant.

'Now that the security guards are properly impressed, Al and I can take it from here. Hang around the area as a show of force for about thirty minutes to intimidate anyone dumb enough to resist. And stop that helicopter on the ground if it attempts to lift off. Then at my signal head back to Colonel Hargrove's field command.'

'You have a welcoming committee,' said the pilot, pointing to the landing pad.

'My, my,' said Giordino, squinting in the bright sunlight. 'It looks like our old pal, Captain Brunone.'

'And a squad of his goons,' Pitt added. He tapped the pilot on the shoulder. 'Keep your firepower aimed at them until we wave you off.'

The pilot hovered half a metre from the ground, keeping his rocket launchers and Chain gun pointed at the waiting security guards. Giordino dropped lightly to the concrete pad and then helped Pitt step down to favour his leg. They walked over to Brunone who stiffened as he recognized them and stared in astonishment.

'I did not expect to see you two again,' said Brunone.

'I'll bet you didn't,' muttered Giordino nastily.

Pitt stared hard at Brunone, reading an expression in the Captain's eyes that Giordino missed, an expression of relief instead of anger or fear. 'You almost look happy to see us.'

'I am. I was told no one ever escaped from Tebezza.'

'Did you send the project engineers and their wives and children there?'

Brunone shook his head solemnly. 'No, that travesty occurred a week before I arrived.'

'But you knew about their imprisonment.'

'I only heard rumours. I tried to investigate the matter, but Mr Massarde pulled a wall of secrecy around it. Anyone connected with the crime has vanished from the project.'

'He probably slit their throats to shut them up,' said Giordino.

'You don't much like Massarde, do you?' said Pitt.

'The man is a pig and a thief,' Brunone spat. 'I could tell you things about this project — '

'We already know,' Pitt interrupted. 'Why don't you quit and fly home?'

Brunone stared at Pitt. 'Those who resign from Massarde Enterprises receive funerals within a week. I have a wife and five children.'

In for a penny, in for a pound. Pitt had a hunch he could trust Brunone. The Captain's cooperation could prove valuable. 'As of now, you're no longer in the employ of Yves Massarde. You're working for Pitt and Giordino Industries.'

Brunone thought over Pitt's proposal, more like a statement of fact, for some time, eyed the hovering helicopter that had enough firepower to level half the project, and then studied the resolute and supremely confident looks on Pitt and Giordino's faces. Then he shrugged. 'Consider me hired.'

'And your security guard force?'

For the first time Brunone grinned. 'My men are loyal to me. They hate Massarde as much as I do. There will be no protest over a change of employers.'

'Cement their loyalty by informing them their pay has just been doubled.'

'And me?'

'Play your cards right,' said Pitt, 'and you'll be the next managing director of this establishment.'

'Ah, now, a first-class incentive. You can be assured of my full cooperation. What would you like me to do?'

Pitt did a sideways nod of his head toward the project's administration building. 'You can begin by escorting us to Massarde so we can give him the sack.'

Brunone suddenly hesitated. 'Forgotten General Kazim, haven't you? He and Massarde are partners. He won't sit by and see his share of the project go elsewhere without a fight.'

'General Zateb Kazim is no longer a problem,' Pitt assured him.

'How can that be? What is his present status?'

'Status, status?' Giordino replied in a mocking tone. 'The last time anybody saw him he was drawing a lot of flies.'

Massarde sat behind his massive desk, the steady, watchful blue eyes reflecting benign displeasure, as if the surprise appearance of Pitt and Giordino was no more than a passing annoyance. Verenne stood behind him like a loyal disciple, face scowling in disgust.

'Like the avenging furies of Greek mythology, you never cease to plague me,' Massarde said philosophically. 'You even look like you ascended from the underworld.'

There was a large antique mirror on the wall behind the desk with a baroque gilded frame crowded with fat cherubs. Pitt looked into it and he could see Massarde had made an accurate assessment. He was in stark contrast to Giordino who was reasonably clean and intact. Combat suit tattered and filthy from smoke and dust. Bloodstained rips and tears revealing bandages on the left arm, shoulder, and right thigh, a gash that ran from cheekbone to chin, face sweat-streaked and haggard, if he could have found a street to lie in, Pitt thought he could pass for a hit-and-run victim.

'Ghosts of the murdered who torment the wicked, that's us,' Pitt retorted. 'And we've come to punish you for your evil ways.'

'Spare me the droll humour,' said Massarde. 'What do you want?'

'The Fort Foureau hazardous waste project for starters.'

'You want the project.' He said it as if it were an everyday occurrence. 'Then I must assume your brazenness indicates General Kazim failed in recapturing the escapees from Tebezza.'

'If you're referring to the families you forced into slavery, yes. As we speak, they're all on their way to safety, thanks to the sacrifices laid down by the UN Tactical Team and

605

the timely arrival of an American Special Operation Force. Once they arrive in France they'll expose your criminal acts. The murders, the hideous atrocities at your gold mine, your illegal waste dumping operation that has caused thousands of deaths among the desert peoples, enough to make you the world's number one criminal.'

'My friends in France will shield me,' he said firmly.

'Don't count on your high connections in the French government. Once the public outcry hits your political buddies, they won't admit to ever having heard of you. Then it's a nasty trial and off to Devil's Island or wherever the French send their convicted criminals nowadays.'

Verenne clutched the back of Massarde's chair, hovering like one of the flying monkeys over the Wicked Witch of the West. 'Mr Massarde will never stand trial or go to prison. He is too powerful; too many world leaders are in his debt.'

'His pocket, you mean,' said Giordino, moving over to the bar and helping himself to a bottle of mineral water.

'I am untouchable so long as I remain in Mali,' said Massarde. 'I can easily continue to operate Massarde Enterprises from here.'

'I'm afraid that's not possible,' said Pitt, circling for the kill. 'Particularly in light of General Kazim's well-deserved demise.'

Massarde stared at Pitt, his mouth slowly tightening. 'Kazim dead?'

'Along with his staff and about half his army.

He looked then at Brunone. 'And you, Captain. Do you and your security guards still stand with me?'

Brunone shook his head slowly. 'No sir, in light of current events, I have decided to accept Mr Pitt's more attractive offer.'

Massarde exhaled in a long, defeated sigh. 'Why on earth would you want control of the project?' he asked Pitt.

'To set it straight and attempt to repair the environmental damage you've caused.'

'The Malians will never permit an outsider to take control.'

'Oh I think government officials will come around once they're told their country will receive all profits from the operation. Considering Mali ranks as one of the poorest of poor nations, how can they refuse?'

'You'd turn over the world's most technically advanced solar waste project to a bunch of ignorant barbarians to run it into the ground?' asked Massarde in surprise. 'You'll lose it all.'

'Did you think I slithered in on your slime with the intention of making a financial killing? Sorry, Massarde, there are a few of us around who aren't driven by greed.'

'You're an idiot, Pitt,' Massarde said, rising from the desk in rage.

'Sit down! You haven't heard the best half of the deal yet.'

'What else can you possibly demand besides control of Fort Foureau?'

'The fortune you've got stashed away in the Society Islands.'

'What are you talking about?' Massarde demanded angrily.

'The millions, maybe hundreds of millions in liquid assets you've accumulated over the years from your shady manipulations and ruthless business transactions. It's a matter of record you don't trust financial institutions or follow usual investment practices, nor do you have your money socked away in Grand Cayman or the Channel Islands. You could have retired a long time ago and enjoyed a good life and invested in paintings or classic cars or villas in Italy. Or better yet, you might have become a philanthropist and shared your inventiveness with needy charities. But greed begets greed. You can't spend your profits. No matter how much you hoard, it's never enough. You're too sick to live like normal people. What you don't keep in Massarde Enterprises for acquisitions, you hide somewhere on a South Pacific island. Tahiti, Mooréa, or Bora? My guess is one of the lesser-inhabited islands in the chain. How close to the truth am I, Massarde?'

He had no reply to make on how close to the truth Pitt was.

'That's the deal,' Pitt continued. 'In return for giving up all control of this project and revealing where you've hidden your ill-gotten gains, I'll let you board your helicopter along with your stooge, Verenne here, and fly free wherever you wish.'

'You are an idiot,' Verenne snapped hoarsely. 'You don't have the authority or power to blackmail Mr Massarde.'

Unnoticed by the others, Giordino stood behind the bar and spoke softly into a small radio transmitter. The timing was near perfect. There were only a few moments of silence before the Eagle helicopter suddenly appeared outside the office window, hanging menacingly in the air with its deadly armament seemingly poised to blow Massarde's office into dust.

Pitt nodded at the hovering aircraft. 'Authority no, power yes.'

Massarde smiled. He was not a man who could be cornered without a fight. He seemed to have no fear at all. He leaned across the desk and said evenly, 'Take the project if you will. Without a despot's backing like Kazim, the stupid government will allow it to deteriorate and become abandoned scrap like every other piece of Western technology that's come to this godforsaken desert. I have other projects, other ventures to replace this one.'

'We're halfway home,' said Giordino coldly.

'As to my wealth, don't waste your breath. What's mine is mine. But you're right about it being on an island in the

Pacific. You and a million other people could search a thousand years and never find it.'

Pitt turned to Brunone. 'Captain, we still have a few hours of afternoon heat left. Please gag Mr Massarde and remove his clothes. Then spread-eagle and stake him to the ground, and leave him.'

That jolted Massarde badly. He could not comprehend being treated as brutally as he had treated others. 'You cannot do this to Yves Massarde,' he said savagely. 'By God, you're not – '

His words were broken off as Pitt backhanded him across the face. 'Tit for tat, pal. Except you're lucky I'm not wearing a ring.'

Massarde said nothing. For a few moments he stood there motionless, his face masked in hate and turning white from the beginning sensations of fear. He looked at Pitt and saw there was no reprieve, because there was an emotionless coldness about the American, an utter lack of compassion that negated the slightest possibility of escaping the ordeal. Slowly he removed his clothes until he stood white-skinned and naked.

'Captain Brunone,' said Pitt. 'Do your duty.'

'With pleasure, sir,' replied Brunone with obvious relish.

After Massarde was gagged and securely staked on the baked ground outside the administration building under the merciless Sahara sun, Pitt nodded to Giordino. 'Convey my thanks to the men in the chopper and send them back to Colonel Hargrove.'

Upon receiving the message, the pilot of the chopper waved and dipped his craft toward the battlefield. Now they were alone with their own creative devices, relying on an enormous amount of bluff.

Giordino looked down at Massarde and then at Pitt with a curious glint in his eyes. 'Why the gag?' he asked.

Pitt smiled. 'If it was you roasting in the sun out there,

how much would you offer Brunone and his men to escape?'

'A couple of million bucks or more,' answered Giordino, admiring Pitt's finesse.

'Probably more.'

'Do you honestly believe he's going to talk?'

Pitt shook his head. 'No, Massarde will suffer the tortures of the damned and go to hell before revealing where he's hidden his wealth.'

'But if he won't tell you, who will?'

'His closest friend and confidant,' said Pitt, gesturing at Verenne.

'Damn you, I don't know!' Verenne's voice was a despairing shout.

'Oh I think you do, maybe not the exact location, but I think you could put us within spitting distance.'

The shift of his eyes, the fearful expression was evidence enough that Verenne knew the secret. 'I wouldn't tell you anything if I could.'

'Al, while I take advantage of Massarde's fancy quarters and clean up, why don't you escort our friend to an empty office and persuade him to sketch out a map to Massarde's private money vault.'

'Sounds good to me,' Giordino said casually. 'I haven't drilled any teeth for nearly a week.'

59

Almost two hours later, after a shower and short nap, Pitt felt almost human again; the biting soreness from his wounds was almost bearable. He was seated at Massarde's desk in a silk robe at least two sizes too small that he'd found in a closet containing enough clothes to open a men's store. He was probing through the drawers of the desk, studying the Frenchman's papers and files when Giordino walked through the door, pushing a white faced Verenne in front of him.

'You two have a nice chat?' asked Pitt.

'Amazing what a great conversationalist he can be in the right company,' Giordino acknowledged.

Verenne looked around through wild unfocused eyes that seemed to have lost all contact with reality. He slowly moved his head from side to side as if he was clearing away a mist. He looked on the verge of a nervous breakdown.

Pitt studied Verenne curiously. 'What did you do to him?' he inquired of Giordino. 'There isn't a mark on him.'

'Like I said, we had a nice chat. I spent the time describing in vivid detail how I was going to dismember him millimetre by millimetre.'

'That's all?'

'He has a great imagination. I never had to lay a hand on him.'

'Did he pinpoint Massarde's island cache?'

'You had the right idea about it being owned by the French, but it's almost 5000 kilometres northeast of Tahiti and 2000 southwest of Mexico. Truly the backside of beyond.'

'I don't know of a French island in the Pacific off Mexico.'

'In 1979, France assumed direct administration of an atoll named Clipperton Island after the English pirate John Clipperton, who used it as a lair in 1705. According to Verenne, its land mass is only about 5 square kilometres with a 21-metre promontory as its highest point.'

'Any habitants?'

Giordino shook his head. 'Not unless you count a few wild pigs. Verenne says the only remnant of human activity is an abandoned lighthouse from the eighteenth century.'

'A lighthouse,' Pitt turned the word over slowly. 'Only a slick, wily pirate like Massarde would think of hiding a treasure near a lighthouse on an uninhabited island in the middle of an ocean.'

'Verenne claims he doesn't know the exact spot.'

'Whenever Mr Massarde anchored his yacht off the island,' murmured Verenne, 'he always took a boat ashore alone, and only at night so no one could observe his movements.'

Pitt looked at Giordino. 'Think he's telling the truth?'

'I am, I swear to God!' Verenne implored.

'Could be he's just a natural-born storyteller,' said Giordino.

'I told the truth.' His voice came like the pleas of a child. 'Oh God, I don't want to be tortured. I can't stand pain.'

Giordino stared at Verenne fox-like. 'Or then again, he might be a naturally gifted actor.'

Verenne looked stricken. 'What can I do to make you believe me?'

'I'll be convinced when you inform on your boss. Supply his records, names, and dates of his victims, every filthy business deal he ever created, expose the guts of his entire rotten organization.'

'I do that and he'll have me killed,' Verenne croaked in a frightened whisper.

'He'll never touch you.'

'Oh yes he can. You don't know the power he wields.'

'I think I have an idea.'

'He won't hurt you half as much as I will,' said Giordino menacingly.

Verenne sank into a chair, stared at Giordino with a sweat-moistened face, with fear-widened eyes that carried the faintest flicker of hope as he turned and trained them on Pitt. These men had stripped his chief of all dignity, of all arrogance. If there was a chance of saving his life, he knew he had to choose.

'I'll do as you ask,' he moaned softly.

'Let me hear it again,' Pitt demanded.

'All records and information on Massarde Enterprises, I will turn them over to you for investigation.'

'That includes unrecorded records on illegal and immoral activities as well.'

'I will supply what isn't on paper or computerized.'

There was a brief silence. Pitt stared out the window at Massarde. Even at that distance he could see the white skin had turned a deep red. He rose stiffly from behind the desk and put a hand on Giordino's shoulder.

'Al, he's your project. Extract every shred of evidence out of him you can.'

Giordino put his arm around Verenne, who cringed. 'We'll have a real friendly rap session you and I.'

'Work on the names of the people Massarde victimized or murdered. Those first.'

'Any particular reason?' Giordino asked curiously.

'When the time is right for a voyage to Clipperton Island and a search proves successful, I'd like to set up an organization to use Massarde's stashed wealth to pay back those he hurt and the surviving families of those he killed.'

'Mr Massarde will never permit that,' Verenne muttered hoarsely.

'Speaking of our favourite villain,' said Pitt, 'I think he's baked in the oven long enough.'

The front of Massarde's body looked like a shellfish after it had been broiled in a pot. Already he was in excruciating agony, his skin blistering. By the next morning it would begin to peel in huge strips. He stood there without support between Brunone and two impassive guards, motionless, his lips drawn back like a snarling dog, his reddened face contorted in rage and hate.

'You cannot do this to me and live,' he hissed. 'Even if I'm killed, I have devised methods to make those responsible pay.'

'An avenging hit team,' said Pitt dryly. 'How foresighted of you. After cooking in the sun, you must be tired and thirsty. Please take a chair. Al, bring Mr Massarde a bottle of his special French mineral water.'

Massarde very slowly eased into a soft leather chair, his face suddenly taut from agony. Settled finally in a comfortable position, he took a deep breath. 'You are fools if you think you can get away with this. Kazim has ambitious officers who will quickly step into his place, men who are as vicious and cunning as he was, and who will send a force to bury you in the desert before the next sun.'

He reached for the bottle of water held out to him by Giordino and swallowed its entire contents within seconds. Without being asked, Giordino handed him another.

Pitt couldn't help but admire Massarde's incomparable nerve. The man acted as if he was in complete control of his situation.

Massarde finished off the second bottle and then looked around his office for his personal secretary. 'Where is Verenne?'

'Dead,' Pitt said tersely.

For the first time Massarde looked genuinely surprised. 'You murdered him?'

Pitt shrugged indifferently. 'He tried to stab Giordino here. Stupid of him to attack a man carrying a gun with a letter opener.'

'He did that?' Massarde asked warily.

'I can show you the body if you like.'

'Not at all like Verenne. He was a coward.'

Pitt exchanged glances with Giordino. Verenne had already been put to work and was under guard in an office two floors below.

'I've got a proposition for you,' said Pitt.

'What deal could you possibly make with me?' snarled Massarde.

'I've had a change of heart. If you promise to mend your crooked ways, I'll let you walk from this room, board your helicopter, and leave Mali.'

'Is this some sort of joke?'

'Not at all. I've decided the sooner you're out of my hair, the better.'

'Surely you can't be serious,' said Brunone. 'The man is a dangerous menace. He'll strike back at his first opportunity.'

'Yes, the Scorpion. Is that what you're called, Massarde?'

The Frenchman did not answer, but sat in sullen silence.

'Are you sure you know what you're doing?' asked Giordino.

'There will be no argument,' Pitt said harshly. 'I want this scum out of here, and I want him out now. Captain Brunone, escort Massarde to his helicopter and see that it lifts off with him on it.'

Massarde rose shakily to his feet; the sunburned skin was tightening and it was with only an agonized effort that he could stand straight. Despite the pain he smiled. His mind was churning again. 'I will require several hours to pack my things and personal records.'

'You have exactly two minutes to get off the project.'

615

Massarde swore, bitterly and vilely. 'Not like this, not without my clothes. My God, man, show some decency.'

'What do you know about decency?' Pitt said dispassionately. 'Captain Brunone, get this son of a bitch out of here before I kill him myself.'

Brunone didn't have to order his two men. He simply nodded and they hustled the wildly cursing Yves Massarde into the elevator. No word passed between the three men in the office as they stood at the window and watched the humiliated mogul roughly shoved aboard his luxury helicopter. The door was closed and the rotors began to thump the hot air. In less than four minutes it had disappeared over the desert to the north.

'He's heading northeast,' observed Giordino.

'My guess is Libya,' said Brunone. 'And then on to hidden exile before recovering his loot.'

'His final destination is of no consequence,' Pitt said, yawning.

'You should have killed him,' Brunone said, his voice sharp with disappointment.

'No need to bother. He won't live out the week.'

'How can you say that?' asked an astonished Brunone. 'You let him go free. Why? The man has the resilience and lives of a cat. He's not about to die from sunburn.'

'No, but he *will* die.' Pitt nodded at Giordino. 'Did you make the switch okay?'

Giordino grinned back. 'As smoothly as decanting wine.'

Brunone looked confused. 'What are you talking about?'

'Tying Massarde down out in the sun,' explained Pitt, 'I wanted to make him thirsty.'

'Thirsty? I don't understand.'

'Al here, emptied the bottles of mineral water and refilled them with water contaminated by chemicals leaking from the underground storage vault.'

'It's called poetic justice.' Giordino held up the empty bottles. 'He drank almost 3 litres of the stuff.'

'As his internal organs disintegrate, his brain will be eaten away and he will go mad.' Pitt's tone was ice cold, his face chiselled in stone.

'There is no hope for him?' a dazed Brunone asked.

Pitt shook his head. 'Yves Massarde will die strapped to a bed, screaming to escape his torment. I only wish his victims could be there to see it.'

PART FIVE

The *Texas*

60

June 10, 1996
Washington, D.C.

Two weeks after the siege of Fort Foureau, Admiral Sandecker was seated in a conference room at NUMA's headquarters in Washington at the head of a long table. Dr Chapman, Hiram Yaeger, and Rudi Gunn sat alongside, staring into a large TV monitor embedded in one wall.

The Admiral motioned impatiently at the blank screen. 'When are they going to come on?'

Yaeger was holding a telephone to his ear while studying the monitor. 'The satellite should be downlinking their signal from Mali any second.'

Almost before Yaeger finished speaking, a picture flickered and settled onto the screen. Pitt and Giordino sat together behind a desk piled with file folders and papers while facing into a camera. 'Are you receiving us all right on your end?' asked Yaeger.

'Hello, Hiram,' answered Pitt. 'Nice to see your face and hear your voice.'

'You're looking good here. Everyone is anxious to talk to you.'

'Good morning, Dirk,' greeted Sandecker. 'How are your injuries?'

'It's afternoon here, Admiral. And I'm healing nicely, thank you.'

After Pitt exchanged friendly greetings with Rudi Gunn and Dr Chapman, the Admiral launched the discussion. 'We have good news,' he said enthusiastically. 'A satellite survey of the South Atlantic, computer analysed only an hour ago, shows the growth rate of the red tide as falling off. All of Yaeger's projections indicate that the spread is slowly grinding to a halt.'

'And not a week too soon,' said Gunn. 'We've already detected a 5 per cent drop in the world's total oxygen supply. It wouldn't be long before we'd all begin to feel the effects.'

'All automobiles from every cooperating nation in the world were within twenty-four hours of being banned from the streets,' Yaeger lectured. 'All aircraft grounded, all industrial factories shut down. The world was a hair away from coming to a standstill.'

'But it appears both our efforts have paid off,' acknowledged Chapman. 'You and Al, finding and burning the source of the synthetic amino acid that stimulated the dinoflagellate population explosion, and our NUMA scientific team discovering the little critters are fussy about reproducing if they're subjected to a one-part-per-million dose of copper.'

'Have you found a significant drop in the contamination streaming into the Niger River since we shut off the flow?' asked Pitt.

Gunn nodded. 'By nearly 30 per cent. I underestimated the migration rate of groundwater from the hazardous waste project south to the river. It moves more rapidly through the textured sand and gravel of the Sahara than I originally projected.'

'How long before the pollution reaches a safe level?'

'Dr Chapman and I are predicting a good six months before most of its residue has flowed into the ocean.'

'Cutting off the pollutant was a vital first step,' Chapman spelled out. 'It gave us extra time to air drop copper particles over large areas of the tides. I think it's safe to say we've turned the corner on an eco-disaster of frightening consequences.'

'But the battle is far from over,' Sandecker reminded him. 'The United States alone produces only 58 per cent of the oxygen it consumes, oxygen mostly created by plankton in the Pacific Ocean. In another twenty years, because of the increase in auto and air traffic, and the continuing devastation to the world's forests and wetlands, we'll begin to use up our oxygen faster than nature can replenish it.'

'And we still face the problem we're currently experiencing of chemicals poisoning the oceans,' Chapman followed the Admiral. 'We've had a bad scare, but the near tragedy with the red tides has demonstrated how critically close human and wildlife are to the last gasp of oxygen.'

'Maybe from now on,' said Pitt, 'we won't take our air supply for granted.'

'Two weeks have passed since you took over Fort Foureau,' said Sandecker. 'What's your situation with the operation?'

'Pretty damned good, actually,' answered Giordino. 'After cutting off all incoming waste shipments by train, we've kept the solar reactor burning day and night. Another thirty-six hours should see all industrial contaminants that Massarde hid away in the underground storage vaults destroyed.'

'What have you done about the nuclear waste storage?' asked Chapman.

'After they had a brief rest from their ordeal at Tebezza,' Pitt replied, 'I asked the original French engineers who supervised the construction of the project to return. They agreed and have since assembled Malian work crews to continue excavating the storage chamber down to 1.5 kilometres.'

'Will that depth keep high-level waste safe from earth's organisms? Plutonium 239, for example, has a half-life of 24,000 years.'

Pitt smiled. 'Unknowingly, Massarde couldn't have selected a better place for the deep burial of waste. The geology is very stable in this part of the Sahara. The rock beds have been undisturbed for hundreds of millions of years. We're nowhere near crustal-plate boundaries, and far below existing groundwater. No one will have to worry about the waste affecting life ever again.'

'How do you intend to contain the waste after it's stored underground?'

'The safety criteria the French waste experts have created are stringent. Before burial in the deep rock it will be encased in concrete and then in a stainless-steel cylinder. This is surrounded by a layer of asphalt and a cast-iron enclosure. Finally, a backfill of concrete is poured around the container before it is embedded in the rock.'

Chapman grinned from ear to ear. 'My compliments, Dirk. You've put together a world-class waste disposal site.'

'Another bit of interesting news,' said Sandecker. 'Our government and that of Mongolia have shut down Massarde's hazardous waste projects in the Mojave and Gobi Deserts after surprise inspections by a team of international waste investigators found them to be substandard and unsafe.'

'The Australian outback installation was also closed,' Chapman added.

Pitt sat back and sighed. 'I'm happy to hear Massarde is out of the waste disposal business.'

'Speaking of the Scorpion,' said Giordino, 'how's his condition?'

'He was buried in Tripoli yesterday,' replied Sandecker. 'CIA agents reported that just before he died, he went insane and tried to make a meal of a doctor.'

'The perfect ending,' Giordino muttered sardonically.

'By the way,' said Sandecker. 'The President sends his warmest regards and thanks. Says he's going to issue a special citation of merit for your achievement.'

Pitt and Giordino turned to each other and shrugged indifferently.

Sandecker chose to ignore the display of distaste. 'You might be interested in knowing that for the first time in two decades, our State Department is working closely with the new Malian parliament. Much of the improved relations were due to you turning all profits from the project over to the government to aid their social programmes.'

'It seemed the proper thing to do since we couldn't profit by it,' said Pitt benevolently.

'Any chance of a coup by the army?' inquired Gunn.

'Without Kazim, the inner core of his officers fell apart. To a man they crawled on their knees and swore undying allegiance to the leaders of the new government.'

'It's been almost a month since any of us have seen your ugly faces in person,' Sandecker smiled. 'Your job is finished in the Sahara. When can I expect you back in Washington?'

'Even the turmoil and mess of the nation's capital would look good after this place,' muttered Giordino.

'A week's vacation would be nice,' Pitt answered seriously. 'I have to ship something home and take care of some personal business. And then there's a little historical project I'd like to investigate here in the desert.'

'The *Texas?*'

'How did you know?'

'St Julien Perlmutter whispered in my ear.'

'I'd be grateful for a favour, Admiral.'

Sandecker made an act of shrugging condescendingly. 'I guess I owe you a little free time.'

'Please arrange for Julien to fly to Mali as quickly as possible.'

'With Julien weighing in at 180 kilograms,' Sandecker looked at Pitt roguishly, 'you'll never get him on a camel.'

'Much less induce him to trek over blistering sand under a blazing sun,' Gunn joined in.

'If I'm right,' said Pitt, staring through the monitor at them in amusement, 'all I'll need to get Julien to walk twenty paces across desert terrain is a bottle of chilled Chardonnay.'

'Before I forget,' Sandecker spoke up, 'the Aussies were overjoyed at your discovery of Kitty Mannock and her aircraft. You and Giordino are national heroes according to the Sydney papers.'

'Do they have plans for a recovery?'

'A wealthy rancher from her home town has agreed to fund the operation. He plans to restore the plane and hang it in a museum in Melbourne. A recovery team should be at the location you provided by tomorrow.'

'And Kitty?'

'A national holiday when her body is returned. I was told by the Australian ambassador that contributions are pouring in from all over the country for a memorial over her proposed grave site.'

'Our country should contribute too, especially the South.'

Curious, Sandecker asked, 'What is our connection with her?'

'She's going to lead us to the *Texas*,' answered Pitt matter-of-factly.

Sandecker exchanged questioning looks with the NUMA men around the table. Then he refaced Pitt's image in the monitor and said, 'We'd all be interested in knowing how a woman who's been dead for sixty-five years can pull off that little trick.'

'I found Kitty's logbook in the wreckage,' Pitt replied slowly. 'She describes her discovery of a ship before she died, an iron ship buried in the desert.'

61

'Good lord!' Perlmutter uttered as he peered out the helicopter's windshield at the sunrise illuminating the dead land below. 'You walked through that?'

'Actually, we sailed across this section of the desert in our improvised land yacht,' Pitt answered. 'We're flying our trek in reverse.'

Perlmutter had flown into Algiers on a military jet, and then caught a commercial airliner to the small desert city of Adrar in southern Algeria. There, Pitt and Giordino had met him shortly after midnight and escorted him aboard a helicopter they'd borrowed from the project's French construction crew.

After refuelling, they headed south, spotting the land yacht just after dawn, lying forlornly on its side where they had left it after their rescue by the Arab truck driver. They landed and dismantled the old wing, cables, and wheels that had saved their lives, lashing the pieces to the landing skids of the helicopter. Then they lifted off with Pitt at the controls and set a course for the ravine that held Kitty Mannock's lost aircraft.

During the flight, Perlmutter read over a copy Pitt had made of Kitty's logbook. 'What a courageous lady,' he said in admiration. 'With only a few swallows of water, a broken ankle, and a badly sprained knee, she hobbled nearly 16 kilometres under the most wretched conditions.'

'And that was only one way.' Pitt reminded him. 'After stumbling on the ship in the desert, she limped back to her aircraft.'

'Yes, here it is,' said Perlmutter, reading aloud.

Wednesday, October 14. Extreme heat. Becoming very miserable. Followed ravine southward until it finally opened out into a wide, dry riverbed, I estimate about 10 miles from plane. Have trouble sleeping in the bitter cold nights. This afternoon I found a strange-looking ship half buried in the desert. Thought I was hallucinating, but after touching the sloping sides of iron, I realized it was real. Entered around an old cannon protruding through an opening and spent the night. Shelter at last.

Thursday, October 15. Searched interior of ship. Too dark to see very much. Found several remains of the former crew. Very well preserved. Must have been dead a long time judging from the look of their uniforms. A plane flew over, but did not see the ship. I could not climb outside in time to signal. It was travelling in the direction of my crash. I will never be found here and have decided to return to my plane in the chance it has been discovered. I know now it was a mistake to try and walk out. If searchers found my plane they could never follow my trail. The wind has blown sand over it like snow in a blizzard. The desert has its own game, and I cannot beat it.

Perlmutter paused and looked up. 'That explains why you found the logbook with her entries at the crash site. She came back in the vain hope the search planes had found hers.'

'What were her last words?' asked Giordino.

Perlmutter turned a page and continued reading.

Sunday, October 18. Returned to plane but have seen no sign of rescue party. Am pretty well done in. If I am found after I'm gone, please forgive the grief I've caused. A kiss for my mum and dad. Tell them I tried to die bravely. I cannot write more, my brain no longer controls my hand.

When Perlmutter finished, each man felt a deep sense of sadness and melancholy. They were all moved by Kitty's epic fight to survive. Tough guys to the end, they all fought to suppress their glistening eyes.

'She could have taught a lot of men the meaning of courage,' Pitt said heavily.

Perlmutter nodded. 'Thanks to her endurance, another great mystery may be solved.'

'She gave us a ball park,' acknowledged Pitt. 'All we have to do is follow the ravine south until it opens into an old riverbed and start our search for the ironclad from there.'

Two hours later, the Aussie recovery team paused in their task of carefully dismantling the weathered remains of Kitty Mannock's old Fairchild airplane and looked up as a helicopter appeared and circled the ravine containing the wreckage. Smiles broke out as the Aussies recognized the missing wing and landing gear tied to the chopper's landing skids.

Pitt eased back on the cyclic control and brought the craft to a gentle landing on the flat ground above the ravine to avoid covering the recovery workers and their equipment in a tornado of dust and sand. He shut down the engines and checked his watch. It was eight-forty A.M., a few hours shy of the hottest time of day.

St Julien Perlmutter shifted his bulk in the copilot's seat in preparation for his exit. 'I wasn't built for these contraptions,' he grumbled as the full blast of the heat hit him upon exiting the air-conditioned cabin.

'Beats the hell out of walking,' Giordino said as he surveyed the familiar ground. 'Believe me, I know.'

A big, brawny Aussie with a ruddy face climbed from the ravine and approached them. 'Allo there, you must be Dirk Pitt.'

'I'm Al Giordino, he's Pitt.' Giordino gestured over his shoulder.

'Ned Quinn, I'm in charge of the recovery operation.'

Pitt winced as Quinn's huge paw crushed his hand.

Massaging his knuckles, Pitt said, 'We brought back the parts of Kitty's aircraft that we borrowed a few weeks ago.'

'Much appreciated.' Quinn's voice rasped like iron against a grinding wheel. 'Amazin' bit of ingenuity, using the wing to sail over the desert.'

'St Julien Perlmutter,' said Perlmutter, introducing himself.

Quinn patted an enormous belly that hung over a pair of work pants. 'Seems we both take to good food and drink, Mr Perlmutter.'

'You wouldn't happen to have some of that good Aussie beer with you by chance?'

'You like our beer?'

'I keep a case of Castlemaine from Brisbane on hand for special occasions.'

'We don't have any Castlemaine,' said Quinn, mightily impressed, 'but I can offer you a bottle of Fosters.'

'I'd be much obliged,' Perlmutter said gratefully as his sweat glands began to pour.

Quinn walked over to the cab of a flatbed truck and pulled four bottles from an ice chest. He brought them back and passed them around.

'How soon will you be finishing up?' asked Pitt, moving off the subject of brew.

Quinn turned and stared at the portable crane that was preparing to lift the engine from the ancient aircraft onto the truck. 'Another three or four hours before she's snugly tied down and we're on our way back to Algiers.'

Pitt pulled the logbook from his shirt pocket and held it out to Quinn. 'Kitty's pilot log. She used it to record her final flight and tragic aftermath. I borrowed it for reference on something she found during her ordeal. I hope Kitty wouldn't have minded.'

'I'm sure she didn't mind at all,' said Quinn, nodding down at the wooden coffin draped in the Australian flag with the cross of St George and stars of the Southern Cross. 'My countrymen are indebted to you and Mr Giordino for clearing up the mystery of her disappearance so we could bring her home.'

'She's been gone too long,' said Perlmutter softly.

'Yes,' Quinn said with a touch of reverence to his rasping voice 'That she has.'

Much to Perlmutter's delight, Quinn insisted on supplying their helicopter with ten bottles of beer before they said their farewells. To a man, the Aussies climbed the steep bank to express their thanks and heartily shake Pitt and Giordino's hands. After he lifted off the helicopter into the air, Pitt circled the wreckage once more in tribute before turning and following Kitty's footsteps toward the legendary ship in the desert.

Flying in a straight line over the meandering ravine that had taken Kitty days of painful struggle to limp through, the jet helicopter reached the ancient riverbed in less than twelve minutes. What had once been a flowing river surrounded by a green belt was now little more than a wide barren wash surrounded by unstable sand.

'The Oued Zarit,' announced Perlmutter. 'Hard to believe it was a thriving waterway.'

'Oued Zarit,' Pitt repeated. 'That's what the old American prospector called it. He claimed it began to go dry about a hundred and thirty years ago.'

'He was right. I did some research on old French surveys of the area. There once was a port near here where caravans traded with merchants who ran a fleet of boats. No telling where it stood now. It was covered over by sand not long after the unending drought began and the water sank into the sand.'

'So the theory is the *Texas* steamed up the river and became landlocked when the river ran dry,' said Giordino.

'Not a theory. I found a deathbed statement in the archives from a crewman by the name of Beecher. He swore he was the only survivor of the *Texas*' crew, and gave a detailed description of the ship's final voyage across the Atlantic and up the tributary of the Niger where it became stranded.'

'How can you be sure it wasn't the ravings of a dying man?' asked Giordino.

'His story was too incredibly detailed not to believe,' Perlmutter said firmly.

Pitt dropped the helicopter's speed as he stared down at the dry wash. 'The prospector also said the *Texas* was carrying gold from the dying Confederacy's treasury.'

Perlmutter nodded. 'Beecher mentioned gold. He also gave me a tantalizing clue that led to Secretary of War Edwin Stanton's secret and still unopened papers – '

'I think we have something,' interrupted Giordino, pointing down through the windshield. 'Off to the right. A large dune that spills out from the west bank.'

'The one with a rock embedded on top?' asked Perlmutter, his voice rising in excitement.

'You got it.'

'Break out the Schonstedt gradiometer Julien brought from Washington,' Pitt ordered Giordino. 'As soon as you set it up, I'll make a pass over the dune.'

Giordino quickly unpacked the iron-detecting instrument, checked the battery connections, and set the sensitivity reading. 'Ready to drop the sensor.'

'Okay, approaching the dune at an airspeed of 10 knots,' replied Pitt.

Giordino lowered the sensor on a cable leading back to the gradiometer until it dangled 10 metres beneath the helicopter's belly. Then he and Perlmutter intently studied the needle on the frequency dial. As the helicopter moved slowly over the dune, the needle wavered and the sound amplifier began to buzz. Suddenly the needle pegged and then shot to the other side of the dial as the sensor passed over the magnetic polarity from positive to negative. In unison the buzz rose to a shrill shriek.

'She's off the scale,' Giordino shouted jubilantly. 'We've got a king-size iron mass down there.'

'Your reading could be coming from that circular brown rock on the dune,' cautioned Perlmutter. 'The desert around here is teeming with iron ore.'

'Not a brown rock!' Pitt whooped. 'You're looking at the top of a smokestack coated with rust.'

As Pitt hovered over the mound, no one found the right words to say. Until now, deep down, they had wondered if she existed at all. But there was no uncertainty in their minds now.

The *Texas* had surely been rediscovered.

62

The first flush of exhilaration and elation soon died when a survey of the mound showed that with the exception of 2 metres of smokestack, the entire ship was covered by sand. It would take days for them to shovel through the avalanching sand to reach inside.

'The dune has marched over the casemate since Kitty was here sixty-five years ago,' muttered Perlmutter. 'The wreck is buried too deep for us to penetrate. Nothing but heavy excavation equipment can clear an entrance.'

'I believe there is a way,' said Pitt.

Perlmutter looked at the enormous size of the mound and shook his head. 'Looks hopeless to me.'

'A dredge,' snapped Giordino as if a light clicked on inside his head. 'The method salvagers use to remove silt from a wreck.'

'You read my mind,' Pitt laughed. 'Instead of a high-pressure hose to excavate, we hang the chopper overhead and let the air surge from the rotors blow away the sand.'

'Sounds rather half-assed to me,' grumbled Perlmutter thoughtfully. 'You won't be able to exert enough downward thrust to move much sand without lifting us into the sky.'

'The slopes of the dune rise sharply to a peak,' Pitt pointed out. 'If we can level the summit by 3 metres, she should see the top of the ironclad's casemate.'

Giordino shrugged. 'Can't lose by trying.'

'My sentiments also.'

Pitt hung the helicopter over the mound and applied only enough power to keep the craft in a static hover. The force of the air from the rotor whipped up the sand below in a frenzied swirl. Ten, twenty minutes, he held the chopper stable, fighting the buffeting from the down draught. He could see nothing; the induced sandstorm hid all sight of the dune.

'How much longer?' asked Giordino. 'The grit must be playing hell with the turbines.'

'I'll blow the engines to scrap if that's what it takes,' Pitt answered with bulldog determination.

Perlmutter began to see visions of his ample body becoming a ten-day feast for the local buzzards. He felt nothing but pessimism about Pitt and Giordino's mad brainstorm, but he sat quietly without interfering.

After thirty minutes, Pitt finally hauled the helicopter into the sky and off to one side of the mound until the cloud of sand and dust settled to the ground. Every eye peered downward. The minutes that followed seemed endless. Then Perlmutter let out a bellow that drowned out the whine of the turbines.

'She's clear!'

Pitt was seated on the side of the cabin opposite the dune. 'What do you see?' he yelled back.

'Iron plates and rivets of what looks like the pilothouse.'

Pitt shoved the chopper to a higher altitude so he wouldn't disturb more sand. The cloud had finally drifted away and settled, exposing the ironclad's pilothouse and about 2 square metres of deck over the casemate. It seemed so unnatural for a ship to be lying under a desert, it materialized like a giant sand monster out of a science fiction movie.

Less than ten minutes later, after Pitt landed the helicopter, and he and Giordino heaved a labouring Perlmutter up the sides of the dune, they found themselves standing on the *Texas*. The pilothouse rose clear, and they half expected to find eyes peering back at them through the observation slits.

There was only a light coating of rust on the thick iron

that shielded the wood of the casemate. Gouges and dents from the Union navy's guns were still evident on the armour.

The entry hatch on the rear of the small structure was frozen shut, but it was no match for Pitt's wiry strength, Giordino's thick muscles, and Perlmutter's weight as it squeaked in protest at being forced open. They stared at the ladder that dropped into the darkness, then stared at each other.

'I think the honour should go to you, Dirk. You put us here.'

Giordino removed a backpack slung over his shoulders and passed out maximum optic flashlights that could illuminate a basketball court. The interior beckoned, and Pitt flicked on his light and stepped down the ladder.

The sand that had sifted through the eye slits covered the deck almost to the tops of Pitt's hiking boots. The wheel stood frozen in time as if patiently waiting for a ghostly helmsman. The only other objects he could see were a set of speaking tubes and a high stool lying on its side in a sand-filled corner. Pitt hesitated at the open hatch leading down to the gun deck for a moment, inhaled deeply, and dropped into the darkness below.

The instant his feet touched the wooden deck he crouched and turned completely in a circle, beaming his light into every corner of the immense enclosure. The great 100-pound Blakely guns and the two 9-inch, 64-pounders sat half immersed in sand that had flowed past the shutters of their open gun-ports. He walked over and stood beside one of the Blakelys, still solidly mounted on its huge wooden carriage. He had seen old Mathew Brady photographs of Civil War naval cannon, but had never conceived their monumental size. He could only marvel at the strength of the men who once manned them.

The atmosphere of the gun deck was oppressive but surprisingly cool. It was also eerily empty but for the guns.

No fire buckets, no ramrods or shot and shell. Nothing littered the floor. It was as though it had been stripped clean for a dockyard refit. Pitt turned as Perlmutter awkwardly climbed down the ladder followed by Giordino.

'How odd,' said Perlmutter, gazing around. 'Are my eyes failing or is this deck as bare as a mausoleum?'

Pitt smiled. 'Your eyes are fine.'

'You'd think the crew might have given it a lived-in look,' Giordino mused.

'The men on this deck and these guns battered half the Union fleet,' exclaimed Perlmutter. 'Many of them died in here. It doesn't figure there isn't a scrap of their existence.'

'Kitty Mannock mentioned seeing bodies,' Giordino reminded him.

'They must be below,' said Pitt. He aimed his light beam at a stairwell leading down into the ship's hull. 'I suggest we begin with the crew's quarters forward and then work back through the engine room toward the stern and the officers' quarters.'

Giordino nodded. 'Sounds good.'

So they moved on, numbed by an awe of the unknown. The knowledge that she was the only completely intact ironclad from the Civil War with remains of her crew still on board only deepened an almost superstitious reverence. Pitt felt as if he was walking through a haunted house.

They slowly moved into the crew's quarters and came to an abrupt halt. The compartment was a tomb of the dead. There were over fifty of them frozen in their final posture when overtaken by death. Most had died while lying in their bunks. Although there was water to drink from the dwindling flow of the river, the shrunken stomachs of their mummified corpses told of the disease and starvation after their food ran out. A few were sitting slumped around a mess table, some crumpled on the deck. Much of their clothing was stripped off their bodies. No sign of their shoes or a trace of their sea chests or personal belongings could be seen.

'They've been picked clean,' murmured Giordino.

'The Tuaregs,' Perlmutter concluded wearily. 'Beecher said that desert bandits, as he called them, had attacked the ship.'

'They must have had a death wish to attack an armoured ship with old muskets and spears,' said Giordino.

'They were after the gold. Beecher said the Captain used the Confederate treasury gold to buy food from the desert tribes. Once the word spread, the Tuaregs probably made a couple of futile assaults against the ship before getting smart and laying siege by cutting off all food and supplies. Then they waited until the crew starved or died off from typhoid and malaria. When all signs of resistance disappeared, the Tuaregs simply walked on board and pillaged the ship of the gold and everything else they could carry. After years of scrounging by every nomad tribe that wandered by, nothing is left but the crew's bodies and the cannon that were too huge to haul away.'

'So we can forget about the gold,' said Pitt thoughtfully. 'It's long gone.'

Perlmutter nodded. 'We won't get rich this day.'

There was no temptation to linger in the compartment of the dead. They moved aft and into the engine room. Coal was still heaped in the bins and shovels hung beside the scuttles. Without moisture to cause corrosion, the brass on gauges and fittings still had a faint gleam under the bright glare of the max optic flashlights. But for the dust, the engines and boilers looked to be in first-class operating condition.

One of their light beams caught the figure of a man sitting hunched over a small desk. A yellowed paper lay under one hand next to an inkwell that had spilled when he had slumped into death. Pitt gently removed the paper and read it under his flashlight.

I have done my duty to the last of my strength. I leave my sweet, faithful engines in prime condition. They beautifully carried us across the ocean without missing a stroke and are as strong as the day they were installed in Richmond. I bequeath them to the next engineer to move this good ship against the hated Yankees. God save the Confederacy.

Chief Engineer of the *Texas*,
Angus O'Hare

'There sits a dedicated man,' said Pitt approvingly.

'They don't make them like him today,' Perlmutter agreed. Leaving Chief Engineer O'Hare, Pitt led the way past the big twin engines and boilers. A passageway led into the officers' quarters and mess, where they found four more undressed bodies, all reposed on bunks in their individual cabins. Pitt gave them little more than a passing glance before stopping at a mahogany door mounted in the aft bulkhead.

'The Captain's cabin,' he said definitely.

Perlmutter nodded. 'Commander Mason Tombs. From what I read of the *Texas*' audacious fight from Richmond to the Atlantic, Tombs was one tough customer.'

Pitt brushed off a tinge of fear, turned the knob, and pushed open the door. Suddenly, Perlmutter reached out and clutched Pitt's arm.

'Wait!'

Pitt looked at Perlmutter, puzzled. 'Why? What are you afraid of?'

'I suspect we may find something that should remain unseen.'

'Can't be worse than what we've already laid eyes on,' Giordino argued.

'What are you holding back, Julien?' Pitt demanded.

'I — I didn't tell you what I found in Edwin Stanton's secret papers.'

'Tell me later,' Pitt muttered impatiently. He turned from Perlmutter, shined his light through the doorway, and stepped inside.

The cabin would have seemed small and cramped by most contemporary warship standards, but ironclads were not built for long weeks at sea. During the fighting along the rivers and inlets of the Confederacy, they were seldom away from dock for more than two days at a time.

As with the other quarters, all objects and furniture that were not attached to the ship were gone. The Tuaregs, having no skills for handling tools and wrenches, had ignored any fixtures that were built in. The Captain's cabin still retained bookshelves and a mounted but broken barometer. But for some inexplicable reason, as with the stool in the pilothouse, the Tuaregs had left behind a rocking chair.

Pitt's light revealed two bodies, one reposed in a bunk, the other sitting as though slumbering in the rocking chair. The corpse in the bunk was lying on its side against the bulkhead naked, the position the Tuaregs had crudely shoved it in when stripping away the clothes and bed covers and mattress. A thicket of red hair still covered the head and face.

Giordino joined Pitt and closely studied the figure in the chair. Under the bright glare of the max optic light, the skin reflected a dark brown shade with the same textured leather look of Kitty Mannock's body. It had also mummified from the dry heat of the outside desert. The body was still clothed in old-fashioned one-piece underwear.

Even in the sitting position it was evident the man had been quite tall. His face was bearded and exceedingly gaunt with very prominent ears. The eyes were closed as if he had simply drifted off to sleep, the brows thick and strangely short, stopped abruptly as if clipped at the outer edge of the eye. The hair and beard were jet black with only a sprinkling of grey.

'This guy is the spitting image of Lincoln,' Giordino remarked conversationally.

'That *is* Abraham Lincoln,' came Perlmutter's subdued voice from the doorway. He slowly sank to the deck, his back against the bulkhead, like a whale settling to the seabed. His eyes were locked on the corpse in the rocking chair as if hypnotically fixed.

Pitt stared at Perlmutter with concern and obvious scepticism. 'For a renowned historian, you've taken a wrong turn, haven't you?'

Giordino knelt beside Perlmutter and offered him a drink from a water bottle. 'The heat must be getting to you, big buddy.'

Perlmutter waved away the water. 'God oh God, I couldn't bring myself to believe it. But Lincoln's Secretary of War, Edwin McMasters Stanton, *did* reveal the truth in his secret papers.'

'What truth?' asked Pitt, curious.

He hesitated, and then his voice came almost in a whisper. 'Lincoln was not shot by John Wilkes Booth at Ford's Theater. That is him sitting in that rocking chair.'

63

Pitt stared at Perlmutter, incapable of absorbing the words. 'Lincoln's assassination was one of the most widely recorded events in American history. There were over a hundred witnesses in the theatre. How can you say it didn't happen?'

Perlmutter gave a slight shrug of his shoulders. 'The event occurred as reported, only it was a staged deception planned and carried out by Stanton using a near look-alike actor made up to appear as Lincoln. Two days before the fake assassination, the real Lincoln was captured by the Confederates and sneaked through Union lines to Richmond where he was held hostage. This part of the story is backed up by another deathbed statement by a captain in the Confederate cavalry who led the capture.'

Pitt looked thoughtfully at Giordino, then back at Perlmutter. 'This southern cavalry captain, his name by chance was Neville Brown.'

Perlmutter's jaw dropped. 'How did you know?'

'We ran into an old American prospector who was looking for the *Texas* and her gold. He told us about Brown's story.'

Giordino looked as if he was waking from a bad dream. 'We thought it was a fairy tale.'

'Believe you me,' said Perlmutter, unable to keep his eyes from the corpse, 'it's no fairy tale. The abduction plot was hatched by an aide of Confederate President Jefferson Davis in an effort to save what was left of the South. With Grant tightening the noose around Richmond and Sherman marching north to strike General Lee's army of Virginia from the rear, the war was lost and everyone knew it. The hatred for the secessionist states in Congress was no secret.

Davis and his government were certain the North would exact a terrible tribute when the Confederacy was totally defeated. The aide, whose name has been forgotten, came up with the wild proposal that by capturing Lincoln and holding him as a hostage, the South could use him as leverage to strike an advantageous deal for surrender terms.'

'Actually not a bad idea.' said Giordino, settling on the deck to take a load off his feet.

'Except for old nasty Edwin Stanton. He queered the deal.'

'He refused to be blackmailed,' said Pitt.

'That and other reasons,' Perlmutter nodded. 'To Lincoln's credit, he insisted Stanton join his cabinet as Secretary of War. He believed Stanton was the best man for the job despite the fact the man disliked Lincoln intensely, even sneering at him as the "original gorilla." Stanton saw the President's capture as an opportunity rather than a disaster.'

'How was Lincoln abducted?' asked Pitt.

'The President was known to take a daily carriage ride through the countryside surrounding Washington most every day. A Confederate cavalry troop, dressed in Union cavalry uniforms, and led by Captain Brown, overwhelmed Lincoln's escort during one of the outings and smuggled him across the Potomac River and into Confederate-held territory.'

Pitt was having trouble putting the pieces together. An historical event he had fervently believed as gospel was now being revealed as a fraud, and it took all his willpower to keep an open mind. 'What was Stanton's immediate reaction to Lincoln's abduction?' he asked.

'Unfortunately for Lincoln, Stanton was the first to be notified by survivors of Lincoln's bodyguards. He foresaw the panic and outrage if the country learned their President had been captured by the enemy. He quickly covered the disaster with a cloak of secrecy and created a cover story. Going so far as to tell Mary Todd Lincoln that her husband was on a secret mission to General Grant's headquarters and wouldn't return for several days.'

'Hard to believe there wasn't a leak,' said Giordino sceptically.

'Stanton was the most feared man in Washington. If he swore you to secrecy, you'd die silent or he'd make sure you did.'

'Didn't the situation become exposed when Davis sent word of Lincoln's imprisonment and his demands for favourable surrender terms?'

'Stanton was shrewd. He guessed the Confederate plot a few hours after Lincoln was captured. He alerted the Union general in command of Washington's defences, and when Davis' courier crossed the battle lines under a flag of truce, he was taken immediately to Stanton. Neither Vice-President Johnson, Secretary of State William Henry Seward, nor any other members of Lincoln's cabinet were aware of what was happening. Stanton secretly replied to President Davis' terms and soundly rejected any negotiation, suggesting that the Confederacy could do everyone a favour by drowning Lincoln in the James River.

'Davis was stunned when he received Stanton's reply. You can imagine his dilemma. Here he sits with the Confederacy going up in flames around him. He has the leader of the entire Union in captivity. A high-ranking member of the United States government tells him they don't care a damn, and as far as they're concerned they can keep Lincoln. Davis suddenly began to see the very real possibility he might be hanged by the victorious Yankees. With his great plan to save the South from going down the sewer, and not about to have Lincoln's death on his hands, he temporarily got rid of his nemesis by ordering him put on board the *Texas* as a prisoner. Davis hoped the ship would successfully run the Union navy blockade, save the treasury gold, and keep Lincoln out of Union hands as a pawn for future negotiations when calmer heads than Stanton prevailed. Unfortunately, nothing went right.'

'Stanton stages the assassination and the *Texas* vanishes with all hands and is presumed lost,' Pitt concluded.

'Yes,' Perlmutter acknowledged. 'Imprisoned after the war for two years, Jefferson Davis never spoke of Lincoln's capture for fear of Union anger and retaliation against a South struggling to rise to its feet again.'

'How did Stanton pull off the assassination?' asked Giordino.

'There is no stranger story in American history,' Perlmutter answered, 'than the plot that supposedly took Lincoln's life. The astounding reality is that Stanton hired John Wilkes Booth to direct and act in the hoax. Booth knew an actor who was close to Lincoln's height and thin body. Stanton took General Grant into his confidence and together they gave out the story of their meeting with Lincoln that afternoon, and Grant's turning down the invitation to go to Ford's Theater. Stanton's agents also drugged Mary Todd Lincoln so that by the time the fake Lincoln appeared to take her to Ford's Theater she was too muddled to see through the substitute who was made up to look like her real husband.

'At the theatre the actor acknowledged the standing applause from the audience who were just far enough away from the presidential box to not detect the bogus President. Booth did his act, actually shooting the unsuspecting actor in the back of the head before leaping to the stage. Then the poor dupe was carried across the street with a handkerchief over his face to deceive onlookers and then died in a scene directed by Stanton himself.'

'But there were witnesses at the deathbed,' protested Pitt. 'Army doctors, members of his cabinet, and Lincoln's aides.'

'The doctors were friends and agents of Stanton,' Perlmutter said wearily. 'We'll never be sure how the others were deceived. Stanton does not say.'

'And the conspiracy to kill Vice-President Johnson and Secretary of State Seward? Was that part of Stanton's plan?'

'With them out of the way, he would have been next in line as President. But the men Booth hired bungled the job. Even so, Stanton acted somewhat like a dictator the first few weeks after Johnson took over as President. He conducted the investigation, the arrest of the conspirators, and directed a lightning-fast trial and hanging. He also spread the word across the nation that Lincoln had been murdered by agents of Jefferson Davis as a last desperate gamble of the Confederate war effort.'

'Then Stanton had Booth killed to keep him from talking as well,' Pitt surmised.

Perlmutter shook his head. 'Another man was shot in the barn that burned. The autopsy and identification were cover-ups. Booth got away and lived for a number of years, eventually committing suicide in Enid, Oklahoma in 1903.'

'I read somewhere that Stanton burned Booth's diary,' said Pitt.

'That's true,' replied Perlmutter. 'The damage was done. Stanton had inflamed public opinion against the beaten Confederacy. Lincoln's plans to help the South back on its feet were buried with his double in a grave in Springfield, Illinois.'

'This mummy in the rocking chair,' whispered Giordino, staring in rigid awe, 'sitting here in the remains of a Confederate warship covered by a sand dune in the middle of the Sahara Desert is truly Abraham Lincoln?'

'I'm positive of it,' answered Perlmutter. 'An anatomic examination will prove his identity without doubt. In fact, if you'll recall, grave robbers broke into his tomb but were caught before they could steal the body. What was not revealed but quickly concealed was that the officials who prepared the body for reinterment discovered they had a substitute on their hands. Word came down from Washington ordering them to keep quiet and to fix it so the grave could never be opened again. A hundred tons of concrete were poured over the coffins of Lincoln and his son Tad to prevent future ghouls from desecrating the grave, so they said. But the real truth was to bury all evidence of the crime.'

'You realize what this means?' Pitt asked Perlmutter, 'don't you?'

'Do I realize what *what* means?' he muttered dumbly.

'We are about to alter the past,' Pitt explained. 'Once we announce what we've found here, the most tragic event in United States history will be irrevocably rewritten.'

Perlmutter stared at Pitt in near horror. 'You don't know what you're saying. Abraham Lincoln is revered as a saint as well as a humble man in American folklore, history books, poems, and novels. The assassination made him a martyr to be revered through the centuries. If we expose Stanton's fake assassination of him, his image will be shattered, and Americans will be the poorer for it.'

Pitt looked very, very tired, but his face was set and his eyes bright and alive. 'No man was admired more for his honesty than Abraham Lincoln. His moral principles and compassion were second to no man. To have died under such deceitful and unconscionable circumstances was against everything he stood for. His remains deserve an honest burial. I have to believe he would have wanted the future generations of the people he served so faithfully to know the truth.'

'I'm with you,' Giordino affirmed steadily. 'I'll be honoured to stand next to you when the curtain goes up.'

'There will be a negative uproar,' Perlmutter gasped as if a pair of hands were around his windpipe. 'Good God,

Dirk, can't you see? This is a subject best left unknown. The nation must never know.'

'Spoken like an arrogant politician or bureaucrat who plays God by denying the public the truth under the misguided ploy of national security, not to mention the crap about it not being in the national interest.'

'So you're going to do it,' Perlmutter said in a stricken voice. 'You're really going to cause a national upheaval in the name of truth.'

'Like the men and women in Congress and the White House, Julien, you underestimate the American public. They will take the disclosure in stride, and Lincoln's image will shine brighter than ever. Sorry, my friend, I won't be talked out of going through with it.'

Perlmutter saw it was no use. He clasped his hands on his global stomach and sighed. 'All right, we'll rewrite the last chapter of the Civil War and stand in front of a firing squad together.'

Pitt stood over the grotesque figure, studied the ungainly long arms and legs, the serene, weary face. When he spoke, it was in a soft, barely audible voice.

'After sitting cooped up in here for a hundred and thirty years, I think it's time old Honest Abe came home.'

64

The news of Lincoln's discovery and the Stanton hoax electrified the world as the body was reverently removed from the ironclad and flown back to Washington. In every school of the country, children memorized and recited the Gettysburg Address as their grandparents had.

The nation's capital pulled out all stops on celebrations and ceremonies. Five living Presidents stood in the Capitol rotunda and paid homage at the open casket of their long-dead predecessor. The speeches seemingly went on forever, the politicians climbing over each other to quote Lincoln if not Carl Sandburg.

The sixteenth President's mortal remains would not go to the cemetery in Springfield. By presidential order a tomb was cut into the floor of his memorial immediately below his famous white marble statue. No one, not even the congressional representatives from Illinois, considered protesting the interment.

A holiday was declared and millions of people across the country watched the festivities in Washington on television. They sat transfixed in awe at actually seeing the face of the man who had led the country through its most difficult times.

Little else was shown from morning until night as regular network programming was temporarily rescheduled. News programme anchor persons had a field day describing the event, while other newsworthy stories fell by the wayside.

Congressional leaders, in rare display of cooperation, voted funds to salvage the *Texas* and transport her from Mali to the Washington Mall, where she would be preserve and placed on permanent display. Her crew was buried in the Confederate Cemetery in Richmond, Virginia, with great pomp and a band playing *Dixie*.

Kitty Mannock and her plane returned to Australia where she was glorified and given a riotous down-under welcome. She was entombed in the Military Museum in Canberra. Her faithful Fairchild aircraft, after restoration, was to sit beside Sir Charles Kingsford-Smith's famous long-distance aircraft, the *Southern Cross*.

Except for a few photographers and two reporters, the ceremony honouring the contributions of Hala Kamil and Admiral Sandecker for their efforts in helping halt the spread of the red tides and preventing the projected extinction of life almost went unnoticed. The President, between speeches, presented them with medals of honour awarded by a special act of Congress. Afterward, Hala returned to New York and the United Nations, where a special session was called to pay her homage. She finally succumbed to emotion during the longest-standing ovation ever given by the General Assembly.

Sandecker quietly went back to his NUMA office, worked out in his private gym, and began planning a new undersea project as if every day was the same.

Though they would not win, Dr Darcy Chapman and Rudi Gunn were named as candidates for a joint Nobel Prize. They ignored the hoopla and returned together to the South Atlantic to analyse the effects of the mammoth red tide on the sea life. Dr Frank Hopper joined them after being smuggled from the hospital and carried on board the research ship. He swore he'd recover faster back in the saddle, studying the toxicity of the red tides.

Hiram Yaeger received a fat bonus from NUMA and an extra ten-day paid vacation. He took his family to Disney World. While they enjoyed the attractions, he attended a ᵉminar on archival computer systems.

General Hugo Bock, after seeing that the survivors and relatives of the dead from the now legendary battle of Fort Foureau received commendation medals and generous financial benefits, decided to resign from the UN Tactical Team at the height of his reputation. He retired to a small village in the Bavarian Alps.

As Pitt predicted, Colonel Levant was promoted to General, presented with a United Nations peace-keeping medal, and was named to succeed General Bock.

After recovering from his wounds at his family manor in Cornwall, Captain Pembroke-Smythe was promoted to Major and returned to his former regiment. He was received by the Queen, who presented him with the Distinguished Service Order (DSO). He is currently posted with a special commando unit.

St Julien Perlmutter, happy that he was wrong at seeing the American public take the reappearance of their most esteemed President and the belated exposé of Edwin Stanton's treason in stride, was fêted by numerous historic organizations and honoured with enough awards to fill one wall of his house.

Al Giordino tracked down the cute piano player he met on Yves Massarde's houseboat in the Niger. Fortunately, she was unmarried and for some inexplicable reason, at least to Pitt, she took a liking to Giordino and accepted his invitation to go on a diving trip to the Red Sea.

As for Dirk Pitt and Eva Rojas . . .

65
June 25, 1996
Monterey, California

June marked the height of the tourist season on the Monterey Peninsula. They drove their cars and recreational vehicles bumper-to-bumper over the scenic Seventeen-Mile Drive between Monterey and Carmel. Along Cannery Row, the shoppers were shoulder-to-shoulder as they alternated between buying sprees and dining in the picturesque seafood restaurants overlooking the water.

They came to play golf at Pebble Beach, see Big Sur, and take pictures of sunsets off Point Lobos. They wandered through the wineries, stared at the ancient cypress trees, and strolled along the beaches, thrilling to the sights of gliding pelicans, the barking of the seals, and the crashing waves.

Eva's mother and father were becoming immune to their spectacular surroundings after having lived in the same cottage-style house in Pacific Grove for over thirty-two years. They often took for granted their good fortune at living in such a beautiful part of the California coast. But the blinders always came off when Eva came home. She never failed to see the peninsula through the eyes of a teenager, as if viewing her very own car for the first time.

Whenever she came home she dragged her parents out of their comfortable routine to enjoy the simple beauties of their community. But this trip was a different story. She was in no condition to push them into a bike ride or a swim in the brisk waters rolling in from the Pacific. Nor did she feel in the mood to do anything but mope around the house.

Two days out of the hospital, Eva was confined to a wheelchair, recovering from her injuries suffered at Fort ᵮoureau. The wasted body, drained by her ordeal in the mines at Tebezza, had been rejuvenated by hefty helpings of healthy food that had added an inch on her slim waistline with the addition of too many calories, a condition exercise could not cure until her fractures knitted and the casts came off.

Her body was slowly mending, but her mind was sick from not hearing a word from Pitt. Since she had been airlifted from the ruins of the old Foreign Legion fort to Mauritania, and from there to a hospital in San Francisco, it was as though he had fallen into deep space. A phone call to Admiral Sandecker had only assured her that Pitt was still in the Sahara and had not returned to Washington with Giordino.

'Why don't you come golfing with me this morning?' her father asked her. 'Do you good to get out of the house.'

She looked up into his twinkling grey eyes and smiled at the way his grey hair never stayed combed. 'I don't think I'm in shape to hit the ball,' she grinned.

'I thought you might like to ride in the cart with me.'

She thought it over for a while, and then nodded. 'Why not?' she held up her good arm and wiggled the toes on her right foot. 'But only if I get to drive.'

Her mother fussed over her as she helped load Eva into the family Chrysler.'Now you see she doesn't hurt herself,' she admonished Eva's father.

'I promise to bring her back in the same condition I found her,' he joked.

Mr Rojas teed off on the fourth hole of the Pacific Grove Municipal Golf Course along fairways that stretched around the Point Pinos Lighthouse. He watched his ball drop into a sandtrap, shook his head, and dropped the club in its bag.

'Not enough muscle,' he muttered in frustration.

Eva sat behind the wheel of the cart and gestured to a bench perched on a lookout over the sea. 'Would you mind

Dad, if I sat out the next five holes. It's such a beautiful day, I'd just like to sit and look at the ocean.'

'Why sure, honey. I'll pick you up on my way back to the clubhouse.'

After he helped her settle as comfortably as possible on the bench, he waved and drove the cart on down the fairway toward the green with three of his golfing buddies following in another cart.

There was a light mist hanging just over the water, but she could see the sweeping shore of the bay as it curved into the town of Monterey and then swept in a near straight line northward. The sea was calm and the waves moved like burrowing animals under the great fields of kelp. She inhaled the air, pungent with drying seaweed draped on the rocky shore, and watched a sea otter's antics as it cavorted around the kelp.

Eva looked up suddenly as a squawking sea gull glided overhead. She slowly turned her head to follow its flight and suddenly found her eyes locked on a man standing slightly to the side and behind the bench.

'You and I and the Bay of Monterey,' he said softly.

Pitt stood smiling in delight and immense affection as Eva stared at him for a long moment in uncomprehending joy and disbelief. Then he was beside her and she was in his arms.

'Oh Dirk, Dirk! I wasn't sure you'd come. I thought we might be finished — '

She broke off as he kissed her and looked down at the gleaming Dresden blue eyes now misting with tears that crept down her reddened cheeks.

'I should have contacted you,' he said. 'My life has been chaos until two days ago.'

'You're forgiven,' she said joyously. 'But how in the world did you know I was here?'

'Your mother. Nice lady. She sent me here. I rented a golf cart and drove around the course until I saw this poor little lonely waif with a parcel of broken bones staring sadly at the sea.'

'You're a nut,' she said happily, kissing him again.

He slid his arms under Eva and carefully picked her up. 'I wish we had time to watch the waves roll in, but we have to be on our way. My God, but all this plaster makes you heavy.'

'Why are we rushing off?'

'We have to pack your things and catch a plane,' he answered as he lowered her into the golf cart.

'Plane, a plane to where?'

'A little fishing village on the west coast of Mexico.'

'You're taking me to Mexico?' she smiled through the tears.

'To board a boat I've chartered.'

'For a cruise?'

'Sort of,' he explained with a grin. 'We're going to sail to a place called Clipperton Island and look for treasure.'

She said to Pitt as he drove the cart into the parking lot by the clubhouse: 'I think you are the most sneaky, beguiling, and crafty man I've ever known —' She broke off as he stopped beside a strange-looking car with a bright fuchsia paint job. 'What is this?' she asked in amazement.

'An automobile.'

'I can see that, but what kind?'

'An Avions Voisin, a gift from my old pal, Zateb Kazim.'

She stared at him blankly. 'You had this shipped over from Mali?'

'On an Air Force transport,' he answered casually. 'The President owed me big. So I made a simple request.'

'Where are you going to park it if we're catching a flight?'

'I talked your mother into storing it in her garage until the Pebble Beach Concours in August.'

She shook her head in disbelief. 'You're incorrigible.'

Pitt held her face gently between his hands, smiled down at her, and said, 'That's why I'm so much fun.'

Inca Gold

Clive Cussler

THE INTERNATIONAL
NO. 1 BESTSELLER

A desperate call for help from a stricken archaeological expedition brings Dirk Pitt to a sacred well high in the Andes. What he discovers as he attempts to rescue two divers lost in its perilous depths leads him into deadly confrontation with a ruthless band of international art-thieves, who plunder ancient sites for their precious arte-facts.

Dirk Pitt's extraordinary adventures take him to the fabled Lost City of the Dead, lead him in search of a Spanish galleon washed miles inland by a giant tidal wave centuries before, and eventually set him on the trail of a fabulous hoard of Inca Gold. But Pitt will need all his skills and tenacity simply to survive as he races to track down the sacred site – before the richest prize known to man is lost to the world for ever. . .

'Clive Cussler's hero Dirk Pitt is made of strong stuff, handling the improbable with nerves of steel . . . he is one of the best adventure heroes around.'   *Today*

'Clive Cussler is the guy *I* read.'   TOM CLANCY

ISBN 0 00 647909 X